BLACK LIGHT: CELEBRITY ROULETTE

BLACK COLLAR PRESS

BLACK LIGHT: CELEBRITY ROULETTE
An Anthology of the Black Light Series

BY

USA TODAY AND INTERNATIONAL BESTSELLING AUTHORS
Renee Rose, Livia Grant, Maren Smith, Jennifer Bene, Measha Stone,
Maggie Ryan, Sue Lyndon, Lesley Clark, Dani René

Black Light: Celebrity Roulette
Renee Rose, Livia Grant, Maren Smith, Jennifer Bene, Measha Stone,
Maggie Ryan, Sue Lyndon, Lesley Clark, Dani René

Published by Black Collar Press
Don't miss a release! Sign-up for our newsletter here!

EBook ISBN: **978-1-947559-08-0**
Print ISBN: **978-1-947559-10-3**

Cover Art by Eris Adderly, http://erisadderly.com/

The authors of Black Light: Celebrity Roulette would like to dedicate this book to our very own Maggie Ryan, her daughter, and her brand new grandson, Cormac. Cormac was born during the editing process of putting this complicated boxed set together. There were scary complications, but everyone is doing well and Maggie and her family were in our thoughts the whole time this incredible set of stories was coming together. With that, we'd like to say CONGRATULATIONS on your healthy, new grandson Maggie!

HOW HIGH WOULD YOU BID FOR A FANTASY NIGHT WITH YOUR CELEBRITY CRUSH?

What's inside this anthology?

Celebrity Roulette Introduction

Black Light is back for the 3rd year in a row with nine *__brand new__* sexy stories set in their new West Coast club! This year you're invited to celebrate Valentine's Day VIP-style as Black Light combines their annual kinky game of BDSM roulette with a celebrity charity auction. Three hours of fun. Five hard limits.

We've loaded the wheel with naughty new kinks for our couples as they play to win a free month at the exclusive club... but there's more than money on the line when hearts get involved.

Drama, fame, and fantasies await if you're brave enough to spin the wheel!

Publisher's Note: If you've checked out the previous Valentine Roulette anthologies, then you already know the high stakes for these daring couples. If you haven't spun the wheel with us yet, what are you waiting for? Each set is full of completely new, edgy, stand-alone BDSM romance stories! Dive in and enjoy this one of a kind anthology, full of tempting dominance and tantalizing submission.

~

Guarded by Renee Rose

Guarding pop star Scarlett A wasn't just a job to me, it was a mission. Losing that position cut deep. That's why I put a second mortgage on my house for one night with her. Tonight she's going to discover a different side of me. I'll be the boss. And she'll be the one on her knees begging.

RENEE ROSE is a *USA Today* bestselling author and a naughty wordsmith who writes BDSM and spanking romance novels. She's hit #1 on Amazon in multiple categories in the U.S. and U.K., is often found on the list of Amazon's Top 100 Erotic Authors.

~

Switched by Livia Grant

Two dominants in one game of submission is one too many. Will the spin of the wheel melt Mistress Ice or will Master Nolan get switched… literally.

LIVIA GRANT is a *USA Today* bestselling author who lives in Chicago with her husband and two sons… one a young man, the other a furry rescue dog named Max. Well-known for her deep, character-driven plots, & incredible ensemble casts, she writes one hell of an erotic romance.

~

Determined by Maren Smith

Claire was determined. Determined to win male-model Adam Butler for her first BDSM scene. And especially, determined to finally know what a spanking feels like. There's only one problem: this is Black Light and on Roulette night, nothing goes as planned...

MAREN SMITH is a *USA Today* bestselling author with more than 20 years' worth of books in print. She is well known for both her slightly twisted sense of humor and her unhealthy love affair with coffee.

~

Hooked by Jennifer Bene

A ballerina, a soloist, and Wyatt Strickland's obsession. Vanessa is the girl of his dreams. Perfect. Too perfect for a man like him, but if there's a chance to get her hooked, it's Roulette. And Wyatt isn't going to miss his chance.

JENNIFER BENE is a *USA Today* bestselling author of dangerously sexy and deviously dark romance. From BDSM, to Suspense, Dark Romance, and Thrillers--she writes it all. Always delivering a twisty, spine-tingling journey with the promise of a happily-ever-after.

~

Pressure by Measha Stone

Michele was comfortable staying in her little box, nicely hidden from view. Except the universe had other plans, and so did Egan. Nothing like a little pressure to set her heart on fire.

MEASHA STONE is *USA Today* bestselling author from the western suburbs of Chicago where she lives with her husband and children, who are just as creative and crazy as her. Her vanilla writing has been published in numerous literary magazines, but she's found her passion in erotic romance.

~

Surrender by Maggie Ryan

As a chef, Ronan is used to having his every command obeyed--without question. Under his mastery, Carnegie will learn how to savor the pain and pleasure in life--one lick at a time.

MAGGIE RYAN is a *USA Today* bestselling author and #1 international bestselling author in Victorian, Historical, Contemporary and Western Romance. She loves to write stories that take a reader on a journey, one they can disappear into, to experience what might have been or what is to come!

~

Cherished by Sue Lyndon

She's a newbie. Innocent. Sweet. F*cking adorable. If calling him 'Daddy' makes her stammer and blush, just wait until he gets her into the nursery...

SUE LYNDON is a *USA Today* bestselling author who writes steamy D/s romance in a variety of genres, from contemporary to historical to fantasy. She's a #1 Amazon bestseller in multiple categories, including BDSM Erotica and Sci-Fi Erotica.

~

Jazzed by Lesley Clark

Jazz has everything she's ever dreamed of - fame, money, and all the attention that comes with it which means she has to hide parts of herself, and she needs a place to be free. Michael has met all of his goals, but it isn't enough... can one night and three spins of the wheel give them both what they need?

LESLEY CLARK is a bestselling author who is first and foremost a wife and mother. She has been an RN for the last twelve years and truly enjoys taking care of her patients, but she loves to spend her downtime writing stories with hot alpha men and sexy, sassy ladies that will keep you on the edge of your seat from start to finish.

~

Control by Dani René

For far too long I've craved to control her pleasure, to own her body. And now, I finally get my chance.

DANI RENÉ is an international bestselling author and proud member of the Romance Writer's Organization of South Africa (ROSA) and the Romance Writers of America (RWA). She is a fan of dark romance that grabs you by the throat and doesn't let go. It's from this passion that her writing has evolved from sweet and romantic, to dark and delicious.

~

Celebrity Roulette Conclusion

~

A Note from Black Collar Press:

Every book you are about to read happens on the same night, during the same event at the Black Light BDSM club. Valentine Roulette has its own set of rules outside of normal play, and the nine daring couples in these books were brave enough to sign-up.

But before you can decide if *you* are brave enough to spin the wheel, continue reading to find out more about Valentine Roulette, and this year's event *Celebrity Roulette* ...

CELEBRITY ROULETTE
INTRODUCTION

Jennifer Bene & Livia Grant

EVENT PLANNING SESSION

*W*alking into the meeting room, Jaxson only gave a cursory glance at the people gathered around the table as he dropped into the head chair, setting the folder of reference docs in front of him. Chase took the seat to his right a second later, while the chair to his left remained empty — a heavy reminder that they'd left Emma at home with Khloe and the twins.

"Sleeping well, I gather?" Miguel asked, grinning when Jaxson stared at him.

"Just great," he deadpanned. "Look, I don't want to be here any longer than you all do, but we have to get this year's Valentine's event settled for Runway West and Black Light West."

"Sounds good to me, we've got four lockers malfunctioning at the Runway entrance that I'd like to get squared away before tonight." Their head of security, Miguel Martinez, was always working. Something Jaxson definitely appreciated, especially since he was the same way.

Or, he used to be. *Dammit.*

"Then let's get to it." Scanning the faces, Jaxson settled on Elijah Keaton, their West Coast Dungeon Master. "Did you get the chance to talk to Spencer?"

"Sure did, and I think I'm up to date on the decisions you made on the call last week for the changes to the Roulette procedures this year." Elijah yawned, almost cracking his jaw as he leaned back in his chair. "Still sounds like one hell of an event. Is it true you had someone land on diaper play last year?"

"Yep," Chase answered, grinning.

"Yes, that's true, and these events tend to get very intense very quickly." Jaxson couldn't help but remember their lawyer Connor Lambert trussing up Ella Castle in such devious ways that *he* had even seen the appeal. Just not enough to actually want to try it with his own subs. Rubbing his eyes, Jaxson continued. "And, really, that's one thing we're concerned with here at our West Coast location. With our clientele we may need to—"

A huff came from the petite blonde a few seats away as Madison noticeably rolled her eyes.

"Do you disagree, Madison?" Jaxson was in no mood for this shit. Even if their tiny club manager was doing a great job, it didn't mean he had the patience for her California-girl attitude at the moment.

"I do," she began, leaning forward so she could meet his eyes with a confidence more than half the male employees failed to have. "You've had us working to make these clubs, like, *the* destination for the affluent and celebrities here in Cali, and from what Elijah has shared with me Black Light has totally had the same success that Runway has in recruiting."

"Elijah shared the membership list with you?" Jaxson questioned, wondering why it would be relevant to Madison's job. The Dungeon Master grumbled, and Jaxson couldn't help but ask a follow up. "You and Ms. Taylor have frequent chats about Black Light?"

"Have you spent much time with her? She shows up to ask about something, and then never stops talking!" Sitting up, Elijah scrubbed a hand over his face. "Sharing the information is the only way to get her to shut up since I can't fit her with a ball gag. And she's signed the NDA, and already knows about the club, so... let's just say it's for my sanity."

The answer was almost enough to make Jaxson smile, even though he felt like roadkill. There wasn't enough coffee in the world to battle the sleep deficit he'd racked up, but it was nice to have a Dungeon Master with less of a territorial stick up his ass than Spencer Cook did as DM at their East Coast location. That conference call had been exhausting.

Madison sighed, rolling her eyes again. "Look, having an awareness of our crossover attendance has done wonders for understanding both the people and financial flow from one club to the next. Seriously, *so* many members of Black Light begin their night at Runway before moving downstairs, and that's important to know!"

"That's actually pretty awesome. Have we looked into that on the East Coast?" Chase asked.

"I totally talked to Maxine when we first set it up, and she's doing it in D.C. too. Obviously, we're handling the lists personally so that Runway staff aren't aware." Madison smiled like a pageant winner, and as he scanned her quickly he noticed she was in another perfectly put together designer outfit. If he had to bet, he would have guessed the flowy, floral print top was Dolce & Gabbana. As much as he hated to admit it, even though she looked and sounded like the Valley girl she was, she knew what she was doing with the business side of things.

Which was a gift, since he and Chase had been focused on Emma and the twins.

"All right, I get it. What was I even talking about before this got side-tracked?" Jaxson glanced at Chase, but his lover seemed to be at a loss as well.

"You were incorrectly assuming that due to our clientele we need to, like, treat them with kid-gloves or something." Madison maintained the smile as she not-so-subtly insulted him.

"Well, please, since you're an expert in BDSM... enlighten me." The caustic retort wasn't exactly out of character for Jaxson, but normally he tried to be less of an asshole in these meetings. Or, at the very least, he thought about it.

A pretty blush hit Madison's cheeks, only growing brighter as several of the dungeon monitors at the end of the table chuckled.

"Listen, I'm not claiming I'm an expert in that, but I do know from experience that having people assume things about me due to my name, or what I look like, is totally fucking irritating. If someone is a member of Black Light, we have to, like, at least give them the courtesy of believing they know what they're getting into."

"As annoying as it is, I have to agree with her," Elijah chimed in, leaning his head to the side to stare at him.

"So, our Black Light West members aren't going to have any issues with spinning implements that leave marks? Humiliation? ABDL?" Jaxson asked, doubt staining his voice.

"Look, from what Spencer told me, everyone gets to choose some limits. And from my experience, a sub is a sub no matter how many figures in their bank account." Elijah shrugged, glancing at his DMs for a moment. "I mean, hell, you know Khloe Monroe is here with Ryder practically every damn week. She's a fucking A-list actress, and he plays rougher than most."

"Jax..." Chase said softly, leaning a little closer over the corner of the table. "How many people would have put us in these categories when we were still modeling? I mean, sure, you're always dominant and hot as hell, but an actual Dominant Sadist? Pfft. We can't make assumptions, babe."

"Point made," Jaxson acquiesced, reaching over to wrap his hand around Chase's knee. Squeezing, he couldn't bite back the smile when Chase wiggled and gave him a heated glance that meant *some* action might happen tonight — if they could both stay awake, and the twins weren't crying. Groaning, he sat up straight and flipped open the folder in front of him. "Okay, before we dive completely into the details for Roulette this year, let's just make sure Runway is good for Valentine's Day. Where are we with the plans?"

"Well, we've had *so* many people asking us to do another masquerade event that we've looked into doing sequin masks in, like, red, black, and pink. That will also be their swag for the event, and Avery has partnered with the bar for some kick ass new drinks we can highlight for the night." Tapping her iPad, Madison started scrolling through something on the screen. "Based on our last decoration budget, we can make Runway totally *scream* Valentine's without being, like, gaudy about it. And the masks are super cheap, but will let everyone feel special."

"That sounds—"

"Oh!" Madison continued, talking over Jaxson's attempt to reply. "And I'm super excited because my friend's brother-in-law worked with DJ Yellowtail at this party a couple of months ago in Ibiza, and he hooked me up with a connection, and Yellowtail is totally down to play Runway for Valentine's."

"Am I supposed to know who this is?" Jaxson asked, but Chase had already gasped.

"Are you sure? I thought he wasn't touring outside of Asia and Europe right now?" Chase looked excited, which meant it was probably a solid booking for the event even if Jaxson had no idea who the DJ was. Then Madison matched Chase's joy with a high-pitched squeak of glee.

"Oh my God, so, *get this*. Apparently, he is going to be in a movie this year — like, not a big part, but he's in one — and so he's been to L.A. a few times. Lately, he's been stopping over for a day or so on layovers because he just wants to party." Madison was grinning, oblivious to the stare levelled at her from Elijah, or the nudges and low laughs from the DMs behind her. "He's only done, like, a handful of guest spots during shows here in L.A. and *none* of them had him listed. We'd legit be his first L.A. booking and with his name alone on the event we'll pack this place by ten o'clock!"

"Is he within budget?" Jaxson asked, already wishing he was done with the discussion.

"If we have DJ Yellowtail, who cares what he'll cost?" Chase was *definitely* excited, which softened Jaxson's irritation a little. Making his subs happy was always on his mind, and the way Chase's eyes shined he knew he'd be agreeing no matter the price tag. Laughing, Chase added, "Hell, even I want to sneak out of Black Light for a minute that night just to see him."

"See? Also, like I'd mention him if I hadn't already handled the budget?" Madison grinned, scrolling on her iPad again. "I already explained the kind of people who would be in the audience, since he's *clearly* looking to expand his reach here in Cali, and he's already accepted. I've just been waiting for this meeting to send over the contract."

"Fine. As long as we're in budget." Jaxson waved a hand, not wanting to waste any more time on the relatively uncomplicated upstairs event. Although, the quiet *yes!* from Chase made him happier than he cared to show to the other people at the table. "Is there anything else for Runway we need to think about?"

"I've already contacted some of the part-time guys to see if they'd be willing to pull a shift on Valentine's, and they've accepted." Miguel answered, reciting everything from memory since he'd arrived with only a pen and a blank sheet of paper. "So, we'll have extra security on site, and the valet company is going to have dedicated manpower to deal with the influx of hired cars, limos, and ride share we always have at the bigger events. They'll keep the cars moving."

"Great. So, are we ready to address Black Light's Roulette event now?" Jaxson asked, waiting to see if anyone else wanted to annoy him, but even Madison kept her mouth shut. "All right. This is our first Roulette event at Black Light West, and while we're doing something similar to last year's for our East Coast club this year... there have been some suggestions made for how we can make it feel new and different here."

Chase took the cue and picked up the explanation. "Right. We know that Runway West's biggest attraction is the opportunity to rub elbows with various celebrities. From actors, to athletes, to musicians, etcetera. But, while we've provided a secure place to play for those members, we haven't leveraged that side of things as much with Black Light West."

"Why would it matter who's watching them get paddled?" Elijah asked, doubt staining his tone.

"That's just it. Roulette is our largest annual event on the East Coast, and we had people asking about this year's the day after the last one ended. It's become a major thing for the members of the club to attend, and a goal for many of the single members to participate in. I mean, according to Spencer, we've already had over thirty inquiries and we haven't even posted the guidelines and rules for this year!" Chase laughed a little, and Jaxson remembered their surprise when that bit of information had been revealed on the call. The event really had taken off, which was good, but it put a lot of pressure on their West Coast location.

"That didn't answer my question. Why would it matter if some famous member is in the audience? I mean, that's a regular occurrence at Black Light already and I haven't seen anyone getting off on that more than any normal exhibitionist would." Elijah yawned again. "It seems stupid to advertise what already happens here on a regular basis."

"True. But what if for Roulette... they could get paired *with* one of the celebrities?" Chase smiled as everyone in the room sat to attention.

"That *is* interesting," Madison said, almost to herself.

"It is," Jaxson agreed. "Chase and I have had a few people reach out asking if we'd be replicating Roulette here on the West Coast, and so we already have a few 'celebrity' names in the ring for it."

"In the ring for what, exactly? The random chance that the roulette wheel pairs a member with one of a handful of celebrities and not just another member?" It was one of the Dungeon Monitors speaking, and even though Jaxson recognized the man, he couldn't place his name.

"Actually, that's the part that Emma figured out," Chase said, voice glowing with the pride they both felt for their deviously smart and beautiful wife. "We always do the sign-ups online, and instead of having the roulette wheel pair off the couples for the night, we have members bid to win the right to play with a particular celebrity during Roulette."

"That's a nice way to make a quick buck!" Elijah laughed, and several of the DMs laughed too.

"Having the money go straight to Black Light won't draw in as many participants. We could totally pick a charity for the funds we'd raise," Madison suggested, clearly thinking about how fast the bids could go up considering their members, an issue they'd debated with Emma as well. But donating the excess to a *charity?*

"Fuck that, we're not doing this event for free. Spencer said that it was a good night for the bottom line, and — as Madison is constantly talking about — we have to watch the finances for both clubs. Handing all the money to charity is just stupid."

Sighing, Madison swiveled to face Elijah head on, not backing down despite the man's intense gaze. "Celebrity tournaments are done *all* the time, and it's really not complicated. We'll still totally make money on food and beverage, plus the event attendance fee, and then we just take an administrative fee from the bids to cover us. Like, we could just do the five percent we did at the Las Dunas Golf Tournament in 2016, and then the *rest* goes to charity."

"What fucking charity wants a BDSM club to donate?" Jaxson snapped.

"It can be an anonymous donation, Mr. Cartwright-Davidson." Madison's calm response was a verbal check to Jaxson's attitude, and he took a deep breath, frustrated that he hadn't thought of the obvious answer.

Fuck, he really needed some sleep.

"All right, then does anyone see an issue with the concept of Celebrity Roulette?"

"Sounds like it's just a kinkier version of a bachelor or bachelorette auction. They do those for charity too and it's never an issue," Miguel added.

"Only issue I'm seeing is making sure we have enough *celebrities* willing to sign up. The DMs and I can talk to some of the more adventurous single members when they're in." Elijah rubbed at the five o'clock shadow on his cheek. "How exactly are we defining celebrity for this thing?"

"It's way more than actors," Chase spoke up. "We're talking about singers, musicians, models, athletes, dancers — the list goes on. I mean, this is L.A. We're not exactly in short supply."

"You haven't asked these members to submit to a stranger and a random selection of BDSM activities before," Elijah mumbled, but it was more than loud enough for everyone to hear.

"You already argued that we can't make assumptions about our members' willingness to participate, didn't you, Elijah?" Jaxson asked, and the man grumbled. "Right. So, the plan is that we'll have a type of silent auction online in the weeks leading up to Roulette. Celebrity participants will have a photo and a brief bio, including whether they're dominant or submissive, and we'll let our members bid for the opportunity to play with them."

"How many are we aiming for?" Elijah asked.

"About fifteen couples is where we've capped it before, and it seems to work well." Jaxson skimmed the notes he made, ignoring the headache already pulsing behind his left eye. "Winners will be notified before the event, but the contestants won't know until they're brought on stage to spin activities."

"And we'll inform the runner-up on the bids in case someone drops out at the last minute," Chase added.

"Yes, and there will be some West Coast only rules for the event." Jaxson looked over the list, wondering if the length was going to deter members from participating... but they'd already agreed on the other call that certain issues had to be dealt with. "Normally we require all members to be out on the floor at all times, but the layout of this location adjusts things a bit. Participants will be allowed to use the themed rooms as long as the observation window is kept active. We'll turn off the ability for private use for the night."

"That sounds like fun," one of the DMs commented, grinning as he nudged the man next to him.

"That's the point," Jaxson deadpanned. "Now, since we have so many separate spaces here at Black Light West, we're going to have a pretty full bar area at the beginning of the night. We'll probably need to rent a stage to elevate the MC and the activity roulette wheel so everyone can see, and that's only going to reduce the space further."

"Why are you using the bar area?" Madison asked, and he shot her a look that usually had people backing down. *Dammit, she's like a blonde, chatty version of Maxine.*

Groaning, Jaxson took a slow breath. This was why he'd hired her, wasn't it? "Where would you put the activity spins, Madison?"

"We can use the movie theater," she answered quickly, the gears spinning fast behind her eyes just as Jaxson's began to turn on the possibility. "It's got a lot of seating, we could add some standing bar-height tables along the walls to accommodate more people. If we had some extra waitstaff on hand they could bring snacks and drinks in there, and the stage would fit a lot better in there without removing the bar space as a calm space."

"And it would be much less of a fire hazard," Miguel said, shrugging. "Really, it's the only option in Black Light."

"Actually, that would be pretty fantastic. The theater is right off the main play area, and would let people filter back and forth without causing a traffic jam." Chase was nodding as he spoke, and Jaxson had to admit it was the best solution.

"That's settled then, we'll host the spins for activities in the theater. And just to make sure we get through everyone before the eight o'clock start time, we're going to officially kick off the event at 7:15." Several groans came from the room, and Jaxson raised his hand to silence them. "Stop it. We've always done an eight to eleven time block, but for the last two years on the East Coast we've failed to give the full time for play. This is the same change we've made for that event, and I'm not changing my mind."

"Fine," Elijah groused, bracing his elbows on the table. "Spencer also said that you decided to use house safe words only, right? That's something I push for in the dungeon anyway, because my guys and I can't do our jobs if we don't know what to listen for — and fuck if there aren't nights it's hard to remember what weird term I'm supposed to be keeping my ears open for when we're busy."

"Yes, for Roulette it will be the standard red, yellow, or green. Obviously, you guys just need to be listening for red." Several of the DMs gave him a look like it hadn't need to be said, but Jaxson didn't want any confusion, or overstepping boundaries in a scene. And on the topic of overstepping boundaries... "There is one rule I want to be very clear on, all employees are banned from participating in play the

12

night of Roulette. This has nothing to do with anything I've heard about you guys here at Black Light West, it's purely based on the last two years of Roulette. The safety of everyone is important on any night, but Roulette is always busier. It will be more chaotic, and the activities being spun can put a dominant out of their experience level. That means every dungeon monitor, bartender, waitstaff, etcetera, will be focused on their job, and not stepping in to play with a submissive."

"My guys don't interfere," Elijah said defensively.

"Like I said, this isn't about this location. And I'm not saying you all can't connect with a sub on another night, but for Roulette it's banned." Waiting until he had the eye contact of the five dungeon monitors at the far end of the table, Jaxson continued. "The consequences for violating this rule will be severe, up to and including termination. Is that understood?"

A chorus of mumbled agreements came from them, and Elijah nodded. "I agree with you on the potential safety concerns. I'll want to review the list to make sure we have a DM on site that can support each of them."

"Good." Jaxson was about to move on when Elijah smirked and crossed his arms.

"Just out of curiosity, does this have anything to do with that drama last year with the cell phone? One of your DMs was involved in that mess, wasn't he?"

Clenching his jaw, Jaxson nodded, but it was Chase who answered. "Yes, Garreth is one of our DMs on the East Coast and he's a good dom, but he was just the most recent one of our employees to get caught up in the event. And the so-called-dominant that broke the rules was banned that night, and now he's in jail for the shit he did to his submissives."

"Whoa, what?" One of the DMs sat up straight, alarm making his eyes go wide. "You guys turned him into the cops? For a cell phone?"

"No," Jaxson growled, struggling with his anger as he remembered the things Noah Carver and Garreth had told him about what the bastard had done to those women. "Ethen O'Dowell is in jail for beating the hell out of his submissives, raping them, coercing them into contracts to steal everything they had, while keeping them trapped out on his property. *That* is why the bastard is in jail."

Everyone was silent for a moment, and Madison had turned a sickly pale while Elijah turned red in anger. "He was a fucking member?" the man growled.

Shifting his gaze to the Dungeon Master, Jaxson was satisfied to see the rage simmering there. "We didn't know anything about what he did off premises until one of his subs ran, and Hadlee is the woman Garreth is with now. It was when his other sub escaped that we got the full picture, and now he's in prison."

"Only two fucking years…" Chase muttered, and Jax reached over to grab his lover's hand, gripping it tightly.

"That's all?" Elijah asked, his voice a growl.

"He took a plea deal for five years, eligible for probation in two, which included dropping charges against his ex-submissive Kitty, and Noah Carver." It was only because Chase squeezed his hand that Jaxson was able to keep his own frustration and anger from boiling over. Just the thought that some submissive could be walking around in either of their clubs, terrified and vulnerable, made him sick.

"Wait, is that Carver the whip expert?" A dungeon monitor asked.

"The very same. He and Kitty were together, and he thought she was at Ethen's house. From what I understand, Noah showed up and gave him a taste of his own medicine." Jaxson squeezed Chase's hand until he thought his sub would protest, but Chase barely blinked. It showed just how much the three of them loved each other that his subs let him lean on them when he needed it. "However, I want to be clear, that if any of you suspect that kind of abuse happening here at Black Light, you'll report it to Elijah, and he and I will look into it. Noah is lucky he's not in jail for assault charges."

Elijah nodded, glancing at his DMs. "Absolutely, guys. You don't take shit into your own hands, got it?"

They agreed, but one of them still looked angry. That man spoke next. "Still, how is two years fair for torturing two women?"

Madison scoffed, the color having returned to her cheeks a bit as she glanced at the DM. "Are you kidding? There are rapists that barely get six months. Two to five years is a solid sentence for our justice system."

"It was four women, but only three pressed charges. Still, unfortunately, Madison is correct. We're lucky he'll be off the streets for that long." Jaxson shifted in his seat, suddenly aware of the fact that Madison was the only woman in the room. A room full of men with sadistic tendencies, and he had to swallow down the bitter lump in his throat as he acknowledged just how brave she was to speak up when she wasn't even in the lifestyle. Ethen O'Dowell was the worst kind of monster in his world. Hiding behind BDSM to justify his violence to both the submissives and himself. That wasn't a good dom. Hell, that wasn't a dom at all — he was just an abusive asshole.

And he'd been dragging his *Menagerie* in and out of Black Light for months before the ban.

"Like I said before, the expectation is that if you suspect abuse, you bring it to Elijah's attention. He'll get us involved, and we'll look into it." Jaxson watched as several of the DMs studied the wood grain of the table.

"If that happens, I better be in the loop," Miguel Martinez said seriously. "I'll get it handled one way or another, and the cops may or may not be involved."

All eyes swiveled to their head of security, and the fact that he used to work at The Office with a group of men like Ryder Helms meant that Jaxson had no doubt he could handle something if necessary. *Buried-in-an-unmarked-grave kind of handled.*

"Let's hope we never have to deal with it here at Black Light West, okay?" Jaxson said, trying to deflate the tension of the room. Skimming the notes in front of him, he grasped for something to talk about that didn't involve abused women and legal issues.

Chase squeezed his hand, and Jaxson finally remembered to ease back on the death grip he'd held on his lover. Releasing him, he watched Chase flex his fingers and smile. "Look, Roulette is going to be a lot of fun. It always is! You're going to see some entertaining battles of wills, some really hot scenes, and after the eleven o'clock mark, you can seek out Elijah if you want to play with one of the guests."

The man shrugged solemnly, but Chase continued with that light-hearted smile that always made Jaxson think of the sun.

"Also, if you're still worried about people wanting to participate, the prize has always been a free month of membership. Follow the rules, finish the night, and that's money back in their pocket. And, as dungeon monitors, you have the opportunity to award an extra week of free time for particularly inventive or entertaining scenes."

"Like what?" One of the monitors asked.

"Well, our first year we had one of our lawyers play out an intense scene involving a dunk tank and water-based breath play. I think Alexander and Sienna each got two bonus weeks, didn't they?" Chase asked, glancing at him.

Sighing, Jaxson nodded. "However, we have limited it to *one* bonus week. We're not running a charity here."

"Apparently we're just donating to one," Elijah snarked, and a few laughs rumbled around the table, breaking the heavy tension.

"Apparently we are," Jaxson agreed, smiling a bit at the thought. "I'll ask you all to look into some charities and email over your suggestions. Emma, Chase, and I will pick one before the sign-ups are posted."

"So, if you guys are going to be here this year, who is running Roulette on the East Coast?" Elijah asked.

"Actually, our friends Cash and Samantha Carter have volunteered." Chase laughed. "Cash has always liked the lime light, and Roulette is one of their favorite events. But Emma, Jax, and I are going to record a quick video welcoming people to the event before he starts it."

"Does that mean you're MC'ing the West Coast event?" Madison asked, and Jaxson saw the tension in Chase's shoulders as his sub straightened. Always attuned to his responses, Jax stayed silent to see whether last year's punishment for not speaking up had taken or not.

If not, they had a pretty collection of canes back home to remind his lover.

"Well…" Chase started, glancing at Jaxson as if he'd answer the question for him. *No chance, babe.* Clearing his throat, Chase wiped his hands on his pants, and then pushed a hand through his blond hair. "I mean, I'm open to the idea, it's just—"

"I don't think that's necessary," Madison interrupted cheerfully. "I'm more than happy to MC the event. You two are totally exhausted from being daddies, and, like, it's not the first time I've MC'd an event. Super easy."

Saved by the Valley girl. Jaxson smirked as all the tension left Chase, his sub immediately grabbing onto the offer. "Are you sure? I mean, it's a lot of work. You have to be on *all* night."

"Totally!" she answered with that pageant winning smile, bright blonde hair bouncing as she waved a hand at Chase.

"Yeah, she'll totally fit in with the members showing up dressed like that," one of the DMs mumbled, but they all laughed quietly, and even Elijah was smirking. They were entertained by the idea, and while Jaxson liked the idea of letting Chase relax with him and Emma to enjoy the night… the picture of pretty, peppy Madison in front of the BDSM crowd didn't exactly work.

"I'm sorry, did you say something?" Madison asked, turning to stare daggers at the man who just grinned back at her.

"Nope," he answered, and her cheeks turned bright pink as she turned back to face Chase.

"I've been down to Black Light a number of times, and I'm not an idiot. I have the experience for this, Elijah and the DMs need to be focused, and unless you have some secret volunteer in your back pocket then I'm your best bet." She kept her chin up, but Jaxson's gaze was drawn to her tightly clenched hands, knuckles white as the DMs continued with their quiet jabs.

"Quiet," he snapped, shooting a look at the DMs that appropriately chastised them into silence. Looking her over, he used every one of his dom instincts to evaluate her. She may not be a sub, but she was still easy to read. Madison was nervous, more than a little embarrassed, but he was sure that was because of the dungeon monitors. If her fingers weren't intertwined so tightly, he was sure her

17

hands would be shaking, a result of the adrenaline spike from their mocking challenge. "You understand that you'll be required to discuss various activities on the stage, and that any of your personal beliefs about them can't show on your face, much less be voiced?"

"Like I would ever—"

"I'm going to need to hear a *yes*, Madison," Jaxson cut her off, not realizing the dominant edge to his voice until her blush darkened, and she replied softly.

"Yes, sir." Madison swallowed, and he saw Chase turn to look at him out of the corner of his eye. His husband had seen the same thing he had in that moment, and it meant a lot of things that they didn't have time to address in that moment. All that really mattered was that it seemed Madison would fit in better in Black Light than they may have guessed. "I'm really happy to do it," she added, attempting to fill the silence.

"Then I think we'd all very much appreciate if you would MC, as long as you adequately cover your responsibilities for the night," Jaxson answered, smiling when he heard Chase let out a tense breath.

"Thank you so much, Madison. I can't even tell you how nervous I've been about this, and I've been trying to think of someone who could fill our shoes like Cash and Samantha are on the East Coast." Chase's voice sounded strained, and Jax glanced at him to see his sub's eyes welling with emotion. "We've just been under so much stress this past year, and now we have the twins at home, and getting to just sit with my husband and wife and *enjoy myself* is the biggest gift you could have given me. I just — really, thank you."

Madison's tension faded as she reached past Miguel to touch the table when she couldn't quite reach Chase's hand. "Aww, Chase! Like, I am always willing to help when I can! For real."

"Like I said, we are grateful Madison, and it's nice to have that settled." Looking at Chase, he lowered his tone. "Although there are *other* things I'll be addressing later."

"But I took the help!" Chase argued, and Jax's hand was in his soft blond hair, craning Chase's head back with a sharp jerk before he'd even finished the complaint.

"Did I, or did I not, explain to you last year that if you have concerns, that my expectation is for you to bring them to me?" His tone was stern, serious, and full of the dominance that always made his sub melt.

"You did, sir," Chase said through a tense throat, only exaggerated by the angle of his head, but Chase knew better than to move and ease the strain.

"And what happens when you keep something from Emma and I?" he asked, enjoying the flush in his submissive's face, already imagining what he would do once they were home.

"Punishment." There was no tremor of fear in Chase's voice, in fact, it was softened by the rampant need that turned it into almost a purr. *Fuck, they all needed this.* Chase's mistake had his dom-side already turning over the various options for punishment. He'd make both of his subs strip, have Emma hold Chase's hands as he bent over the end of the bed, where he'd use the punishment paddle... or a cane again. A reminder for his masochistic husband that continuing to keep his mouth shut over the Roulette proceedings would leave his ass sore in more ways than one. Just as his mind started to wander to the vision of Chase licking Emma to completion while he slammed into him from behind — Elijah cleared his throat.

"That's right," Jaxson growled, releasing his hold on Chase's hair, watching as his sub's eyes loosely focused on his. Pupils already dilated, just as caught up in arousal as he was.

This meeting needed to end.

"Shit," one of the DMs mumbled, and the predatory smile on Jaxson's face wasn't fading. Slipping into his dominance had been better than any cup of coffee. He felt wide awake now.

"I'm going to summarize our decisions so we're all on the same page, and then I'm ending this meeting so I can go handle my naughty submissive." Jaxson may have switched back to his professional voice, but his cock was already tenting the front of his slacks under the table as Chase shuddered beside him.

"Sounds like a smart idea, boss," Elijah answered, grinning as Chase focused on the table.

Looking around the table, he saw half the DMs smirking, Madison was *still* blushing while watching Chase with more curiosity than he'd expected, and Miguel was simply smiling. Enjoying the front row seat to the dynamic he'd been around more than enough since the day he was hired.

"So, we've all agreed that Celebrity Roulette will be the Black Light West event for this year. Members will bid on celebrity participants until a few days before the event so that we have time to notify the winners and the runner-ups. We'll choose a charity for the bidding, but will keep an admin fee. Standard club safe words only, 7:15 start time, and no employees of Black Light will quit working to involve themselves with a sub. Have I missed anything?" Jaxson asked, eager to grab Chase by the back of the neck and walk him back to the pool house they'd made their own.

"At the risk of earning a larger punishment, sir, we did move up the number of limits to five this year because of the additional activities." Chase was quiet, keeping his voice soft and submissive, and the sound made Jaxson's balls tighten.

"That's true, we'll have it listed on the sign-up form. Anything else?" he asked, forcing his eyes to roam the table instead of Chase's body.

"Uh, this is more a request than anything you missed." One of the DMs spoke up, shrugging as he continued. "But my brother and I make implements, equipment, stuff that several of the members have started buying or placing orders for. If we're doing a silent auction before the event for the participants, could we also do one during the event for BDSM stuff? Have some of our items up for bid?"

"What's your name?" Jaxson asked.

"Tyler," the DM replied, sitting up in his chair. "My brother is Brian."

"Does Brian work here?" he asked, and Tyler shook his head.

"Nah, he works part-time at a couple of other clubs when he's got the time, but he's a firefighter. Schedule isn't consistent enough for a steady gig, and the membership fee here is more than a bit out of his range." Tyler shrugged, but now that Jaxson's brain was awake his mind was firing on all cylinders.

"Elijah, see what we can do about getting him *here* part-time instead of whatever clubs he's working at. It's always a good idea to have someone trained in emergency care on site." Jaxson wasn't asking, but Elijah didn't seem bothered by it. He just nodded, and glanced at Tyler to say something quietly.

"As for the on-site silent auction, I think that's a great idea. Work with Madison to get it organized. I'm sure we have enough connections with suppliers and craftsman in the industry to stock the auction well, and it gives them free advertising at Black Light." Jaxson scanned the room again, trying to think of anything else they might have left off, but now all he could imagine was the sounds his subs would be making soon enough.

"I think we have everything settled for now," Madison replied, tucking her iPad back into her large Hermès bag.

"All right then, everyone out." The command got everyone moving, and there was no doubt it was an order. Dom-voice had turned back on without Jaxson even thinking about it, and he pinned Chase to his seat with a look as everyone filed out around him.

"Sir—"

Jaxson leaned forward and caught Chase by his throat, squeezing just enough to silence him and feel the rapid pulse under his fingers. "Oh no. You're going to be quiet until we get back to the house, and then you're going to tell Emma what you kept from us while she strips you. Then you're going to take her clothes off, and you're going to bend over the bed and present your naughty ass for punishment. Do you understand?"

Chase nodded, his cheeks red, and his cock already hard in his pants. Grinning, Jaxson stood and pulled him up as well. Kicking the chair out of the way, he pushed him back to the wall, crowding him as his sub let out a quiet groan of need.

"After I cane your ass, I'm going to watch you lick our gorgeous wife until she comes over and over." The need in Chase's eyes was vibrant, and he let that predatory grin spread as he leaned closer until his lips brushed Chase's ear. "And if you're a very good boy, I'll fuck you while you taste Emma."

Another groan, louder this time as Chase's knees almost buckled, but he held him firmly. Nodding insistently, Chase bit down on his lip to keep from speaking.

"Good boy," Jaxson growled and switched his grip to the back of Chase's neck, pushing him to the door so they could walk back to the house. As close as it was on the club property, it still felt way too far as they headed to the exit, and he couldn't wait to get his subs in position for a real session. They might be exhausted new parents, but there was nothing quite like a little reminder of roles to give everyone the break they needed.

Hell, Khloe kept saying how much she loved the twins, maybe watching them for the night would satisfy those urges for a while.

And then — sleep. For all three of them. With Emma between him and Chase, completing them like she always had.

VALENTINE'S DAY EVENING

"*M*adison! Telephone!"

Madison was running late. She didn't have time to deal with the media. News outlets and entertainment reporters had been ringing the phone off the hook to Runway for the last few weeks, anxious to get the scoop on that night's epic Valentine's Day event.

The last thing they needed was more publicity.

They hadn't sold tickets in advance. She wouldn't be making the same freaking mistake again. They would be getting the ticket sales out of the way weeks earlier next year.

Nalani Ione, the property's head of housekeeping and one of the handful of their employees to live on property, stepped up to where Madison had been reviewing the table of welcome swag. The beautiful Polynesian woman reached out to pass the wireless phone set to her boss.

"Like, who is it? I need to..." Madison cut herself off mid-sentence and glanced around the expansive foyer. Several of the part-time employees they'd hired for the popular Runway event were setting up the crowd-organizing stanchions to keep the crush of attendees from turning the wrong direction when they walked in the front doors.

She kept her voice soft as she leaned in to finish her sentence. "...

get changed and downstairs. I don't know what I was thinking offering to MC the event at Black Light on the biggest night Runway is gonna have since, like, we opened."

Nalani smiled softly. The women had gotten to know each other better the last few months. Unlike Madison, Nalani was more comfortable staying in the background, but she had proven she could totally step up into the spotlight when necessary. "It's the chief of the Beverly Hills Police Department. I tried to see what he wanted, but he says he'll only talk with you," her assistant for the night answered apologetically.

"Shit." She took the phone and answered with the agitation the jerk on the other end of the phone deserved. "What is it now, Doug? Did one of our patrons jaywalk this time? Or maybe they drove one mile over the speed limit?"

"Cut the crap, Madison. This is serious," the older voice groused.

"It's, like, always serious with you. You should be thrilled Runway is such a huge success. I'm sure the added revenues for the city are helping pay your bonus check this year."

"Are you kidding? Any added revenue is eaten up by the overtime I have to pay out to cover the traffic problems in the blocks surrounding the mansion. The damn city council never should have changed the zoning to allow a public business in a residential neighborhood," he whined like a child.

The bastard found a way to fit that complaint into every conversation they had. She didn't have time for repeats.

"Is that why you called? If so, I suggest you take this up with the city council. I'm busy."

"Oh, believe me, I've tried. That cocky bastard Jaxson Davidson has a lock on every last one of them. I don't get it. He's a real prick."

"It's Mr. Cartwright-Davidson, and you're just jealous." Madison grinned, understanding that since all but one of the city council members were now regulars at Black Light, they would not be in a hurry to threaten their sexual playground. Handing out those free memberships had been some of the best money the trio had spent.

The bark of laughter at the other end of the phone annoyed her. "Yeah, right."

"Is this why you called? To let me know my boss is a prick?"

The head of police got serious again. "No. I called to warn you that you have exactly fifteen minutes to clear the traffic jam surrounding your property before I give the green light to start passing out tickets for impeding traffic to the hundreds of cars clogging the streets around your property."

Madison glanced at the clock on her cell phone. Shit, it wasn't even five-thirty yet.

"We aren't opening the gates until five-thirty tonight. The party doesn't start until seven."

"Wrong. You're gonna open the gates now and start moving the crowd along. Residents are calling complaining that they can't get to their home. There are cars and limos double and triple parking close to your gate, making it impossible to pass. And there are people trapped trying to get in and out of the Beverly Hills Country Club."

"Why are you calling me with this? You should have called Miguel Martinez. He's in charge of security."

"Yeah, right. We all know you're in charge of everything and everyone there, except maybe Jaxson Davidson, and that bastard isn't answering his phone. I tried him first."

"It's Jaxson Cartwright-Davidson and that's because he pays people to handle shit like this."

"Exactly. So handle it. You have fifteen minutes." The call ended abruptly.

"Dammit."

Nalani had stayed nearby, knowing Madison would be turning Runway over to her and Avery for the night soon anyway. And unfortunately, this particular problem was impacting both Runway and Black Light. "Well?" she prompted.

"You need to call Miguel and let him know we need to open the gates and start clearing the traffic jam from the neighborhood."

"Okay, I can do that," Nalani replied, still completely calm.

"At least the weather is cooperating. I still don't want to let partiers inside too early tonight until we are ready, but they can start lining up at the front door." She took a deep breath and resumed her action item list. "Make sure Miguel gets men out directing traffic, too. Not just at the gate, but in the streets surrounding us. Thank God we had DJ Yellowtail sleep in one of the guest rooms last night. Give him a heads up that, like, we want him to start early. Oh, and we need to let Avery know to move the catering timeline up. And…"

"Stop! I can handle this stuff. You need to head up and get changed. We both know a good portion of the cars fighting to get here are heading down to Black Light anyway since the event is supposed to start at seven-fifteen. Let Avery and me handle things up here tonight."

It felt wrong to be dumping so many problems onto the woman, but even so, there was no way Madison was going to bow out of her mistress of ceremonies duties that night. She'd been looking forward to it for months. Her pulse quickened at the promise of the sexual adventure ahead of her. Acknowledging she would let Nalani take charge, Madison handed her the phone. "Thanks again, for jumping in to help out up here tonight."

"It's a great change of pace for me. I'm actually having fun." Nalani's brown eyes twinkled.

"That's good. I won't be able to keep my cell phone with me tonight so you'll have to call down to the bartenders and have them find me if you need anything."

"Just go. We've staffed up and have everything organized. I'm sure all will go smoothly and if not, we'll let you know."

Madison leaned in for a quick air-hug that ended up little more than their shoulder's bumping before she took off at a fast pace towards the open, winding staircase that was the focal point in the foyer of the mansion. Her high-heeled pumps clicked on the marble as she rushed up.

Since her own home was just a ten-minute drive from the mansion, Madison rarely had occasion to stay over at her place of employment, but she'd decided to make an exception tonight. Not just because she would be working as MC for Black Light until late, but more-so because it was Valentine's Day and she had high hopes for her own romantic end of the holiday... if Trevor McLean cooperated.

She used her electronic master key to open the heavy door to her suite. Despite already taking one shower that day, Madison headed straight to the large bathroom where she'd dumped all of her belongings earlier in the day. Catching a glimpse of herself in the long mirror, she had to smile at the transformation she planned on pulling off.

After turning on the water to warm, Madison starting stripping the designer, floral business suit off, not stopping until she'd removed even the lacy bra and panty set from Victoria's Secret. She stepped directly into the spray of steamy water, anxious to wash her straight-laced businesswoman persona down the drain for the evening.

Tonight, she would be assuming a new and improved role.

Mistress Madison.

She'd done her research and couldn't wait to make her grand entrance at Black Light that evening. While she'd popped downstairs occasionally after the rush at Runway died down, it had always been quick visits as an employee.

No, more like a *voyeur*.

Tonight would be different. She would not only be participating, but in many ways, she would be the center of attention—a place she was ordinarily very comfortable. But tonight would be more exciting. Naughty.

And she couldn't wait.

She spent the next hour or so transforming herself. When she finally stood before the full-length mirror on the back of the bathroom door, her reflection shocked even herself.

Gone was her flowing blonde hair and conservative, feminine business suit, replaced by the most sinful outfit she had ever worn. She'd spent a small fortune on her makeover, yet the second she saw the results, she knew it had been worth every single penny.

She started at the floor, inspecting the thigh-high black leather boots with three-inch spiked heels. The small jeweled buckles at the ankle and top added just a splash of fashion that would twinkle in the unique lighting of Black Light.

Moving higher, the skin-tight, faux-leather bodysuit hugged every inch of her curves. She'd purposefully chosen the one with long sleeves and a high neck, not because she was too shy to show off her body, but because it fit the Mistress Madison persona. Regardless, this outfit fit her like a second skin, leaving nothing to the imagination. The design lifted and showcased her ample breasts and highlighted her hourglass figure. She turned ninety degrees so she could admire the way the unique material shimmered as the suit clung to the curve of her ass, extending just a few inches down her legs. That left about four inches of her tanned skin peeking out above her boots.

The transformation of her face and hair had taken some practice. She'd spent hours on Tumblr studying the hair and makeup of women in various BDSM accounts, and had settled on pulling her long flowing hair up into a high and tight pony tail, blow drying the thick strands until they were pin straight and hanging far down her back. It worked perfectly with the thick eyeliner—black, smoky eye shadow— long, fake eyelashes—and deep crimson lips.

Topping it all off was the thin riding crop she grasped in her left hand.

Hello, Mistress Madison.

As if they knew she was finally ready, her cell phone beeped with an incoming text from Elijah. *'Gsts arriving. Jax looking 4 u. Chase gonna throw up if not here soon.'*

Madison smiled at the typical Elijah text, always abbreviated. At least she could understand this one. She shot off a reply: *'On my way,' and then set her phone on the counter.*

She'd be leaving it here in her room since electronics weren't allowed in Black Light. Grabbing the electronic keycard and tube of lipstick she'd need, she tucked them into the only place she could carry anything—jammed between her leg and the inside of her high boots.

With a deep breath, she took one final look in the mirror and gave herself an impromptu pep talk. "You've totally got this, girl."

28

~

MINUTES LATER SHE STEPPED INTO THE SMALL ELEVATOR THAT WAS THE fastest route to Black Light from the third floor. In addition to using her electronic keycard to identify herself, the elevator also required her retinal imprint before it would acknowledge the basement as its destination.

Madison used the short ride down to calm her nerves. She could hear the pounding music that had already started at Runway as the elevator passed the first floor, heading into the bowels of the mansion.

When the doors opened, the dim lighting of the sex club stood out in stark contrast to the brightly lit lift. As the elevator was located away from the normal entrance in the bar of the club, she saw just a few people as she stepped into the open play area.

No one seemed to pay much attention to her until she arrived at the drawn velvet curtain that separated the dungeon room from the bar area. As soon as she pulled the fabric aside, she came face to face with Elijah.

It was in that moment she wished she'd snuck in her cellphone just so she could have captured the dumbstruck look on her co-worker's face as he recognized her.

"Eh... Madison?"

While most women, including herself under most circumstances, might feel sexually harassed by the feral look on the Dungeon Master's face, tonight Madison took his stunned silence as he ogled her as the highest compliment. It was too tempting to fuck with him. She reached up with her right index finger, placing her long, pointed fingernail under his chin to close his slack jaw. "You look surprised to see me. I told you I was on my way down."

"Yeah, but... I didn't... I mean... never seen..." His rambling trailed off as he shook his head, trying to pull it together.

"I'm headed to the theater. Get back to work, Elijah," she demanded, taking off before the DM snapped out of his haze and realized she'd just dommed the Master Dom.

She grinned as his mouth slid open again, too stunned to come up with a retort before she was moving around the curtain.

The bar area was already almost full of people and it wasn't even seven yet. They still had fifteen minutes before the event would start.

Madison felt the eyes of the crowd on her as she pushed her way through the members. The space was condensed enough that everyone already bumped against each other. The closer she got to the theater, the more hands she felt brushing against her as she weaved through the bodies, while trying not to look too hard for Khloe Monroe. It wasn't necessarily that she wanted to run into the A-list actress, but she knew that where Khloe went, Trevor McLean wouldn't be too far behind.

She needed to let her obsession with the burly bodyguard go. They'd gone out a few times, but then he'd had to travel to the East Coast for a few months when his boss had to be in New York... and they hadn't stayed in touch. He'd played the gentleman, insisting they keep things casual, and in theory she'd agreed — but the longer he'd been gone the less she liked the arrangement. With Ryder and Khloe back in Cali, she had high hopes of picking up where they'd left off tonight.

"Holy shit, bossman wasn't kidding." The comment had come from one of the dungeon monitors, Tyler. He was blocking the entrance to the theater and didn't move without making her an offer. "I'll let you use that crop on me any time, baby."

Falling deeper into her Dominatrix persona, Madison stepped closer until their chests brushed. He was a good eight inches taller than her so she had to crane her neck back to meet his eyes. Feeling empowered by the nature of the club, Madison dressed him down. "That's Mistress Madison to you. I'm nobody's baby."

She didn't miss the widening of his eyes or how his breath caught as he answered with a soft, "Okay."

"Not okay. Say 'yes, ma'am.'"

The normally dominant man finally snapped out of his temporary stupor at her transformation, but he continued to play along. "For tonight I'll call you whatever you'd like if it will get me a date after the event."

She let the sly smile play on her lips as she crushed his hopes. "I have plans, but thanks."

"Lucky bastard." Finally remembering they both had work to do, Tyler stepped aside and ushered her in with a grand sweep of his arm. "After you, ma'am."

Madison felt powerful. I mean, like, she wasn't a pushover on a regular day or anything, but tonight was different.

And she liked it.

A hint of disappointment threatened to cloud her happiness when she realized Trevor wasn't there yet to admire her new persona. She was going to be sorely disappointed if she ended up in that king-sized bed alone later. She wanted Trevor McLean, and by God, tonight was the night she would seal the deal.

"It's about time you got here. We expected you thirty minutes ago." It was her boss, Jaxson, dressing her down. The only indication that he even noticed her metamorphosis to Dominatrix was a quick up and down of her outfit. Unlike the other men she'd encountered, he clearly only had eyes for his husband and wife, which made her like him that much more.

"I'm here in plenty of time. Anything happening I need to know about?"

Jaxson took a stack of notecards out of his suit-jacket pocket and handed them to her. "Here's your cue cards and notes on the contestants. We were moving stuff around on the stage and I didn't want them to get knocked off and put out of order."

"Thanks," she said as she reached to take them from him. "Where are we with the arrival of the contestants?"

"Per the last update from security at the gate, all are accounted for but one, although some are still walking in from the parking lot. It was a good idea to use the golf carts to help ferry people tonight."

"Yeah, we have the carts. Why not use them?" The small talk was making the butterflies in her tummy flutter. It had been a long time since she'd felt the jitters before being in front of a crowd. It didn't take a genius to figure out it was because she was out of her element tonight, but she'd done her homework. Now that she was down here, she just wanted to get things started as soon as possible.

"Madison! You look amazing! I almost didn't recognize you."

She turned to find that Chase and Emma had joined them from the other side of the theater. She wasn't sure which one of them looked better. The few times Madison had spent any time around the new parents, they had looked so wiped out. But not tonight.

The trio had come to play.

"Emma! Chase!" They did an awkward group hug as she gushed over them. "I was hoping you'd be here tonight."

Chase grinned as he pulled out of their hug. "Are you kidding me? We wouldn't miss roulette. I'm really looking forward to just being a spectator tonight. Thanks again for taking on the MC role."

Before Madison could reply, Emma whistled an unladylike catcall before adding, "This outfit is going to have many men, and probably a few women, here fighting over you before the night is over."

She chuckled as she added, "There better not be any fighting. I don't want to have to use my crop." She waved it around for good measure, hoping she didn't look as inexperienced as she felt.

"Don't kid yourself. Most of the people here would love nothing more than to feel your crop across their bare ass," Chase teased.

The pleasant sexual anticipation she felt settling low in her abdomen reminded her that she wasn't at Runway tonight. She gripped the leather tightly in her hand in an attempt to hide how her hands had started to tremble. What the fuck? She needed to keep control.

Trying to stay focused on her friends, she changed the subject back to them. "I don't think I've seen all three of you here together since you had the twins. You must be happy to have a night off parenthood."

She noticed the flash of panic in Emma's eyes just as Chase wrapped his arm around his wife's waist and hugged her to him.

It was Chase who answered. "It's kind of a big night for us. It's the first time we let the nanny take the twins over to my mom's house alone. They are going to spend the night there... away from us... and Emma is..."

"Freaking out," the beautiful brunette finished.

Chase tried to comfort her. "They are in good hands. And my mom is on cloud nine."

"But, I just don't see why she couldn't have come to our house and then be there when we get home tonight."

The crack of Jaxson's paddle-like hand against Emma's curvy ass was loud enough to tell anyone around them that it hadn't been a love tap. Like a ninja, he moved in close on Emma's other side—the men sandwiching their wife between them as he delivered his lecture. "We've discussed this. Alicia and Andrew are almost six months old and we haven't had even one single night alone, with just the three of us in the house, since we brought them home from the hospital. If it isn't our parents or friends visiting, there's a nanny or a security guard or a chef." Jaxson paused, his frustration shining through in his continuing rant. "For one fucking night I wanna be able to walk naked through the house. I'm going to enjoy using every fucking implement in our toy chest that's been gathering dust on my subs' sexy bodies. You're both gonna be able to scream as loud as you want to as I pound out my pent-up sexual tension on you both. Got it?"

Madison smiled through her beet red face at the lusty look on Chase's face as he actually swayed at his dominant's stern promise.

"Well alright then. How long do we have to stay before we can head home?" Chase asked, a naughty grin on his tan face.

Emma was less convinced. "You promised I can call for an update after we leave the party, right?" she asked, genuine anxiety in her voice.

Jaxson's face softened, leaning closer to talk against her ear. With the crowd pressing in around them, Madison almost missed his promise. "Of course you can call for an update. I know you won't be able to relax and have any fun unless you know everything is going okay."

Emma turned, tears in her unique violet eyes. "I love you, you know that?"

"I'll remind you of that the next time my asshole gene rears its ugly head." Finally, Jaxson had a smile on his face.

Emma stood on her tippy toes to plant a kiss on her husband's lips before informing him, "I happen to love your asshole gene."

Madison probably should have felt like an interloper witnessing the very personal exchange between her bosses. Instead, she felt privileged to be allowed into their inner circle. With the paparazzi as rabid as ever, the trio worked hard to keep their private lives private. Knowing the great lengths they went to warmed Madison's heart to see how much they trusted her. Not just with running their club, but with keeping their most exclusive secrets.

"So, you have any last minute questions?" Chase prompted Madison, bringing her back to the pressing crowd piling into the too-small room.

"Yeah. Is someone sending all of the celebrities up to the front now before we start, or will I have to call them and wait for them weave their way through the crowds? I mean, like, it's bad enough we'll have to wait for the winning bidders to come up to the front when I call them."

Jaxson answered with a nod behind her. "It looks like Tyler has most of them up there to your stage left, already. I can see now we're going to have to move this out into the main room next year. It's getting too crowded in here and it's hot as hell, and we haven't even started yet."

The words weren't even out of his mouth when a loud screech filled the packed theater. All eyes turned to the aisle along the right side of the room where a circle of people were looking down at the floor of the aisle. Madison and the trio moved in unison towards the crowd to try to find out the source of the sobbing that was cutting through the din of excited chatter.

"My ankle! I think it's broken, you bitch!"

She couldn't see who had screamed the curse, but Madison had a perfect view of the smirk on the face of a woman who had been sitting in an aisle seat since she'd arrived to the theater. She looked familiar, but Madison couldn't quite place where she'd seen the sour looking woman.

"Well, maybe you shouldn't have worn such slutty 'fuck-me' pumps. You clearly can't walk in them."

The injured woman wasn't taking the insults being flung at her. "This is low, even for you, Carrie. You tripped me with your umbrella on purpose, you jealous bitch!"

The already pressing crowd was getting downright dangerous in the confined area. Several dungeon monitors had moved in and worked to clear some of the spectators to prevent a trampling. Only once they had succeeded in moving some of the members did Madison get a look at the crying woman on the floor. She recognized her immediately as one of that night's winning bidders.

Kneeling next to the woman, Tyler inspected a swollen and red circle on the outside of Stephanie Reynolds's ankle. "I hate to say it, but we're gonna need to get you to the hospital for x-rays. It looks like you could have a break here." He touched the area of her injury and her wails of pain filled the room.

"I don't care, I'm not leaving! I won my night with Carlos Ferrara fair and square and I'll be damned if she's gonna try to pull a Nancy Kerrigan on me to try to take my spot." The crying woman shouted so all could hear.

It was in that moment the umbrella owner's identity came back to her. She was Carrie Boughten, the president of baseball MVP Carlos Ferrara's fan club. She had made a complete ass of herself during the bidding process, arguing with the staff of Black Light several times when she refused to accept the answer that no one, including presidents of fan clubs, got to automatically win a bid on one of their favorite celebrities. The bidding between these two women for the popular MLB pitcher had been some of the most heated. Stephanie, the winner, had literally won by putting in a bid only one dollar higher than Carrie's less than a minute before the auction ended.

In light of the current evidence, Madison had no problem believing the smirking woman had intentionally injured her competition in order to take her place in roulette. Madison didn't have to inject her thoughts, though, because Tyler had things under control.

"I've been standing at the stage keeping an eye on things and I had a perfect view as this woman purposefully hit her ankle with her umbrella." The dungeon monitor looked at Jaxson for direction. "Want me to call the police to have her booked for assault?"

"Assault? Are you kidding me?" Carrie balked as Tyler's threat finally wiped the smug smile off the bitch's face. Immediately, she jumped to her feet to get up in the large DM's face.

"I heard my name. What's going on here?"

Madison couldn't see the man speaking from behind her in the crowd, but she knew from Carrie's suddenly bright smile that it was Carlos himself.

"Hello, Carlos. We were just sorting out who would be the winning bidder to play with you tonight." The sickly-sweet tone of the perpetrator was laughable.

"Hello, Carrie. I didn't expect to see you tonight. I was pretty sure my threat to get a restraining order the last time I caught you trying to break into my property had gotten through to you." He groaned. "I'm not even that into BDSM, but I had to join an exclusive club like Black Light just to get the hell away from you following me whenever I leave my house. How the fuck did you even find out about tonight's event?"

"I'm the president of your fan club. I know everything about you, Carlos. It's my job," she bragged.

"Well, consider yourself fired. You've gone too far this time." He pushed forward and kneeled down beside the injured woman on the floor. "Are you going to be okay?"

It was Tyler who answered. "We should get her ankle checked out. It could be broken."

The handsome, bearded baseball player squatted down to be closer to the injured contestant. "I'm Carlos. What's your name?"

Despite her injuries, the attention from her chosen celebrity lit up her tear-stained face. "Stephanie."

"Nice to meet you, Stephanie." Carlos moved closer and

effortlessly scooped the crying woman up into his arms. "Looks like you just lost one couple for tonight, Jaxson. I have a driver and a car waiting outside. I'll see that Stephanie makes it to the hospital and gets checked out."

Jaxson countered, "We have staff that can take her."

Carlos was already on his feet when he answered. "No need. There is no way in hell I'd play with Carrie anyway and I feel bad I didn't press charges earlier. I knew she was nutso."

The packed crowd that had pressed in to catch the drama parted like the Red Sea to make a path for the tall athlete to weave through to the exit.

Jaxson turned to one of the security guards who'd shown up to help. "Follow behind them to the hospital. Stick with them and make sure she is well cared for." Expanding his comments, he spoke to the wider group of people surrounding the point of drama. "And I'd like everyone who witnessed the assault to submit a short, written statement with what you saw. I promise your identities will be kept confidential, but I want to be sure to document the events so we can hold Ms. Boughten responsible for her actions tonight."

Miguel, the head of security joined the crowd at that moment. "My guys filled me in. I'll be happy to escort Ms. Boughten upstairs and outside. I have a police officer waiting to take her downtown for some questioning."

The dark-haired woman started shrieking as security clamped onto her arms and began dragging her out. "Are you crazy? You can't treat me like this! I've done nothing wrong!"

Madison could hear her shouting even after they were out of the theater, and Jaxson tried to bring order to the room. "Sorry for the early drama, folks. I promise the rest of the night will have less of an 'assault and battery vibe' and more of a 'naughty sub gets punished' feel."

His barb was met with good-natured chuckles as club members turned back towards the stage, anxious to get the real show started.

"Well, that was exciting," Madison noted.

"That's one way to put it," Chase answered under his breath, finally releasing Emma who he'd pulled into his arms protectively while they were unsure what was going on.

"Let's get this show on the road. It's after seven now. I want us all to debrief at the end of the night just in case Stephanie Reynolds decides to sue us."

Madison shook her head, trying to shake off the drama and get back into a party frame of mind. As MC, she would need to help lift the more somber mood that now blanketed the too-hot room. She needed to get everyone focused on sexy fun as soon as possible.

Weaving her way through the pushing crowd to get back to the small stage at the front of the long room, she psyched herself up with each step she took, consciously letting the dominatrix persona she had chosen for the night wash over her. She had her short leather crop lead the way, swishing into small crevices between the bodies, lightly slapping the flesh it met until a path opened for her to slide through.

By the time she stood on the stage facing the excited crowd, she was once again Mistress Madison. Jaxson, Chase and Emma had followed her and her boss moved behind the microphone stand.

"Time to get this party started!" Jaxson called out. The PA system squeaked feedback and he moved back a few inches to avoid a repeat.

"Thank you all for coming tonight. As I think everyone knows, this is our first Valentine Roulette event here on the West Coast, but the third annual event is already halfway over on the East Coast. I spoke with the host there for tonight, Cash Carter, about an hour ago and he let me know that they had to start turning members without pre-bought tickets away at the door because the club was reaching capacity. I love hearing how much our members enjoy roulette night, and I hope you're all just as excited."

Jaxson waited until the smattering of excited applause died down before taking his eyes off the crowd. Then he turned to his left as he continued. "Chase, Emma, and I are extra excited to share tonight with you here at Black Light West."

He paused and while she couldn't see his face from her angle behind him, she could feel the sexual tension emanating from the trio.

As the pause extended, catcalls from the crowd broke out, pulling Jaxson back to his speech.

"Sorry, I got a bit lost there looking forward to all of the naughty things I plan on witnessing from our participants, and the dirty things I'll be doing to my husband and wife later tonight."

The crowd laughed as he cleared his throat and got back to business.

"So welcome all. Members. Guests. Contestants. Voyeurs. Tonight is about letting loose. Experimenting. Trying new things." He then turned towards the grouping of celebrities that Tyler had gathered together at the edge of the stage. "And a special thanks to our celebrities that agreed to play in tonight's event. As I think everyone is aware, we tweaked roulette just a bit for our West Coast club, and for the first time added the auction component. We are still compiling our final numbers, but I'm very proud to announce that we will be donating over three-hundred thousand dollars to charity." The room burst into a raucous round of applause.

Once the racket faded, Jaxson continued addressing the celebrity contestants. "Because of your willingness to play with some very generous fans, battered women and children of Southern California will receive funds to help them as they try to get their lives back on track after being in abusive situations. Emma, Chase, and I chose a women's shelter charity intentionally to help shine a light on the stark differences between our chosen consensual BDSM lifestyle and abusive relationships."

A supportive round of applause once again had Jaxson pausing.

"So, without further ado, I want to introduce everyone to our Mistress of Ceremonies for the night, Madison Taylor. You may recognize her as the manager of Runway upstairs where she runs a very tight ship. Tonight, she is our own Mistress Madison."

Her pulse had been pounding harder as her boss spoke, but when he finally turned towards her, a broad smile across his face, Madison knew she was on. Taking a deep breath, she stepped forward to take her spot behind the microphone stand. Jaxson was kind enough to lower the mic over a foot to get it to the right height before he moved to the side to join his husband and wife.

"Good evening, ladies and gentlemen, and thank you for coming. Like, I know it's hotter than hell with us jammed into the theater together, so let's get this show on the road so we can all spread out." She turned to the celebrities to finish her thought. "And I know you're all very anxious to find out who has won the honor of playing with you tonight."

She returned her gaze to the crowd as she continued. "But I'm sure that the people most anxious to get rolling tonight are the winning bidders. Not only do you have the excitement of unknown play to look forward to, like, I know how fun it is to finally meet your favorite celebrities! Tonight is a unique opportunity for you to get to know your play partners on a deeper level than most fans ever get to.

"So, before I start matching our couples and having them spin for their first kink, let's review some basic rules to make sure everyone is on the same page. First, I'll be calling each celebrity up here in a random order and then I'll announce his or her winning play partner. If for some reason the winner is not available, we did invite the runner-ups to be here tonight. Each couple will then drop a ball into our modified roulette wheel, which will determine their first scene for the night.

"The wheel has thirty-seven different kinks on it ranging from rather normal sexual kinks like spanking, or one of my favorites, oral sex—" Madison abruptly cut herself off, losing her train of thought as she felt the panic fluttering in her chest. *Shit.* She totally hadn't meant to say that. She could feel the full-body blush betraying how uncharacteristically nervous she was. Dammit, she just needed to stay focused and avoid adlibbing.

Madison cleared her throat and forced a smile so she could continue. "There are also more advanced kinks on the wheel like knife and needle play. Each contestant was given the opportunity to list five hard limits from the wheel that they could opt out of. If the wheel lands on any of the hard limits for either partner, we'll spin the roulette wheel again until a scene is decided. Couples will need to stay in that scene for a minimum of thirty minutes and then they can decide if they want to continue there, or return here to the theater to give the wheel another turn. Couples can drop a new ball as often as every thirty minutes if they so choose, but remember, you take a chance of rolling a kink you may not like as much," she warned. "Play will end at eleven. Any partners still together at that time will each win one free month of membership at Black Light.

"A couple other housekeeping reminders. We are using house safe words tonight for all play. That means the standard traffic light system of green, yellow, and red will be observed by all playing couples so our dungeon monitors will be able to, like, keep everyone safe.

"Now, for those of you here to watch, that doesn't mean you don't get to have any fun yourselves. We hope you will all disperse to watch your favorite scenes while enjoying the free-flowing champagne and appetizers.

"Not to leave you out of the auction, we have several tables filled with BDSM themed items set up out in the bar area. Everyone is invited to bid on the items throughout the night and the highest bidder for each item at eleven will get to take their winning item home when they leave. Like, be generous as we will be adding all proceeds from tonight's silent auction to our charity total.

"Now, as you know, we have the three specialty rooms that normally house schoolroom or nursery play, heavy-duty dungeon play, and medical or clinical play. Tonight, we may need to either share these spaces or even convert the rooms into alternate play areas depending on the luck of the wheel. Couples are encouraged to get creative, using the platforms in the main club area to set up your scenes or even the spaces around the pool and steam sauna. Don't worry though, the dungeon monitors will be helping contestants find locations and props for their scenes."

Madison looked down at her cue cards for the first time, making sure she wasn't forgetting important details. She picked up her instructions by adding, "You'll be happy to know we also invested some of the proceeds from tonight's event to expand on the costumes and props available to all members going forward. We also hired an award-winning make-up and costume designer duo to assist with everything so please stop by and see them if you need help with your scenes.

"For those of you watching, we have a special treat for you. As you know, Black Light West has its own Red Light District. If you are here without a play partner but still find yourself... well..." Madison's voice quavered. Dammit. She could feel the blood rushing to her face with embarrassment. Exactly what she didn't want to happen, but she took a breath and forged ahead. "If you find yourself in need of relief, there will be several holes for your use along the Red Light wall on your way to the back of the club."

She hated how she glanced down again, not to check her notes this time, but to avoid the heated looks coming her way from the crowd. She felt like such a newbie in front of the experienced BDSM crowd. When she looked out at them again, she was ready wrap up her comments when she saw two people sliding into the very back of the room.

Actress Khloe Monroe and her handsome, yet scary, Dom Ryder Helms had arrived.

Overwhelming disappointment crushed in as she noticed Trevor McLean was not with them. She'd been so looking forward to seeing him again that the realization that he hadn't come had unexpected tears clouding her vision. She'd been too forward the last time they'd seen each other months before. He was avoiding her. There was no other explanation. And the truth hurt.

Jaxson clearing his throat to her left brought her back to the moment. She'd have plenty of time later to lick her wounds of rejection. She needed to get through the pairings first.

She swallowed the lump in her throat and tried to smile even bigger. "So, like, before I start matching up our couples, does anyone have any questions?"

A question came from the grouping of celebrities. "Yeah. After we're matched, do we go get started or do we all have to stay here and start at the same time?"

Damn. She'd meant to include those instructions. *Stay calm.*

"Great question. We'd like all of our couples to stay here in the theater and then once we've matched you all, I'll do an official start and everyone will be free to get started after that. I'll be staying in the theater all night and be here if you choose to re-roll. We'll also have some sexy BDSM scenes and movies projected on the big screen for those of you wanting to stay and keep me company."

When no one else asked a question, Madison moved on to announce the first match. "All right! Like, let's get this party started by matching our first couple.

"Egan Mendez is up first! Egan if you would join me here on the stage."

Madison had her cue cards sorted in the order she planned to call the celebrities up. She'd spent a ton of time sorting out the order — men and women balanced — dominants and submissives balanced — types of celebrity professions balanced. Egan would be the first of many musicians being auctioned off that night.

The tall rocker joined her as she read his bio to the audience, although they would have to be half dead to not recognize the man who was regularly on the cover of the tabloids.

"And with a winning bid of just over $29,000 is Babygirl Michele!" Madison had expected the winning bidders to be jumping out of their seat to rush the stage with excitement, so the fact that she saw so many people scanning the room trying to figure out who Michele was surprised her. "Babygirl Michele, if you'll come up to the stage for your spin."

She was about to call the name again when she heard a girl about halfway back call, "She's here," while waving an arm in the air to point towards the friend next to her. From this distance it looked like Babygirl was having second thoughts on her bid. Madison was grateful she'd put the info for the runner-up bidder on the same bio card so she wouldn't need to fumble if someone backed out.

Just when she thought she might need to call for the backup bidder the winner pushed to her feet and started making her way through the crowd. Once on the stage, Egan grasped her hand and said "Nice to meet you, Babygirl Michele."

Their handshake went on so long a smattering of chuckles from the audience filtered up to the stage as the pair spoke quietly to each other. Once the couple joined her at the wheel, Egan urged her, "I think we can spin now."

Madison handed the marble to the shell-shocked looking submissive and gave the wheel a turn. They watched the ball bounce until she could finally announce, *"Dom's Choice!"*

She waited until the couple had made it down the opposite set of steps before moving on to the next celebrity. She'd put this next couple close to the beginning just so she could get it over with. The sooner she could get the blowhard celebrity out of her sight the happier she would be.

"Everyone will recognize our next celebrity as a beloved TV doctor from several dramas when we were kids."

More like before I was born.

"Let's welcome Robert McCauley to the stage."

The crowd broke out into polite applause as the grey-haired man in a ridiculous leather outfit climbed the stairs. It wasn't that Madison had anything against his age. What she did object to was the jerk's insistence on being treated as if he were the reigning king of Hollywood. He'd been the only celebrity to provide a long list of demands they'd had to meet just to get him to participate in roulette. It had gotten so bad that she would have kicked him out of the event if Jaxson had agreed.

She'd just opened her mouth to announce the winner when the asshole slipped his arm around Madison's waist, pulling her towards him hard enough that she almost tipped over.

The second she regained her balance, she grabbed the short crop hanging from her belt and whipped it up, slapping it against the leather covering his protruding stomach.

"Hands to yourself, there, Robert. Like, if you want to play with me, I'll be doing the dominating. Don't forget, I'm Mistress Madison tonight."

The crowd broke out in hoots, hollers, and laughter. She saw the flash of anger in the Dom's eyes before he plastered a fake smile on his reddened face. Her heart pounded. She didn't want to create a scene in front of the entire club, but she was damned if she was going to get manhandled by a guy older than her own dad.

Turning back to the crowd, she tried to get them back on track. "I didn't think so. Now, like, why don't we ask Lady Anita to come take her place on the stage? She paid $9,000 to be your play partner tonight."

As they waited for an older woman to join them from the back of the theater, Madison suppressed the smile she wanted to show knowing the asshole was the celebrity that had earned the least amount of money for the event. He didn't know it yet, but he'd have to listen to the rest of the pairings and realize every other celebrity drew in significantly higher amounts.

The icing on the cake was Lady Anita rolling 'watersports' as their first kink and listening to each of them chastising the other for not putting watersports on their hard-limit list.

"Well now, that was fun!" Madison grinned as they moved off the stage. "Let's move on and invite the amazing Vanessa Novak to join me. Vanessa is our only dancer in tonight's event. She is a soloist with the Dudorov Ballet here in L.A. Now, I'd like to welcome our winner to the stage with a winning bid of $27,000… Wyatt Strickland!"

Madison waited for a handsome man to join them on the stage. As soon as he arrived, he captured his sub's hand and gallantly kissed it while the crowd waited.

"Well, it looks like these two are already, like, totally hitting it off!" She held out the small marble to Vanessa, inviting her to drop it into the spinning wheel. "Ready to see how you're going to start the night, Vanessa?"

The shell-shocked celebrity answered, "Right, yeah I am."

After the ball dropped, Madison announced to the crowd, "*Impact Play!*"

There was a murmur in the enclosed space, but Madison heard her low, "Thank, God."

"Sounds like Vanessa got what she wanted." That brought a few laughs as she moved on. "All right, let's get our next celebrity paired up."

Glancing down at her next card, she announced, "Our next celebrity contestant is the one, the only, Trenton Banks! As we are all aware, Trenton has starred in dozens of action movies. If you haven't seen at least one of them, then shame on you! The lucky submissive to place the winning bid of a whopping $52,000 on Trenton Banks is...Sunshine! Come on up, Sunshine, and you can spin the activity wheel."

Madison was excited that socialite Serena Hawthorne, aka Sunshine, had joined Black Light. A celebrity in her own right, Serena's line of handbags was some of Madison's favorite bags.

As soon as the couple was together, she heard Trenton say, "Nice to see you again, Sunshine."

"Errr... hi, Mr. Banks." Only Madison and Trenton were close enough to see the full body blush consuming Sunshine.

"Ready to spin?" she asked them. They hadn't stopped looking into each other's eyes and Madison sensed there was already some magic going on between them. "I'm like, so happy you two matched up. You look so cute together!" Turning to the crowd she added, "Don't they look cute together, folks?"

More whoops and cheers from the crowd while they moved to the wheel. Sunshine looked so nervous as she handed her the marble that Madison did a quick wink, trying to keep her calm. They stood together watching until the wheel came to a stop.

"ABDL!" she shouted. Madison felt herself blushing remembering the photos and stories she'd found on the Internet during her research for tonight. She might have spent a bit more time than necessary researching the Adult Baby Diaper Lover kink.

She glanced at the limits card before confirming, "And that isn't on either of their hard-limits list so have fun!"

Madison waited a few seconds before moving on and asking the next celebrity to join her. "I'm so excited to welcome the first of two celebrity chefs participating tonight. I'm sure you have all seen Master

Chef Ronan Bellington whipping up amazing dishes on his high-rating cable show and, if not, perhaps you've eaten in his five-star restaurant. Tonight, he will be dominating one lucky submissive. Chef Ronan, please join me."

Madison glanced at the pool of dwindling celebrities and could see the handsome Chef still scanning the crowd, looking like he hadn't heard a word she'd said. She called him again in her best principal's tone, "Ronan Bellington, please report to the stage immediately."

It seemed that the smattering of chuckles finally caught his attention and he glanced up at her. "Well, praise the Lord. I thought you'd gone deaf," she said, shaking her head as the crowd laughed louder. "I'll repeat, I'd like to ask our celebrity chef, Ronan Bellington, to join me."

The Dom was finally in motion and was next to her quickly. "Ronan, it's my pleasure to announce that your lucky winner with a bid of $23,000 is Andrea Carpenter," Madison said, looking out into the crowd. "Andrea if you'd come join us—"

"Over my dead body! You take one more step, young lady, and I swear you won't be sitting for a month." A voice that was decidedly not a female's rang out even as a woman in the front row froze mid-step. The crowd chuckled again as the woman turned to see a man storming up the aisle from the back of the theater.

"Steven? What are you doing here?"

"What does it look like? I'm here to take you home."

"But I won him," she said, turning to gesture toward the chef. "I paid over twenty thousand dollars..."

"I don't care if you paid a million. There is no way in hell I'm going to let another man touch what's mine," Steven growled.

Andrea appeared unsure whether to be flattered or insulted. Her mouth opened and closed several times before she planted her hands on her hips and finally said, "What happened to our agreement that we each get a hall-pass? You know I said I'd look the other way if you and that model, Gigi Hadid, wanted to... well, you know and you said I could—"

"Again, I don't give a rat's ass what I said then," he thundered as he finally reached her. The room didn't seem to take a breath as he moved to stroke a finger down her cheek. "What's important is what I'm saying right now. You've got to choose. Three hours with some man who might be able to make you the fanciest cake in the world but doesn't know that your favorite is a simple white cake with strawberry icing. He doesn't know that your favorite color is green or that you are allergic to cats but are willing to take shots just so you can adopt a kitten. And I can damn sure promise you that he doesn't know that you make these little squeaks when you are about to come apart in my arms... So, what's it going to be, Andrea? Him or me?"

"You," she said without a moment's hesitation.

"Right answer," he said as he stepped forward, picked her up off her feet, and tossed her over his shoulder.

"Wait!" she said, planting her hands against his back and arching up. "What about the chef? I was going to ask for some cooking tips."

"For fuck's sake, Andie, he's in a sex auction, not a contestant on *Iron Chef!*" The crowd laughed.

"What a waste of money. I should have spent it on your cookbooks," she called back to Ronan.

"Don't worry, Andrea," Madison said. "I'll be in touch about returning your winning bid."

"Don't bother," Steven called out. "Give the money to charity." A single swat silenced Andrea's protest at the loss. "Consider it my fee for being stupid enough to fall for that hall pass shit."

Madison tried not to let the chaos sidetrack the event as the crowd laughed. "Like, no one can ever say these events are boring, right?" she said, drawing the attention back to the stage. "Shall we continue?" She checked her card again for the name of the second bidder before announcing, "Congratulations, Carnegie. As the runner-up, would you please join us on the stage?"

When no one moved in the audience, she found herself wishing she'd invited the back-up to the back-up. It was going to suck if there was no one who would partner with such a great celebrity.

Apparently, Ronan agreed as he stepped to the front of the stage and announced, "Carnegie, not only did Andrea bid on me but then kick me to the curb, but now you don't want me either? Are you telling me that no one wants to play with me?"

Several hands began waving wildly in the crowd and cries of "I'll play," "Pick me," "Hell, we'll share," rang out as women began to stand and try to step into the game.

"No!" a woman towards the front said, the single word drowning out the other voices. "He's mine!"

Ronan stepped up to meet her as she approached the stage. "Thank you for not leaving me stranded," he offered. He took the white ball from Madison and dropped it into Carnegie's free hand before leading her the final few steps to the large roulette wheel.

Madison spun it, and waited for the ball to drop into place before announcing, "And it looks like *Medical Play* is our winner. Unless, of course, either one of you marked it as a hard limit?"

Ronan asked his sub for the night. "Is it?"

"Huh? Is what?" She was clearly still in shock for having to step in and play.

"As much as I'd love to play doctor with you, I need to make sure you didn't mark that as one of your hard limits," he said.

"Not a hard limit. I'm all yours, Chef."

"It's Doctor," he corrected "Hmmm, you seem a bit flushed, Miss…"

"Bishop," the winner replied.

"Miss Bishop," he said. "I can hardly wait to get you up on that exam table."

They started moving off the stage as Madison congratulated them, "It looks like they're going to have a lot of fun tonight."

Madison knew who was next without looking at her cards. Jed Major was one of the sexiest Doms participating that evening, at least by her standards. She'd always had a thing for musicians anyway, and if she'd had the opportunity to bid, she'd have put all her money down to play with the sexy singer.

"I can't tell you how excited I am to call the amazingly talented rocker Jed Major up to the stage as our next celebrity Dom! You know him as the front man for Original Sinners." She watched as he gracefully climbed the stairs to come stand next to her. The rocker towered over her so she had to crane her neck to look up at him. "So good to see you here this evening, Jed." She fought to keep her voice steady and not turn into a silly fangirl in front of the audience.

"Thank you," he replied with a nod before looking out at the audience.

"All right!" She cleared her throat and tried to get back on track. "And the winner with a bid of $85,000 for a night with the amazing Jed Major is..." She glanced down at her card just to make double sure before adding, "Kaelin Le Blanc!"

"What?" Jed questioned, scanning the crowd.

A beautiful young woman made her way to the stage while in a stare-down with Jed. Once she'd climbed the steps, Madison congratulated her and added, "You're welcome to step up to the wheel and take a spin for your activity for the night."

The marble took a few extra bounces before settling in a slot. "And it's a *Roleplay Wild Card*—Dom's choice! Wishing you both a fun-filled evening."

She watched the couple leave the stage before glancing down to prepare for the next match, letting the audience know, "This is where we were going to pair off Carlos Ferrara, but as we all witnessed just before we got started, he is currently driving the winning submissive to the hospital to have her ankle checked out, so we will skip over Carlos.

"Scarlett A requires no introduction. I know you all have watched this two-time Grammy-award winner these last few years on *The Song*, and you can sing along to the twenty-two chart-topping hits she had as lead singer of Spider. She's now going solo, and I understand will be releasing a new album this year, is that right?"

The red-headed singer nodded, giving the crowd a small wave as she joined Madison on the stage.

"And tonight, Scarlett will be submitting to..."—she paused for dramatic effect— "Master Lincoln! He paid an impressive $30,000 to dominate Scarlett tonight."

As soon as he joined the ladies on the stage, the singer said his name under her breath. "Lincoln."

"That's *Master* Lincoln to you, sweetheart." His voice was commanding and it made Madison's pulse spike. She could only imagine the effect it had on the singer.

"Scarlett listed hard limits as blood play, needle play, edge play, and water sports. Spin the wheel and throw your roulette ball, Scarlett. Let's find out what your first adventure will be."

She waited for the ball to come to a rest before announcing, "*Whipping!*"

As the couple made their way towards the back of the room, she called the next celebrity to the stage. "Like, I'm very excited to introduce our next celebrity, philanthropist Heather Graham who is our only celebrity to indicate she would be happy to be dominated by either a man or a woman dominant. I'm sure she'll be excited to find out that Mary Reardon beat out a lot of other bidders by bidding $19,000 to get her chance to play roulette tonight. Mary, please join us here on the stage."

The spin of *electrical play* seemed to excite both women as they headed down to watch the remaining pairs be matched.

"Next up on our auction block is the international fitness model whom we've all seen gracing the covers of fitness magazines. Welcome Adam Butler!"

Madison tried not to drool as she watched the handsome Dom climbing the steps to come stand next to her. She was briefly distracted by how great he smelled, until she finally remembered to ask his partner to join them. "And the winner of the auction for Adam Butler with a bid of $31,000 is..." she paused, drawing out the suspense before calling, "Claire Allerton!"

Once again, they had a shy submissive on their hands. When no one stood up, Madison shielded her eyes from the spotlights in the theater and called out again, "Where are you Claire?"

Finally, a woman sitting about half way back stood. "There you are! Come on up here."

The new couple spoke quietly for a moment as Adam reached to grab Claire's hand. "Here you go." Madison smiled, handing Adam her list of hard limits. "You might want to read these over."

He skimmed the list and then encouraged them to proceed with, "Wonderful. Let's find out what we're doing."

"I'm going to spin the wheel. When you're ready, just give the ball a toss." Madison announced as she heard the model asking the sub questions.

"What are you hoping for?" When she didn't respond he started guessing as the ball bounced around on the wheel. "Breast torture? Shibari? Electric shock? Does a certain Little someone need to be put on her knees while she calls me Daddy tonight?"

With each suggestion, Madison could see the submissive blushing a darker shade of pink. He continued to taunt her with suggestive ideas until Madison could see the wheel slowing. "Here is comes!"

Adam called out like a gambler on the casino floor in Vegas, "Come on, anal! Come on, spanking! Someone needs to go home with a red-hot, well-used bottom."

When the ball finally rested on the wheel, Madison called out, "Consensual non-consent!"

Madison bit her lip before she internally added, *'the thing I'd like to try with Trevor McLean.'*

The happy couple took off down the stairs as she glanced down at her cards. "Next up, we have Jazz! Lead singer of the rock band The Scarlet Letter!" Once Jazz was on the stage she continued, "And our winning bid of fifty thousand dollars came from Dr. Michael Adams!"

A tall Dom was quick to get on the stage, greeting his sub for the night with a simple, "Hello, Pixie."

"Time to spin!" she called as she handed the white ball to Jazz. It took the celebrity a few long seconds to throw the ball in, but it quickly fell into a slot. "Like, their first scene for the night is *teacher/student role play!* I'm sure that will be fun!"

The next two couples flew by quickly as she matched up Genevieve, a celebrity chef, and a morning news anchorwoman, Francesca.

"We're almost done with our celebrity pairs! Next up is Cassandra

Moreira, an international model who totally walked the catwalk at New York Fashion Week last year, but is spending Valentine's with us this year!" Madison smiled at the beautiful woman who climbed the stairs in killer heels with absolute grace. Her natural curls formed a dark, shiny halo around her head and she offered a bright smile as she waved at the trio.

"Hi, Cass!" Chase shouted excitedly, waving back as the audience chuckled. "You look amazing!"

"Thanks!" she whispered back, laughing as Jaxson gave her a wave as well. "Emma you better let me meet the babies before I leave town!"

"Obviously," Emma replied, and Madison almost smacked herself for forgetting they knew each other from Jaxson and Chase's modeling careers. Still, she had to keep the night on track because it was almost eight o'clock.

"And the winning bid of $32,000 came from Logan Chisholm! Please join us on stage!" A handsome blond man was already approaching the stairs when she saw him. In an expensive suit, he approached with a smirk, not even offering his hand. As the two squared off, both sizing each other up, Madison shrugged to the audience. "All right then, like, let's see what they spin!"

Cassandra took the ball without hesitation, tossing it in as soon as Madison set the wheel in motion.

"Eager to get started?" Logan asked.

"More curious if you'll be able to keep me entertained," she replied, laughing and turning to wink at the trio, where a few more laughs buzzed. The wheel slowed, the ball bounced a few more times, and then Madison's stomach tensed. *Whoa.*

"*Fisting!*" she announced, surprised to see Cassandra's expression hadn't lost her challenging smile, while Logan looked much happier.

"Shall we?" Logan waved towards the edge of the stage and Cassandra nodded, almost as tall as the man as they were led off stage.

Suddenly, she was down to the last celebrity of the night. Piper Kole was unique in the event for many reasons, not just because she was being paired last.

"And our final celebrity for the night is Piper Kole, better known as Mistress Ice here at Black Light. Not only does she have the distinction of being our only female Domme playing tonight, but more importantly, she is our celebrity who drew the highest bid. Everyone please put your hands together to thank Nolan Boeing for his very generous bid of one-hundred thousand dollars!"

As the crowd's cheers and applause thundered in the small room, Madison glanced to the sidelines, expecting to see Piper and Nolan joining her, especially since they'd been standing near each other the entire time she'd been pairing up the matches for the night. From this distance, she couldn't hear what was being said, but anyone watching could see Mistress Ice was not happy as she'd turned and was dressing down the man several inches taller than her even in her high boots. Since she was scary enough when she was happy, Madison had to question Master Nolan's strategy of pissing his Domme for the night off even more.

She tried to give them time to sort their argument out, but finally had to resort to calling them again to join her on the stage. A minute later they finally complied.

"We're down to, like, just one more roulette spin before everyone can get their first scenes started. Which one of you will be throwing in the marble to choose your first stop for the night?"

She held the marble out in their direction, but neither of them took the small ball. Nolan asked Piper, "Are you okay with me tossing it in, Mistress, or would you like to do the honors?"

"Oh, please do," the Domme quipped.

Madison spun the wheel and Nolan threw the ball in. She had to smile at the look of panic on the normally dominant man's face when it stopped on ABDL. "Both of our contestants have ABDL play listed on their hard limits list. Please roll again."

Next the wheel stopped on, "Watersports."

Both Nolan and Piper answered in unison, "Hard limit."

Madison held out the marble to him for a third roll, but Piper snatched the ball instead. "Clearly, you need some help here. I'll drop it this time."

The ball bounced around more than ever before finally coming to a rest on the wheel. It spun hard until finally landing on, "Knife play!"

She glanced at the clock against the back wall and was pleased to see she'd wrapped things up perfectly. It was only five minutes before eight and time for the couples to start on their first challenge.

"I can see our couples are excited to get started. So let Celebrity Roulette officially begin. Everyone have fun and play safe!"

GUARDED

A Black Light: Celebrity Roulette Novella

By

Renee Rose

CHAPTER 1

 incoln

Congratulations, Lincoln, your bid for dominating Scarlett A at the Black Light Celebrity Roulette won!

I read the email four times before I believe it, my heart pounding harder than it did in six years of combat. Or running the Boston Marathon.

The money has been transferred from your account but your partner will not know who won the bid until our event.

The cardiac palpitations are one part victory, one part gnawing fear over my own mental state. Or is it my financial state?

Because, yeah. I've lost my ever-loving mind.

Bidding thirty grand for one night with a pop star? Worse—with a former client? Thirty grand I had to take a second mortgage on my L.A. condo to afford?

Certifiably nuts.

But that's what Scarlett A does to me. The uber-famous, beautiful, talented, kind-hearted pop star who I had the honor of protecting for thirteen months, has me risking everything just to get near her again.

And now I definitely sound as nuts as the loonies I used to keep from intruding on her personal space. The fuck-nuts who sent her boxes and crates of designer clothes, shoes, purses, cosmetics. All because they worship the glittering ground she walks on.

Because hip hop legend Scarlett A is all that. And more.

And I've seen a side of her few know.

Saw so much she fired my ass.

It was the night that changed everything for me.

My life. The way I fuck. Who I am. And it's why I need to see her again. To take this thing full circle back to the woman I would kill or die for.

And not just in the client/bodyguard capacity.

I have something to give Scarlett.

I just don't know if I can make her see it.

~

SCARLETT

SIGNING UP FOR THIS EVENT MIGHT HAVE BEEN A HUGE MISTAKE. I'M hanging out with the rest of the celebrities up for auction in Black Light's version of a green room. The Black Light has always been discreet--both the D.C. and the new L.A. location. But putting myself up on stage—allowing myself to be auctioned off to the highest bidder —could be a colossal mistake.

The Scarlett A image requires me to be a powerhouse. I'm the queen of hip hop and I consistently demand to be treated like royalty. Letting people see me as a bottom—a submissive even—could ruin my brand.

You know how these things go. Two hundred people see me on my knees with a collar and a leash tonight and then it's a whisper here, an under-the-breath joke there, and I'm the TMZ Richard Gere-gerbil story of the decade.

"I need a drink," I mutter to no one in particular, although I've been sober for three years now.

"Right?" The woman next to me says, tightening the laces on her corset.

"Let me." I walk around to the back of her, where the laces are pulled unevenly and work my way up until the entire thing squeezes the breath out of her. "Too much?"

"No, it's perfect. I like to get swoony when things get exciting." The tiny bleach-blonde throws me a wink. "I'm Genevieve, by the way."

I grin. "I know. I watch *Cooking with Gen* all the time."

The blonde in the corset blushes. "Really? Scarlett A watches *me*? I'm totally fangirling because I've been singing along to you since high school when you were with Spider."

High school? Ouch. Okay, now I feel old. I don't often think about my age--it's just a number, after all--but at forty-six, I'm twice the age of the singers I judge and coach on the television hit show *The Song*. I've been a famous music star for half my life now and I still feel like I'm just getting started. Like I need to conquer the world.

"Are you a top or bottom?" Her eyes fall on my soft leather collar. I'm wearing a corset, too, only mine is a satiny hunter green to bring out the green of my eyes. I'm wearing a matching green thong and a white pair of thigh-highs. White stripper heels complete the outfit.

"Bottom? Really?" she answers her own question. "Wow. Cool."

I unwrap a lollipop, which is part of my outfit and take a lick. It gives me something to do with my hands and keeps my mind off the craving for a drink. "Surprised?"

"Honestly? Yes. But I shouldn't be. Strong women like to submit, too."

"Yes," I say simply, trying to keep my mind from hopping down the rabbit hole of debating if I'm actually strong, or just playing the role that goes with the persona.

No, I'm strong. I divorced Ted. Finally had the courage to break up

Spider. Put myself in rehab. I replaced the substance addiction with sexual. Still chemical, really. I need pain to let go. Release my mind from the constant bonds of pushing harder, never believing I'm good enough.

Discovering the Black Light was a godsend. A place where I get everything I need in a totally discreet environment. Before they opened the L.A. location, I used to fly out to D.C. twice a month just to get my ass whipped.

Heh. The things we do to stay sane, right?

"Okay, celebrities, it's time to head in so we can get started. Let's have all of you head up towards the stage," Emma, one of the owners of the Black Light says after swinging the door open wide.

I take a hard suck of my lollipop and strut forward. "Me first."

❧

SCARLETT

THE CROWD WHISTLES AND CHEERS AS THE AUCTIONED CELEBRITIES sweep up near the stage. Jaxson, Chase and Emma, the three owners—and a lovely throuple—give an opening speech, then introduce the MC Madison Taylor. I try to distract myself by staring directly into the lights. I wish to hell this was a music concert, because then I'd know exactly what to do. It would be my show, I'd take the mic and work the crowd.

But this? Submitting in public? On stage, even? This is not comfortable territory for me. I work the lollipop with my tongue like my life depends on it, make love to it like my master's cock. Might as well give them the show they're after, right?

Madison starts announcing the winner for each celebrity. I zone out until she calls my name. "Scarlett A requires no introduction. I know you all have watched this two-time grammy-award winner these last few years on *The Song*, and you can sing along to the twenty-two chart-topping hits she had as lead singer of Spider. She's now going solo, and I understand will be releasing a new album this year, is that right?"

I smile and nod to Madison, waving to the enthusiastic crowd.

"And tonight, Scarlett will be submitting to..."—she pauses for dramatic effect—"Master Lincoln! He paid an impressive $30,000 to dominate Scarlett tonight." She goes on to say how much I fetched, but I'm not listening.

My gaze snaps to the left where a huge, far-too-familiar figure emerges into the ring of lights.

Fucking hell.

Lincoln.

My former bodyguard.

My heart pounds and I'm pretty sure all my blood rushes to my feet, because I get wobbly and light-headed.

Nothing shows on his inscrutable mask—did it ever?—as he strides confidently toward me, his eyes glued to my face. He's as beautiful and imposing as ever. Way over six feet tall, with broad shoulders permanently thrown back in that military stance he wears so well. He's in a grey fitted t-shirt that shows off every muscle, and a pair of black slacks.

I stare with my mouth open, cherry lollipop gone still on my tongue. When he reaches me, I rasp out his name without meaning to. "Lincoln."

"That's *Master* Lincoln to you, sweetheart." His voice is deep and commanding. He never used it much when he worked for me, but every time he did, I swear I felt it right between my legs. Like he had that exact resonance to set off vibrations in my nether regions.

Right now, I'm way less turned on than I am freaked out.

Because if Lincoln Wall paid—what did Madison say? *Thirty grand?* —for me, then we have a problem. A very big problem.

He's out for blood.

~

LINCOLN

. . .

SCARLETT GOES PALE AGAINST HER WILD MANE OF RED HAIR. SHE PIVOTS away from me, tosses the long locks over one shoulder and struts to the roulette wheel. If I didn't know her so well, I might have missed the wobble in her step.

I fall in behind her and when she reaches the wheel, band one arm around her waist. Protecting her will always be my first instinct, so I'm sure as hell not going to let her trip or faint up here on stage. Yanking her soft form back against my already swelling cock, though? That's a pure show of dominance.

She makes a tiny *oohmph* that gets my dick harder. Lord, I have dreamed of making this woman scream for too many nights now. When she sends me a glance over her shoulder, though, I see fear there.

I dial back a degree of roughness.

"Shh," I murmur in her ear, letting my hand slide up from her toned belly to cup her tightly constrained breast. I thumb over her nipple to distract her from whatever's making her nervous.

The MC announces, "Scarlett listed hard limits as blood play, needle play, edge play, and water sports. Spin the wheel and throw your roulette ball, Scarlett. Let's find out what your first adventure will be."

She tugs the wheel to get it started, then tosses her ball in. The seconds seem like years as the ball dances, bouncing around until it finally settles into a groove.

"*Whipping!*" Madison announces.

My grip on her breast tightens. "Perfect," I purr. "It's always best to start with the punishment, don't you think?"

It takes me a second to note that she's not breathing. "Exhale," I command, my lips still at her ear. I bite the outer shell, harder than a nip.

She releases her breath with a slight sigh.

"Good girl."

This time when she looks sidelong under her lashes, there's speculation in her green gaze. She doesn't know what the hell I'm up to. Good.

I'll keep it that way.

For a while.

At some point, though, before this night is through, I'm going to have to lay my cards on the table, which is never easy for me. I prefer to show my feelings with actions, rather than words, but I realize that the habit often bites me in the ass. Especially where women are involved. Especially where Scarlett is involved.

I take her elbow when Madison finally releases us and guide her off-stage, steadying her as she walks down the stairs. It's a familiar role. Not that I ever played her escort, but I always kept close, within arms' reach, so I could catch her if she stumbled.

"What is this?" she whisper-shouts at me when we reach the floor.

I whirl her around to face me. The power exchange is different this time—I'm not her hired boy, and she needs to remember it. I tilt my head and cock a stern brow. "What did you say?"

Her throat bobs in a swallow. "What are you doing here, *Master?*"

"I'm doing what needs to be done." Yeah, like I said earlier, words aren't my gift. Sue me. We find a place to stand in the periphery to watch the rest of the matching and roulette spins.

I take her elbow again and pick up my bag of toys where I left it before I guide her to a spanking bench on a small platform in the main open area of the club.

I lift my chin toward it. "Bend over, beautiful."

She's not afraid of this part. No, she practically throws herself over the bench, like it's her refuge in the storm. A safe place.

I get it. I've played a lot over the last year. Every chance I could get, so I could learn how to give a sub exactly what she needs. I understand how freeing surrender must be. Especially for someone like Scarlett, who feels like she must always be in control.

I buckle her ankles, then walk around the front of the bench to fasten her wrists.

She twists to lift her head. "What is this about, Lincoln? You came to humiliate me?"

I finish buckling her second wrist. "Are you into that?"

She huffs. "Why are you here? Why are you doing this?"

I wrap my fist in her hair and tug her head back.

"--Master Lincoln," she adds immediately, already guessing what I was going to admonish her for.

"Yes. *Master Lincoln. Master. Sir.* Any of those will work. You address me without respect? There will be consequences."

Her eyes dilate and a tiny shudder runs through her. I know from my experience at Black Light I pushed the right button.

I walk behind her and stroke her ass. The tiny scrap of fabric between her legs is soaked. If I wasn't certain of my affect on her before, I am now. I slip my fingers under it and rub her dewy slit. Her pelvic floor lifts, muscles tightening and fluttering in response to my touch.

"Aw, baby." I give her ass a resounding slap. "I like it when you soak your panties for me." Even though I already have full access to her ass for whipping, I tug the G-string off. I need to see everything tonight.

Tonight Scarlett will be bared to me. Every part of her—body and soul.

CHAPTER 2

 *carlett*

I CAN'T FUCKING BELIEVE LINCOLN IS HERE.

The man's presence has always done crazy things to me. Just looking at his oversized fit body makes me hot and fluttery. The strong silent thing gives him mystery. Makes him a sort of blank slate for all kinds of freaky fantasies.

I wanted to jump my bodyguard every day he worked for me. And maybe even a little after I got rid of him.

But getting rid of him was a must. There was no way I was going to be able to live with the humiliation of what he'd seen.

But I just can't figure out what his game is. Did he turn into one of my crazy stalker fans? I know the guy didn't just have thirty grand lying around ready to piss away for one night getting even with me. And anyone who wants revenge this bad...must be seriously deranged.

But it's hard to think because my body is already in total submission mode. Being restrained, my bare ass and pussy up on display, has me creaming for anything from Lincoln. And from what I've seen so far—the man knows what he's doing.

Which is *such* a turn-on.

Jesus. He really did match all those fantasies I had about him taking me rough.

Something cold drips between my cheeks.

Shit. He's lubing up my ass. I didn't land on the anal sex, but I guess if he's dom, he can do whatever the hell he wants unless I safe word.

A hard cool plug presses against my anus. I force myself to exhale and relax my tightened sphincter muscles to let it in. A groan falls from my lips as he stretches me wide. Instead of pushing past the thickest part and letting bulb seat, he backs out, stretches me again, fucking me with the wide bulb.

"Oh-oh," I groan. My belly flutters, inner thighs start trembling.

"Nothing like starting things off with a good ass fucking, is there?" Lincoln has his lips up against my ear again. I shiver at the sensations, my pussy clenching on air.

"M-master Lincoln," I manage to say, straining to keep my train of thought. "Where did you get the money for this?"

"Second mortgage," he answers evenly.

"You want to punish me." It's not really a question. I already know the answer.

He shoves the plug all the way in, making me mewl before it seats and becomes far more comfortable. When he leans down to my eye-level, the corner of his mouth ticks up. "Oh I definitely want to punish you."

I'm shaking all over. Not just from pleasure. There's a little fear here, too. But I'm in Black Light. There are security guards everywhere. And all I have to say *red* and everything ends.

"You want revenge."

"Revenge?" Surprise tugs his brows. He wraps my hair up in his fist again and lifts my head. "No, princess. Not revenge." We're forehead to forehead, his cinnamon breath warm on my lips.

As always, I can read absolutely nothing on his smooth, cool mask.

The guy could very easily be one of those Buckingham Palace guards who never crack.

"I don't need revenge. I want my job back."

Well.

Thankfully, he releases my hair so I can duck my head and hide my confusion. For some odd reason, tears prick my eyes.

He wants his job back?

He went to these lengths to get his job back.

And then it hits me.

He's here because of me. Well, no—I mean, duh. Of course he's here because of me, but the reason he became a dom is because of me.

No, that's too ludicrous to imagine.

But how else? If he was a dom before I let him go, then he would've understood what he walked in on. He wouldn't have tried to kill my play partner, nearly costing me a lawsuit.

So after I let him go, he would've had to totally devote himself to learning the art of domination. Because he seems quite skilled. Of course, he was in Special Forces. Maybe torture was a skill already ingrained in him.

And that thought should *not* excite me so much.

And then he gets busy on my ass, and I lose all ability to concentrate.

He starts with a leather paddle, light and slappy, a great warm-up tool.

Yes, this man definitely knows what he's doing. He doesn't hold back. It's not too much--the leather slapper is forgiving, but he's certainly not one of those doms who fears I can't take it. My whole ass warms up under the slaps, which he concentrates on my sit spots. Every once and awhile he smacks the butt plug, driving it deeper inside me.

My body purrs as the heat builds, endorphins start to flow. And with the sense of well-being comes all the sexier memories of my former bodyguard. The time he answered his hotel door in nothing but a small towel around his waist. Lord, that body! Tattoos wrapped around solid muscle. He is a perfect specimen of manliness—a freaking stallion. I remember the time we got stuck in a throng outside a club in the Big Apple. I tripped but instead of falling, found myself swept up into his arms and carried like a princess out to the waiting car.

It was hard not to swoon.

He stops spanking and pumps the plug in and out of my ass.

I am seconds from orgasming when he stops.

I bet he knew that, too.

He slaps between my legs. "You need to come, Red?"

"Yes," I moan, excited that he might let me.

"Too bad."

Damn.

"You won't come until I give you permission."

Yeah, this man definitely has government-trained torture skills. *Delicious.*

He runs a calloused hand over my twitching ass. "Redheads mark easily, don't they?"

I don't answer because I assume the question is rhetorical.

"I bet you'll look good in stripes."

Excitement simultaneously zips up my spine and down my inner thighs. My toes curl in my platform heels.

He slaps my pussy again, then gives my clit a far too short rub.

I moan and wiggle my ass. He steps away and out of my periphery I watch him draw a cane from his bag.

Oh shit.

That's a happy *oh shit,* of course. I love to hate the cane. It's seriously painful. In the best possible way. He is definitely planning on tearing my ass up tonight. And that shouldn't do all kinds of fluttery things to my belly, but it does.

One of the edgier memories of Lincoln surfaces. The time I woke him up in the middle of the night.

·　·　·

I HAD INSOMNIA—A NORMAL OCCURRENCE FOR ME—AND I DECIDED I wanted to go for a walk. We were in my L.A. mansion. He was asleep in his room and I touched his shoulder.

His hand flashed out and closed around my throat before his eyes even opened.

I think I screamed—as much as was possible with my throat being crushed—and he released me.

"Oh fuck," he muttered in that guttural voice of his. He returned his hand to my throat and stroked the bruised skin as he blinked rapidly, eyes already sharp and focused. "I'm so sorry."

I remember realizing he must have terrible PTSD from his service. I wondered why I hadn't even considered the things this man had seen already in his young life. "I didn't mean to scare you," I said in a rush. "I just wanted to let you know I'm going for a walk. I didn't want you to wake up and freak out."

He scrubbed a hand over his face. "The fuck you are."

I narrowed my eyes. "I'm sorry?" He never spoke to me that way. I mean, he hardly spoke at all, but when he did it was always business-like and respectful.

He gave his head a shake. "I'm sorry." He swung his legs out of the bed and stood up, towering over me in nothing but his boxer briefs. "I meant I'm coming with you. Of course. That's my job."

I shrugged but my heart thudded from almost being choked to death. Or maybe it was from the sight of his nearly naked body. And despite the fact that I had to shut it down, I was turned on by his bossy response. To hide it, I tossed my hair and marched out, waiting at the front door for him to throw on his clothes and shoes and follow.

His jaw clenched tight and his shoulders were stiff as he trailed a half step behind me. I power walked, trying to release the pent up anxiety that kept me from sleep, but my brain couldn't go anywhere but on thoughts of him. I could feel the tension radiating from him and it distracted me.

"Are you pissed that I woke you up? Because you didn't have to come," I finally snapped.

"No," he exploded. "God, no."

I stopped and faced him, hands on my hips. "What's the problem, then?"

He scrubbed a hand over his stubbled jaw. "I can't switch out of lethal mode easily once it's triggered," he admitted, like it was a flaw. "And I can't fucking believe I choked you. It's unforgivable. I understand if you're not comfortable with having me as your guard anymore."

My heart bled for him. A wounded warrior. He may not have debilitating physical wounds, but the psychological ones would always be there.

"You have PTSD?" I asked softly.

He let out a soft chuff. "Probably. Not an official diagnosis." Then the walls flew back up. "Nothing that normally affects my job performance," he said stiffly.

I took his hand and squeezed it. "It's all right. I think breath play is hot."

From the way his brows dropped to confusion, I could tell he had no idea what I was talking about.

I laughed. "Don't worry about it. I'm fine. And I don't need another bodyguard. I like you."

For a moment, I swore I saw something vulnerable and raw flit over his face, but in a flash it was gone, again. My ready warrior back at arms, mask in place, ready to defend me.

I TRY TO RECONCILE THAT VULNERABLE YOUNG MAN TO THE ONE WHO just circled in front of me. He sure as hell knows what breathplay is now.

He lifts my face with my hair again, eyes searching my face. He doesn't ask how I'm doing, which I appreciate. I can't stand when a dom goes soft on me. He does offer me a sip of water, which I also appreciate. It dribbles down my chin, but cools my tongue and lips. He puts the cap back on the water with finality. "Time for your caning."

My ass clenches at the word.

Hell, yes.

LINCOLN

. . .

So far, so good. Scarlett's lush body is hella responsive and turning her on gets my dick harder than stone.

It's funny I never knew about this world before her, because as soon as I slipped into the role of dominant I discovered how much it fit me. In this world, my economy of speech is a tool. My size and strength work a power all their own. My natural alpha tendencies shine. Hurting a woman?

That took a little getting used to, but once I got a taste of how satisfied it made them, it became an addiction.

That doesn't mean I got addicted to turning women, in general, on. No, it's all been for Scarlett. I had to figure out this world so I can meet her in it.

And now that we're here, I realize how foolish I was. What did I think? She'd get one taste of me and beg me to be her personal dom? Invite me back to her mansion as a live-in fuck toy?

What the hell was I thinking telling her I wanted my job back?

That's not what I want. I want everything from her. Want to give all of myself to her. Not an employee.

A lover. A partner. A fucking soulmate. And yeah, I don't even believe in that soulmate shit.

Sweet, generous, beautiful Scarlett. The woman who is in constant creation, who works herself to the bone, who gives and gives to her friends who take and take.

But she doesn't even know me. When I worked for her I rarely opened my mouth, rebuffed all her attempts to draw me out. So this is as much as I'm going to get. Thirty grand for one night of pleasure with her.

Yeah, I'll take it.

I stand behind her and perfect my aim with the cane. *Swish.* I lay the first stripe just below the start of her ass crack, above the butt plug.

She jerks in her bonds, ass squeezing and wriggling.

I rub her slippery folds to reward her for enduring the pain.

She sighs and collapses again, limp.

I lay down another stripe, just below the first one.

"Ahh," she cries out.

Another caress of her folds.

I aim below the plug and lay three quick strokes down her ass.

She screams this time and her right leg starts shaking uncontrollably.

I stroke down her thigh, squeeze the calf. "Shh. You're doing so well. I slide two fingers inside her and pump them a few times, then pull out and slap her pussy. "Good girl."

The shaking subsides and I grip the cane again with my dominant hand. "Three more," I announce. I know she loves pain, but the way she marks so easily slightly alarms me. I sure as hell hope she knows about arnica.

Scratch that. I will personally be applying arnica to her ass. Repeatedly.

I make the last three count, slow and methodical, one right under the next, the last two on the backs of her thighs where it hurts the most. She jerks and cries out for each one, pants and sobs.

I love the sounds. I want to let her come, but it's still too soon. This first scene needs to set the tone for the rest of the night, and she needs to be clear on our role reversal. I'm in charge of her tonight. I will take care of her completely, but she submits to me.

I walk around to the front of her bringing my cock to mouth level. "You need to come, baby?"

"Yes, master," she gasps, the words tumbling out so fast they blend together.

I unbutton my pants and free my aching cock, giving it a few rough jerks. "Suck me dry and I'll think about it."

She lifts those striking green eyes to my face. They're dilated and glassy. Good--she's in full submission mode. And I've never seen a more beautiful sight in my life. Her lips part immediately, like she's dying to get that lush mouth on my cock.

I groan, a bead of pre-cum leaking out before she even touches me. When I shove forward into her mouth, she sucks eagerly, even though

I purposely bump the back of her throat. I slowly draw back out and she hollows her cheeks, pulls hard. I pop out and her tongue emerges from her mouth: wet, velvety, ready. I rub my wet dick over her tongue, her mouth. The moment I inch forward, she closes her lips around my dick and starts sucking again, that clever tongue swirling around the underside of my cock.

Christ.

I'm not going to last long. This woman's gives chart-topping head. My breath comes in faster and I grip her hair to use her as a fuck-hole. It's unbelievable pleasure. Waves of heat pour through my body, my thighs start to shake, muscles tighten everywhere.

"Fuck, Scarlett. Fuck, fuck, fuck." She's going to draw more words out of me tonight than I've spoken in a month.

I pump into her mouth faster, harder. I'm making her gag and choke, but it doesn't dampen her enthusiasm. The woman was born to be a service submissive.

Heat spikes at the base of my spine, my hips snap. "I'm gonna come," I croak. She lifts her eyes to my face, sucking harder, with more enthusiasm as I lose control, shoot my load down the back of her throat.

I release my tight hold on her hair and start to caress her head, massaging away the sting, stroking her ear, the side of her face, the back of her neck. "Fucking amazing, Red. So good."

She licks me clean and I reluctantly pull out. She smiles up at me, smug in her knowledge of what she just did to me.

I unbuckle her wrists. "I bet you think I'm going to let you come now."

Her smile droops.

I give a minuscule shake of my head. "Not yet, baby. You still haven't earned it."

CHAPTER 3

carlett

I AM LITERALLY GOING TO DIE IF I DON'T COME SOON. EVERY NERVE IN my body zings, every cell is activated and ready. I'm hot and trembly. I'm needy. Desperate, even. My ass throbs, anus is stretched and full in the best possible way. And my pussy? Sopping wet.

But it seems Lincoln has other plans for me. Which only turns me on more.

Damn him.

He unbuckles my ankles straps. If he thinks I can move, he's sorely mistaken.

Oh! Apparently he understands because he rolls me right off the bench and into a blanket in his arms. His long legs carry us swiftly to a couch, where he settles with me on his lap.

It's a position I never dare allow myself to fantasize about. A cuddle. I feel warm and cared for and cherished.

I don't let people take care of me. I'm the one in charge. Even with Ted I was the one who had to mother his ass all the time. Had to finally stop trying to take care of him and leave when I finally realized his addictions were insurmountable.

Like when Lincoln told me he wanted his job back, the inexplicable urge to cry rushes forward, making my nose sting, building pressure in my cheekbones.

He sees it, which terrifies me, but all he does is cup my face and slowly stroke my cheek. His expression is still completely neutral, as always, but the gesture says it all. He sees me. He has me.

He opens the bottle of water and puts it to my lips, jerking it away when I try to hold it myself.

I allow him to baby me, dribble water into my waiting mouth, cradle me in this soft velour blanket.

"Hey," he says softly, his blues staring into my greens.

Wow. He initiated a conversation. Right when I feel vulnerable and cracked open and want to hide my face in his chest. Which isn't me. I don't come here to cry on a man and get held. I come here for the pain.

"Hey," I mumble back and my stupid face gets warm. It's really hard for a redhead to hide a blush.

I lean my cheek against his solid chest—not quite hiding, but not able to maintain eye contact. His heartbeat is strong and steady, like him. He smells of fresh soap and the outdoors—like a forest at dawn. I turn my head and nip his pec and he chuckles, a deep, rumbling sound.

"That didn't take long."

"What?" I lift my eyes. Are we actually going to have a conversation?

"You already had enough with the aftercare?"

I grin, because a) it's so weird to hear him talk about BDSM stuff like he's an expert and b) yeah. I'm definitely done and ready to move on to do anything that gets me my orgasm. Because I'm still burning for it. Hot, itchy—hell, I'm practically feverish. I've never been one to back down from a goal. I wouldn't have become a star if I had. "What do I have to do to come?"

His lips twitch. "Submit."

I roll my eyes and thump his chest. "Asshole."

This time, I'm rewarded with a big smile, his straight white teeth gleaming like he's a toothpaste model. "Apparently, I didn't punish you enough." There's a wicked gleam in his eye that sends a zing straight to my lady parts. My nipples tighten, clit throbs.

As if he knows it, he pushes the blanket off my shoulder and cups my breast, shoving the molded cup of the bustier down and strumming my pebbled nipple. "You like punishment, don't you, beautiful?"

I answer by rocking my pelvis in his lap, rubbing against his erection jutting into my hip.

"Now who's playing silent?"

My lips part. Truly, I'm shocked to hear him tease me the way I teased him the entire 13 months he worked for me. Yes, I counted them. Now that I'm back in his presence, I realize just how much I miss him. He may not say much, but his presence conveys so much protection, warmth, strength. I always felt safe when he was at my side—and not just physically safe. Emotionally. I felt stronger when he was around. Like I could do anything. It's been fucking hard since I fired him. The new guards have done their job and I've hated them for not being Lincoln.

"I may have made a mistake," I blurt, reaching out to touch his lips. They look so soft compared to the rest of him, I can't resist. They are. And he immediately takes one of my fingers into his mouth, drawing it deeper, sucking on it. He watches my eyes as he swirls his tongue around it the way I swirled around his cock. When he's finished, he nips the tip of my finger and lets it go.

"You definitely made a mistake." There's no amusement now. Still the promise of punishment, though.

Yummy.

I like him stern.

I like him commanding.

He squeezes my entire breast roughly, then drags his hand down my belly to cup my mons. I push into his hand, moaning wantonly.

Please. Give me what I need.

"I didn't land on edging, Master. You want me to beg?"

"Oh, you'll beg, sweetheart. I guaran-fucking-tee it. But first I need to take care of that ass of yours."

He scoots to the middle of the couch and flips me face down over his lap.

Okay, more punishment, then.

I'm down.

But he doesn't spank me. Instead, he rubs some kind of cream over my ass. Quite the thorough aftercare. "You look like you bruise easily and I don't want you hating me tomorrow."

Every time he speaks, every time he offers an explanation, I'm amazed to hear it. Finally I get inside this guy's head. And so far, it's all good.

He starts twisting and pumping the butt plug, slowly. My pussy turns molten. I part my thighs and hump his hard lap. He slides several fingers inside me and pumps them, too, alternating with the butt plug. Waves of heat flush through me with the strength of a hurricane. An earthquake. Hell, Lincoln is a force of nature himself, able to topple this middle-aged star with a single touch.

"Please, Master. Please," I plead. I really need this. I mean, *really* need this.

He finds my G-spot and my hips jerk and dance under his touch.

"Oh God, please, Lincoln--Master--sir."

"Come for me, Scarlett." His deep voice enters my bloodstream, races to my core. Everything erupts as my orgasm blooms. Full body ripples shake me as my pussy clenches and squeezes his fingers, anus tightens around the damnable plug. I explode. Shatter. Disappear.

Float.

~

LINCOLN

. . .

I DIDN'T GET TO SEE SCARLETT'S FACE AS SHE CAME. THAT'S A SITUATION I definitely have to rectify. Next time she's going to be beneath me, squirming and screaming my name when she hurtles over the edge.

Even though I just came—*down her throat*—I'm hard as stone again hearing her climax. I want to hear those needy sounds from her a million times more. I want to be the guy who keeps her on edge and then takes her to Shangri-la every fucking time.

She lies, limp as a rag doll, over my thighs and I ease my fingers out of her and put them in my mouth, tasting her.

Then I grip the plug. She protests with a tiny mewl as it leaves her body. I drop it in a plastic bag in my duffel to clean and sterilize later.

I pull her panties out of my pocket, where I'd tucked them earlier, and bend her feet toward the ceiling to slide them on. I don't want anyone seeing her perfect pussy but me. I get them partly up her thighs, then slap her ass. "Lift."

She complies, pushing her delectably striped ass in the air.

When I have them on, I nudge her off my lap. "Kneel for me, princess."

"Mmm." She slides off my legs to kneel prettily at my feet. Bliss radiates from her lovely face, and the way she looks up at me nearly makes my heart stop. So open. So trusting. Not a look I've seen on her before.

I was already willing to slay dragons for her, now the need to protect her is stronger than the urge to breathe. I run my thumb lightly down her cheek. "You look beautiful."

She continues to stare up at me, eyes wide, barriers down. Searching. She's still trying to figure me out. She still doesn't know how much I care.

Fuck.

I sure as hell don't know how to tell her. Words get stuck in my throat. They get swallowed back down. It's like I swore some oath in this lifetime, along with not spilling my government's secrets, never to speak the secrets of my heart, too.

I want to tell her I missed her. I want to ask how she's been. Not the news I can—and do—find on the internet about her. That she agreed to let Taylor Swift cover one of her old Spider songs, or that she's going to do a song with the Chainsmokers. No, I want to know how she's been. How her sister's doing. The word on the little nieces she loves the stuffing out of. What's the latest with her circle of friends—the ones who practically lived at her mansion—filled the place with gossip and love.

I'm right in front of her and I still miss her because I long to be back in her life. Seeing her first thing when I wake up in the morning with her rumpled hair and a coffee mug in her hand, last thing at night when she flits around the place restlessly in a sleep shirt and socks, trying to get herself wound down enough to sleep.

Hell, if I'd ever let things get physical with her, I would've made damn sure she slept like a rock every night. I'd fuck her into oblivion.

But sleeping with clients was against the rules. And fuck if I don't honor my position and the job I swore to do. She came damn close to getting me to crack once.

It had been one of those nights she couldn't sleep and a storm rolled through L.A. Lightning, thunder—the whole bit.

She loved it. She came running out, eyes wide and excited like a child, her pouty lips rounded into "oohs" and "ahhs."

"Let's go dance in the rain, Lincoln," she said, slipping on her flip flops.

I'd cursed inwardly, because my client was in nothing more than a thin sleep shirt—no bra, no pajama shorts—and if anyone saw her it would be all over the tabloids. But it wasn't my job to police her, just to protect her, so I stayed silent and followed her out.

She hadn't left her property—thank fuck—but had just danced around in her yard, spreading her arms wide and lifting her face to the sky.

It was beautiful and sweet. One of the few moments when Scarlett seemed truly happy since I'd started working for her. By the time she was ready to go in, we were both soaked through to the skin, and believe me, Scarlett could've won any wet t-shirt contest in any state in the union. The fabric of her pale gray shirt stuck to her breasts, molding around their perfect form. Her nipples were

81

hardened bullets, and damn if she didn't want to shoot them right at me.

I opened the door for her and she fell into me, laughing, fisting my wet shirt.

"You'd better take this off." She rolled the hem of my shirt up to bare my abs, the lower edges of the tattoo I got after my first tour to Afghanistan.

"You didn't have to come out with me," she breathed, lifting her wet face up to mine. She flattened her palms on my bare skin, slowing sliding them up under my shirt to my chest. Her nails scraped lightly over the hair there sending a zing of electricity straight to the base of my spine.

My cock was already hard from watching her dance in the rain and she found the bulge of it with her belly. I don't remember what she said after that. There might have been words, but my brain blanked out because she started rubbing her wet breasts over my ribs, her belly over my cock.

I didn't mean to, but one of my hands snaked down and cupped her ass.

And—oh fuck! It felt so perfect in my palm. I squeezed and lifted, yanked those sinful hips right up against my groin. She bit my chest, lifted her lips for me to kiss.

But then reason kicked in.

"Scarlett," I ground out. I remember my voice sounded about two octaves lower to my own ears. Like some other guy was speaking. "There is nothing I want more than to fuck you right now." I squeezed her ass again, guided her in another lift and drag down my raging hard-on. "But if I do, I'm gonna lose my job. And I'm really fucking fond of this job."

It was the truth, but somehow the wrong thing to say.

I released her and she stumbled back, a little pissed. A little embarrassed. "Whatever," she sang out like she didn't care at all, but I felt like the biggest ass ever. She sashayed away, into her bedroom and I heard the sound of the shower running for over thirty minutes afterward.

I stayed in my wet clothes, punishing myself. Listening to the water run and imagining she was using the shower head between her legs to relieve the pressure. I squeezed my cock hard through my wet slacks and imagined it was me in there with her, giving her exactly what she needed.

Instead of dripping in the hallway, my sense of honor sagging, heavy with regret.

I want to tell her now, how I wished I had acted. How I wished I had broken protocol one time in my life to bring her pleasure.

But even now, I can't speak. Can't let myself ruin this moment. Because what happens if I tell her how much she means to me?

She's going to freak out and assume I'm another one of the crazies who stalk her.

No, better to bide my time. Convince her to give me my job back, promise I'll take care of her needs if she does. This time I won't follow company rules. And then maybe I can show her my feelings. I don't fucking know how, but I've got to try this. It's literally the only shot I have at getting near her again.

CHAPTER 4

 *carlett*

I'm pretty blissed out from subspace. The whipping and the orgasm might be the best I've had at Black Light, and that's saying a lot, considering the two clubs are the only place I've gone to get my rocks off for the last few years.

I'm sure it has nothing to do with the fact that they were delivered by Lincoln.

Yeah, right.

Only if *nothing* means exactly everything.

I'm still marveling over the fact that Lincoln is here and knows exactly what he's doing. It's like having a real-life boyfriend suddenly turn into the character from the smutty romance novel you've been reading.

It seems almost too good to be true.

But I still can't figure out Lincoln's angle. This isn't just some dream-to-life fantasy for me where I rubbed the genie's lamp and got my perfect dom.

No, Lincoln wants something, too and I need to understand what it is. It can't be just his job. Is this a long game revenge plan?

No. Lincoln doesn't seem like the revenge kind of guy. Of course, how do I know? He never talks. I have no idea what goes on inside that handsome head of his. All I really know is that he suffers from PTSD and is quite capable of a deep level of violence.

I really think if I hadn't stopped him that night, he would've killed Joe.

He rubs his thumb over my lower lip now and I have to fight the urge to climb up, straddle his lap and kiss him. Why have we never kissed? It seems wrong on every level that I don't know how his lips taste.

Of course, I'm not in charge here, so I wait for his instructions.

"Looks like you're ready for more," he observes.

He's right. I wonder what he sees that gives me away. But of course he knows. It's not just luck that he manages to play my body and each scene like a champion. He's a smart, well-practiced, observant man.

Suddenly, the thought of him practicing on other women has my stomach clenching. Did he have sex with them? Did any of them mean something to him? Does he have a regular play partner?

No.

I know he doesn't.

Or maybe I just fervently hope he doesn't. Because deep down in my bones, I know Lincoln belongs to me.

That's why he's here. That's why he spent his life savings for a night with me.

He was mine and I stupidly gave him away.

My mistake, but easily rectifiable. He already told me he wants back in.

"Yes, sir. I'm ready," I tell him, excitement for the next scene starting to dance in my veins.

He stands and gently pulls me up by my elbows. "Throw that ball again, Red. Let's find out what's next for you."

It's ridiculous the flutters of excitement his words bring, but it might be about the wicked look that accompanies them. Like he's going to torture me more, and enjoy every minute of it.

Lord, if this man was my live-in dom?

I'd never have trouble sleeping again.

My mind spins with fantasies of him suspending me from the ceiling in my bedroom and whipping me every night to put me to bed.

And just like that, I'm wet again.

I let him guide me back up to the stage where Madison publicly greets me.

"Our celebrity Scarlett A is back up on stage to spin again. So, Scarlett, how was your first scene?"

I grin and turn around and bend over to model my whipped ass. The crowd nearest the stage cheers and applauds. I take the mic. "Master Lincoln is a very skilled dominant," I say. "But he's off-limits, ladies. I'm claiming him for myself."

The crowd laughs and Lincoln steps up closer to me, cupping my throat from behind. "Do you do the claiming, Red? Or do I?" he growls in my ear.

I soak my panties. "Y-you do, Master," I manage, shifting to twitch my inner thighs together. I'm so horny for him I could die.

"That's what I thought."

Sexy, sexy man.

I love the way he talks to me.

He tightens his grip, although he's nowhere near to choking me. "You may have been my boss once, angel. You may be my boss again. But right now, I'm the only one in charge."

More melting.

More creaming of my panties.

"Yes, sir."

"Good girl. Now throw that ball and land something I can work with."

Of course I have no idea what he can or can't work with, but I'm dying to find out. Madison ushers us to the roulette wheel and I give it a spin, then throw my ball in.

"What's next for Scarlett A?" Madison muses as it bounces around and finally settles. "Shibari!"

I twist to look over at my shoulder at Lincoln. Shibari's pretty specialized. Only doms interested in the intricate rope work learn it. It's definitely not something you could improvise, even if you were an Eagle Scout, and I strongly suspect Lincoln was.

A small smile plays on his lips, though.

Okay. *Shazam.* He knows what he's doing.

I'm mostly impressed at how dedicated he must've been to have learned all this in the year since I let him go. But nigglings of worry also try to rear their heads. These are signs of a man obsessed.

I push the nervous thoughts away.

Maybe he just got curious after I fired him. Wanted to find out what it was all about and discovered he had an affinity for it.

I just wish I knew for sure.

Lincoln loops an arm around my waist and guides me off the stage.

"Do you have rope?" I ask.

He turns and cocks a brow.

"--Master?"

"You topping from the bottom?" Merriment dances on his normally blank face.

I grin. "Would it get me spanked?"

His chuckle lights me up from the inside out. "You'd better believe it, angel. Smacking your ass is a pleasure I'm eager to repeat."

And just like that I'm falling in love. All I ever craved from this man was a little flirtation.

No, that's a lie. I definitely craved much more, but would've been happy with a tease and a wink.

He guides me toward a wall, away from most of the activity. He drops his bag and unzips it, producing a long length of rope. "Turn around," he instructs, but guides me with his large hands before I can comply. I face the wall. He unlaces my bustier in the back. "The problem with shibari is that I want you naked for it."

I'm not quite sure what the problem is because I want me naked for it, too. He finishes loosening the corset until it comes completely apart and drops at my feet.

"I want you in nothing but my knots, but I'm not crazy about everyone else catching you that way, see?"

Something warm and sticky floods my chest. I should see it as possessive. Jealous, even. But I don't. All I hear is chivalry. He's always been fiercely protective, even without expressing himself.

I remember the way he'd glare at paparazzi when they got too close. Or the frown between his brows when I did anything he deemed unsafe—like going outside without shoes, or answering my own door.

Of course, I remember what he did to Joe.

He leaves me facing the wall as he starts winding his rope around me. I'm not surprised that his fingers move deftly. There's no stopping to think, no unwinding and starting again. Lincoln knows exactly what pattern he's making and how to execute it. He winds it around my chest and arms until he's created the center of a flower over my sternum, with bands of rope securing my arms to my sides. My breasts are caged and displayed with loops of rope above and below my nipples, forcing them to jut out.

It's beautiful. *I'm* beautiful. And being immobilized sends me straight back to sub-space, exactly where I love to be. This is the space where I don't have to keep striving, don't have to worry that I should be doing something more, that I'm not enough. When I'm here, when I'm under a master's control, all I have to do is surrender. Everything becomes pleasure. Release. Freedom.

Lincoln hooks his thumbs in my panties and slides them down my hips. I step out of them and he winds the rope between my legs, one loop on each side of my pussy and between my buttocks.

When he ties the final knot and rotates me to face him, I nearly combust from the heat in his eyes.

～

LINCOLN

. . .

FUCKING PERFECTION.

The sight of Scarlett trussed up in my rope does all kinds of things to me. The need to claim her nearly overwhelms me. I flash a feral smile. "How is it?"

"Delicious," she breathes.

I grin. Beautiful woman. So turned on by my work.

I pick up my bag, grip the knots in the back and use them to propel her through the crowd. She's in nothing but her thigh-highs, heels and my rope, but the knots provide a covering of sorts. A visual dressing and framing for her most intimate parts.

"You're about to get yourself fucked into tomorrow, Red," I murmur behind her as we weave through the appreciative bystanders who make way and admire.

She throws a glance over her shoulder. "Oh goodie."

The great thing about rope is that it gives you handles. Makes it easy to arrange your submissive any way you want her. Right now I want her on her back.

Legs spread.

I find a free sofa and swivel her down on it. Her eyes widen at being dipped suddenly, but her smile is pure delight. The anticipation in her eyes makes my cock strain against my pants.

I drop to my haunches in front of the sofa and spread her knees wide. "I've been dying for a taste of this pussy, Red. And now I get to feast on it to my heart's content, don't I?"

"Yes, Master." Her fingers wiggle at her sides, like she wants to reach for me. She jerks when I lick into her, her thighs closing around my ears. I push them back open and pin her pelvis down. With my thumbs, I part her outer lips and trace around the inner ones with the tip of my tongue.

"Lincoln."

I would correct her for not calling me Master, but I love the sound of my name in that quavering voice, so thick with desire. I flick her clit with my tongue a few times, then affix my lips over it and suck the little bud until it stiffens.

"Lincoln...Master...*yes*," she encourages.

I stiffen my tongue and penetrate her with it, lick her from anus to clit and back again. She writhes and moans beneath me.

"Lincoln." She picks her head up from the sofa, straining to catch my eye.

"Yeah, baby?"

"Master, may I please come?"

"No, Red. Fuck no. You don't come until I do, and that's not gonna happen until you've learned everything there is to know about taking my cock." I don't usually talk so crudely. Hell, I don't usually talk much at all, but I've had to up my sex talk game as a dom. It's part of setting the scene.

It seems to ring Scarlett's bell, because her pupils dilate and she arches her hard nipples toward the ceiling.

I stand up and unbutton my pants, take my dick out.

Scarlett licks her lips, watching, hips bucking in a silent invitation.

I fish a condom out of my pocket and roll it on. "Give me a green." I'm 99.9 percent sure she wants this, but I'm not asshole enough to fuck her without total consent. Especially not in a situation like this where I literally hold all the power.

"Green. Green, give it to me, Lincoln."

I grab her ankles and lift them in the air, swatting her ass a few times.

"Master!" she squeals. "Master Lincoln. I'm sorry!"

"Better." I lower her pelvis back down and push her knees toward her shoulders. "You want this cock?"

She's trembling beneath me, her ripe body beyond ready for me. "Yes, Master."

"You gonna take it until I'm done?"

"Yes, yes, Master. Give it to me."

My grin must be wolfish as I shove into her.

She cries out, her muscles tightening around my dick. She's tighter than I expect, considering how wet and plump her folds are. My eyes roll back in my head at the sheer pleasure of being inside her.

She's bound, immobilized, but she still manages to lift her pelvis to meet my strokes, grind her clit down on my shaft when I shove deep.

Her glassy gaze stays glued to my face, which has the effect of making me feel like a goddamn superhero.

It's intense and glorious. And also like coming home. Every thrust feels so right. Like our bodies were made for each other. Like my dick knows its sole purpose now.

I ride, taking her hard, plowing deep.

She mewls and cries out beneath me, her desperation to come clear in the needy keen of her voice.

I reach between our hips and rub her clit with my thumb and her mouth flies open, back arches.

"Not until I say," I warn, but I'm almost there myself. My balls tighten up, thighs bunch.

I slam in harder and harder, flesh slapping flesh. "Fuck, yes, Scarlett. You feel so damn good. I'm going to come."

"Master, please?"

"Wait for it," I growl, but I'm already catapulting off the ledge. I slam deep inside her and shoot my load. "Now, baby."

Her muscles seize around my cock, squeezing and releasing as she screams my name.

"That's it baby," I murmur against her lips. "Say my fucking name. Who owns you right now?"

"Lincoln," she pants. "Lincoln, Lincoln, Lincoln."

I claim her mouth, twisting my lips over hers and fucking her with my tongue. Her muscles flutter again around my cock, an afterquake no doubt inspired by the kiss.

Satisfaction burns through the aftermath of lust, helps clear my head. I stay inside her and she rocks her hips, taking me deeper in slow thrusts as we kiss like our lives depend on it.

When we finally unlock lips, she's panting, cheeks flushed pink, hair a fiery halo around her on the sofa.

"Fucking beautiful. I want to see you come like that another thousand times tonight."

Her husky laugh goes straight to my dick, making it surge again inside her. I pull out and remove the condom, disposing of it in another plastic bag in a garbage can beside the sofa.

I get my cock tucked away and zip my pants back up, then sit down on the couch and arrange Scarlett on my lap. She leans back in my arms, resting her head on my shoulder and tucking her face into my neck. I trace patterns lightly over her bare thighs, loving the way I make her quiver with each touch.

"Sweet thing," I murmur. The endearment slips from my mouth, even though I've never spoken the words before in my life. But it's an acknowledgement of truth. Scarlett is precious to me.

If only I could figure out how to tell her without totally freaking her out.

~

SCARLETT

LINCOLN LIFTS THE BOTTLE OF WATER TO MY LIPS AND DRIBBLES SOME into my mouth. I'm nestled into him, drunk with endorphins.

"You need something else, baby? Chocolate?"

I perk up at the word *chocolate*. It is my favorite treat. After I gave up partying, coffee and chocolate became my new addictions. Of course they don't help with the insomnia situation.

Lincoln reaches down to his duffel bag and produces a container of dark chocolate covered almonds. He snaps the lid off and pops one in my mouth.

"Mmm mmm." I purr approvingly. All my senses are heightened and the flavor practically explodes in my mouth. Like almost orgasm-worthy.

The memory of Lincoln producing chocolate at various times in the past surfaces now. He'd wrap up my half-eaten bars and bring them along when I went out, producing one exactly when I needed it most. Like after the paparazzi frazzled me to smithereens and I wanted to curl up in a ball and rock myself until my heart rate came down. Suddenly Mr. Calm and Collected would pull out a bar of chocolate, break off a square and silently offer it to me while we rode in the back of a limo. Or after we boarded a plane, and I needed something to do with my hands.

Or when too many friends took over my house and I hadn't had quiet time in days.

"Did you bring this for me?" I ask when he pops a second one in my mouth.

"Yes."

"Because you remembered I love chocolate?"

"Yeah."

Always with the single word answers. The man drives me insane.

For one moment, I wonder if Lincoln has feelings for me. *Real* feelings.

That night—the night it all ended—I attributed it to his PTSD. But what if his violence stemmed from something else? From genuine rage at the thought of me being hurt? From a genuine desire to see me avenged for any suffering I incurred?

We were in D.C. I stopped there after singing in the Macy's Thanksgiving Day Parade in New York for the sole purpose of visiting Black Light. It was before they opened one in L.A., and I had to get my fix on the East Coast.

I'd brought a guy back to my hotel room that night. I don't know why—I never do. I usually just get my rocks off at the club and leave. But the club was crowded that night. We couldn't find a free spanking bench or anywhere to set up a scene, and I was horny as hell. Joe, my play partner, had suggested we go back to my hotel room. I wasn't afraid, because well, I have a bodyguard.

Little did I know my bodyguard would lose his mind.

Of course Lincoln knew nothing about Black Light or the kinds of things that went on there. I had him drop me off at the psychic shop where the secret entrance was and told him to wait in the car. When I emerged with Joe and asked to go back to my hotel, he didn't comment. Lincoln retired to the room next to mine, as always.

Joe handcuffed me to the bed and used a crop on my ass. I guess I must've screamed too loud. Maybe I even screamed no--I don't know.

Sometimes things come out of my mouth. It doesn't mean I want the play to stop.

When Lincoln burst in, Joe had one hand around my throat as he fucked me.

And that's when Lincoln lost his shit.

Joe literally flew across the room and hit the opposite wall. I don't even know how. And then Lincoln proceeded to smash his face in repeatedly.

I screamed and screamed for him to stop.

Finally I yelled, "It was consensual—consensual, you idiot. I liked it!"

That's when Lincoln finally heard me. Or my words got through. He slowly dropped Joe to the floor and turned to me, horror scrawled across his normally impassive face. "It was consensual?" he mumbled.

I was sobbing, my wrists torn open from yanking on the cuffs to free myself. "Yes, you idiot. Jesus. Call an ambulance, I think you killed him!"

Remembering it now, I'm sorry for calling him an idiot. He didn't deserve that. He hadn't understood and he needed to save me. Hell, the guy thought he was being my hero. Instead, he lost his job.

The same twisty pain I've felt in my chest every time I think about Lincoln since that night burns. I want to apologize, tell him I forgive him.

Before I can figure out how to broach the subject, his body goes stiff beneath mine. Without a word—big surprise—he picks me up and sets me down on the sofa, stalking away, hands balled into fists.

And that's when my whole night turns upside down.

Lincoln picks a guy up by his throat.

The women around them scream and back away.

Security rushes over.

I struggle to get up from the sofa without the use of my arms. *"Lincoln!"*

Seriously, what the fuck?

"Give me the bottle." His lethal growl is low but unmistakable.

I can't figure out what the problem is. The guy is holding an ordinary water bottle.

"I know there's a camera in there," Lincoln snarls.

Camera? No one is allowed any recording device in Black Light. No phones, no cameras. It's one of the reasons I feel safe here. No photos. No paparazzi.

Oh shit. Did I have a photo stalker?

The guy's feet dangle above the floor, his face turning purple. He tries to say something but his words come out garbled.

I manage to get to my feet and toddle over. All traces of submission are gone now. I'm furious, and being naked and tied up only makes me more angry. "Lincoln--*hey!*"

One of the Black Light security guys shouts for Lincoln to stand down, but—just like the night he nearly killed Joe—Lincoln's not listening. Definitely not answering.

It takes two of the Black Light security guys to tackle and wrestle Lincoln away from the guy, and even then, he slips their hold and punches the guy in the nose. He tackles him to the floor and grabs the faux water bottle out of his hand. Then he smashes it against the guy's skull, cracking it open and revealing electronics inside.

"Lincoln, no!" I scream.

Not that I don't want to do the same thing to the asshole, but I know from experience Lincoln is dangerous when he's in attack mode and I don't want to end up with another lawsuit or—God forbid— have to bail him out for murder.

"What in the fuck is going on here?" A guy I vaguely recognize appears. Beside him stands a tall, model-esque beauty in heels and a slinky red dress.

Something about his authoritative tone makes Lincoln turn and listen, and then I realize how I know him. It's Victor Jannakos, the owner of the security company where I get my bodyguards. He's Lincoln's boss.

Victor's partner—maybe wife, I'm not sure—rushes to my side. "Let me get you out of these ropes, Ms. A." she murmurs, fumbling with them. "Actually, let me get you away from this shit storm." She touches my back and hustles me away from the chaotic scene of shouting, angry men, into the women's locker room.

"Holy shit, what just happened back there?" the woman asks. "I'm Mariana, by the way, director of Personal Protection Security. You're a client of ours."

"I know," I say but my focus isn't on her. I'm staring at the door as if I might see through it—find out what the hell is going on.

Mariana resumes her attempt to get me free, but she doesn't know where to start and she makes no headway in loosening even a single knot. "Shit, I just need a knife or a pair of scissors," she finally admits.

"Just get Lincoln," I say. "He'll untie me."

I need to see him. Need to know he didn't kill anyone. Find out what exactly happened.

"Do you want to see him?" she asks dubiously. "What was he even doing with you? Wasn't he the bodyguard you fired last year?"

"Yes," I mumble. My lips feel numb, my stomach is in knots and for some reason, my eyes start to burn like I'm going to cry. Maybe it's the memory of the heartbreak last time this happened. The pain and the guilt and the shame around having to fire the best employee I've ever had.

Just then a heavy fist pounds on the door.

Lincoln.

I know it's him even though it could easily be any other number of alpha males out there.

He doesn't wait for an answer, just pushes through the door, heading right for me. The other women in the locker room yelp and shout.

"Where in the hell do you think you're going?"

"You can't go in there, buddy."

Victor and one of the Black Light security guards follow him in, but he ignores them both, just beelines it straight for me, holding a blanket.

A blanket.

He nearly kills a guy out there, gets tackled to the ground, is confronted by his boss and security and he heads straight here, to the women's locker room, with a blanket.

He wraps it around me, tucking it into the knots above my breasts so I'm fully covered, and starts to unwind the rope. Working blind under the blanket.

"Lincoln, what happened?" I demand, but I stand docile under his touch, still trusting him implicitly.

"Tell me you didn't bid on her." It's Victor, Lincoln's boss. And he looks uber-pissed.

Lincoln doesn't answer, just bends his head and unravels knots, working around me in a circle.

Mariana looks at me. "Did he?"

I nod, mutely.

Victor crosses his arms. "Why?"

"Yes, why?" Mariana asks.

Lincoln doesn't answer.

I pin him with a stare. "Yes, Lincoln. Why? Tell us what made you put a second mortgage on your house for one night with me."

It's a challenge. A dare.

Maybe I'm being a little mean.

But Lincoln still hasn't given a satisfactory answer and I really need to know. The ground I'm standing on is way too shaky. I like Lincoln. A lot.

I loved partnering with him tonight.

I've missed the hell out of having him around.

But the bottom line is, I still know very little about him and his motives. And he won't open up. I really need to know--what is this all about?

∼

LINCOLN

. . .

FUCKING HELL. THIS IS MY WORST NIGHTMARE. A WHOLE AUDIENCE waiting for me to spill my guts.

I swallow around the tight constriction in my throat.

Give me a rifle and tell me to eliminate an enemy from 400 meters away. Send me into enemy territory on a suicide rescue mission. But please, not this.

Am I supposed to bare my soul here? Confess the depth of my feelings for Scarlett? Explain exactly why I spent the last year learning to be the best dominant I could be?

Fuck. She's going to think I'm a whack-a-doodle obsessed fan. They all will.

"I just want my job back," I force out over numb lips.

Something closes in Scarlett's face and I know I fucked up. Royally.

"Are you fucking kidding me?" Victor demands. "That is entirely unacceptable. Seriously, Lincoln. You have me really questioning your sanity right now. This is beyond unprofessional, it's downright invasive." He turns to Scarlett. "Ms. A, under the circumstances, I think this evening's pairing should be terminated immediately. Lincoln--" He turns back to me-- "You need to leave the premises right now if you hope to keep your employment with Personal Protection."

I seek out Scarlett with my gaze. My hands are clammy, my heart thunders in my chest. "Is that what you want, Red?"

She doesn't move, doesn't speak. The silence stretches into an eternity. Then, finally, she says, "Yeah, I guess that's best."

My stomach plunges to my shoes.

"I mean, unless you can give a better explanation..."

Four pairs of eyes focus on my face. Actually more like ten, because all the women in the locker room are listening, too.

"Yeah, I can," I force myself to say. But then nothing more comes out. The air in the room becomes stifling. I can't breathe.

This is fucked up. There's nothing I can say to Scarlett that will explain my behavior. I literally have no words.

"Nevermind," I mutter. I turn away because if I keep looking at

Scarlett's face, I'll never be able to leave. And they all want me gone right now.

Somehow, I make it out to the main room, pick up my duffel bag, retrieve my phone from the lockers, and leave.

CHAPTER 5

 *carlett*

As soon as Lincoln walks away I realize I made a mistake. I tried to force him into explaining himself, but he's not a man with the gift of gab.

And really, he called my bluff. I didn't want him to go.

But I'm buck naked except for the blanket—*heart-squeeze*—he brought me. I can't very well go chasing after him. I can't even leave this locker room.

I turn to Mariana. "Um, would you mind—"

"I'll get your clothes," she says decisively. There's a reason she's Director of Personal Protection. "Where are they?"

"Um..."

I realize I'm not so sure I want to redress in my costume for the night. Maybe I should just slip on the dress I came in and leave.

Well, either way, I still need to retrieve my clothes. "Against the far wall, I think. Unless Lincoln picked them up." My brain suddenly feels totally foggy.

A knock sounds on the bathroom door. Victor and the security guy already left.

My heart jams up in my throat. Did Lincoln come back?

When Mariana opens the door and speaks to the security guy, I'm flattened by disappointment.

Of course he didn't come back. I sent him away. Like an idiot.

Again.

When Mariana turns she's holding my outfit. "Lincoln asked the guard to bring this to you," she says softly.

I blink, hard. "That was nice of him." The lump in my throat grows bigger.

I walk to my locker and pull out the clothes I arrived in, getting dressed. "I think I screwed up," I admit out loud. Mariana's still there, like she's decided to be my personal bodyguard, even though I have Martin, a guy from her company, waiting for me in the car outside.

"You didn't do anything wrong," Mariana says immediately.

"No, I mean, I wanted Lincoln to stay."

She narrows her eyes, studying my face. "You did? Why? His behavior seems way off beat. Very sketchy."

"I know. But...if I go by his actions, not his words, he's never been anything but honorable and upstanding."

It hits me, suddenly, how much his actions can speak for him. And yet I let his words—or lack of them—drown out what I know in my gut.

Lincoln's good. He cares about me. Maybe he even loves me—who knows?

And I don't know if I can say I love him—I mean, if I go by words, I hardly know him at all. But if I go by his presence? His energy? His actions?

He makes me feel good. Special. Cherished, even. I was happier when he was around.

And if I go by tonight?

The man fucking rocked my world.

He was a dream dom to the core.

I let out a shaky laugh. "Did you ever read Shel Silverstein when you were little? *Where the Sidewalk Ends?*"

"Of course," Mariana says with a surprised chuff.

"Remember that poem 'Deaf Donald?' Where Talkie Sue keeps trying to get him to say he loves her but all he can do is sign it?"

Mariana goes still, like she realizes where I'm going with this. "Yeah. And she ends up leaving him, even though he was saying he loved her all along."

Tears prick my eyes. "Yeah. Exactly. I think that's maybe what I just did."

Her face goes soft. "Lincoln loves you." She says it like a statement, not a question. "Of course he does. That's why he was ready to kill for you."

"Yeah." Misery and happiness simultaneously loop through me, twisting around each other in a tangle of emotion. "The thing is, I have crazy people claiming they love me all the time. Sending me shit and acting nutty and obsessive. So him showing up tonight put me on guard, you know? It seemed a little over the top, you know?"

She nods.

"But he wasn't weird or possessive or crazy at all." I chew the inside of my cheek. "He was perfect." My voice breaks on the last word.

"If he cares, then he didn't really walk away." She speaks with so much certainty, that I have to cling to her words with hope.

"Right." I bob my head, grabbing my jacket and heading toward the door. "Oh." I stop and turn. "Um, could I have his number?"

Mariana laughs. "Of course. I'll have to look it up, but I will text it to you in the next ten minutes. Promise."

"Great." I pull open the locker room door and slip out, hoping no one will notice my hasty exit.

~

LINCOLN

. . .

102

Rather than get in my car and drive back to my doubly-mortgaged condo, I take off walking. My body needs to move and I need to clear my head.

Or maybe I'm just not willing to leave when Scarlett's so close.

The night she fired me I was lost in a fog of shame and self-loathing. I went to the hospital with her date—the guy I nearly killed —and answered questions from the police.

I called Victor right away, so he'd hear it from me first. He called back just as the police finally let me go-, which was probably due to some magic he'd worked with them.

"I'm so fucking sorry," I said right away, the phone pressed to my ear as I walked outside to call an Uber. "I misread the situation."

"I know, Lincoln. Listen up. You're not going back to Scarlett's hotel or her place in L.A.. I'll get your replacement to pack up your personal belongings from the mansion."

I stopped walking, ice sluicing through my veins. "No."

"Scarlett doesn't want you to come back. She's not filing a complaint against you, though. And she offered to cover any lost wages you incur between jobs."

"Fuck." I shoved my fingers through my closely-cropped hair. "I didn't even get a chance to apologize."

"I will pass your apologies along. Of course you understand. Tonight left a bad taste in everyone's mouth. It's better to wipe the slate clean. I'll get you reassigned as soon as I have a new job for you. Go get a room at a new hotel and do not try to contact Ms. A. Understand?"

"Yes, sir," I answered, and I obeyed, like I always do.

Because if Scarlett wanted me gone, I couldn't force myself on her.

Now, though, it feels like I made a mistake. That night and this one.

I need to at least try to tell her what she means to me. Then, if she still wants me gone, I'll go.

I turn around and walk back to Black Light. I don't have a goddamn clue what I'm going to do or say when I get there, I just know I have to figure it the fuck out.

Because if I don't, I will regret it until the day I die.

I get back to Black Light, and by some miracle, they let me in. I head straight down the steps and barrel into the room, nearly knocking down a woman trying to leave.

"Scarlett." I catch her arms and steady her. "You're leaving."

She stares at me, wide-eyed. "What are you doing here?"

"Listen, I know you asked me to leave. And I will. But first I need to tell you something."

I release her arms—not because I want to, but because it's the only right thing to do. She takes a step backward.

"What is it?"

Is her voice shaky? Fuck, I hope I haven't upset her.

I force myself to speak. "Scarlett, I came tonight… I'm here because I'm in love with you." The words tumble out, one on top of the other. "And I don't mean I'm in love with Scarlett A, the pop star. I mean, I'm in love with *you*. The person standing in front of me.

"And I fell in love with her little by little, day by day. Watching the way she fluffs up all her friends, makes sure everyone's happy, even when they forget to ask about her. When they take too much. Stay too long.

"I'm in love with the woman who spontaneously makes up songs for her nieces, who takes them to Disneyland seven days in a row, even though crowds are her biggest nightmare.

"I'm in love with the woman who never stops. Who answers every fan's tweet, who stays up all hours of the night writing songs, playing chords, always working. The woman who asks about her housekeeper's children, who remembers the staff members' birthdays.

"And I lied to you tonight, when I said I wanted my job back." I scrub my hand across my jaw. "I mean, I do. If you'll take me back, I'm there. But I want more than the job. What I really want, Scarlett, is to be the guy who makes you scream at night. The one you turn to when you need your release. Or when you just need to be held. I want to be your man, Red."

I stop talking, trying to escape the feeling that I said way too much, that I'm hanging out in the wind with no chance of finding my footing again.

Scarlett stares at me with those expressive green eyes, but for once I have no idea what she's thinking.

I try to back peddle. "Or you could forget all that and just give me the job."

She smacks my chest, tears glistening in her eyes as she laughs. "Yes."

I snatch her up against my body, one arm around her back, the other in her hair. "Yes, what?" My voice sounds hoarse.

"Yes, I want you back. As my bodyguard..."

My heart dives.

"Bodyguard with benefits?" She lifts her gaze to me, and damn if the vulnerability there doesn't make me want to blow up mountains to protect her. "I've missed you so much, Lincoln. Nothing felt right with you gone. The new guy drives me crazy. I can't stand having him around. I don't even feel like *myself* without you around. You may not have said much, but I always felt your support. Your amusement. Your empathy. I knew I had you on my side no matter what." She shoves her hair back from her face. "And tonight was amazing. I definitely want more of this side of you."

Holy shit.

I claim her mouth, kissing her hard, yanking her hips up over my hardening cock. She yields to me, fully, parting her lips for my tongue, kissing me back. Her arms loop around my neck and she runs her nails through the hair at the back of my head.

I lift her thigh and she jumps, straddling my waist.

I walk out with her, lips still locked until right before we reach the outer door, then I reluctantly lower her to the ground. "There might be someone else with a camera out there, wanting to get a picture."

She climbs back up on me. "I don't care." She bites my ear.

CHAPTER 6

 *carlett*

LINCOLN GETS RID OF MY CURRENT BODYGUARD AND TAKES THE KEYS, saying he'd be driving now. I text Mariana, who had texted me with Lincoln's number to let her know the situation, since she's boss to both of them and needs to know the score.

I get nervous on the way back to my place. Or rather my thoughts take over where my body and heart were leading. Uh, how exactly does this work, when he's my employee but I want a dom?

Of course, Lincoln's as quiet as ever. It wouldn't bother me, except that things feel unsettled.

I chew on the inside of my lower lip. "I'll reimburse you for the auction cost," I offer.

He shoots me a sidelong glance. "Fuck that. No. I like the idea of paying for you every month for the next ten years."

I let out a surprised laugh. "Yeah? That's--" I break off and shake my head unable to produce a word that matches his level of crazy. "Well, there may be a signing bonus for taking this job."

Lincoln stops at a light and twists to face me, putting a knuckle under my chin. "You trying to remind me who's in charge, Red?"

I flush, because that's exactly the part I'm trying to work out in my head. "No, I mean--"

"Listen up. I'm not guarding you for the money. I'm guarding you because I don't trust anyone else to do the job. Because I need to. And I take the job of protecting you very seriously. That may mean some changes, baby." The light changes and he starts driving again, weaving through late night L.A. traffic easily.

"What changes?" There's a smile on my face because suddenly, I don't have to be in charge. Lincoln isn't waiting for direction or leadership from me. He has a plan. He's going to execute it.

"I'll be putting you to bed at a decent hour every night, making sure you get good sleep. If that means you need your ass whipped before bedtime, I'm gonna be the guy to do it."

My pussy clenches, thrills running through me. Not just sexual, but something deeper. Warmer. The sense of being cared for.

"What else?" My voice is pure maple syrup. I reach for his thigh and squeeze.

The corners of his mouth curve up as he takes the exit toward my mansion. "I'm gonna kick your friends and your sister out when they overstay their welcome. And you will be restricted to ten hour days. No more." He arches a brow meaningfully.

I grin like a little fool. "I can live with that."

"Good." He slides a glance over at me. "You can be alpha anywhere in public. Anytime you need to be. But in the bedroom, I'm in charge."

I melt a little more. I'll be a mushy puddle by the time he peels me out of this car. "Yes, sir," I murmur.

He cracks a real smile and when he looks at me, his gaze is filled with warmth.

"I never got my last roulette spin," I say, not to complain, but to let him know I'm still up for more play, if he is.

"Hmm. We'll call it *dom's choice*, then."

I smile. "Isn't it always?"

He answers with a wink, and then the quiet between us is warm and easy.

Lincoln, my strong, silent warrior. Capable. Dominant.

Perfect.

EPILOGUE

incoln

I FIND SCARLETT PERCHED ON THE COUNTER IN THE BATHROOM, replying to tweets.

"Hmm." I make my voice sound disapproving and she startles and jumps down, hiding the phone behind her back. "Looks like someone's breaking the rules."

She tips her head back to look at me. Her cheeks flush, lips part invitingly.

I fist her hair and tug her face up even more. "I think someone's getting punished tonight."

Scarlett gets punished most every night, so this isn't anything earth-shattering. She can't sleep without the release, and I consider it my duty to make sure she sleeps soundly. So the bedtime ritual almost always involves some pain, then some pleasure, then pulling her against my body for sleep.

I cup one of her breasts, flattening it, squeezing. She's wearing nothing but a tank top and panties, looking cuter than should be legal. She's gone a little babygirl on me, which I didn't expect.

Scarlett had been playing at total pain slut before I moved back in. But now she's embracing my protective dominance and letting go of her need to control. There's more laughter, teasing, fun. There's giggles and tickling and over the knee spankings.

And yes, I still tie her up and fuck her hard about every other day.

I lean down and bite her ear. "Bad girl. Go to the bedroom and take off your clothes."

She scurries out, excitement flushing her cheeks.

I give her a few minutes, then enter to find her naked, bent over the edge of the bed with her legs spread wide.

Beautiful woman.

As always, I suffer from feeling too full. Too satisfied, even in my hunger for her. I can't believe I'm here, privileged enough to the be the one Scarlett let into her life. Into her bed.

I walk over slowly, making a noisy production out of unbuckling my belt and pulling it from the loops.

Her back tenses, a slight shiver running through her.

I smile, knowing how much she loves this. The evidence of her arousal is already there, glistening between her legs.

I wind the buckle end of my belt around my hand to shorten the length, then swing. I use it lightly at first to warm her up, then slap harder, leaving red weals on her porcelain skin.

She jerks and moans under the strokes, breathing heavier, but not protesting.

I lighten up again. It's not just about inflicting a little pain and being done with it. Scarlett needs time for it to build, time to be in this space, time to get used to the pain, and then to be challenged. I whip her for twenty strokes lightly, then go harder again.

Now she's ready.

She's whimpering and whining into the bedsheets, pleading with me for it to be over.

I drop the belt and run my palm lightly over her heated ass. "You know what happens when you disobey."

"Yes, sir."

"What?"

"I get my ass fucked."

"That's right, Red. You get your ass fucked hard, don't you?"

She moans.

I grab the lube from the bedside table and drip a generous amount between her cheeks. I'm harder than stone—which is pretty much a normal occurrence any time I'm near Scarlett. I free my erection and rub lube over it.

I slip into her pussy first, teasing her a few times before pulling out.

"Noooo," she moans.

"You know what you're getting," I remind her. "Pull your cheeks open for me."

She complies and I prod her anus with the head of my cock without applying pressure. Just greeting the hole I'll be punishing. She's good about holding still, trying not to resist.

She's had plenty of anal training—anal sex isn't really punishment, it's pleasure, but I like to frame it this way because it turns her on.

I press forward and wait for her to open. She pushes back and I slide in, filling her slowly.

"Uh ung." She moans and sucks in a shaky breath.

"That's right, Red. I'm filling your ass with my big cock right now. And then I'm going to fuck you long and hard."

"Yes," she breathes. "Please, sir."

Hell, yes. I start to lose control when she acts so fucking needy. I reach around and cup her throat, stroke the slender column as I bump her ass with my loins.

"Oh God, yes, Lincoln."

I use my hold around her throat to lift her head, make her arch up. With my other hand, I reach around and pinch her nipple. She cries out, the pitch of her voice desperate.

"I'll bet you're hoping I'll put my fingers in your pussy, aren't you?"

Her response is incoherent. Good. She's just the way I want her. Completely lost to me. Blind with need. Desperate.

I release her nipple and slide my fingers under her hips, rubbing her clit. She screams. Her pussy's sopping wet.

My balls tighten up. Commanding her body, wringing out her orgasm, never fails to make me lose control.

I shove my fingers into her slick channel and pump harder and faster. She's screaming my name. I shout hers.

The room tilts and slides. I come in her ass and she comes on my fingers.

"Lincoln. Lincoln." I don't know how long she's been croaking my name.

"Yeah, baby?" I pull out and get a washcloth to clean her up. When I'm done, I flop on the bed and pull her up into my arms.

"What, angel?"

She nuzzles her face into my chest. "Nothing. I just need you."

She needs me. I love this woman.

I stroke her hair. "I need you, too, Red."

"When are you going to ask me?"

I go still. "Ask what, baby?"

She lifts her head and peeks at me. "Did you want to marry me?"

Pretty sure my heart stops beating.

Fuck, yeah, I want to marry her. But I haven't worked up the nerve to ask because I wasn't sure she wanted it. She's already been married once—unhappily. And I stand so much more to gain in a legal commitment than she does.

I flip her on her back, straddling her waist and pinning her wrists to the bed beside her head. My lips hover, centimeters over hers. "Marry me, Red?"

"Yes." Her eyelids flutter. She smiles.

"Yeah? You really want to?"

She laughs and struggles against my hold. I don't budge. "Of course I do. Don't you?"

I indulge in a taste of her lips. "I don't need a marriage certificate to tell me what I already know."

"What's that?"

"That you belong to me."

112

She kicks her legs.

"That nothing in the world would ever take me away from your side."

Her eyelids droop and she turns her wrists in my hands to hold my fingers.

"That I've been sworn to you from the moment I met you."

She pulls my head down and delivers happy kisses all over my face. "I love you, Lincoln."

"I love you more." I claim her mouth, covering her body with mine, showing her all the ways I worship her.

The End

ABOUT THE AUTHOR

USA Today **Bestselling Author Renee Rose** loves a dominant, dirty-talking alpha hero! She's sold over a half million copies of steamy romance with varying levels of kink. Her books have been featured in USA Today's Happily Ever After and Popsugar. Named Eroticon USA's Next Top Erotic Author in 2013, she has also won Spunky and Sassy's Favorite Sci-Fi and Anthology author, The Romance Reviews Best Historical Romance, and Spanking Romance Reviews' Best Sci-fi, Paranormal, Historical, Erotic, Ageplay and favorite couple and author. She's hit the USA Today list five times with various anthologies.

Grab six free books for FREE here.

Please also follow Renee on:
BookBub | **Facebook** | **Amazon** | **Instagram** | **Twitter** | **Goodreads**

SWITCHED

A BLACK LIGHT: CELEBRITY ROULETTE NOVELLA

By

Livia Grant

CHAPTER 1

iper

"THIS MEETING HAS GONE OVER. WE NEED TO WRAP THINGS UP. I'M late for another appointment." She kept it to herself that she was late for a date with a lounge chair next to her swimming pool.

Piper Kole sat at the head of the long conference table in the movie studio's upscale boardroom. Four pair of anxious eyes were on her, waiting for her instructions as the production meeting came to a close.

Damn she was tired. Just once, she wished one of the men in their expensive suits and designer shoes would fucking get a backbone and take charge. But the thought was fleeting as she shivered at the thought of losing control over even the smallest decisions in her life.

"John, you're in charge of the marketing action items. Peter, get back to me tomorrow with the updates on the location changes we discussed. Frank, I want the revisions to the contracts over to me by courier no later than noon tomorrow. We need to wrap contracts up if we want to hit our target to start filming in three weeks. And

Jorge," she said turning to face the man closest to her. "Get the fucking catering contractor under control or I'll find someone who can."

"Yes, ma'am, Ms. Kole. I'm on it."

"Dismissed," she said, sounding more like a high school teacher than an international superstar. As if to prove her point, the men who worked for her all jumped up and scrambled to quickly leave the boardroom, afraid of being grilled by their boss for their continued incompetence. She'd fire them and get replacements, but since she'd already done that the year before, she was reluctant to go through the hassle again. And the women she'd hired before them had been worse. Sure, they may have been competent, but they had also been jealous, backstabbing bitches.

Why was it so damn hard to find good employees?

Her long sigh hinted at her near exhaustion, but as a certified workaholic constant fatigue went with the territory.

"You know it's your fault they all act like emasculated eunuchs around you, right?"

Piper jumped as a deep voice spoke from directly behind her. She didn't need to swing around to see who it was. That voice was permanently etched in her brain, right alongside other flashbacks she'd like to eradicate from her memories. "Nolan, how unpleasant it is to hear your voice again. You really need to warn me when you'll be in town so I can avoid coming into the studio."

His soft chuckle didn't jive with the normally awkward standoff usually wedged between them.

Piper gathered up her iPad and files, stuffing them into her oversized Prada bag before pushing to her feet. She needed to get the hell out of there. When she spun to make her exit, a wall of handsome smugness blocked the door. At six-foot-three, Nolan Boeing emanated power with his mere presence. Most women melted into a pool of goo at the slightest attention from the powerful movie executive. But for a woman like Piper who had worked hard to control her own destiny in the cutthroat entertainment industry, a business known for lucky breaks, he represented danger. The neatly trimmed dark beard he'd grown since she'd last seen him only added to his powerful profile.

"If I didn't know better, I'd swear you were trying to avoid me, Ms. Kole."

"It took you long enough to get the message," she deadpanned. Her insult didn't faze him in the least, which only reminded her that he was the antithesis of the men who had just run from the room with their tails between their legs.

"And here I thought you were only avoiding me because I watched you scene with your rent-a-boy at Black Light two weeks ago."

Piper's heart rate bumped up a notch. She'd counted on his discretion to avoid having this conversation. Glancing nervously around the conference room to ensure they were indeed alone, Piper finally took a step closer, leaving only a few charged inches between them. "I don't know what you're talking..."

"Cut the crap, Piper. I know you saw me watching you play with your boy of the week."

She fought to keep her breaths even, refusing to let him see the affect he had on her.

"Looking for some tips, maybe? Like what you saw?" She forced a playfulness into her banter, despite them both knowing full well they weren't playing around.

They were already too close, so his step closer had her wanting to flee. Only through sheer willpower did she remain still.

"I loved the leather bustier you had on." He was close enough she could feel his warm breath on her cheek and smell his clean masculine scent. She could feel her resolve melting under his heated gaze. Desperation to end this encounter warred with her reluctance to touch the wall of muscle standing between her and a safe exit. He wasn't the only one who'd done some spying at Black Light. Unwanted memories of his toned, shirtless torso flexing as he'd wielded a flogger across the flesh of a restrained submissive pushed Piper's anxiety higher.

Unwilling to take this particular trip down memory lane, she risked making things worse by placing her palm in the center of his chest, crushing his designer tie and dress shirt as she tried to shove him aside. She worked out daily. She was a strong woman, so the fact that he didn't even sway under her pressure pissed her off.

Realizing she wouldn't move him, Piper snapped her hand back. "I'm not doing this. Not here."

"Fine. I'll meet you at Black Light tonight at nine. We can pick up the conversation then." The asshole had the audacity to smile, lighting up his dark eyes. She hated that she missed the small dimple that always appeared in his chin when he smiled, now camouflaged by his sexy beard.

"You're delusional. And I'm done with Black Light."

"Uh-ha. You didn't look like you were done last time."

"What the hell is that supposed to mean?" She moved her hands to her hips, impatience getting the best of her.

His smirk turned to a full grin. "I noticed the boy you were playing with failed to… finish things up to your satisfaction."

Her right palm itched, desperate to feel the sting from slapping that smug smile off Nolan Boeing's handsome face. She had to settle for a parting shot. "Have you been watching the news, Mr. Boeing? There's this little movement going on you might have heard about. It's called MeToo. Are you really going to sexually harass me like this in the studio's boardroom?"

She scored a small victory when her words wiped the smirk off his tanned face.

But her victory was short lived.

Nolan closed the gap between them, grabbing her biceps to hold her captive, but stopping just short of pulling their bodies together. She hated that she had to crane her neck back as he towered over her, their faces just inches apart. She tested the grip he had on her, trying to wiggle away, but his hold was too strong.

"Don't threaten me, Piper. I'm not some pimple-faced fan who'd sell their soul for an autograph or a few minutes of your time." His words piqued her anger. She put both palms against his chest and pushed away from him as hard as she could. She may have broken free, but she was under no delusion; it was only because he'd released her.

"I'm leaving."

"Running away from me again?"

She scrambled to think of anything to say that might finally break the tenuous thread she'd always felt between them. "Are you so insecure you can't take no for an answer?"

Nolan leaned in closer to talk softly against the shell of her ear. "Are you so insecure you have to keep hiding behind this ice queen facade?"

In her silence, Nolan got the last word. "I look forward to one day melting the ice queen. See you at Black Light, Piper."

CHAPTER 2

olan

"GOOD, YOU'RE STILL HERE. I WAS HOPING I'D CATCH YOU TONIGHT."

Nolan had just taken the last swig of his bourbon when the club owner, Jaxson Cartwright-Davidson, slid onto the bar stool next to him. The bartender, Susie, quickly placed what looked like a glass of soda in front of her employer without being asked.

Nolan wasn't in the mood to shoot the shit. In fact, he wasn't in the mood to do anything other than wallow.

"Bring my friend here another one, will 'ya, Susie? Put it on my tab," Jaxson instructed.

"But... Mr. Boeing has already had his two-drink limit, sir."

"We'll let him slide by for tonight since he isn't playing."

"Yes, sir. Whatever you say." The attractive bartender with her pixie-cut hair and skimpy uniform turned to grab the bottle of Booker's and pour a jigger of the top-shelf booze in his empty glass. Only after she left did Nolan raise his glass.

"Thanks for the drink, but I know why you're here and the answer is no."

"You couldn't possibly…"

Nolan cut him off with a raise of his hand. "Elijah already gave me the full court press. I'm not participating in the roulette event. I don't need the free month's membership."

"Of course you don't, but I'm sure you like doing good deeds for charity," the club owner countered.

"I give plenty to charity," he answered after his next swallow of smooth, burning liquid. He had a nice buzz going. He reached to take his phone out of his suit jacket pocket to call for a car, but then remembered that, like everyone else in the club, he'd had to check his phone in a security locker. What a pain in the ass.

"Where's your sense of adventure?" Jaxson prodded, not giving up easily.

"I just got back from a mountain climbing jaunt with some of my old college buddies. My sense of adventure is alive and well."

"Come on. Can't you do us a favor? I know you can snap your finger and have a play partner whenever you'd like, but this would really help us out. We had a last minute withdrawal of a celebrity and we've already opened up the online bidding."

"You must be scraping the bottom of the barrel hitting me up. I'm hardly a celebrity, at least not to the general public."

"Don't sell yourself short. I know you usually stay behind the scenes as an executive producer and financier on projects, but you've made a name for yourself in the film industry. And more importantly, you're a damn fine Dom. Any submissive would be lucky to win a night of play with you."

Nolan nursed his drink, trying to avoid being rude, but there was no way in hell he was going to scene with a stranger doing God-only-know-what kink. He was sure there was nothing that could change his mind.

"Come on. We even got Piper Kole to sign up. You aren't going to let her show you up, are you?"

Surprised, Nolan inhaled too quickly causing the last drops of liquid heat to sputter as he coughed. Jaxson hadn't missed the effect the news of Piper's participation had on him.

"I've seen the way you watch each other play. I've even seen the stories in the gossip rags about you two having a past. What better way to spend some time with her than to both be celebrity Doms? You can have your own side bet on who can take their submissive for the night closer to the edge without pushing them over."

"As fun as that sounds, I'm just not interested. I'm not even sure I'll be in town that week," he lied, trying to think of somewhere, anywhere, he would need to be other than California.

"Well, shit. I was hoping I could change your mind." Jaxson took the last swig of his drink and pushed to his feet before he said his goodbyes. "Looks like I better head up to the office and start making some calls then. Thanks for nothing, asshole." His insult was accompanied by Jaxson's good-natured slap on his back, telling Nolan the gruff club owner wasn't going to hold a grudge.

After he was alone again, he let his thoughts drift to the news that Piper Kole would be in attendance on Valentine's Day. He knew she'd been avoiding coming to the club since he'd cornered her in the studio conference room the week before. He'd come to the club for a nightcap all week in hopes of catching his favorite Domme in action. Tonight, like the other nights before, he'd be leaving disappointed.

Would he really need to wait until Valentine's Day to see her in action again? The idea depressed him, which only pissed him off even more.

Why the hell couldn't he just shake off the magnetic pull he felt to the ice queen of Hollywood? Even as he thought it, he knew the answer deep down.

Warm memories flooded back from years past. From a time when Piper Kole was new on the scene and she had been anything but an ice queen. She'd been outgoing... vibrant. He was certain every one of his colleagues would think him crazy, but he'd seen it with his own eyes.

The woman known as the ice queen had a hot, melty center that he'd had the pleasure of dipping into only once. They'd shared one extraordinary night years before. He'd woken up to an empty bed and a few days of the brushoff before she'd left town for a few months to film in Europe.

He'd hoped to whisk her away and sort things out when she'd returned to Hollywood, except the woman who'd come home from Europe was a whole new Piper Kole. The ice queen had swallowed her whole and he'd been shut out of her life like everything and everyone else.

Refusing to spend more time rehashing a past he would rather forget, Nolan pushed to his feet and headed towards the exit. Once he got his phone back, he pulled up his Uber app to call for a car. He knew he was too buzzed to safely drive and he had zero desire for a repeat of the near DUI he'd almost got over ten years before. He'd been fortunate enough to get a friendly cop who had recognized him and let him slip through with a stern warning. He'd pledged to take that gift to heart and had never driven even close to drunk since.

The drive to his house in the canyons of Beverly Park, just north of Black Light, only took fifteen minutes. He was losing his buzz already as he keyed in his security code at the dark entrance to his empty house. A pang of something close to loneliness invaded at the quiet stillness that greeted him.

His ex-submissive, Diane, had moved out over a year before. Ironically, it wasn't her that he missed the most when he got home each night. Why the hell did she have to take Sadie with her too? Their energetic pup had been who he missed the most after their rather short relationship had ended. Maybe he should just break down and get a new dog.

He was contemplating the idea as he walked through the dark house. Knowing he was in way too much of a reflective mood to try going to sleep, he beelined it to the full bar at the edge of the great room. Only after he poured himself a double did he walk to the floor-to-ceiling wall of windows.

The view of the California hills with the City of Angel's lights twinkling in the distance relaxed him. This was exactly how he enjoyed ending most nights. Reflecting on the day... alone.

Even thinking it, he knew if he could transport Piper Kole beside him, he would. He'd love to get her alone... here... at his home. He'd throw her over his shoulder like a caveman and carry her to his dungeon in the basement. He'd strip her bare and tie her naked body tight to his St. Andrew's Cross... perfectly round ass out. His cock twitched at the thought of using every one of his impact toys on each delectable inch of her body until he cracked through her icy exterior. He would so enjoy the pleasure of watching her melty insides spill out all over his playroom as he drove her to one screaming orgasm after another... something those pitiful submissive boys she liked to play with could never do.

He shook his head, knowing he was delusional to have such thoughts. Piper Kole had made it clear to him, and anyone else who cared to pay attention, that she had no desire to be melted. On the contrary, she much preferred cutting those around her with her shards of sharp ice... often taking the form of sharp knives, one of the Domme's favorite kinks.

How could he get her out of his system once and for all? Maybe he should plan on being in town for Valentine's Day after all. Like Jaxson suggested, he could volunteer to play that night too. She'd have to talk to him then. Maybe he'd finally push her to have the hard conversations they needed to in order to put the conflicting memories he had of her to bed once and for all.

Giving in to temptation, Nolan crossed to his favorite chair, plopping his shoes on the ottoman and reaching for the iPad on the end table next to him.

He'd visited the Black Light private website many times. As a member, he entered his encrypted login credentials and waited until the home page splashed on his screen.

They'd updated the site with the marketing blurb for the upcoming Valentine Roulette event. Photos of the featured celebrities available to bid on started scrolling by, changing every ten seconds. A brief bio tagline labeled each photo, along with the ability to click and find out more about each participant.

He recognized most of the celebrities, either from meeting them at the club or seeing them in the tabloids or news. A celebrity chef...

Major League Baseball player... professional ballet dancer... rock stars... models...

He was beginning to think Jaxson had pulled his leg when a picture of Piper Kole filled his iPad. It was one of her popular marketing photos. He touched her picture to stop the rotation from moving to the next participant.

God, he hated this photo of her. It didn't jive with the real Piper he liked to think he knew. In it, she had her long, dark hair pulled back into a severe, high ponytail. Her sexy lips were curved in a barely-there smile. Some talented make-up artist had used silver and blue hues to turn her warm blue eyes into icy orbs. He preferred to remember those blue eyes boiling over with passion as he'd pounded her to not one, but two, orgasms in their single night together.

Piper Kole was gorgeous by almost anyone's standards, but Christ she had never been more beautiful as when she'd lost control in his bed that night.

Nolan scrolled lower, reading through the distinguished bio of the international veteran movie star, director, and producer. She was Hollywood's rare version of a trifecta, and as such, was by far the most famous participant in Celebrity Roulette. He hated to admit that it bugged him that she would clearly rather play with a complete stranger that she could dominate than spend a few minutes with him catching up over a drink.

Scrolling lower, he glanced through several photos of Mistress Ice, as she was openly referred to, while in several intense scenes at Black Light. He'd watched her in action and as a dominant himself, he recognized her need, and skill, with controlling her submissives. But that's where the comparison ended.

He'd met and talked with many dominatrixes over the years. He respected and supported them completely in the BDSM community. It's how he knew how different Piper's style of control was.

Most dominants, himself included, got sexual satisfaction from pushing their subs to the edge and then enjoyed watching them soar through subspace, bringing them equal measures of pleasure and pain. Even when playing with someone new, there was still an intimacy... a trust… between partners. He loved to feel the yin and yang. The push and pull. Dominance and submission.

He'd been given the gift of reconnecting with Piper again when Black Light had opened last spring. He'd had the opportunity to watch her from afar and he knew without a doubt that she wasn't interested in the push and pull of dominance and submission in her scenes. He'd watched her choose to play only with men ten years her junior who were eager for any little scrap of time they could spend with the famous movie star. Men she could completely control. They took what scraps she gave them, and remarkably — unlike most dominants — she rarely took pleasure for herself.

Maybe she really has turned to ice and doesn't need passion.

He was too tired to figure things out tonight. Closing the iPad case and setting it aside, Nolan rose to head to bed. He'd sleep on it and call Jaxson the next morning if he decided to change his mind and play after all.

CHAPTER 3

 iper

PIPER'S DRIVER TURNED THE SUV TO THE LEFT JUST INSIDE THE property's entrance gate, taking them straight to the night's event. She usually entered Black Light through Runway. She'd found making brief appearances at the popular dance club was a nice way to keep up the required exposure celebrities like her needed while being able to control the environment as much as possible. Jaxson and Chase had a phenomenal setup in Runway and Black Light. As celebrities themselves, they understood the pressures of controlling the media, banning unwanted electronics from the premises.

But tonight was different. The knot in the pit of her stomach was proof of that. She was rarely nervous, but there was no other way to describe her current state of mind. Why the hell had she let the men talk her into participating in their Celebrity Roulette event? She sure as shit didn't need the help in finding play partners. She had a long line of handsome submissive men on speed dial, ready to play, or rather ready to submit at a moment's notice. And as Black Light was exclusive and private, she couldn't claim to be participating for the publicity.

Too fucking late now. A security guard was opening the car door next to her and helping her exit onto the brick walkway that would lead through the grounds of the mansion to the secret entrance of the private BDSM club. She grabbed her bag of toys she always brought with her to Black Light just before exiting.

"Good evening, Ms. Kole. We've been expecting you," the man in the black suit welcomed.

"Hello," she replied a bit too sharply.

She was already slipping into her Mistress Ice persona.

Most women would be insulted at the moniker, but Piper wore it proudly, just like the body-hugging leather mini-dress and thigh-high, high-heeled, black boots. She'd chosen a dress that showcased her bare, muscular arms. Unlike many women, she loved her arms. She should. She worked out daily to keep them toned... strong.

She'd also worn her favorite piece of jewelry, a half-inch wide ring of ice-white diamonds that circled her left bicep. The piece had cost her a small fortune but was worth every damn penny.

At five foot ten, Piper was able to easily keep up stride-for-stride with the security guard accompanying her through the winding garden towards the unmarked entrance to Black Light. They passed a golf cart headed back towards the parking lot. The driver, another security guard, slowed as if to stop to offer them a ride, but she shook her head slightly and he gunned the gas, passing them.

An awkward silence fell over the duo once they were alone in the garden. The only sound besides their footsteps on the brick was the rhythmic thwack of the riding crop she'd attached to her wide leather belt as it slapped against the leather of her outfit.

The February evening air was cool so the whoosh of warm air that hit them as they entered the building was welcome, but the line of patrons waiting to check in with the security desk was not. She'd left her phone in the car, not wanting to deal with the lockers. Why hadn't all of these people done the same?

"What time is it?" she asked her escort.

"It's just seven now, but I promise they won't start without you, Miss Kole."

She had opened her mouth to ask if there was some way she could go around the line, when a voice from behind stopped her in her tracks.

"Good evening, Piper."

Keeping her eyes forward, she grimaced inwardly. "Nolan. I should have guessed you'd be here tonight. You're turning out to be quite the little voyeur, aren't you?" After she spoke, she regretted acknowledging that she'd come to expect him to be hiding out in the shadows, watching her scene.

"Not tonight, I'm afraid. Tonight I'll be playing just like you." He dared to step up next to her as if they were together.

She took a step forward as she answered. "That surprises me. You don't usually like being in the limelight like most celebrities here tonight. You've always been more a 'stay behind the scenes' kinda guy."

He spread his arm wide, letting her step up to the check-in point ahead of him as he answered. "Yeah, well I thought I'd make an exception tonight. After all, it's for a good cause."

She assumed it was because they were both participants and it was already after seven that the security guard, Brian, didn't do more than a quick check for their membership cards before waving them through. She tucked her card back into the side compartment of her toy bag as they were both whisked through the relatively empty social area of the club, past the bar, towards the packed to the brim theater.

"I'm going to go first to make a path up to the stage for us. Stick close," their club escort instructed.

Piper stayed as close as she could as they pressed through the throng of spectators. She noticed Nolan brushing against her back several times in the crush of the crowd. As always, she felt the electricity that seemed to spark between them.

The temperature in the room was oppressive with wall-to-wall bodies pressed together. Extra chairs had been brought in, but the majority of the crowd was on their feet. She was relieved when their escort stopped just short of the stage where a small group of vaguely familiar looking people milled about looking as nervous as she felt.

"Hello, Piper. I was glad to see you'd signed up to play tonight as well. I was afraid I'd be the only really famous participant."

It was a good thing she wasn't prone to laughing easily or she would have probably made an ass of herself snickering at the boasting statement by the has-been Robert McCauley. He may have been the hottest leading man in a TV drama in his day, but she had to admit his day was long gone. "Never fear, Robert. Looks like there's a good showing here," she nodded in the direction of the others including Scarlett A, the famous rock star and then to Ronan Bellington the hugely popular celebrity chef.

The much older man, with an obvious toupee, leaned in close enough that she caught a whiff of his stale breath, luckily overpowered by his Old Spice aftershave. "Well, they aren't of our caliber now, are they?"

The asshole was bold enough to reach out and touch her arm with an intimacy he didn't deserve.

This. Right here. It was just one of the many reasons why she had taken her sexuality into her own hands years before. Piper took a deep breath, reminding herself that he wasn't one of her submissives. As much as she'd like to, she probably shouldn't grab her crop and whip his offending hand.

Showing restraint, she reached and clamped her hand over his, squeezing hard enough to turn his sleazy smile into hilarious open-mouth shock. Not wanting to make a scene, she leaned in close to talk intimately against his ear. "You seem to have forgotten that I am not Piper Kole tonight. My name is Mistress Ice and I don't recall giving you permission to touch me, Robert."

She pulled back so he could see her stern scowl, and resisted chuckling at the older man's quick submission, snatching his hand away from her as if her skin was now on fire.

"Um-well, sorry." He took a step back, crashing into the back of one of the other celebrities waiting for the show to start. Stumbling away, he added, "Good luck tonight, Piper… I mean Ice…Mistress…"

She finally let the grin fighting to escape shine as he scurried to the other side of the group.

Her grin didn't last long.

"Well done, Mistress." Nolan's compliment was delivered against the shell of her ear. She suspected he was being careful not to physically touch her, which ironically only made her wish he'd sucked her earlobe into his mouth instead.

Not knowing what to say, she ignored him and Jaxson luckily chose that moment to take the stage with Chase and Emma. He flipped on the microphone to welcome the crowd.

"Time to get this party started!" Jaxson called out. The PA system squeaked feedback and he moved back a few inches so avoid a repeat.

Piper found it hard to concentrate on the club owner's words knowing Nolan Boeing was responsible for the heat she felt at her back. As Jaxson handed the mic over to the MC for the night, Piper fought to pay attention to anything other than the uncomfortable heat surrounding her — and she didn't mean from the temperature in the room.

She forced herself to pay attention to the kickass MC, Mistress Madison, as she ran the crowd through the plans for the night. She had to give Jaxson props for his choice of MC. Not only was Madison witty and engaging, she represented the small percentage of women dominants in the room well, controlling what could have been a chaotic process with ease.

It was a relief when the pairings began, giving Piper the distraction she needed to keep from getting more nervous. She wished she'd requested that she be paired with her submissive first so she didn't have to look out into the crowded room, wondering who out there had spent the money to play with her that night. She saw several men she'd scened with before trying to catch her attention. She hoped it was one of them as she might actually have some fun.

Getting paired with someone inexperienced would be a nightmare. She'd found that most men who thought they wanted to submit to a dominatrix really just found the idea hot. When it came to actually being submissive, many choked, not really enjoying the experience.

As the group of remaining celebrities started to dwindle, her wandering mind took a darker turn. Which one of the women in the crowd would be submitting to Nolan Boeing?

The second she thought it, her mind revolted, trying valiantly to reject giving a fuck about the answer. He could play with whomever he wanted.

Fine. She'd admit that Nolan was one of only a handful of men who somehow had the ability to make her want to shed her icy exterior, if only for a few hours. It didn't help that her body seemed to remember the one passionate night she'd spent in his bed. It had been years ago. Ancient history. Pre-Mistress Ice. Pre-Henry Winston.

God-dammit. Not tonight.

She would not allow thoughts of a man that had changed the trajectory of her life in every possible way to intrude on an evening that was supposed to be fun. Thank goodness it wasn't just submissive men whom she dominated. She took control of her wayward thoughts and pushed all negativity out with the same ruthlessness she used on play partners.

When the celebrity pool was down to just her and Nolan, he stepped up next to her. As the only Domme in the auction, she suspected that they were leaving her as the last celebrity for the night. Proving to herself, as much as him, that he wasn't affecting her, she leaned to her left to whisper, "So you want to make a bet on who can make their submissive cry first?"

"Oh Piper, you're on."

The words had just left his mouth when she heard her name being called from the stage.

Wait. What had Madison just said? They were down to only one? She forced herself to pay attention to the stage in spite of the sexually charged glare on Nolan's face as he watched her.

"And our final celebrity for the night is Piper Kole, better known as Mistress Ice here at Black Light. Not only does she have the distinction of being our only female Domme playing tonight, but more importantly, she is our celebrity who drew the highest bid. Everyone please put your hands together to thank Nolan Boeing for his very generous bid of one-hundred thousand dollars!"

W.T.F.

She spun to face Nolan while taking a step away from him, trying to put distance between them.

"Wait. You said you were a celebrity tonight!" she accused, sure he could hear her heart pounding in her chest.

"Wrong. I said I was playing tonight. Which I am." He closed the distance between them again and leaned in to speak against her ear again. "With you, Piper. Or should I call you Mistress Ice?"

CHAPTER 4

olan

CHRIST, SHE WAS GORGEOUS. HE WISHED HE COULD HAVE SNUCK HIS phone in to capture the look of shock on Piper's face as she realized she'd be forced to play with him for the next three hours. He'd done the math, and already considered the five hundred and fifty dollars a minute he'd be spending to play with Piper to be a bargain.

The crowd's cheers had died down, yet Piper hadn't moved towards the stage. Nolan held out his crooked arm, inviting her to join him on the stage, but she remained frozen. Mute.

He leaned closer again to talk to her privately. Well, as privately as he could with a room packed full of spectators, all staring at them. "Come, on, Piper. It's just one night. A few hours, actually." When she didn't answer, he tacked on, "You owe me."

"I don't owe you shit, Nolan," she spat.

Apparently he'd found the words to unlock her silence. Titters of laughter made the rounds with those closest to them. Daring her wrath, he stepped closer, pulling her stiff body into his arms to talk to her alone. "You're right. You don't owe anyone anything. I just meant that after all these years, I'd like to see if we can get a little closure is all."

"There is nothing to close. There was nothing open in the…"

He squeezed her hard enough to let her words trail off. "Don't you dare. You can pretend there isn't anything still happening between us if you want, but I'll be damned if you're gonna minimize what we had together that night."

"Do you hear yourself? It was one fucking night. A one-night stand."

"Bullshit. I…"

Mistress Madison calling them to the stage again cut off his rebuttal. "Mistress Ice, please report to the stage with your submissive for the night in tow."

He took a deep breath before leaning closer again. "This is your chance, Piper. I signed up knowing that tonight you'll be in charge. If you won't meet me on my turf, I'm putting down my Dom hat and am offering to submit to you for the next three hours." He paused, unsure if he should continue, but knowing this was just the first of many submissive things he'd hopefully be doing that night, he added a vulnerable truth. "That's how much I want to be with you."

He couldn't see her eyes, but he felt her tense muscles relax slightly in his arms. He caught her as she wobbled on the too-tall heels of her sexy boots. For a brief second, he enjoyed the feel of her against his body and then it was gone. Her hands were on his chest, pushing him away.

Most men would hate the flash of anger in her eyes, but Nolan preferred the heat of anger to her more common icy glare.

"You'd better watch what you ask for, Nolan. I'm not sure you can handle what I'm gonna dish out tonight."

"Bring it on, Piper."

She paused long again, continuing their stare-off until he finally knew he'd won at least a small victory. "Mistress. From now on, I'm Mistress Ice." When he didn't acknowledge her instruction, she barked louder. "Say it!"

This was it. He'd been so sure he'd be able to submit for three short hours, yet now that the moment to start had arrived, Nolan felt uncharacteristically nervous. It wasn't like he was the most hard-ass Dom in the world, but at no point in his sexual history had he felt the need to submit sexually, or otherwise, to a woman. Still, he took a deep breath and dove in with gusto. "Yes, ma'am, Mistress Ice."

The spark of victory in her eyes brought him surprising satisfaction. She didn't take his offered arm, but instead diverted around him and headed towards the few steps that would take them to center stage next to Madison at the roulette wheel.

He felt all eyes on them as they took their places. He'd never been shy at Black Light before, but he was only then realizing how different it felt coming into the scene as the submissive. A twinge of excitement for the unknown edged up his pulse as he avoided making eye contact with the other dominants in the room who were at that moment thinking he'd lost his ever-loving mind.

"We're down to, like, just one more roulette spin before everyone can get their first scenes started. Which one of you will be throwing in the marble to choose your first stop for the night?"

Madison was trying her best to keep things moving along by holding the small object out to him, but when Piper didn't take it, he turned to her and asked, "Are you okay with me tossing it in, Mistress, or would you like to do the honors?"

"Oh, please do," she quipped.

Nolan ignored her temper, grabbing the marble just as Madison spun the wheel. He held the small bauble, saying a silent prayer it would land on something good. He was smart enough to know that his idea of good and bad fluctuated greatly based on if he were in charge of the scene or not.

He about had a heart attack when the wheel landed on ABDL. There was literally nothing he could think of that could have been worse as the night's activity than baby/diaper play.

It was Madison who saved the day. "Both of our contestants have ABDL play listed on their hard limits list. Please roll again."

Feeling like he'd dodged a bullet, Nolan dropped the marble in a second time, this time landing on something barely better. Madison yelled, "Watersports."

Both Nolan and Piper answered in unison, "Hard limit."

Thank God.

Madison held out the marble to him for a third roll, but Piper snatched the ball instead. "Clearly, you need some help here. I'll drop it this time."

The ball bounced around more than ever before finally coming to a rest on the wheel. It was still spinning too fast for Nolan to read the activity. He had glanced up to watch Piper just as Madison yelled out, "Knife play!"

Conflicting emotions invaded. Compared to the first two rolls, this was an immensely better choice, but since knife play was one of Piper's favorite kinks, he might be a bit out of his league.

The grin on her face let him know she thought the same thing, particularly when she retorted, "Who knows. Maybe by the end of the night I'll make you cry like I do most of my other subs."

Dream on, Piper.

"Let's see how long you can hold out without using your safe word, shall we?"

Shit.

CHAPTER 5

 iper

DAMN HIM. NOLAN HAD FUCKING BLINDSIDED HER. WHAT AN IDIOT SHE was for not realizing this could happen, although in her defense, Nolan Boeing was such the ultra-dominant in everything he did, she would have never guessed he'd even consider bidding on her.

Just thinking about it pissed her off. He was incapable of submitting to her. The next three hours were going to be a fucking train wreck. The best she could hope for was to teach Mr. Boeing a valuable lesson about staying in his lane once and for all. It was a damn good thing this event was raising money for a worthy charity or she would seriously consider backing out.

Willing herself to stay calm, she crossed back to where they'd been standing earlier to retrieve her bag of tricks — as she had dubbed her toy bag years before. Despite her brain's anger, an unwelcome excitement sparked deep in her belly at the thought of using some of her toys on Nolan's athletic body.

As they were at the front of the room, they had to wait for the crowd in the theater to disperse before they could weave their way to the exit. Each of them avoided talking as she let Nolan take the lead, pushing them through the throngs who'd stopped in the social bar area and through the red velvet curtain.

That's where he ground to a halt, stopping to let her catch up. Already several other couples were setting up scenes on the small platforms dispersed around the room. Since their roll didn't have something to do specifically with themed rooms, Piper wanted to scene in the open space where the most people could watch her humiliate Nolan. He'd decided to play a dangerous game with her and he would soon be paying the price for that.

Public humiliation.

By some miracle, the biggest stage in the corner of the main club was still open. Piper waved a dungeon monitor down on her way there.

"Hey, Santiago. Do you have a padded table you can bring to this platform? One with restraint rings?"

"Yes, ma'am. I'll just need a minute or two. I'll be right back."

As the guy took off at a jog towards the back hallway, Piper took a deep breath and turned to face off with Nolan.

"Strip. Now."

The grin on his face as he loosened his tie and started seductively unbuttoning his dress shirt felt like he was mocking her. Piper turned her back on his display to sprint up the three steps to wait for the DM to return. There was a small table where she laid down her bag. One by one, she started pulling out the tools of her dominatrix trade, laying everything out on display. Paddles, crops, and canes. Clamps, weights, and pinchers. Rope, handcuffs, and collars.

She glanced back to find Nolan standing bare-chested, watching her with interest. She pulled her knife kit out next, sure to show him the full set in their protective case. His face didn't register fear, but then again he'd been expecting that. Time to bring out the unexpected.

She saved her favorites for last, pulling out the cock cages, rings, and torture devices one by one, stopping to show each to her unlikely submissive. The room was humming with activity so she had to speak louder than she wanted to when she addressed him. "What are you doing just standing there? I gave you a command."

Their eyes met, linking them across the distance. She hated her uncontrolled reaction to the hungry look in those eyes.

Determined to keep control, she tacked on, "I didn't give you permission to look at me. Eyes down until told otherwise."

His—"Yes, Mistress"—caught her off-guard.

She was glad he'd followed directions and looked at the floor, missing her checking him out as he unbuckled his belt and started to slowly lower his pants. Santiago chose that minute to return, pushing the folded, padded table on wheels for easy transport. Within minutes he had the table setup and locked in place in the center of the stage, ready for use.

"Sub, get up here!" she shouted, aggravated that he seemed to be stalling.

To his credit, Nolan grabbed up his shed clothes and headed up the steps to meet her without complaint. He'd already complied with more commands than she'd have thought he would.

When he was down to just his boxer briefs and socks, she commanded, "Leave those on."

"Afraid to see my impressive package again?"

There it was. His sass.

"Naw. I'm gonna cut those off you," she retorted.

That shut him up.

"Up on the table. Face up," she directed.

When he hesitated, she offered him an out. "Sure you don't want to just safe word now and call it a night?"

Her taunt sparked Nolan's quick retort. "I'm not gonna make it that easy on you, no. I paid a shit-ton of money and I'm not leaving until I get my money's worth."

Piper forced even breaths as she replied. "Oh, I'm ready to give you your money's worth all right, starting right now. Get your ass on the table, Nolan."

He opened his mouth to argue back, but she reached out and clamped her hand over his mouth.

"Silence. I like my subs quiet. The only thing I want to hear from you for the rest of the night are your cries of pain or the word red when you're ready to put an end to this nonsense. Got it?" She watched a bevy of emotions flittering through his grey eyes. He was struggling, as she knew damn well he would. "Admit it. You can't do this. You can't act submissive to save your life."

Their stare down stretched out until she was sure he was going to safe word and they could both go home and forget this night ever happened.

"You're right. I'm sorry, Mistress." He turned then and climbed on the table, moving into position and leaving her standing in frustration.

Fine. They were in a battle of wills, but she had the upper hand, and she'd use it to break him and this obsession he had once and for all.

Piper grabbed his right wrist first, roughly pulling his arm up and out to the corner of the long table and reached to pick up one of the pairs of handcuffs she'd brought. She could have chosen to use rope, or the padded cuffs, but those would be more comfortable. She wanted to make Nolan as uncomfortable as possible to bring this disastrous night to an end fast.

Once she had the cuff on his wrist, she attached it to the closest ring at the edge of the table. She could feel his eyes on her again, watching her every movement as she returned to the table to pick up the next pair of handcuffs. She took a minute to look through her bag, pulling another important tool out before returning to her sub for the night.

As soon as she placed the blindfold over his eyes, Nolan used his free left hand to try to stop her. She quickly diverted to restraining his left hand next, leaving him helpless when she put the blindfold back, pulling the elastic band at the back of his head to make sure it stayed in place.

She felt better the second he could no longer watch her. Keeping her cool around Nolan Boeing was difficult on a normal day, and there was absolutely nothing normal about today.

Piper grabbed one of the metal ankle cuffs from the table and returned to affix it to Nolan's right ankle. She pulled his dress sock off first to make sure the tight metal would be as uncomfortable as possible later when she was making him writhe on the table.

And he would be writhing, of that she was sure.

Desperate for the night to end before she lost this battle of wills with Nolan, Piper took her time, moving to his final ankle and slowly subduing her submissive to the table.

She felt lighter once he was secured and blindfolded. Pausing a minute just to take a few calming breaths at the foot of the table, she let her gaze rake up and down the restrained man now at her mercy.

She couldn't help but admire his physique. Toned and tanned all over. She wasn't sure exactly how old he was, but he had to be at least ten years older than her. While she normally chose to play with men younger than her, she had to admit that there was something really sexy about the salt and pepper smattering of chest hair that Nolan sported. While he may not be showing the rock-hard abs that some of her younger submissives often had, he did manage to have the same sexy happy trail of hair that led the way under the elastic waist of his boxers.

For the first time that night, Piper got excited at the unexpected opportunity Nolan had provided her by agreeing to be her submissive even for a few hours. While she had no intention of allowing him to break down the protective wall she'd constructed around her heart, there was absolutely nothing stopping her from breaking him of his unhealthy obsession with her, and she could have some fun while doing it.

It was time to get started. Piper went to the prep table and reached into her bag to pull out her elbow-length, black satin gloves she loved to wear during knife play. She pulled the gloves over her manicure before reaching to open the wooden case that held the top-end set of knives and blades she used in her scenes.

She was relatively certain Nolan was a novice when it came to knife play, which would work in her favor. His uncertainty of what to expect would heighten his fear. She tested her theory by picking up her favorite fixed-blade knife. It had a custom carved base with several small ice-white diamonds inset in the design. She'd sharpened the three-inch stainless-steel blade herself that afternoon in hopes of getting to use it in roulette.

Piper stood on Nolan's right side silently watching him. With each breath he took, his pulse was increasing because his exhales were becoming shallower... faster. If she were honest with herself, she had to admit her own pulse had crept up as well. It always did when she held a knife against a submissive, getting off on the feeling of life-and-death power she held in her hand. One small slip and she could end his life, and they both knew it.

"I know you're trying to psych me out, Piper," he complained, his tone not nearly as cocky as it had been just minutes before.

She was happy he couldn't see her smiling. "Is it working?"

"Not even..." As soon as he started to answer her, Piper pressed the dull edge of the blade against his right nipple, cutting off his words mid-sentence. She dragged the blunt side across and lower.

"You were saying something?" she teased.

When he didn't answer, she changed the knife's position so that the sharp point poked at the toughened skin of his areola just hard enough that she knew he would feel the cold steel. Moving at a snail's pace, Piper moved the knife lower, trailing the tip through the patch of chest hair to his flat stomach.

"I wouldn't breathe too deeply if I were you, sub. I'd hate to accidentally cut you instead of your shorts."

Like most newbies to knife play, she watched him hold his breath, too afraid a slight movement might draw blood. And then, like all inexperienced subs, he eventually ran out of air and had to draw in a deep breath that raised his chest. She was ready for it, moving the knife perfectly so that the point of the blade pressed the perfect depth to scare him without drawing blood.

"God-dammit, say something, Piper."

With practiced speed, Piper used her free right hand to slap the inner part of his right thigh. As expected, he jumped with surprise, pressing the point of the blade against his chest harder than before.

"Naughty submissive. What is my name tonight?" she lectured through her grin.

"Mistress," he hurriedly supplied, anxious to please her.

Damn, this was turning out to be a lot more fun than she'd expected.

"Good boy."

Most true submissives lived for positive affirmations from their Dominant, but she knew those two words would grate on Nolan. Still, she admired his restraint at not complaining.

Getting back to work, she pulled the point of the blade lower down his stomach, over his belly button, only stopping when it hit elastic. She paused again, letting the vulnerability of the moment wash over Nolan. Letting it sink in that she currently held a razor-sharp object just an inch from his manhood and there was absolutely nothing he could do to stop her from turning him into one of the eunuchs that he enjoyed comparing her normal play partners to. Well, other than screaming, red, of course.

She always got high on the power rush of subduing a submissive on a normal night, but tonight was special… unique. Nolan may have come here willingly, and even paid good money to play as a submissive, but she knew the man well. Submission would never come naturally to him, making it that much more rare and precious.

With a quick flick of her wrist, her knife sliced through the waistband of his shorts, splitting them open down the crotch. Like she was opening a birthday present, Piper used the tip of the knife to flick each half of the shorts to the side, exposing Nolan's impressive cock and balls to Piper and the growing crowd of spectators.

Using the tip of her gloved finger, Piper slowly dragged the satin from tip to base, letting him feel the vulnerability of his exposure. His flesh expanded with her touch, but she withdrew before he could truly get hard. As soon as she sensed him relaxing, she moved the knife into motion again, quickly slicing the remaining boxer short material on his legs until the tattered material lay on the padded table, her submissive fully naked before her.

"I want to thank you, sub. This is actually turning out to be a lot more fun than I'd expected. I'm just gonna grab the rest of my knives and I'll be right back," she taunted seductively.

It was too quiet for most of the spectators to pick up on it, but Piper grinned at his soft, "Shit."

Yep, she'd be home drinking a nightcap by ten.

CHAPTER 6

olan

HE COULD DO THIS. HE'D THOUGHT LONG AND HARD ABOUT THE consequences of bidding on Piper, running through every scenario and still deciding it was worth it to get close to her again, if even for a few hours. His goal: to get closure. To understand why she had thrown away something that had felt so special to him years before. He didn't buy her explanation that it had merely been a one-night stand to her.

But, as he felt the cold metal lightly dragging across his chest, a niggle of doubt started to wedge into his brain. It obviously didn't hurt. On the contrary, it felt kinda nice. But it was freaking him out that she was jumping around on his body, letting the sharpness touch him in the most unexpected ways. It was... unsettling.

He focused on the only thing he could control—his breathing. He tried to keep his breaths steady as she would tickle him one minute, and scratch him the next. He doubted she'd draw blood, but they hadn't discussed it.

And he hadn't put Blood Play on his hard limit list.

With his eyesight cut off, his hearing was trying to compensate. Lucky him, he picked up on the slapping sound of a couple not far from them having sex. Not just sex. The submissive was being pounded almost brutally hard and screaming for her Dom to let her come. Despite his best attempt, he could feel blood rushing to his cock. Unfortunately, Piper noticed too and chose that moment to park the tip of her knife directly at the end of his now growing shaft. With each centimeter of growth, the pressure against his cock increased until he was in pain.

"Piper..."

"Wrong name, sub." Her reminder was accompanied with a slap that made him jump, pressing his most tender skin against the knife hard enough to draw out a shaken shout. The accompanying giggles of mirth from Piper made his pain worth it... almost.

"I haven't given you permission to get a hard-on. As a newbie sub, you might not be aware that my submissives are only allowed to get hard, and especially only come, on command." Her voice had gotten softer, telling him she'd returned to her supply table.

Her next comment was against his ear. "Lucky for you, sub, I'm a good trainer. Let me show you."

Her gloved hands felt heavenly as she cupped his balls for a long moment. Her gentle massage had started to feel good when he felt the first softness wrapping around the base of his cock. At first, he thought she had circled her fingers around him, but then another row was added a bit higher. And another. It couldn't be her fingers. And shit, it was getting tighter. Fuck, much tighter.

"In case you were wondering, I like to call this little cock and ball torture trick a Mummy. I'm wrapping your poor little cock in rope, like mummification. Be grateful I use soft rope the first time. Future training will be with increasingly rough jute rope." She had started circling down with another layer, this time adding his balls in the rope confinement as she continued. "I've tried all kinds of chastity devices on my subs, but there is really nothing better than a Mummy to train naughty boys to keep their cocks to themselves."

Damned if she wasn't using the sexiest voice as she delivered the horrifying explanation. Her voice alone was responsible for more blood rushing to his family jewels. It only took seconds to understand the true deviousness of her plan. As his cock grew, the rope constricted tighter, cutting off circulation. It was the damnedest thing, but within minutes he could swear he could feel his pulse as his encased cock throbbed against the rope.

Nolan had been so focused on worrying about the state of his poor manhood that he'd lost track of where Piper was. The cold line of steel laid lightly across his jugular reminded him quickly of exactly how much control he'd given up to her.

"You're doing better than I thought you would, sub." Her compliment was unexpected. Hearing the playfulness in her tone instead of her normal disdain for him almost made playing the switch for the night worth it.

Maybe his plan was working.

"Too bad you'll spend the entirety of the night with this rather impressive tool in training."

Okay, maybe not.

The only place he wanted to put his *tool* was in her wet pussy.

He tried to force himself to pay attention to Piper instead of the throbbing ache below his waist, but loud cries of pain from a punishment scene happening nearby distracted the sadist in him. Fuck if his cock wasn't getting strangled by the damn rope.

Piper was moving the knife again. It didn't necessarily hurt, but he felt her scratching the top layer of his skin as she trailed the tip of her weapon from shoulder to his fingers on the right and then moving it in reverse on his left side.

The tip of the knife jumped back to his neck and started to slowly slalom down his chest, weaving around his nipples, abs, and belly button before training lower. She'd attached his legs a foot or two apart at the end of the table so he couldn't even close his legs. He instead had to hold his breath as her knife trailed around his bound groin area before moving in long strokes up and down each leg multiple times. There were moments that she'd hit a ticklish spot and he'd have to fight not to laugh. The next stroke she'd press deeper and he'd feel his skin getting scratched enough to hurt.

Nolan lost track of time as he played pincushion for Piper. Having never played as a bottom before, he wasn't sure what to expect, but one thing was clear. There was something to be said about being helpless and at Piper's mercy. He was glad she'd tied him down and blindfolded him. It gave him the perfect reason to just let go and experience.

He'd fallen into a trance-like state so the sudden yank of the rope wrapped around his cock jarred him to attention. Holy Christ, she was pulling the rope hard and fast. He could feel his penis spinning in a small circle as row after row was quickly unwrapped.

While her pulling didn't necessarily hurt, the blood rushing back into his numb manhood fucking hurt like hell. It was like she was sticking hundreds of needles directly into his cock, like when he would sleep on his hand wrong and it fell asleep. Once the limb woke up, blood rushing to it felt like getting stabbed. He'd normally shake out his hands until the pain receded, but there would be no shaking out his penis.

"Jesus Christ!" he shouted when the pins and needles sensation got too much.

"Nope. Mistress Ice," was her answer. She rewarded him by taking his blindfold off. Even though the room was dimly lit, he had to squint to focus on the scenes happening in the main room nearest them.

"You've done well so far, sub. In fact, you're doing better than I'd thought you would."

"Have I earned a reward?" he dared ask as she started to release his right hand.

As she leaned across him to unlock his left handcuff, she asked, "I'm not sure. What exactly did you have in mind?"

Her face was just inches away when he felt his arm regain movement. Nolan shook his hands to get the circulation flowing again as he debated his answer. When she hovered over him from above, her ice-blue eyes warming slightly, he decided to go for it.

"This." His mouth was on hers in a heartbeat as he reached up to grab her ponytail, using it to anchor her to him. Piper fought like a wildcat the first few seconds, pushing against his chest to escape with no luck. But once he succeeded in thrusting his tongue into her mouth her flailing reduced to half-hearted objection.

He'd kissed many women since their last kiss, but damn if he couldn't shake a feeling of coming home. Despite her control over the scene, he felt like the universe had shifted back into place.

He had to finally release her when they needed to come up for air. Christ, he loved the fresh apple smell of her shampoo as she lingered, placing her head on his shoulder while they each caught their breath. He was glad she'd released his hands so he could stroke her bare arm within his reach.

"That was…" he started.

"You just had to fucking ruin it, didn't you!" she shouted, pushing off his chest and stepping out of reach.

He quickly pushed to sit up, trying to get to her until he remembered he was still restrained at the ankles.

Piper had turned and was rushing to throw all of her laid out toys back into her leather bag. He could see she was really upset and he felt like shit for screwing up the intimacy they'd achieved during the knife scene.

"I need to go to the ladies' room. As you've just reminded me, you're a Dom and know how all this stuff works so you can get your own damn legs free. Get dressed… or don't. I don't care. If you still want to keep going, I'll meet you back in the theater in ten minutes."

She didn't wait to let him answer. She just threw the bag's strap over her shoulder and took off down the stairs, running away from him in her characteristic cold-shoulder way.

"Piper! — Mistress!" he shouted, but she was too far away to hear his softer, "I'm sorry."

Fuck.

CHAPTER 7

iper

STUPID. STUPID. STUPID.

Piper pushed through the throngs of spectators milling about at the bottom of the steps, heading to the ladies' room as fast as she could. She would be damned if she was going to let them see the Ice Queen cry. It was bad enough that she was fighting to hold back tears, but having a witness to them would be unacceptable.

She pushed open the swing door to the ladies' room and was grateful there wasn't a long line. It was early enough that not that many people needed a break yet. There was a small group of women gabbing in front of the mirrors, and she rushed past heading to the farthest stall, slamming and locking the door just in time.

Hot tears fell down her cheeks as she sat on the toilet, still fully dressed. She leaned forward, her elbows on her knees, head in her hands, and forced herself to take long, deep breaths.

She was overreacting. She knew it, but it didn't mean she could stop the involuntary panic when it decided it wanted to stop in for a visit. She'd been doing so well. She'd learned to power through even the most powerful of triggers.

So, what the hell had just happened?

She leaned up to spin the toilet roll, ripping off a good amount and using it to blow her nose, using a still-clean corner to dab at her eyes in an attempt to keep her mascara from running into a hot mess.

In and out. Deep breath after deep breath. With each one, she felt marginally better until she was able to finally think about what had just happened.

She'd let her guard down. Unbelievably, she had started to really have fun dominating Nolan. He'd been surprisingly pliant, for a dominant himself. Once he got past the initial resistance, he'd responded to her lead beautifully, lulling her into thinking he could possibly be a switch... like herself.

It was her deepest secret. One that Nolan Boeing had already caught a hint of years before. Of course, she hadn't been a switch when they'd met. She'd merely been a young, naive actress with big dreams.

"Piper? You still in here?"

What the hell? It was Nolan calling out to her. Had he actually had the balls to come into the ladies' room?

She heard the group of women by the sinks answering him, letting him know she was still in one of the stalls. She held her breath, waiting for him to just go away. Instead, she heard him asking the women to check on her, as if she were some kind of child who needed supervision. Even if he meant well, his concern grated on her, sparking her dominance back to life.

She was the fucking Ice Queen.

Ice queens don't cry.

Shaking herself mentally, she stood, smoothing down her leather mini-dress before blowing her nose one last time. Piper closed her eyes, taking deep breaths and mentally running through the empowerment chant she repeated internally fifty times a day.

When she opened the stall door, Mistress Ice walked out. Since she didn't pee, she didn't bother washing her hands.

The three ladies had stopped talking to turn towards her as she approached. She just whisked past them, letting them know, "As you can see, I'm just fine."

She didn't make it two feet outside the ladies' room before Nolan was beside her. He'd been waiting right next to the exit. She saw no need to stop for him so she kept walking in the direction of the social room.

"Hold up, Piper," he said, clamping his hand down on her right elbow, trying to stop her.

She yanked her arm free and kept going. "I don't think so. Not unless you're going to tell me you're dropping out?" she asked, hopefully.

Nolan finally succeeded in pulling her to a stop. Just one more way he insisted on controlling her, and not the other way around. With little choice left, she swung to confront him in the middle of the bar.

"What?" she demanded sharply.

"It's just... I wanted to... apologize. I'm really sorry."

"That's nice. And what exactly are you apologizing for?" she prodded.

"For kissing you. I know I overstepped."

Her own thoughts on the matter were still muddled. She probably should have stayed in the bathroom longer to sort through her feelings, but she was anxious to get this night over and then never have to see Nolan Boeing ever again. She'd need to cancel her membership to Black Light, which made her sad, but it couldn't be helped.

"I'm not upset that you kissed me. I'm upset that you disrespected me. I don't play games, not even at Black Light, and you're treating this just like a continuation of the normal game you insist on playing between us."

Nolan's face flushed red. "I resent that. I'm not trying to play any kind of game." He paused, obviously frustrated before tacking on, "I've never thought what we have was just a game."

Piper scoffed in his face. "What we have? We don't have anything, Nolan," she lied. She was an actress, after all. If she could win an academy nomination for playing a serial killer, she should sure as hell be able to fool one measly man with her acting skills.

She wanted to break their visual showdown so badly, but she refused to be the first one to look away. He flinched first, releasing her arm and running his now free hand through his dark brown hair nervously. If nothing else, she was getting to see a whole new side to Nolan tonight. She wished it would make things easier for her, but when he chose to apologize again, it only made things worse.

"Well, like I said, I'm sorry I overstepped. You're in charge tonight. I forgot that for a minute. I'm really trying my best with this whole switch thing. I'd like to roll for another scene."

She watched him closely for signs he was lying, but then chastised herself. Nolan Boeing may be many things, but a liar wasn't one of them.

There was almost nothing she wanted more in that moment than to go home and lick her wounds in private. Unfortunately for her, one of the few things she might want more was standing in front of her. In that moment, she finally knew why she was feeling so emotional. Tonight would be her last chance to get a taste of what she'd walked away from years before. The kiss had reaffirmed that.

He waited a full minute to let her think through her options.

"Fine. Let's go back to the theater and roll for our next activity, but you'd better keep in mind who's in charge this time."

"Yes, ma'am," he answered, and it didn't even sound condescending.

The theater was only a quarter full, yet the temperature still seemed oppressive to Piper. They had Secretary playing on the big screen, the volume turned down low.

Madison greeted them as they hit the stairs, "Welcome back. Ready to roll for your next activity?"

Nolan hung back, letting her go up first. Piper reached out to take the marble while Madison chatted on.

"Hope you're having fun. Don't forget to stop in and grab some snacks between your scenes. Like, Avery made the best appetizers tonight."

As nice as she was, Piper wasn't in the mood for chitchat. She cut the MC off, asking, "What time is it anyway?"

Madison pointed at the newly installed digital clock at the back of the theater. "We installed a couple clocks around the club. You must not have been in a position to see one of them. It's only nine-fifteen. You have plenty of time remaining for more fun."

"Oh goody," she snarked.

Nolan chose that moment to reassert himself, stepping up behind her to pull her back against his chest and talk against her ear. "I wish the night would slow down. It's going too fast for me."

Why the hell couldn't he just stay the dominant asshole he usually was?

She thrust the marble at him. "Here, sub, you roll."

Piper kept her eyes on the spinning wheel to avoid making eye contact. She needed to get her ice back and quick.

"Bondage!" Madison exclaimed, checking the cards in her hand before adding, "And neither of you put that on your hard limit list. Have fun."

Nolan ushered Piper down the stairs and up the left side of the theater, his hand at the small of her back. He just couldn't help himself. That was such a Dom thing.

So why wasn't she calling him out on it? Mistress Ice would never let one of her normal boy subs get away with that shit. More likely, she'd have him crawling on a leash behind her like a trained pet.

The answer was simple. Because as fun as their earlier scene had been, it was impossible for her to see Nolan for anything other than the larger-than-life Dom that he naturally was.

The next scene should be fun. Not.

They were almost to the velvet curtain that would lead to the playroom when they met a waitress with a round bar tray full of champagne flutes. Piper flagged her down, grabbing one flute and drinking it on the spot. She replaced the empty on the tray and grabbed two more from the tray.

"Sorry, Ms. Kole, but participants are only allowed two drinks tonight."

"Never fear, only one of these two is for me." She turned and handed the second one to Nolan before adding, "I got one for my submissive as well."

"Of course," she acknowledged with a nod and then scuttled off to push booze on others.

Piper had almost finished the second glass a few seconds later when Nolan started waving to catch the attention of another waiter across the bar. As the server approached, she noted he had a tray of appetizers. Each had a toothpick with colorful confetti attached at the end.

Nolan didn't ask what she wanted. He just took charge and loaded up a napkin with a variety of finger foods.

After the waiter moved on, he picked up a bite-sized potato skin and held it up to her lips. When she didn't open her mouth, he scolded her. "If you're going to down champagne that fast, you need to get some food in your stomach."

She opened her mouth to argue and he had the audacity to shovel the whole bite in. After she swallowed, she confronted him. "You just can't help yourself, can you?"

"What? You need to eat."

"No. I don't. And it isn't your decision."

"But... we aren't in a scene."

"Of course we are. Never mind." There was no good trying to explain her struggle to him. How as a woman in Hollywood she'd learned she had to be the Ice Queen just to keep any semblance of control over her own life. No matter how successful she became, there was always some powerful man waiting in the wings to tell her what to do, or undermine her, or pay her a fraction of what she was owed.

"Hey... it's just a few appetizers," he answered, almost as if he were reading her mind.

Tug-o-war. That's what this night felt like. Push and pull. Back and forth the power swung between them. Well, she needed to grab it and hold on tight if she was going to get through the night without losing it.

"Finish up. We have a bondage scene to get started," she snapped.

She'd meant for him to eat the fucking food, but instead he picked up a bite of white cheese and held it to her lips.

Had he been the Dom that night, she was sure he would have ordered her mouth to 'Open,' but tonight he said, "Please," instead.

The polite asshole.

She ate as he shared the napkin full of food with her.

"Ready now?" she asked.

"Yes, ma'am," he grinned, lighting up his grey eyes. She suspected his dimple would be showing if he had shaved. As it was, the close-trimmed beard was sexy as hell.

Back on the main club floor, they found the only place open for play was the same stage they'd been on before. Most of the spectators had moved on to watch other couples, but she wasn't under any delusion. Once they started playing they would draw another crowd.

Before she climbed the stairs, she waved at Santiago who was on duty across the room. He hustled over to her to see how he could help.

"Do you have another spanking bench hanging out around that isn't in use yet? Either that or some other piece of furniture I can use for a bondage scene?"

"Let me go back to the dungeon room and see if all of them are in use there or not. I'll be right back."

Piper climbed the stairs and pulled her bag off her shoulder, setting it back on the original table. Taking a deep breath, she channeled her inner Domme. "Time to strip again. I'd tell you to take your boxer-briefs off this time too, but, well, I know you're going commando now. "

Nolan started unbuttoning his shirt.

"You owe me one pair of Tommy John's," he complained as he bared his upper half.

Piper chuckled. "Yeah, right. You can afford to bid a hundred thousand fucking dollars for three hours of play but you can't afford to replace a pair of underwear? You should have bid a few bucks less." It still blew her mind when she thought about it.

"I would have paid more." His statement startled her.

She found herself looking back at him to gauge if he was teasing her, but she found he was dead serious. The fluttering in her lower abdomen caught her off guard. It passed quickly, yet still pissed her off. She refused to act like some delicate flower swooning at some flattering thing her prom date said.

Lucky for her, Santiago returned with another dungeon monitor that she didn't recognize. They were carrying a heavy wooden spanking bench that was exactly what she was hoping for. They may have rolled bondage, and she would certainly enjoy restraining Nolan again, but what he didn't know was all of the fun things she had planned for him after he was completely immobile and at her mercy again.

CHAPTER 8

olan

NOLAN COULD ALREADY TELL HE'D RATHER BE RESTRAINED ON HIS BACK instead of this humiliating position—on his hands and knees, draped over the wooden spanking bench, his head closer to the ground than his bare ass.

If nothing else, tonight's experiment was proving to be very educational, not just in regards to learning more about what made Piper Kole tick, but more because it gave him a glimpse into the motivations of his previous submissives. If he was unsuccessful in his quest to get Piper back in his bed, he was at least learning tips for better domination in general.

And if he were honest with himself, the first knife scene had been hotter than hell. He could truthfully say he'd sign up for that kink with Piper again any time. As was her usual style of domination, the sexuality had been subtle, but that's partly what made it so fucking hot.

He was less sure how this bondage scene was going to end up. It wasn't the bondage part he was worried about. It was what his Domme would do to him once she had him at her mercy again. She'd already secured his ankles and shins to the padded ledge where he was kneeling.

The length of his torso rested along the padded top of the custom-made furniture. It at least provided decent support for the awkward position. He was repositioning his hands on the handles near the floor in front of him as Piper kneeled next to him, two padded cuff-restraints in her hand.

With expertise, she attached the leather cuffs to his wrists and then used a carabiner to latch each limb to its restraint ring. He couldn't resist pulling on one. The test confirmed he wouldn't be getting up anytime soon.

Nolan suspected she was stalling because she left him restrained there, ass-out and on display, for almost five minutes. In between the sounds of other scenes going on around them, he could hear her rummaging through her duffel bag, placing items back out on the table. Part of him wished he could see what she was doing, but the bigger part knew it was best to just go into this scene blind like he had the last one.

Her first touch was to squeeze his balls, hard. They were still tender from being mummified the hour before. He groaned, but managed not to call out until he felt something clamp around the top of his sack, strangling his balls in a tight constriction. Whatever the hell she'd put there stayed even after she stood and he could hear her footsteps going back towards the table.

He was fine, he reassured himself. He took a cleansing breath, exhale out.

About all he could make out of Piper was the bottom part of her fashion boots. He traced her through his peripheral vision as she paced back and forth around the stage. He was curious about what the hell she was doing, but since he was trying his best to be a good submissive, he held his questions.

He didn't need to wait long for answers. Out of the blue, he heard the whish of a crop or cane just before he felt the line of fire across his ass. The strike hadn't been necessarily hard, but it sure as hell woke him up. He held his lips together tightly to keep from making sound. He didn't want to give her the satisfaction in their ongoing game of wills.

Determined to get a reaction out of him, Piper's next strike was a bit lower and twice as hard. The good news was he now knew she held a crop and not a cane, which would have hurt worse. The bad news was he'd seen her wail on one of her play partner's asses with her crop until he'd been reduced to crying out yellow for her to stop.

He wouldn't put it past her to try to break him in the same way. In some ways, it was her style. He'd known that when he'd bid to play with her. No backing out now.

By the sixth strike, he accidentally let a groan escape. He couldn't help it. She'd started crisscrossing her strikes over previous lines of heat. By the tenth connection, he let out his first shout of pain. It was short, and not very loud, but it still felt like he'd lost the most recent battle of wills they were involved in. Piper must have thought so too, because she walked away behind him and returned to her stash of implements on the table, leaving him to figuratively lick his wounds.

When Piper returned to her position behind, she surprised him by gently palming his ass cheek in her satin gloves, intimately massaging his punished skin. Pain and then pleasure—the hallmark of their lifestyle.

Splat!

The sound of paddle on ass broke through the rhythmic music before the pain registered in his brain. Holy fuck, that hurt. Gone was her thin crop, replaced with what felt like a wide leather paddle.

Splat!

Yep, a leather paddle for sure. He only made it to three before calling out on this implement.

Piper's tinkling laughter brought conflicting emotions. He loved to hear her happy—really happy. He just wished it could be under different circumstances.

"In case you were wondering, I'm going to give you a little taste of each of my punishment implements while I have you as a captive audience. Consider it my Valentine's Day gift to you."

Splat!

Nolan took a deep breath through the worst of the pain before squeezing out, "It's not too late to get me flowers!"

Her hearty laughter was her real gift. She rarely laughed, and never in his presence. It helped him power through the next four swats until she struck lower on his upper thighs.

"Shit!"

"Oh goodness, don't do that."

It took him a minute to understand what she'd meant. This time it was his turn to laugh, just as the eighth paddle landed.

He sucked in his breath, determined to take whatever she dished out, hoping it would finally clear the air between them. Her satin gloves caressing his bottom again gave him hope, only because he'd watched her scene many times and he'd never seen her comforting her play partners. Piper preferred to play only with masochists. Subs who needed the unending pain to reach their highest highs.

That was not him and she knew it. Like her, he was a sadist, preferring to be on the other end of the paddle, yet tonight was proving to be an eye opener for the Dom. Ten years ago, he'd have walked out of the club before submitting to Piper, or any Domme for that matter. Tonight, he was secure enough in his own masculinity to hand over power for the night.

Nolan focused on the satin, enjoying the softness as it moved lower, encasing his semi-flaccid cock hanging down between his legs. Still tender from its earlier abuse, the softness felt heavenly as Piper slowly stroked his cock from head to base again and again. He closed his eyes, enjoying the attention as she gave him an impromptu hand-job. As great as it felt, he'd much rather have her release him so he could put it deep inside her instead.

"Fuck yeah," he encouraged her as he neared his climax, now short of breath.

"How'd you like to stick it in?" she asked.

"Christ, yes. Unbuckle me. I'll be..."

Holy mother of God.

"What the fuck?!" he shouted as a cold, wet object pierced his asshole, quickly filling him with an uncomfortable pressure.

"You're acting surprised. I asked you if you wanted me to stick it in," she asked sweetly.

"Take it out, Piper. You know damn well I thought you meant me in you," he demanded.

"Well that's just not going to happen, now, is it? I'm the Domme. I'm afraid that means I get to do the fucking around here."

To make her point, she pulled whatever the hell it was she'd shoved up his ass out and then shoved it back in even deeper this time. He'd never been into ass play, at least not when it was his ass involved.

Piper's tinkling laughter was back again. "I was so relieved to see you didn't mark Anal Play on your hard limits list." To make her point, she pulled the dildo out and shoved it back in again.

"Stop! You know I meant I'm not against *giving* anal. I didn't say I'd be okay on the receiving end," he complained.

"Well, I'm throwing it in as a bonus present tonight. I'm just generous like that."

Another thrust and he shouted, "I'd still rather have the flowers!"

"Oh don't be a baby. This is the smallest anal trainer I own. It's barely thicker than one of my fingers. Be glad I'm not putting Big Bertha into service. Now that would be a life changer."

"Fucking great..." he added.

At last, the pressure in his bowels was gone. She'd removed the anal trainer.

"Fine, if I can't have any fun fucking your ass, then I'm going to have to go back to wailing on it. Your choice."

Thwack!

Shit, that hurt like hell. He looked back over his shoulder to see a long, heavy, wooden paddle ready for the next swing.

Christ, it was so wide that it only took two swats to cover his whole ass. He suddenly had a flashback to his one and only visit to the principle's office in high school where he and his best friend had each received six of the best for destruction of school property after a Halloween prank gone wrong. There had been nothing sexual about that encounter, but he had to admit his rock-hard cock seemed to be enjoying itself immensely.

Damn traitor. Maybe he had a drop of masochist in his blood after all.

He was more than ready for the short break she gave him after the fifth swat. His ass was throbbing and he suspected he might end up with a bruise or two as a souvenir of their time together.

The arrival of two dungeon monitors carrying yet another piece of BDSM furniture reminded him he was still very much on display on the main stage of Black Light. He'd played there before, of course, but those nights he'd been in control. There was a strange vulnerability in waiting, not sure what would happen next.

Piper didn't keep him waiting long. She knelt next to him, her long, dark ponytail coming into his view as she unhooked first his right and then left arm before moving back and undoing his legs. He'd been in the stretched position long enough that it took him a bit to push up and off the spanking bench. Once on his feet, he stretched and twisted, trying to get feeling back into his limbs.

"What's the matter, you getting to be an old man? You weren't in position that long," she taunted.

He glanced around, looking for one of the clocks Madison had told them about. Ten-twenty-five. Shit, the night was going by way too fast. He had worried he'd be ready to quit in the first few minutes, but despite even having a damn dildo shoved up his ass, he still felt like he was getting his money's worth.

"I was in that position for almost an hour, thank you," he defended.

"Like I said, not very long."

Nolan caught her eye and he loved seeing the spark of humor where only ice usually lived. Looking uncomfortable, Piper glanced away, barking her next order.

"Get your ass on the seat of the chair. I don't have all night."

Her words were meant to push him away, but her body language said something else entirely. She lingered next to him, only inches separating them. The dungeon monitors were long gone, yet she wasn't enforcing her control.

He was close enough to see her shallow breathing. She was as nervous as he felt and that made him smile. There was something special happening between them. There always had been. He just needed to convince her to let her guard down long enough to let him inside.

Taking a chance, he ignored her command, closing the last inches between them and taking her into his arms. He'd worried she'd object, but someone else beat her to it.

"No fair! You aren't worthy to be with Mistress Ice! You're supposed to be a submissive... following her every direction like I do! I should have won the auction!"

Piper pressed against his chest until he reluctantly released her. Together they both swung to see who was shouting at them from the front row of spectators. Nolan recognized the heckler as one of the subs Piper had dominated at Black Light in the past. He was obviously not taking being replaced well.

Nolan couldn't care less what the guy thought about them, but Piper's push away and sudden stiffness told him she didn't agree.

"I can't do this..."

He grabbed her arm to hold her near him. "Do what? I'm having fun and I think you are too, Piper."

The heckler was close enough to hear them as he renewed his objection, "Her name is Mistress!"

Nolan ignored the asshole. "Don't let him rattle you."

She shook her head, mumbling, "This isn't right. I should be treating you like everyone else."

"Fuck that. We have a history."

Anger flashed in her eyes. "What history? You think because we fucked once that I owe you something?"

He tried not to feel hurt that she spoke of their one special night together as if it had been her equivalent of a trip to the dentist. "You don't owe me shit, but you sure as hell owe it to yourself to have a little fun in life instead of treating every interaction you have like it were a declaration of war." He paused before adding, "I'm not the enemy here."

She renewed her struggle in his arms, forcing Nolan to grab her other arm, holding her tight and commanding. "Look at me, Piper."

It took her several long seconds to comply. When she did, he could see her confusion. He wanted to say something magical to bring back her happiness from a few minutes before.

"Right is what you and I decide it is, Piper."

The tears swimming in her eyes told him he'd missed the mark.

CHAPTER 9

iper

WHAT A DISASTER TONIGHT WAS TURNING OUT TO BE. SHE FELT LIKE THE biggest failure. Years of work honing her Mistress Ice persona were going down the drain with every minute that passed in Nolan Boeing's presence. How right she'd been to avoid him for the last few years. She was pretty sure he was her kryptonite.

Nolan still held her close. She could tell the jerk wanted to pressure her into talking about their feelings, something she didn't like to do in the best of circumstances, let alone on the floor of Black Light.

"What is it you need, Piper? Talk to me."

She hated the fucking tears that were blurring her vision.

"Control. I feel out of control," she whispered truthfully.

She had to fight to get him to let her right arm go free so she could swish at her eyes in time to prevent a tear from falling. It was bad enough that Nolan witnessed her weakness. She would not crack in front of the rest of the club.

"I'm sorry that I'm a terrible submissive."

"Honestly, I can't believe you even tried. You've never struck me as a switch."

He thought pensively before answering. "I can be that for you—a switch."

"That would imply that I could switch for you, too. That's just not possible."

"You haven't even tried."

She barely heard his reply because the sub, Ryan, in the front row was making a scene, trying to get those around him to complain about Nolan as well. Out of the corner of her eye she saw Santiago and the other DM coming to subdue the heckler, pulling him along towards the velvet curtain exit.

Feeling panicked, she tried to regain control. "This isn't the time or place for this conversation. We still have a little over a half hour left of the challenge. Maybe we should call it quits."

"No," Nolan demanded.

"Don't look now, but your inner Dom is showing again."

She hadn't meant to say something funny, but it just sort of slipped out when he was around. The smile that lit up his face went straight to her core. God, she needed to get laid, and by someone, anyone, other than Nolan Boeing. She needed to find someone else who could make her forget the feelings he stirred in her. Someone she wouldn't lose control around.

"Maybe you should punish me for being a bad sub," he challenged her playfully, grasping her ass in his hands.

"Maybe you should stop topping from the bottom."

"Touché."

In the distance she heard someone calling, "Thirty-minute warning."

Surely she could hold it together for thirty more minutes. Then they could win the challenge and she could leave and never have to come back again. Or maybe she could just spend some time out on the East Coast. She could play at Black Light in D.C. where no one would know about how bad she'd fucked up tonight.

Piper took a deep breath and tried to reassert her control. "Ass in the chair, Boeing. Now."

The pupils in Nolan's grey eyes flared, but he released her as he acknowledged the command. "Yes, ma'am."

They each moved into motion, and her sub-for-the-night sat in the tall-backed wooden chair. She'd used this piece of custom furniture only once before and knew it was the perfect way to end her time with Nolan.

Grabbing her stash of soft nylon rope, Piper got to work setting up their final bondage scene of the night. She started by connecting Nolan's ankles to the rings attached on the outside edge of the front legs of the chair. Next, she tied his wrist cuffs to the heavy metal ring at the top of the back of the wood chair. As it was patterned after a king's throne, it meant his arms were pulled awkwardly above his head.

For the third time that night, she had Nolan Boeing tied and at her mercy. In one way it made her feel powerful… but the heat of his gaze as he followed her every movement made her feel more like prey.

Being his prey wasn't what scared her.

What scared her the most was that for one night, she was so fucking tempted to let him catch her.

Shaking her head, she reminded herself she had a job to do.

Kneeling at the side of the chair, Piper reached beneath the wooden seat and unlatched the locks under Nolan's ass—locks he knew nothing about.

She watched his face carefully as she pulled the trap door that would remove the middle front two-thirds of the chair. Like a trap door opening, Nolan's cock and balls free fell into the sudden opening between his legs. Before he knew what was happening, she stood and pulled his right leg out. The chair did as it was designed, splitting the remaining seat into two parts, forcing a submissive's legs wide apart.

God she loved how his impressive cock and balls hung down, swinging between his legs. Unable to resist, she pulled her light crop from her belt hook and started tapping his family jewels lightly with the tip of the crop.

He jumped, trying to escape the intermittent harder flicks of her punishment implement. Despite the pain she was delivering, she watched as Nolan's cock filled, growing hard again, in spite of the painful attention.

To his credit, he didn't cry out as she slowly increased the strength of her strikes.

"Christ, I want you, Piper," he begged.

Clearly she wasn't getting her message across. She grabbed a pair of clover nipple clamps and unceremoniously snapped them onto each of his nipples.

"Fuck!" he shouted through the pain.

That's better.

"You aren't going to scare me away, you know," he gritted out when he could finally talk.

What the hell was this guy's problem? Why couldn't he just get the message?

Fine.

She rummaged through her bag and found her set of incremental weights. "Let's see how you handle a bit more weight, shall we?" she taunted.

His only acknowledgement as she added weights to each of his nipples was a long, low hiss.

After the weights stopped swaying, he needled her back. "Is that all you got, Mistress?"

Shit. Okay, he asked for it.

Her next trip to her bag had her locating her metal set of cock rings. She wanted to see how well Mr. Boeing would do with a thirty-minute hard-on that would never deliver him the relief she knew he was angling for.

His look of unease as she kneeled in front of him upon her return to the chair quickly changed to excitement when she boldly grabbed his cock in her right hand and started jacking him off. She'd had her gloves on when she touched him last time, and she was happy for this chance to stroke his velvet hardness without the satin barrier between them.

She wouldn't say it out loud. He didn't need anything else making his head get any bigger, but his cock really was flawless. Perfectly long, sufficiently thick, and soon to be steely hard. And unlike the younger men she most often played with, she suspected he would have the kind of staying power that would leave her walking funny the next morning.

"That's it. The only thing that could possibly feel better is if you'd climb on my lap and go for a ride."

"Sorry, but I had something else in mind."

When he was almost fully erect, Piper held her left hand up to show him the simple circular metal cock ring. It didn't take her long to slide the metal down his shaft and squeeze it into position at the base of his cock. She then resumed sliding his length until the ring pinched the base of his manhood uncomfortably.

"You know you don't need to use that, right? I don't have any problems in that department."

She smiled despite herself. "Oh, I'm sure you don't. It's not for you, it's for me."

He didn't seem to have a retort for that on the ready. Several long minutes went by with her on her knees, jacking his shaft harder and faster until her arm started to ache. Knowing this would be her only chance, Piper gave her arm a rest by leaning forward and licking his shaft lightly from base to tip like a lollipop, letting her wet tongue linger a bit longer at the tip, playing lightly with his aching cock.

"Shit, that feels amazing, but please, take the fucking ring off now."

She looked up from his lap, her tongue swishing across the sensitive tip of his manhood before grinning. "You act like I'm going to let you shoot your wad. You must not have been paying attention when I said it earlier, so let me properly set your expectations. You will not be coming tonight."

His quick grin unsettled her.

"Want to make a little wager?" When she remained silent, he

tacked on, "You agree to go on a real date with me if both you and I come by the time we leave here tonight."

"I don't date," she scoffed.

"That's why I'm making it a bet."

As tempting as it sounded, her need for control kicked in just in time. "You're on. Now, what's my reward when I win?"

"A weekend away with me at my place in Palm Springs." He actually kept a straight face as he said it, the jerk.

"Or better yet, I win and you leave me alone… once and for all. No sneaking up on me at the studio. No more sitting behind me at premiers. No sitting in the wings watching me here at Black Light." She hated the shard of pain that bounced back at her when she saw the hurt in his sexy grey eyes. And that right there was why she needed to win. He made her feel things she didn't want to feel. They were not good for each other. Every decision they'd ever make would forever be a power struggle.

"That's not what you want, Piper." He sounded so damn sure.

"Oh really? And you think you know me better than I know myself?"

Nolan waited until they were staring into each other's eyes before he answered with complete confidence. "Absolutely."

"Too bad. That's the bet. Take it or leave it."

"Oh I'll take it." *What a cocky bastard.*

Piper had to get to work. They had limited time left and she understood with a welcome certainty what she needed to do.

Pushing to her feet, she crossed to her toy bag, reaching in and coming out with the dozen pinching clothespins she liked to carry. They were all linked in a zipper by one thin rope for fast, excruciating removal.

Nolan's only acknowledgement that he might regret his over-confident bet was the holding of his breath as she kneeled in front of him and started attaching the twelve clothespins all across his scrotum. With each clamp she attached she regained a small measure of control. She had him exactly how she wanted him, at her mercy.

So why didn't she rejoice in the knowledge that she totally had the upper hand in their little wager?

It might have something to do with the wetness she felt rubbing between her own legs. Yes, mastering men turned her on. That's why she chose to be Mistress Ice.

But only she knew just how different tonight's scene was—how close she was to letting Nolan try to melt her ice.

"Eyes," she ordered when he closed his eyes.

When his grey gaze met hers she realized her error, because his orbs were absolutely smoldering with the heat that always spread like wildfire between them.

"I'll repeat. You aren't going to scare me away. No matter what you do to me," he reminded her.

Wanna bet?

Piper knelt again, pulling Nolan's legs back together before reaching under the seat to pull the trap door back up. She was purposefully rougher then she needed to be, making sure to jar her sub's tortured privates as much as possible. A sub's groans of pain as their cock and balls were battered about usually made her feel powerful.

Today, they brought guilt.

She hated guilt, which was too fucking bad, since he'd boxed her into a corner now.

"Ten minute warning," the shout came from near the velvet curtain.

Time was closing in on them. She should be rejoicing that the end of this misguided attraction between them was only minutes away from final annihilation and then things could finally get back to normal.

Instead, a cloud of anxiety moved in like a fast-moving fog, threatening to make her lose sight of the right end goal. Before she could second-guess her path, Piper leaned forward, taking Nolan's cock in her hand, fisting him faster and faster until he begged her, as she knew he would.

"Take the fucking ring off now, Piper."

"Sorry, that would be way too easy, now wouldn't it. I think I'd rather take these off."

Her words were accompanied by her hands sliding up under her own short dress and coming back out with her tiny, thong underwear. Edging him closer to his fall, Piper held her panties up close to his nose, ensuring he would take a nice, long drag of the drug that would be his downfall.

"You smell like heaven. I can't fucking wait to taste you too. Untie me, Piper." He dared to try to Dom her.

"Such a naughty sub. We still have at least eight minutes. Until eleven, I'm in charge here, remember?"

"Please, at least take the fucking cock ring off and climb on."

She glanced down at his now purplish colored cock that was throbbing from pent-up need. Her heart rate tripled the second she swung her right leg over his legs, leaving her straddling his lap. With him tied completely immobile, there was no doubt that she was in control as she reached under her mini-dress and moved his rock-hard cock into position.

Piper stood on her tippy-toes, placing the tip of his shaft against her wet pussy. Her cleavage was at the perfect height to smother his face as she leaned closer to him, enjoying the slide of his cock back and forth through her pussy folds, ensuring she got wetter and wetter by the minute.

"Five minute warning," Santiago shouted.

The warnings had started to feel like the countdown to a bomb exploding, only it would be the confusing push-pull relationship they'd always danced around that would be imploding tonight.

Unable to stall any longer, Piper let gravity pull her body down, impaling herself in one thrust on his steely cock. She tried not to think about how fucking perfect it felt. She forced herself to be brave enough to look into his eyes as she let an intimacy she rarely felt wash over her. She knew the intimacy had an expiration date that was fast approaching, so the least she could do was enjoy it while it lasted.

"Christ, this feels as good as I remembered, Piper."

She silently agreed with him, lifting herself and falling again, letting him fill her even deeper. Moving her boots to the rung that ran along the chair a few inches off the floor, she was able to gain better leverage to lift and fall harder and faster until she was riding his shaft at a gallop.

The sound of additional spectators crowding in to watch them as one of the last couples still in an active scene brought mixed emotions. She was an exhibitionist, normally, but there was nothing normal about tonight. Yet, she knew the spectators would play an important role in how tonight would end.

Shifting to lean back had the tip of his heavy cock hitting her g-spot again and again, making her fly higher and higher until she could think of nothing else but chasing her orgasm. Their bodies slapped together loudly as she felt the first tingles of her climax.

"You're so damn beautiful. I can't wait to watch you come all over my cock."

Her body chose that moment to oblige him as she let herself fly. Piper closed her eyes, letting the white explosion of pleasure wash through her. From head to toe, her entire body felt her release. She fell forward, her head on his shoulder as waves of contractions squeezed his still hard length lodged deep inside her.

"Good girl." He had the audacity to praise her as he nuzzled his lips into the crook between her shoulder and neck, kissing and nibbling her intimately. For one insane second, she contemplated changing her end plan, but then Santiago called out, "Time!" and like Cinderella, the magic ran out.

Their eyes met as she sat up, his dick still like steel inside her.

"I'm still here, Piper."

"Time's up, Nolan. You lose."

"Don't be ridiculous. Untie me and I'll help you come again and again."

She knew he spoke the truth, which was why she had no choice but to push to her feet, letting his hardness slip from her body. The wet plop when his cock slapped against his torso as their bodies separated was what the end of the game would sound like for her when she relived this night later in the privacy of her bedroom. There, she'd finally be free to let the tears she was holding back fall. It was time to remind him who he had bid a shit-ton of money to play with that night.

Piper stood tall, smoothing the scrunched-up skirt of her dress down to cover herself. She tried to ignore the drip of warm cum sliding down her inner thigh. It would be the only souvenir she would have of this one night together.

Feeling generous, she picked up her smashed panties from his lap and held them up for his inspection.

"Thanks for a good time tonight, Nolan. It was unexpected, but it's over now. I'm going to leave these with you as a small souvenir." His eyes flared with the shock she had expected. It was finally dawning on him just how much control she had over him.

"Piper... untie me, baby."

She smiled, sadly. "You just won't learn, will you? I'm no one's baby. Not even yours."

"Don't do this... Not after all the progress we've made tonight," he begged.

She forced a sickly-sweet voice she despised. "We did make progress, I agree." Piper looked him in the eyes and delivered her deathblow. "Thanks for the nice orgasm, but I won. You lost."

"Piper! God-dammit come back here!"

"Maybe now you'll believe I really am Mistress Ice." She took a step backwards. "I'll expect you to honor our agreement from now on, which means this will be goodbye." Her voice faltered on the last word, with her goodbye coming out as a strangled cry. His totally shocked face swam before her, tears threatening to ruin everything.

She needed to leave. Immediately.

She dropped the panties into his lap as she spun and rushed down the steps to the stage. She couldn't stay here even one minute longer. Thank God they were at Black Light where she knew he'd get the help he needed to get loose. It grated against her Domme code of ethics to desert her submissive without making sure he was safe, but she reminded herself he wasn't a sub anyway.

Piper used the last of her strength to rush to Santiago. She pulled him close and spoke into his ear.

"I have to get out of here. Do me a huge favor. Wait five minutes and then go let Mr. Boeing out of his restraints. I'm leaving all of my toys. Pack them up and I'll pick them up some other time… or not."

The dungeon monitor's face looked horrified when he realized what she was actually asking him to do. "Don't you think you should… I mean, he is your responsibility," the DM rightly pointed out.

"I know, but I just can't. I have an emergency. I need to leave."

Looking as uncomfortable as she felt, he finally agreed. "Okay, I'll make sure he's taken care of."

She took off at a jog through the pressing crowd yelling a short, "Thank you!" over her shoulder. The last thing she heard before she dodged through the velvet curtain was Nolan screaming her name as loud as he could.

She suspected it would be a sound that would haunt her for a long time to come.

CHAPTER 10

olan

"I THINK WE SHOULD TAKE YOU IN FOR X-RAYS. IT COULD BE BROKEN," Elijah warned.

"Fuck that. Just wrap it up. I need to get the hell out of here."

Only now was Nolan's blind rage starting to simmer into a burning fury. He'd signed up prepared to be sexually submissive for the night. He hadn't signed up to have his fucking heart ripped out and then trampled on center stage by the only woman he'd ever cared enough to put aside his own dominant needs just to try to give her what she needed from him.

Elijah stepped away and Nolan watched as one of the dungeon monitors finished wrapping his right hand. It hurt like a sonofabitch, which was fine by him. It gave him something else to think about besides the bone-crushing ache in the pit of his stomach when he remembered the final look on Piper's face as she'd turned and left him on stage.

"I heard you did a real number on one of our best spanking benches."

Just great. Jaxson had joined them in the men's locker room. Could they possibly add any more Doms to come witness his humiliation?

"It was either punch that or track down Piper and strangle her. I'll pay to replace the bench," he offered as the DM finished up the wrapping and prepared to leave.

"That won't be necessary. I'll use some of the hundred thousand you bid to replace it," Jaxson offered.

"Gee, thanks. I didn't think I could possibly feel worse than I did a minute ago. I appreciate you reminding me I paid a goddamn fortune to have my balls beat, physically and figuratively, in front of the entire club."

"Sorry man, but you have to admit it was always a long shot with Piper."

Nolan couldn't really argue the point, especially knowing how the night had turned out, yet there had been long moments during their play where he was absolutely sure he was connecting with her. The real her. Not the Ice Queen.

If Piper Kole thought they were through, she had another thing coming.

As if he had read his mind, Jaxson sat on the bench next to him and held out a cell phone. When Nolan didn't take it, Jaxson reached and dropped the phone into the pocket of the thick Black Light robe Nolan was wearing.

"I know you don't have your phone in the club so use mine. I looked up her personal cell phone in our club records and added it to my contact list." He paused and then added, "Call her. You weren't imagining things. I watched you scene for a while tonight and there was definitely something there."

"Oh, there's something, alright. Anger and resentment."

"Maybe, but I also saw how scared she was."

Nolan laughed at that one. "Yeah, right. She looked real scared as she laughed in my face and left me tied up like a total chump."

Jaxson sighed. "I didn't see her leave. I was in the back hallway, but

Brian told me she was crying when she passed through security like a bat out of hell, and the guard in the parking lot said she lost her shit when her SUV was boxed in and she and her driver couldn't leave right away. All of that doesn't seem like the actions of an Ice Queen."

For a hot second, Nolan let his guard down to hope again. Then he remembered the shitty feeling of watching her turn and leave him— his hard cock still dripping with her juice, tied down and humiliated. "Thanks, but I've had enough rejection for one night. I think I'll just go home and get drunk and lick my wounds in private."

"If you say so," Jaxson added as he stood. "Just in case you change your mind, I'll leave my phone with you. Drop it off with Brian in security on your way out, but don't wait too long. The screen will only be unlocked for another three minutes or so."

The club owner didn't bother saying goodbye. He just left as quietly as he'd arrived.

Nolan was finally alone. He leaned forward, his elbows on his knees and his pounding head in his throbbing hand. His balls ached from the abuse they'd taken and he was pretty sure he had a nice bruise forming on his right asscheek.

And still, it was his heart that hurt the worst. What kind of black magic had Piper used to wrap him so firmly under her spell? He'd come wanting closure, and would leave with his heart ripped open and raw.

Fucking hell.

He so wanted to resist letting her see how much she'd decimated him, but at the last second, he reached in the pocket and grabbed Jaxson's phone. It was just going to sleep as he saw it. He ran his finger across the screen just in the nick of time to keep it alive.

True to his word, Jaxson had left the contact record up on the screen for Piper Kole. He knew he probably could have tracked her private cell number down through one of his contacts at the studio, but it would have taken time. Time he wouldn't want to waste.

Taking a deep breath, Nolan pressed the cell number on the screen and held the phone to his ear. His heart raced as the call rang several times. He wasn't surprised at all when it went to voicemail.

This is Piper. Leave a message.

Short. Demanding. So Piper.

"Piper..." It was all he got out before freezing. What the fuck did he want to say? He should scream at her. Call her names for making a fool out of him. He took so long, he wasn't even sure if it was still recording when he finally spoke. *"Piper, it's me. I know you think this is over, but you're wrong. We're just getting started, you and me. You can try to run away again, but unlike last time, I'm not gonna let you shut me out. Not without a fight. So get ready. I'll give you a few days to lick your wounds, but then I'm gonna track you down and we'll hash things out, one way or another."*

He pressed END before he could say something even more stupid. The adrenalin had left his body, and he was crashing fast. He picked up the pile of his crumpled clothes and headed to the door of the locker room. Thank God he'd pre-ordered a car for the ride home. He was in no condition to drive. About all he was fit to do was drink enough booze to numb his aches, physical and emotional.

The End – For Now

ABOUT THE AUTHOR

USA Today bestselling author Livia Grant lives in Chicago with her husband and two sons... one a young man, the other a furry rescue dog named Max. She is blessed to have traveled extensively and as much as she loves to visit places around the globe, the Midwest and its changing seasons will always be home. Livia started writing when she felt like she finally had the life experience to write a riveting story that she hopes her readers won't be able to put down. Livia's fans appreciate her deep, character driven plots, often rooted in an ensemble cast where the friendships are as important as the romance... well, almost.

- Livia's Website: http://www.liviagrant.com/
- Facebook: http://www.facebook.com/lb.grant.9
- Facebook Author Page to Like: https://www.facebook.com/pages/Livia-Grant/877459968945358
- Twitter: http://www.twitter.com/LBGrantAuthor
- Goodreads: https://www.goodreads.com/author/show/8474605.Livia_Grant
- Instagram: https://www.instagram.com/liviagrantauthor/

DETERMINED

A BLACK LIGHT: CELEBRITY ROULETTE NOVELLA

By

Maren Smith

CHAPTER 1

*H*er hands were shaking. That was the first thing Claire Allerton noticed when she shrugged out of her coat, folded it neatly, and lay it in her changing locker. That she was shaking all over was something she didn't notice until after she closed and locked her personal things up for the night. She stood for a full count of sixty, her eyes closed, willing her heart to stop panicking.

She was a woman who spent the whole of her adult life making important, impactful decisions for a company that rocked the world of architectural design at least once per fiscal quarter or she wasn't doing her job. They called her 'The British Bitch,' but only occasionally to her face. Right now, her current decision wasn't going to rock any world but her own, but she could already feel the repercussions. They were gut-tying, heart-stumbling. Knee-weakening. She'd put her last bid in three days ago. The only thing capable of stopping it all now was a safe word, but Claire was determined — that word would never cross her lips. She wanted this just too much.

Breathe in. She inhaled. *Breathe out.* While it was all still in her control to do so, while it was still her decision to make.

She still couldn't believe she had won the auction. All those nights of watching the site, wondering if she'd bid enough, if she should add more. But no, Claire yet again assured herself. She never lost. God knows she'd bid enough on this one event to pay an entire year's membership at this club. Black Light wasn't cheap. Not in D.C., and especially not in L.A., where the sun, surf, and celebrities abounded.

And just like that, images of Adam Butler — *the* Adam Butler — flashed through her mind. Again. Looking just like he did on last month's cover of *Male Fitness and Fashion*, with his living room window and a wooded backdrop behind him, relaxing in workout sweats, his signature six-pack abs all oiled up and glistening. That man was nothing short of heaven in the carefully-sculpted flesh. And he was kinky. That had been the proverbial icing on the spank-cake right from the first time Claire had walked into Black Light's dungeon play area in time to see him, play bag in hand, walking out. He hadn't been alone then, but for the life of her all Claire remembered about the woman who'd left with him that night, was the bright red, welted state of her ass, barely covered as it was by the black thong and bustier she'd been wearing.

More than anything, Claire had wanted her ass. Not that Claire didn't also have a very nice ass — she hit the gym five days a week, no matter what was happening at the office, and never missed booty day — but she had wanted those welts. She'd wanted the pinkness, the lingering burn that had no doubt still been sizzling beneath her skin when they got... wherever, and he put down his bag, pulled her into his arms, grabbed her ass in both hands and squeezed. God, she had wanted that.

She had wanted it so badly that when Black Light announced that this year's Valentine Roulette event would include an online celebrity auction — and she spotted Adam's name on the list of volunteer victims — she'd known what she wanted. She'd cashed out a savings bond, second-guessed herself for seventy-two of the most grueling hours of her life, then as soon as someone had outbid her, she'd cashed out another one and put it all down on a chance to scene with the mouth-wateringly good looking, professional model, amateur bodybuilder, King of the Spanking Benches, Adam Butler.

Now here she was. Silently freaking out in Black Light's changing room, while several women around her laughed and talked and changed out of their street clothes in preparation for what promised to be a fabulous night for those who'd put down enough money. No more second-guessing now. Three days ago, the owners had contacted her to say she was the highest bidder. From this moment on, all Claire had to do was get her act together, find a seat in the theater area, and wait for her name to be called when Adam — in all his kinky man-model glory — stepped up onto the stage.

She'd never felt so out of control in her life. She kind of hated it; it was somewhat exciting. Tonight was destined to culminate in her very first red-hot, vigorously spanked ass. A chill danced across her shoulders, but she refused to squirm. No more hesitations. No more self-sabotaging excuses. Claire opened her eyes, lifting her chin as she stared at her closed locker. She was ready. She was also determined, and when she was determined she always got her way. Both in and out of the boardroom.

Always.

Smoothing her hands down over her trim stomach and hips, letting her uncharacteristic nervousness hide in a last-minute check to make sure the lay of her little white dress was correct, she walked out of the locker room, past the club office and out into the main mingling area. The click of her heels on the marble tiles was almost completely drowned out beneath the deep-bass thump and club-music grind blaring over the speakers. Someone would turn it down once the action started, but it was always loud beforehand and already the bar was hopping. Naked but for a pair of sparkling pink heels, a speedo, and a collar, his trayful of drinks balanced in his hands, a server wound his way through the crowd of mingling onlookers. Falling into his shadow meant less pushing her way through the crowd as she made her way to the stage. Claire couldn't help herself. Already the roulette wheel was calling her. Spanking was one of the cards on that wheel. So was flogging, caning, and whipping, but it was the one marked spanking that was on Claire's mind.

Anticipation shivered through her, felt most keenly across the surface of her bottom beneath the thin cover of her short, white dress. Almost overwhelmingly, most of the women here were dressed in black — black leather, black sequins, little black dresses, corsets, lingerie, bras and panties, collars and cuffs. Here and there, she spotted a flash of hot pink or scarlet, sinful red. It was impossible to see everyone in a crowd like this, but so far she was the only one dressed in virginal white. That was all right. She liked standing out, and in this dress, she certainly accomplished that.

This was a barely-there dress, meaning there was cloth enough only to cover what needed to be. Backless and sleeveless, twin spaghetti straps tied behind her neck to keep the spartan 'V' of her loose top covering both breasts. Her incredibly short skirt was split to the hips on both sides. Instead of skin-tight, the shiny satin fabric draped her form, showing off her curves to their absolute best advantage. As she turned from the stage, she knew she garnered her fair share of hungry looks, but her eyes were on the lookout for one man, and one man only. A chill hardened her nipples, heightening their sensitivity to the subtle scraping as the dress caressed her walking movements.

She made her way to an empty seat near the front, avoiding two gentlemen Doms who attempted to catch her eye. Hers were locked on the front of the room, and the podium where all of the action was getting ready to start.

She wasn't the only one worrying herself into a state of anticipatory panic. The soundproofing in this room had reduced the outside bar music to little more than thumping pulses, but this was not a silent theater. Snippets of conversations kept filtering in around her own insecurities. From the group of men two rows behind her chair, laughing as they speculated on which lady celebrity would go for the highest bid; from two women in different parties, who suddenly realized they'd put bids on the same man. The woman who hadn't won politely wished the other luck. How many women in this room had she beaten out, Claire wondered, her chest already so tight that her heart couldn't seem to keep a steady beat. Almost as fast as that worry crossed her mind, the noise from the outer room diminished as the theater's doors were closed, effectively hushing all the scattered conversation around her too. The lights above dimmed. Those focused on the stage zeroed in on club manager Madison, the MC for the evening, in a halo of plum, red, and Black Light's signature black-light glow as she took center stage alongside Jaxson Cartright-Davidson, and his lovers.

"Time to get this party started!" Jaxson called out. The PA system squeaked feedback and he moved back a few inches to avoid a repeat.

Claire tried to focus on the words the retired model was saying, but her thoughts kept wandering, her eyes searching for the first sign of Adam until Jaxson wrapped up his welcome speech.

"So, without further ado, I want to introduce everyone to our Mistress of Ceremonies for the night, Madison Taylor. You may recognize her as the manager of Runway upstairs where she runs a very tight ship. Tonight, she is our own Mistress Madison."

As the petite MC took the mic, she knew she was one step closer to meeting her Dom for the night. She waited anxiously as she listened to Madison going through the rules and taking questions from the packed-in crowd. She felt like she was going to jump out of her skin when the MC finally acknowledged the grouping of celebrities that had taken their place stage left, next to the few steps that would take them center stage when their name was called. She scanned the group until her heart stopped.

God, there he was. Oh, and he looked even better than he did on the cover of *Fitness and Fashion*. He was fully clothed, something that only rarely happened in the workout mags. He'd traded in comfortable, flexible spandex for black denim and a midnight t-shirt that could have been poured over him it fit so well. His thighs were thick as tree trunks as he planted himself in that line of men and women that, as far as Claire was concerned, just could not compete. The strap of a big, black playbag was slung over one shoulder. Biceps bulging, he waited with an easy grin for the cheers and applause to die down, and all Claire could do was sit in silent panic, so in awe that she couldn't even clap as each new winner was paired off.

"Next up on our auction block is the international fitness model whom we've all seen gracing the covers of fitness magazines. Welcome Adam Butler!" Madison called out, clapping along with the audience.

Oh God. She pressed damp palms flat against her thighs, letting the fabric of her skirt absorb all her useless anxieties as Adam stepped out of the dwindling line to take centerstage.

"And the winner of the auction for Adam Butler, with a bid of $31,000 is…" Madison was an awesome, if sadistic, MC. She drew out the tension and all Claire could do was sit there, her nails digging into her legs as she drew in a breath, "Claire Allerton!

Her stomach hit her toes and her panic hit the roof. Claire waited for that half-feared, fully-expected 'just kidding, folks.' Maybe even followed by a smattering of laughter, but it never happened. She really had won. Voyeurs in the audience were applauding. Her heart was racing so hard it hurt.

Madison shaded her eyes from the brightness of the lights. "Where are you, Claire?"

On shaking knees, Claire rose.

"There you are!" Madison beckoned. "Come on up here."

She went, but her eyes were locked on Adam—his warm smile, that crinkle of laugh lines that appeared like tummy-tingling magic at the corners of his piercing grey eyes as he walked to the edge of the stage and simply hopped off it.

"Evening," he greeted as he held out his hand. His biceps were even bigger up close.

"Hi." She hardly recognized that shaky voice as her own. She was a woman accustomed to making half-million-dollar decisions on the spur of a moment, either on the phone with business contacts overseas or in front of board members and stockholders. Her voice never shook like this. Right now, she sounded breathy and scared.

Taking her hand, Adam gave her fingers a squeeze and leaned in to whisper, "Don't worry." The incomparable delicious scent of sandlewood and coffee accompanied him. "It's my first time too. Depending on what we're doing, I'm sure one of us will be gentle." The corner of his mouth turned his knowing smile crooked. "Or maybe not. I guess we'll have to see."

She melted.

"Here you go." Madison handed Adam a copy of Claire's submissive preference and list of hard limits. "You might want to read these over."

"I get to be on top," Adam noted straight off, and his smile broadened as he read through the sparse information the club provided. "Wonderful. Let's find out what we're doing."

He squeezed her fingers again and, floating on a sandlewood and coffee-scented cloud of disbelief, she turned to the roulette table, marked with its colorful display of kink options instead of numbers. Her gaze found spanking again. Her sex twitched and her womb burned a little hotter. She'd just put a hell of a lot of money down on a night with Adam Freaking Butler, at a Black Light event, surrounded by her fellow members. And yet, all of a sudden, having him know she'd spent the last however many months it had been since she'd first seen him sceneing with that other woman fantasizing about having him smack her bottom until she was gasping and groaning and undulating her hips upon his knee, not like a bad girl, but like a woman in heat — it was all too much. Too intimate. She looked away before he could guess what she was staring at.

Every sultry nerve ending she had was firing in overdrive as Adam slipped in even closer. "What are you hoping for?"

She shook her head, unable to say it.

"I'm going to spin the wheel," Madison said as she handed Claire the ball. Claire couldn't move, she stared, frozen in the face of all these clearly spelled out possibilities. "When you're ready, just give the ball a toss."

"I know what I'm rooting for," Adam said, clapping his hands and rubbing briskly as she stepped up to the wheel.

She knew what she wanted, too. As Madison spun the wheel, Claire held out the ball and closed her eyes. The friction tab clacked furiously. The writing on the wedges was a blur, so it was useless to try aiming. She simply let the ball drop and held her breath as the wheel caught and spun it.

"Around and around she bounces," Adam murmured, the low tenor of his voice sending chills dancing up her back, especially where his breath brushed the naked skin of her nape. "Where is it going to land, do you think?"

The ball was whirling and the wheel just starting to slow.

"Breast torture?" Adam suggested.

Her nipples peaked, though her mouth ran instantly dry.

"Shibari?" he mused. "Electric shock? Does a certain Little someone need to be put on her knees while she calls me Daddy tonight?"

Claire had to remind herself to breathe. Her skin was crawling, tingling, and shivering. Where his chest brushed the back of her arm, she swore she felt actual, physical sparks leaping out of him to pinball wildly through her. Spanking was a black pie-wedge of hope still spinning too fast to make out. It hurt her eyes to try, so she closed them. Twisting her fingers along the split seam of her skirt, she crossed them.

"I haven't flogged anyone in a while. Flogging could be fun," Adam continued, as if he didn't even know the chaos his very nearness was putting her through. "Whipping too, maybe. Foot worship? I'll admit, I've never had anyone suck my toes before. I'm not really sure about that one."

She'd never had her toes sucked either. It wasn't her kink, and yet the idea of being made to get down on her knees in front of Adam, of staring up past the bulge in his dark jeans as if she weren't at all aware of it… damn if her knees didn't just weaken at the thought. Claire almost went down.

His hand found the small of her back, both steadying and branding her with the heat of his touch. "Not yet," he said, amusement playing opening in his tone. "When I want you on your knees in front of me, I'll put you there."

The wheel was slowing fast.

"Here it comes," Madison said, more for the benefit of the raptly watching audience.

Her chest was strangling her. It was all she could do just to keep breathing and her heart felt like it would explode.

"Come on, anal," Adam cooed. "Come on, spanking. Someone needs to go home with a red-hot, well-used bottom."

Her whole body shivered, but not out of revulsion. Far from it. Was Adam planning on sex with her, even if they didn't draw that on the wheel? It wasn't one of her limits. Sex could definitely be on the table, but never in her wildest dreams had she dared to think about it. His cock, standing high and hard, thrusting out from his body as if seeking for her.

She startled when the ball dropped, thunking loudly into its fated slot. For a miniature span that seemed to go on forever, the room was completely silent... silent apart from the ticking of the still-slowing wheel.

"Consensual non-consent!" Madison announced.

Her breath sucked completely out of her and, shoulders sagging, Claire opened her eyes. She stared at the wheel as if it had just betrayed her. It and, in particular, the little white ball sitting so defiantly in the wedge marked 'consensual non-consent.'

"I was going to suggest that next," Adam said, surprise underlying his words. "Is that on the list?"

He consulted the slip of paper he'd been given, but Claire already knew it wasn't. Restricted to only five slots, when one had the very real risk of needle-play, fisting, blood play, and golden showers to contend with, 'non-con' hadn't made the list. Frankly, it hadn't even occurred to her as a possibility.

"No, it sure is not," Adam pronounced. Folding up the paper, having read it all again, he stuffed it into his back pocket and smiled at her.

All she'd wanted was a spanking, Claire had just enough trembling presence of mind to think — *what had she gotten herself into?*

CHAPTER 2

"Sour apple crown for you," Adam said, setting a glass in front of the woman who'd bought him at Black Light's celebrity auction. "Bourbon neat for me."

Tugging at his jeans, he nudged his playbag further under his barstool before sitting down next to Claire. That he'd been able to secure two barstools, side by side at the end of the bar on an event night like this, was phenomenal good fortune. He was glad of it, though. His poor assigned-subby looked a little shell-shocked.

Cupping his drink in his hands, he watched as she accepted her own. The best part of a seat like this in so crowded a place was, everywhere he turned all he could see were other participants of the evening going over their pre-scene negotiations. Anticipation was thick in the air, even among those groups made up only of voyeurs. People were laughing, talking, taking bets on who they thought might tap out first tonight and who might survive all the way to the end. One man unlucky enough not to win his auction was loudly complaining to the long-suffering server who'd just brought his drink about how he'd been 'robbed,' of all things. As if that could happen. The server managed not to roll her eyes where the complainer could see it, but she definitely seemed not to share the irate man's deprived opinion.

"Thank you," she said softly. Yes, definitely shell-shocked.

Claire was not a new member. He'd seen her at Black Light a few times, but she was a member in passing to him. He hadn't talked to her, apart from a nod, a smile or a quick 'hi' as they crossed paths. He hadn't known her name before tonight, and he certainly hadn't scened with her, but maybe he should have. She was pretty. Long blonde hair and legs that went on forever. On her, that dress was nothing less than magic, poured over the curves of her breasts, leaving her sides and back bare and a deep 'V' between her breasts that dipped so far down her stomach that if he leaned just a little bit closer, he might get a glimpse of things below her cleavage.

Not that he would. He wasn't a creeper. He wasn't going to do that. Especially since in just a few minutes she would be his. Consensually non-consensually his. What in hell was he going to do with her? Oh, he'd played rough before certainly, but nothing as extreme as the plans now tickling at his brain.

She raised her eyes to him for the first time. "Have you ever done this kind of play before?"

"Nope." Honesty was always the best policy, but he relaxed in his chair and hoped his body language conveyed only confidence in his abilities to make what seemed strange and scary good for her. "Have you?"

She shook her head.

"What sort of play do you normally enjoy?" he asked.

Was that a trick of the club lighting, or did her brow just buckle and her mouth flatten in the faintest cringe?

"Well…" she hedged. "I had a massage once."

It took every ounce of will he possessed not to drop his drink on the table. "You've never played before?"

"I helped in a food scene once and I watch a lot." Her mouth flattened again, this time defensively. "Don't think I don't know what that look is."

"What look?" he immediately tried his best not to have one.

"That one." She scowled. "I know where I am, and I'm more than old enough to know what I want."

Abandoning his drink, he immediately held up both hands. "I apologize. I didn't mean to sound as if I thought — I don't know — like you didn't belong here, somehow. I'm just a little surprised and a lot in awe. To go from a massage to, in effect, a take-down scene is one hell of a leap. Right off the deep end. Into a fast-running river. Full of sharks."

"I'm more than old enough not to like melodramatics, too."

"Have you met some of the Doms in this place?" he countered. "Comparing them to sharks isn't being melodramatic. It's being kind."

She frowned, her eyes flashing. Even in the careful atmosphere of the club's low-light interior, when she leaned toward him over their small section of bar, he could tell she had pretty eyes. A lovely shade of hazel that only got prettier when sparking full of half-concealed ire. "Thank you for thinking you have to look out for me, but I'm a big girl and I can look out for myself."

"Of course, you can." He loved it when submissives thought they could do that better than the Dom they were handing that care over to. Showing them how much better it could be simply to let go always struck him a little like foreplay. Still, he needed to make sure she knew what she'd signed up for, and the best way to do that would be to spell it out. "I'm sure you can. Let me just ask you this: Have you ever *seen* a take-down scene? Because, in essence, that's what we're going to be doing."

She blinked back at him. She had a great poker face. That half-concealed ire earlier had completely disappeared. Now she showed nothing, zero fear or apprehension. "I don't know. I might have. What is a take-down scene?"

"Forced compliance," he pressed. "A simulated rape. A flogging or spanking done for punishment instead of fun, where you know the submissive is being taken well across the line of what he or she can bear, but still it goes on. A dozen strikes, two dozen more, and the Dom is still going hard with zero safe words being cried out because it's been negotiated. Nothing will stop it, not until the Dom decides he's done. It's the kind of scene where the voyeurs are cringing and it becomes almost too painful to watch. You can't imagine how the poor submissive keeps going. Her back is so welted, her ass is hamburger, and now she's being fucked. Brutally, in fact. You can feel the echoes of every thrust stabbing all the way up into your own gut, and you're holding yourself so tense that you're actually sore from the strain of it the next day."

A single pulse of muscle along her delicate jaw showed the minute clenching of her teeth, but that was as close to expressive as she let herself get. Her eyes betrayed nothing. "Is that what we're going to do?"

"You tell me." Folding his hands around his bourbon glass, Adam leaned toward her and lowered his voice. This wasn't really a conversation for anyone who might be close enough to eavesdrop. "Have you ever thought about it?"

"It?" she echoed.

"Yes, whatever your particular 'it' might be, have you ever thought about being *forced* to take it. Physical; sexual — I promise I won't judge, but I am going to ask. The fewer misunderstandings between us, the better both our chances are of enjoying the hell out of this." He could tell some part of this was getting to her, and that it was not an entirely unpleasant prospect.

Her cheeks were flushed the faintest pink, her breathing was shallow and her nipples were taut. Adam kept his gaze on her face, but those darling jewels were poking out against her dress. It was enough to make a man's mouth water.

"Have you ever in your quietest, darkest, kinkiest moments thought about something being done to you that — though it soaks your panties in a heartbeat and your fingers can't help but doing a little walking in the middle of the night — you would never actually want it to happen to you in real life? Something you've always wanted to try, if only you could work up the courage to tell someone about... someone you could trust to make it good for you. Something dark. Something you know you're going to like, even when you won't like it. Something you want... deeply, sexually... even when you know you won't want it. Not while it's actually happening. Especially not when you know you shouldn't be turned on by it."

Her nipples beneath that thin virginal seductress's dress could not have been any tighter. He wondered if she knew that. He wondered also if she was aware of just how noticeably she was trembling. He could see it — not in her lovely face. No, her carefully composed expression was as cool as any he'd ever seen. Rather, he could see it in her shoulders, in the vibration playing along the loose wisps of her golden hair, and in the grip of both hands on her shot glass, white-knuckled though it was.

"Come on, sweetheart," he coaxed. "If not here and now, when will it ever be safer to bring such a fantasy to life. We have to do something. So why not make it something that already turns you on?"

She worried at her lips, the tip of her tongue dipping out to moisten before her teeth caught the bottom bow between them. "All right," she said, and though it might have been a trick of his eager imagination that made her sound a bit breathless, there was no denying the shiver that brought a rush of goosebumps everywhere he could see bare skin. "Sometimes I like to imagine being made to"—she ducked her head, conscious of those close enough to listen in as she confessed—"to *take* things."

He didn't for a second think she meant theft. "From a lover, or a stranger?"

Those hazel eyes of her turned almost green with arousal right before she looked away. "He's not someone I know."

"Are you kidnapped?"

Her breasts rose, heaving against the barely-there cover of her dress and, though she tried to hide it, she shivered again. Then she shook her head. "I never really worked out a plot for it."

"Of course not."

"More like... I've done something stupid and—" She stopped, her trembling lips unable to finish, but that was all right. He had imagination enough to finish that train of thought.

"And now he" –Adam smiled before correcting himself— "*I* am going to teach you a lesson you'll never forget."

"Like a weird amalgam of father, lover, protector and friend," she said. "All rolled into one."

One had to listen closely to detect the faint tremble underlying those words, but Adam heard it. "I can be those things."

"But it's not always sexual," she hastened to add.

Which meant sometimes it was and from the blush stealing across her cheeks, before spreading outward, moving down the graceful column of her neck to color the pale of her chest above those heaving breasts, it was definitely sexual things she was thinking about now. He shifted in his own chair, feeling that twitch of interest like the slow pull of female fingers stroking all down the length of his stiffening cock.

"What were you hoping you'd spin on that wheel?" Adam heard himself ask just as the club lights dimmed above them, altering the atmosphere throughout all of Black Light. Sending ripples of heightened anticipation running through the crowd of voyeurs—a silent summons that the other participants of tonight's event that hadn't already headed deeper into the club promptly obeyed. Adam felt that change rippling through him as well, tightening his abdomen and spreading across his shoulders and down into his arms. Though he never took his eyes off Claire, in the periphery, he was aware that the other contestants had already wrapped up their negotiations and hurried off to lay claim toward whatever equipment fit their needs the best.

Claire didn't take her eyes off him either. Again, the tiny, pink, bewitching tip of her tongue peeked out to wet her lips. His own itched to know her taste.

"I don't know," she finally said, a lie if ever he'd heard one. She hiked her chin, almost defensively, but that was okay. Let her try to keep her secrets. Before the night was over, he would pry them from her one way or another.

Glancing at the clock, he knew they had to get moving. "Well, I'm sure we'll find out."

"Okay," she replied quietly.

For the first time, staring back at him, Adam detected a glint of apprehension. She conquered it quickly, hiding her emotions behind a blink and a steadying breath. Raising his glass, he toasted her. "To jumping off the deep end."

Her gaze was everywhere but on him as she took that toast and downed her drink. Two swallows and it was gone. Pressing her hand to the back of her mouth, no doubt bracing herself through the burn, she stood up. "Where do you want me?" she asked, calm, cool, and resolute.

"I'm sure we'll find a place if we start walking," Adam replied, snagging his playbag from under his stool. He liked her poise. He really liked her determination, although her mask on what must have been a snake's nest of nerves twisting and twining inside her was slipping. Her hands were her biggest betrayers. Despite the hike of her chin as she climbed up from her chair, turning with damn-near regal posture as she surveyed the crowd before picking her way through it, those traitorous little hands tugged at the sides of a skirt that didn't need it and then slid down satin-shining falls to wipe the damp from her palms.

She had a damn fine ass. One he had no problem at all following, at least far enough for him to get a feel for where she was heading and for him to pull together a plan. The bar was well behind them and the naked pool within sight when he suddenly abandoned his tail on Claire and cut away from her. Swinging the weight of his playbag to his other shoulder, he forged a new path, quickening his pace so he could get ahead of her while using the crowd for cover. *Father, lover, protector, friend...* Heated hunger licked to life along with the alcohol burning in his belly. He didn't know Claire, but he could be those things for her.

Long enough to fulfill a fantasy, anyway.

CHAPTER 3

Claire had just reached the first of the platform stages before the tickles of self-doubt finally defeated her. She had no idea where to go. The pool with its bondage pillars were to her right. She could smell the chlorine and squiggles of refracted light rippled on both the wall and ceiling above and behind it. No one was over there yet, nor did she want to be the first. But then, the platform stages looked too busy. A whole slew of people followed like herding cattle up the far steps, heading down the long hallway that stretched from the medical dungeon all the way to the classroom. At least one pair of contestants must be back there already and anticipation was high that the scene would be hot. It would be standing room only around the two-way mirrors tonight. God, she didn't want to be back there, either.

What did that leave? Claire didn't know and that flustered her. She couldn't remember the last time she'd let herself not know the answer to even the smallest of problems. Which is exactly what this was, a problem so miniscule that it hardly ranked as one and yet, in this place and in this moment, suddenly it felt insurmountable.

Feigning a smile, she turned to ask Adam where he wanted her. This was the sort of problem a Dom ought to shoulder, anyway, but she froze when she found he wasn't there. She did, however, have her own stream of following voyeurs. That was unnerving. She doubted this many people were interested in watching her play, so it had to be Adam who was drawing their interest. If Adam took her dress off — Jesus, she was going to be naked in front of all these people. They were going to watch everything he did to her.

Which was going to be... what, exactly? She had no idea. Consensual non-consent covered a lot of things, most of which she'd only ever entertained in... what had Adam called it, her darkest, most private fantasies? What had possessed her to tell him the things she had? What if he used them against her? Because, of course, he would. None of the things he'd asked had been random questions; he'd been negotiating their scene. Even as she'd opened her mouth and let those damning little details fall from her lips into his waiting ears, she'd known he was going to do — she shivered — all of it.

Her clit was too keyed up, too scared to pulse or throb. She felt electrified, on the verge of actual zinging shocks straight out of her pores. Stiff as they were, her nipples ached and the minute scraping of her dress as she breathed only made that aching worse. And Adam wasn't even with her anymore.

She spun around, sweeping over those now forced to wait on the steps while the people ahead of them filtered out of the way. She couldn't see him there. Nor was he among the watchers gathered by the pool, where naked swimming was usually a guaranteed thrill on any other night but this one. A pair of her fellow players were nearing the stage now — a Dom and a Domme. Claire knew them only in passing. Sparing them only a glance, it was hard to tell who was stalking whom as they walked among the bondage posts, still talking at this point.

"You're kidding, right? *This* is where I find you?"

Claire jumped at the sharpness of Adam's voice, lashing at her from behind, a place he certainly hadn't been only a moment before. She whirled to find him looming over her, his handsome face skewed into a frown of disapproval.

Blinking, Claire almost stammered. "I beg your pardon?"

Catching her by the arm, he dragged her sideways, tucking her up into the shadow of a vacant platform as if to keep his scolding private. Except, he didn't lower his voice at all and the burn of public embarrassment scalded from her tensing stomach all the way up into her face as he said, "Have you any idea what kind of place this is? Or what kind of women come here? What the hell were you thinking?"

He was roleplaying. Taking everything she'd told him by the bar and using it now to create the scene they'd have to perform in order to abide by the rules of Black Light's Roulette event. And yet, embarrassed as she was to admit it, Claire almost didn't realize this was his intent. Not until she'd yanked her arm back out of his too-tight grip and squared herself against him. She'd never tried roleplaying before. She felt silly and self-conscious, and she caught herself twice alternately tugging at her dress or eyeing the crowd. Her stomach knotted; she was out of her element and she didn't at all like the feeling.

"I-I-I..." She snapped her mouth shut, swallowed hard to silence that traitorous stammer. "Go away."

Face burning, she wasn't at all sure if she was roleplaying or not when she turned her back on him and tried to walk away, but he didn't let her get more than a step before he grabbed her arm again.

Yanking her back around, this time he pinned her against the platform with his huge hands gripping the edge of the floor and the whole of his trim, muscular body holding her captive. It was hard to tell just by looking at his picture on a magazine cover, but he was tall — many inches taller than she was, even in two-inch heels — and the sheer size of him was breath-taking. She was not a short woman, but standing next to him, he made her feel small.

"Go away," he echoed back. "After everything I've done for you, that's how you're going to talk to me? Go away?"

"I have a right—" she hissed, but stopped when he grabbed her jaw. His hand was huge and his fingers weren't gentle, but nor were they as rough as they could have been when he gave her a controlled shake.

"You have only the rights I give you," he snapped. "Until you repay what you owe me, you're mine. That was the deal, Claire, and you agreed to it." He released her, suddenly, abruptly. Shoving back off the platform, now it was his turn to present his back to her. "Go home. I'll deal with you when I get there."

But of course, she couldn't go 'home.' They didn't live together. The long dormant submissive within her could tremble to obey all she wanted to, but Claire's options were limited. What was she supposed to do now, fall to her knees and try to plead her way out of trouble? Get sassy? Or maybe sultry... should she attempt to seduce? Why did there have to be this many people watching her right now?

'For God's sake, get it together,' she scolded herself. She was the British Bitch. Act like it!

Her chin hiked and her back stiffened. "No," she defied, forcing herself to swallow back the awkwardness and drawing on her strengths in the boardroom, because never in a million years would she have allowed anyone to control her there.

Adam played his part perfectly. The look he gave her could have withered even the brattiest sub. "I'll give you one chance to correct yourself," Adam said, low and slow, all but growling. "Then I'm going to do it for you."

Claire almost forgot they were role-playing. It was a good thing she didn't have an opponent like Adam at work, or she'd never be able to keep her mind on her job. Her belly warmed, that heated flow melting down to pool in her now throbbing sex. She stammered all over again. "I-I said no."

He turned back to her, a mountain of cool-eyed disapproval.

"I am not a child. I won't be treated like one."

"No," he agreed, his voice no longer projecting, but certainly loud enough for the growing crowd around them to hear. "You are a responsible adult, but in a place like this, as you're about to discover, when it comes to defiance, the disciplining of both is pretty much the same."

Claire knew he was going to grab her now. She couldn't count the number of times she'd envisioned this moment — imagined over and over how it would happen, what it would feel like, being seized by the arms and yanked in close — her faceless, nameless, non-existent

Dominant angry but in control of himself and determined to mete out the harsh but loving discipline she both craved and deserved. And yet, when it actually happened, she was so physically, mentally and emotionally unprepared for it that she almost blurted the club safe word.

Instead of grabbing her by the wrist or the elbow, in a flash, Adam had her by the hair at the back of her head. As it turned out, it was a far more effective hold than her imagination could have produced. In less time than it took her to suck a startled breath, he had her dancing up on tiptoes, grabbing his wrist in both hands to ease the pressure, and stumbling in gasping obedience toward the nearest sofa.

"W-wait!" Claire flailed, grabbing for balance, but when he threw himself down on the center cushion, he pulled her down with him, tossing her with effortless precision across his lap. He did it like a man who'd had plenty of practice, and all Claire caught was an ineffective fistful of decorative throw pillow before her kicking legs were pinned and his restraining arm was locked down across the small of her back, hugging her hips in tight.

Holy shit! Her eyes grew huge. She was lying sprawled across a man's knee. She was going to get spanked! *Adam Butler* was actually going to spank her the way she'd always wanted him to.

"You're damn right about one thing," Adam said, cool air sweeping up the back of her legs as he ripped her dress out of his way and yanked the white lace of her panties as far down her thighs as his own scissoring legs would allow. "You are not a child."

The flat of his hand caught the full center of her right bottom cheek, jolting her up over his lap, widening her eyes and her mouth that much more. She'd envisioned this moment, literally, for years. Starting in her teens, she'd played it out hundreds of times. Thousands, even. Sexy spankings, disciplinary spankings. Spankings given by hard, but loving hands. Hands that felt nothing of the pain they imparted. Hands attached to men impervious to the cries, and pleas, and eventually to the tears as she broke down.

But imagining it was a very different thing to feeling it. The heady clap of his palm flattened her naked butt, driving in a sting so ferociously sharp that the shock of it radiated up her back and down her legs, driving her feet to kick and her hands to snap back in helpless defense of her vulnerable flesh. He only caught her wrists again, pinning them together in the small of her back.

"That was a mistake," he commented mildly. After that, the rise and fall of his hard hand continued without mercy or pause. And he was right, she was not a child and he did not spank her like one. He did not start off easy, gradually building in intensity to help her take the pain. He started off hard. As hard as it would be if this were a real argument, a real situation… a real spanking.

And it really hurt. The sting was overwhelming. It swallowed every sense, every nerve. Every instinct she had was thrown into the fight to break free, except his hold was stronger than she was and reinforced by his vastly superior experience. This wasn't a fight; she was floundering. Unable to buck, kick, or even twist and rock her hips, all she could do was scrape the floor with the toes of her high-heel shoes and claw the air with useless fingers.

And squeak. Gasping and panting, she bit back her cries through tightly gritted teeth because if she opened her mouth even the smallest bit, she'd be shrieking. Maybe even begging, and Claire didn't beg any more than she cried. Not in real life. Only in her fantasies. Only when she was being held like this, with the hurt growing and deepening into the kind of pain that soon grew overwhelming.

"Is it everything you thought it would be?" Adam challenged, pausing to shake out his hand.

Claire barely heard him above the rasping of her own breathing, the amplified echoes of which she could hear as if on speakerphone trapped within the pulsing of her own head. That same pulse was beating out a similar tattoo within the confines of her aching ass. It became more than just hurt. Flames were igniting in the pain, heating her wounded flesh until the burn was almost as agonizing as the sting had been. Only now it refused to be restricted to just her ass. No, the fire was spreading, branching out, traveling to places he hadn't spanked — her chest and back, around her hips, beneath her belly where the hardness of his muscular thigh kept digging into her abdomen like a wood plank.

Between her legs. God, of all the places she most wanted not to burn, that shadowy vale was it. But that was where the fire caught on most viciously, devouring its way through her flesh as if she were made of dry timber.

She couldn't handle it. She tried to get up, but his arm across her back locked around her waist, jerking her that much more firmly over his knee. He tightened the vise-grip of his thighs now too.

"We're not done," he said, the flat of his hand coming once more to rest on the naked curve of her ass. "We're not anywhere close to done... unless you've got something to say to me? A safe word, perhaps? Because that's the only way you'll be getting off this lightly or this soon."

Lightly? Claire stared at the couch cushion just inches from her nose, her submissive soul both panicking and... calmed. It wasn't over yet? Of course, it wasn't. They had to go until 11 pm, three full hours of this. Or at least, thirty minutes of this, after which she could cry enough and beg they roll something else on the roulette wheel. What if she rolled something worse? Somewhere in the labyrinthine dark of this place, she heard the snap of a whip, and the cry of its victim. This was just a spanking —something she'd always wanted. Maybe not *quite* like this, but now that she was warmed up for it, the wounded pulsing in her bottom meant he could keep right on spanking until the proverbial cows came home. Let Adam do his worst. It would never again be as bad as those first few swats had been.

"I'm sorry, did you say something?" Adam asked, mockingly, "or was that just a stray whimper?"

Somewhere in the shadow of onlookers, a man chuckled.

Whether it was that laughter, Adam's teasing, or the idea that he thought she couldn't take whatever he could dish out, Claire didn't know, but it pricked her carefully-buried insecurities first and then her Bitch's temper.

"It was a snore," she sniped back, loud enough for the audience to hear. If he wanted to embarrass her, she could more than return the favor. "Be a dear, wake me when you decide to get started for real."

More than one person was chuckling now. Adam wasn't one of them. Twisting back her head, she met his frown with one of her best 'shark in the boardroom' smirks.

He cocked an eyebrow and very softly, for her ears only, asked, "Are you sure this is the role you want to play?"

She kept her tone low now too. "If you can't take it, then stop dishing it out. I already told you, I'm not a newbie. I can take care of myself, but if you don't feel 'dom' enough for the job, I'm sure any number of people here tonight would be happy to show you how it's done."

"I see." Glancing out into the shadows to someone she couldn't see from her sprawling angle over his lap, he asked, "Would you mind handing me my bag? I dropped it over there, quite foolishly thinking I wasn't going to need it."

Claire twisted, first one way and then the other way, but his restraining arm blocked her from seeing anything. Not until a near naked woman in a leather bustier and collar waded out from the shadows to hand him a heavy-looking duffel bag.

"What are you doing?" Claire asked, as he thanked the girl and sent her back to her Domme's side.

"Don't worry about it," Adam said, letting the bag drop on the floor by both their feet. "You just go on back to sleep. I have a feeling you're going to need all the rest you can get."

The click of a zipper jumped down metal tracks an instant before Claire heard him dig down through a rustle of plastic bags and the jostle of wood and metal objects. A low rumble of dominant approval rippled through the shadowy audience at whatever he withdrew. He had her pinned in such a way that Claire couldn't twist back far enough to see anything, but she knew the cool, flat business end of a hairbrush-sized paddle when she felt it tap the upper swell of her right butt cheek.

Leaning down, Adam softly whispered to the back of her head, "Are you awake yet?"

214

Someone laughed.

Shit.

She knew a stupid decision when she made one, but — utterly boxed in — Claire let out a long, rattling, unladylike snore.

As it turned out, she was not as far past the worst as she'd thought. Perhaps it was because enough time had passed since his last swat that all her battered nerve-endings were once more awakened to the renewed swats of pain now snapping and biting at her ass, as if with razor-sharp teeth all agonizingly honed. Or maybe this was just the raw difference between what the flat of a man's hand felt like, versus light, unyielding wood. Whatever it was, Adam took her from snoring to shrieking in three sharp snaps of his wrist.

"Oh look!" he declared above her bucking and wailing. "We're awake!"

She wasn't just awake, she was on fire! With the club safe word dancing right there on the tip of her tongue, locked behind tightly clenched teeth because no way was she going to let him break her. Not after what he'd said. Not over a spanking — especially not when he was giving her exactly what she'd asked for. Exactly what she'd always fantasized about.

Someone else was going to have to call Red. Someone else was going to have to be the first submissive to wimp out and go home a loser, because it would not be her. Never. No matter how much it hurt, burned, snapped and bit as he spanked and spanked and spanked, stripping her of her ability to be silent. She shrieked through gritted teeth, wails without words to obscure the purity of her pain-filled banshee's song. He took away her ability to hold still — every inch of her moved as if with a life all its own. Her head thrashed. Her fingers raked and clawed the air, her feet drumming the floor as her hips flinched and humped and twisted in an effort to find some magical place upon his knee where the hairbrush-paddle could not find her.

It was useless, a complete waste of energy and effort. It found her no matter how she moved — found and punished her, over and over again until she couldn't even think. Every part of her, every breath she took and move she made was a reaction to — or in anticipation of — the never-ending rain of swats pouring down on her from above.

Until it stopped. Suddenly.

Above the rasp and gasp of her own ragged breathing, Claire could hear the slightly heavier than normal labor of Adam's breaths as well. She was making him work at holding her down. It was not effortless for him; she was wearing him out. Hell, maybe tonight would be the first time in Black Light history that a submissive made a Dom call red. Ha! And she'd be the one to do it. The British Bitch in her liked that.

"What have we learned?" Adam asked the back of her head.

She could almost hear the smirk in his tone. Sweating and panting, she ached and burned. Not just in the flesh of her throbbing ass, the fiery sensation was everywhere. It was coursing through her veins, filling up her molten pussy, engulfing her clit in a pulse of such wanting that she could feel all the echoes of it radiating out into the rest of her. Her breasts felt heavy with it. Whoever knew such pleasure could come from pain? She might be the one getting spanked, but in that second she had never felt more powerful or more in control.

She smiled. "I guess I've learned how easy it is to wear you out." His smirk faded as hers grew. "You should hit the gym more. I'm surprised how easy this is."

Startled laughter barked from several watchers in the audience. Again, Adam didn't join them. It seemed to take a moment for him to find the humor in her sassy comment, but when he did, his rumbling chuckle came back dark and dangerous.

"Buckle up, Buttercup," he growled when she giggled. "Daddy's going to take you to school."

CHAPTER 4

*A*dam dragged Claire up off his lap by her hair. He needed to hit the gym more? *He* needed to hit the gym more? He damn near lived at the gym. He knew what she was doing. She was relaxing, discovering her inner brat, letting go and exploring her submissive self for maybe the first time ever. There was something incredibly pride-building in knowing he was the one taking her through this journey. And yet... *he needed to hit the gym more?!*

Claire stumbled, but his grip on her arm and her hair kept her from falling. She was still laughing — giggling, really — at him. He shook his head. He was going to have to do something about this, but what? He was making this up as he went along and frankly, role-playing wasn't his strong suit. Which wasn't to say he couldn't play the part when the situation warranted it in real life, because he loved domestic discipline. In his mind, that was simply a meeker version of a 24/7 Master-slave relationship, which was right up his alley and his personal goal for all his future relationships. But actual role-playing — just acting; spinning a punishment scene out of sheer fantasy — that wasn't his thing. After a while, it started to feel like an unprepared scene to him. The only thing working to his advantage right now was how well he knew Black Light and, in particular, the Red Light District of the club.

Tucked away in the back of the club, the Red Light District was simply the partitioned hallway that ran from the VIP elevator, all the way down the length of the back wall, behind the stage, until it met up with the two-way mirrors at the school-themed dungeon playroom. Gothic in its dark décor, the light sconces played a shadowy game of leapfrog with bondage rings, glory holes and face-hiders. Tonight, this hallway would provide the only sexual release members not allowed to participate tonight would find at Black Light. It was no surprise to him that most of the glory holes and one of the 'hiders' was already occupied. Claire, on the other hand, seemed incredibly surprised. Her breath caught from the moment he muscled her up the steps and she caught her first glimpse of a naked woman, bent over a padded plank with her head trapped on the other side of an identity-hiding hole. Her hands were cuffed to rings in the plank. A small arrangement of implements — a flogger, paddle and cane — were arrayed on hooks on the wall beside a small green light. It was the responsibility of the DM on duty to flick that light to red if the safe word was called. Directly above the head-entrapping hole was a chalkboard on which had been written: *Bad girl. Use and abuse.* Already someone was.

"Keep walking," Adam said, giving his fistful of her hair a gentle shake.

She stumbled forward, but her eyes never left the woman or Domme standing just behind her, oiling up the length of the horse-cock strap-on she was readying.

"Holy shit," Claire hissed, trying to duck as they passed by and catch a better look at the other's predicament. "I've never been back here. Is she stuck like that?"

"There's a DM attendant on the inside," Adam explained, enjoying her shaken composure. "When someone sticks their head through, he buckles them into a wooden collar. From that point, the submissive is stuck, unable to withdraw until his or her Dom allows it, or the safe word is used. Would you like to meet him?"

Too late, Claire slammed her expressionless mask back into place. "No, thank you."

"Isn't that too bad," Adam mocked. "Because suddenly, this looks like a nice place to play."

She took one look at the unoccupied plank and hole he dragged her to and locked her legs, rearing back so hard that she crashed into his chest. He caught her there, hooking his arm around her waist to hold her tight and still, with her head reared all the way to his shoulder. She gave the plank, hole and bondage rings the same dubious, closed stare that he remembered from the bar.

"Do you have something to say to me?" Adam whispered in her ear. The heat of her burning hot ass was searing straight through both her clothes and his, branding the whole of his crotch with her fiery heat. It was arousing, far more so than the idea of putting her in the predicament of being his faceless fuck-doll. But if she was scared, honestly scared, he'd find another place to play.

Claire rolled her lips together, nostrils flaring as she breathed in quick, shallow breaths through her nose. She didn't answer.

"We put enough time in on that spanking, we could go spin the wheel again if you want to," Adam offered. "Or maybe, somewhere beneath that tickle of fear you're trying so hard to pretend isn't there, maybe there's an even bigger tickle of curiosity begging to be fulfilled. Let's play a game, Claire."

The tip of her bedeviling tongue dashed out to moisten her lips just before she shot him a nervous, side-eyed look. "What kind of game?"

"It's called Tit-For-Tat. I'm going to tell you something and then you're going to tell me something. We're both going to be brutally honest — no lies, no pretenses, no games."

"Then what?"

"That depends on what you tell me, but I promise I'm going to do exactly what you say you want. How does that sound?"

She hesitated, staring at that hole. "It sounds like a trap."

He couldn't help it. He grinned, loving the steel in her that dared a

219

near-joking reply when she was so obviously unnerved. "Do you want to play?"

Holding her tight, he couldn't help but feel her shiver. Reluctantly, Claire whispered, "Sure."

"I'm going to tell you exactly what I am going to do at this station, all right? No surprises, no deviations."

Her gaze slid from the hole to him. He held her so close that when she turned her head, he could almost have kissed her without really moving. A pucker of his lips and he could have pressed one to the very tip of her nose. A slight tilt of his head, and he could have brushed her cheek or stolen the softest taste from her trembling lips.

"Okay," she whispered again, only the slightest quaver giving her away.

"I'm going to bind your wrists behind your back and, do you see that ring on the wall just above the chalkboard?"

She stole the quickest glance at it, and nodded.

"I'm going to tie you to that, forcing your arms up behind you until you have no choice but to bend over. It won't be comfortable, but I know how to do it without injuring you. The plank is going to be your safeguard. Even if you lose your balance, it's going to keep you steady. Now, after that, what I do is entirely up to you."

Confusion narrowed her eyes. "What do you mean? Up to me, how?"

"For as long as your head is on this side of that hole, I'm going to punish you. Your back, your legs, your ass, your pussy — any part of you that I'm inspired to strike, with any item I'm inspired to use. Flogger," he said, loving how her blush deepened as she caught on to what he was saying and her eyelids fluttered. "Belt, paddle. Cane. Hand. Whatever I want, however hard or fast, or soft and slow I want for as long as it takes to find your limits, Claire. And don't think for a second that I won't find them. I promise, I'm going to introduce you to limits you didn't know you had before this is over. Or—"

Her fluttering eyes met his again. The hazel hue had deepened to a sultry green. She was aroused, whether she wanted to admit it or not. Maybe even whether she knew it or not.

"Or?" she whispered.

"Or you can put your head in the hole, in which case I'm going to do everything I can to pleasure you. My fingers, my tongue. I absolutely guarantee I am going to glove up and put my cock in you. Your pussy, your ass. I'll use butt plugs, dildoes, a strap-on in order to double penetrate you, and my vibrating wand. I am going to deny you orgasm after orgasm, until you're sobbing with need, and then I'm going to make you cum hard and fast, until you don't think you can manage it, not one more time. Until it fucking hurts and you're begging me not to make you do it anymore."

Her whole body shuddered deeply, laying bare all the expression her face tried to deny him.

"Brutally," he told her. "Honestly. That is exactly what I am going to do. Or…"

Again, he let that word hang until she echoed, "Or?"

"Or you tell me right now you don't want to do either, and we'll go spin the wheel for our next activity. The choice is entirely up to you." A ghost of a smile tugged at his mouth. "At least until you make one."

He loved how high and pert her nipples were as she stared at the padded plank and considered her options. He didn't for a second think she was as scared or uncertain as she looked, not anymore. If her nipples could be believed, he knew there had to be a measure of intrigue circulating within her. His hand was on her belly. It would be such a short journey for his fingers to travel down over and under the curve of her mons, between the lips of her sex and check. The spanking had turned her on. She had to be just as wet as wet could be. Dripping, even. She'd positively soak his fingers, something he couldn't wait to feel.

Pure anticipation tickled up his back and across his shoulders, bringing a wave of goosebumps with it. He had no idea whose benefit it was for when he said, "Who knows, maybe we'll spin controlled orgasm next on the roulette wheel. Or cock worship. Or anal play"— her shiver fed his—"and end up right back here anyway, with you staring at the restraints and me thinking about all the delicious things I'm going to do once I get you in them."

Snapping her eyes shut, she turned her head away. Her indrawn breath was the shakiest he'd yet felt her take, but her voice—oh, how calm and steady she sounded when she said, "Tie me up."

He didn't know what she did for a living, but she should have been an actress. She was that good.

Dropping his playbag on the ground by their feet, Adam took out a length of purple rope. One round of predicament bondage coming right up. It had been a while since he'd practiced his ropework. Hopefully, he still remembered his basic knots.

CHAPTER 5

*T*he ropes looked soft and smooth until they were on her, binding her hand-to-forearm behind her back. The tension ran up her biceps into her shoulders. It didn't hurt when he bent her over that narrow support ledge that culminated in a dark wall hole just inches from her face, but it did keep her from being able to move much. Especially once he tied the other end of her rope to the bondage ring high up on the wall above her and then secured the thick leather strap around her waist, buckling it to rings on both sides of the ledge. He kept the strap loose but she was trapped all the same, unable to pull backwards without hurting her shoulders, unable to twist sideways, unable to move in any direction except face-first into that dark unknown on the other side of the wall.

It wasn't completely dark in there. The eerie glow of black lights provided just enough illumination for her to see movement — the DM probably — passing back and forth in front of her hole. She could hear sucking sounds, soft moans that correlated with what was going on two stations to her left. A man dressed in wolf-pack leathers, complete with a master's cap and vest, was bellied up to a glory hole with his pants open and his cock shoved inside. His hips were barely moving. Holding onto a shoulder-high bondage ring for support with one hand, he had a remote control in his other. While Claire watched, he clicked it and through the hole in front of her, Claire heard a hitching gasp and muffled moan. The sucking resumed with renewed enthusiasm. He or she, whoever was servicing that particular hole, was going to need it. Behind her current patron, two other wolf-pack men were lined up, waiting their turns.

"Remember your safe word," Adam said, reclaiming her attention with a touch of his hand. His bare hand. On her tender, bare ass. Her legs tightened and she locked her lips against an involuntary mew as he caressed her. "Remember, you also have a choice. Your ass belongs to me... until you put your head in the hole."

He gave her right bottom cheek a squeeze, his broad fingers finding and digging into all the sore spots. She locked her lips tighter, squirming. God, it hurt, but in a good way. Such a good way.

"Then your ass really will be mine. It's..." He consulted his wristwatch. "...almost nine o'clock. We've two hours left to go. We'll begin gently." He chuckled. "More or less."

Even bound as she was, Claire jumped at the crispness of his first open-handed slap to a bottom as well-spanked and tender as hers. The heat was slow to re-ignite, but so was the swatting pace he set. By the third slap, the flames were licking up under the hurt once more and Claire was melting into them.

Swat after swat, the hurt muted and the fire grew, spreading out through her until all she could feel was the hurt, the steady pulsing throb, and fire. He swatted, then caressed, and then swatted harder, only to cup and squeeze and caress a little bit more.

The woman two stations down, moaned as she attended the cock now slowly thrusting into her suckling ministrations. It was all Claire could do not to moan along with her, because damn if the wanton pressure to come wasn't building up between her own trembling legs. It was hard to ignore it. The swats kept her grounded, but the caresses — oh God, she wanted so badly for him to touch between her legs, but his fingers skimmed from one cheek to the other, never touching where she ached most to feel it.

The padded edge of the ledge on which she lay stopped

aggravatingly short at the edge of her pubis, so she couldn't even shift how she lay to apply discrete pressure, either. Not without pushing her head up into that hole, and she wasn't ready to give him that satisfaction. She could take whatever he could give. She could wear him out if she tried.

A particularly hard swat landed lower, missing most of her bottom to clap the top of her left thigh. Her sit-spot. That oh-so tender stretch of flesh that couldn't help but encounter a chair when next she tried to sit. That place where the curves of her bottom met leg and which held onto punishment's sting the longest. Adam rubbed the hurt in, but all Claire could think was how very close his fingers now were to other, more demanding places. If he spread them out wide, he could have touched the outer folds of her pussy. He could have felt her wetness, the mortifying evidence of just how badly she wanted this… and him.

But just for one night. This night.

She could take it. Claire arched as he caught the sit-spot on the other side. His hand slid — *Jesus!* — and her back arched, head straining back as she felt the full press of his palm glide across her naked pussy. He stopped, the heat of his flesh radiating into her sex.

She would not sob out for him to just stick it — something, anything — in her. The British Bitch never weakened, cried or gave in. Not when the market was down. Not when the boss was pissed, and certainly not when Adam's touch vanished from her desperate sex.

Claire bowed her head, all but pressing her forehead to the padded ledge in an effort to keep from saying something she knew he could easily make her regret. Something that would just as inappropriately betray how badly she wanted his hand back between her legs. Braced as she was for disappointment, what she wasn't braced for —what no amount of will-power or tightly rolled lips could stifle — was the sharp force with which his clapping hand caught her naked sex.

Hips tucking and twisting, Claire threw back her head with a shout. The strap around her waist creaked as she threw herself into a mini, squirming revolt that died in absolute ineffectiveness. She couldn't break free of the strap and the rope that bound her wrist-to-elbow refused to let her hands fly free in defense of her throbbing pussy.

"Fuck!" she shouted, and would have bit the leather padding beneath her if only her teeth could have got a grip. It hurt, but this was more than hurt. It was agony and ecstasy and the raw, aching desperation for more that she couldn't — wouldn't — give voice to, because she was already the noob in his eyes. The last thing she could afford to be was the first submissive to give in. As if that should even matter, the grown-up, intellectual, professional side of her brain interjected. But, damn it, it did!

In a few hours' time, when she walked back out of this place, she could live with whatever mental fallout there might be to finally experiencing her first spanking. The fun, embarrassing and even painful parts—she would man up and she would deal with it, because that was what she did. She could live with humping his knee and riding his hand in front of a bunch of strangers. With whimpering and maybe even crying a little bit as she gave in to the roller coaster of emotions that his spanking physically was taking her through. What she didn't know was if she could live with crying and pleading and begging him to please just put something inside her, in public, because she had never anticipated this. She wasn't prepared — how did someone even begin to prepare — for this, and the last thing she wanted was for it to stop.

"Fuck," she growled again, but it came out more like a sobbing moan because his hand had returned to her pussy. Caressing her boldly now, slipping his fingers through the silken folds of her sex to soothe the hurt he had created.

"Not yet, honey, but I will." He found her clit and circled it, amplifying her throbbing desire. "At least you're not snoring now, are you?"

Claire had no ready response. She couldn't think beyond gasping out her loss when he abandoned both her clit and took his caressing hand away. Last to go was his thumb, which followed the seam of her pussy all the way up between her buttocks, pausing at her anus, pressing as if he would enter her there before disappearing.

"First punishment," he said instead.

She heard the rustle of his bag, followed by the flick of a plastic snap on top being popped open, then closed. A faint medicinal smell that should have been familiar flowed on the air around her. His hand appeared over the top of her head, waving his glistening fingers in front of her nose to let her smell. It was minty, white, but too smooth to be toothpaste.

"You have until the count of three to safe word," he warned.

"What is that?" Claire asked.

"My own special compound," he replied.

Her eyes widened. He did this enough to have his own compound? What few times she'd seen him play here, she'd never seen him do much more than spank. Well, he'd dripped candlewax on a submissive once. She'd squeaked and squirmed around, but it was watching him spank that really turned Claire on.

It really turned a lot of submissives on. It was the number one thing his partners requested of him. Not just because he had six-pack-abs, but because he had six-pack-everything and looked damned good holding them pinned across his lap.

Claire shivered. "What kind of compound?"

"Cooling and burning. It's a little bit of peppermint oil and Tiger Balm, and a few other things. If you've ever played with Bengay, it's like that but a little more intense. Also, once it goes on, I can't undo the damage until it's run its course, which works well in non-con scenes. Still, it's chemical play, so you'd best make up your mind. One..."

She'd heard about Tiger Balm and Bengay being used to heighten sex play. She'd even seen it once. A Domme had donned gloves before smearing a hefty dollop of Bengay all over her submissive's balls and ass, and even on the condom-wrapped strap-on she'd then used to fuck him with. From that poor sub's initial teeth-gritted grunts to his eventual howls, it must have been intense.

"Two..." Adam warned, while Claire stared into the shadowy abyss of the reverse glory hole.

She wasn't going to safe word. She knew it, even if he didn't. But it was nice of him to give her a warning and an option. Considering the type of scene this was, he didn't have to do either. Her job was simply to endure, but did she really want to endure chemically-induced burning on her genitals?

Maybe the better question was, did she want to give up?

Pressing her forehead against the leather padding, Claire rolled her lips tight so she wouldn't make a sound. Bound in this position, all she felt was her own vulnerability.

"So be it," he said, his tsk of sympathy utterly belied by his cheerful tone. "Deep breath, now. When the intensity hits that point where you don't think you can bear another second of it, try to keep in mind my compound has a short lifespan. It'll only burn its most hellish for about twenty minutes, and all residual effects should disappear after a couple of hours if you don't rub anywhere. No later than tomorrow morning if you do."

"Twenty minutes," she echoed. That long? Could she do twen—too late. With a cool, wet splat, he slathered everything on his hand up the inner slope of both her thighs until his hand was solidly on her pussy. She sucked air, but could no more than flinch while he worked the wetness into her, smearing her outer folds, her clit, stabbing two fingers into her to rub the compound up inside and ending at last on her asshole, where he spent no more than a few seconds, working the residual gel all around her puckered rim, before a thrust of his thumb imbedded it inside that as well. He was nothing if not thorough.

"Oh my God," she gasped, as his thumb fucked her with impartial roughness, pumping in and out a half-dozen times before withdrawing. He gave her bottom a slap, as if to say, all done, and with a rubbery snap, took off his gloves and tossed them into a nearby trashcan.

Claire stared at the wall before her, hardly moving or breathing, straining for the first heated signs of the hell he'd promised. Her thighs tingled, strangely cool everywhere the compound had touched her. Not just cool, but cold almost. Noticeably cold. Maybe he'd used the wrong compound, and why did that strike her as kind of disappointing?

228

She was just debating whether she ought to tell him or not when she heard the clink of his belt buckle coming undone, followed by the hiss of supple leather being pulled free of pants loops.

"Don't worry," Adam said, moving to her side so she could better see as he palmed the buckle and wound his belt around his hand. When it reached a manageable length, he patted her hip. "We're going to get there, I promise."

Where? To hell, she had time to wonder, before he drew back his arm and, with a sharp downward swish, swiped his belt across her ass.

It wasn't hard. Tender as she was, it didn't have to be when all he struck her with was the last few inches, and he wasn't finished yet. He kept the belt swinging, back and forth across her ass, and he moved with it, never striking the same place twice, letting each leathery snap bite new spots all over her flinching backside. From the crack of her ass to the backs of her thighs, and all the way around the curves to her hips, he not only deepened the blush of pain that already stained her, but he deepened the wanton fire.

It stung, but it felt good. More than good, Claire melted into each swish and snap and the tingling up the inside of her thighs intensified, growing colder as it spread.

"Mm," Claire turned her cheek to the ledge padding. Her eyes closed, her eyebrows quirking as the chilly tingle sank into her clit and anus at the same time. The rest of her pussy was slower to follow. It had to be the cool air brushing across her bottom each time the belt tip smacked her. Or was that the compound, just now starting to work?

"Mm," Claire whimpered again, turning her face into the padding, pressing her forehead hard until she could feel the solidness of the wood underneath, because the tingle was starting to feel like needles now and the cold was damn near icy, but also with licks of fast-growing flames igniting all around her back passage. "Mm."

It was on her clit now too, burning. Scalding her. Searing and tingling and branding her everywhere he'd smeared that devil's ointment on her sensitive skin. It was shocking how fast it went from nothing, to coolness, to hellfire.

"Okay," she half-laughed, starting to get alarmed. "I think I feel it now."

"You *think* you do?" Adam inquired. "Well, let's just make sure, shall we?"

Gone was the gentle back and forth rhythm of his belt. In a sudden swipe, he lashed her ass with the full force of his arm and the supple leather that had felt so good up until then, caught both her cheeks together, hugging her flesh in its biting grip and amplified the heat until it blazed lava hot.

Claire yelped, snapping open her legs as far as they would go, waggling frantically to put out the fire.

It was all the invitation Adam apparently needed. Shifting both his aim and his swing, he brought the length of his belt whipping up between her legs, laying a single branding stripe against her exposed pussy lips. She'd have shrieked all over again, but when that biting snap flicked her clit, it stole her breath. Her shout warbled, dissolving into a hoarse, crow-like cawing. She snapped her feet up, waggling her ass, lewdly humping the end of the ledge as if in the throws of the hottest passion.

Oh Jesus, the heat! The minute she snapped her legs together, she thrust them far apart just as quickly, but the bonfire refused to be expelled. It was lava. It was a living, molten monster thrusting and throbbing and burrowing its way inside her. No matter how she moved — there was no relief and oh, what a show she must be presenting. The more frantically she humped and waggled, the worse the heat grew and the more Adam seemed to take it as a personal invitation to snap her pussy with his belt. When she squeezed her legs together, his attention returned to her ass but the slightest touch of skin on skin made the fire unbearable.

"Get it off!" she ground through gritted teeth. "Oh, my God, you're killing me!"

"Are you giving up?" The kiss of his belt gentled once more, returning to that back and forth swish across her ass and thighs, smacking so lightly it barely registered above the burning of the compound. The weight of his hand came to rest on the small of her back, soothing her with gentle circular caresses.

The Bitch never quit anything, no matter how hard or how ferociously her skin was broiling off her. God! She thumped her forehead against the padding, groaning. He had her diapered in an oven — that was what this felt like. And it wasn't stopping!

But it would. Twenty minutes, he'd said. She could do anything for twenty minutes.

"I can wipe off the excess," Adam said cheerfully. "I can even put some neutralizer on it, although it doesn't really stop the burning. Nothing can help that now, I'm afraid, but time." He checked his wristwatch. "If you're not at the worst of it yet, you will be soon enough." He patted her hip again. "Still, if you're done, you're done. Just say the word."

Claire growled, drowning in molten lava and the sweat now beading up on her own body. She didn't think she was moving, but the squeak of her belly sliding on the ledge padding said otherwise. Impossible as it was to hold still, moving made the fire worse.

She'd paid *how much* money for this? She was insane!

"Tell you what," Adam said, "just because I admire your perseverance, how about a little ice?"

Who the hell brought this man ice and when had he stolen a quiet second to ask for it? Claire twisted, but all she saw was Adam, with his belt draped over his shoulder and a bar glass dripping with condensation in his hand. He fished out an ice cube. Common sense said that would soothe the heat, but that mocking twist of a smile on his lips suggested otherwise. She knew why, too, the second he slipped that ice cube up between the burning lips of her labia, into her hellishly throbbing pussy. The ice did not put out the fire. It turned the burning cold, and hell took on a whole new dimension of discomfort.

"Oh my God!" Claire arched as high as the waist strap and her wrist bonds would allow. Everywhere the ice touched her, the cold stabbed her with frozen needles. Everywhere it didn't, the fire was ravaging.

His body heat was unbearable. The cup of his hand against her pussy was torture in a way both impossible to bear and, God help her, weirdly erotic. Not just because of where he was touching her, but because of the tingling, throbbing, raging pressure of her own bloody heartbeat, thundering through her clit and radiating out through her in waves that made her stupid nipples think this hell was somehow sexy.

The throb in her anus was the worst of all. He'd long since taken his thumb away, and yet her body still felt him embedded in her. With each fiery, pressure-pulse, her ass became that much more convinced that what she was feeling was really him, stabbing that digit in and out of her. Stoking the fire hotter one deep pump at a time, only now he was using more than just his thumb. Now it was his cock, longer and thicker, almost more than she could take. The pulses were telling her he was doing all those things he'd promised wouldn't happen with her head on this side of the hole. It tried to say that he was balls-deep inside her, the girth of his pounding cock stretching her to the point of rawness as he fucked her.

While she burned. In hellfire. And now in ice, too.

And there was nothing she could do about it. Nothing except endure.

Endure the icy needles as he rubbed that melting cube all over her clit. Once it was gone, the frozen needles instantly melted back into flaming agony, but only until he got another cube. This one he placed against her anus, circling her flaming back entrance and driving her straight to the point of tears.

"I love the sounds you make." He pushed the cube into her as deep as his finger could go. The melting ice was cold comfort while his finger pumped slow thrusts in and out of her, and his body heat took her to blazing new levels of torture. He chuckled. "If it's any consolation, I took my gloves off too soon. My hands are killing me."

His hands were killing him? His *hands*?! What about her ass?!

Consumed in raw, pulsing hell, Claire was moving before she knew what she wanted to do. She threw herself forward, thrusting her head through the hole in the wall into the shadows of the narrow room beyond. It wasn't giving up, she told herself. She was sharing.

The fiery agony between her legs, but still. The British Bitch would be so proud.

"Hello, sweetheart," said the DM stationed on the other side of the wall as he came toward her. It was hard to recognize a man by his knees and shoes, but his voice was not instantly familiar and she couldn't look up. When she tried, the back of her neck butted up against the top half of the wooden collar the DM was already sliding down on its wall-tracks. He brought the bottom half up under her chin and quickly locked the two halves together.

Having the collar affixed to the wall grossly restricted her movements, but she was relieved not to have to carry the weight of it on her neck. Unfortunately, it also covered the hole, dimming the light creeping in behind her and muffling all sound, including Adam's voice as he massaged her ass. "Did someone think she was going to get away or is this my Valentine's present?"

He gave her a swat, his hand bouncing off her fiery backside before he reached under her, delving between her legs to catch her clit between oven-hot fingers. He rolled, the flames of his touch all but killing her.

"Someone must be playing with peppermint," the DM chuckled, ruffling Claire's hair. "You smell like a candy cane."

And she burned like the devil, but let it not be said that Claire Allerton didn't know how to share. God, this was going to hurt. Her, probably more than him, at least at the start. But if his hands weren't immune to the effects of his compound, then chances were good the rest of him wouldn't be either.

"Let's see how you like it," she muttered, as he lay his belt across her back and bellied up behind her. His hands cupped her hips pulling her ass back into the sizeable bulge now tenting the front of his jeans. "Welcome to hell."

And who knew, she might just wear him out yet.

CHAPTER 6

*L*et it not be said Adam couldn't admit to his mistakes. This particular one, he knew, as he rolled the condom down over his high-standing cock, was going to be a painful one. But that wasn't going to stop him from making it. With any luck, it wouldn't stop him from enjoying it, either.

"He's going to regret this," someone in the audience laughed, not quite low enough to count as whispering.

There were strict rules against interrupting scenes at Black Light, and in particular during tonight's events. If he weren't right now perched on a cock's thrust of getting some of the hottest — both literally and figuratively — action he'd had in a long time, Adam might have paused to lodged an official protest. As it was, he merely tossed back over his shoulder, "If you're not man enough to take it, you shouldn't be dishing it out."

This was so going to hurt. Without giving himself time to dwell on it, Adam saddled up to the brightly-spanked ass now quivering before him, zeroed in on the honey-well of glistening pussy folds weeping peppermint-scented tears and musky female arousal, and stabbed his way home.

Her body was so hot and so tight, and from the moment he thrust deep inside, she welcomed him with the kind of heavenly squeeze most women reserved for those last moments before orgasm struck.

"You want to come?" Adam reached for her shoulders, gripping hard and pinning her down, though bound as she was that wasn't necessary. She wasn't going anywhere, but he wanted her to feel his ownership as he took his prize. Before he was done, he wanted her to feel conquered. She wouldn't be able to hear him through the wall, not with that heavy wooden collar buckled into place. He couldn't hear her either, but he liked to imagine she was now one of the women moaning on the other side of that wall. He couldn't help himself. He rolled his hips, pushing his cock as deep into her as it could go. "I'm going make you come until you don't think you can anymore."

Until it hurt to come. Until she was sobbing, crying out into the abyss for him not to make her do it, not one more time. He wondered if he'd be able to hear it. Probably not, but the DM on duty tonight would likely tell him all about it later on. Laughing under his breath, Adam began his assault.

The inner quake of her thighs grew steadily more violent. He could feel echoes of it in the fluttering muscle spasms that engulfed his steadily pumping cock. He shifted his grip from her shoulders to her breasts, reaching under her far enough to seize her by the nipples and squeeze. Her hips arched back, her pussy clamped down hard as her knees buckled. The ledge kept her from falling. It kept her at the perfect height as her feet came so high up off the floor that he felt the bumping of her heels against the backs of his thighs and then at his waist. If she used them to push him away, he'd slap them back down again and take his belt to her bottom as a warning, but she didn't. No matter how hard Adam rolled and tweaked and pulled back on her tight, little nipples, she stayed right where he wanted as he pounded into her.

Stabbed into her.

A slow drag out of her body, until only the very tip of him remained, and then a deep ramming thrust all the way home again. Until he was all the way inside. Until he could feel her low, guttural grunts of impact all the way up through his cock and into his tightening balls.

His tight and starting to burn now balls. Oh yeah, he could definitely tell where the protection of the condom ended, because from his belly to his thighs, across all the tender flesh in between, his flesh was heating up.

"You little bitch," he marveled, just beginning to wonder if she'd chosen this moment to stuff her head in the hole, not because she was so aroused that she couldn't take it anymore, but as a way of sharing this fiery experience with him. Letting go of her breasts, he gave her ass a slap and then withdrew. "Let's see how you like this."

Revenge was a dish best served hot, as his balls could now attest. But he was still in charge, and he wasn't about to let her have anything close to the last word on this particular matter. Not tonight. Not in front of all these people.

Hell, not even if he had her alone in his apartment, tied facedown to all four corner bedposts with a pillow under her ass and a hood over her head. That would almost be preferable. At least then, he could hear her moans and lusty screams, especially when he bent, sinking his teeth into her butt cheek so she would know this wasn't yet over— that she sure as hell hadn't won — and followed it with a crisp slap to the other side of her ass. Purely so it wouldn't feel neglected.

His cock, belly and thighs now convinced he was standing way too close to an open fire, he delved down into his bag for a few more toys. The vibrating wand was his first choice. The most complicated to set up, all he had to do was find the electrical outlet in the floor just under this station, plug it in and turn it on.

"Hold this for me." Giving her no warning, he stuck his finger in her ass, loving how she jumped and arched her hips. She even danced a little on her tiptoes and when she did, he shoved the handle of the wand under her belly, letting her own body weight pin it where the vibrating head would do the most good. Two slight adjustments to the angle and Adam knew he'd found her clit when her thighs tensed even tighter, shook even harder, and back up on her tiptoes she jerked.

"Oh no, you don't." He unbuckled her waist strap long enough to tighten it all the way down.

Now it didn't matter how hard she kicked or strained, she'd lost what little leverage she'd have. There would be no more arching, no more wiggling her sexy ass back and forth. She was caught, the wand was on her, and the sliding knob that controlled both the speed and pulse variations was positioned on the cord instead of the handle. Which put it in his easy reach.

"Let's see how you like this." He turned the controller, upping the speed from the lowest continuous hum to a steady, intermittent beat. Bound behind her back, her hands clawed empty air as she strained against the ropes. "We like that, do we? Well, it's about to get even better."

Patting her hip, he dug through his playbag until he found a deep purple Crown Royale bag. Inside was his collection of anal plugs — metal for ease of sanitation, varying sizes to accommodate any experience level. Having had his thumb in her twice, Adam knew she was tight. The small would have been easier for her to take; he chose the next size up for Claire. Wet as she was, shaking like this, a little extra pain would probably be the spice she needed to send her straight over the top into her first hard orgasm. If not, well... she deserved a little something for sharing her suffering with him.

Ripping open another condom, he gloved the butt plug. He didn't need any extra lubricant. Not only did the condom come drenched in its own, but between his compound and Claire's own state of arousal, she was more than wet enough. Still, he slid the plug into her pussy, giving her a few practice thrusts so she would know what was coming next.

"Say 'ah' for me, baby."

From the glory hole two stations down, he thought he heard the distant high-pitched whine of Claire's muffled cry. Were her lips tightly pressed? Was she fighting to keep her composure as he fit the nose of the plug to her back entrance and gradually increased the pressure until her body gave in? Her feet kicked up all over again, this time leveling their protests at him, but the plug was firmly seated and he wasn't about to take it out again.

Two hard swats to her ass were enough to settle her down. A slap to each heel had her feet back on the floor, but he noticed her toes remained tightly curled. This was not a pain response. She was enjoying this.

While her toes scraped the floor, he took hold of the butt plug's base and pulled it sharply back out of her, just to invade her again. And again and again, repeatedly, fucking her ass while that tell-tale whine behind the wall grew higher in both pitch and volume. At last it erupted in a full-throated shout: "Please!"

Please stop? Please harder? Adam rammed the plug deeply home, sinking all four fingers into her pussy instead. She fit him like a glove, shaking and clenching and so very wet. Sopping, sloppy. The kind of wet that left puddles on the floor as he forcibly fucked her with his fingers, spanking her weeping pussy with every vigorous thrust. With all the force of his arm. Until that scream of please was being repeated and she positively drenched his hand with a flood of orgasmic release.

He slapped her pussy with her own juices, before slamming his cock back into her. The heat of her ass scalded his belly. The heat of her fluids spilling down his thighs were like flashes of branding irons burning away his skin. His balls were dipped in hellfire itself, but he fucked her the way faceless fuck-dolls should be taken — hard and fast and with all his concentration now locked on his own impending release. On the vise-tight squeeze of her pussy seizing as she came yet again, sobbing out another muffled plea.

This wasn't a mistake, it was an addiction. One he wasn't eager to end and which he tried to make last as long as possible. He'd made a lot of promises at the start of this. He tried to live up to some of them, but each was a new torture and he wasn't at all sure who was suffering more. With the butt plug embedded deep inside her, yes, she was writhing and panting to the incredible fullness of being taken two ways at once. But, God, he could feel the butt plug too, encroaching on his territory and making the already tight confine of Claire's pussy tighter. He could even feel the vibration of the wand, but that heady tremor was nothing compared to the spasmodic shake and squeeze when she came.

And came.

And God, it was going to be the death of him. This was heaven's call, right here — squeezing, pulling, milking at his shaft at a time when he should be doing everything he could to extend the duration, not aiming for completion this early in the game. Of course, coming this early had its benefits too. There was still plenty of time left in the event to rest, recover, and then go again. He always lasted long on the second round. And just because he was resting, well... that didn't mean she would be. He still had his strap-on. He had his Bad Dragon dildo with the prickly spines down the base of the shaft, and his violet wand with insertable heads for both her puss and her ass, and a separate tens unit with nipple attachments that would have had her climbing the walls, if only he didn't already have her tied down.

That was it. The last mental image he could bear before the tightening of his balls erupted in shivering spasms of his own. He rammed into her, letting the softness of her yielding sex absorb the force of his erupting passion. Heated drops of sweat tickled his shoulders. Head falling back, he held himself pressed as deep into her as he could reach, the heady beating of her heart dragging out the shuddering spasms right down to the last glorious spurt.

Struggling to calm his heavy breathing, Adam waited to pull out until the twitching was completely gone. Dropping the used condom in the trash, he bent to kiss the small of her back. She smelled like a well-fucked woman.

He quirked a smile, then checked his watch and gave her a nipping bite on the hip. "We're not done yet, baby."

He picked up the tens unit with its metal-tipped nipple clamps and both phallic conductors — the long, curved vaginal dildo and the short, thick anal one as well. He suspected this might be more fun for him than for Claire, and oh well. That was the nature of non-con, wasn't it? It was, in fact, part of the excitement. And although a fine line to walk, it would be interesting to see if he could make her toes curl even during the worst of what he was about to do.

Taking hold of the base, he pumped the butt plug in and out of her, slowly at first to bring her back out of the languid aftermath of her orgasm and back into the role of fuck-doll. He built his strokes up, pumping harder and deeper until her initial flinches of discomfort as the widest part of the plug forcing her open eased and her hips began to rock along to the motions he'd set.

"There's a good girl." Removing the plug, he promptly placed the cool metal end of the anal insert to her relaxed opening. "Say ah."

He slowly pushed it in. This was thicker than the plug; already she was working harder to relax, taking what he gave her. He inserted just enough to make sure it wouldn't accidentally slip out. Holding it in place, he turned the tens unit on, giving her the first jolting shock.

He heard her startled gasp through the wall. "Oh my fucking God!"

"Now that I have your attention..." Chuckling, Adam set the tens unit to pulsing, slow but rhythmic, shocking her once every few seconds. Not too strong, not too painfully. Although from the sounds he heard coming through the glory holes around them, when he slid the length of that anal device all the way into her, Claire disagreed.

She squealed even louder when he nosed the other insertable in past the folds of her pussy, the wetness of her body meeting the first electrical snap all down the length of that metal dildo. "Are you ready? We're going to play a game. Every time you come,"— adjusting the angle of the wand to make firm contact with her pussy, he changed the pulse from a steady beat to the next highest setting—"I'm going to turn up both the power on the wand and the tens unit. If you can go ten minutes without coming at all, then I'll turn everything off and let you rest a moment before we start again. If you come too many times, you're going to make me hard again. When that happens," he tsked, "I don't care how much it burns, I'm going to fuck your ass. Are you ready?"

Her thighs were shaking. The sounds on the other side of the wall were constant, breathy squeaks. High-pitched desperation that tickled his inner Dom. It was the perfect answer.

"Deep breath," he said, taking an insertable in each hand. "Let's make your little body sore."

~

"TIME!" THE SHOUT OF SANTIAGO, THE DUNGEON MONITOR ON THE main floor, hit them. The lights came on, banishing out the dungeon gloom and raising swells of applause from those observers who'd stayed to the end.

Claire knew some of that applause was aimed at her. Even from the heights on which she was soaring, she recognized the clapping, both from those outside the wall and from the DM sitting on a folding chair near her head, with all her hair swept up in his hand so he could keep a constant check on her pulse, her breathing, and the garble of words that by the end of it she was sobbing, even as she writhed under the waves of yet another orgasm.

The biting zaps to her nipples abruptly ceased. So did the vibrating of the wand, and for the first time in what felt like forever, the sensation was not immediately followed by the flat of his hand, spanking her ass, her pussy or directly on her clit. She was exhausted. A limp and wrung-out rag, tied to a padded ledge with her head in a hole. Adam's faceless fuck-doll. And God, had he taken advantage of that. Her pussy... her ass... every inch of her body felt utterly used.

"You, little girl," the DM rumbled as he unbuckled the wooden collar, "were fantastic."

Sweat poured from her. She was so thirsty, despite the nearly empty water bottle tucked up to the wall practically underneath her chin. Adam had passed it through a vacant glory hole over an hour back and at intervals of every ten minutes or so, all activity would stop while the DM fed her sips.

Her clit was so sore. Her ass — she groaned when Adam caressed her, one last groping squeeze on her fire-engine-red flesh before the collar was removed and he helped her ease back out of the hole. She tried to sit down on the ledge, but she was still flying and so unstable that she didn't even realize Adam was lowering her to floor until her butt bumped the wooden planks of the flooring.

With her back propped against the wall and the scent of sex and leather still heavy in her nose, Claire drifted in subspace. Only coming down when Adam, chuckling, took her hands and physically put a cold drink into them.

"Five sips," he said, cracking the bottle open for her. "Are you allergic to peanut M&Ms?"

She looked at him. "Allergic?"

"Your throat gets tight," he said, laughing. "You can't breathe…"

Claire melted. "Yes, please."

"God, if it weren't a violation of everything I believe in, I would so love to take you home right now." Laughing, Adam dug through his bag for the M&Ms. He put those in her hand too. "Be glad I'm not a jerk. You're going to be sore enough tomorrow as it is."

She was sore now. Wonderfully, deliciously sore in all the right places, including those she hadn't known that she had before tonight.

"Do you have a ride home?" Adam asked, physically putting two candies in her hand and bringing her hand up to her mouth.

"Gonna call a cab," she said, drowsing as she chewed.

"I'd offer to drive you home myself, but I don't want you to feel pressured. Still…" He fished his wallet out of his back pants pocket. "Five sips," he reminded, and she took a few before accepting the business card he handed her. "Take this. The moment you get home, you're to call me so I know you're okay. If you should have any questions or concerns, or even if you just want to talk, call me. If you hit subdrop"—he gave her a bottom-tingling look that made both her stomach and her pussy tighten—"call me. That's something I need to know about and if you pull that submissive thing where you think it's not important enough to bother me with, I'm honestly, legitimately, going to be upset. So let's just not go there. I'm serious; call me."

"Okay," she sighed.

"Sip."

She sipped.

"Eat."

She opened her mouth and he put another candy in it. Pulling her knees up to her chest, she rocked from side-to-side. Now and then, she bumped up against him. He felt good sitting beside her. Everything felt good when she rocked on her tender, tender bottom.

"At the risk of sounding like a broken record," he said. "If your pussy and ass are so sore you can't bear the slightest touch…" Pausing long enough to cast her a roguish wink, he added, "Call me, I'll come over and happily do it all over again."

Grinning, Claire closed her hand upon his business card, holding it to her chest as she stole another sip of her water. Adam Freaking Butler had given her his card. He wanted her to call him.

Maybe she would, too… if she could come up with a good reason. That was something he didn't yet know about her. She could be awfully determined when she wanted to be.

And when she was determined… she always got what she wanted.

The End

ABOUT THE AUTHOR

Fortunate enough to live with my Daddy Dom, I am a Little, a coffee whore, pain slut, administrator at two of my local BDSM dungeons, resident of the wilds of freakin' Kansas (still don't know how I ended up here) and submissive to the love of my life. An International and USA Bestselling Author, I have penned more than 120 novels, novellas and short stories, and am the author of the Masters of the Castle series.

CONNECT WITH ME

- Visit Maren Smith's blog here: http://badgirlscorner.blog
- Friend me on Facebook here: http://facebook.com/Maren. Smith.10
- Follow me on Twitter: @authmarensmith
- Friend me on Instagram: maren_smith
- Follow on Bookbub: https://www.bookbub.com/profile/ maren-smith
- Visit me on Tumblr: https://www.tumblr.com/blog/ authormarensmith

HOOKED

A Black Light: Celebrity Roulette Novella

By

Jennifer Bene

CHAPTER 1

 anessa

Staring at the computer screen, Vanessa couldn't even type her damn name in the box at the top. The cursor just blinked, mocking her. Taunting. She felt like a fake, and that feeling only grew as she switched back to the other tab in the browser. The tab where she'd been scrolling through the ballet company's online photo gallery for the last thirty minutes — which had only resulted in her headache turning into a throbbing ice pick just behind her left eye. Another sip of coffee didn't ease it, and finishing this cup would only guarantee she'd be up half the night. And for *what?*

This was stupid.

The entire damn idea was stupid and ridiculous and pointless.

If she hadn't been two Moscow Mules in last Friday, she would have laughed and told Miles he was crazy, but... it was like he'd planned the whole thing out. The sadistic DM had found her at the end of the night, parked at a table in Black Light's bar, tipsy and happy from chatting with Kelsey. Completely unaware of the freight train of ill-intent barreling towards her in the form of the tall, handsome dungeon monitor. She'd actually smiled when he'd walked up to them, she'd even patiently listened to the DM's suggestion to sign up for Black Light's crazy auction idea — but before she could turn him down Kelsey was already squealing with excitement and agreeing on her behalf. She'd tried to decline politely, tried to say no more directly, and even told Kelsey to shut the hell up even though that *never* worked.

Then, somehow, between finishing Moscow Mule number two and the arrival of number three, the two troublemakers had actually convinced her that she counted as some kind of celebrity.

Right.

The actual conversation was still some kind of fuzzy blur, like it had happened in a dream — or rather a nightmare — but it happened. And now she was supposed to fill out this bio page so that she could be humiliated when absolutely no one bid to be her Dom for the night on Valentine's. Fucking fantastic.

A tinkling chime came from her phone and she glared at it as Kelsey's name popped up on the screen. Her friend had already caused enough trouble, so she was in the proverbial doghouse for the week. Maybe the month depending on just how badly the bidding went. Still, at the hundredth irritating chime she picked it up and read through the messages. Of course, she was asking about the bio so she could see if her maniacal scheming had paid off yet.

Huffing, Vanessa tapped out a response: *'No, it's not done. I'm emailing them back to cancel.'*

The text had barely gone through when her phone started ringing. Declined.

It rang again. Declined again.

On the fifth round of this game she answered with a small scream of frustration. "I am not doing this, Kelsey! Stop harassing me about it!"

"You *are* going to do this, girl. You're overthinking this like you do everything, just fucking fill out the bio and then enjoy the night!"

"It won't be very fun when I'm the only idiot on the list with no bids because no one has a fucking clue who I am and this whole Celebrity Roulette thing is supposed to have — oh, hmm, let's see... what could these people actually want? That's right CELEBRITIES!" Shouting the last word actually helped a little, especially since Kelsey seemed to be stunned into silence for a moment, but it didn't last.

"What the fuck, Vanessa!" Kelsey groaned. "How many times do I have to remind you that you are amazing? Like, really fucking amazing! Hell, even if they don't know what you do they're going to see your picture and bid anyway."

"I said *no*. Just stop pushing me on this. Please?" Sighing, she reached for the glass of water behind the coffee and took a drink to ease the pinched feeling in her throat. "I know you're trying to do the best friend thing and be all supportive and encouraging, but this isn't the time for that. I like going to Black Light and I really don't want to humiliate myself with this and never be able to go back."

"Would you care to explain how you think this is going to *humiliate* you?" The sarcasm was practically dripping from her best friend's tone and it made her angry all over again.

"God dammit, Kelsey, I already told you! I have no place on a list of 'celebrities.' There are going to be actresses, singers, *real* celebrities up on this crazy auction site and if anyone at Black Light, other than you, even knows what *fouetté* turns are... well, I'll gladly eat my last wrecked pair of pointe shoes because this is fucking stupid and you know it."

"That would be really gross," Kelsey said just as she started laughing. "I mean, I've seen your nasty shoes after a month of class and that's probably a hospital stay just waiting to happen."

"Fuck off," she growled. Leaning back in her chair to stare at the ceiling, she let her eyes trace the familiar water stain that looked a little like the continent of Africa... if it had a swollen bulge at the top. Rubbing her eyes to try and ease the headache that Kelsey was only making worse, she forced a deep breath into her tight lungs. "Listen, I'm being serious. Best friend clause, you can't make me do this. They'll find someone else to fill the spot."

"Maybe, but they won't have *you*. You're a fucking soloist at the Dudorov Ballet, Vanessa. You are literally living the dream of millions of little girls across the country. Hell, you're living *my* dream! So, whether you want to admit it or not, you're a celebrity. Get over your shit and fill out the damn bio." Laughing a little, Kelsey's voice grew quieter. "God knows if I were in your pointe shoes I'd be filling it out."

"Kelsey..." Vanessa felt her chest tighten a little further. Five minutes before she would have sworn that her friend couldn't have said anything to convince her to go through with the stupid event... but then she'd played the one card she *never* did. The simple fact that while they'd both come to L.A. from the Nevada Dance Company, and both originally claimed a coveted spot with a smaller company, only Vanessa had received a renewal contract for the corps de ballet the next year. Kelsey never blamed her for it, in fact she was her biggest cheerleader, but Vanessa still felt guilty.

And it was the guilt that did her in.

"Fine, I'll fill it out."

"Seriously?!" Kelsey's voice was shrill with either excitement or shock, or a mix of both, and then she cheered. "You deserve this! You get so few nights off and I know you don't get to play as much as you'd like to, and of *all* people you need the fucking stress relief. Oh my God, I am so excited! Is it too early for me to bet how much cash you'll rake into this thing?"

"I am totally going to regret this," Vanessa grumbled as she returned her gaze to the screen where the photos of the principal dancers still mocked her. "You know what? Since this is all your fault anyway, pick a photo from the gallery on Dudorov's website for me to upload."

"Done and done! There's that one of you doing a *développé* from last year's workshop that will show off just how fucking hot and flexible you are."

"Ha. Ha." Rolling her eyes, Vanessa settled down to scroll through the list of potential hard limits, but all the words seemed to blur together. "I can't believe I'm doing this."

"Shut up and just recognize that other girls are going to be super jealous when they see your fit as fuck bod." A clatter came from the other side of the phone, followed by a round of curses and the yowl of Kelsey's cat, Marvin. "Here it is. I'm going to touch up your pic in photoshop, fix the lighting so the Doms can see just how good your ass looks in tights."

Vanessa laughed as she picked the first five limits to make her stomach flip flop, and then scrolled back to the bio section. "You're so lucky I love you, Kelsey."

"Whatever, you're lucky that *I* love *you*, but that's what best friends are for, right?"

"Right." Smiling despite her nerves, Vanessa tried to be even a fraction as positive as Kelsey was... but as she propped one foot up on the stool beside her all she could think of was the thousand reasons why no one would want her.

And if no one bid, then it wouldn't matter how much her best friend loved her, because she'd never be able to show her face at Black Light again.

CHAPTER 2

 *yatt*

Black Light's social area was too crowded and too loud, but at least Wyatt had claimed the end of the bar where he could enjoy his Manhattan... and watch the door.

He'd arrived in the private parking lot before some of the staff, hours early, which had avoided the insane traffic jam that had apparently occurred, but the early arrival hadn't actually helped him much. Sitting in the car waiting for the club to open as he re-read Vanessa Novak's online bio a dozen more times was neurotic even for him. He couldn't even use the excuse that it was to ensure he'd memorized each hard limit, because there was no way he could forget that short list: *blood play, watersports, vacuum table, sensory deprivation, and age play.* It had told him a few things about the dancer he hadn't known, including her likely claustrophobia, but none of those kinks interested him anyway. Still, he kept re-reading the page, looking at the picture of her in that very impressive ballet

254

position, and thinking through the remaining list of kinks they might spin.

He was halfway through his second online article on *erotic cupping* when Brian finally saved him from himself by waving to let him know security was open. The man had cracked a few jokes about him being impatient for the event, but it's not like he could deny it. Roulette had been all he could think about since the auction had first gone live.

So, he'd been the first member inside the club, which had afforded him his favorite people-watching spot at the bar before the crowd descended. However, the only person he was watching for tonight was Vanessa, and all he was doing was staring at the damn door. Every time it opened, he tensed, and as the minute hand crept towards 6:30 she still hadn't arrived.

"You're always so fucking impatient," he muttered under his breath, berating himself as he tugged his sleeve back over the watch and forced a deep breath. He needed to get his shit under control before the event started.

Easier said than done, Wyatt. You're a goddamn basket case.

It was hard to tell if the rapid rate of his pulse was due to the dense crowd, or finally getting the chance to play with her. Not that it actually mattered why his heart seemed to be drilling through his ribcage, because the auction part was finally over. Everything was decided, and Wyatt had won the chance to spend the evening with her for just twenty-seven thousand dollars. He'd been prepared to spend a lot more, twice that or more if necessary — but the ignorance of others had always been to his benefit.

The other dominants would see their mistake when he made Vanessa soar.

Another sip of his drink brought the sweetness of the Rittenhouse Rye along with a slight steadying of his nerves. It helped that many of the patrons were moving into the theater where the Roulette event would kick off, and it was tempting to follow and find a good seat near the stage — but then he might miss her arrival.

Not worth it.

Absolutely not worth it.

If he'd understood the rules of the event correctly, which he was sure he had, then she didn't even know he'd won her auction. Right now, he was just another face in a suit. Just another Dom. So, this would be the last time he could observe her before she knew him, and after they played tonight she'd decide if it would ever happen again.

Shit. No fucking pressure there.

The temptation to simply walk away flashed through his mind — which gave a whole new meaning to *risk averse* — but the idea faded just as quickly. There was no way in hell he could step aside and let someone else play with her. He'd done that on too many other nights, missing chance after chance to approach her, and he wasn't going to lose this one. He'd invested in this opportunity, planned for it, prepared for it, and well... high risks led to some of the highest returns.

Sure, there was a lot of pressure during Roulette, a larger audience too, but his experience and the gear bag at his feet weighted the odds in his favor. Plus, the roulette wheel could give him some challenging scenes, some interesting kinks, and that was half the fun of Roulette, right?

Right. This was a gamble, but it was a gamble he was more than prepared to take for the chance to impress her. Fuck the risks.

He felt more focused as the clock on the wall passed 6:30. She'd be there, she was too much of a professional to be late, all he had to do was keep his mind busy by planning another potential scene. This one involved handcuffs and his favorite thick, unforgiving leather strap. Her sweet yelps of pain were echoing in his head when the door opened again and the world tilted.

For just a moment it was like someone had switched off the sound in his ears. No noisy crowd, no clatter of glasses and bottles... just her. Even through all the people standing around, Vanessa Novak shined like she always did. Gorgeous in a skin tight, dark dress that barely brushed the tops of her thighs. The neckline was high, however it was so damn short that it turned into a tease — but the real killer were the thigh highs that had his cock waking up in his slacks.

"You're going to want to wipe the drool off before they call your name, dude." Elijah chuckled as he stepped in front of him, momentarily blocking his view of Vanessa. "You got it bad for her, huh?"

Wyatt managed to keep his tone casual as he fought the urge to wipe his chin. "I'm looking forward to playing with her tonight, if that's what you mean."

"No, I *mean* that you looked like a kid in a fucking candy store the second she walked in." Glancing over his shoulder, Elijah blew out a breath slowly as he shook his head. "Of course, who can blame you? She's very pretty and one hell of a masochist."

"Vanessa is beautiful..." Wyatt's fingers tightened on the glass in his hand as Elijah lifted a brow at the correction. "And I'm well-aware that I'm a lucky man to have won the auction."

"Yeah, like I said, you've got it bad." The man chuckled as both of them tracked her across the bar until she disappeared into the theater. "At least you finally had the balls to go for her."

Turning to the Dungeon Master, he kept his voice cold and quiet. "I can be patient where it matters, Elijah."

"I've noticed," he replied, more serious for a moment as he turned that appraising stare on him. "Hope she knows how lucky *she* is that you won."

"Right." Wyatt laughed softly at the idea, because knowing how to wield a flogger the right way wasn't a unique skill in this place. There were much more interesting Doms she could have spent the night with, ones that had developed a name for themselves with flashy scenes and over-the-top displays. That just wasn't his style. A scene had to be intimate, purposeful — even if he got creative with it. "Honestly, I think I'm going to consider tonight a success if she's willing to play again on another night when the whole damn club isn't watching."

"Don't worry about that, dude." Elijah slapped him on the shoulder, hanging on to squeeze in a friendly way. "The DMs here like you because you always respect the subs you play with. Vanessa will see that and so will everyone else."

"Shit." It was the only word that escaped his tongue as he tried to push down the surge of anxiety. If there was a polar opposite to an exhibitionist, he'd claim that title, but it wasn't like he had a choice. The clubs had been his only outlet for years. Black Light at least had the extra security that guaranteed he wouldn't get outed at work, but the idea of an extra attentive audience tonight still made his stomach churn.

"Seriously, you won't even think about it the second you touch her." Elijah grinned and stepped back. "I think this is where I wish you 'good luck' and remind you that all participants need to get their ass into the theater."

"On my way now. Thanks, Elijah." Wyatt offered a smile as the man waved and walked toward the curtain. Finishing his drink, he lifted the toy bag over his shoulder and joined the ragged line of people heading into the theater.

The crowd was thick as he walked in, but he just tightened his grip on the strap of his bag and focused on the air near the ceiling. The very warm, stifling air, because this room was too fucking packed. No way in hell it would pass a fire inspection. Still, he needed to get closer to the stage, and that meant weaving through the people along the edge of the room. A dozen *excuse-me*'s later and Wyatt had snagged a spot by the wall, close enough to the stage to not have to make a long, awkward walk when his name was called.

He'd just taken his first deep, calming breath to handle the crowd when a woman screamed —and not in a fun way. Someone wasn't starting the event early, this was real. Ignoring the rush of panic, he instantly scanned for Vanessa.

Please, be okay... just be safe... where the fuck did she go?

As shouts filled the air, Wyatt finally saw her. Almost directly opposite him, against the other wall, Vanessa was craning her head trying to see what was going on. Her dark hair was pulled high on her head, which left the elegant line of her neck exposed. A man passed by her, pushing through the crowd towards the commotion closer to the back of the theater, but Wyatt had already put that out of his mind. It would be handled, and since Vanessa was safe it didn't really matter.

Focusing on her was better than any breathing technique on earth, it was like the crowd faded and the tension melted out of him.

Others may not have known the absolute perfection that had been available during the auction, but they would see. By the end of the night, they'd regret not bidding on the ballerina who had a pain tolerance they couldn't imagine — not like he would have let any of them win.

No, Vanessa was about to be his for the night, and he had so much in store for her.

CHAPTER 3

 anessa

"Can you believe that shit?" Cassandra rolled her eyes. "People can be so cruel to each other, you know?"

"Totally. I really hope that girl is okay," Vanessa replied, turning back to face her new friend.

"Carlos carried her off, so I'm sure she's feeling better already. I know I'd be on cloud nine if that hunk was rescuing me." Laughing, Cassandra leaned against the wall. "So, you said you're a ballerina?"

"Yeah, I'm with the Dudorov Ballet here in L.A." Tucking a stray strand of hair behind her ear, Vanessa struggled not to make a self-deprecating comment. On the ride over, she'd called Kelsey for a pep talk, which she'd got — but her bestie had also threatened her and made her swear on their friendship that she wouldn't say *a single fucking negative thing about being in the ballet*. Still, standing next to rock stars, models, and actors wasn't making it easy.

"Ugh, I'm so jealous! I was in ballet as a kid and never could get my feet to do what I wanted them to, and you're in incredible shape!"

Cassandra talked with her hands, waving them around as she continued. "I'm absolutely going to look you up when I go home and I'll totally come to one of your shows."

"Oh, you don't have to do that! Really, it's not—"

"Pfft, don't be ridiculous. I need some culture in my life. I think the last ballet I went to was in Italy last year and I was totally impressed by the skill and the fucking *power* of you guys. You're just giving me an excuse to not hide in my apartment when I'm here in town." Rolling her eyes again, she tugged on the bottom of her silver top before smoothing out the black mini-skirt. Both looked designer, and probably were considering she was a model and friends with the owners of the damn club. Her warm brown skin made the bright silver pop, but she didn't even need it. Cassandra was a fucking Amazon goddess with full lips, high-heels, and gorgeous natural curls in a halo around her head that just made her look even taller. By comparison, Vanessa felt boring and uninteresting in her dull navy dress — despite how kind the other girl was being. "Look at your freaking arms! Do you work out every day?"

"Kind of, yeah." The blush was burning in her cheeks, but Vanessa couldn't ignore just how infectious Cassandra's energy was, it was inspiring. "I mean, we have class five days a week, so that's about six hours a day and—"

"What! You dance for *six hours a day?*"

Vanessa laughed and shrugged. "Yeah, it's really the only way to keep your skills sharp enough. Some of the moves can be dangerous if you're not completely confident in your ability, you know?"

"I believe that. I think the second you step into the limelight, people feel like just because they can look at you on a stage or in a magazine that suddenly your job must be so easy." Her eyes rolled again. "As if everything on the planet is pure genetics when it's only *part* of what makes people successful."

"I agree! I can't imagine all the stuff you had to do to become a model."

"Basically, learn to become a contortionist and not eat fries every time I want them." Another round of laughs was shared, which just seemed to annoy the jerk actor, Robert McCauly, who'd insulted them both when they'd tried to say hello.

"That sounds… miserable." Vanessa kept laughing, and it felt good. Like all her paranoia about not being bid on, or anyone caring who the hell she was, was finally fading. "I swear, I try to eat well, but if I skipped my Friday pancakes I'd probably have to stab someone before noon."

"Oh my God, pancakes sound incredible." Leaning close, Cassandra whispered conspiratorially, "What do you say, if our Doms end up being a bust, that we find an all-night place with pancakes and catch up after?"

"I'm in," she replied, grinning as Piper Kole was escorted up to the little gathering of celebrities — none of which really touched her level of renown. "Whoa, look at who showed up. I was starting to think she'd backed out."

"Ditto. Still can't believe she's here. I almost never get to come to Black Light, and it's crazy to me that she's a Domme. I just saw her in *The Park Connection* last year!" Cassandra's eyes were wide, and Vanessa chuckled.

"Well, get ready. I've seen her play here before and they don't call her Mistress Ice for nothing."

The last words she spoke were almost obliterated by Jaxson Davidson opening the event with a loud, "Time to get this party started!"

Cassandra nudged her, clearly excited, and they both turned to listen as Jaxson finished speaking, and then a petite blonde in a hot leather catsuit stepped up to the mic. That would have been a smarter outfit to wear, or at least something sexier than the little party dress that she normally wore tights under because of how short it was. Still, it didn't really matter what she was wearing because she probably wouldn't be wearing it for long — and leather would be a bitch to get out of anyway.

Zoning out on the woman's valley-girl voice, Vanessa looked out at the different men in the audience trying to imagine which one had actually bid on her. A few people went up on stage to get paired off, spinning different kinks, but none of that was intimidating. If anything, it was more likely that the Dom she got would think she was more fragile than she was... it was her normal issue at Black Light, but it didn't mean she wouldn't have fun. The only thing that really bothered her was that they were announcing the winning bids out loud.

To the whole audience.

Fuck.

Now she really wished Kelsey had been able to come tonight. At least then she would have been able to give her an epic side-eye for convincing her to do this when her bid was a thousand bucks or something. Just a fraction of the tens of thousands that had already been announced.

"Girl, you're up!" Cassandra patted her arm, a bright smile on her face as she pointed to the stage, where Madison was waiting. "Good luck! And remember, even if he's no fun... pancakes!"

That made Vanessa laugh and she whispered a quick, "Thanks! Good luck to you too!" Then she hurried up the steps to the stage as Madison continued talking.

"—soloist with the Dudorov Ballet here in L.A. Now, I'd like to welcome our winner to the stage with a winning bid of $27,000... Wyatt Strickland!" The words left the woman's mouth, but didn't fully sink in as a handsome man in a suit slipped past the people crowding the right side of the room. His cheeks were flushed, probably because the room was hot as hell, but... so was he.

When Wyatt Strickland stopped in front of her, he took her hand in his and actually kissed it like a fucking prince. She was staring at short-cropped, light brown hair as his lips brushed her knuckles and then he stood tall. Hazel eyes, more brown than green, kept her attention and she couldn't understand why this man had bid so much money on her.

"Well, it looks like these two are already, like, totally hitting it off!" Madison held out a white ball and tilted her head towards the roulette wheel on the table. "Ready to see how you're going to start the night, Vanessa?"

"Right, yeah, I am." Taking the ball, she tried to look a bit less stunned as Madison sent the wheel spinning. Vanessa let the pale marble roll off her palm and into the roulette wheel, which clicked as it whirled around, the ball bouncing and clattering until it finally slowed, bounced again, and landed.

"Impact play!"

"Thank, God," she mumbled under her breath, and Madison laughed.

"Sounds like Vanessa got what she wanted." The audience laughed too with a few loud cheers mixed in before Madison stepped closer to the mic. "All right, let's get our next celebrity paired up!"

Wyatt offered his hand, palm up, as a small smile tilted his lips. "If you like, we can wait over by my bag until the event starts."

"Sure." Nodding, she slid her hand into his and let him lead her off the stage. Her brain was still trying to catch up, and it wasn't exactly easy as he tucked her in front of him by the wall. Not only had he spent a small fortune bidding on her, but he had his own bag of toys, was hot, and smelled like something both masculine and seriously delicious. It didn't make sense. "You really bid on me?"

He glanced down at her with a strange look on his face. "Of course it was me, what do you mean?"

"Shit, I— uh, I just mean that it was a lot of money and it surprised me." She shrugged. "That's all."

"Why would that surprise you, Vanessa?" His question was soft, but his voice was somehow still powerful. Even through the noise of the crowd talking and Madison on stage, she heard him so fucking clearly. As if she wasn't off-balance enough, he reached up to cup her cheek, tracing just under her lip with his thumb. "Just a quick reminder... tonight, when I ask a question, I expect an answer."

"Yes, sir." The response was automatic, but with him teasing her bottom lip with his perfectly manicured thumbnail there was no chance she could remember the fucking question that had prompted it. "What was the question, again?"

He chuckled and adjusted his hold to pinch her chin and lift it. "I

264

asked you why it would surprise you that I'd bid to spend the evening with you."

"Oh." The heat wasn't just in the room, it was singeing her fucking cheeks too. "Yeah, I really can't answer that. Sir."

He smiled again, tilting his head a bit as he turned and pressed her back against the wall. It was half a second later when she recognized the gentle pressure of his hand on her throat. "Are you trying to bait me into a punishment, or—"

"SHIT! NO! FUCK, THAT'S NOT IT. I JUST PROMISED MY BEST FRIEND I wouldn't say anything negative about being in the ballet, and so it's not that I don't want to answer you and I swear I'm not a brat or anything, it's just that she made me swear on our friendship and so I'd answer you, but it would betray her and she kind of wins on who I owe more allegiance to. Sir." Sucking in a deep breath she shrugged a little. "Sorry."

Humor flashed in his eyes, a slight crinkling at the corners before he nodded. "I think I understand." His thumb stroked up and down the column of her throat, but his grip never tightened, there was just a little more... pressure. "You think because you're in the ballet that you're somehow less than the other celebrities involved in the auction?"

"Well, they're actual celebrities, so... there's that." A quiet laugh almost escaped her lips, but then his grip really did tighten. Higher on her throat now, just under her jaw, and he used the hold to tilt her head back again until his face filled her view.

"Let me add on to your friend's requirements. While we're playing tonight, you won't refer to ballet, or yourself, in a negative way or you'll earn a punishment, and it will be one you don't enjoy. Understood?"

"Yes, sir," she whispered, practically breathless, but that had a lot less to do with his relatively gentle hold on her throat and a lot more to do with the arousal currently buzzing through her bloodstream and concentrating the pulse between her thighs.

"Wonderful." He removed his hand and smiled again. "Thank you for your trust."

"Trust?" she echoed.

"Yes. Not every sub will let you touch their throat like that without proving yourself first, establishing the trust. I appreciate that you gave me that on faith alone. You trusted that I would keep you safe, and I swear that I will." Wyatt's smile changed a bit, widening into a grin that made him seem a lot less serious, more... playful. "That doesn't mean I won't hurt you, though. I admit that I'm looking forward to pulling some of those sweet cries from your lips myself."

And, boom.

The pulse between her thighs turned into an all-out fire, which didn't help the fact that she already felt too hot in the stifling room. "You've, um, seen me play here before?"

"Many times, but I saw you several times at the Dudorov Ballet before Black Light ever opened." He hadn't stepped back, still standing close enough that it wouldn't even take a step to be against his chest, and that was more than tempting. "I'm curious, where did you play before this?"

"Stone Door, it's not a big place." *Did he say he'd seen her dance?*

"I think I've heard of it." He glanced at the stage and then back at her. "Time's about to start, Vanessa. Once it does, I expect you to call me sir and follow my directions. If there's something you don't want to do—"

"I'll say yellow, and if I need you to stop I'll say yellow-yellow." She laughed until he caught her by the chin again, holding her firmly.

"No. Let's be clear, if you need to safe word, you will use the proper club safe word, which is *red*. I know you're a masochist, Vanessa, however, I don't care about winning the free month if you feel unsafe for a single second. Am I clear?"

"Yes, sir," she whispered, staring up at him with more hope than she wanted to admit to herself. If Wyatt was as intense as he seemed before play even started, then maybe... just maybe, he'd actually take her to the edge. "I wasn't trying to be disrespectful. It would just be nice to not dip into my trust fund for a month. Sir. And I already showed you that I trust you to keep me safe, right?"

He passed his thumb over her mouth as he smiled again, making her lips tingle. "You did show me that. And I'm hoping I'll learn more about you tonight as we play, but it will be on my terms."

"Okay." She nodded and he stepped back, his touch abandoning her as he turned his attention to the stage. It took Vanessa a moment longer to stop staring at his profile, but then she looked at the stage as well. Piper Kole was talking to some guy that she'd seen around the club before, but she could have sworn he was a Dom. *Weird.*

Maybe he's a switch?

"I can see our couples are excited to get started. So, let Celebrity Roulette officially begin!" Madison called out over the microphone, and her next words were almost swallowed by the applause and cheers. "Everyone have fun and play safe!"

"Ready?" Wyatt asked, picking up the bag by his feet before flashing that playful grin again.

"Yes, sir," she answered with a smile, and she really felt excited. Because while she'd never live her complaining down when it came to Kelsey, she also didn't think she'd be needing pancakes at 11 o'clock.

CHAPTER 4

 *yatt*

GUIDING VANESSA THROUGH THE SHIFTING CROWD IN FRONT OF HIM felt like something out of a dream... or more likely one of the numerous fantasies he'd had over the past few weeks. Or months, or since the first time he'd seen Vanessa strapped to the St. Andrew's cross and belted until she made the most perfect sounds.

Fuck.

He was already getting a hard-on, and all he'd done was give her a few corrections, a few rules, and... touched her. Goddamned Elijah had been right, because the second he'd held her cheek it was like the crowded room had melted away. There was just Vanessa and the sweet little breaths she'd taken as she'd tried to explain all of her negative thoughts. Almost nervous, whereas he'd finally felt calm.

Although, she'd probably been most concerned with who the hell had won access to her body for the evening. Based on the way her eyes had dilated when he pressed her to the wall by her throat, she seemed to be pleased with whatever she saw in him — which was a huge relief. Likely, for both of them. Still, he'd struggled to keep his hands off her once he'd crossed that line. Her skin was so damn soft, her lips so perfect, and he knew that every inch of her body was stronger than she looked at first glance. He also knew that she craved the pain, to be pushed, and he'd watched her walk away disappointed from scenes before while he'd cursed himself for not having the balls to be the one to approach her first. Wyatt wasn't afraid to stripe her ass, to make her scream.

In fact, he was looking forward to it.

They finally made it out of the too-narrow entrance of the theater, and he gently guided her to the right, back to his favorite spot by the bar. People would disperse, find their places for play or voyeurism, but he'd already made arrangements so there was no need to rush. He just needed to get the ball rolling.

"So... *impact play.*" Vanessa was grinning, clearly excited as she turned to face him, and he couldn't help but return the smile.

"Yes. Any favorite implements you'd like to tell me about?" He chuckled when she lit up. "No promises that I'll use them, but data is always useful."

"Yes, sir. I guess a tawse? Or any strap really. And once I'm warmed up, I sort of love-to-hate the cane." She laughed a little, and he had to take a breath so he wouldn't picture those beautiful lines forming on her ass. Just being this close to her was already giving him some concentration issues, and he needed to find Tyler. Now.

"Thank you for telling me... it's good to know what you respond to best." *Right.* He couldn't have come across any stiffer in response to such a fucking hot confession, but if he got any stiffer behind his slacks it was going to be flat-out embarrassing. "I'll be right back. Just stay here, I need to find one of the dungeon monitors."

"Okay, sure." She muttered a curse. "I mean yes, sir. Sorry."

Winking, he stepped away from her before he touched her again, which would just end up delaying everything. Still, he couldn't resist teasing her. "Tsk tsk, Vanessa. Play time *has* started."

"Shit."

He chuckled as he turned to scan the room, walking forward both to gain a little breathing room and to look for Tyler in the swarm of people still congregating in the bar area. Half the people were swarming around the silent auction, but through the crowd he saw Kaiden and headed his way, but a different DM stepped in front of him first.

"Wyatt?"

"Yes?" he answered, trying to remember the man's name, but he couldn't place him even though he looked familiar.

"Finally! I'm here to help you get set up for your scene. Where is—"

"Thanks, but I actually need to find Tyler. He and I have been working on something special. I appreciate the offer though." He looked around, trying to spot the guy, but the DM beside him started laughing quietly.

"Yeah, man. I know. I'm Dave, Tyler's brother. We built your little contraption together, and Tyler's busy being Elijah's bitch right now, so... you're stuck with me." Shrugging, the man spread his arms. "Sorry if I'm a disappointment."

There wasn't any real apology in Dave's voice, but he understood why. He obviously knew more than Wyatt did about the plan for the night. Offering his hand, Wyatt smiled. "No offense meant, Dave. I can come off a bit cold when I'm focused, but I appreciate the help."

Dave shook his hand. "I get it. I saw Vanessa on stage, and it seems like she's already interested in you. Does she have any idea what you put together for her?"

"None at all." Grinning, Wyatt turned to find her still standing where he'd left her by the bar. "I just hope she likes it."

~

VANESSA

She couldn't quite believe what she was looking at as she stood on the main floor of the play area. Others had already begun to gather around, just as surprised — or curious — as she was at the strange piece of furniture that had taken three men just to haul up the steps.

It was a ballet barre.

There was no other way to describe it, even though it was free-standing and in the process of being secured to one of the platforms. Turning to look at Wyatt, she couldn't read the placid expression on his face. "Did you *make* this?" she asked, unable to keep the shock out of her tone.

"Well, no. Tyler and Dave made it, but I did commission it." A wrinkle appeared between his brows as he glanced over at her. "Does it bother you?"

Vanessa opened her mouth to answer, and then snapped it shut. She'd almost said yes, but it wasn't quite true. When she'd first seen it, and recognized what it was, she'd felt more confused than bothered. Really, she was still more confused than anything, because the barre looked incredibly out of place inside the club and she had no idea what Wyatt had planned. "It doesn't bother me, sir. I mean, I know the rules said we needed to get into our scene and stay in it for at least thirty minutes, and while I'm fine if you want me to do a little ballet for you... I'm not exactly prepared."

"Yes, well..." He smiled a bit, glancing down at the floor for a moment before he looked up at the men finishing up *whatever* they were doing. "While it would be delightful to see you perform up close, that's not what tonight is about. So, asking for it would be unreasonable."

Laughing, Vanessa turned to face him completely. "You paid $27,000 for me, I don't think *unreasonable* applies to any request."

Wyatt's smile disappeared and suddenly his hand was in her hair, fingers tightening until pinpricks of electric light skittered across her scalp as he bent her head back. "I didn't buy you, Vanessa. I bid in a charity auction for your *time*, not you."

"Yes, sir," she whispered. Realizing she'd grabbed onto his suit jacket, she let go and dropped her arms to her sides. "I'm sorry, sir."

"It's all right. You're always curious, and you make too many assumptions, but you're still a good girl." A hint of his earlier grin returned to his lips as he lifted a hand to trace her mouth. "This is where you have to trust me, Vanessa. Can you do that?"

"Yes, sir."

"Thank you." Wyatt plucked at her bottom lip before he released her and then turned to crouch beside his bag. "Please undress, you can leave on your bra for now."

"And my tights, sir?" She tried to keep her tone even, but her voice still wobbled — and Wyatt didn't miss it. That keen gaze found hers and held for one beat, two, and she was worried he was going to ask her *why*, but instead he just nodded.

"All right. You can keep them on for now." He returned to digging through his bag. "The bows on the back are a nice touch, by the way."

"Thank you, sir." Relief coursed through her as she toed off the heels and then reached back to tug the zipper down.

"You're all set, Wyatt. Catch our attention if you need anything, okay?" One of the dungeon monitors walked down the steps of the platform and moved towards them, but he veered closer to her as he saw her twisting to grab the zipper from a different angle. "Want a little help?"

"I've got it," Wyatt answered for her, standing immediately to find the little metal pull and glide it down her back. His fingers barely brushed her skin as he spoke over her shoulder to the DM. "Thanks, Dave, I've got it from here. But if you could send Dominic over that would help."

Chuckling, Dave gave a little salute and started to walk away. "Cool. I'll send him your way. You two have fun tonight."

Wyatt didn't say anything else as he reached the bottom of the zipper. Instead, his hands slowly glided up her sides to grasp the small cap sleeves.

She took in a slow breath as he slid them off her shoulders, but he continued holding onto the fabric so that his knuckles trailed along her arms as the dress moved down inch by inch — and then he let it drop. Warm hands found the bare skin of her hips, pulling her back against him where the bump of his erection against her ass was unmistakable.

"You are breathtaking," he whispered against her neck, close enough that she felt the movement of his lips on her skin.

"Thank you, sir." A tremor of excitement buzzed through her

272

muscles as he skimmed one hand around to her stomach, pressing her back more firmly.

"I noticed you didn't list intercourse as any of your hard limits…" The heat of his exhale over her neck was more than distracting, and she felt her own breath hitch as he began to draw tiny circles on her skin with his thumb. "I want to clarify, was that on purpose or an oversight?"

"What?" she whispered, caught up in his overwhelmingly gentle touch. It felt strangely intimate, even though she was vaguely aware of the small audience they'd gathered and the buzz of conversation all around her. Then his hand moved a little lower, his thumb plucking at the lace-covered edge of her underwear, and she held her breath as she waited for his fingers to slip inside.

"Did you mean to leave intercourse on the table for tonight? Or did you only skip it to avoid other kinks that worried you?" His lips brushed the sensitive spot just behind her ear as he continued. "I want the truth, Vanessa."

The truth. That would be a lot easier to identify if her mind wasn't so damn scattered by arousal, anticipation, and nervous energy — but it was. Every thought that came into her head seemed to crash into another and send them both careening off. Still, she knew what he was really asking. It wasn't just whether she'd accidentally forgotten to check vaginal and anal intercourse on the list, it was if she'd be open to either of those things tonight. With him.

But it was something he didn't even have to ask. The rules had been clear that anything not on the hard limits was fair game, and she'd prioritized appropriately. Of course, there was always the safe word…

That was it.

He wanted to know, now that they'd met, now that his hands were on her and the hard ridge of his cock was pressed against her ass, if she would consent to sex with him — or if she'd safe word. For some reason, that made her even more brazen than usual and, without a word, she tucked her thumbs into her underwear and pushed them to the floor.

Wyatt's breath caught, which she probably wouldn't have noticed if he hadn't been nuzzling just behind her ear at that moment. "Vanessa?"

"It wasn't an accident. Sir. I consent." A grin took over her face as he slipped his hand lower and cupped her between the legs. Nothing more, no probing fingers, just the slightly more insistent press of his erection against her now bare ass and the heat of a shuddered exhale against her throat. She leaned her head back on his shoulder and whispered, "Do you think we *have* to start our scene right now?"

"Fuck," he growled, and she shifted her hips forward, into his hand. Wordlessly begging for *something*, anything more than these gentle, almost chaste touches. Finally, one finger slid between her lips, barely exploring, but it confirmed just how wet she already was. His groan echoed the small noise that escaped her throat, but then a voice came from too close.

"Excuse me, Mr. Strickland?"

"God dammit, I should have done this sooner," Wyatt grumbled, but he removed his hands from her in an instant, and she felt the chill of the room the second his heat left her back.

"I apologize, sir. I have the things you sent ahead." A thin man with dark hair and a flamboyant outfit was standing to their side, looking like a 1970's version of Pirates of the Caribbean. "It will only take me a moment to fit Ms. Novak so that you can get to your scene."

"Fit me for what?" she asked, still reeling from the incredible tension she'd felt under Wyatt's control, but then she saw the woman standing behind him with a small pushcart covered in boxes and a pile of pale pink cloth. "Oh my God."

"Do you know your size, miss?" the man asked, but she ignored him to turn and face Wyatt.

"You got me pointe shoes for tonight?"

He shrugged, looking almost as flustered as she felt, but his voice came out steady. Almost stern. "It's what I'd like you to wear."

"But these are Bloch Eurostretch pointe shoes! They're like a hundred bucks a pop, and there's got to be over ten boxes here!" She stared at the narrow, tan boxes and walked over to grab one. "If you wanted me in pointe shoes there are way cheaper options."

Wyatt's expression went placid once more, blank, and he crossed his arms. Silence reigned for a moment as he continued to stare and her stomach did a little flip-flop.

She almost cursed as she dropped the box back on the little cart. "Sir, I—"

"Oh, no. It's too late to add that on." Wyatt turned to the man and spoke quickly. "Thank you for keeping these safe, Dominic. Please fit her for the shoes and ballet skirt while I get our scene set up. As Ms. Novak just reminded me, we're already behind schedule on beginning our *impact play*."

Before she could apologize, Wyatt had already grabbed his bag from the floor and walked up the few steps to the top of the platform, leaving her with a grinning Dominic and the wide-eyed woman blushing beside the cart.

"Well, that was exciting." Dominic laughed and clapped his hands together. "It's okay, love. We'll have you fitted quickly so you can go apologize. Can you tell me your size?"

"In Bloch? I'm a 5.5 X." Sighing, she accepted a pink ballet skirt from the woman and pulled it on, surprised to feel how well it fit. Not digging into her waist, nor at risk of falling off.

"I totally guessed your size right!" She cheered, reaching out to swish the edge of the skirt that only brushed the tops of her thighs. "You know, I have to admit, that's a hot look. *Especially* without the underwear underneath." She winked and handed the correct box of shoes over to Dominic.

"It is, Annie, but like Mr. Strickland said — they are behind. It's already almost 8:20 so we need to hurry." He flipped the lid off the box and held out one of the shoes. "Quickly, love, show me where you like to attach your ribbons and I'll sew them in for you. Don't worry, I swear I know what I'm doing."

Sighing, Vanessa pointed, explaining a little about how she did it herself, and when Dominic rushed back to the cart she moved to the base of the stairs to watch Wyatt. He'd already removed his suit jacket and was busy digging through his bag again, laying out various implements along the edge of the platform and looking very good as he did it. Damn it all, she wished they hadn't been interrupted. No matter what the roulette wheel said they were supposed to be doing right now, it had been nice to feel him pressed against her. Touching her. Even just his quiet voice in her ear had been enough to let her start slipping into that submissive mindset where everything else fell away.

But, no. They'd been interrupted and now he was irritated because she'd mouthed off. Mood killed. All because she couldn't keep her mouth shut and say thank you like a normal person.

Fuck, fuck, fuck.

Great job, Vanessa.

Now her mind wasn't quiet at all. No, her head was spinning, a million questions passing through as she watched Wyatt start to roll up his shirtsleeves. He was keeping everything so close to his chest, which just made her want to know more. Plus, it felt strange to realize just how much he seemed to know about her — right down to her favorite pointe shoe for performances — while she knew nothing about him.

If Kelsey was here she'd probably be mumbling about how that was just one more piece of evidence proving she was a celebrity. Or that those concerns didn't really matter because he was hot and she'd lucked the fuck out on a bidder... which was very true. And she'd fucked it up spectacularly.

Rolling her eyes, she almost turned directly into Dominic who was holding up the beautiful Bloch shoes with ribbons sewn into their proper place. Surprised, she managed a small laugh. "Wow, you did a great job, Dominic!"

"Why, thank you." Dominic bowed with a flourish before standing with a big grin. "Go ahead, love, get them on so you can have your fun."

Sitting on the floor, Vanessa appreciated the small skirt, because it was just long enough to fall between her thighs and avoid the direct shot several audience members would have received as she bent one knee to start tying the ribbons on.

"I know you guys tend to do all kinds of crazy things to your shoes to get them comfortable, but just remember tonight is more about the look. Okay?" Dominic seemed worried she'd start cutting at the sole, burning the edges, and breaking it in while sitting on the floor of Black Light and the idea made her laugh under her breath.

"I understand what this is all for. I just hope he's still interested after I was so ungrateful." She finished tying on the second set of ribbons and held out her hand for him to help her up.

Dominic glanced up at the platform and then winked at her as he pulled her upright. "Oh, I think he's still very interested. Why don't you remind him what you can do, eh?"

Right. Wyatt hadn't invested so much in bidding for her time, the barre equipment, and the shoes, if he wasn't a fan of the ballet. He'd seen her perform at the Dudorov, knew so much about her... but he'd never seen her up close or when she was just having fun. With a big grin, she spun away from Dominic, going en pointe for a quick *bourrée en couru*, before pirouetting and then shifting into an *arabesque*. Turning to face the platform, she couldn't hide her smile as Wyatt stared, mouth slightly open as she did an *échappé* and then worked her way through other moves as she curved closer and closer to the foot of the steps, finishing the brief improvised routine with a *jeté*. A leap that brought a round of applause from their gathered audience, and a smile to his face before she curtseyed and dropped into a kneel at the bottom step.

Vanessa kept her head bowed as her heart raced, already feeling how the stiffness of the shoes had strained her feet — but that was nothing new. All that mattered was whether or not she'd fixed her faux pas and un-ruined their night.

"That was... incredible." Wyatt's shoes came into view on the stairs, and she raised her eyes to see him smiling. "Thank you, Vanessa. Now, I think we need to get you on this platform and some marks on your ass before Elijah gets irritated with us, don't you?"

"Yes, sir!" she answered, happy to know that he didn't hold a grudge. Vanessa took his offered hand and climbed the steps, once again impressed by the beautiful craftsmanship on the free-standing barre. Two light wood poles hung at the correct heights between large wooden triangles. She traced one of the bars in awe. "Wow... this looks so beautiful. And seriously heavy."

"Tyler did tell me it was going to be a bitch to move around, but I was more interested in how secure it would be."

"Secure?"

"For all the terrible things I'm about to do to you." That grin was back, and he stepped forward to catch her by the back of the neck, his fingers slowly weaving into her hair before they tightened into a fist. "Now, be a good girl, Vanessa, and put your hands on the top bar."

CHAPTER 5

 *yatt*

THIS WASN'T A WET DREAM, BUT IT MIGHT AS WELL BE.

Vanessa Novak had actually danced for him, up close, on the fucking floor of Black Light. When he'd bid on her, he had hoped to see her use all that power and grace to show him a few moves, especially once she had the shoes… but she'd done much more than that. Vanessa had performed what could have been a solo in any ballet lucky enough to feature her. And now she was bent over with her hands on the barre, her bare ass peeking out from under that pale pink skirt like she'd pirouetted straight out of one of his fantasies. Distracting as hell, and he was having trouble getting his brain back in gear for the scene. Hell, half the people standing around the platform were still stunned into silence. But he'd known before the night even started that Vanessa would impress them — he just hadn't expected it to be with her skills as a dancer. It was a good thing, though. Nice to see them looking at her in awe instead of just leering at another beautiful woman on display tonight.

That wasn't what he wanted for her. It wasn't what she *deserved*.

She deserved to be cherished, to be seen for all the talent and skill she had and be respected for it… but she also needed to be treated like the little pain slut she was. And *that* made this more like a wet dream than anything else, because tonight he had the privilege to be the one wielding the implements.

The dark leather cuffs on her wrists made his cock twitch, and although she could stand up all the way he had ordered her to stay bent at the hips, her feet in one of those ballet positions as if it were a habit she couldn't break. Fighting the urge to chuckle out loud, he just smiled. "Spread your feet a bit."

"Yes, sir," she answered, jumping her feet out *en pointe* for a moment before dropping her heels to the floor.

Oh, yes. The pointe shoes had been worth the expense.

Plus, he planned on just donating the other sizes to one of the schools that worked with underprivileged kids, so… it really was a good investment either way. Some positive karma, and an incredibly hot submissive to torment, complete with a fantasy-validating outfit.

Who says money can't buy happiness? Or, at least a few hours of it…

Focus, dammit.

"Such a good girl." He stepped up behind her and flipped the little skirt onto her back, exposing her ass and just a hint of the pretty pink folds he'd barely brushed before Dominic had interrupted them. He'd get his chance again soon… very soon, but first he needed to make her scream. "What's your safe word, Vanessa?"

"Red, sir." She shimmied a little, her ass wiggling, and he allowed himself the chuckle.

"That's right." Bringing his arm back, he landed a spank that wouldn't have been considered a warm-up by anyone. Vanessa gasped, and he delivered another. His hand was already stinging, but he got to admire the perfect outline of his hand on her olive skin for a moment while she whined and gave another wiggle of her round ass. The audience perked up, drawing closer as he braced his other hand on the small of her back and continued his version of a warm-up for the masochist.

Wyatt hadn't tried to keep count of each swat, but by the time her ass was a vibrant pink he estimated it had been... a lot. His own hand fucking hurt, but it was worth it to deliver the first marks skin-to-skin. To feel her body jerk with the impact, to feel the heat of her ass. It was more personal, but it would never make Vanessa Novak scream or cry.

"How you holding up?" he asked, grinning as he lifted his suit jacket off the implements he'd hidden.

"Just fine, sir." Her voice was breathy, and he glanced back in time to see her shifting her weight from foot to foot in a futile attempt to ease the pink marks that had her ass glowing. She'd barely made a peep during the spanking, but as he picked up the double loopy johnny he couldn't help but grin. She'd said she liked leather, and maybe he'd reward her with it... but first he'd get her to make all those pretty noises he'd been jealous of in the past.

"I'm so glad," he said softly, running his fingers over the warm skin on her ass before resting his palm on the small of her back again. "Hold position for me, or you'll just add more to this."

"Add more to—" The first swat of the loopy johnny cut her off, and one of her hands came off the bar, accompanied by the lovely clatter of chain keeping her tethered. "Fuck!" she cried out, shaking her head as she held position.

Impressive.

"You've had a bit of trouble since the event started remembering to call me 'sir,' but I have a feeling this is going to help. Don't you?" Another snap of the vinyl-coated steel loops formed twin curved welts on the round of her ass, so beautiful that before she could even answer he landed another strike a little lower.

~

VANESSA

"Sir!" she whined, not even sure what she wanted to say, she just

281

needed to make *some* kind of noise as the next lash of the demonic implement set her ass on fire. "Oh God, oh *fuck...*"

"So pretty. Especially when they overlap." Wyatt was definitely enjoying himself as he delivered another wicked strike, and then another, and another. Vanessa had her teeth clenched against the urge to let go of even more obscenities with each spike of pain, but she knew she had to hold on. This was the path of coals, the suffering before nirvana, and Wyatt was the first Dom she'd played with at Black Light that had ever come out of the gate this strong. Even the spanking had been harder than she'd expected. He might be quiet, soft-spoken, but she'd sensed a darker side to him that hid behind his clean-cut appearance. An edge when he'd first held her by the throat and looked almost... *hungry.* For this.

"Fucking hell, please, sir!" The whimpers were impossible to bite back as the implement wrapped to the bottom of her ass. "What the hell is that thing?"

"This?" Wyatt taunted, delivering another hard swat that brought the sting of tears to her eyes, causing her to arch her back in a desperate attempt to ease the rising wave of pain. "It's called a double loopy johnny. I think they used to use something like this as a rug beater? Personally, I think it works very well on a submissive's ass. Especially when that submissive is a masochist who thinks that she has the right to criticize how a Dom chooses to spend his money."

He punctuated the reprimand with another brutal strike, and she screamed, "I'm sorry, sir!"

"That's good." Wyatt's voice held a sadist's joy for his work, but at least the fucking loopy johnny didn't slice through the air again. Instead, she felt his hand stroke down her welted ass, squeezing just a little too hard to be soothing as he spoke again. "Tell me, how far down on your thighs can you hide marks?"

"What?" She tried to look over her shoulder, while also keeping her feet planted where he'd told her to, but it wasn't easy. "Sir?"

"Your ass is going to be black and blue by the end of the night if I don't get to spread things around a little. So, how far down your thighs can the marks go before it might cause an issue during your practices?" He slid his hand down and pinched her sit spot. "Here?"

Vanessa hissed air in through her teeth, because she was quite sure one of those last strokes had hit that exact spot, which made her affirmative pointless. Still, she had to answer. "That's fine, sir."

"Good. What about here?" This time Wyatt pinched a couple of inches down, still painful enough to make her squirm, but she nodded. "And here?"

The next pinch was halfway down her thigh and she wavered. There were a few pairs of tights thick enough to hide marks, but in class they couldn't wear the more casual ballet onesies that would have the shorts-style bottom. "I'm sorry, sir, but..."

"No?" he asked, his voice light and unconcerned.

"No, sir."

"That's all right, we know it hurts more up here anyway." Without warning, he laid the loopy johnny across her sit spot, the lower arc of fire coming just to the point she'd agreed. Sometime after the scream, amidst the cursing and whining, she recognized the skill it took to apply an implement with that level of accuracy — and she appreciated it, and his concern for her privacy.

It was just hard to say that aloud when she was digging her already ragged nails into the wood of the barre as another lash landed, perfectly placed. "Fucking shit, fucking hell!"

"What's wrong, Vanessa? Did that sting?" he mocked.

She opened her mouth to snap at him, but he was suddenly beside her, tilting her chin up with a firm grip, and all of the vitriol at the tip of her tongue seemed to fade away. Wyatt looked... different in the middle of a scene. His eyes were alive with energy, his cheeks a shade brighter, and the grin he wore spoke of devilish plans that left her utterly speechless.

"God, you're beautiful," he whispered as he brushed a thumb over the damp trails on her cheeks before dragging the lingering taste of salt over her lips. "I think you're ready to fly now. You want me to bring you over the edge, Vanessa?"

"Sir?" she whispered, fuzzy headed as she stared into his hazel eyes, vibrant and clear.

"Do you want me to whip your ass with a strap until you fly off into subspace?"

"Please, sir?" she begged, holding onto the eye contact like a lifeline as he bit his lip and let out a low groan.

"Say it again," he commanded as he dropped the evil implement to the floor and crouched — face to face, eye to eye, while he traced his thumb just under her lip. "Now."

Swallowing, she obeyed. "Please, sir."

A hungry growl rumbled in Wyatt's chest as his touch turned rough, fisting her hair, and then he kissed her. Hard. It was fiery, burning brighter than any of the flashes of pain she'd felt before. All she could do was hold onto the barre as their tongues clashed. Unable to stifle the moan that hummed in her throat, Vanessa gave in. To the kiss, to the heat, and to Wyatt. Everything buzzed as he nipped her lips, her tongue, before diving deep into the kiss again. All she wanted was for him to touch her again, to finish what they'd started, because the cool air between her thighs said she was more than ready for him to do whatever he wanted to her. She just needed *more*.

As if he'd heard her internal pleas, he suddenly pulled back and she whined, meeting his gaze where the black of his pupils had almost completely swallowed the mesmerizing mix of brown and green. Proof that he wanted her just as much, even as he pulled back further.

"Dammit, you're dangerously distracting." Wyatt laughed, hazel eyes blazing as he swept her hair out of her face and bit down on his lip again. "You still want to fly?"

"Whatever you want, sir," she whispered, and he groaned and stood. The erection pressing against the front of his pants promised a lot of fun. 'Soon,' she promised herself, but first he was going to try and put her over the edge into subspace. She just had to actually let go.

Wyatt walked away towards his toy bag, and Vanessa took a deep breath. Pain was a fleeting thing, something that just had to be accepted, walked through to get to the other side. Kelsey knew better than anyone that it was something you did every day as a dancer, but whereas Kelsey had always been able to translate that into an easy stride into subspace at clubs — she always said that Vanessa fought it. That she didn't let go of the constant stream of thoughts in her head long enough to, well... fly.

Butter-soft leather stroked down her spine and she almost purred, twisting to see the strap in Wyatt's hand as he took up position on her opposite side this time. It was thick, and she knew it would thud and sting in the best ways. Another deep breath and she relaxed, letting her muscles go soft, ready and waiting.

"All you have to do is take it, Vanessa. Nothing more. Just focus on the sensation." His voice was warm as he trailed the leather over her ass, back and forth, a thrumming buzz along already hyper-sensitive nerves. "You've already made my night, beautiful, all you have to do now is breathe."

The first lash from the strap hurt because it overlaid so many welts, but it hadn't actually been very hard. Still, she whined as the next came just below, back tense, she forced her hands to relax on the bar.

"That's it. Focus on the warmth of the leather, the snap, and ride the wave. You're such a good girl, Vanessa..." Wyatt's voice was soft, a lulling hum that bled into her ears and she held onto it.

With her next breath, the strap cracked against her ass, bringing with it a spike of sweet torment that slowly spread into the heat of her skin. The next lash melted into it, along with the next, and the next, until each pulse of pain shimmered along her nerves. A sultry buzz that inched up her spine, along her ribs, wrapping around to her front until she could only hear the whisper of leather cutting through the air and the pop of it landing as her breaths grew slower.

Such a good girl...

A hazy purr filled her mind, lost in the ebb and flow of each new lash as his words echoed in her head. *Good girl. Breathe.* She obeyed, breathing in light that stretched to the tip of every nerve ending. Shining and golden. Everything was perfect, a delirious drone of sensation that wrapped her in bone-deep warmth and a feeling of safety. A place to let go and fall without fear of a crash.

A place to fly.

Vanessa floated, content to be lost in the darkness behind her eyes — but then there was the pulse. It started out small, a tiny thrumming beat between her thighs as all the warmth and golden light burning her blood in the best of ways found a home. Then it grew stronger, more insistent, a needy *thump thump thump* as her clit pulsed with each beat of her heart. She tensed as the zing of pleasure spread fast, finding the points of her nipples trapped inside the soft fabric of her bra, and moving on until it drew a soft sound from her throat.

Another snap of leather filtered into her ears, and everything amplified. Blurry sensations coming into sharp focus as she heard Wyatt's quiet voice. "Just let it happen. I'll catch you. I promise."

The pounding pulse between her thighs had her pulling her legs together, squeezing as she wrapped her arm over the barre. The pop of the strap came again, but there was no pain. Everything was bright, and good, and as her muscles trembled she felt the next surge and didn't have the energy left to fight it.

It crashed over her, an overwhelming wave of perfect pleasure that made everything tense and tight for a breath before it all shattered. Sending sparkling shards of magic through every inch of her body. Ecstasy, delirium, chaotic wonder — and then she was gone.

Flying, floating. Blissful.

CHAPTER 6

 *yatt*

VANESSA HAD TRANSITIONED INTO SUBSPACE SLOWLY. WITH EVERY SWAT from the strap her muscles had tensed less and less, and he'd carefully watched every breath expanding her ribcage. Watched the marks form and blossom on her bright red backside, knowing that as she went quiet there was no way she'd stop it — it was all up to him.

To take care of her. To guide her. To help her fly.

And there was nowhere else in the universe he would rather be.

The marks on her ass from the loopy johnny had eased into dark, curved bruises as he watched her relax, letting the pain flow through her while she took tiny steps closer to the barre until she could put her arms on it. Then she'd rested her head on her forearm, no longer fighting it, just breathing deeply with barely a hitch from a random swat. He'd kept the strikes on the round of her ass, ignoring the raging hard-on behind his zipper, because she was more important than any fleeting orgasm.

He was going to be the Dom that took her to subspace in their first session. It was the earliest soft sound of pleasure, instead of pain, that ensured it. Guaranteed that she'd remember this, remember tonight, remember *him*.

She'd started to squirm, shifting her weight as those quiet moans grew louder, as her feet pulled in and she squeezed her thighs together. Wiggling her ass in the most tempting of ways while she rocked forward and back with each new lash of the leather. Then... then he could have sworn she came. Back arched, head up, eyes closed with her pretty mouth open as that quiet, gasped cry left her lips.

He'd been so entranced he almost hadn't stepped forward in time to catch her around the waist as she dipped back down, knees almost buckling, but she was too strong to really fall. Vanessa would have been fine even if he'd stood back to enjoy the sight — but feeling the tiny tremors running through her was worth missing the view.

It hadn't taken more than a few seconds to release the safety latch tethering the cuffs to the chain, and then she was in his arms. Yet, none of it felt real. The intoxicating power he'd felt as she'd trusted him, submitted, screamed and cried out through the pain while never showing a hint of fear. It had been his dream for the night, his fantasy, but part of him had refused to let him really hope. She could have walked away, refused him, or simply gone along with the event without really being present.

But she was in there. *Here.*

Vanessa Novak was curled in his lap, in his arms, dazed and floating in subspace, with the heat of her welted ass pressed against his erection. He cradled her, shifting until he could lean back against one of the legs of the makeshift barre, as he accepted the attention from the small crowd. Smiled and nodded at the light applause, the knowing nods of several doms he recognized — because they understood. They knew what kind of gift she'd given him, and as he leaned down to kiss her hair, he couldn't help the stupid grin that took over his mouth.

"Thank you," he whispered, but she didn't stir and he was fine with that. The night was barely getting started. There would be plenty of time for more fun, to talk with her, and to *maybe* deal with the steel rod that had taken up permanent residence in his pants.

'Later,' he promised himself as he carefully leaned forward with her to grab his suit jacket. Settling back against the barre, he draped it over her and smiled as she burrowed into his chest. She looked just as perfect up close as she did from afar. Better, because now he noticed the small mole high on her left cheek, close to her hairline. He could smell the lingering scent of her perfume, her shampoo, and the erection damning smell of her arousal.

She'd been wet when he'd dared to dip a finger through her slit, and he would have bet another ten grand that she was soaked now. But… not yet. Not now, when he could feel the steady rise and fall of each breath against his chest. This was a different kind of perfection, and it was one he wouldn't dare ruin.

VANESSA

Everything was soft and warm as she drifted towards consciousness, comfortable and relaxed. It wasn't until she heard a shrill, feminine cry that her brain came back online and Vanessa remembered exactly where she was napping.

Inside Black Light. At Roulette. With Wyatt.

Prying her eyes open, she found herself in Wyatt's lap. Felt his arms around her, his jacket covering her, and… well, not *everything* was soft. Blushing, she sat up and met his gaze. "Hi."

"Hi there." He grinned and shifted to sit more upright, keeping her in his lap. "How are you feeling?"

"Um…" Vanessa trailed off as she turned her thoughts inward, recognizing the dull ache of the welts on her ass, but there was also the bone-deep relaxation that always followed subspace. It was impossible to suppress the grin that spread across her face. "Pretty fucking amazing, actually. Sir."

Wyatt laughed. "I'd say that's good then." His hand moved to cup her cheek gently, and then he stroked the soft pad of his thumb across her lips. He was so focused, so close, and for a second she thought he was going to kiss her again. *Hoped he would kiss her?* Maybe. It didn't matter though, because after several breaths passed, just as she was about to lean in, he turned away. "I think Tyler wants to say hello... and probably remind us to keep playing."

"Oh?" she asked, trying not to sound disappointed as she sat up completely and scanned the room until she saw the DM standing near Elijah — but they were both looking at her. "Did we do something wrong? Sir?"

"No, beautiful. You were absolutely perfect." He pressed a kiss to her hair in a mockery of what she'd craved moments before, but he soothed the regret with his next words. "You were such a good girl."

The grin returned as she felt him nudge her to stand, and Vanessa reluctantly took the suggestion. Every mark on her ass woke up as the bruised muscles shifted, but she didn't reach back for them as he stood and shook out his jacket. "Thank you, sir."

"It's the truth. You were remarkable." Wyatt draped the jacket over the barre before he wrapped his arms around her again, so much more confident with his touches as one hand slid down to cup her ass and squeeze until she hissed air between her teeth. "Just checking to make sure those still hurt."

"They do." Vanessa laughed and looked up at him. "What's next?"

"I think we check the roulette wheel, at least if you're willing to take a chance on me again, and—"

"Of course I am! Oh shit," she cursed herself for interrupting him. Worse, that had sounded more than a little desperate and she hadn't even ended it with, "Sir."

"Well, I'm glad you're as excited as I am to continue our night." Wyatt winked, and then landed a sharp spank to her ass that made her gasp from the spike of pain. "Let's go spin again, and then you're going to have juice and some fruit before I find new ways to torment you."

"Yes, sir." She was prepared to follow him across Black Light, but he took her hand instead, interlacing their fingers as they walked down the steps. Across the room she saw Cassandra tied down on a spanking bench with a tall blond man wielding a paddle behind her. She wasn't trying to stare, but she was pretty sure that she saw the low lights catch on the silver of a butt plug.

'Hope she isn't going to want pancakes at the end of the night,' she thought as she watched the man land another swat with a loud pop.

"You two going for another scene?" Tyler asked as he intercepted them.

"That's the plan," Wyatt answered, offering his free hand to shake Tyler's. "Thanks for the barre, man. You guys do great work."

"Thanks, it was a fun challenge." He crossed his arms, scanning the room before looking her over. "You holding up, Vanessa?"

"I'm fantastic. Just excited to see what the wheel gives us next."

"Hopefully lady luck is on our side again," Wyatt added.

"Well, you've certainly set the bar high for the rest of the night — if you know what I mean." Tyler laughed at his pun as Wyatt groaned.

"That was bad," Vanessa said through a laugh.

A much harder spank landed on her ass, bringing each welt into brilliant agony for a flash, before it finally faded as she bit down on the whine. Wyatt and Tyler were both looking at her expectantly, but Tyler wasn't able to keep a straight face as he broke into a quiet chuckle. "Wanna rephrase that, girl?"

"I'm sorry, sir," she answered fast, dropping her eyes to the floor, which made it easier to hide the thrill she'd felt race up her spine from Wyatt's swat. He had such an easy dominance when he wasn't holding back, resisting the urge to do what came naturally — but little things kept slipping through, and she wanted more of that. More of the real him under the quiet exterior.

She just had to somehow show him it was okay.

"We're going to head to the theater to spin again, but please let your brother know I'm very grateful for the work you did on such short notice. I'll definitely pass the word." Wyatt accepted Tyler's slap on the shoulder as the DM moved past them.

"Thanks, man. You two have fun. I'm sure you'll have your sub's mouth in check before the end of the night." Tyler was laughing as he veered towards Cassandra's scene.

"We will." Wyatt replied, and she nodded as she tore her eyes from the blond man who now had a hand busy between her new friend's legs. "Ready?"

"To get my mouth in check, sir?"

"Well, I plan to try." He smiled and she squeezed his hand as they walked towards the curtain.

"I'll try too, sir."

"Good girl," he answered, facing ahead once more, which made it easy to study his profile.

Not that it was hard to focus on Wyatt, even amidst the carnal chaos of Black Light. He was handsome, kind, and had absolutely made her *fly*. His word, but she liked that description of subspace, especially since — with him — it made sense. The whole scene had felt like coming to the edge of some high place, inching closer and closer. Teetering towards an abyss, a threatening emptiness, but when she'd finally fallen… she'd soared.

And then she'd woken up in his arms.

Squeezing his hand harder, she spoke quietly, "I meant to say it before, sir, but that scene was amazing."

Wyatt looked at her like he was surprised. "Really?"

"Are you kidding?" Vanessa laughed, pushing the hair off her forehead. "I don't think I've ever hit subspace that quickly, *or* that easily. I usually suck at it." Rolling her eyes, she huffed and took one last glance at the play area before they passed through the curtain into the bar. She was mid-step when Wyatt suddenly spun her around, and her back hit the wall next to the doorway, his free hand on her neck.

"Tell me what you forgot, beautiful."

"Sir," she replied, swallowing against the slight tension in her throat as she met his eyes. "I'm sorry."

"All the welts on your ass *should* be reminder enough, but I guess not." He sounded serious, but he was still smiling, not angry at all, and then his gaze fell to her mouth just as his tongue traced his lower lip.

A teasing brush before his eyes lifted to hers again. "Tell me why you think you suck at subspace."

"It's stupid, sir. I shouldn't have mentioned it."

"I'm glad you did." His thumb glided just above her racing pulse, which wasn't helping as he continued to push. "Try and explain it to me. The words don't have to be perfect, Vanessa."

"It's just... I don't know. My head is always spinning, sir. It's too chaotic and I can't just let go and absorb the pain, even though I know that's what I need to do. Even when everything starts to numb out I just keep... *thinking*." She shrugged as if that would explain her weird BDSM issues. "Kelsey does it so easily, and I really don't know why I can't."

"Kelsey is your friend, right? The one you're always here with?" There was something odd in his tone as he spoke, but she nodded. "Well, have you talked to her about it?"

"Of course. We tell each other everything, but her answer is always that I 'fight subspace'... which isn't actually helpful when it comes to fixing it, sir."

Wyatt released her throat, but he was still close enough to smell the warm spice of his cologne as he said, "She's right." Then he tugged her off the wall, pulling her towards the entrance to the theater while her brain tried to catch up.

"Wait, what?" Vanessa tried to tug his hand so he'd stop and explain, but he kept walking. Dragging her behind him. "Sir, please, what do you mean *she's right?* I just hit subspace with you!"

"Yes, you did."

"But—"

Before she could argue further, they stepped inside the theater and Wyatt marched them up the middle path through chairs and tables. Most of the audience had spread out across the club, but more than a few people were sitting around inside. Too much of an audience to continue that conversation, even though everyone seemed to be focused on the wall-to-wall movie screen. Drinking and talking as Maggie Gyllenhaal crawled across the floor in *The Secretary*. The rest of Vanessa's questions left her head as Wyatt led her up the steps to the stage and Madison faced them.

"Are you guys, like, wanting to spin again?" The pretty blonde was excited, and her California-girl voice made her seem less intense than her outfit had first suggested. It was actually the muscular hottie standing nearby, paying very close attention, that made approaching her a bit intimidating. Fortunately, he seemed to only have eyes for her. "Come on, let's do this! You totally don't want to waste the night, right?"

"No, we don't," Wyatt answered with a charming smile as he stepped forward and pulled her up to the wheel with a gentle tug. "Ready to see what your next torment is?"

"Haha." Vanessa looked up at him and couldn't hide the grin when he raised his eyebrows. "Sir," she added as Madison handed her the little white ball and set the wheel spinning.

Wyatt moved behind her, resting his hands on her hips as he whispered, "Be a good girl and get us something fun."

She was about to say something snarky when he nipped her earlobe and the shock of it made the ball bounce out of her hand and into the wheel. It almost bounced right back out, but managed to clatter and jump until it started to spin with the roulette wheel. As the spinning slowed, she started to see different phrases in the whirling text, and then it finally landed. On *needle play*. "Oh shit."

"Whoa," Madison said softly, looking up with eyes as wide as Vanessa's probably were.

A quiet laugh buzzed against her ear, and then Wyatt kissed her neck. "I think you're lucky I'm not into stabbing pretty submissives with needles. It's on my limits list."

"Thank, God! You're not kidding. I'm very lucky." Staring at the marble sitting by those two words had made her feel more than a little squeamish, and she didn't realize why the space around her had gone quiet until she felt a sharp spank light up every welt Wyatt's handprint had just vibrantly outlined. Groaning, she turned around and he caught her face in a gentle grip.

"Well?" he prompted.

"Shit. Sir! I'm sorry I forgot, sir." Wetting her lips with her tongue, she tried her best to look contrite. "I swear I'm trying."

"Don't worry, I'll get your mouth in order once we find out exactly what kink we get next." Wyatt's wicked grin had her staring as Madison held out the white marble once more.

"Sounds like you better spin," Madison said, laughing as she placed the ball in her hand.

"Right." Vanessa turned to face the roulette wheel once more, focusing more on the heat of Wyatt's body against her back than the terms spinning too fast to read. Tilting her hand, she let the marble fall and closed her eyes to focus on Wyatt's fingertips holding tight to her hips. Pulling her back, pressing her to the hard ridge of his erection that made more promises than anything the wheel might produce.

"Anal play!" Madison announced, her voice bright and cheerful. "That's not on either of your limits lists."

"No, it is not," Wyatt replied, a seductive edge to his tone that summoned that pulsing heat between her thighs again as his lips brushed her ear. "Looks like your ass is going to get a bit more punishment tonight, beautiful."

"I guess so, sir," she whispered. Madison winked at her and then turned around to talk with the hottie who was still completely focused on the leather-clad MC for the night. But Vanessa's mind was already spinning with possibilities.

"Come on. Time is ticking!" Wyatt's excitement was contagious as he took her hand once more and led them towards the steps.

"Already have a plan for the spin, sir?" she asked through a laugh, and his bright hazel eyes met hers as he glanced over his shoulder.

"Oh, I've been planning for tonight for a while now." The confession kept a smile lingering on her lips as she followed him past the audience members still distracted by *The Secretary* playing behind them.

There were so many questions she had for him, so many things she wanted to know before the end of the night. And step one to getting the answers she wanted? Get her damn mouth under control, and start saying 'sir.'

Maybe then he'd kiss her again. *Maybe then he'd do more than kiss her.*

It wasn't like she was shy. She wasn't playing coy, but he was playing his cards too close to the chest. So locked down that she felt like she was only catching glimpses of the real Wyatt, and that made it easy to decide what her goal would be for the night.

She was going to lure Wyatt Strickland out of his shell.

No matter what it took.

CHAPTER 7

 *yatt*

"You want someone there to help out? Weston is good and—"

"I appreciate the offer, but I want this to be more intimate than that." Wyatt smiled as Dave gave him an appraising look. "Look, I'm not new, and I'm not doing anything dangerous. But, if Weston could be around the main floor while I'm getting her set up that would be helpful. I can flag him down if I have a question."

"All right, bro. I'll go take care of the platform for you. The barre will be in storage whenever you're ready for us to deliver it. Cool?"

"Thanks." Wyatt shook the DM's hand, but his attention immediately shifted as Vanessa appeared by the women's locker room. She was perfect. Walking across the bar area with that ridiculously short ballet skirt fluttering at the tops of her thighs, those pretty pink ballet slippers carrying her straight out of a fantasy — and he couldn't decide which urge was stronger. The protective urge to cover her up so that everyone would stop staring, or the much more tempting urge to pick her up and set her beautifully marked ass on the bar so he could spread her legs and finally taste her.

He definitely wouldn't care about the attention with his head buried between her thighs.

"Sorry, did I take too long, sir?" Vanessa asked, and Wyatt had to shake himself out of yet another daydream about her.

"Not at all. They just brought over the apple juice and this fruit and cheese plate." Nudging the plate a little closer to her seat, he tried to keep his eyes up as she slid onto the high barstool. The slight wince as she settled onto her bruised ass made him smile. "Sore?"

"Are you surprised, sir?" she replied, smiling back. "Honestly, it's the kind of ache I like a lot. Means I had fun. You did too, right?"

"Of course," he answered, fighting a laugh. "Just being your Dom for the night easily puts this in my top five nights of all time."

A pretty blush touched her cheeks as she popped a grape between her lips, chewing as she toyed with the glass of juice. "May I ask a question, sir?"

"As long as you get some sugar in you, absolutely."

"Why did you bid on me? I mean… you mentioned you'd seen me at the Dudorov before, sir, but…" Vanessa trailed off, taking a sip of the apple juice as she once again studied the small plate of fruit and cheese.

"But?" he prompted, fighting the anxious tension building between his shoulder blades.

"But is that honestly why you bid on me, sir?" she asked softly, taking the opportunity to steal a strawberry that was a bright red against the pink of her cheeks.

He shook his head as he watched her. "You really don't see how special you are, do you?"

"I'm not—"

"I'm going to stop you from saying that before you get yourself in trouble with me *and* your friend Kelsey." Smiling to gentle the chastisement, he searched his mind to find a way to explain how he felt about her without… coming across completely creepy.

Not. Easy.

Wyatt took a deep breath and blew it out slowly. "I've been going to the ballet since I was a kid. My parents were major supporters of several companies in the area, and my mother actually danced for a few years when she was young. Now, I admit that when I was a teenager I did not appreciate being dragged to the ballet for an evening of forced culture, but even back then I was always impressed by the performances — even if I didn't admit that to my parents.

"My mom made sure I understood how hard they worked, the hours and years dedicated to it, and it had an effect on me. Even after I grew up I kept going to the ballet, got my own memberships, and I think I liked the Dudorov so much because it was smaller. It made each performance seem more personal, and they do so much with the sets."

"We have a pretty amazing set design team," Vanessa added quietly, before taking a drink of the juice. Then her eyes went wide and she almost choked on it. "S-sir! Shit," she cursed and coughed. "Sir, sorry."

He chuckled and snagged a grape from the plate. "It's okay, beautiful. You caught yourself. And I agree, the Dudorov really puts effort into the sets, and I think it's why it became one of my favorites. I see each ballet a few times, sometimes more if work is more stressful than usual. It's where I can let my mind go and just dissolve into the performance." Wyatt shrugged, unable to hide his grin. "At least, when I'm not seeking out a BDSM club for a different kind of stress-relief."

"And you've seen me dance at the Dudorov, sir?" There was doubt in her voice, but he tried not to take it in a negative way. It was clear to him that Vanessa didn't see herself like he did. She couldn't see how incredible she was, how talented and graceful and beautiful.

Sighing, he touched her chin to make her meet his eyes, enjoying the dark stare that so easily captured his attention. "I saw you perform last year. The night you subbed as the Lilac Fairy in Sleeping Beauty."

"Oh. Tori had the stomach flu that night, it was her role. I mean, you really should have seen her do it, she's a principal dancer and—"

"I did see her perform it. The night I saw you dance as the Lilac Fairy was the second time I'd been, and you were much better than her." Wyatt raised his hand when he saw her warming up to argue, and then he pointed at the juice. "Finish that, and listen to me. I'm not just saying that to stroke your ego, Vanessa. Your performance was so clean, every move so sharply performed that the whole audience was amazed. I wasn't the only one staring as you moved across the stage, doing every single move Tori had performed, but better. You know, there was this little piece of paper in the program announcing the change when I arrived, and as soon as I could dig it out to find your name... I saved it."

"You did?" she asked, and the look of surprise on her face wasn't disgust or fear so he ignored the lack of 'sir' for the moment.

"I did. And then when the Dudorov did The Nutcracker at the holidays I was disappointed to learn that you weren't a principal dancer, because even before I saw you here at Black Light I knew you were special." Grabbing for his water, he took a long drink and wished it were something a lot stronger. There were so many ways this discussion could go wrong, and he was trying to choose each word carefully. *But he could still fuck it all up.*

"Why haven't you approached me here then, sir? I mean, if you've seen me here, if you liked my dancing that much... why not at least talk to me?"

"Because we both suffer from the same issue," he answered with a laugh.

"Huh?" Vanessa stared, holding a half-eaten strawberry in her lap as if she'd forgotten about it. Leaning forward, he gently took her hand and moved the strawberry to her lips, and his cock twitched in his slacks as she bit down and swallowed.

"We both think too much," he answered, and then he kissed her. Tasting the sweetness of the fruit, the ripe burst of flavor on his tongue as she instantly parted her lips to let him in. Sinfully decadent, like every inch of her, and his earlier fantasy of spreading her out on the bartop returned in full force.

Fuck, you have to rein it in.

Breaking the kiss, he pressed his forehead to hers for a moment before pulling back completely. Hands back in his own space, but his heart was racing and Vanessa looked dazed too. "I'm sorry, I—"

"If that's what not thinking too much is like... I think I can do that, sir." Vanessa smiled, and then chewed on her bottom lip as she shrugged. "And, for the record, I wish you'd approached me before tonight. Most Doms play too careful with me, like they're afraid I'm going to break."

"It's because you look delicate, but they don't know what it takes to be a ballet dancer. My mom told me just how hard it is, and I'm sure it's why you have such a high pain tolerance." Tossing back the last of his water like a shot, he was about to stand up when Vanessa grabbed his arm.

"Wait, sir. Can we talk for just a few more minutes before we get into... whatever scene you have planned?"

Checking the curtained doorway to the main floor, he debated whether or not Dave would seek him out to let him know the scene was ready, but a good part of him didn't care if Elijah got pissy. Hell, if they said they weren't playing by the rules and failed them out of the event, then he'd just buy her a damn month so she didn't have to touch the trust fund she'd mentioned. Settling back on the stool, he nodded. "Sure, we can wait a little more."

"Thanks. Um, I... I just wanted to..." Vanessa groaned and grabbed a slice of the cheddar. "Dammit, I don't know what I'm saying, sir."

"Just ask. I've already thoroughly embarrassed myself by telling you I've been watching you here at Black Light and stalking your performances at the Dudorov, so what do you have to lose?" *I just left out the other things.*

She laughed and shook her head. "No. It's... nice to have someone other than my best friend appreciate my dancing. I guess I'm just curious why you didn't approach me here. Did I come across stuck up? Because I never meant—"

"Trust me, that's not it." He groaned under his breath and stared at the ceiling like the universe might provide him some kind of support. "I know it's not exactly the sexiest thing to admit to someone, but I get pretty fucking anxious in crowds, especially around new people. Every time I've seen you in the club I'd start to get the nerve up to talk to you, but your friend Kelsey is always right beside you. And on the nights when she'd gone to play with a dom, someone else always gets to you before I can untie my tongue enough to even contemplate approaching you."

"Really, sir?" she asked with what looked like genuine surprise and *not* pity.

"Yeah. So, now that my ego is as bruised as your ass, are there any other questions you have?"

"Just one. Was it through the stalking that you found out my favorite pointe shoe for performances? I mean, you can't exactly pick up Bloch at your local Target." She was smiling, which was a good sign.

"Surprisingly, that was not a result of any light stalking. It was from a link in one of the membership emails from the Dudorov. There was an article where they interviewed a bunch of the dancers about their habits, and you answered a question about your rituals before a performance, which included your favorite pointe shoe."

"I remember that now." She laughed a little, shaking her head. "That doesn't sound like stalking to me."

"Right, well..." Wyatt groaned because he could feel the need to confess swelling up. *Shit.* "I may have bribed someone at the Dudorov to make copies of your practice videos. For me."

"What?" she asked, and this time that look was definitely a little more concerned.

"I was just... fuck, I don't have a good excuse for it. After I saw you perform as the Lilac Fairy, I saw you here at the club, and I just wanted to see more of you. I—"

"Okay, well..." Vanessa smiled, releasing a little burst of laughter. "I admit that is much more like stalking. *Light* stalking, sir."

"Thanks?" he answered, cursing himself for being such a creep when all he'd had to do was fucking talk to her. "Listen, I swear that's as far as it went. No hiding outside in the bushes or anything."

"That would be hard considering I'm on the second floor." She winked, actually winked, and he finally took a breath. It was a fucking miracle that his confessions hadn't sent her running for the hills — or more likely a dungeon monitor to report him as a psycho. "Well, I'm taking it as a compliment. After all, you're the only one who wanted me enough tonight to bid."

"Not true, beautiful." Wyatt sighed, still at a loss for why she couldn't see how perfect she was. "There were others bidding, I just outbid them to the point that they gave up, because there was no way in hell I was letting someone else get to you first tonight." He grinned. "And *that* counts as insulting yourself, so I'll be handling that in our scene."

"Dammit," she groaned and shifted on the barstool a little. "Sorry, sir."

"Nothing like a punishment to wipe the slate clean. Come on, I want to show you what I have planned next."

"Yes, sir," she answered, hopping down from the stool to follow him. As he led them towards the main floor, he made himself focus on the list of things he needed to do so she'd be safe, instead of their incredible kiss and the lingering taste of strawberry on his tongue.

CHAPTER 8

 anessa

"Sorry, sir. I actually do have another question though, or maybe it's a request," Vanessa said as they climbed the steps back to their platform. It was the same one as before, only the barre had been replaced by a narrow table with a smooth, black, padded top.

"Okay, as long as you let me get to work so we don't get the DMs interfering," Wyatt answered as he unwound loops of pale pink nylon rope. He smiled at her when he noticed her staring, but she knew better than to ask what he had planned. He'd reveal it when he wanted to, and that was part of the excitement humming under her skin.

"I just— I want to know something about you. You know *so much* about me, and I have not had the chance to do any light stalking. So, I'd just like to know something about you. Anything not ballet related, like… what do you do for work?"

"I'm a CFO for an IT infrastructure company." He chuckled, twirling his finger in the air slowly to make her turn around.

"What does that even mean, sir?" she asked, more than confused because the only thing she understood was that he was involved with finance.

"I handle the financial side of things for the company. We streamline data center storage by leveraging software to integrate computing and storage functions." Wyatt grinned as she groaned.

"That didn't help."

"Well, I always have to use google for ballet moves, so we're even there," he replied, laughing low as he tied a knot that pulled her backwards slightly, and then he pinched her thigh right where a mark had bruised. "You forgot to address me as sir, naughty girl. But I'm going to get your mouth in check before the night is over. Lift your arms for me."

"Shit. I really am trying, sir." She obeyed, raising her arms a little as he wrapped a doubled-over length of rope around her ribs, adjusting it to keep it flat as he moved. "Can I ask another question, sir?"

"I feel like I'm being interrogated," he replied, and she turned to look at him over her shoulder, concerned. But he grinned and nudged her so she faced forward again. "I was kidding. Go ahead, ask away. I'm busy anyway."

"What did you do with the recordings? The ones you got from the Dudorov?" Vanessa had tried to keep her voice light, but he froze. "Sir?"

"I… watched them." He answered softly, and then tugged the rope firmly. She could feel the heat of his body against her back, the warmth of his breath as he exhaled against her ear. "And that is the end of that conversation unless you want to safe word?"

A blush burned Vanessa's cheeks as realization dawned on her, and she bit her cheek to keep from grinning, or letting out an awkward laugh. After a moment, she managed a submissive, "No sir. I'm fine exactly where I am."

"Good girl." Wyatt nipped her skin, sending a rush of chills over her skin before he stepped back. He pulled at the clasp of her bra, giving her plenty of warning before he unhooked it and then she took over sliding it off her arms and to the floor. Picking a spot on the far wall, she put her arms back on her head so he could wrap the rope above her breasts to finish the chest harness.

Exactly how this was going to fit into *anal play*... she wasn't sure yet, but as long as she kept obeying he seemed to be comfortable talking to her. And since his admission he seemed so much more... relaxed.

"You're pretty good at this, sir. Is shibari one of your favorites?"

"Thanks," he said, and she felt the tug as he did something with the rope between her shoulders. "And I like it, but I'm no expert. I mostly just like whatever makes my submissive make pretty sounds."

Another sharp pinch to her ass made her yelp, and he chuckled as he moved around in front of her to weave the pair of ropes through the front of the chest harness.

"Tell me if any of this pinches at all, okay?"

"Yes, sir," she answered, watching his hands as they deftly worked the rope up over her shoulder. On someone else, the harness would probably look a lot sexier, but her breasts were barely an A-cup on a good day, and she almost wished she'd asked him to leave the bra on. At least with Victoria's Secret giving her a boost, she looked like she had more up top.

"Out of questions already?" he asked, walking behind her as he threaded the rope through again, keeping his hand between the moving rope and her skin. Protecting her, like a good Dom should. And Wyatt was *absolutely* a good Dom.

"No sir, just concentrating," she answered, smiling when he stepped around to her front again. "Sir."

"That was close." Wyatt slowly slid his fingers into the hair at the nape of her neck, tightening his fist as he brought their bodies together. His tongue traced his lower lip again and she leaned up on her toes for a kiss without thinking, but he stopped her. Sending stinging sparks across her scalp as he held her tightly, lips just a few inches from his. "Naughty girl. Are you trying to distract me?"

"No, sir," she whispered, whining as he ran his free hand up her thigh, and teased her with a brush just above her slit. "Please?"

"God, I do love the way you beg." His hand slid lower, cupping her between the legs just like he had at the beginning of the night — but he didn't wait this time. One finger parted her lips, stroking slowly through the growing wetness, and she bit down on the whine as he stopped just short of her clit. "So beautiful…"

Her eyes opened, and she felt her brows draw together just as he tilted his head.

"What's that about?" he asked, taunting her with another deft stroke of his finger that skipped her clit completely. "Answer me."

"Nothing, sir— AH!" The reply had barely left her lips when he spanked her between the legs. Once, twice, three times. Her skin stung, and instinct demanded she pull her thighs together, but Wyatt blocked her.

Then he bent her head back sharply, forcing her to meet the steel behind those hazel eyes. "Answer me. Why did you make that face when I called you beautiful?"

"Sir, I didn't mean anything by it." Another sharp swat on her pussy that had her whining and lifting onto her toes. "Sir!"

"Don't lie to me again, Vanessa. Last chance, what were you thinking about when I called you beautiful?" Wyatt wasn't angry, but he did sound abso-fucking-lutely serious. *This* was the real Wyatt. The one that had climbed the corporate ladder, that needed control, that got off on pain from the sadist's side of things.

She just had to hope that answering honestly wouldn't send this version of Wyatt back into hiding. Vanessa took a deep breath, steeling herself as she shifted her focus from his intense gaze to the light brown of his hair. "I just thought that a chest-tie like this would look better on someone who… someone who looked different than I do. Sir."

"Are you referring to these pretty tits?" he asked, just before pinching one of the nipples between thumb and forefinger, hard enough to have her back arching as the sudden pain spiked and then spread across her breast. She whimpered, nodding because it was too hard to form words with her teeth clenched together. "I happen to like the way your breasts look, especially in this pink chest harness I've got you in. In fact, I've spent weeks imagining just what these pert little nipples would look like..." His fingers tightened further, twisting the bud trapped between them until she choked on her next cry. "Wondering just what kind of sweet noises you'd make when I did exactly this."

"Sir!" She whined louder as he twisted his fingers just a little more.

"So, do you think there's something wrong with my opinion? With what I find beautiful?"

"No, sir!" she shouted, fists clenched tight at her sides, driving her ragged nails into her palms as he held her there for one brutal moment longer — and then he let go. She sagged as the tension faded, and a heady rush flooded through her bloodstream. It was almost enough to make her dizzy, but Wyatt's fist in her hair was an anchor. Something to focus on as he grabbed her cheeks, making her meet his eyes again.

"Every woman looks different. No two are the same, and each are beautiful in their own way. If you put yourself down, and therefore insult *my* taste in women again, I'm going to make sure you regret it. Do you understand?"

"Yes, sir," she answered through shuddering breaths, unable to separate the rising flood of arousal from the anxious concern that she'd actually upset him with her stupid reaction to being called beautiful.

What fucking woman wouldn't want to be called beautiful?

She was so goddamned backwards, and for the first time that night she was grateful that Kelsey had suddenly had to fly back to Nevada to be there for her baby nephew's arrival. If her best friend was there, she'd never let her live down insulting her body in front of the man who had paid twenty-seven thousand dollars, and God only knew what else on other stuff, just to spend the evening with her.

Chewing on her lip, Vanessa finally gathered the courage to really meet his eyes again. "I'm sorry, sir. I won't do that again."

"Damn right you won't. Your ass already has plenty of marks, you don't want to earn any more." Wyatt took a slow breath, and then nodded to himself as he slapped the top of the padded table. "All right, time to get up here. I'm going to tie you up so you're exactly where I want you."

"Yes, sir."

"Good girl." He said it just as she moved onto the table, but he never stopped touching her. Making sure she didn't fall, helping her shift until she was flat on her stomach. It made her feel better, the constant contact, the reassurance that he wasn't upset with her, but all of that went away when he said, "I'm going to take your tights off so that the rope won't slip."

She tensed as he reached for them, burying her face against the padded top to hide her expression, but he was too fucking observant. His hands froze with the tights bunched behind her left knee.

"Have something you want to share?" he asked, and she cringed. There was absolutely no good answer to that question that wouldn't result in some kind of punishment. "Vanessa. Answer."

"I don't think I can answer that, sir."

Wyatt sighed, coming around to the side of the table so that he could see her face. "No punishment, as long as you explain honestly why you just went stiff over me taking your tights off."

"I..." Her voice trailed off, but she closed her eyes and forced the rest out on the quietest of whispers. *"...don't have pretty feet. Sir."*

"Would you feel more comfortable if I just cut the tights, and left the shoes on? Because I'm not comfortable putting rope over the tights, they could slip." Leaning closer, Wyatt brushed a thumb over her cheek, waiting until she opened her eyes. "I think you're forgetting that my mother used to dance. She was self-conscious too. Broken toes and all the insane shit you guys do to yourselves to dance so gracefully. I get it, and I won't push you on it. All right?"

She nodded, fighting the swell of emotion in her chest as she choked out a soft, "Yes, sir."

"Good girl," he answered, standing upright again to walk over to his bag. This time, she turned her head to follow him, watching as he took out a knife that sent a warm hum through her bloodstream. Wyatt faced her and narrowed his eyes. "You like this, don't you?"

"I think you're too good at reading people, sir." She smiled as a grin spread across his face.

"We don't have time for edge play tonight, but I think if we get to play again I know exactly what I could do with this knife." As if Wyatt knew exactly how to distract her, he dragged the sharp side of the blade down the back of her thigh, a carefully controlled scratch that made every muscle in her body go still. "Oh yeah... I think you'd like that a lot. Am I right, beautiful?"

"Yes, sir," she answered, nodding as she felt him pull the tights away from her leg, and then she heard the blade slicing through the material with ease. There was no question she'd want to play with Wyatt again. On a night when the rest of the people at Black Light were more distracted, when he wasn't having to follow the whims of a roulette wheel — although he hadn't started with the *anal play* the wheel had chosen yet. That idea kept her distracted until Wyatt dropped the thin strips of black fabric onto the platform beside the table.

"Very good. Now, what I want to do is tie your arms behind your back in a box tie. Basically, elbows bent at about ninety-degrees. Then I'm going to link each of your ankles separately to loops I'll put in the rope on your arms. Do you think you'd have any issues in that position?"

"No, sir. I'm pretty flexible."

Wyatt chuckled behind her. "Right, that was a pretty stupid question."

While she watched, he gathered more of the pink rope into his arms, but he suddenly dropped it to the floor beside his bag. "What's wrong?" she asked, propping herself up on her elbows.

"Changed my mind about the order of things. Up on hands and knees for me," he commanded, gesturing upward. As she moved into position, his eyes slid over her, the erection tenting the front of his pants more obvious in the lighting above the platform. "Okay, now scoot back a little, and then spread your legs a bit more."

She obeyed each command, so focused on Wyatt's expression that she barely registered the presence of others around the platform, able to see everything she had on display. "Sir?"

"You're just... so fucking gorgeous. And I know just the thing to make you stay exactly where I want you." That wicked grin was back as he pulled a small sack out of his bag and opened it to reveal a shining, silver anal hook.

"Fuck," she muttered, and he just grinned wider.

"Don't worry, I'll help you take it." He grabbed a little bottle of lube out of the bag and then moved behind her. "Ever used an anal hook before?"

"No, sir." Vanessa focused on relaxing her muscles, mentally preparing as the cold lube touched her ass. He spread it around the entrance of her ass with one finger, and then another. Massaging, pressing firmly, until he slid one finger easily past the tight ring of muscles.

"You're doing so well, just relax..." Wyatt spoke quietly, in almost the same soothing tone he'd used as he'd guided her into subspace. Yet, as his finger slid back and forth in her ass, she kept shifting. That changed to outright wiggling when he pressed a second finger against the hole and pushed.

"Sir..." she whined as he pushed past the barrier of muscles with a stinging stretch, opening her further.

"Oh, you can beg, Vanessa. You know I like to hear it, but you're going to take this anal hook." He wasn't going for soothing anymore, that delicious edge was back in his tone as he held the cold, steel hook against the small of her back. "Push back. Now."

She obeyed, clenching her teeth as she felt both of his fingers move inside, scissoring, making way for the larger ball on the end of the damnable anal hook.

"I think you like being a naughty girl, Vanessa." A third finger pressed at her ass, and he laughed low behind her as her hips swayed. "That's right. Dirty girls take things up their ass, and you're going to like it, aren't you?"

Her breaths came faster as she bent forward, leaning on her forearms, because this was different. Wyatt had been a gentleman most of the night, only giving her peeks at this side of him, but as he forced that third digit inside, burning, stretching her until she let out a keening whine — she was more aroused than she had been all night.

"Say it, Vanessa," he demanded, thrusting his fingers in and out as the ache dulled and spread out. "Say you like it."

"Yes, sir. I like it." Panting, she forced deeper breaths as her body adjusted to the ache of his thick fingers moving back and forth.

"Like what, Vanessa?" A click, and then more cold lube joined his fingers as he pumped them back and forth, occasionally spreading them just enough to bring a new zing of pain that quickly faded into the ache. "Naughty girls get punished if they don't obey. What do you like? I want to hear it."

"I like taking…" Her voice trailed off and he forced his fingers in harder in response. Whimpering, she arched her back and obeyed. "I like taking it up the ass! Sir!"

"God yes," Wyatt groaned, sliding his fingers free, but a second later the hook replaced them. More lube, and she clenched her teeth as he pushed the cool, metal ball part of the way in, but then she tensed. A sharp spank on her welts made her gasp, but Wyatt wasn't playing the gentleman right now. He put more pressure behind the hook as he spoke quietly. "You're going to take it, Vanessa. You're going to take this hook deep in your ass, and then I'm going to tie it to that pretty pink chest harness so that it stays nice and taut. That way, even after I tie your hands behind your back and tether each of your ankles into position, you're going to keep this ass right where I want it. Because do you want to know what I'm going to do once you're all trussed up with this pretty silver hook inside you?"

"Sir?" she prompted, barely able to focus through the pounding arousal between her thighs that was only amplified by the intense feeling of the anal hook.

Wyatt leaned forward, his body weight adding pressure to the metal ball until it finally started to stretch her open at the widest point. A vibrant ache, piercing and dull at the time same, as he whispered, "Then I'm going to finally taste you. And once I have you

312

squirming and begging, then I'm going to fuck this pussy that's already soaking wet and needy."

The hook slid inside her just as he said the last words, and she squirmed as the cool metal settled inside. An odd sensation because it had no give, no forgiveness with each twitch of her muscles. "Oh my God," she groaned against the table as Wyatt slid the hook back and forth, until finally seating it completely.

A sharp swat to her ass made her whine, and she found him grinning when she opened her eyes. He was crouched by his bag, tearing open packs of alcohol wipes to clean his hands, and then he stood tall. "Do you have any fucking idea how hot you look right now?"

"No, sir," she answered through clenched teeth, still trying to adjust to the feel of the hook.

"Straight out of a fantasy, beautiful." Wyatt's grin spread as he approached, bringing the ropes with him. "Just like a fantasy..."

CHAPTER 9

 *yatt*

AS HE THREADED THE ROPE THROUGH THE ANAL HOOK, HE *MIGHT* HAVE pulled harder than necessary once or twice — but listening to Vanessa whine was like some kind of highly-addictive drug. Just when he thought he'd had enough, he wanted just one more hit. One more squeak, one more whimper, one more muttered curse that told him just how she was feeling.

"Come on, upright. Hands on your head." Winding his fingers in her hair, he tightened his hold and pulled her upright, watching as her muscles twitched and shifted until she was kneeling upright. "You like feeling that hook in your ass, don't you? Dirty, little slut…"

Vanessa had her eyes closed, her face aimed at the ceiling as if it would somehow ease the tension on the hook, but he heard her shallow breaths. He could see the rapid pulse firing along the column of her neck, and there had been no ignoring the wet shine of her cunt that developed as soon as he'd started talking to her like this.

Apparently his beautiful ballerina liked a little degradation, which worked for him just fine. In fact, the whole scene was giving him blue balls, and he still had so much fucking ropework he wanted to do. First things first, though. "You're going to tell me if this hurts too much, understand?"

"Yes, sir," she groaned as he pulled the pale pink rope up her spine, finding the right tension before working it through the back of the chest harness to form an attractive knot. Then he wound the two pieces of rope around the front, under her breasts, forcing her to turn slightly to accommodate him — but really it was just to hear another squeak as the hook moved inside her. Putting her back in the proper position, he finished securing the hook, and checked the tension of the rope.

"How does that feel?"

"Just fantastic, sir." The reply was dripping with sarcasm, but it just made it an easier decision to slip the little nipple clamps from his pocket as he walked around into her line of vision. "Oh shit."

"Yeah. I was actually debating putting these on, but since you're still struggling with that mouth of yours..." He grinned when she actually lifted a hand as if to stop him. "Hands behind your back, naughty girl."

"Yes, sir," she said through clenched teeth as she lifted her chest just a little higher from the position. Her breasts were perfectly sized for her body, just another thing that made her beautiful, and he was going to make sure she remembered that he liked them the entire time they were in this scene.

Pinching one nipple, he rolled and twisted it until she whined, and then he laid the little rubber coated bars on each side of it, sliding the locking mechanism upwards to trap the little bud. He moved slowly, waiting for her to really cringe before he stopped and left it in place. They were small nipple clamps, without the more aggressive pincher-style clips that could cause damage once she was back on her belly. Still, the dangling black beads looked beautiful against her olive skin and the pink rope. "One down, one to go."

"Sir..."

"Tsk tsk, Vanessa. Don't argue *now*." Pinching her other nipple, he couldn't hide his sadistic joy as she whimpered. Locking the second clamp in place, he tugged the first one, making her gasp. "You just begged for me to put that hook in your ass like a good little whore. You should be saying thank you."

"Oh, thank you *so* much, sir." It was clear in her eyes that she knew the mistake she'd made, but it was too late. Without warning, he forced her down to the tabletop roughly. She gasped loudly, but he'd kept his hold on the chest harness to ensure the hook didn't pull the wrong way. Still, from her perspective, she'd suddenly gone from vertical to face down in an instant. Hissing air through her teeth, she wiggled that round ass of hers and muttered a soft, "Fuck."

"Not yet. I have to get you all tied up first. Patience, Vanessa." He was probably pushing his luck, but as he pulled her arms back, she didn't fight him at all. She held position where he placed her as he gathered more rope and the paramedic scissors. Leaving the scissors on the floor at the edge of the table, he couldn't help but smile at how compliant she was. Waiting obediently as he wound the forearm tie through select parts of the chest harness until both arms were bent in a beautiful box tie. *Perfect.* "Don't move."

"Haha, sir," she replied, deadpan, and he couldn't help but laugh quietly. Vanessa Novak was better than he could have ever expected. Not just incredibly talented, more than just beautiful, she was also funny, and vulnerable, and a fantastic submissive whenever he could get her to stop overthinking everything.

"I'm glad you find me funny." Snagging a length of rope, he pocketed the last few things he'd need and caught one of her ankles just as she was swinging them back and forth above her ass. "Personally, I think I have a great sense of humor. Not sure my subs always feel that way though."

Making his point, he tweaked the rope connected to the hook, chuckling as Vanessa squirmed.

"Alright, so talk to me while I'm getting you all tied up. Why did you pick ballet?" He'd warmed up his rope skills as he'd worked, so the first tie on her ankle didn't take long at all, and he swatted her ass when she stayed quiet. "Answer me. You don't want to know what I can do with that anal hook, little whore."

"I don't know. I just always loved to dance, sir." She wiggled a little and as he spread her thighs wider to get her positioned where he wanted, and he could smell her arousal. It was so fucking tempting, but he just had one more damn tie and then he could taste her.

"Why did you stick with it though?" he asked. Trailing his fingers up her other calf, he held onto the pointe shoe, squeezing firmly. "With all the consequences of pushing your body that hard, to make your body capable of doing all those *jetés, arabesques, pirouettes,* and *bourrée en couru?* Strong enough to do a *développé?* Why keep going?"

Just as he straightened her leg out, she twisted to look at him over her shoulder, and showed just how flexible she was as she bent her leg back towards her body with inhuman grace. She grinned as she let her leg relax into the proper position for the tie. "Showing off your knowledge, sir?"

"You think I wasn't going to look up the proper term for that incredible move from your bio?" He chuckled as he started the last tie, pushing the desperate ache of his cock to the back of his mind. "Come on, answer me."

"I guess I do it for the same reason everyone does things that are hard, sir." Vanessa relaxed back onto the table, resting her cheek on the padded top. "It makes me happy. Just this pure rush of turning your body into a piece of music... there's nothing else like it."

Wyatt paused as he threaded the last ropes through the loops, spending more time than he needed to ensure the ropes were straight, and the decorative knot the same size as the others. It wasn't complicated, but what she'd said was important — and it deserved at least a moment of attention before he lost all higher-level thinking skills. "That's a beautiful way to describe it."

"Thank you, sir," she replied softly, and he stepped back to admire her for a moment. Trussed up and laid out like a feast, Vanessa Novak was every inch the fantasy he'd imagined. The pale pink rope matched the tiny ballet skirt, which was flipped up above her ass and held in place by the shining steel of the anal hook. Smooth, olive-toned skin was everywhere, except for her ass where the dark loop-shaped bruises and the broad welts from the strap still showed.

"Almost ready, naughty girl." He grinned as he palmed the little bullet vibe. "How are those nipple clamps feeling?"

She adjusted, rolling each of her shoulders until she finally relaxed against the tabletop again. "Achy, sir."

"Ah, someone seems to have learned to watch their tongue." Grabbing her by the hips, he pulled her backwards slowly until she was right where he wanted. "You know, after all of your little protests" —he traced a finger down through her slit, barely touching her clit— "you are very, very wet."

"Please, sir," she begged, and he almost threw the rest of his plan out the window just to feel her wrapped around his cock, but he managed to take a deep breath and slide two fingers exactly where he wanted to be. The soft moan she released was absolute fucking torture, but the best kind. "Oh God, yes, please?"

"Such a good girl." Curving his fingers down, he started to thrust slowly, searching for that certain spot where he'd feel her body react.

And then a shout came from the main stage area, "No fair! You aren't worthy to be with Mistress Ice!"

Fucking hell, really?

"What's going on?" Vanessa asked, lifting her head, and Wyatt wanted to put a ball gag on whoever the fuck had just shouted. He'd had her so close to letting go of all the busy thoughts in her head, and then—

"Her name is Mistress!" The idiot at the front of the small crowd shouted again. Wyatt could see Santiago moving in to drag the fucker away from the scene, but that wasn't going to fix the problem with *his* submissive.

"It's okay, baby. Just an idiot trying to interrupt Mistress Ice's scene with Nolan, and that's a mess neither of us need to pay attention to." Wyatt realized what he'd said and froze with his hand on her ass. *Dammit, fuck!* He'd called her 'baby' on reflex, just trying to soothe her concern, and he did not need any other distractions when everything was about to go according to plan. "I think what we're doing is much more interesting."

"But what—" Before she could continue, he flipped the little vibrator on and held it directly to her clit. Her whole body jerked, which also meant the anal hook got a nice tug, and a few seconds later Vanessa wasn't doing anything other than grinding against the little vibe. "Sir, oh my God, please!"

Kneeling at the edge of the table, he dragged the bullet up to her pussy, teasing her entrance before he pushed it inside. She instantly bucked again, and he listened to her moans escalate as he leaned forward and dragged his tongue from clit to hook.

"Fuck, sir! *PLEASE!*" Her shout drew attention, and he could hear the buzz of people moving closer, but he didn't care at all as he tasted her. He alternated between focusing on her clit until he could feel her thighs trembling, and then dipping his tongue inside her cunt. Sweet and tart, a taste that was going to haunt his fucking dreams if he never got to touch her again, which was the wrong thing to be thinking. But, as if she knew just what he needed, the next time he focused on her clit she suddenly came hard. Crying out, shuddering, and he licked her again and again, until she was whimpering, pleading, and her words made it into his ears. "Sir, please, fuck me, or let me taste you. Please let me taste you? God, please, just something."

Definitely not an offer you ignore.

Standing, he saw her twisted slightly so that she could see him, and the bright flush in her lips and cheeks made his decision for him. "You want to taste me, beautiful?"

"God, yes," she moaned, hips shifting because the little bullet vibe was still going, and he followed the cord to the tiny plastic control in his hand. Grinning, he left it in, setting the control box on the small of her back, and then he turned her on the table so he could have access to either end of his bound ballerina.

There was nothing graceful about fumbling with his dress belt, but her eyes lit up when he slid it free from the loops. "Such a little masochist. Like belts?"

"Yes, sir," she answered, but her eyes were focused a little below where his belt had been. "Please?" she begged again, and he groaned.

"You're going to fucking kill me if you keep begging like that." Moving closer, he opened his pants, slowly sliding the zipper down, and then he used both hands to sweep the hair back from her face, winding it into one hand to help keep her head up. Then he shoved his boxers out of the way and finally wrapped his fist around his cock. It was a full body shiver, only made worse by the way Vanessa wet her lips and opened her mouth. "I'm in control. Got it, little whore?"

"Yes, sir!" With her mouth open, tongue waiting for his cock, it was a goddamned miracle he didn't pop off like a teenager. The only hope he had was for him to stay in control, and that meant easing in. Slow.

An electric shudder moved up his spine as he first slid over her tongue, so wet and warm when she sealed her lips around his shaft, and he tightened his grip as he eased back and forth just the first couple of inches. Still, Vanessa was moving her tongue along every hypersensitive ridge, and he could feel the buzzing hum of her moan as her hips started to wiggle again. "Jesus..." he groaned, pushing in deeper.

He'd bound her for the fun of it, to restrict her movement and force her to rely on him, to trust him, to submit so that she could let go. But he had not planned appropriately on what the visual would do to *him*. His hips twitched forward, seeking more, and he lost all hope of going slow. Wyatt fed her every inch she could take, testing the back of her throat, and even pushing for just a moment until he felt her swallow and almost came.

"Bad girl," he growled as he jerked his hips back. Staring down at her swollen lips, the bright flush in her cheeks, and the defiant little tongue that she held out as if taunting him to try again, he shook his head. "I'm not coming down your throat, little whore. I'm about to fuck you, any objections?"

"No, sir," she answered, grinning, and he dug in his pants pocket for a condom. Holding up the wrapper so she could see it before he let go of her hair.

The walk around the damn table was the longest of his life, as was the suddenly complicated process of getting the fucking foil wrapper to open so he could slide the condom on, but then he was standing behind her. Hands on Vanessa's hips as he tugged her over the edge of the table just enough to let her lay her head down. "Ready?" he asked, tugging the little vibe out of her to palm it.

"Please, sir!"

As if he needed her to beg right now, any more of that and he'd need to gag her just to last long enough to enjoy it. Next time he'd let her suck him earlier in the night. *That would have been smart.* Unless there wasn't a next time? *You're thinking too much.* He needed to focus on her enjoying this so there could be a next time. *Shut up, shut up, shut up!*

There was only one way to get the anxiety to go away, and Elijah had told him that trick at the beginning of the night. She was soaking wet, which made it easy to line up and push forward. Each inch was perfection, and when he pulled back and thrust deep everything went quiet.

No one else. Just her. Unbelievable and absolutely perfect.

CHAPTER 10

*V*anessa

"God yessss," she moaned as he slid inside her, filling her in a way the little vibrator couldn't. That had been a tease, a taunt, and this was… this was everything. Each full thrust shoved the anal hook deeper, and the double penetration was mind-blowing. "Sir, please! More?" she cried out, begging, unabashed.

"Come for me," Wyatt growled, and then she felt the buzzing bullet slide through her folds before it found her clit just as he slammed in, forcing his cock and the hook in at the same time — she didn't stand a chance.

The orgasm hit her hard, blanking her mind with bright ecstasy for one glorious moment until it fractured and sent light careening to the end of every nerve ending, only to grant a million tiny explosions that had her straining against the ropes. Whimpering and moaning as she shivered, slowly becoming aware of her body again, only to find Wyatt still moving inside her. The perfect size to give her that little ache with each deep thrust, but no pleasure-distracting pain. It was all good, all wonderful, raw joy as he teased her with brushes of the vibe against her clit. Taunting her as she murmured pleas for… something. "Sir, oh God, please, please!"

"Such a good girl, Vanessa. So beautiful, come on. Come again." The little bullet found its mark once more, and she couldn't tell if the cry made it past her lips, or only existed in her mind, because everything seemed to invert. It wasn't as powerful, but it was still too much. Overwhelming chaos storming through her nervous system, a shining wave of pleasure that stole the air from her lungs and left her blood humming. Just... absolute bliss, capped off with the incredible feeling of his cock jerking deep inside her as Wyatt groaned behind her.

She was still shivering as he rocked against her ass, all of the welts a flickering memory of sensation, but she was very aware of his warmth draped across her back. The gentle kisses brushed across her back, her bound arms, as she lay limp and satisfied on the table. "Thank you, sir. Thank you..."

"You're incredible," he whispered against her spine, and then she felt him stand up, the warmth leaving her completely as he stepped back.

"Sir?" she twisted, trying to see him, and then he stood upright again and she saw Weston walking away from them. "Is everything okay?"

"Of course, beautiful. Let's get you out of all this." Wyatt started to rub her arms, and then she felt the medical scissors sliding between her skin and the rope.

"Wait! You don't need to destroy the rope!" Twisting, she saw him glance at her with a serious expression on his face and she sighed. "Sir, I just don't want you to waste the rope."

"Didn't we talk earlier about not telling a Dom how to spend his money?" The fleeting seriousness left his face as he chuckled. "I do not have the energy to untie all this, I'm cutting it. It's my choice, because I want you in my arms and comfortable faster. Got it?"

"Yes, sir," she answered, laying her cheek against the padded table as he continued cutting rope away. She had to admit, it took a hell of a lot less time to be free of the ropes as he deftly cut pieces and unwound them.

"Alright, up on your knees and lean back towards me a little."

She obeyed, still focusing on the pretty rope marks pressed into her skin, until she felt him tug at the anal hook and instantly tensed. "Sir—"

"Vanessa, relax. Now." The stern edge of his voice had her submitting, even though she closed her eyes as she felt him slowly pull the hook free. It hurt again as it passed the widest point, but his quiet, "Now push," freed her of it.

"God, my ass hurts," she grumbled, listening to him chuckle just before a warm cloth passed between her legs, and then over her tender ass.

"I'm definitely enjoying the view," Wyatt replied. "And I'm sure it only partially has to do with all of these gorgeous marks, or that the hook made your ass sore."

"I can hear you trying not to laugh, sir." She attempted to sound serious, but when Wyatt smacked her ass and laughed anyway, she ended up laughing as well. Post-orgasmic hysteria, or something. Sitting up on the padded table, she watched as he tossed random implements in his bag, piling the rope in one spot, and then Weston handed him a robe and he held it open for her.

"Come here, beautiful. There's still a few minutes left." With that kind of invitation, she couldn't have resisted even if she wanted to. The robe was fluffy and warm, like it had recently been in a dryer, and as soon as they walked the few steps down to the main floor, Wyatt scooped her up.

"Showing off again, sir?" she asked, grinning as he settled onto an empty couch near their platform and tucked her into his lap.

"I'm well aware I have nothing on the guys you work with. I'd need to go to the gym more than once a week if I wanted to lift you like they do, but yeah, I was showing off a bit." Wyatt brushed her cheek, and then dragged his thumb just below her mouth. "And I really want to kiss you again."

"I'd like that, s—" His lips were on hers before she could finish agreeing, their tongues warring as she held onto his shirt, trying to pull him closer to her. But he understood, like he seemed to understand most things about her, and he held her tighter.

They'd already had sex, but now they were making out like teenagers, on a couch in the middle of Black Light, and it was somehow still thrilling. In a different way, not necessarily better or worse, but she did like being able to touch him.

Although, the rope bondage had been fucking hot.

Wyatt was a unique mixture of quiet and intense. He was absolutely a sadist, but also an absolute gentleman. A conundrum that she wanted to know more about, even as time was ticking down.

He nipped her lip and pulled back from the kiss. "You're thinking again, aren't you?"

"Yeah." She shrugged, and then groaned. "Shit, sorry, yes, sir."

He laughed, light and easy. "Play is over, beautiful. No need."

"Oh, okay." She tried to smile, but knew it was going to come across awkward so she dropped it and looked to where the crowd was gathered by the main stage. Piper was riding the guy who had bid on her, and he was tied to a fucking chair. Pointing, she spoke quietly, "Whoa, look at that."

Wyatt turned to glance at the stage, and then he made a snorting sound. "I would have bet money *that* would have never happened, but apparently I would have lost."

"Huh?"

"That's Nolan. Some bigshot guy in movies, but he's definitely not a switch." Wyatt shrugged. "Or maybe he is, I'm not judging. I've just had some conversations with him here at Black Light, and I wouldn't have thought he'd be into it."

"Maybe he's exploring," Vanessa suggested, but she tore her eyes from the blatant voyeurism and caught Wyatt's eyes. "Can I ask you something?"

"Of course," he answered, smiling at her as he tucked hair behind her ear.

"Earlier... you said that Kelsey is right about me fighting subspace. But I hit it with you, I swear—"

"I know you did, that wasn't why I agreed with her." Wyatt leaned back on the couch, the smile still lingering on his lips like the discussion didn't bother him at all.

"Then why say that?"

"Because you're like me," he replied, and then dropped his head back to take a deep breath. "How do I explain this… it's that you can't just let go and turn your brain off. You're too wound up, too focused, too driven — so it doesn't happen easily. You fight subspace, because giving up control is scary."

She felt a flush in her cheeks, embarrassment or some similar emotion. It was like he was accusing her of being a bad submissive, even though she knew that's not what he meant. Really, the problem was she didn't understand what he meant at all. Frustrated, she sighed. "But I didn't fight it with you, right? Or, did I?"

"At first you did, but then I figured out how to help you let go." He leaned forward to kiss her, just a tease compared to their make-out session, but it left her lips buzzing when he broke it. "You just need the right distractions, Vanessa. The right set of circumstances so that your only solution is to release all those busy thoughts, all of that mental chaos, and let things happen."

"Like the kiss, and the bondage."

"Exactly." He nodded, slowly interlacing their fingers before he snuck a mischievous glance at her. "And the degradation, you respond very well to that."

"Thanks, I think?"

"It's just another kink, and I happen to find it very hot. No trouble at all to call you a dirty little slut when I'm bending you over for something fun." Wyatt laughed and she did too, because it *had* been really hot.

"Good to know that you're willing to do that." She relaxed against his shoulder, tracing his fingers with one of hers. "So, what's your trick? How do you tune it all out so that you can, you know, be a Dom?"

"Usually… I don't. I mean I can't turn it off completely. There's this constant hum, and it can be distracting, but it usually only affects me. If I ever feel like it's affecting my attention on the sub, I'd just stop a scene. But that's only happened once or twice, mostly because of other people's loud scenes in a place like this, and I don't think it will be a problem anymore."

"Why not anymore?"

"Well, I hope it won't be, because—" Wyatt stopped as they called out the end of the event, but she touched his cheek to make him look at her again.

"Because... what?"

"Well, I mean." He shrugged. "Tonight was busy because of Roulette. Just complete chaos all over the club, but... every time I touched you my head just went quiet. And since I'm hoping we'll play again, hopefully more than once, then it wouldn't be a problem anymore because I'd be with you."

"So, I help you let go?" Vanessa smiled.

"You have no idea, beautiful. No idea." Wyatt smiled back and kissed her, and he had just snuck his hand inside her robe when they heard a man shouting.

They broke the kiss just in time to see Piper Kole walking quickly across the main floor as Nolan shouted at her to come back. Santiago intercepted her, but she barely paused to talk to him before she hurried through the curtain.

"What the fuck is going on?" A familiar voice asked, and Vanessa turned around to see Cassandra holding together her torn silver top, but the rest of her clothes seemed fine. Still, as Vanessa looked over the man standing beside her she was definitely curious about what had happened between them. "Is that dude still tied to the chair?"

"Looks like it," Wyatt answered, laughing softly.

"No idea what's going on. But I just saw Piper Kole run out of here a minute ago, and they were paired up for the night." Vanessa shrugged, watching as Santiago climbed the steps to the stage, trying to calm a raging Nolan.

"Idiot shouldn't have volunteered to be at the mercy of Mistress Ice. That chick is hardcore."

"This is Michael. He bid on me, and I've convinced him to take me out for pancakes since it looks like you're hanging out here for a bit." Cassandra grinned. "Am I right?"

"Yeah, I'm going to hang out with Wyatt. But leave me your number with the security desk, and I'll text you so we can hang out. Okay?"

"Hell yes! That is going to happen. Now"—Cassandra nudged the blond man beside her—"this guy promised me pancakes." He'd looked bored the entire conversation, but he lit up when he looked at her.

Yeah, they definitely needed to talk about their evenings.

"Talk to you soon, Cass. Enjoy the pancakes." She waved a little as the beautiful model walked towards the curtain with Michael.

"Bye, girl!" Cassandra called over her shoulder.

Once they were alone again, Wyatt touched her chin and grinned at her. "You're choosing me over pancakes?"

"Long story," she answered quickly, brushing the topic off even though the story *wasn't* that long. "Let's go back to this whole thing where you say I help you let go and relax?"

"Yes?" he asked, still grinning.

"I just want to hear more about my calming effects on you."

Wyatt laughed, and shook his head. "Oh, Vanessa, the very last thing you do is *calm* me." Holding her cheek, he leaned close. "You make my head quiet, and that's something I used to think was impossible. But, it's like I said... when I touch you, all that chaos, all that *thinking* just stops. I can just *be*."

"Wow," she whispered.

"Yeah, I agree 'wow' pretty much nails it. So, I'm sure you can see why I'm hoping we get to play again. Soon?" he asked, using the same charming smile that seemed infectious because a second later she was smiling too.

"That sounds like you're asking me out on a date."

"And if I were asking... what would you say?" He shrugged a shoulder. "Theoretically, of course."

"Theoretically, I'd say yes, and I'd ask you to bring that knife of yours."

"Christ," he growled, pulling her into another burning kiss that made her lips buzz and her skin hum, and then he broke it just as quickly. Half-laughing as he met her gaze. "I really should have done this a long time ago."

Vanessa nodded, unable to fight the laugh. "Yeah, you really should have…"

"Well, great. Come here and kiss me so I stop thinking about it." Wyatt shifted her so she was straddling his lap, and she felt a lightness growing in her chest as he smiled up at her.

"I think I can do that," she answered, kissing him again. Even as she heard the buzz of people leaving around them, and the bright lights clicking on, none of it seemed to matter as Wyatt separated the front of her robe. A sharp tug on her nipple made her gasp and she saw his smile.

"I really do love the noises you make. Want me to take these clamps off?"

"Nah, they're fine for now." Vanessa wrapped her hand over his, squeezing so that his grip on her breast tightened and the delirious zing of the clamps shot straight between her thighs. She rocked her hips and he groaned.

"Want to continue this at my place?" he asked, tweaking the other clamp with a sharp twist that pulled a soft moan from her. "Was that a yes?"

"As long as I make it to class in the morning." She smiled when his eyes lit up.

"I can do that. Ten o'clock?" he asked, and she laughed.

"You really are a bit of a stalker, aren't you?" Grinning, she watched his expression flicker for a second before she kissed him. "It's okay, I kinda like it."

"Naughty girl," he purred against her lips before claiming her mouth again, and just like he'd said it made her spinning thoughts slow. Every brush of his thumb across her aching nipples turned down the volume on the rest of the world until it was just them.

Perfect.

The End

ABOUT THE AUTHOR

Jennifer Bene is a *USA Today* bestselling author of dangerously sexy and deviously dark romance. From BDSM, to Suspense, Dark Romance, and Thrillers — she writes it all. Always delivering a twisty, spine-tingling journey with the promise of a happily-ever-after.

Don't miss a release! Sign up for the newsletter to get new book alerts (and a free welcome book) at: http://jenniferbene.com/newsletter

Connect with Jennifer:
- Website: https://jenniferbene.com/
- Facebook: https://facebook.com/jbeneauthor
- Author FB Page: https://facebook.com/jenniferbeneauthor
- Twitter: https://twitter.com/jbeneauthor
- Instagram: https://www.instagram.com/jbeneauthor
- BookBub: http://www.bookbub.com/authors/jennifer-bene
- Goodreads: https://www.goodreads.com/jbeneauthor

PRESSURE

A BLACK LIGHT: CELEBRITY ROULETTE NOVELLA

By

Measha Stone

CHAPTER 1

"Michele, I have to tell you something." Corrine pulled on Michele's elbow.

Michele's concentration was on the room, distracted by all the people in attendance. People who'd really made a name for themselves. She recognized a few of the Hollywood elite, and several musical gods and goddesses. They put everything out there for the world to see, their talent, their faces; while Michele hid quite nicely on the inside cover of her paperbacks.

"Shell." Corrine pulled harder, dragging Michele back a step.

"Shit. Corrine." Michele held her drink steady, watching to be sure she hadn't spilled any of her wine. White and sweet. Just like she liked it, and she didn't want to spill it all over the floor before she had a chance to have a sip. "What's wrong?"

Corrine eyed the bar. "I think we should sit down."

"I've never seen you so antsy. You'd think you were playing tonight. Relax. We're just going to watch. Live wildly, vicariously, through these brave men and women playing tonight." Michele sipped her wine and let out an easy breath. She'd been so right not to sign up for the event. She'd be a twisted up mess if she were one of the participants waiting around for the matching to begin.

It was better this way. Have a fun evening being the voyeur. No expectations to be ruined. No hopes to be dashed. Yes. This was definitely the way to spend Valentine's Day.

"Corrine, slow down." Michele laughed as she all but chased her good friend to the bar. When she caught up to her a flicker caught her eye.

Egan Mendez stood fifteen feet away. The wine glass slipped from her grip, but thankfully she'd already been poised to place it down and it didn't break.

Corrine caught it before it fell over. "Michele! What's— oh."

"I knew he was playing tonight," Michele told herself. It wasn't a surprise to see the lead guitarist of Tanked standing mere feet away from her. She'd seen him before, playing in the dungeon or chatting up a beautiful woman in the bar. Definitely no surprise. And she'd seen him on the list of celebrities auctioned for the evening. But she couldn't help the butterflies throwing themselves around her internal organs every time she looked his way. She adored his talent. So raw, so passionate. Just watching him play the guitar was entertainment enough, she could put the music on mute and just watch him play.

"Michele." Corrine pulled her attention away.

"What is it?" Michele snapped. "You've been nervous all day." Michele picked her drink back up and gulped it down.

"You know how you said you were thinking of signing up for the game tonight?" Corrine snatched the glass from her when Michele tried to wave down the bartender.

"Shit, Corrine. I wanted another glass. It's my relax time." Michele reached for it only to have Corrine slide it down the bar away from them.

"You have to listen to me. And you have to remember that we've been friends since forever. And you have to remember that you said you love me unconditionally. Remember that."

Michele laughed. Corrine usually got a little dramatic about things. Being an actress, Michele forgave her for it, but she was pulling out all the stops tonight. "Okay, I remember all of that. What's up? And can you stop cock-blocking my wine glass?"

Corrine shook her head. "No, you already had two glasses."

"So?" Michele's gaze wandered back toward the spot she'd noticed Egan. He'd moved on. Her heart sank a bit. Whatever woman had won the bid for his playtime tonight was lucky. She'd watched him in scenes. He played harder than she did; he was definitely a sadist. Which turned her on in theory, but she couldn't let go of the baby girl tendencies she had.

Feeling the power of a man through his stern rules and care for her filled her with love. She couldn't imagine being with anyone that wouldn't hold her accountable and be a guiding light in her life. And yet, at the age of twenty-seven, she was still alone. Maybe it was time to face up to the fact that men liked to spank her, loved playing daddy in role. but when it came time to going home she was just too needy.

"So, you had two glasses. You can't have any more," Corrine said, remaining as evasive as ever.

"Corrine. The two drink rule is for the participants. Not the people watching," Michele reminded her and started to wave for the bartender again.

"Oh, look. The theater's open. Let's go get our seats. They're gonna start soon!" A chipper high-pitched voice came from beside Michele.

She noticed everyone starting to file into the theater room. "Come on. I'll get another drink after they've all been paired. We can figure out where we want to sit to watch after." Michele reversed roles with Corrine and tugged on her elbow.

"Michele, wait. I really have to explain something."

"You can tell me once we have good seats!" Michele pulled her along and maneuvered through the crowd.

Michele had spent her first evening at Black Light in the theater room. It wasn't that she was new to BDSM, she'd been quietly active in the scene since college, but she'd never embarked on any public play before. Watching the movies playing in the room for the two hours she'd given herself for her first outing had left her with more than a slick pussy. She knew she needed the real thing more than ever.

But the room had been mostly empty when she'd been in it the first time. Now it was packed. Chairs had been added to the room in addition to the recliners usually there. A stage was at the front with a microphone stand and, of course, the large roulette wheel.

For a moment she wished she'd submitted the application for the party, but once she caught a glimpse of Egan standing near the stage ready to be called up for his spin, she knew she'd done the right thing.

A woman dressed in a killer black leather dress stepped on stage signaling the opening remarks were coming. Michele didn't recall seeing her around the club before, and with a body like that, Michele would have remembered.

"Michele." Corrine leaned over to whisper in her ear as the crowd simmered down to hear the opening remarks by Jaxson Davidson, the owner. "You know how I'm always telling you that you need to get out of your box a bit. That maybe the guy you're looking for isn't right in front of you, but maybe you need to like, reach out and grab him?"

Michele turned to look at Corrine. "And you know how I'm always reminding you that I've accepted I'll always be on my own? That I'm perfectly fine just playing when the need strikes?" They'd had this argument too many times to count, and the pairing was starting. It wasn't the time to rehash old topics.

"Yeah, but sometimes you just have to dive in, you know, jump then check?" Corrine's eyes darted to the stage. Her usual laid-back appearance was long gone, leaving her with wildly large eyes and a look of pleading in her expression.

Michele's stomach tensed. "Corrine. What did you do?"

"Egan Mendez is up first..." the MC said, drawing Corrine's attention.

"Listen. I did it because I love you." Corrine hurried to say while the MC continued to introduce Egan.

"What did you—"

"Babygirl Michele. If you'll come up to the stage for your spin." The MC's voice carried over the crowd. Michele's heart stopped. Not paused, not stuttered. Stopped. Cold beat.

"Michele," Corrine hissed, knocking her out of her stupor. Her heart started again. Not a strong beat, but at least she hadn't actually died. Although, turning her stunned attention to the stage and seeing

Egan's eyes surveying the crowd for his submissive for the evening, made her wish she had.

"Corrine."

"She's here." Corrine waved her hand in the air and gave Michele a shove, then pushed on her until she stood. "It's okay, Michele, go. You can yell at me later."

Michele stood on shaky legs. Two drink minimum. Corrine had insisted she wear the dark blue dress with the flowing skirt. And she'd been rambling nonsense most of the night. How could Michele have missed the guilt on Corrine's face when they sat down in the theater?

Michele made her way through the aisle of patrons. She'd just explain to Egan, to the MC lady — *what did she say her name was?* — that a mistake had been made. It would be fine and Egan could be paired up with someone that he'd want to actually play with.

Good plan.

Solid plan.

Only when she stepped on stage, and Egan flashed that warm grin of his at her, her mouth stopped working.

"Nice to meet you, Babygirl Michele," Egan said reached out his right hand toward her.

She took his hand in hers and stepped around him so their linked hands hung between them. A soft bout of giggles came from the audience and Michele looked to the MC for an answer. She only smiled back at Michele with a warm grin.

Egan wiggled his fingers a bit and repositioned his grip on her hand.

"Oh," she said quietly. He'd meant to shake her hand not take it. "I'm sorry." She tried to release him, but he held tighter.

"Too late. You're mine." He winked down at her and moved his gaze to the MC. "I think we can spin now."

Michele took the small white ball from Madison — she remembered her name now — and hovered over the spinning wheel. All thoughts of quitting and running off the stage, and back to the safety of her apartment, drained away as the wheel spun before her. She tried to find the words, tried to find where she wanted it to land.

Closing her eyes, she tossed the ball into the wheel and listened to the ball bounce from spot to spot.

"You can open now," Egan whispered in her ear. She shook her head. Absolutely not. He chuckled and squeezed her hand again. It shouldn't feel so good to have his hand in hers. So warm, so intense. She was going to kill Corrine. *If she survived the night herself.*

"Dom's Choice!" Madison called out.

CHAPTER 2

*M*ichele's hand tightened in his when Madison called out the activity.

"Do you have her limits list?" Egan asked.

"Like, of course!" Madison handed over a piece of paper to Egan. "Don't forget and come back to spin again after thirty minutes if you want a new activity."

Egan nodded. "Thanks."

Michele seemed preoccupied with staring into the crowd. Her eyes narrowed from the lights shining on them, but he could sense she was searching for someone.

Something was off here. He'd caught the look of shock on her features when Madison had called her name. He didn't know she was Michele at the time, he'd just spotted her in the crowd. She caught his attention, and then when Madison called her name, her surprise was evident.

"We need to get off now," Egan said softly and gently tugged her to follow him. She seemed so small compared to his large frame. Her head barely came up to his shoulders. He was used to being the tallest in a room, and hovering over his partner, but she had a softness to her that was refreshing compared to the usual women he played with.

341

They stepped off the stage and walked toward the back. They had a little time to chat before the games began for the evening, and he wouldn't waste it.

As he pulled her to the back of the room, she let go of his hand and spun to face him. "I have to, uh, talk to someone. I'll be right back. Promise." She didn't meet his eyes when she rattled off the words and was gone before he could ask any questions.

He watched her shuffle through the crowd of people, still watching the stage, and come up to another female. The girl she'd been sitting with.

Another sub was called forward to the stage, but Egan's eyes were glued to his partner. Her hands were waving in the air, and the other girl shook her head, looking down with guilt written all over her face.

Egan stepped back from a small group of women wiggling their way past him. When he looked back at Michele, she was shaking her head, and it looked like she stomped her foot. He couldn't help but smile at the image. She definitely had a bit of a little hiding inside her — not usually his thing, but he found her too adorable to disregard her so easily.

A bout of laughter drew Egan's attention back to the stage. They were almost done with the pairings. When he searched out Michele again, she was slinking her way back to him with her friend behind her. Both looked like they were on their way to the principal's office.

He crossed his arms over his chest and waited. Whatever was about to take place he had a good sense that he probably wasn't going to like it. No matter how much he was enjoying the blush on Michele's cheeks as she stepped up to him.

"Hi," she said on a hard exhale.

He laughed. "Hi again."

"We have a small problem." She looked behind her and glared at her friend. "Get up here." Reaching out, she snagged the woman's arm and pulled her forward.

"Who is this?" he asked in a firm voice.

"This is Corrine. She's been my friend forever — a fact that has saved her life this evening, otherwise I would definitely consider

342

killing her right now." Michele kept her eyes planted on her friend who looked as though she were saying serious prayers for the floor to open up and eat her alive.

He shook his head. "I'd prefer it if you'd focus on me while talking to me," he said.

She swung her gaze up to meet his. He didn't miss her throat as she swallowed along with the little fluttering of her eyelashes. He made her nervous.

The devil on his shoulder enjoyed the sight immensely.

"Sorry." She dropped her hand from Corrine's. "There's been a misunderstanding."

"Okay, go on," he prompted.

She looked back at Corrine who gave the impression she wasn't willing to speak up.

"Corrine," Michele ground out. "Thought it would be a good idea that I participate tonight. Even though I had decided not to make a bid. She submitted the application and did the bidding. Corrine actually won you tonight. Not me."

"Not me. You. It was all your information!" Corrine finally piped up.

Egan took a long breath and tried to process the information. "So, you didn't sign up for tonight?"

"Right," Michele said.

"She wanted to, but she just chickened out. She panicked," Corrine hurried to add.

"So you don't want to play tonight?" This wasn't exactly how he'd planned to spend his evening. He'd agreed to be auctioned off for the night because he wanted to have a casual night. Valentine's Day always came with so much expectation. With Black Light Roulette, the only expectation was to have a fun filled evening of play. And he got to earn some money for charity. Win-win.

"She does," Corrine interjected.

"I want to talk to her right now. Corrine, I'd like you to go find a Dungeon Monitor and bring him over here."

"Why?" Corrine asked, obvious fear lacing her words.

"Because I need to talk to one of them. And you've created a little problem here." He hadn't unfolded his arms, and he wasn't easing up his glare on her. She'd really made a mess here, and they needed it cleaned up before anyone had any fun.

"Okay, sure." Corrine shot Michele a quick glance, maybe hoping she'd step in and help, before walking off.

"She meant well." Michele's tone softened once Corrine was out of sight. "She didn't mean to mess everything up. She wanted to warn me sooner, but I wasn't really giving her the chance—"

"So this is your fault?"

"Well, not really, no. She was afraid I'd back out if she told me before we got here, then I made us behind schedule because I was finishing a chapter, and I can't just stop until it's time to stop, so I was an hour late getting to her house. Then when we got here, I just wanted to unwind, so I went to the bar and got some wine. Then she caught up to me—"

Egan moved his hand to her mouth, pressing the tip of one finger against her lips. Her words had poured out so fast he couldn't catch up.

"She signed you up, you were late because you were reading, and then you were drinking?" He listed the events as far as he knew them.

"Writing. I was writing, not reading. But otherwise yeah."

He nodded, still confused but starting to understand.

"How many drinks did you have?"

"Just two. I should have realized when she cock-blocked my third glass, but I didn't think she'd do something like this. I mean, she's always saying I need to look outside the box for someone. That I shouldn't just keep playing with the same people time after time, but I didn't think she'd actually go behind my back and do something like this."

He was still grinning at the term cock-block being used in reference to drinking, as well as that language being dropped from such a pretty mouth, when Corrine showed up with Tyler in tow.

"Hey, Egan. What's up?" Tyler asked with a nod.

"I'm not entirely sure, exactly. But it seems Corrine here signed

Babygirl Michele up for tonight's event without her knowledge. She found out about it when Madison called her name," Egan explained, thinking he'd gotten the gist of it right.

Tyler raised an eyebrow. "You signed her up?" He settled his glare on Corrine.

"I was only trying to help." Corrine's tone became defensive.

"So all the information on her sheet is false?" Tyler pressed.

"No! I used her information. I mean, she had it all up there already. She'd filled everything out already, but she hadn't submitted it. When I borrowed her laptop it was there, so I— well, nudged."

"Not nudged, Corrine, you shoved. You threw me off a cliff, not nudged. Nudging would be to leave the application where I could see it," Michele spat.

Good girl. Stand up for yourself.

"Fine. I shoved. But you needed shoving!" Corrine argued back.

"Okay, so we have her information but no consent," Tyler stated. "She didn't consent to be here, so she didn't consent to play."

Michele readjusted her stance. Egan studied her for a long moment while Tyler lectured Corrine on all the rules she'd broken.

"We may have to revoke your membership—"

"Tyler, wait. Hold on a second." Egan put his hand out to stop the conversation. Corrine looked properly guilty and remorseful, and kicking her out of Black Light forever wouldn't help the situation. Egan turned to Michele and placed his hands on her shoulders. "Do you want to play tonight? Stick to the activity we rolled up there?" When she started to refocus her gaze, he caught her chin and held tight. "Eyes here, young lady, nowhere else."

He'd been right. Her lips parted and a soft gasp escaped when he used the term young lady. The light blush blossoming on her cheeks made his dick ache. So fucking sweet. She'd make a beautiful crier, too. He knew it.

"Now. Do you want to play?"

"Yes. I do," she said. Her attention remained on him, but he could see the struggle. She wanted to look away. She'd find out that it didn't always matter what she wanted, but for right now he gave her a reprieve.

He released her and stood straight again. "What can we do?" he asked Tyler.

Tyler moved his glare from Corrine to Egan. "Well, I guess we'll just draw up another consent package. Get her signatures on all of them and then she's yours. But what about this one?" He jerked a thumb at Corrine.

"I really was only trying to help her," Corrine said with her chin thrust out.

"Corrine." Michele stepped in when it seemed Corrine was going to keep talking. "Maybe it's better if you just go home for tonight. Can't that be enough, that she doesn't get to stay?" Michele asked Tyler.

"You want me to ground her from Black Light as punishment?" Tyler asked with a twist of his lips. Obviously, he wasn't too turned off by the idea. "I'll have to report all this to the owners. It will ultimately be their call, but yeah. I think that's a good start."

"I'm not leaving you," Corrine said to Michele.

"You thought she was safe enough with me to pair us without her permission, but now you're objecting?" Egan said with force.

"I'll be fine. I'll take a cab home, and I'll call you the second I get in the cab," Michele promised.

Corrine sighed. She was beat, and she knew it. "Fine."

"Okay. Babygirl, if you'll follow me, we have to get more papers for you to sign," Tyler said.

"Just Michele is fine," she interjected with a fresh blush. "You don't have to call— I mean that first part..." Her eyes darted to Egan. "It's just a nickname, my name's Michele."

"I'm sorry, Michele. Really," Corrine said again, stepping between Egan and Michele.

"I know. We'll talk later." Michele hugged Corrine.

"Michele, you go with Tyler. I'm going to get my things. When you're done with him meet me over at the tables behind the curtain,"

Egan instructed. He had a solid plan in place already because he'd had the time to prepare, unlike her.

Her eyes went wide. "What are we playing with?"

"Dom's choice." Egan winked. "The limits on this list, they are yours, right?" He handed her the paper to let her look them over.

"Yeah, these are all mine. She wasn't lying. I did have everything filled out I just didn't submit it." She handed the paper back to him.

"Okay, then. Off you go with Tyler, and meet me there. They're done with the pairings and will be starting before you get done." Egan caught Tyler's attention. "If you need me, come get me."

"Will do. Let's go, Michele." Tyler motioned for her to follow him as he walked off.

Egan watched her leave the theater room. The gentle sway of her hips, the sweet way she looked back over her shoulder before she left the room, all of it dangerous. The angel on his shoulder chanted *RUN*. She was too damn pure for the likes of him.

But the devil on his left laughed.

It was her purity he wanted to devour.

CHAPTER 3

*C*orrine really didn't know when to stop pushing. Michele finished signing the last of the consent forms and handed the pen back to Tyler.

"I'm sorry about all this," she said. *What a way to make a first impression.* Tyler probably thought she was crazy to have a friend like Corrine, and Egan most likely only agreed to play with her out of pity. After all, he didn't have a choice in who his playmate was for the night. He knew that going in, she understood that, but now that he'd gotten stuck with her because of Corrine's meddling he probably wished he hadn't bothered.

"Don't worry about it. You didn't do anything wrong as far as I can tell. I just want to be sure you actually want to play tonight. I don't want you to feel pressured." Tyler folded the papers.

Did she? All the reasons she didn't submit that application still applied. But Egan was already waiting for her. Corrine had gotten booted from her favorite club for the night. It would be rude not to go forward with it.

"No — I mean, no, I'm not feeling pressured. I do want to play. I was just nervous, that's all." She wouldn't confess the full truth of it. No one wanted to hear all of that.

Tyler nodded. "Okay. Well, at least your friend did use all of your actual information."

"Like I said, she just submitted the application I had filled out and abandoned. She's a good person, well-meaning, but misguided." *How many times had she said those words about Corrine?*

Tyler raised his eyebrows. "Some guidance would probably help her, I agree." He blinked a few times, like he'd just realized what he said. "You better get going. Egan's waiting and the play officially started a minute ago."

Michele nodded and left the office. Her stomach clenched with every step she took. Once she passed through the velvet curtain, she could see couples were already starting to get into their scenes, and the onlookers were milling around the space. She paused for a moment to take several deep breaths.

She couldn't do this.

She'd been stupid to even consider it.

She should have left with Corrine and apologized to Egan. That's what she should have done. Instead, she stood five feet away from the play space he'd prepared trying to keep her anxiety from making her cry, or worse.

"Michele." Egan's forceful voice pulled her out of her own swarm of thoughts. He stood at the foot of the table, his hands on his hips, his eyes boring into her. Then he frowned.

Not exactly the best start to a scene with a new partner. A new partner she'd been eyeballing for weeks.

Of course he was frowning. He'd been stuck with her for the evening.

"Come here," he said moving his gaze to the spot on the floor before him. She hadn't moved. She thought she had.

With another deep breath, she managed to get her feet to do what her brain wanted. When she was an arm's length away from him she stopped, clenched her fists, and looked up at him. Well, at his chin. His eyes were too beautiful, too distracting. His chin, however, was a reasonable place to stare while she said what she wanted to say.

"Egan. I'm really sorry this happened. And I completely

understand if you'd rather get another partner for tonight." She wished she'd worn the larger dress. The one Corrine corralled her into wearing was too form fitting to have a man staring down at her.

"I had no idea who won the bid, Michele. I wasn't expecting anyone in particular, so even though Corrine was wrong with what she did, it doesn't really change anything for us. Unless you don't want to play. I would understand that, but you have to be the one to pull the plug because it's not going to be me."

'It's for charity,' she reminded herself. Of course he'll keep her to play, otherwise they may not get the money for the charity.

"Okay, no— I mean, no, I don't want to pull the plug." What the hell was she saying? Her mouth and her head were definitely not on the same page.

"Good. Now, I'm pretty sure I was clear I want your eyes on me when we talk." He hadn't moved. Hadn't raised his voice, yet her chest tightened, and her stomach dropped at least a foot.

Clenching her jaw, she raised her gaze to meet his.

Yep. Too damn distracting.

She still preferred to focus on the dark stubble covering his chin to staring into the creamiest brown eyes she'd ever seen. It was like looking at a lake of milk chocolate.

"Sorry."

His left eyebrow rose up.

"Uh, sir? Sorry, sir?" she amended. Was she supposed to call him sir right away? The other men she'd played with hadn't asked for it. One had wanted to be called Daddy straight away. She hated using the title with someone she didn't know well enough to have earned it. Using it made it feel wrong. Unnatural. Just one more reason for Egan to be better off playing with someone else. Someone more his speed.

He brushed her hair back and cradled her face with his hands. "I'm not too much into protocols. But I do like the sound of that word on your lips." He ran the pad of his thumb over her bottom lip.

"Okay," she breathed. "Sir. Okay, sir." It wasn't going to be easy to remember to say it, not when he touched her like that and sent all the sparks through her body.

He chuckled. "I've seen you before." He narrowed his eyes. "I can't place it though. What do you do?" He hadn't released her yet, and the longer his fingers caressed her cheeks the harder she had to focus her attention.

"I'm an author. I write books."

He let go of her and stepped back, snapping his fingers. "Michele Walsh!"

Her mouth dried. He knew her?

"Yes, well, that's my pen name, yeah." She nodded.

"I love psychological thrillers. I've read almost all of your books." He smiled, a little crease popped up along side his lips. If the man got any more attractive her eyes would cross.

"You did?" She managed to keep her head on track with the conversation, but barely.

"You have some twisted little thoughts." He tapped her forehead. Twisted didn't cover half of it. Depraved was a better word. At least that's what her agent told her. Thankfully, there were enough thriller readers out there that enjoyed the gruesome mindfuckery she wrote to keep her well-fed and housed.

"I suppose." She was much better at the written word. Talking had never been her strong suit. Give her a computer, a dark room, and a glass of wine, and she'd find all the words she needed.

"I meant that in the best way possible," he said, leaning down until he was close enough that she could feel his breath on her face. She liked that, feeling him so close.

"Right. Of course." She nodded. Compliments weren't her thing either. Speaking and compliments, not in her armory. Deflection and hiding, those were her best combatant tools. "Thank you!" she finally sputtered.

She was mucking this all up! Talking to people she didn't know always made her sound stupid. She said the wrong thing, in the wrong tone, looked the wrong way. Exactly why she didn't hit the damn submit button.

His eyes narrowed and his lips pressed together into a thin line. "I have some pretty twisted ideas, too," he said.

351

"Oh?" She swallowed back the little squeak bubbling to escape. He was doing it again, staring at her, making all the nerve endings in her body tingle. How the hell was she going to handle him touching her?

"Any changes to that list they gave me? Now's the time." He ran the tip of his middle finger down the length of her nose.

"No. I think that was it," she whispered. Her heart was doing a damn conga line in her chest, it was a miracle she'd even heard him.

"Good." He straightened up. "I want you to take off that pretty dress, and any underwear you have on, and lay on the table. Tits up." He didn't stick around to be sure she started to move. Instead, he turned and walked away.

She let out a long sigh of relief. Air filled her lungs easier without him standing so close and her mind cleared.

"Now would be a good time, Michele." His firm voice carried to her, and she got moving.

She whisked the dress over her head and dropped it on the chair near the table. It was then she remembered what she wore beneath it. A pair of full body Spanx. Nothing says *take me daddy* like a nude colored elastic fat crusher.

There was no sexy way to get out of the thing. *Heaven knows it was no easy feat getting into it.* She growled to herself as she unzipped the front. Corrine needed more punishment than just being kicked out of the roulette night. No, she needed to experience some serious humiliation.

"Need help?" Egan stepped behind her and placed his hands on her bare shoulders. Instant fire exploded on her face.

"No. Uh, maybe I should go change in the bathroom." She pointed to where she could escape his gaze but he shook his head, abolishing any hope she had of reserving some dignity.

"I think here's fine." He leaned against the table, folding his arms over his chest again. Already towering over her because of her lack of height, his new stance only enhanced his dominating presence.

She toyed with the idea of disregarding him all together and just hightailing it to the washroom. It wasn't that long of a run, she was small, could maneuver through the crowd better. She might make it.

352

"Whatever little plan you're concocting in that sweet head of yours, you can forget it. I'll catch you within two strides and then you'll have to have a spanking before we can get to the fun."

Her pussy clenched at the word *spanking* the same way a mouth drooled when a steak appeared.

"Maybe I'd like a little spanking," she teased. Or at least she tried. He didn't smile.

"You'll get all the spankings your ass can handle, but first you have to get out of that." He plucked the elastic band running over her shoulder.

She pinched her lips together and glared up at him, wishing her thoughts were as organized as his. It wasn't fair, throwing her off with all his hotness and authority.

Stomping her foot, she turned away from him in a huff and began the indelicate dance of wiggling out of the elastic tube covering her body. He wanted to see it, well there. She rolled it, pushed it, yanked it from the bottom hem until it finally released her hips and fell to her feet.

With an exaggerated sigh she swooped down to grab it then threw it on the chair with her dress.

"That little fit was cute, but if you do it again, I'll pull you over my lap and spank you until you beg me to stop — and then I'll start all over again." His breath heated her earlobe with his statement.

"It wasn't a fit," she argued quietly.

"You're a little, aren't you?" he asked, grabbing her elbow and turning her around to face him.

She wouldn't look at him. It wasn't that she was embarrassed about her play habits. She enjoyed taking on the little role, she loved being cared for. It was who she was, but he wasn't a daddy. He was a domineering sadist that took up too much room in the space they were playing in.

"Not right now, I'm not." She decided to edge the conversation. She already had a hell of a lot going against her, she didn't need age play fantasies to be added to the list.

"Hmm, you're right. Right now, you're my plaything. And it's time to start. Up on the table like I said. Tits up." He patted her bare bottom and motioned for the table.

She'd forgotten she was naked. But she remembered now.

"Nope. No covering. Up on the table."

CHAPTER 4

*E*gan walked around the exam table to his tray of goodies. He did his best to keep his eyes on the line-up of implements and toys, but he snuck a peek at the delicious body laid out on the table for him.

Watching her wiggle out of that elastic suit had probably been the most adorable thing he'd seen a woman do. And, oddly enough, it was as arousing to him as seeing her completely naked. She probably didn't think so, since she'd taken the effort to stuff herself into that contraption, but she had a body he could stare at for hours. And if they had more time, and were at his own house, he'd tie her up on the cross and do just that. Except for when he'd walk over to pinch a nipple, or bite her hip, anything to get the sweet sound of her squeal.

"Arms over your head, Michele," he said as he ran his fingers over the wartenberg wheel handle. Rolling Dom's choice had been a gift. He would get to let his sadistic demons play while still giving her a chance to enjoy her role.

He wasn't a daddy. Not by any means, but he could still give her what she needed.

Once she had her hands where he wanted them, he grabbed her wrists and fixed them in the restraints. He could feel her eyes on him, warming him with all the questions boiling in her mind. Answering them wouldn't be much fun, and she hadn't actually voiced them yet.

He made his way to her feet, letting his gaze linger on her tits, and not caring that she could see him. Egan wrapped his arms around her waist, shifting her down and positioning her with her ass on the edge of the table.

"Put your feet flat on the table," he ordered knowing it would be a bit uncomfortable. It was the discomfort he enjoyed most. Watching her struggle with her footing while she obeyed his directions lightened his heart. He didn't make any move to help her. It made the accomplishment all the more arousing when she found a good position and she looked to him for his approval.

He fucking approved.

Keeping his stare on her, he reached down and pulled up the leather straps he'd connected to the table. He brought a strap over her chest just above and another one just below her breasts and secured them in place. Her tits were nicely trapped, and she wouldn't be able to wiggle away from the sensations he wanted to deliver. Her eyes widened and he almost chuckled. Seeing that little flicker of fear hardened his cock and sped up his heart.

When her gaze finally locked on his, he smiled. She was delectable, so ready for the corruption he would bring her. He collected two smaller restraints from his bag and used them to bind her calves to her thighs. She couldn't straighten her legs at all. It would make keeping her feet on the table slightly easier, but not more comfortable.

"Now you're completely exposed to me." He grinned, moving her feet to the corners of the table.

Her cheeks reddened, but she didn't say anything. He could sense the tension in her body; if he plucked her would she make the same sound as his guitar?

"Seems so," she said under her breath, but he heard her. He leaned forward between her legs. One of the advantages of being taller than most, he could easily reach parts of her body from his current position without having to move around much.

"Did you want to repeat that?" he asked in a low voice just as his lips wrapped around her pert nipple.

"Uh, no... I'm good," she said on an exhale.

He bit down, dragging his teeth until her nipple pulled free of his grasp. Her sharp inhale played sweetly in his mind as he moved to the untouched nipple.

"Definitely have nipple sensitivity," he said, glancing up at her from the valley between her breasts. With her arms stretched over her head, her breasts were pulled taut, giving him the perfect amount of tension. "I should make a note." He laughed and bit down on her nipple, flicking his tongue over the little bud before once more dragging his teeth upward and letting go.

A little squeal escaped her this time. Soft, more of a purr.

"On a scale of one to ten, one being *meh* and ten being extremely arousing, what was that?" he asked, putting on a serious expression and hovering over her face. Her lips were parted, little puffs of air came out. He'd barely gotten started, and she looked ready to burst already.

"Seven," she said. Her brow wrinkled, like she'd just said something wrong and wanted to take it back.

"What has you worried, beautiful?" he asked, rubbing away the wrinkles of her forehead with his thumb.

"Nothing. I'm fine," she said and smiled up at him. Except he knew that smile. He'd seen it plenty of times on the faces of music executives who weren't man enough to say if they actually liked something or not. They'd just wait until the band filed out of a meeting and call their agent to give the bad news.

"If you can't be honest, how can we play?" he asked seriously. He enjoyed playing, but he didn't do games. Not even with women as hot as the little number he had tied down to the table.

"Was seven too high?" she asked softly. The weight of her concern seemed to tighten her muscles.

"Was seven accurate?" he asked with raised brows.

"Yes, sir."

"Then no, it wasn't too high or too low." He ran his fingers along her collarbone. "We spun Dom's choice, and my choice is to play with these tits and then make you come harder than you ever have."

Her nostrils flared with a hard breath and her cheeks puffed out. He didn't bother suppressing his chuckle.

"How have I not noticed you before tonight?" he asked, more to himself. He had to have run into her before. The club was large, but surely he would have seen her before tonight.

"I'm unnoticeable I guess," she said softly. It wasn't a joke. She meant what she said. No merriment of a tease in her eyes, no little wrinkle around her mouth like she was waiting to giggle. It was simply her reality.

Being the lead guitarist in one of the most popular bands in the country didn't give him many moments of peace. The only time he wasn't noticed was when he was alone at home. And even then, there was usually a photographer lurking at the gates.

"I see you now, though." He narrowed his lids and leaned further until his nose touched hers. "Really see you, and it's going to be a real eye opening night for you, too, sweet girl."

When he stood to full height her wide eyes followed him, but she didn't speak. With her arms pulled tight over her head, her breasts were pulled upward, her stomach elongated. He rested his hands on her knees and watched her quietly, wondering what was whirling around that head of hers.

He wasn't lying, he had read nearly all of her books. She had a dark mind. He was on her mailing list, but he wasn't going to tell her that, though.

He had sinister thoughts as well; the difference between them was he lived his out. And now that he had her strung up tight, he could play with her all he wanted.

He left her for a moment to gather more toys. He opened and closed the nipple tweezer clamps over her face so she could see them clearly.

"The tips are made of rubber. They'll pinch, but not too badly," he assured her as he pulled a nipple upward and fixed the clamp in place. She sucked in her breath sharply at the bite, and he smiled.

"How is that, sweet girl?" He picked up the handle of the clamp, moving it up and down, which in turn twisted her nipple. She squirmed and snapped her eyes shut.

"I asked a question," he said firmly, knowing she'd react. She enjoyed the power dynamic; he read it in her eyes. Rules and obedience, she probably got wet just hearing a dominant tone. Which worked well for him, since he got hard using one.

"It's fine."

He tsked. "Uh uh, I want a number. Remember one is *meh* and ten is *ohmygod, I'm gonna come right now*." He changed up the wording he'd used before and got the exact reaction he wanted. Her tense lips curled a bit at the edges. She was softening.

"A six," she whispered.

He leaned closer to her face. "Open those pretty eyes, sweet girl," he ordered.

Her lids fluttered open, and she seemed surprised to see him so close.

"Do you want me to put the other one on?" he asked showing her the clamp in his hand.

She bit down on her lower lip. Michele had herself firmly planted in one box and was having trouble moving outside of it. That was fine. He'd help her. And he'd have a shit ton of fun doing it.

"If I have to repeat a question one more time, I'll pull your legs up and spank you until your ass glows. Do I make myself clear?" Punishments were hot in theory, but he hadn't delivered a real one in years. It seemed that would be changing tonight.

"What did you ask me?" she asked sheepishly. The woman wasn't playing a game, she really couldn't remember. He studied her expression then shook his head.

He grabbed the other nipple and placed the clamp firmly in place, pulling the handle up until her nipple stretched and she was squirming.

"Did you not hear me?" he asked, staring down at her.

She shook her head. "No, I mean, yes I heard you, but I was— I lost my train of thought. You were looking at me," she said in short bouts of energy as he twisted the handle to the right.

"So, this is my fault because I was looking at you?" he asked, amused and delighted, but still trying to understand her. He could usually read women pretty easily, but Michele was locked up tight. She didn't let much past her walls.

"No! Ouch!" She squirmed when he twisted the handle the other way.

"I wasn't paying attention! It's my fault!" she yelled when he increased the pressure by twisting a bit further.

"Yes, it is your fault. Because who's responsible for your actions, me or you?" He released the clamp and lightly trailed his fingertips down the length of her torso, going further and further down until he reached the small patch of dark curls that hadn't been swept away by a blade.

"Me. I am," she said, blinking hard.

"That's right. Now. Since you couldn't answer that question, answer this one. Do you want me to lick and suck on your pussy while I fuck you with my fingers and make you come?"

Her entire lower lip disappeared between her teeth. When it looked like she wasn't going to answer, he gripped the curls in his fingers and pulled.

She cried out. "Yes! I'm sorry, Yes!"

"You're sorry that you want me to eat your pussy?" He laughed, releasing the curls and petting them back down. Fuck, she felt sweet in his hands. She took the pain and twisted it around until it was pure and innocent. The perfect light to his dark.

"I'm sorry I didn't answer fast enough. I was thinking." She was honest to a fault, he'd give her that.

"Thinking what?" he asked, moving around her, never moving his touch from her body as he kicked a stool in place between her thighs and took a seat. He looked up the length of her, through her partially spread legs. Slipping his hands between her knees, he pushed them down to completely expose her pussy to his ministrations.

She couldn't see him well, he knew that and loved it, with her head bent to see and her chin tucked into her chest. She gave up and laid her head back, staring up at the ceiling.

"I was trying to figure out what the right answer was." She sighed.

"The right answer is the truth. Always. I don't have a premeditated script in my head, and you shouldn't either." He ran his thumb over the hood of her pussy, pulling it back to expose her little clit.

"Right," she said, but she didn't convince him.

"You think there's a wrong answer?" He stilled his hand.

"There's always the wrong answer," she said with more force. It seemed, he'd struck a little nerve.

"Explain," he ordered and slapped the inside of her thigh for good measure.

She heaved out an annoyed sigh. "There's always an answer you want to hear, then there's the answer you weren't expecting. And if I give the wrong answer, not the one you expect or the one that makes this work better, then it won't be fun for you. And if it's not fun, you'll stop. And I will have messed up the whole fucking night." She made a sound like a growl and planted her feet flat on the table, snapping her knees together "Like I just did."

Egan sat quietly for a moment.

"Let me up," she said after the silence between them continued to stretch out. "I'll pay for your next month's membership. I knew this was stupid. I knew I'd fuck it up. And I did. Just let me up," she said again tugging on the binds.

A dungeon monitor circled their area, watching them carefully. She hadn't said the safe word, but it seemed she was teetering pretty damn close.

Egan stood up from his spot and made his way toward the head of the table. Without touching her, he leaned over her face, squaring his gaze with hers.

"Are you safe wording?" he asked. If she was, he'd let her down, help her dress, and call it a night. As unsettled as he felt, he'd let her walk away. This wasn't right, though. This wasn't the way the night was supposed to go.

It was supposed to be frivolous fun. A fun night of fuckery. Yet, here he stood in front of her wanting to both hug her tight and take his belt to her ass at the same time.

She didn't hide from his gaze, for the first time all night she stared right into his eyes without blinking. The strong woman he'd seen stick up for herself to her friend was back.

"I don't want to, but I've really messed this up, haven't I? I shouldn't have said all that." She shook her head.

"It's what you meant though. And I said to always tell me the truth," he replied. "You put a lot of pressure on yourself, don't you?"

"What do you mean?"

"If you don't do exactly what I want even if I haven't told you what that is, I won't have any fun and the whole scene will just die. Right? That's what you think? So, you think you have to be perfect. Say the right thing, the right way, at the right time to make it all perfect. I have no part in it, it's all on you. How can you have any fun if you're playing both the submissive and dominant part?" He rested his palms on her knees.

"I don't know. I manage." Her stare wavered. He pinched her chin and pulled her head back.

"I think you've managed to have enough fun to convince yourself, but you've never really let yourself go, have you? Really put yourself in someone else's care. Even for a scene." He studied her face, the little freckles dotting her nose, the small scar on her left cheek. He wanted to know how she got the scar.

She opened her mouth and snapped it shut again. "I don't know how to answer that."

"I think that answers it perfectly." He let go of her chin and straightened to his full height. If she wanted to safe word, he wouldn't stop her. "Give me the next few hours. Don't worry about what you think I want you to say. I'm not going anywhere. All I want from you is honesty and an open mind."

"I already—"

"Earned a damn hard spanking. Yes, you did. But we'll take care of that after we finish here. I think we have to stay here for another ten minutes at least, and I'm not done playing with you." He folded his arms across his chest.

"But I—"

"Unless you're going to safe word, I suggest you drop your knees to the side like I had them. You've earned a punishment for getting out of position without permission, but like I said — later."

Her brow furrowed, and she looked around. Couples were still playing in their scenes. Plenty of moans and groans played in the background.

"You didn't ruin anything," he said softer when she still looked torn. "Just try for me. Ignore the bullshit telling you that you've done it wrong and said it wrong, and focus on me. I'll tell you if you've done something wrong. Only me. Give me that."

With a shaky breath she nodded and wiggled her feet to a better spot on the table and spread her legs for him again. An open invitation.

"I'm not stopping unless you safe word," he said, walking back to his stool. "Be a good girl for me now, take everything I'm going to give you, or you'll earn a harder punishment. Understand, sweet girl?" He sat on the stool, scooting up to the table.

"Yes, sir," she whispered.

CHAPTER 5

She'd come so close to screwing up the whole evening. Michele stared off at the ceiling doing her best not to berate herself into the next millennium for edging so close to the fire. No doubt any other man would have seen her for a crazy fool and let her stomp off the scene.

"Get out of your head, sweet girl." Egan's voice dragged her from the dungeon of self-doubt. "How are these nipples doing?" he asked very matter of factly as he reached up her body and played with the clamps.

The pressure intensified, and she let out a long breath. She'd never been a fan of pain, but this was different. Seeing the excitement in his features when she withstood the burn morphed it into an easy throb of pleasure.

"Okay."

"Number," he prompted

"Five." He moved the handles again. "Seven when you do that though," she admitted, feeling her pussy clench in sync with the new sensations in her tits.

"Good, girl." He leaned down and kissed her between her breasts.

"Such a sweet girl. Let's make you scream." He winked up at her and twisted the handles on both clamps.

Even if she wanted to tease him by holding back, she couldn't. He seemed to know exactly how to play her, how far to turn the clamps before releasing. She cried out from the sudden burst of sensation and whimpered when he took it away. He gave her another wink.

"Sweet, sweet, Michele." He kissed her again, this time above her navel. She wanted his lips on hers, but knew it wouldn't happen. Real kisses had meaning, and it was too much to even allow herself to fantasize about. She'd take what he gave and that was it. The evening had never been about finding her one and forever.

His mouth moved down lower, pressing his warm lips to her belly, and lower again just above her pubic hair, and then landed right on her clit. She fisted her hands and sucked in all the air her lungs would hold.

So long.

It had been so fucking long since she'd had anyone's lips on her pussy. She curled her fingers around the edge of the table, pressing her lips closed to muffle her moans as his tongue began to swirl around her clit.

"Definitely a sensitive little clit," he muttered. She felt his fingers on her, spreading her pussy lips open. Her toes curled, and she clenched her eyes waiting for it.

"Oh fuck!" She gasped as his tongue casually licked her from her entrance to her clit. "Fuck," she cried out.

"Let's see how your cunt feels." His words penetrated through her own sounds just before two fingers plunged into her entrance. She arched her hips, and bit into her lower lip.

None of the men she'd played with touched her like this. Brush a finger over her sex, yes, rub her clit hard until she came while over their lap, absolutely, but never did they take so much time to explore and devour her.

"Oh! God! Egan!"

His fingers worked in and out of her, curling just enough to stroke the embers into a full blazing inferno.

"That's it, so good, such a good, sweet girl. Come hard for me, can you do that? Show me how beautifully you can come?" His fingers plowed harder into her.

His tongue lashed over her clit, hard then soft, around and around then flicked this way and that. The pressure was too much.

Her body tensed, her thighs shook.

"Fuck!" she screamed, arching her hips up at him, and pressing her chin into her chest until she could see down her body. His mouth was wrapped around her clit, his fingers kept working their magic and her hips gyrated against him.

As the harsh waves ebbed into a soft current of pleasure she threw her head back and sucked in air. His tongue slowly eased off, and his fingers withdrew. She opened her eyes to see him licking himself clean and grinning at her.

"Very good girl." He winked again.

She released the table, working her fingers until the stiffness eased out. "Can I put my legs together yet?" she asked softly. She couldn't look at him, in a minute maybe, when her body stopped humming so loudly.

"Eyes on me," he instructed. The stool scraped along the floor when he stood.

She wasn't quite ready, but she remembered what he said. She needed to put herself in his hands, at least for a little while. And since he didn't run screaming after she'd broken down, she could do that, it wasn't too much. She could handle it.

"Good. Now breathe with me, in… out… in… out… good, keep going. In… out… in…" She met his pattern, bringing her heart rate back down to normal, and the racing thoughts subsided. All she concentrated on, all she could think of, was matching his breath. His eyes never left hers. They were completely in sync.

"Off comes one." He said. "Breathe… in… out…" The clamp on her right breast was removed, a fire ignited but she gritted her teeth and kept her focus on him. "Fuck, that was beautiful." He smiled. "And the next one… Breathe, Michele, breathe for me, sweet girl. Yes, in… out…" The second clamp was removed, and she only winced at the burn. His fingers replaced the clamps, massaging her breasts while he kept his breath even with hers. "Gorgeous." He grinned.

Her cheeks heated, and she turned her head to the side, unable to hold his gaze any longer.

He released the straps across her chest and helped her sit up, but made her stay on the table while he put away the clamps. She noticed a whole row of toys. He'd had a whole set up, ready to go, and she'd probably messed it up for him with her minor breakdown.

"I'm sorry you didn't get to do what you planned," she said, scratching her knee. Two days ago she'd tripped on the way up the stairs and cut herself. A new scab had formed, and she picked the edges of it while watching him.

He shrugged. "What makes you think I didn't?" He opened a black satin bag and started tossing the instruments inside.

"You're a sadist. So, it makes sense that you have all those clamps and those pokey wheels," she said.

"I like to have everything ready in case I change my mind on what I want to do. It's freeing to be unscripted like that. Here we don't have to live up to the expectations of a large crowd or reader base. We get to just play and enjoy each other. Free of judgement."

Her body eased from her self-imposed tension. He didn't think less of her for getting frazzled, he'd simply changed course and kept them on track. And all she had to do was put herself in his hands.

Freeing. His words nailed it perfectly.

He looked over his shoulder at her for a long moment then went back to cleaning up his toys.

"I think the half hour is up." She filled the silence.

He tossed the bag into a larger duffle bag on the floor. A monitor stepped up to him. "We'll clean this station. If you want to go spin for another activity better get up there, there's a line."

Michele hopped off the table and snatched her dress off the nearby chair. She had it halfway over her head when she heard Egan respond.

"Actually, I think we'll stick with Dom's choice." His voice had an edge to it now. The softness he'd used when calling her beautiful was gone. "Just need a new station."

Michele's head popped through the neckline of the dress in time to see Egan hoisting his duffle over his shoulder and frowning at her.

"What?" she asked, looking down at herself. Had she put the dress on backwards?

"I didn't tell you to dress." He wiggled a finger at her. Her panties and Spanx were still on the ground, at least for the moment. Egan snatched them up, then grabbed her elbow. "Yes, a new station."

"My shoes." She pulled back on him.

"I'll bring them over," one of the staff members offered. *Great*. How nice of him. Didn't he see that she needed to break the momentum of the moment?

"Egan?"

He didn't so much as look back at her, just continued to pull her through the room until he found an empty station. A spanking bench.

Once he dropped his bag at the foot of the bench he gingerly flung her around until her ass bumped against it. With both hands he hoisted her up easily from the ground and plunked her on the edge.

"Stay," he said with a finger pointed at her. She nodded, not that he seemed to need her agreement. He was already squatting down at his bag rifling through it.

"Can't we talk about this? I mean, I'm not sure we really talked about any sort of punishments." She scratched at the stubborn scab on her knee again. He looked up at her from his bag, caught her action and reached up to stop her.

"Don't pick at that." He pushed her hand away from it and went back to his digging expedition. Maybe what he wanted wasn't in the bag. Maybe he'd forgotten whatever it was and they could march up to the roulette wheel and get another activity. Like sex. Yes, she'd prefer that to whatever he was searching for.

She'd played spanking with guys. Even role-played punishment spankings, a lot of daddies liked to do that. But she'd never been actually punished before. Egan didn't look like he was going for something easy like a little hand spanking, either. And he didn't give off the role-play vibe.

"So, maybe we should just go roll again." She put her hands on the edge of the bench, ready to jump off, but the glare he shot up at her froze her.

"Don't. Move." He pointed at her again. That damn finger. That damn long, strong finger that had some sort of magical power, because the moment he put it in her direction she couldn't do much else but obey.

"I was only saying, we're just playing so it—" Her words died off when he had an aha-moment and pulled out the thinnest wooden paddle she'd ever seen. A ruler length, or a bit more, with multigrain coloring — this was a handmade paddle. Not something bought from Spencer's gifts at the mall.

He tucked the bag under the bench. When he stood up again, he was standing right in front of her, his hip pressed against her knee.

"Even when *just* playing, there's punishment for disobedience. Isn't that right?"

She knew the answer to the question, but she wasn't quite sure she was ready to be punished by him. He was severe.

Playing with men she didn't have any level of a crush on had been easier. She still had to battle off the nagging reminders to make sure the Top was getting exactly what he wanted so she could get what she needed, but the intensity hadn't been so high.

"Well, I suppose. But you didn't say I couldn't get out of position," she pointed out while staring at the devil in his hands.

"Did I really need to? I also didn't say to put on your dress, but you did anyway," he retorted. Okay, she'd give him that one.

She dug her thumbnail into her thigh through her dress.

"Tell me what you're worrying about," he ordered.

Moving her gaze from the dreaded paddle to meet his eyes, she let out a long breath. Keeping herself so walled off was getting exhausting.

"What if I can't take what you give me?" She pointed at the paddle. "It looks wicked."

His right eyebrow arched. "Oh, it is. That's why I only use it for punishments. It was buried at the very bottom of my bag because it's been a long time since I've had to pull it out."

So much for helping to alleviate her concerns.

"Oh." *What else was there to say to that?* He'd just confirmed what she was worried about.

"All you need to think about is what you did wrong, how you will do it differently in the future, and take your punishment as best as you can." He ran the back of his hand along her cheekbone. "So many worries for such a sweet girl. Let me take this one, okay? I'll do the worrying about this punishment, and you just concentrate on what I said. Okay?"

When he touched her like that, she believed him. She needed to remind herself this was all just for fun. After the night was over, they'd go their separate ways. She'd go back to her writing cave, and he'd go back to touring with his band. He'd find any woman he wanted whenever he wanted, and she—well, she'd hang around Black Light on nights she needed a decent scene.

"I'll try," she agreed.

"Good girl." He pressed his lips to her forehead. "Now, off with the fucking dress. You aren't allowed to put it back on until we're done for the night. Understand?" He lowered his chin and glared down his nose at her. The squirming in her stomach was automatic, and so was her nod.

"I understand."

"Once you're undressed, up on the bench. Grab hold of the handles and keep your ass high in the air. I will cuff you down if I need to, but I'd rather you took your punishment without it." He stepped away, giving her room to hop down and follow his instructions.

She kept eyeing that damn paddle.

It was going to kill her.

She'd never sit again.

She'd probably safe word within the first three swats.

CHAPTER 6

*E*gan readjusted his cock in his jeans while Michele had her head covered with her dress. Watching her move brought a lightness to his chest. She didn't have the grace of a supermodel, and she probably wouldn't be asked to join dancing with the stars anytime in her life, but she had a carefree air about her. Most women probably would have unzipped the dress and let it slip down their body and step out.

Not Michele.

She pulled it up by the hem over her head and wrestled to get out from the sleeves. Not as entertaining as the dance she did to get out of that damn elastic thing women insisted on wearing, but it still worked for him. She was real.

The most real he'd come across in L.A. since he'd started in the music business. He loved playing in the band, always had, but he was tired of the same plastic Barbie dolls hanging around. And most of the women in the scene with him were angling for more than just a good flogging. They wanted into his life, well, his bank account was more like it.

Black Light helped save him from a lot of that, but still, he wanted something more from his play partner. He was tired of fake gasps, or women who swore they could take more than they could because they were trying to prove something to him. Michele had real fears and they were written all over her face.

As much as she wanted to hide from them, he could see her demons front and center. It was refreshing to see such truth opened before him.

She glanced at him through lowered eyelashes before climbing onto the bench. He moved behind her, letting her have a moment to herself to collect her thoughts. He didn't need much more time with her to recognize that her mind was both her best attribute but also her greatest enemy.

"I'm not a hard man to obey, Michele." He rested his left hand on the small of her back. Her naked, round, beautiful ass was propped up high for him. She wanted to please him. "When I put you in a position do you think you should get up without asking?" He pressed the thin paddle to her ass, the chill of the wood would draw her attention from wherever her mind was at the present moment.

"N-no." She shook her head. He waited to see if she would look over her shoulder at him. She didn't.

Good girl.

He pulled the paddle back.

"That's right," he said and brought the narrow paddle down on her ass. It was long enough to cover both of her cheeks. She groaned at the impact. He'd gone soft with the first stroke. Easing her in.

She was scared of the pain because she hadn't experienced it before, at least nothing like he planned to give her.

"Have you been punished before, Michele?" he asked and pulled the paddle back again.

"N-no. Well, not as an adult," she clarified. He brought the paddle down again, harder this time, pressing the wood into her ass to help keep the sting at a minimum. He hadn't lied. The thin, narrow wooden paddle was wicked. It stung like hell. But he knew how to keep it tolerable until he wanted it not to be anymore.

He delivered another swat, watching her bottom bounce with the impact as the light pink started to appear beneath the paddle. She moaned a bit, but wasn't giving him the indication she couldn't handle more.

The next swat came hard, and he lifted it straight away from her ass, letting the sting fully impact her mind. She yelped and tossed her head back. He gave her another and another until her feet were wiggling, and she made the most delicious hissing sounds.

"I want obedience. I want your best effort. I want all of your focus when I have you under my control. Do you understand that?" He delivered another hard strike, right to her sit spot. The light jiggle of her ass cheeks from the impact made his cock strain against his zipper.

"Yes!" Her left leg kicked out, straightening behind her and almost hitting him.

He paused. "Did you just try to kick me?"

"Oh my God, no! I wouldn't! I didn't!" She looked back at him with full panic brimming in her expression.

"Feet down and stay down," he said moving more to her side and pulling her hips until they were pressed against his body. Wrapping his arm around her waist he held her fast and began to really deliver the punishment.

It had been a while since he'd meted out discipline, but he hadn't forgotten how. He restrained her while he continued to spank her and tuned out her cries and promises to be good.

They always promised that when the spanks got harder.

No. He watched her ass. Watched as the little pink deepened beneath the paddle. He ran his tongue over his lips as she wiggled her feet, but didn't kick back out. She was doing so fucking good.

"I'm sorry! Egan! Please! I'm sorry!" Her body was tense beneath him. *Not done yet.*

He controlled the strength of his swats. It wasn't the force that hurt, it was the sting, and well-placed smacks lit her ass up. She hissed and cried out, but she wasn't near the breaking point yet. He wouldn't take her there, either. Not tonight. Not when he couldn't cradle her in his bed all night long. No. This was just a little punishment.

"I swear. I'll do exactly like you say. I won't move. I promise!" she called out, but she still wasn't letting go.

He continued. Not an inch of her delectable ass was neglected. He tossed the paddle to the floor and used his hand. Feeling the heat of her skin against him and delivering harder spanks, he peppered her ass and tops of her thighs.

"Oof! Egan!"

"You think I'll just give up here? Not gonna happen," he said, readjusting his grip around her waist and continuing with the spanking. She'd taken more than he thought she would, but not as much as he knew she could.

Her body stiffened at his comment, and he paused for a moment. She sniffled. A little, gentle sound, but he heard it.

Now they were getting somewhere.

He began spanking her again. Not hard, not delivering the sting anymore, but just giving her the sensations. He wasn't going to let her wall herself off from him.

Slowly her body relaxed, her muscles unclenched.

"There you are. Good. Let go." He continued to concentrate on her sit spots until she let out a hard sob. After three more well-placed smacks, he stopped and rubbed her red, blotchy ass. It looked worse than it was. He didn't see anything to indicate she'd bruise, but she'd be sore for the rest of the night.

He unwrapped his arm from her waist and rubbed her back. Her head was pressed against the bench.

"Breathe, baby. Breathe." He whispered into her ear. "You did so fucking good, sweet girl. So good." He wiped the hair from her face. Tears streaked her cheek and he wiped them away with his fingers. "Such a sweet girl."

She sniffled.

"No one's ever—" She blew out a long breath. Her cheeks puffed when she did it and he didn't even try to hide his chuckle.

"I'm sure they didn't. But I did, and I'll do it again." He pressed his lips to her cheek, wanting to kiss her. Really kiss her, but she wasn't ready. Or maybe he wasn't.

Maybe he wasn't being truthful with himself. He'd said this was a one-night thing. Separate lives after tonight. Just like any other play night for him. But this girl was under his skin. And in the best ways. He wanted to kiss her, to taste her, to capture her energy. And he wanted to hold her and cradle her and care for her. And he wanted to tie her up, and hurt her, scratch her, spank her, pinch her and then cradle her all over again.

"Come on up." He helped her off the bench and wrapped his arms around her. She fit so neatly into his body, melting right into him. He rested his chin on her head. "You did great, Michele."

"It hurt so much."

He chuckled. "It was supposed to. How do you feel now?" He ran his hands over her back.

She sighed. "Clean."

He paused for a beat. "Clean?"

"Yeah, like fresh." She shook her head, bumping his chin. "That doesn't make any sense. You'd think I could use words better considering I'm a fucking writer."

He held her tighter. "I'm no good at free style. When we're just jamming away, it's harder for me to play without music already in my head. I'm no good on the fly. So, I get what you mean."

She pushed back from him. "Really? I've seen you play, you always look so free, so taken over by the music."

A warmth exploded in his chest knowing that she'd been in one of the audiences. "I am. I mean, I feel the most free when I'm playing, but I can't just make it up like other guys do. I have to have the music in my head already written."

"Huh." She smiled. "I never would have known."

"So, you've been to a concert?"

"A few. I like watching you play." A blush blossomed on her cheeks, like she'd just given him another secret of hers.

"The guitar? Or have you watched me play other times, too?" He wouldn't pass up the chance to make that soft pink bloom into a full red.

"I've seen you play here too. Lots of times." She let him go and pulled out of his embrace.

"And?"

"And, it was different than the guys I played with. They were, well, they play-acted. I suppose that's what daddies do, but it wasn't real. When I watched you... it seemed like more. At least for you. Some of those women you were with—" Her nose scrunched up like she'd just tasted something sour.

He laughed. "Yeah. You aren't wrong about that."

She began to rub her ass, but he pulled her hands forward, holding them in his own. "No rubbing. I want you to feel that the rest of the night."

A frown took over her lips. He couldn't hold himself back anymore. He kissed her.

The best damn kiss he'd ever had. Her hands flattened on his chest, and his fingers entwined in her hair. When his tongue touched her lips she opened for him, taking him in, demanding he enter. She matched his energy and urgency. Her fingers curled, fisting his shirt in her hands.

And fuck, when she moaned. His cock nearly burst in his pants.

It wasn't just warm and sweet. It was intense and real.

Like everything with her.

CHAPTER 7

*M*ichele stared at Egan. The warm tingle still fresh on her lips from his kiss, and she couldn't get enough of looking at him. He'd walked her to the wheel again. They were going to spin for the last part of their evening together.

She would be happy to keep playing with Dom's choice. He'd made so many good ones.

Well, aside from the punishment. That was both a good and bad decision. She hadn't thought she'd be able to handle it, the sting was so fierce that the pain radiated up her entire body. But when he wrapped his arm around her waist, when he never broke contact with her, it made everything he was doing to her worth it. And when she'd broken down, he hadn't seen it as a weakness. He didn't stop and pull back. Instead he'd pushed her through to the very end.

It had been one of the best and worst moments of her life.

And in a short time, she'd be giving it up.

"I'm going to go get you a bottle of water. I'll be right back," he kissed her head and handed her his duffle bag. There were three couples ahead of them in line to spin. The air was filled with electricity and excitement. She wished Corrine hadn't had to miss it.

"You're with Egan tonight, right?" A tall blonde thing, thinner than any Barbie Michele had played with, stood before her with her sticklike arms folded over her chest.

"Uh, yeah," Michele said. Her neck hurt from looking up at the woman. She had to be wearing three-inch heels. *Her arches must be wrecked.* "He just went to get some water," she added, nodding toward the direction he'd gone. Suddenly very much aware of her nudeness, she folded her arms over her chest.

Michele wanted her dress back. Or a robe. Anything to cover up everything she didn't have going for her. Short, stout, she might as well grow a spout and be done with it.

"Okay, thanks." Miss Universe wanna-be, spun around, flicking her long locks toward Michele and missing her face by mere inches before she stalked off.

Michele blinked a few times. Not three-inch heels, more like five. Michele barely kept her balance on a pair of one-inch wedge sandals. The couple spinning finished and stepped off stage, moving everyone up a spot.

Michele spotted Egan talking with Miss Universe-on-steroids. He had two bottles of water in his hands and a smile plastered on his face. The blonde tipped her head this way then that way, keeping one hand on her hip and her over inflated chest puffed in his direction while she talked.

Not needing to see anymore, she turned around to face the line. She was next to go up.

"Hey. Here you go." Egan appeared beside her with the water.

"Thanks." She snagged it from him and twisted the top off, downing half the bottle before coming up for air. He was grinning at her when she recapped the bottle. "What?"

He shook his head with a little laugh. "Nothing, sweet girl. It's our turn." He gestured toward the wheel and placed his hand on the small of her back.

"You do it," she said to him and pointed at Madison holding the little ball.

"Okay." He took it from their MC and dropped it as soon as the wheel started spinning.

"Hoping for anything specific?" Madison asked with a smile.

Michele looked off stage. The blonde had disappeared. At least Michele wouldn't have to imagine her watching them together. Judging.

"No, not really," Michele answered as the ball plunked into a seat.

"Edge play," Madison announced.

"Great." Michele tried to sound enthused, but couldn't she catch a break? Couldn't that damn ball have dropped into a play that she'd had some experience with?

"Scared?" Egan took her hand and squeezed.

She looked up at him, ready with a burning retort that died on her tongue when she saw the concern in his eyes. "No, not so long as it's with you," she found herself saying.

He squeezed her hand again. "Good. I think we'll use that lacing table I saw earlier." He led her back into the play area.

Michele kept her focus on his hand touching hers. When she was able to focus, the panic rising up dissipated. And she wanted to make this last bit of time with him the best it could be. For him and for herself.

When they got to the table, it was already taken so he stopped to look around the area for something else. "Well, the cross is open." He pointed to the St. Andrew's Cross.

"I'm too short," she said when he tugged her in that direction.

"No such thing," he replied without looking at her.

When they arrived at the area, he took the duffle bag from her and dropped it on the floor. She walked over to the cross, stood with her back to it, raising her arms to mimic the X. "See? I can't reach." She looked up at the metal rings protruding from the arms. *Nowhere near them.*

He stopped looking in his bag to look up at her. With a laugh he continued his search.

She huffed and dropped her arms.

"Just the thing." When he stepped up to her he had two bundles of rope in his hands. "I'll just drop the ring down for you." He tucked the rope beneath his arm and started putting on the cuffs. "I'm beginning to think you've been playing with some real newbies," he said while buckling the second cuff.

"I never ventured very far from what I was used to," she admitted. "Which is why Corrine did what she did. She wanted me to start playing outside my box, and I wanted to stay tucked up nice and warm."

"With daddies that would give you a little ass spanking and send you home?" he asked while looping rope through the high ring.

She felt her cheeks heat again. He was quite good at that, making her blush. "Yeah."

"You definitely have some little tendencies, but I can't picture you with a daddy. Like a real daddy, baby girl stuff." He worked the rope through another loop. She watched him, amazed at his workmanship. Double knotting her gym shoes was the best she could do.

"I'm not sure what I am, to be honest," she said softly. "I'm not even sure I'm submissive sometimes."

"Why?"

"Well, I'm horrible at following rules. Like, horrible. The moment I have one, I go out of my way to break it. It's bad." She hadn't admitted that to anyone before. Not even with the few boyfriends she'd tried having a kink relationship with. They'd accused her of it, but she'd denied it to the death — of their dating.

Egan moved to the other ring and made the same set up with the rope. "Well, that tells me you like the spankings, the punishments. You want to feel his dominance, and when you don't, you misbehave to force it." After he finished tying off the second rope, he turned around to face her. His eyes were fixed on her. Not an ounce of judgment in them.

"That would make me a brat right? Or topping from the bottom?" She stepped to the cross, taking her position with her back against the wood of the beams.

"Well, maybe. But not for the same reasons. I wouldn't say brat. Or at least I haven't seen any of that tonight. And you didn't try to top from the bottom either. I'd say you just take control when you feel it's not being held by the other person. Like if he's not dominant, then you step in and try to make it work the way you need it." He'd perfectly explained every failed relationship she'd ever had. It was the reason she stopped dating and just came to the club to get a scene in when she wanted one.

"And my little tendencies?"

He picked up her wrist and worked the rope through the ring of the cuff, getting her properly strung up for whatever he wanted to do with her.

"They are adorable." He grinned but didn't look at her. "Wouldn't change that for the world."

She didn't respond to that. How could she?

He finished getting her trussed up and stood back to check his handiwork. "Perfect." He winked at her and headed back to his bag.

"Edge play—that's like knives, right?" she asked, suddenly getting her head back in the game.

"Not always. Sometimes. But what do you think about breath play?"

"I-I don't know," she answered, shaky.

"I'm guessing that would be a soft limit on your limits list if you could have put it, is that right?"

Her stomach twisted. "Yeah."

"Then that would be the edge, right? A little outside your comfort zone? We'll play there."

"But—"

"If you get scared, tell me. If you need to stop, use your yellow color and we'll slow down. Okay?" His voice soothed her. If she had been willing to trust him with a knife, she needed to trust him with this.

"Okay. Yeah." She tugged on her restraints. "I suppose it would have been better to ask questions before you tied me up."

He laughed light heartedly and zipped up his bag. When he came back over to her, he had a vibrator in one hand.

"Gonna take my breath away with orgasms?" she quipped, suddenly feeling much more brave with him.

The right corner of his lips curved up. "Oh, sweet girl, you have so much coming your way. It's going to be wonderful to witness."

"Promises, promises," she teased.

He sucked in air through his grin and laughed. "Oh, you play brave, but you'll see." He flicked on the vibrator. "Spread those thighs for me, sweet girl."

She walked her legs apart and was rewarded with the sweet sensations of the vibe on her clit. She rested her head on her arm and grinned at him.

"Feels good?" he asked, stepping closer to her.

"Yeah, real good." She arched her hips toward the vibrator wanting more pressure.

He wrapped his arm behind her neck. "Good. Take a deep breath."

She barely had a chance to before his hand came from behind her and covered her mouth and pushed against her nostrils. All air cut off. She wiggled as panic took over.

"Look at me, Michele." His face was there, right in front of her. "You're okay. How's your pussy feel?"

His thumb moved, letting air flow through her nose. She inhaled a deep breath with relief only to have it taken away when his thumb came back down.

"Pussy feels good, right?" he asked, running the vibrator through her folds and back up to her clit.

The fight for air and waves of pleasure warred for control.

Her lungs burned.

"There we go." His hand moved away from her mouth.

She sucked in breath, feeling as though she'd just run across the room.

"Feel the vibrator," he said, kicking up the speed.

"Oh!" She became enraptured by the good sensations, the blossoming of utopia between her legs.

"Focus on your pussy. You're going to come like this for me," he announced and pressed his hand against her mouth and nose again. No warning, all air just cut off.

Her eyes went wide, and she started to fight to get free of his hand, but he was holding her tight. She felt his own breath, washing over her as he leaned closer.

The vibrator moved and it was electric. Her orgasm ripped through her body, blindsiding her.

She screamed beneath his now cupped hand as the force of her release rocketed her. Her throat strained but she didn't care. If she didn't let out the pressure, she'd die. Wave after wave, her body was rung out when they finally faded into silence.

Her head hung from her neck. She gasped for air. Tears streaked her face. Where the hell had they come from?

But he was there. Egan pushed her head back and kissed away the tears.

"Fuck, baby," he growled, capturing her lips with his own and taking her breath away again. This time, she craved it, she wanted him to take everything from her. Every worry. Every feeling. Everything, and leave her feeling just like this forever.

"Egan," she said when he released her lips. "Please." She wrapped one leg around his hip. "I need you. Please."

She could barely breathe, her heart was ready to make its debut through her ribs, and her body ached. Especially, her pussy. She felt empty and abandoned. She needed him.

"Are you sure?" he asked, studying her face.

"If you don't fuck me, I will never forgive you. I'll kill you off in my next book."

CHAPTER 8

*E*gan didn't need to be told a second time. He made sure she was good standing on her own feet, then went to his duffle to get the condoms he kept on the inside pocket.

"No fair! You aren't worthy to be with Mistress Ice! You're supposed to be a submissive..." A male's voice carried from somewhere else in the room. Egan paused to look around. That wasn't a cry of passion, that voice had anger.

More commotion and yelling, but the DMs jumped in and got it under control quick.

Egan put his attention back where it belonged. On his girl. He made his way back to her, grabbing her chin and kissing her until his own lungs wanted air.

"What was that?" she asked breathlessly looking over his shoulder where the commotion happened.

"Nothing that we need to worry about," he said. "Hold this with your lips." He put the condom between her lips and waited for her to hold it before letting go.

His hands went to his belt, and he quickly shucked off his jeans and boxers. He ripped two buttons off his shirt getting it off, but he didn't give a fuck. He'd buy a new one.

"Thank you." He plucked the condom easily from her lips and opened the package, rolling it down his length. Fuck, just the little bit of sensation caused his cock to jolt in his hand.

"Now, Egan." She glared at him.

"I think that might be the topping from the bottom you were talking about." He lifted her left leg and spanked her pussy three times. She hopped on the other foot, which got her nowhere with her wrists still bound.

"Ow! Shit!" She tried to twist away, but he still had her leg.

"Are you going to be my good girl now?" he asked, stepping closer and hooking her knee around his hip.

She licked her lips. "Yes. I'll be good."

He laughed. "I don't think I believe you, but I wouldn't mind another reason to spank that ass of yours." He reached around her and grabbed her ass cheek, purring when she cried out. "Fuck! That sound!" He pressed the head of his cock at her entrance.

He squeezed again and when she yelped, he plunged his cock upward into her hot, wet channel. She cried out again, but with satisfaction. He held onto her ass cheek as he pulled back and plowed forward again.

"My ass... oh, fuck... Egan." Her head rolled back as her pussy gripped him. Even with the condom keeping them apart, he could feel her heat. So much heat. He hoped she burned him so he'd feel it for the rest of the week.

"Fuck, baby... sweet girl. Such a sweet girl." His mouth found hers, and he kissed her. He let go of her cheek and used both hands to cup her ass, lifting her from the ground. He pressed her against the cross and plowed into her harder and harder.

She broke the kiss, sucking in air and moaning with each thrust.

"Yes! Fuck, yes! Harder, Egan. Fucking harder!" she screamed at him, nipping at his ear when he didn't do what she demanded. He bit down on her shoulder and her hiss drove him to the brink.

"Come again, Michele. Come with me."

"Yes! Yes! Now! I have to come right now!" she yelled.

The cross creaked from their motions but held steady. It didn't stop him from fucking her hard. Her ass hit the beams, pinning his hands between her and the equipment.

She let out an animalistic growl and her pussy clenched his cock. He thrust once more, it was too much, he couldn't hold back and his own release washed him away in the epic waves of pleasure.

When the air finally came back to his lungs, and his ears tuned into the room, he heard her heavy breathing beside his ear. She was resting her head on his shoulder.

"Sweet girl." He kissed her shoulder and gently slipped from her, lowering her back to her feet.

"I can't—" she said wiggling her hands.

"I know, gimme a sec." He quickly worked the knots loose on the cuffs and had her down on the floor with him in seconds. She was cradled in his lap, legs wrapped around his waist and her head resting on his shoulder as he adjusted to the hard floor.

"I didn't know it could be like that," she whispered, but he had a feeling she was talking to herself. He ran his fingers over her back and held her until she was ready to move. His cock had softened and the condom needed to be removed, but he'd clean up whatever mess he'd made after she was cared for.

All that mattered at that exact moment was Michele.

She untangled herself from him and gifted him with a shy smile. Serious arousal fed her bravery, but she'd lofted down from her orgasmic high leaving her soft and gentle in his hands again.

"Am I hurting your legs?" she asked, starting to climb off him.

"Nope." He held her around the waist.

"It sounds like the night is winding down." She glanced around the dungeon. "It doesn't feel like three hours went by. It feels like only a few minutes."

He kissed her chin. "Time flies when you're having fun, don't you know that?"

She laughed. "I guess."

Michele tapped his arms to signal she wanted off, and he released her. They both got to their feet, the quiet moment had ended.

He went about disposing the condom and finding his pants while she slipped into her dress.

"My shoes. Where did that guy put my shoes?" she asked looking around the station.

"I have them in my bag." He grabbed the pair of flats from his duffle and handed them to her along with her undergarments he'd kept.

"I think I'll just leave this off." She laughed lifting up the pair of Spanx.

"You don't need those. You're perfect all by yourself," he said pinching her hip lightly through the fabric of her dress.

"Thanks," she said after a long beat. "I'm going to use the restroom real quick." She pointed toward the bathrooms.

"Okay. I'll meet you back here?"

"Yeah, sure." She grinned and headed off. He watched her disappear across the room, losing her in the crowd. He'd forgotten all about the other people. When he was with her, it was just them, no background music, no onlookers. Just him and Michele.

It had been the perfect night.

"Egan, hon. Are you almost ready to go?" Jerrica's high-pitched voice hit him from behind. He dropped the rope from his hands.

CHAPTER 9

*S*he looked well-fucked.

Michele grinned to herself in the mirror. Her hair was unrepairable at this point, so she pulled an elastic holder from her purse and stuffed all of it into a ponytail.

Before heading back over to meet with Egan, she took a detour to where her phone was locked up. As much as she liked the security of Black Light it could be a bit annoying when she wanted to make a quick check on her phone.

She fired off a quick text to Corrine.

Awesome night! Thanks for being so stupid on my behalf!

Michele didn't wait for a response. She put her things back in the locker and went back in to meet up with Egan.

He was still at their station. Ropes still dangled from the cross and his chest remained bare. She hadn't gotten the full look of him while she'd been bound to the cross, but she could see him now. All of him. All his muscles, and the small tattoo on his left shoulder.

But it wasn't the sight of him that made her stomach drop three inches. It was the blonde bombshell from earlier talking to him again. Her hand rested on his elbow.

Michele paused for a deep breath to remind herself this was just a one night thing. They'd been playing a game. It had been fun, but the night was over. They needed to go back to their real worlds now. She'd tasted something sweet, but now it was time to put the treat away and get back to reality — no matter how sour of a taste it left in her mouth.

Egan caught her gaze when she moved closer and his lips widened in a smile.

"I thought you fell in. You okay?" he asked, holding out his hand for her to take.

"Uh, yeah." She eyed the blonde beauty whose entire body stiffened with Michele's presence. Michele started to lift her hand to take his but decided against it. He wasn't letting her call the shots on it though, and grabbed her hand, hauling her against him.

"Egan, hon. We should get going." The woman's clear blue eyes swept down from Egan's face toward Michele. She didn't know what to say. Should she back away and let him go? Just wave and walk away?

"Jerrica, thanks, but like I said. I'm good."

Jerrica's lips thinned, and her eyes darted back to Michele. "Would you mind giving us another second, sweetie?"

Egan's hand held firm. "We're done here, Jerrica. Again, thanks for the invite, but I'm not interested." His voice changed. Not quite rude, but definitely headed down that road. Michele supposed with a woman like Jerrica it was better to be straightforward and bold than to beat around the bush. She wondered if Jerrica would understand subtlety.

Jerrica ran her tongue over her top set of teeth and scoffed. "Fine. Whatever." She made a deliberate show of looking down her nose at Michele. "I guess I overestimated your taste."

Again, her long hair was thrown over her shoulder as she turned on her inhumane high heels and stomped away.

Michele let out her breath in a whoosh. "Well, I don't think she'll forgive you for that anytime soon. You should have just gone with her.

I'm just going to grab a cab home. It's fine." Michele dropped his hand and started to pick up the rope, winding it around her palm.

Egan took it from her. "You're doing that wrong."

She left him to take care of the rope while she dragged a chair toward the second rope still hanging from the cross.

When she climbed on the chair, his hands went to her waist, hoisting her off. A sharp smack to her ass shocked her. "What are you doing? I'll get that."

"Okay. Sorry." She rubbed the already sore ass cheek. "I guess I'll just say goodnight then. It was… fun. A lot of fun." She stuck out her hand for a handshake.

He looked at her hand like it had grown spores and was going to start infecting him with some communicable disease, killing him within minutes.

His hand shoved through his hair, and he let out a loud growl. "It's not supposed to be this fucking hard, you know? You meet a girl you dig, you should be able to just ask her out. But it's not that fucking easy."

He was rambling.

She understood rambling.

She spoke it fluently.

"It looked like she was asking you out, so—"

"You! Not that plastic doll! You!" He laughed and grabbed her by the shoulders. "I want to see you again, and I'm not taking no for an answer."

Michele looked at him straight on, not having an ounce of trepidation in her heart. She supposed that happened once you've known a person in the carnal sense.

"Well, I don't think dating me by force would get you very far. I'm pretty sure there are laws. Even for famous Guitar Hero people."

"Guitar hero?"

"Yeah, that game, you know on Xbox or whatever it's called." She bit her lower lip. "I was joking."

His mouth covered hers, stopping her from any more rambling.

"I'm taking you home. No cabs. You aren't even wearing panties.

390

No. No cab. I'll drop you at home and then pick you up in the morning for breakfast." He pointed to the table where his duffle sat. "Go stand there and wait for me."

"Do you have to go home?"

"What?"

"Do you have a cat to feed or something? I don't really like cats, I'm more of a dog person. I have a dog. A big dog. Her name's Pumpkin. I did not name her."

His chest puffed up with his laugh. It was fucking delicious. "No. I don't have a cat. And I love dogs."

"So... instead of wasting gas going home and coming back..." She walked to the spot where he wanted her and folded her hands in front of her. "Why don't you just stay over?" The space between them was needed in order for her to be bold enough to say it. It also gave her a head start if she wanted to run from embarrassment.

"Depends," he said winding up the last bit of rope and walking over to the table. She watched him, waiting for him to continue but he said nothing as he zipped the duffle.

"On what?" she finally asked when he stayed quiet.

He ran his hand along her cheek, cupping the back of her head and pulling her to him for a kiss. A long, sultry kiss. "Does that dog sleep in the bed?"

She stared at him for a second before she realized what he was talking about. "Yeah, but it's a king. Pumpkin sleeps on the bottom corner."

"Okay then." He slid his arms thought the sleeves of his shirt, leaving it completely unbuttoned, and hoisted the duffle bag over his shoulder.

She didn't ask for clarification from him. He was a dog person. And a guitarist. And even though he wasn't a daddy, there hadn't been a moment all evening that it mattered.

This could all crumble the moment they woke up in the morning. But for the first time, in a long time, she was ready to let the wheel spin.

The End

ABOUT THE AUTHOR

Measha Stone is USA Today bestselling author of erotic romance. She's had #1 top-selling books in BDSM, and suspense. She lives in the western suburbs of Chicago with her husband and children, who are just as creative and crazy as her. Her vanilla writing has been published in numerous literary magazines, but she's found her passion in erotic romance.

Stay up to date on her latest releases, get a sneak peek at current projects, and exclusive glimpses at deleted scenes! Just sign up for her newsletter, and earn a free book, too! http://bit.ly/2B7buwt

- Twitter
- Facebook
- Instagram
- www.meashastone.com

SAVOR

A Black Light: Celebrity Roulette Novella

By

Maggie Ryan

CHAPTER 1

onan

IT WASN'T THAT THE LOW, LONG UNDULATING NOTES OF A MOAN WAS A sound I was unaccustomed to hearing, but to be honest, that particular sound was generally one given by someone wearing far less clothing than the female presently seated at the table. It brought to mind the vision of a woman bound to a St. Andrew's Cross, her body striped with thin red lines, her back arching as a flick of my wrist sent the whip to land another line of fire across her flesh. Or perhaps it was given by a woman on her knees, arms encased in a latex sleeve behind her, the fingers of my hand wrapped around the slim column of her throat... the very throat where my cock was buried, plunging in and out, drawing those soft guttural moans from her. That erotic sound painted the perfect picture of a woman lying naked atop tangled sheets in my bed, her hair fanning across the pillow, her skin flushed and nipples pebbled, legs wantonly spread, pussy lips glistening with both her arousal and my cum as it seeped from her slick slit. That cock-stirring moan was an expression one associated with pure, unadulterated pleasure…

"It's a damn good thing I'm not an insecure man or we'd have a problem."

The statement snapped me out of my thoughts, turning my attention to where Jaxson sat. The direction of his gaze assured me he wasn't even aware that my cock had begun to stiffen at the visions in my head. He only had eyes for the woman he adored. His grin belied his words and spoke of his pleasure in seeing Emma enjoying her dessert.

She looked far less harried than the last time I'd seen her. In fact, the word angelic sprang to mind. Her eyes were closed but I didn't believe it was because she was craving sleep as all new mothers tended to do. The soft curve of her lips told the truth without the need of words… if you didn't count another one of those haunting moans as speech, that is. It was clear that she was in her own world, closing her eyes to simply block out anything that might detract from the enjoyment of the rich bite of chocolate she'd just spooned into her mouth.

I'd heard that mothers had some sort of innate radar that alerted them when their children were threatened, but I'd never actually witnessed that skill being used until now, though it had nothing to do with babies. Her eyes flew open, the violet color flashing as she lifted her spoon in a move to block that of Chase's as he attempted to dip his into her dish.

"Mine!" she snapped, pulling the bowl closer.

"Whoa, she's quick," I said. "Who knew she has the reflexes of a ninja."

"And the skills of a master swordsman when it comes to chocolate," Jaxson quipped, sitting back in his chair, amusement on his face as he watched the two people he loved more than anything… well, except for the two new little ones the trio had added to their family. Andrew and his twin sister Alicia were actually the reason I was here.

· · ·

I'D BEEN AT BLACK LIGHT A FEW NIGHTS AGO AND HAD SEEN JAXSON. THE man who'd made a fortune modeling looked a bit unkempt. The man who, with Chase and Emma, had opened not one but two highly successful clubs, looked like he was about to keel over. It had only taken a few minutes of conversation to learn how much two tiny little human beings could totally disrupt the lives of their adult mommy and daddies.

"Don't get me wrong," Jaxson had assured me, "I'd not change a thing, but well, I had no concept of how much energy babies have. I thought all they did was eat, sleep and look cute. And speaking of sleep, why is it that the very instant you close your eyes, theirs fly open? I swear some days we're not too sure which way is up."

"That's great," I said, pausing to hold out my hands, palms out to ward off the explosion I felt coming at the disbelief I saw in his expression. "I don't mean that your lives are scrambled, but I've been wondering what on earth to get people who I'm sure have every baby doodad known to mankind already. For my gift, I'd love to come over and make you dinner one—"

"You don't need to give us"—Jaxson paused midsentence to give me a long look—"wait... did you say dinner? As in real food? That doesn't come out of a take-out container? Like something that is actually fresh and hot?"

Shaking my head, I shuddered. "It's actually pretty horrifying to even consider why you have to ask me that, but, yes."

"Oh, the take out is fairly recent. Avery has been going above and beyond duty coming over to cook for us occasionally. As much as we appreciate it, I made her stop. She has enough on her plate without feeding us too." He paused and shook his head. "What am I saying? It's not like you aren't busy as shit as well. Still—"

"Don't worry about me," I said, brushing his concern aside. "It's not work when cooking for a friend." When he still looked uncertain, I shrugged. "Well, if you'd rather eat another sorry excuse for a hamburger out of some cardboard carton instead of real food served on actual china and crystal, I suppose I can get you a box of diapers. Then you can explain to Emma how instead of a five course meal—"

"No, no! I'm not about to look a gift horse in the mouth!" he protested. "So, um, what are you thinking of serving?"

I grinned and knew I had him hooked. "Let's see, I think we'll begin with

Gillardeau oysters. They are an extremely select variety from France. I'll serve them with creme fraiche, Beluga caviar and, for a bit of flair, dust them with gold flecks. The second course will be a black truffle sabayon. Truffles are rich and usually accompany an entrée, but I like to pair them in a sabayon and serve them as an appetizer." The look on Jaxson's face had me remembering why cooking was my passion. Just building the menu in my head and describing it had my dinner guest practically drooling. *"After cleansing your pallet with a light but lovely salad of prosciutto with persimmon, pomegranate and arugula, your entrée will be one that is truly in celebration of your twins' birth. Balmoral venison is from the Queen of England's estate and is not served in any restaurant. I'll prepare the roasted loin with boiled pink fir potatoes and sautéed girolles. How does that sound?"*

"That's four."

"Four? Four what?" I asked, his answer not the one of delight I'd expected.

"You said five courses. That's only four."

I chuckled. *"Don't worry, there will be five. No meal is complete without dessert. Do I need to compensate for any food allergies one of you may have?"*

"No, and I don't think any of us really dislike—"

"I assure you, there will be nothing about this meal that you won't like," I said without even a modicum of doubt.

"Everything sounds unbelievably good," he said. *"Hell, just listening to you describe them makes me feel weak in the knees. What are you thinking about for dessert?"*

"I believe I'll keep that a surprise," I said with a grin. *"Consider it a reminder that you not only own the best BDSM club on two coasts, but that you are a Dom. As a fellow Dom, it is my duty to assure you have the energy required to not only keep your partners happy, but take care of those little babies as well."*

"Hell, slap a bowl of ice-cream down in front of me and I'll be thrilled," he said.

"Fuck," I said, shaking my head. *"I had no idea you were this far gone. I promise, dessert will be far more refined than a bowl of ice cream. It will be like waiting for your lovers... knowing they have so much to offer and yet the anticipation of their submission is almost as pleasurable as the actual surrender."*

"When?"

I had to chuckle and we'd agreed on a night.

N<small>OW</small>, <small>GIVING THE THREE A CLOSER LOOK</small>, I <small>WAS GLAD</small> I'<small>D OFFERED</small>. I was sure they had to have an entire nursery full of gifts from their many friends, but let's be real. I couldn't believe that even the cutest matching onesies could compete with the five-course dinner I'd just prepared.

"That was hands-down the best meal I've ever eaten," Chase said, finally setting his spoon down, accepting the fact that he'd lost the battle. "And, believe me, I've eaten in some of the fanciest restaurants around the world."

"It was incredible," Emma agreed, giving her empty bowl a look of longing before releasing her hold. "I'm not as experienced as these two, but that dessert... I'd walk barefoot over hot coals, join that polar bear club where they jump naked in water full of ice, even go through labor without so much as a single peep—"

"Watch it, babe. You know what happens when you lie," Jaxson warned, reaching over to slip his hand behind her head and pulling her toward him to plant a kiss on her lips.

The moan became a muffled squeal when his free hand dropped to give her buttock a squeeze. "Well, even if it earned me a spanking, another bowl of that would be so worth it," Emma said when he released her. Turning to me, she smiled. "What exactly was in that soufflé? I've never tasted chocolate anywhere near that decadent. I don't suppose you can just pick up a few bars at the corner store?"

"Hardly. To'ak chocolate is a bit out of the price range most people would feel comfortable paying," I said.

Jaxson shook his head. "What he means is that it's the most expensive chocolate in the world."

"Oh, Ronan, you shouldn't have," Emma protested.

"I definitely should," I countered. "It's not often I have the honor of cooking not only for a lovely new mother of two, but for people I truly admire," I said, brushing aside her protest, not about to add that

I'd paired the chocolate with Armand de Brignae Brut Gold champagne which is also extremely expensive, not wanting to lessen her enjoyment of the soufflé.

"You truly outdid yourself," Jaxson said. "We can't thank you enough."

"It was my pleasure," I assured him. "My staff are finishing up in the kitchen and we'll get out of your hair. And, Emma, if you just happen to get a craving, send one of your men down to look in the refrigerator. They might find a few leftovers if you need a little snack later."

I just managed not to stagger back a step when she jumped up and threw herself into my arms. "You, sir, are worth your weight in gold," she said.

"Anything for you," I said, extremely pleased she'd enjoyed herself.

"Really? In that case, and at the risk of sounding awfully greedy, will you do us one more teensy little favor?"

"Of course," I assured her. Seeing her entire face light up, I could understand how she'd captured the hearts of not one but two men.

"Let us sell you."

"What? Sell me?"

She giggled, turning to look at her two lovers. "Every year on Valentine's Day, we have a party at Black Light. This year will be the first one out here on the coast and we want to do something a little different. We're going to have an online auction. Celebrities volunteer to be auctioned off. Whoever wins the bid gets to spend three hours doing all sorts of deliciously naughty things with their celebrity of choice."

Arching my brow, I looked from her upturned face to see Jaxson and Chase both give a nod... affirming her story. "As much as I'd love to oblige you, I don't see how it's possible. The new season is about to start so between taping my show and running Savor, I don't have a lot of spare time. Not to mention that Valentine's Day is a pretty busy night for the restaurant business and I'm not sure I—"

"What's being the boss good for if you can't take time for yourself. You've got an entire staff to handle the restaurant," she said, waving her hand in the air to cut me off. "I mean there has to be a half dozen people here helping you tonight. Besides, the money raised is going to charity. You do want to help your community don't you?"

I shook my head even as Jaxson chuckled. "I'd tell her not to hassle you, but she's right. The money you'll raise will go for a good cause."

"And, the past two years have taught us that a lot can happen in those three little hours," Chase added with a grin.

"I'm not sure who'd want to bid on me," I said. "How about I just donate—"

"Oh no," Emma said. "You're hot… and I'm not only talking about being an incredible chef! I know you'll get tons and tons of bids. I promise that—"

I witnessed that radar in action again as she abruptly stopped speaking, her head canting to the side as if hearing something inaudible to the rest of us.

"That's Alicia. I'd better hurry before she wakes Drew," she said, already moving away. Before she ducked around a corner, she turned back. "Thank you so much, Ronan. The only way tonight could be any more perfect would be for you to say you'll put yourself up for auction. Besides, it would make me feel a lot less guilty for stuffing myself full of all that expensive chocolate if I knew that some other lucky lady will get to experience your… *gifts*." This last was said with a soft giggle and a wave of her fingers.

Before I could answer, she was gone.

"And there's our little man," Chase said, standing from his seat to follow as a soft cry wafted into the room. "Thanks, Ronan. Best thing I've ever put in my mouth," he said and when Jaxson slapped his ass, Chase yipped. "Beside my lovers, of course!" I shook his hand and he soon disappeared.

Jaxson stood as well, looking after the two. "To be clear, by *gifts*, she doesn't mean cooking."

"Yeah, I sort of figured," I said.

"But she's right. We would love to have you. As a member, you can always just attend, but in order to play that night, you'll need to be an actual participant. And judging by the way just a moan had your cock

403

stiffening…" He grinned and I just shook my head knowing he wasn't the least bit concerned about Emma straying.

After a moment, he quickly ran through what the night would entail and just the possibilities had me intrigued. Three hours spent with a total stranger, no strings attached… it could be fun. Besides, while Valentine's Day was extremely popular for couples to dine out, as evidenced by the fact that every table at my restaurant had been reserved well in advance, I did have an extremely competent staff more than capable of taking care of the diners.

"Tell Emma I'll do it," I said.

Jaxson nodded, grinned and held out his hand. As I shook it, he said, "I will. Don't forget to go online and fill out the forms. Who knows? You might find someone who makes you as happy as Emma makes me and Chase."

"I highly doubt that," I said, releasing his hand. "You three are the poster children for happiness. And speaking of children, I'll let you get to yours. Congratulations again."

When he left, I returned to the kitchen and within a half-hour, my staff had everything cleaned up and packed away, taking the van with the supplies back to the restaurant. I climbed onto my motorcycle and pulled away, glancing toward the house where the club was housed. I still wasn't sure who exactly participated in these sort of auctions, or about letting some random drop of a ball on a wheel dictate my choice of activity, but what the hell. Some of the best recipes ever created had come from being willing to mix things up a bit.

CHAPTER 2

 *arnegie*

Her hair flew about her like the venomous vipers on Medusa's head come to life, strands slithering over breasts that swayed from side to side, bouncing about as she energetically squeezed his hairy testicles in one hand while bouncing up and down as if riding Dick's dick was some sort of Olympic sport and she was determined to win the gold...

What the hell. *Dick's dick? Snakes? And what's with all the bouncing for fuck's sake?* Not only was that probably the most God-awful line I'd ever written, it was actually causing my ears to ring. Oh wait... the ringing was my phone.

"Saved by the bell," I muttered, jumping up to grab my phone off the bar. "Thank God you called," I said, as I pulled open the door to the refrigerator and bent down to grab a Coke. "The world owes you big time."

"Huh?"

Smiling, I tucked my phone against my shoulder and grabbed a glass from the cabinet. Popping the tab, I continued to talk as I poured my drink. "You've saved millions of people from having to read what has to be the worst opening to a sex scene ever written. I mean, seriously? Who names a character Dick and then talks about his dick and hairy testicles? Crazy right?" Pausing, I took a sip of Coke.

"Or you could consider the fact that it literally grabs a reader by the balls and won't let go." Hearing the voice, I suddenly realized that not only wasn't I talking to Kara, my best friend, but I had absolutely no idea who was on the other end of this conversation. I felt my cheeks flame as heat rushed into them, pulling my phone away to stare at the screen. Sure enough, the number meant nothing to me.

"Um, should I apologize or just hang up and we can pretend this conversation never happened?" I offered.

A soft laugh reassured me that whoever it was didn't think I belonged in a loony bin. "No, please, don't hang up and you don't need to apologize. You really do have me intrigued," she said. "Though it does make my news a little harder to deliver."

Not knowing whether to feel complimented or worried, I sank down onto the couch, pulling a fluffy pillow to me. I'd always found it easier to handle things with something to hang onto.

"What news? Who is this?"

"I'm sorry. This is Madison Taylor. I'm the manager at Runway but am also the MC for our Valentine's party at Black Light?"

"Oh, right," I said, relaxing a bit and then sitting up straighter as the reason for her calling became clear. However, remembering her earlier words, I sank back down, hugging the throw pillow a bit tighter. "I'm guessing by hard, you aren't calling to inform me that I won the auction?"

"No, I'm sorry, but I'm afraid not."

"Damn. I know I should think of it not as losing, but as saving twenty grand, right?" I offered, then corrected myself. "Make that $21,002. But just between you and me, I was really hoping those measly extra two dollars would seal the deal." She laughed and I couldn't help but laugh with her. "Silly, huh?"

"No, not at all. Like it just shows that you are very creative. And since the bid below yours was $21,000, your two dollars assured you would be our runner-up for Chef Bellington."

"Runner-up. What does that mean?"

"It means that we really want you to come and be our guest for that evening. If for any reason the winning bidder is unable to attend or chooses not to participate, you would have the opportunity to do so," Madison explained. I remembered reading something about that in the papers I'd filled out, but hadn't truly given it much thought. I'd been so sure I'd be the winning bidder. Still, it did offer a sliver of hope that though I might not have crossed the finish line first, I wasn't yet out of the race.

"I'm not one to wish another ill—"

Madison laughed again. "Of course not, but I can't say that I blame you. We have a lot of great celebrities, but this one—"

"Is exactly like the name of his restaurant. He's someone to definitely savor," I supplied. I could have regaled her with far more tidbits of information I'd garnered about Ronan Bellington, but... well, even I had some pride. It was one thing to be a foodie. A lot of people enthused about delicious food and the people who prepared it. But this chef? My adoration went deeper than gratitude over how he combined ingredients. From the moment I'd seen him, resplendent in his pristine white chef's coat, all I'd thought about was how he'd look out of it. I had spent many an hour dreaming not about the dishes he created, but how he looked when preparing them in the nude... and how he'd offer me bites from the tines of his fork... when all I really wanted was to take a long lick from his lips down the broad expanse of his chest, over the planes of his rock hard abs and circle the head of his cock, slipping the tip of my tongue into the slit to savor the taste of his...

"Hello? Like... are you still there?"

Good grief, there was something seriously wrong with me. Shaking my head to clear it, I pulled my mind out of the gutter, gulping a mouthful of ice-cold Coke before trusting myself to respond. "Sorry, just thinking. And don't worry. Even if I didn't win, I will come. I'll consider it as research... you know, to fix that God-awful sentence I wrote?"

"So you weren't kidding? You really are an author? That's so fantastic!"

"Well, let's just say I've yet to quit my day job," I said. "Hopefully some day I'll be able to dedicate more than a couple of hours a night to writing. And, of course, rewriting."

"I promise to look you up. Like, I really am interested in learning more about Dick's dick," Madison said. After we both laughed, she turned serious. "One more thing. Runner up or not, you still need to let me know if there is anything you want to change as far as your hard limits go. Once the game begins, your fate will be left to chance."

When filling out the many forms required to bid, this one had taken the most time to complete. I'd actually been a bit shocked at how many activities were listed, including some I had to research. Watching a YouTube video to discover exactly what was the purpose of a *vacuum table* had left me shuddering and quickly checking off not only that box but the ones for *cupping, latex* and *breath play*. While the thought of having my wrists and ankles bound during a scene had my pulse quickening, the idea of being entirely cased in latex, lying on some table where all the air is sucked out making it hard to breathe and impossible to move had my heart hammering in terror. I'd thought the club was generous in allowing each participant five hard limits but with four already gone, I had to give a great deal of thought to my last one. I vacillated between *Sybian orgasm torture* or participating in *ABDL*. Which would I prefer if the ball landed in that slot? Being forced to orgasm multiple times or being forced to wear and perhaps actually required to use a diaper? Right—orgasm won hands down.

Marking off my last box, I hoped I'd made the right choices. I couldn't help but wonder what five my celebrity would choose. Even if his were different than mine and ten activities were removed, a wide variety of things for the roulette ball to land on still remained. I couldn't visualize how a single roulette wheel could hold all the choices. Now though it didn't matter, as I'd not actually won my bid.

The only participating in any of those activities I'd be doing would be to include them in some scene in one of my books. Biting back my disappointment, I kept my voice light and said, "Thanks, but I'm good."

"See you soon then, and thanks again for being so understanding," Madison said. "It will be a fun night regardless."

"Thanks for calling," I said, pushing the end call button a moment later. I sighed deeply, allowing myself a moment of pity and then shook it off. It wasn't the news I'd wanted to hear, but I wasn't one to wallow.

Life was too short, and now that I thought about it, this was actually a far better outcome. I'd get a free night to observe various couples in all sorts of delicious scenes. Ignoring the part of me that was complaining that I should be *in* those naughty little scenes instead of just writing about them, I finished the last of my Coke, set down my glass and picked up my laptop. Repeated tapping on the delete key vanquished Dick's dick into the void and, instead of bouncing about like some deranged version of the Energizer bunny, I had my heroine learning that the man of her dreams was kidnapped by some crazy woman. I might be magnanimous in real life but artistic license and an endless stream of videos on all sorts of kinky things allowed me to plot some truly evil way to assure the woman who dared outbid me suffered greatly. You gotta love fiction... right?

CHAPTER 3

 *arnegie*

I COULDN'T HELP BUT SHIVER A BIT THE MOMENT I DROVE BETWEEN THE
high, wrought-iron gates. Intellectually I knew I was just a few blocks
off Rodeo Drive, but emotionally… the moment my car turned and I
began to pass between the towering trees overhanging the drive,
every ounce of my being was transported to what seemed like a totally
different dimension. Coming to an intersection, I glanced at my notes
and took the turn to the left. Coming around the bend, I pulled up in
front of a man who waved at me to stop.

"Good evening," he said after I rolled my window down. "Your
name, please."

"Carnegie Bishop," I said, passing him the paper showing I was one
of the bidders for the event.

He smiled, scanned the document and then tapped some keys on
the iPad he was holding. "Welcome to Black Light, Ms. Bishop. If
you'll just park over there and follow the walkway, another guard will
direct you to the entrance of the club."

"The path isn't made of yellow bricks is it?" I asked, unable to resist the reference to another walkway that led to a land where wishes thought to be impossible had been granted.

Grinning, he handed me my papers back and shook his head. "Sorry, just red brick."

"Thank you," I said, giving him a wave as I pulled forward. From the number of cars I had to pass to find a spot, either this parking lot was far smaller than the one I normally used when coming to Runway, or this party was going to be very well-attended.

I parked and checked my reflection in the mirror on the visor, observing other partygoers already heading back toward the edge of the lot. I also noticed that my car looked a bit out of place as I'd parked between a silver Porsche 911 Turbo S Cabriolet and a low slung silver Jaguar convertible. At least it would be easy to spot my little red Honda when the night was over. Taking a moment to kick out of my slippers I always wore when driving, I slid my heels on. I finally climbed from my car and giggled as I automatically locked it. A thief would have to be a complete idiot to choose my vehicle over the plethora of luxury automobiles surrounding me. Smoothing my hand down my skirt, I was glad I'd decided that while I was far more comfortable in sneakers or even the heels I wore when working, tonight I'd wanted something a bit more... daring.

In honor of the day, I'd used part of my last royalty check and splurged on a pair of Louboutin's *Pigalle Follies*. The salesperson had assured me that the slim stiletto heels with their open toe had a low curved vamp that would make my legs appear longer. Personally, I didn't really care how all that was supposed to work. All I knew was that the second I put on the iconic red-soled shoes, the multiple colors of the glittered leather sparkled with every step I took. They were the only accessory I'd chosen to wear.

My mother used to throw out nonsensical verses to keep our spirits high when times were bad, but the only one I could think of now, that I felt even loosely fit, was that I'd done the best I could to gird my loins. Though, granted, the advice was thousands of years old and referred to lifting one's long robes to avoid being hindered by

411

them in battle, but... well, it was either that or 'don't let them see you sweat'. And what woman wanted to give sweating even a moment's thought. Not me. Nope, I was going with the whole loins thing... girded or not. Besides, even though my bid hadn't won, and Ronan wouldn't be given an opportunity to enjoy my ensemble, I didn't regret a single penny spent. Losing didn't mean I had to look like a loser.

I managed not to break an ankle as I crossed the lot and followed a few others through an opening in some lush, tall shrubs. The pathway was well lit, meandering through gardens that I was sure would be absolutely stunning in the spring. The bricks led slightly uphill, twisting and turning until the vista opened a little, revealing another guard.

"Welcome to Black Light," he said once I reached him. "Enjoy your evening," he added as he opened a door that could have led to nothing more exciting than a mudroom but I instinctively knew led to somewhere far better. After thanking him, I walked down the long hallway, my heels clicking against the floor, my head swiveling to take in everything I saw. Reaching yet another guard, my papers were checked against a list, I was welcomed once again and directed to one of the lockers off to the side and told to leave my purse, phone, and anything electronic inside. Those instructions were ones I'd been prepared for when I'd learned of the club I'd never known existed beneath Runway, the very popular, far more conventional club that was housed in the magnificent mansion.

The woman who'd shared the secret of the club's existence as well as the upcoming auction, had vouched for me when I applied to be allowed to bid. I'd never planned on being solo when I first visited Black Light, but they say that life was what happened while you were busy making plans. I'd make the best of it, spending a few hours observing. No, not observing... researching, I reminded myself. Maybe I'd take the money I'd saved by not winning and invest in one of those Sybian machines. Could that be considered a business expense? Just the thought of asking my straight-laced accountant had me smiling.

Once I closed the door, there was nothing left but to nod as a final employee instructed me to the theater where the auction would take place, kicking off an evening that I was both anxious and a bit sad about. Anxious in that I could already feel my heart rate picking up and my blood rushing through my veins. Sad in that I knew that no one who wasn't an actual participant would be playing tonight. Reminding myself that I was here to take notes to include in stories where I could make anyone a star... or kill them off with impunity, I went to find a spot where I had a good view.

Stepping into the theater, I was glad I'd arrived a bit early. Though chairs placed around the wall showed they'd obviously brought in extra seating to accommodate their guests, seats were filling fast. Murmuring, "Excuse me, oops, sorry, and pardon me," I finally made it to an empty seat without impaling anyone's toes with the heels of my stilettos. Sinking into the soft, buttery leather, I looked toward the stage that had been set up, but no one had yet made an appearance. According to the paperwork I'd been given, I knew that the celebrities would come in and gather to the left of the stage, and that Madison would be MCing the event, but so far, the only thing on the platform was a table holding what had to be the roulette wheel.

"Isn't this exciting?"

Turning, I saw a woman who instantly reminded me of my overactive character. While she wasn't riding a cock, she was definitely bouncing up and down in her seat.

"It is," I agreed with a smile.

"Of course, it would be more exciting if the celebs were here. I can't wait to see who the lucky bidders are," she said. "Oh, I'm Julie. Please tell me you are one of the bidders!"

"Carnegie, and I'm afraid not," I said.

"Me either," she said, her enthusiasm deflating slightly for the briefest moment before she bounced again. "Still, maybe it's even better. This way instead of only seeing one celebrity, we can see them all." Looking around furtively, she leaned toward me and lowered her tone. "And I want to really *see* them if you know what I mean."

Nodding, I could feel my cheeks flush. Though I knew that the chances of being observed were high seeing as the rules required the observation windows of all rooms be kept active tonight, I wasn't really sure what that entailed and really hadn't considered exactly what that meant until now. What would it be like to know that people were watching? Were seeing everything as a submissive followed the instructions given by his or her Dom or Domme? Could I honestly not only take off my clothes but truly get into a scene knowing I had an audience?

And you're just now thinking about that? Good thing you didn't win!

"Shut up," I hissed.

"Excuse me?"

Realizing I must have spoken out loud, I shook my head. "Sorry, just thinking." I didn't elaborate that just the thought of him unzipping my dress to slide it down, of his fingers reaching to unhook my bra, his eyes locked on mine as he lowered the straps to bare my breasts had my panties dampening and…

"Oh look, they're starting to line up!"

Her exclamation burst my fantasy bubble and I looked to watch a group of people stride toward the stage. I recognized both actors and actresses. I saw producers made famous by their skills in creating blockbusters, nodding to people in the audience. Singers and million-dollar star athletes had also volunteered to be part of tonight's event, but I only had eyes for one. The moment my eyes found him, they locked, refusing to look anywhere but at the man who graced the television screens of many home cooks, encouraging them that they too could produce a meal fit for royalty. God, he was even better looking tonight.

At four inches over six feet, he towered over those celebrities next to him. His black hair had silver strands at his temples that had my fingers itching to run through them. His eyes were startling… the blue so intense the color looked fake. And his body? Let's just say that while I might be hesitant about removing my clothing, there is no way I'd have been able to resist begging to be allowed to remove his. To see what lay beneath. To taste, to touch. To stroke flesh I knew had to be hard… Whoa! Girded my ass. Just the thought of what I was sure would be velvet covered steel had me pressing my thighs tightly together in a vain attempt to stop the flow of my arousal from soaking my panties as I bit back a moan.

"I know," my enthusiastic new friend said. "I feel the same way. Isn't she amazing?"

Not sure how I managed not to gouge her eyes out for even looking at my chef, it took me a moment to assimilate the gender of the pronoun she'd used. "Who?"

"Heather. She's the one on the end. Isn't she just too cute!"

Swiveling my head, I followed her finger where she was pointing at the very last person in line. I didn't immediately recognize her, but as long as it wasn't Ronan she was ogling, we were good to go and I could be generous. "She's very pretty."

"Oh, she is and not only on the outside. I'm not surprised she volunteered to be auctioned. I've read that she does a lot for charity. She not only opens her ranch up, she actually works with disabled children," she said. "I wonder how much she went for."

"I don't know if... ow!"

"Sorry, these aisles are too fucking narrow," a man said as he lifted his shoe off my toes.

"That's okay," I said, standing to allow him more room to squeeze by. After he'd passed, I turned to the side, lifted my foot and bent down to assure that his sole hadn't left some mark on my new shoes. Brushing my fingertips over the shimmering leather, I was glad to see that no real harm had been done... well, if you didn't count the fact that my toes were throbbing a bit.

"Are you all right?" At my nod, she picked up the conversation. "If what?"

"What?"

"You know, you were saying if what?"

"If what what?"

She stared up at me and then asked, "Who's on First?" before breaking into giggles. Her laugh was infectious and soon had me joining her as I had to admit we did sound like a bad rendition of the famous comic routine. After a few moments, she said, "I mean, you were saying you didn't know if and then that big oaf smashed your toes."

"Oh, right," I said, turning to drop down into my chair again. "You were wondering how much your idol went for, and I was saying I don't think we'll ever know."

"Yeah, I'm sure Heather went for a fortune, but she's worth every penny."

Even as I listened while she waxed eloquently about all the good deeds her celebrity was credited in doing, I realized I didn't want *nice*. I wanted hot with a dash of danger and a sprinkle of naughtiness. Nice was for people who were satisfied with a grilled cheese and tomato soup combo. Not that there was anything wrong with the comfort food, but for once in my life I wanted to indulge in something far more decadent... far more spicy... far more... well, I wanted to have an experience that truly lived up to the name of *doing the nasty*. With that admission, I squirmed in my seat and slid my attention back to the man I had been so sure would be the one to give me exactly what I wanted. Just seeing him staring at me had my nipples puckering, my body quivering and... Oh fuck! He was staring at me! Every inch of my skin flushed, and I watched as the corner of his mouth ticked up. Sinking down a bit in my seat, I knew not only was I turning as red as the soles of my shoes, I was positive he knew exactly what I'd been thinking.

CHAPTER 4

onan

If not for the fact that I wasn't a quitter, I'd have found some excuse to pull out of this whole auction fiasco. Anyone on television, movies, theater or hell any of the arts or sports knew that being put on the spot out in the public eye was always a possibility. But assuring someone that their world wasn't going to implode just because the crust on their Beef Wellington wasn't the perfect shade of golden brown or the beef inside had gone slightly past rare was nothing compared to this. Standing here, I couldn't help but wonder if this was how a lobster felt in the tank... waiting, wondering which one of the dozens of people in the room would be the one to buy him.

Jesus... I'd actually allowed Emma to sell me. I was a fucking Dom and yet the simple batting of a pair of beautiful violet eyes and a sweet smile was all it had taken to have me submit. Then again, I couldn't say I was in bad company. I was walking behind a pro baseball player and had already spoken to a very attractive little singer who was burning her way up the charts. And I wasn't exactly the type to worry

417

about what might happen. I was more the type to make something happen. Looking out across the room, I scanned the crowd and when a soft cry rose above the murmuring of a hundred different conversations, I immediately tried to find the source. Movement drew my eye to see a large man passing along the fourth row. With his passage, I saw her. It wasn't that she was standing while everyone around her was seated that had my focus zeroing in on her, it was something tugging at my memory.

I was sure I didn't know her, and yet I was certain I'd seen her before... and not here at Black Light. Make that absolutely positive I'd not seen her in the club before. If I had... well, I'd not only already know her name, I'd know what every inch of that incredible body looked like beneath that little black dress she was wearing. I watched as she bent over and felt my cock twitch at the view of the fabric of her dress molding tighter to the most perfect heart-shaped ass I'd ever seen. What on earth was she doing? She didn't bend over far enough to pick up something she might have dropped on the floor and yet she remained in a half bent position long enough for my cock to lengthen further. Before I could decide what it was that held her bent over, she straightened and began to laugh. It was a sound that had me smiling as well as wondering how the tone would change if she were begging to be allowed to come or pleading for mercy as I striped that ass with my belt.

I watched as she conversed with the woman next to her, unable to hear their conversation but grinned when I realized that she was doing her best to disguise the fact that she was squirming. I would bet my paycheck that she was thinking about something dirty, something a bit wicked... and as much as I loved the culinary arts, I loved a girl who enjoyed being a little naughty even more. When her head lifted and the light fell on her face, I smiled as our eyes met and hers widened. Lips that I instantly imagined stretched around my cock pursed into a perfect little circle, and her cheeks flushed as she slunk down in her chair a bit. If that wasn't the perfect picture of a naughty girl, I didn't know what was.

It took the sound of a commotion to snap my attention to the side.

I could see staff members hurrying to assist a woman who was sprawled on the ground. She'd evidently taken a fall. After what quickly turned into a shouting match, it was clear that her fall hadn't been an accident. Evidently, she'd been the successful winning bidder and someone wasn't happy. Declaring her innocence of purposefully tripping the woman might have been a bit more credible if one of the staff hadn't knelt and pulled an umbrella out from beneath a row of seats. And not just any umbrella. This was one used by golfers to cover both themselves and their bags from rain... meaning it was extra long.

The baseball player standing near me took an interest in the hubbub, excusing his way through the crowd until he reached Madison Taylor. I was too far away to hear what they were saying, but he nodded and moved past her to approach the woman who'd won him. When Tonya Harding's doppelganger was escorted from the theater, it was clear the crisis was over.

While people settled, I turned my gaze back to the fourth row. I was surprised to see that she was standing again, her hand on the back of the chair in front of her. Was she about to bolt? God, I hoped not. Even though the chances of her not only being a bidder but had bid on me were slim, I was determined to at least get her name. This stupid auction might keep us apart for the three hours the game would play out, but that didn't mean we couldn't hook up after eleven. I was glad when the woman next to her took her arm and whatever she said, had her friend turning back. I gave her an encouraging grin when she snuck a look at me before flushing again and returning to her seat. As if my gaze was strong enough to assure that cute little ass remained in her chair, I didn't take my eyes off her as speeches and rules were discussed and the wheel began to spin.

It took a burst of laughter from the audience to draw my attention away from the fourth row to realize the group around me had noticeably thinned. Looking up, I saw Madison looking over at me.

"Well, praise the Lord. I thought you'd gone deaf," she said, shaking her head as the crowd chuckled. "I'll repeat, I'd like to ask our celebrity chef, Ronan Bellington, to join me."

I couldn't care less that the crowd found my attention deficit to be funny. I was far too busy trying to remember where I'd seen her before. And when I watched her flush and an expression of sadness wash across her face at my name being called, I had the ridiculous feeling that I was somehow cheating on her.

Fuck. Where the hell had that come from? Since when did I ever give a moment's thought to anything as archaic as monogamy? I'd enjoyed too many women to count, each one special… for a couple of hours or even the occasional few days we'd share. I was almost forty and had yet to feel even a modicum of guilt in moving from one woman to another. But now as I went to stand by Madison's side and saw the wheel, I again wondered how I could pull out of this whole thing. Perhaps offering to match the winning bid…

"Ronan, it is my pleasure to announce that your lucky winner with a bid of $23,000 is Andrea Carpenter," Madison said, looking away from me out into the crowd. "Andrea if you'd come join us—"

"Over my dead body! You take one more step, young lady, and I swear you won't be sitting for a month." A voice that was decidedly not a female's rang out even as a woman in the front row froze mid-step. The crowd chuckled again, the sound breaking her free from her momentary paralysis. Turning, she watched as a man stormed up the aisle from the back of the theater.

"Steven? What are you doing here?"

"What does it look like? I'm here to take you home."

"But I won him," she said, turning to gesture toward me. "I paid over twenty thousand dollars…"

"I don't care if you paid a million. There is no way in hell I'm going to let another man touch what's mine," Steven growled and I saw heads nodding and listened to murmurs of agreement move through the crowd. Dominants were known to be a bit possessive… not all Doms, of course, as I wasn't, but well… most Doms were.

Andrea appeared unsure whether to be flattered or insulted. Her mouth opened and closed several times before she planted her hands on her hips and finally said, "What happened to our agreement that we each get a hall-pass? You know I said I'd look the other way if you

420

and that model, Gigi Hadid, wanted to… well, you know and you said I could—"

"Again, I don't give a rat's ass what I said then," he thundered as he finally reached her. The room didn't seem to take a breath as he moved to stroke a finger down her cheek. "What's important is what I'm saying right now. You've got to choose. Three hours with some man who might be able to make you the fanciest cake in the world but doesn't know that your favorite is a simple white cake with strawberry icing. He doesn't know that your favorite color is green or that you are allergic to cats but are willing to take shots just so you can adopt a kitten. And I can damn sure promise you that he doesn't know that you make these little squeaks when you are about to come apart in my arms… So, what's it going to be, Andrea? Him or me?"

"You," she said without a moment's hesitation.

"Right answer," he said, causing her to treat us all to a high pitched squeal when he instantly stepped forward, picked her up off her feet and tossed her over his shoulder.

"Wait!" she said, planting her hands against his back and arching up. "What about the chef? I was going to ask for some cooking tips."

"For fuck's sake, Andie, he's in a sex auction, not a contestant on *Iron Chef!*" The crowd laughed.

"What a waste of money. I should have spent it on your cookbooks."

"Don't worry, Andrea," Madison said. "I'll be in touch about returning your winning bid."

"Don't bother," Steven said. "Give the money to charity." A single swat silenced Andrea's protest at the loss. "Consider it my fee for being stupid enough to fall for that hall pass shit."

The crowd laughed again, all eyes but mine watching as he pushed through the door at the back of the room. Make that mine and the woman in the fourth row. Like me she wasn't watching the couple leave. But unlike me, though she was staring up at the stage, she wasn't looking at me. Instead, it seemed she was staring at Madison with eyes as wide as saucers.

"Like, no one can ever say these events are boring, right?" Madison said, drawing the attention back to the stage. "Shall we continue? Congratulations, Carnegie. As the runner-up, would you please join us on the stage?"

It took me a moment to realize that Madison was speaking to the woman who'd captured my attention from the moment I'd seen her. *Carnegie...* an unusual name for an unusually captivating woman. I couldn't wait to discover how she'd come by the unique name. Hell, I couldn't wait to discover a great deal about the woman. I was especially eager to learn what naughty thoughts had her squirming in her seat. Yet... something was wrong. Not only hadn't Carnegie taken a single step, the pretty flush had disappeared, she looked far more shell-shocked than thrilled at the news, and was shaking her head.

I didn't have an inflated ego, but still, enough was enough. Stepping forward, I shook my own head. "Carnegie, not only did Andrea bid on me but then kick me to the curb, but now you don't want me either? Are you telling me that no one wants to play with me?"

Several hands began waving wildly in the crowd and cries of "I'll play," "Pick me," "Hell, we'll share," rang out as women began to stand and assure me that I wasn't totally undesirable. It was flattering but it wasn't what I wanted... nor whom I wanted. But it seemed to do the job as Carnegie's head swiveled to take in the women who'd jumped to their feet.

"No!" she said, the single word drowning out the other voices. "He's mine!"

The Dom in me wanted to assure her that line belonged to the alpha, and yet I had to admit it made me feel good to hear it so emphatically stated. I grinned as women began to drop into their chairs, the only one applauding her choice the one she'd been speaking with, jumping up to give Carnegie a hug before shooing her along. Striding forward, I offered her my hand when she reached the stage. She was a tiny thing, her hand disappearing in mine as I helped her up the steps.

"Thank you for not leaving me stranded," I said, lifting her hand to tuck it into the crook of my elbow before guiding her toward center stage. Accepting the white ball from Madison, I dropped it into Carnegie's free hand, closing her fingers around it and led her the final few steps until we stood beside the large roulette wheel.

Madison began its spinning and as I looked down, I saw that Carnegie wasn't watching the wheel's rotation, but was looking up at me, giving me my first glance at eyes the color of emeralds and gold swirled together. It appeared everything about this woman was unique. But it was her smile that had my cock jerking.

"Shall we play?"

"Absolutely," she said, opening her hand and dropping the ball. Funny how neither one of us looked to see where it would land.

CHAPTER 5

arnegie

"AND IT LOOKS LIKE *MEDICAL PLAY* IS OUR WINNER. UNLESS, OF COURSE, either one of you marked it as a hard limit?"

I noticed the right corner of his lip would quirk for just a moment before his entire mouth followed into the sexiest smile I'd ever seen. And his teeth were so perfect, so straight, that I could feel my nipples hardening just imagining how it would feel to have those pearly whites closing around them before taking a...

"Is it?"

"Huh? Is what?"

He chuckled and the sound jerked me out of the trance I'd descended into the moment I'd heard Madison call out my name. I was sure the fingertip he lifted to run down my cheek must have burned from the heat I could feel rushing into my face.

"As much as I'd love to play doctor with you, I need to make sure you didn't mark that as one of your hard limits," he said.

I took a moment to glance at the wheel, telling myself to get with the program. Seeing the small white sphere resting in the small pocket above *Medical Play* I couldn't help the small shudder that ran through me. Or the smile that I felt spreading across my lips as I realized that the time for fantasizing about Ronan was over… it was time to play for real. Catching Madison's eye, I saw her grinning and swore she even gave me a small wink. Looking up at Ronan, I said, "Not a hard limit. I'm all yours, Chef."

"It's Doctor," he corrected, lifting his hand to press it against my forehead. "Hmmm, you seem a bit flushed, Miss…"

"Bishop," I provided.

"Miss Bishop," he said, sliding his hand down to splay his fingers against my lower back. "I can hardly wait to get you up on that exam table."

I could hear Madison saying something but couldn't seem to make sense of any words, but I didn't really care. All I cared about was the smile Ronan gave me and the weight of his hand against me as he led me away from the wheel that had decided our fate.

As excited as I was that somehow I'd actually wound up with the man I'd been fan-girling over for months, I was also grateful that the rules required that participants remain in the theater until all pairings had been made. I took the time to take several deep breaths. Once my heart rate had dropped a teensy bit, I saw that with every celebrity called up on stage, Ronan used the time it took for the pairing to be made and the wheel to be spun to move us further toward the back of the line. I was about to ask why we were moving when it dawned on me that every adjustment had us closer to the exit door. I dropped my gaze to hide my smile. It seemed that someone was impatient to start our play. When the only person between us and the end of the line was the woman who had been described as being just as pretty on the inside as she was on the outside, I leaned toward her.

"I know you don't know me, but I just wanted to say that you have an admirer out in the audience." She smiled and nodded and I realized that being a celebrity, she most likely had a gazillion fans. "No, I mean, she's a huge fan of your charity work. Something about how you believe that animal therapy can really help children heal from trauma?"

"Oh, yes, it's true," she said softly, her eyes brightening. "Putting a child on the back of a pony and watching their excitement is simply amazing."

I saw her looking out over the crowd and took the opportunity to say, "Fourth row, about ten seats in? The woman with the pixie haircut? Her name is Julie." As if her ears were burning, Julie turned and seeing me... or rather her idol, she gave a little wave, her smile growing much larger when the celebrity waved back.

"Thank you. I'll make sure to introduce myself," she said a second before her name was called and a short bio followed. Suddenly I remembered reading the short bio about her. Heather was a country singer... that explained both the boots she was wearing and her love of horses. I had time to hope the two did connect before Ronan's hand gently pushed me another foot closer to the door. I smiled at a man who seemed to be a bit too interested in us rather than the activity up on the stage.

"Why do I feel like I'm about to make a break for it?" I whispered, glancing around to see if anyone else had noticed we'd separated ourselves from the pack.

"Because we are," he stated. "Be ready to run."

I was debating how to tell him that running was definitely not going to happen in these shoes when he said, "Now!" and grabbed my hand, pulling me out the door.

By the time we'd left the theater, and had walked through the bar in the social area, I was seriously rethinking my choice of footwear. The stilettos might have raised my height by four inches, but that didn't make my stride any longer. I was practically jogging beside him as his long legs ate up the floor. The rapid staccato of my heels grew louder as we stepped onto the marble flooring surrounding the incredible pool. I gave a soft "umph" when I ran into him after he stopped abruptly.

"Sorry."

"About what?" I asked wondering where that had come from.

Instead of answering, he bent and in one smooth move, had me off my feet and cradled in his arms.

"I can walk," I squealed in protest, both impressed that he could so easily lift me and aghast that he'd done so.

"And I could realize that my legs are about a foot longer than yours and that's without those killer shoes."

"I can take them off and—"

"Hell no," he said, shaking his head. "The only one removing any clothing will be the doctor, and that won't include those sexy as fuck heels."

I didn't know what to say, so simply laid my cheek against his shoulder as he continued past the pool and sauna on the right and a row of windows on the left.

"Oh, I heard about those," I said softly, noticing a few men scattered among the women behind the glass.

"What? The rooms or the glory holes?" he asked, not even slowing as he continued down the long hallway.

"Both. It reminds me of the Red Light District in Amsterdam. I can't even imagine waiting inside and wondering if anyone was going to stick their…"

He looked down at me as I stopped speaking and I watched his lip quirk. "You do know that this is a club where a lot of kinky things happen, right?"

"Of course," I said a bit affronted but felt my face heating. "Sorry, it's just that while I can write the words, I seem to have a little difficulty in saying them out loud."

"Write them? You're not some kind of reporter are you?"

"No! I work at a hotel. But I'm also an author."

"Ahhh," he said, grinning.

"Ahhh?" I asked, wondering what he meant by the exclamation. "You do know that people write sexy romance novels, right?"

"I do," he said, his chuckle letting me know he recognized that I'd basically thrown his words back into his face. "I just realized that's how I know you."

"You've read my books?"

"No, but I'll be sure to pick one up. I just meant that you mentioned a hotel, and I remember seeing you at the *Beverly Hills?* You work in special events, right? I've done some appearances there." He gave me a long look and added, "Though I definitely remember seeing you, you didn't attend the actual cooking demonstration. Not a fan?"

"You have to ask?" I said, rolling my eyes. "Would I be the runner up if I wasn't a huge fan? I'm just… a little shy, I suppose."

His laugh rang out to echo down the hall as he turned right and then finally stopped walking to push open a door. "An erotic author who's brave enough to bid on me and be a bit snarky about her craft, but is too shy to even say the word cock. Well, Miss Bishop, let's see if we can't cure you of that malady, shall we?"

CHAPTER 6

 *onan*

ENTERING THE ROOM, I WATCHED HER EYES WIDEN AS SHE LOOKED around. You had to hand it to Jaxson, Chase and Emma. When it came to their clubs, they didn't penny pinch on the details. They'd reproduced an actual exam room right down to the smallest details of glass canisters filled with various items on the counter top and the most important feature of all—a bonafide, regulation size exam table. Setting Carnegie down on her feet, I let her continue to scan the room as I shrugged into a white coat that had been hung with others on a rack against the wall. The moment it settled on my shoulders and I transferred the stethoscope that had been tucked into the pocket around my neck, I was ready.

"Remove your clothing and then climb up here so we can begin," I said. The sharp sound of the slaps I'd given against the paper covering the surface of the table seemed to snap her out of her perusal of the room. Her head jerked to me and her eyes went wide.

"Um… where do I change? Where is my gown?" she asked, looking around as if she thought some sort of privacy screen had suddenly appeared.

"No gown and right here is fine," I said casually, moving to pick up the clipboard tucked into a slot on the wall, prepared to pretend to scan it. I grinned to see an actual form held beneath the clip and that it contained suggestions as to what an exam might consist of. I'm sure it was a help to someone new to the game, but this activity was one of my all-time favorite role-playing scenarios. Still, props helped set the mood. Using the attached pen, I scribbled some notes at the bottom of the form before lifting my head to see that my patient hadn't moved a single muscle.

"Do you need some assistance, Miss Bishop?"

"Uh... no?"

The fact that she formed her response as a question told me that she did need a little push. Arching my brow, I made a point of slowly looking her over from head to toe. Lifting my gaze to her face, I said, "For every second you hesitate in obeying my request, I'll add a minute to how long you'll be holding the thermometer."

She looked a bit puzzled and then shrugged her shoulders.

"This one," I said, moving toward the counter and pulling a long glass tube out of a bin before adding, "in your bottom."

"In my... you wouldn't!" she sputtered, her eyes flying from the thermometer to my face and back again.

"I would," I said, biting back a grin. "And if you go over ten, I'll not take the time to lube it before insertion."

When she still didn't move, I began to shake the thermometer, moving the mercury down the glass tube, knowing she was watching my every move. "Do you remember the safe words?" At her nod, I said, "Then unless I hear the word *red*, I will expect you to remember that while you paid a lot of money to be here, I am not the submissive... you are." Pausing, I waited until she looked at me again. "And, Carnegie, I'm not a Dom who is known for giving quarter when scening. Is that understood?"

Her green eyes were so expressive and were telling me that she was both intrigued and terrified, but ultimately it was her choice. I would gladly lead, but I'd never force a woman. She'd either choose to play or choose to keep her clothes on and walk away. I wasn't about to offer her a third option, and she seemed to accept that as she nodded and turned away. I didn't release my breath until, instead of continuing through the door, her hands lifted to the zipper at the nape of her neck and began to drag it down.

"Good girl," I praised softly, sliding the thermometer back into its holder as I watched that zipper lower, the fabric of her dress parting to slowly display the skin beneath it. Well, well… maybe she wasn't quite so shy after all. The red satin strap across her back told me that this little author enjoyed sexy lingerie. When the zipper finally reached the end of its track, I could see just the barest centimeter of another red strip of satin that formed the waistband of her panties.

She hesitated but my softly uttered, "That's one," had her hands moving to drag the cloth off her left shoulder, followed by her right.

"Wait," I ordered, causing her to look back at me. "Turn around." Another pause had me shake my head and tap my pen against the clipboard, ticking off a mark. "That's two."

A soft mewl of protest was ignored as I waited. "Three."

"Wait!" she said, turning around to face me. "Take it back and I'll turn!"

I shook my head. "You aren't buying a car, Miss Bishop. There are no negotiations here. And seeing as you have already turned, you may continue."

Realizing I was right, she gave a huff and a brief glare. I was hard pressed not to chuckle. I admired a bit of spirit as long as it came with obedience. By the time she gave a final shimmy to push the fabric over her hips and allow the black sheath to hit the floor, she'd earned another two counts. One for hesitating after the dress reached her breasts and another when it reached the top of her mons. But, the slow reveal was so very worth the wait. The red lingerie accentuated the porcelain paleness of her skin. Her breasts filled out the satin cups quite nicely, her protests belied by the fact that her nipples were pushing hard against the satin, straining to be set free, but I was willing to allow them to stay imprisoned a bit longer.

The view only improved as my eyes dropped lower. Her waist nipped in, her hips flared out and a tiny little satin patch was the only thing covering her sex. I wondered if her hesitation had come from worrying that I would see that patch was a much darker red than the tiny strips of satin holding her panties in place. Or did it come with the knowledge that even from two feet away I'd be able to smell the scent of her arousal? From the flush that I watched moving up from her flat tummy over her breasts, up her neck to flood her face, I was willing to bet it was both.

She gave a small jerk as I crouched down. Reaching up, I slid a hand up the inside of her right leg and then splayed my fingers wide against her upper thigh. "Steady," I said softly. "I'm just going to help you step out."

"Oh, okay," she said, managing a wobbly nod as she put her hands on my shoulders and then lifted her feet. Once I slid the dress free, I leaned forward and inhaled deeply.

"Lovely."

"Oh my god," she whispered, her legs quivering a bit as she attempted to press them tighter together. That was fine... I'd have them spread wide soon enough. Standing, I shook out her dress and nodded.

"You may continue." Moving to hang her dress up, I noticed that the hallway outside the window was crowded, dozens of people looking in. I was pretty sure Carnegie hadn't yet noticed and could only hope that her choice of lingerie was just the first glimpse of a woman who was a bit wild beneath that innocent façade. There was only one way to find out.

Turning back, I saw she had drawn her bottom lip between her teeth. My cock jerked as I forgot about everyone except the woman before me. Stepping forward, I reached up and gently tapped her lip with my fingertip. "Release," I said quietly and when she obeyed, the tip of her tongue darting out to swipe along her lips as if soothing the bite, I was done with the prelude to this little act. Reaching around her, I deftly flicked open the clasp of her bra and had it pulled down her arms before she could blink. When her arms tightened against her sides as if to trap the garment's further descent, I shook my head.

"Any more hesitation to obey an order will earn you a stripe across your ass courtesy of my belt." Her eyes widened, her nostrils flared and her lips parted as if to speak, but in the end, she simply nodded, allowing me to pull the bra free.

Her tits were magnificent. The globes were high and firm, a full handful tipped with large nipples that protruded a good half-inch from rose-colored areolas. I brushed my palm across first one and then the other, loving the fact that they stiffened even further and the soft moan the action caused. As a reward, I bent to draw one into my mouth, suckling hard as her arms lifted and her fingers gripped my shoulders. Closing my teeth around the turgid bud, I gave it a nip, my cock jerking at her little mewl of protest. Moving to her other nipple, I repeated the laving as my hand slid down her body to cup a buttock. As I gave the bare flesh a squeeze, I had to send up a note of gratitude to whatever genius had created the thong. A garment that looked sexy as hell and kept a woman's asscheeks uncovered deserved whatever was the fashion industry's equivalent to the Nobel Prize.

I continued to move from nipple to nipple, licking, suckling, nipping the sensitive tips as my fingers slid between her legs and into the practically nonexistent panties, finding the reason for the gusset being saturated. Her pussy was hot, swollen and slick with her arousal. As I ran my fingertips along her nether lips, feathering them over her clit, I could feel her begin to shake. With a final flick of both my finger and my tongue, I pulled away, but only far enough to allow me to bend and scoop her into my arms.

"Up you go," I said, lifting her and setting her down on the table's surface. Before she could protest... or notice the audience our play had drawn, I gently eased her down until she was lying on her back. Not wanting her to come out of her state of arousal, I bent down and again suckled each breast for a long moment before standing and drawing her arms up above her head. It took only a few moments to secure her wrists into leather cuffs, which were attached to the head of the table.

433

"You have beautiful breasts, Miss Bishop," I said, both to remind her of our medical play and to not give her time to protest the restraints. "Let's make sure your heart is nice and healthy," I continued, removing the stethoscope from my neck and fitting the tips into my ears. Lifting the round silver disk, I held it a fraction of an inch above her flesh.

"This might be a bit chilly," I warned, lowering the metal flush against her skin. She gasped but settled as I moved the disk around, pressing it a bit harder and smiling when I was rewarded with the sound of her heartbeat... it seemed to be racing a bit, but I would have been surprised if it hadn't been at least a little fast. Using my free hand, I took a nipple between my thumb and finger, listening closely as I gave the little bud a pinch. Well, well... so it was possible for a heart to skip a beat. I played for a bit, moving the disk around while tugging, twisting, stroking and flicking her nipples until she was squirming. Relenting, I lifted the disk from her and set the instrument aside.

"Your heart sounds lovely."

"Lovely?" she repeated, her nose crinkling. "I don't believe I've ever heard of that medical term, Doctor."

"Have you heard of the term *striped ass*?" I quipped, dropping my hand to my belt buckle.

"Ummm... yes, I believe that's a term you've mentioned before."

"Indeed," I said, grinning as I moved to the end of the table, catching sight of the metal stirrups. "Unfortunately, I have to recant my earlier words. These have to go."

Taking her left foot, I removed her shoe and rolled down the thigh-high stocking before guiding her bare foot into the stirrup that was waiting. I fastened the band of leather around her ankle to assure her foot would remain in place as I repeated the process with her other foot.

Pleased that I'd managed to restrain her without so much as a whimper of protest, I looked up her body and saw her lips were trembling... not in fear but in what appeared to be amusement. When her eyes flicked down, mine automatically followed. The red satin stood out from the white paper beneath her body... panties she evidently thought I'd forgotten to remove. Little did she know that I wasn't one to forget anything that I found important. And believe me, what lay beneath that satin was very, very important indeed.

Her look of triumph faltered as I pushed the stirrups up and out, splaying her legs wide. Moving again, I pulled a metal rolling cart to the side of the table, lifting the cloth cover to see what was beneath, grinning when I saw the implement that my very profession assured I could use with both comfort and skill.

"Is there anything you need to discuss before we begin the exam?" I asked, watching her straining to see what was on the tray, the restraints and her position making it impossible to do so. "Miss Bishop? Any medical conditions I should know about?"

"I don't have a fever, so there's no need to take my temperature," she said, and I couldn't help but hear some chuckling coming from the hallway.

"Do you have a medical degree?" I asked, arching my eyebrow.

"Well, no, but—"

"I didn't think so," I said, "Let's leave the diagnosis to the professionals then, shall we?" I didn't give her an opportunity to state that I was no more a doctor than she. Instead, I lifted my hand, holding my choice of implement where she could see it. And I knew the very moment she did. Her eyes grew as large as saucers when the overhead light caught the metal of the scalpel. A bit of fear was good, a full blown panic attack was not, so when she started to pull hard against her restraints, I reached out and laid my free hand against her abdomen.

"Settle down, you're fine," I assured her. "Is knife play a hard limit?"

"Noooo, but... I don't like... I get sick when I see blood... especially my blood."

I smiled and bent down to brush hair that had tangled a bit with her struggle back from her face. "I promise, no blood. Trust me?" I didn't penalize her for taking a long moment to decide, just continued to gently stroke her face and rub circles on her stomach, watching as her body gave her answer by relaxing before she spoke a soft, "yes."

"Good girl. Just relax. Don't think about a thing except the sensations you feel, the pleasure you will experience. Can you do that?"

"I-I think so."

I was the one to be shocked next as I bent down and gently pressed my mouth to hers, feeling the softness of her lips beneath mine, not pushing my tongue between them just yet, content to simply slide the tip along her plump bottom lip. I wasn't a kisser... well, not a gentle one. When I did kiss a woman, it was to thrust my tongue into her mouth, to bruise her lips, to let her know who exactly was in charge. But now, when I pulled away, I knew I'd kissed Carnegie to both reward her for the gift of her trust and to assure her that I wouldn't abuse it.

I took a second to gather my thoughts and then lifted the scalpel. I began at the hollow of her throat, placing the tip of the blade against her skin and watching her pulse jump. Slowly, I drew it down, thousands of tiny goose pebbles instantly appearing as the cold steel blade glided across her flesh. I watched her chest expand and then freeze as she held her breath the moment I began to circle her left nipple with the blade. I didn't have to look up to know her head was tilted as far forward as she could, her eyes watching every move I made. She could be frightened, but, by God, her nipples had hardened even further, drawing into tight little buds that I was pretty sure could cut glass.

A final slow circle and then the blade slid over the hill and down into the valley between her breasts. As if she understood my reasoning for taking that path, she took a long deep breath before holding it again as the scalpel moved up the hill to circle her right nipple. She didn't breathe again until it was snaking down to circle her belly button. Reaching my ultimate destination, I heard her inhale again and knew she understood that I hadn't forgotten to remove her panties... I simply wanted to remove them in a much more dramatic way. The scalpel was sharp, easily slicing through first one side of the waistband and then the other. With a flick of my wrist, the severed front of the satin flipped down to lay between her legs, baring her to my view.

"Very nice," I said, complimenting both her remaining still and the vision of a nicely trimmed thatch of ginger curls above a very pretty little pussy. Reaching down, I slid the flat of my palm across her mound, purposefully connecting with her swollen clit before taking hold of the ruined panties and easily pulling them out from beneath her when she raised her hips. Lifting them to my face, I inhaled deeply, watching her entire body flush as I did so. "Very nice indeed." I returned the scalpel to the tray and tucked the red satin into my pants pocket beneath the white coat. "Thank you, Miss Bishop. Lifting your hips reminded me that I need to take your temperature."

CHAPTER 7

 *arnegie*

HOLY HELL!

No, that wasn't right. Holy crap? Holy shit? What was the proper response for how I was feeling? None seemed right and yet they all did. Never in my wildest dreams would I ever have believed that I'd practically come from having a knife at my throat. Okay, granted, it wasn't a knife and hadn't been at my throat for long, but still. I'd watched as he circled my nipples with a scalpel! I'd felt my traitorous nipples drawing up, not in terror that he'd cut me, but in pleasure at the sensation that had them pebbling so tight they were throbbing.

And cutting my panties off? I supposed I should be pissed that he'd ruined the bottom half of a brand new set of lingerie, but... well, it was one of the sexiest things I'd ever witnessed. But when he'd lifted them to his face, his fingers holding the soaked gusset as he inhaled, I'd almost come a second time. Even his reminder about taking my temperature only notched back my arousal a tiny bit. I turned my head to see what he was doing and that's when I saw them...

Holy fuck!

I'd totally forgotten that the window was even there, much less that people might be looking in. And though I couldn't make out any faces, from the different shapes and sizes of the shadows, I knew that there were more than a couple.

"Don't." Ronan moved to block my view, reaching out to splay his hand over my stomach again. "They don't exist inside this room. In here, it is just you and me. Relax and trust me to keep you safe. Trust me to make you forget everything but the pleasure I want to give you. All right?"

I took a deep breath and remembered how he'd manipulated that scalpel, how he'd sucked and nipped at my breasts, how his lips had felt on mine when he'd kissed me. Did he realize that he'd already given me pleasure without even making me come? Seeing what he'd brought back with him, I said, "It would be a lot more pleasurable if you'd forget all about taking my temperature."

"Not for me," he quipped. "Besides, I'm sure that you are going to discover that you enjoy a little ass play."

I huffed but wasn't exactly in a position to keep him from proceeding. The only way to stop him from sticking that long glass rod up my butt was to safe word and I sure as hell wasn't going to do that.

"Fine, but make it fast."

"If you wanted fast, Miss Bishop, you would have been a good girl," he reminded me as he moved to stand between my splayed legs. "Five minutes for me to enjoy watching you try to deny that you aren't feeling pleasure."

"Wanna bet?" I said.

"Babe, I'm not a man to take advantage. You might be the very best poker player in the world, but your body is incapable of lying. You can tell me you hate it, but your little nipples look like they are going to pop and your cream has already made a wet spot on the paper, so... I'd easily win that bet if you're still interested in making one?" At my growl, he chuckled. "I didn't think so. Now, I don't want to have you strain your back trying to keep your hips lifted for seven or so minutes—"

"Seven! You said five!"

"That five doesn't start until I've seated the thermometer. It doesn't count the time taken in preparing you for the insertion. Now, be a good patient and scoot down a bit for me."

"Oh, God help me," I whimpered.

"Doctor Bellington will do, and of course I'll help," he said, causing me to shake my head and then squeal as he reached up and taking my hips, pulled me down until my arms were stretched taut over my head and my ass was hanging off the edge of the table. The moment he pulled the thermometer out of the jar where he'd stuck it and I saw a glob of thick clear gel dangling from the tip, I squeezed both my eyes and my buttocks tight. What was even more annoying than his bark of laughter was knowing his amusement came from the fact that my embarrassing position assured the only things that actually closed were my eyes.

"Naughty," he said. "A good patient doesn't try to keep her doctor from doing his duty."

"A good doctor would stop torturing his patient and get on with it," I snapped back. His response was to press some sort of button or lever that had the stirrups both moving further apart and elevating, lifting my ass and to my horror, spreading my buttocks to better expose his target and making me regret my bit of snark as he… got on with it.

"Ever had anything in your ass before?"

"No!"

"Open your eyes, Carnegie," he said. All that happened when I tossed my head back and forth against the table was that strands of my hair flew over my face and something hard landed against my ass.

"Ow!" I squealed, my eyes flying open.

"Good girl," he said, using the hand he'd obviously swatted me with to now rub away the sting. "Remember, any more disobedience will earn you a stroke of my belt."

Fuck! I'd totally forgotten about that little caveat.

"Keep them open. You've got the most expressive eyes I've ever seen. I want to watch them as I penetrate your ass for the first time."

Was that supposed to be a compliment? Before I could decide, I felt something cold against my opening.

"That's freezing!"

"Don't worry, it will warm up soon enough," he said, applying another dollop of the lube, rubbing his fingertip around and around my entrance until the area not only warmed, but began to unclench. At least until the circling stopped and the pressure of his thick finger pushing inside began.

"Just relax, I'm not hurting you," he said.

His earlier remarks that he wasn't a man to give quarter came to mind and really, what choice did I have? He pushed forward, my soft whimper ignored as he began to rotate his finger, spreading the lube around my insides and causing a sensation I'd never experienced to spread through me. I couldn't decide if it was pleasant or not, but as his finger went deeper, my fingers clenched and unclenched wishing they had something to hold onto. After what seemed like an hour, he slid his finger from me and made a smooth transition in an instant, sliding the glass tube in to take its place. I tensed and he stood, reaching over me to cover my hands with one of his. *How had he known* raced through my head as my fingers gratefully grabbed onto the anchor he silently offered.

The glass slid further and further, much deeper than his finger and yet I was no longer as adamant that it be removed. Instead, as it slowly began to withdraw, then push forward… the motion repeated again and again, I gave another whimper.

"That's it," he said softly, bending down to meet my gaze. "Just relax and embrace the sensation. Learn that there is no part of your body that isn't capable of bringing you pleasure." His lips descended to brush across mine again. I wasn't sure how he could tell when five minutes was reached as I hadn't seen any clock, but it felt like only a heartbeat had passed before he straightened and slid the thermometer from my ass.

"About that bet?" he said, looking down at me with a grin.

441

"You're right. You would have won," I said, not above admitting when I was wrong.

He didn't gloat, only checked the thermometer, declaring that I was fever-free. "I guess that flush was just from excitement?"

A roll of my eyes and a snort were my answer. With a final squeeze to my fingers, he moved away to the sink and quickly washed the glass tube, placing it in a countertop sterilizer where he'd also placed the scalpel.

Bringing the tray table with him, he pulled up a rolling stool, returning to move between my legs. "No exam is complete without ascertaining your response to stimuli," he said, obviously having moved back into his role of doctor.

I didn't have to understand exactly what he meant to enjoy the exam as his fingertips began to slide along the seam of my sex. I'd been more than ready to 'respond' ever since Madison had called my name. As he continued, some strokes hard, some soft... some slow, some fast, I truly obeyed his instructions to relax... to just fall into the sensations, to let them become my entire world. The only things that existed were his fingers and his softly uttered sounds that might have been words or simply encouragement to let go. When his fingers slid inside me, thrusting softly as his free hand continued to play over my clit, I couldn't stop the soft moans from escaping.

I whimpered when his fingers left me, feeling bereft, but I didn't arch up until I felt something far larger and far colder begin to press into me.

The combination of a stretching sensation and the sound of metal ratcheting had a light bulb going off. He'd not only inserted a speculum inside me, he was opening it... slowly but steadily forcing the walls of my vagina to open. My attempt to lift up was easily thwarted by his free hand pressing against my abdomen.

"Shh, relax," he said.

"Easy for you to say," I said, moaning as another click had me wondering exactly how far a pussy could be opened.

"Just a few more turns," he said, ignoring my snark. "I need you nice and open so that I can see what I'm doing."

I was about to suggest he might find a pair of glasses would help correct his obvious vision problem when he finally said, "There, that should do it."

The only thing that kept me from snarking, "Are you sure," was the fact that I was panting a bit from the stretch. I was positive that he'd opened me wide enough to stick his whole head inside.

It took a moment for me to realize that my breathing was calming and that his hand was gently making tiny rotations over my tummy.

"I know it seems impossible, but I want you to relax. I promise, if you do, if you trust me, it will be worth it."

Granted, I barely knew this man, and I couldn't exactly explain why I trusted him, but I did. Perhaps it was the fact that he asked me to do so, or maybe it was the small things he'd done like standing to allow me to hold his hand when he was playing with that tube in my ass, or every time he splayed his fingers across my stomach, moving them in gentle circles when I became agitated. Whatever the reasons, I couldn't deny that I did trust him. Taking a deep breath, I nodded and stopped trying to push the speculum from my body.

"Good girl," he said, pressing a brief kiss to the inside of my thigh before lifting his hand from me and picking up... a paintbrush? That couldn't be right. But it was. He was holding a long handled paintbrush that had bristles stiff enough to form a fan-shaped head. It wasn't a brush I'd normally associate with spreading paint across a canvas.

"Don't," he said, looking up to meet my eyes. "Don't overthink it. Just relax and let me take control."

I nodded again, my curiosity piqued. Though I watched as the paintbrush disappeared inside me, at first I wasn't sure if I was actually feeling something or imagining it. When my body jerked, I knew the sensation, though alien, was real. Another stroke drew a soft moan as my entire body seemed to react, to awaken... to crave another pass of those bristles.

"They say that cervical orgasms are far stronger, far more pleasurable than clitoral ones," Ronan said, letting me know that my cervix was the part of my anatomy that was being stroked. He used the brush to reach deep inside me and pleasure me in a way I'd never imagined. I wasn't exactly sure who 'they' were, but oh God, they were right. Whether so light as to have me wonder if I'd actually felt it or long and drawn out, the brush scraping across my cervix, each individual bristle felt in every single stroke was driving me closer and closer to a peak I'd never reached before.

"Please, please let me come."

"No," he said, shaking his head. "It's not yet time."

"It is—"

"Trust me," he said, cutting off my protest. "Trust that holding back, denying yourself will make it so much better when I say yes."

Again, what choice did I have? Nodding, I caught my lip between my teeth and bit down, closing my eyes. I just couldn't keep them open and he must have understood as he didn't order me to do so. I dropped deeper into a pool of pleasure as he continued to paint his masterpiece, the brush working its magic until I was moaning incoherently, arching, my fingers shredding the paper beneath me until suddenly my eyes flew open as I felt his finger breach my anus, thrusting inside. I forgot to even breathe until he said, "Come for me."

It was like I was one of Pavlov's dogs and Ronan's voice was the bell. The moment the command was spoken, I shattered, a scream torn from my very soul as I imploded.

"Shit! Oh God...oh God, oh... oh fuck!"

Not once, not twice, but again and again, my body convulsed, every individual muscle contracting, heat bursting from deep within me to spread out along every pathway, to fill every cell until I felt like my very blood was on fire.

"Ronan!" I screamed again as the brush continued to feather over my cervix. My body jerking as I came so hard my toes curled and my legs began to shake, causing the metal stirrups to rattle.

"Oh my God... I-I'm so sorry," I said, feeling the liquid that had come from me spreading across the table, soaking the paper. "I-I didn't mean to—"

"Shhh," he said softly, bending forward to kiss my stomach. "You did exactly what I wanted. You squirted."

"I did what?"

"Squirted. It's like when a man ejaculates. It's a stronger orgasm and it was absolutely amazing to watch," he said softly. "Was it worth waiting for?"

My body continued to quiver, my nipples to ache, my blood to race and my heart to pound. Was it worth it? I nodded. "Oh yes."

"Good," he said with a grin, slowly withdrawing his finger from my ass and then the brush before releasing the speculum to pull it from my pussy. When I continued to spasm, he softly ran his fingers over my sex as if gentling a frightened animal. When he stroked over my clit, I thought about how he'd made me have the most intense orgasm of my life without even touching the little bundle of nerves.

Within a few minutes, he'd removed the restraints and lifted me off the table but only to set me on the stool he'd vacated. "I can help," I said when I realized he was pulling the soaked and torn paper off the table.

"I've got it. You just recover."

I knew I should protest, but I also knew my legs would most likely collapse if I attempted to stand. Instead, I decided to be a good sub and simply obey my Dom's order. Ronan took his time, washing and dropping the speculum into the sterilizer before discarding the paper and then pulling out a spray bottle from beneath the table. He spritzed the table, the smell alerting me to the fact that it was some sort of cleanser. He wiped down every inch of the stirrups and the table and then used another clean towel to dry the leather. Dropping the towels into a bin, he then lowered the stirrups that had spread me so widely. Grabbing the edge of the paper that was on a roll attached to the head of the table, he pulled it down to cover the surface again. By the time he stepped away, the only way one could tell the room had been used was the fact that he was still wearing the lab coat... well, and I was sitting buck-naked on the rolling stool.

He pulled off the coat, dropping it into the bin as well and then plucked my dress from a hanger and brought it and the rest of my clothes to me. Extending one hand, he said, "Let's get you dressed."

"Oh..." I said. "Okay."

"If you'd rather remain nude, babe, that's fine with me. I don't recall there being a rule that a sub had to be dressed when spinning the wheel."

I looked up. "The wheel?"

"Yes. Unless you opt out, you are still mine for a couple of hours."

Leaping to my feet, I threw my arms around his waist. "I'm not opting out!" His chuckle had me stepping back and plucking my clothes from his hand. "And I'm also not going around naked!"

I dressed while he cleaned the stool with as much efficiency as he had the table. Only then did he offer me his hand. Taking it, we walked to the door and I felt my entire body flush as the sound of applause reminded me that we'd not been unobserved. Before I could deal with that embarrassment, I saw that Ronan was shaking the hand of a guy who had his arm around the waist of none other than Jazz, a rock star who had multiple songs topping the charts.

"It's all yours," Ronan said. "We were a bit messy, but I've made sure it's all clean for you."

"Thanks, I'm sure we'll be messy too."

"Have fun," I said, a bit shocked that I'd even managed to speak. But Jazz smiled and nodded as they stepped into the room and we began to walk back down the hall.

CHAPTER 8

onan

RETRACING OUR STEPS PAST THE GLORY HOLES, I THOUGHT OF HOW I'D
yet to show her my cock much less have her begging to be allowed to
suck it. I'd never held off seeking my own pleasure simply to assure
my partner found hers before. Perhaps it was because I knew we had
time and I wanted her to experience more than a single spin of the
wheel. Still, my mind was churning as we walked.

"Oh wow," she said softly, causing me to glance to the side where
she was looking.

"Never seen someone being whipped before?" I asked.

"No... I mean, I have on videos, but not live," she said. "It looks
both incredibly terrifying and like art in motion at the same time."
The whip snapped forward, cracking against the sub's back. "How is
she not screaming?"

I took time, scanning the scene before responding. "Look at how
she arches after each stroke, how she pushes back to receive the next.

Listen to her soft cries. She craves the pain. It increases her pleasure." When I looked over and saw disbelief on her face, I chuckled. "Don't believe me?"

"I'm not sure. That really doesn't make sense when you think about it."

"Ahhh, but that's the secret," I said. "When you finally stop overthinking and just allow yourself to feel, things that make no sense suddenly do." To make my point, I slid my hand down over her dress, pushing the fabric into the seam of her ass, pressing the pad of my finger against the rosette of her asshole. Her soft mewl and the fact she pushed back against my hand told me she got the message loud and clear. Grinning, I began walking again.

"There, you did it again."

"Did what?"

"I've been wondering about your name. You make the prettiest little sounds. Whether you are whimpering, mewling, or moaning or simply enjoying what I'm doing to you or what is happening around you. It's like you make your own special music. Was your mother a singer? Did she perform at Carnegie Hall?"

She giggled and I added that delightful sound to my list of new favorites.

"She couldn't carry a tune, but she'd get a huge thrill out of being thought of as some famous performer. She worked behind the scenes in Vegas designing and making costumes for the Cirque du Soleil troupe at the Mirage. As for my name, it has nothing to do with performing and everything to do with meat."

"Meat? I'm afraid you're going to have to give me more than that," I said, thoroughly enjoying her story.

Laughing again, she said, "Corned beef to be exact. When she was pregnant with me, Mom started craving pastrami. There is a deli inside the Mirage based on the famous delicatessen that used to be in New York adjacent to Carnegie Hall. Mom went to Carnegie—the deli, not the theater—every day to eat. She was such a regular that they'd already be preparing her sandwich by the time she walked through the door at precisely 11:15. One day, she had just taken her first bite when she went into labor. She wasn't like most women who suffer several hours of labor before the baby comes. The story goes that she didn't even make it from the counter to the door before her water broke. By the time the paramedics arrived, it was too late to transport her to the hospital. I was delivered right there on the deli floor on the stroke of twelve."

"Seriously? That's one hell of a story."

She grinned and nodded. "Exactly and do you know what the best part is?"

Reaching up to tuck a strand of her hair behind her ear, I smiled. "The fact that on that day the most incredible woman was born and given the most unique name I've ever heard?"

I adored the blush that painted her skin, but absolutely loved the smile of pleasure that spread across her face. "Well, thank you for that, but I was going to say that if you ever get tired of cooking and want to pop over to Vegas, I'll treat you to lunch. I got free meals for life as a gift."

"It's a deal," I said, sliding my hand behind her head to cup the nape of her neck. "But I meant everything I said. You are an incredible, unique woman." Bending, I tugged her closer and kissed her... hard. My tongue demanded she let me in and once her lips parted, I swept the inside of her mouth, learning her taste. Only the need to actually breathe had me pulling back, my hold keeping her steady. I loved the way she lifted her fingers to her lips as if expecting to feel them swollen. Sliding my hand down, I planted my palm against her lower back. "Let's go see about a little ball, shall we?"

She grinned and I saw her eyes drop to my crotch. "I said little, babe, like in a roulette wheel." When she giggled again, I just shook my head and walked a little faster, leading her into the theater and up onto the stage.

"From the smiles on your faces, I'm thinking you enjoyed playing doctor," Madison said as she picked up the white ball. "Like enjoyed it a lot."

"A Valley-girl and a psychic," I teased, plucking the ball from her hand and handing it to Carnegie.

Madison laughed and set the wheel spinning. Carnegie dropped the ball and this time we all watched it bounce from place to place, in and out of several pockets before settling in one as the wheel slowed.

"*Wild Card*," Madison said. To clarify, she added, "*Dom's Choice,* lucky you."

"Lucky indeed," I agreed before turning to Carnegie. "If you need to use the bathroom, now is the time to do so while I prepare."

"Oh… okay. What are you going to be preparing?"

"My choice, of course," I said. "That's the fun of spinning *Wild Card*. You'll find out soon enough."

"I could come help you."

"Or you could use the bathroom and come right back here to wait for me," I countered, pointing to the first row of chairs facing the stage. "I won't be long, so don't keep me waiting. If you're not here when I get back—"

"You'll swat me with your belt," she said.

It wasn't the interruption that sealed her fate… it was the rolling of those gorgeous green eyes. But that wasn't something she needed to know at this moment. Instead, I simply nodded and led her down the steps. "I'll be back."

She giggled and when I arched my brow, she shook her head. "I'm sorry, I'm not being ugly it's just that… well, I'm already a little nervous about exactly what you are going to choose and then you say a line made famous by Arnold Schwarzenegger in *The Terminator.*"

Grinning, I pulled her close. "A little fear is a good thing. Keeps your blood flowing, but know this. I'm going to push your limits, but I'm not going to ever harm you, babe."

"I know," she said, leaning in and then lifting onto her toes and kissing my cheek before turning and walking away. I took a moment… or two to simply admire the sway of her hips, not failing to notice a few heads turning to watch as well. Though part of me wanted to bark, "She's mine!" another part knew it simply would make this next scene all the sweeter. I waited until Carnegie disappeared around the corner before approaching the men. After a brief conversation and their assurance they'd spread the word, I turned in the opposite direction to set my plan in place.

~

"THANKS, AVERY," I SAID. I'D GONE UPSTAIRS TO RUNWAY TO FIND HER in the kitchen where it was quite obvious she was busy. Still, she'd not only agreed with my plan, she'd instantly set some of her employees to preparing what I'd need.

"Don't mention it," she said with a grin, looking around to assure we wouldn't be overheard. "I think it's a great idea. Sex burns a lot of calories and the people attending the auction are going to be hungry. I promise you're not going to have to worry about anything but getting your girl ready. I'll make sure everything is brought over to Black Light when the trays are prepared."

"Thanks again," I said, bending to buzz her cheek. "Jaxson told me what a fabulous cook you are."

She scoffed. "Jaxson is just being nice. I'm nowhere near your level."

"Now that I don't believe," I said, popping yet another of the samples she'd plucked from a tray for me to try into my mouth. "These are delicious. Just put the cost on my tab and make sure to add a huge tip to the invoice. I'll—"

"You don't pay for favors... well, not with money. I want an hour or so of your time. No matter how many attempts I've made, I can't get a soufflé out of the oven without it falling. I stopped in to see the twins yesterday and Emma went on and on about the one you served. What better payment than a chance to learn from the master, so if you're open to the idea, I'd love a lesson."

"You've got a deal," I said. "You let me know when your schedule is free and I'll be here."

"Sounds great," she said, turning away as a server paused to get her approval. She looked over each item on his tray before nodding. "Perfect, you can go."

I was following him out when Avery called, "Oh, and Ronan, when you come, don't forget to bring that special chocolate."

"I will and I'll even pop for the champagne," I promised, moving out of her domain and making my way back down to Black Light without being detected. It was time to find my little sub.

CHAPTER 9

arnegie

You do know what they call women who forget they aren't wearing underwear, don't you?

"Satisfied?" I said, staring at my reflection in the mirror above the sink where I was washing my hands. "A woman who is not only having the best night of her life, but is anxious for more? Horny? Take your pick." I giggled and shut off both the faucet and the annoying little voice in my head.

Returning to the theater where they were playing *Secretary* on the screen behind the stage, I settled into a seat to wait for Ronan. The volume was low, allowing my mind to drift as I thought of all sorts of sexy possibilities of what Ronan might be choosing for us to experience. My thoughts were interrupted as couple after couple climbed the steps to the stage to spin the wheel, the ball making the decision of what they'd be playing next for them.

"Sorry, it took a bit longer than I'd planned."

Standing, I gave Ronan a smile, accepting his hand as we started to walk down the aisle. "It's fine. The wheel has kept me entertained. It's amazing how many different..."

I stopped speaking as I realized that something was wrong. Voices had often been a bit amused and even teasing after Madison had announced what activity a couple had spun, but this time, the tone sounded almost demanding. We both turned back toward the stage to see a man stalking across the floor. The smile that had been on Madison's face disappeared as she shook her head at something the man said.

"What did he say?" I asked, unable to hear the conversation.

"I don't know, but something is off," Ronan said. "Stay here." He dropped my hand and had taken a step toward the stage, but when Madison began to turn away and the man reached out and grabbed her arm, a man I hadn't even noticed exploded out of the shadows and was on the stage before I could blink. Ronan stopped walking and then turned back.

"Whatever it is, Trevor's got it handled," he said, taking my hand again.

"He came out of nowhere," I said. "It's like he's more of a ghost than a staff member."

"He's neither," Ronan said. "He's Khloe Monroe's bodyguard."

"The actress?" At his nod, I looked back at the stage to see Madison standing with her hands on her hips as Trevor took control of the situation. "I'd say she's in good hands. I'd sure hate to be on his bad side." Leaving the theater behind, I said, "So what are we going to do?"

"You'll find out soon enough."

"If you need any ideas, I can give you some options," I offered.

"Thanks for the offer, but I've got it covered," he said without even pausing.

"Oh, okay, um... where are we going?"

"You'll see," Ronan answered and looked down at me when I huffed.

"What does that mean?" When he simply grinned, I said, "Didn't your mother ever teach you it's not nice to tease?"

His grin became a chuckle. "Didn't yours teach you that half the fun is in the surprise? Not knowing what's going to happen?"

I rolled my eyes and poked him in his side with my finger. "A woman who eats the exact same thing at the exact same time in the exact same place every day for nine months isn't exactly one to advocate surprises."

He tightened his arm around my waist, pulling me a little closer. "Granted, but I'm a very firm believer that anticipation only adds a bit of spice to the dish." Before I could state that only a chef would use words like spice and dish, he stopped walking. "All right, we're here."

Looking around, I was a bit confused. We'd passed by this way earlier on the way to the medical room, but as far as I knew, this was an area where people socialized enjoying one of the two drinks that the owners of Black Light allowed its members, but was not where any kinky little games were played. "Are we going to have a drink before we—"

"Shh, anticipation, remember. No more talking unless I ask you a direct question or if you wish to safe word."

I gave him a long look and evidently he saw the flare of concern I couldn't control. Reaching out, he cupped my face in his palm. "The entire purpose of a safe word system is to make sure you understand that while you are submitting, you still maintain control. Knowing that all it takes to instantly stop a scene by uttering a single word is meant to allow you to relax... to enjoy the scene your Dom is creating for you."

His touch calmed me far more than his assurance, as I had no doubt that while he was a man who enjoyed pushing the envelope, he'd not ever push me past a point I couldn't handle. "Okay."

"Good, now I know blood play is a hard limit, did you list others on your form?"

Appreciating that he'd taken them into consideration, I quickly told him what limits I'd listed and he nodded. "That's fine, none of those are in my plans. Last thing before we start. Are you allergic to anything?"

"Like what?" I asked wondering why in the world he was asking when a possibility popped into my head. "Well, I'm allergic to hornet stings so if you were planning on going outside—"

"Don't worry, no insects will touch you," he said cryptically. "Is that it? No food allergies?"

Food? Ahhh, I should have known. He was a master chef after all. I smiled and shook my head. "Not that I know of, so feel free to feed me whatever wonderful dish you've whipped up."

He bent down until we were eye to eye. "Babe, the only thing I whip up here doesn't involve food. But I promise you this. Every single bite will be savored," he said cryptically, and at the look in his eyes, a rush of arousal dampened my panties... well, it would have if I'd been wearing any. Instead, my thighs grew slick as I pressed them tightly together. He'd already made me come without touching my clit, so I really shouldn't be shocked that he almost did it again with nothing more than a look and a few words.

"Ready?"

I nodded because I didn't trust my voice, my body already beginning to thrum simply from the look in his eyes.

"Remember, any hesitation, any disobedience and my belt comes off."

My stomach flipped, my blood heating. "Just promise me that even if I'm a very good girl, your belt and your pants will be coming off at some point."

"Ahhh, does my shy little author want to see her Dom's cock?"

My pussy spasmed, another rush of moisture running down my thigh, my body's instant response as I stepped closer, pressing against him, to give him my verbal one. "I was hoping to be allowed to do more than just see it."

I loved the flare of desire in his eyes, and it was wonderfully gratifying to feel his cock jerk against my body, my eyes dropping down to see it lengthening, thickening beneath his pants. His fingertip beneath my chin brought my head up to meet his gaze that was full of heat.

"That's a promise," he said, a huskiness to his voice I'd not yet heard. "But first..." he didn't finish his sentence, letting his actions speak for him as he reached behind me and begin to drag my zipper down.

"Wait... I-I don't think you're allowed..."

"Did I ask you a direct question?" he asked, his eyebrow quirking as the zipper continued to lower.

"Well no, but... the rules... something about off-limits..."

"There is nothing about you that is off-limits to me. Not tonight. I've got a wild card. And if I want to remove your clothes and play with your gorgeous body, then, babe, that is exactly what I'm going to do."

What could I say to that? He thought I was gorgeous. He wanted to play and... *shit!* And a crowd had already begun to gather and this time, there was no darkened window between us. I saw every expression on every face. I didn't say red and yet the zipper stopped lowering.

"Carnegie, just breathe. I've got you." His fingers cupped my chin, drawing my attention back to him, to see the sincerity in his eyes. "Though I honestly believe that if you'll let yourself, you'll totally enjoy what I have planned, I can blindfold you if you prefer."

He hadn't asked if I wanted to stop... and I understood he wouldn't unless I used my safe word. He was the Dom, the one in control, and yet he was demonstrating yet again that submission didn't mean I had no voice, no choice. Reaching out, I placed my hand over his that had dropped to pull a black satin blindfold from his pocket.

"I do and yet I don't. I know that makes no sense, but... no. I want to experience everything." The approval made his grin seem bigger, his eyes lighter, as he tucked the blindfold away.

"Good girl. Now, where were we? Ahhh, yes, I was preparing my platter."

"Platter? What—"

"No question, no talking," he said, pressing a fingertip against my lips. It might have been meant as an admonishment, but all I could think of was how very much I wanted to open my mouth and...

"Naughty," he said with a chuckle as he pulled his finger away... his wet finger, and I realized I'd sucked it into my mouth. My face flooded with heat but he just grinned. "You don't start a meal with the main course." He reached around me to take the zipper tab once again. I didn't pull away, didn't attempt to stop him as I felt him undo the clasp of my bra and draw both it and my dress off my shoulders and down my body. As my skin was exposed, I could feel my nipples pebble... and not just from the air, but from the knowledge that people were watching... were looking at me... at him... at us.

"Beautiful," he said softly as he pulled the dress over my hips and my hands automatically reached out and found his shoulders as he crouched to lift my feet free of the fabric and then removed my shoes and stockings. My hands dropped but before I could cover myself, he took them into his own.

"Don't. Let me look at you. Let them see how stunning you are. Let yourself see how brave you are... give yourself permission to enjoy being the center of attention." He gave my fingers a squeeze before releasing them to slip an arm around my waist, another around my knees and lifted me into his arms.

I wrapped my arms around his neck, feeling a myriad of emotions... the most prominent one being how naughty it felt to be totally nude yet again while this sexy as shit man remained fully dressed as he carried me through a crowd... oh holy hell! How could it have doubled in size without my noticing? And why did it appear they were forming some sort of corridor, parting as Ronan strode forward toward... No! No way was he going to put me... yes, yes he was. Before I could process it, my bare ass connected with the smooth, cool surface of the bar.

"Get me off, I'm going to break the glass!"

"You're fine," he said, ignoring my protest, reaching to turn me sideways and then easing me back until I was lying prone on the surface.

CHAPTER 10

onan

THE MOMENT HER MOUTH OPENED AGAIN, I SHOOK MY HEAD, GRINNING when she closed it but scowled, her eyes doing the talking. My little sub didn't appear to be a fan of her Dom's choice. It was time for a bit of distraction.

Lifting her head with one hand, I swept her hair from underneath, my fingers running through the wavy strands as I spread them like a fan out over the bar. Describing her hair as red would be like stating a sunset was just yellow. Her glorious mane was a mass of gold, copper, russet, and chestnut strands. "You have the most gorgeous hair I've ever seen. The color is as unique as your name. It reminds me of a mixture of many spices: cinnamon, paprika, cumin, and cayenne." Bending forward, I lifted a thick curl, bringing it to my nose and inhaling deeply as her eyes softened, her scowl no longer filling their emerald depths. "Sweet and yet spicy… the perfect combination." I spread the strand out along with the others, and said, "Give me your hands."

She didn't hesitate, lifting her arms to place her hands in mine. I think she expected them to be pulled over her head as I'd done in the medical room, but instead I drew them down to lay them along her sides. Turning her hands, I kissed each palm, watching her fingers unfurl. Satisfied with the position, I gently stroked along her hips, knowing I had a decision to make. Yes, I wanted to put her on display; however, I found I wasn't willing to expose her fully. She was pressing her thighs tightly together, and I could feel her trembling beneath my fingertips.

"Relax, Carnegie. You are doing beautifully. Which is more comfortable for you? To cross your ankles or not?" Understanding that I wasn't going to pull her legs apart and expose her pussy, she slowly relaxed, moving to cross her ankles and then to return them to simply lay beside each other. "Comfortable?" I asked.

She hesitated and I grinned. "Or at least good for now?"

She nodded. "I'm good."

"Then we can begin," I said, turning to give a nod before looking back at her. "As I said, a fine meal does not start with the main course. It begins with a nice variety of appetizers; don't you agree?"

"I-I suppose?"

"As they say, people eat with their eyes first, so presentation is a vital part of any offering. And what better way to proffer your guests their choice of delicious tidbits than to arrange them in a beautiful display... on a unique platter." I saw her gaze flick from me to something to my right and as her eyes widened, I knew she finally understood exactly what wild card her Dom had chosen. Turning, I reached for the first of many items Avery had so graciously prepared for me.

Holding up a shrimp, I turned it a bit, watching her eyes track the slight movement. "Do you know how the cook chooses the precise moment to remove a shrimp from the pan?" Her head shook slightly. "Ever been spanked before?" When her mouth pursed into a perfect little 'o' and her head shook again, I continued. "One knows it has reached the pinnacle of perfection when it's the same exact shade of pink that a Dom achieves with a few strokes of a paddle against a sub's bare ass."

Her eyes were so expressive as they tracked my movement to place it on her abdomen. I continued, arranging each one until they formed a circle around her belly button, loving the fact that she quivered just a bit with the placement of each chilled shrimp. Once the contents of an entire tray had been transferred to their new platter, another server stepped up and I picked up the next item on her tray.

"Some people enjoy the bite, saying they savor the brine," I said as I set it inside the circle. Adding another, I watched her tremble slightly, adjusting to both the weight and the soft abrasion of the shells against her skin. "Others like to simply allow the oyster to slide over their taste buds, straight down their throats." I continued placing the shells until the area was completely covered. Picking up the last one, I stepped up and then placed the shell to her lips.

"However, I believe the only way to properly get the most pleasure is to experience both. Open," I said and when her lips parted, I tipped the shell just enough to allow a bit of the liquid to flow into her mouth. "An oyster's liquor is filtered seawater and offers a robust flavor. It's where the oyster is concealed until that moment it's carefully shucked, exposed to be sucked, to be savored. Taking a small sip of the liquor and letting it coat your tongue not only enhances the experience, but actually compliments the flavor of the meat as you take it into your mouth."

I tilted the shell further and watched as the plump oyster slid onto her tongue. Her lips closed and her eyes darkened as she rolled the meat around her mouth before giving it a gentle bite. When I saw the column of her throat move as she swallowed and gave a soft moan, my cock threatened to burst. And when her tongue came out to lick her lips and she smiled, I knew that without uttering a single word, she'd managed to turn the tables. What I'd meant to be titillating for her, had turned into a cock-tease for me. Clearing my throat, I pulled myself together as I placed the empty shell on the tray and motioned for another server to approach.

"Now here is an item that your guests will appreciate for both its beauty and its taste," I said, using a pair of chopsticks provided to pick up the first California sushi roll. "These are known as *uramaki,* which means 'inside-out'. The rice is on the outside and the nori on the inside, wrapped around the avocado, cucumber and crab."

As I talked, I laid pieces of the roll in a line between the valley of her breasts and then in an arch above each beautiful mound. With the last one laid, I picked up a bowl and added a dollop of caviar to the top of each bite.

Looking up, an orange-red orb held gently in the chopsticks, I said, "Nothing is as satisfying as a firm, round orb between your teeth, rolling it a bit in anticipation of the burst of flavor when you finally bite down." Her smirk told me she still thought she'd won. I fed her the single bead of caviar and then bent forward, opening my lips and then closing them… not around a piece of sushi, but around a pebbled nipple, teasing the plump flesh, flicking it with my tongue until she began to squirm just the slightest. Taking the nipple between my teeth, I gave my head a little shake, communicating both my disapproval of her moving and the fact that two could play this little game. My teeth closed to give the bud the slightest bite… hard enough to draw a moan from her, but not one that threatened to disturb the display I was building. Straightening, I grinned.

"As one is taught in culinary school, it is vital that a chef taste his creation as he works." Using my fingertip, I circled the nipple I'd bitten, watching it draw even tighter. "Tonight, I find that it is my favorite lesson as it allows me to nibble before my guests. And, as a dedicated student, I do want to be thorough." I sampled her other nipple, finding it as delicious as the first. By the time I pulled back, she was breathing a bit hard, her back arching as if wanting to offer me another bite.

"Another lesson we were taught is that a good host embraces the fact that we live in a time where so many people are vegans." Motioning to the next sever, I began to lay thin slices of fresh ginger on her naked body. The spicy aroma complemented her own unique scent of arousal as I began to lay a line of fat, plump blueberries along the seam of her legs, their rich purplish-blue color vivid against her pale skin. Slices of fresh fruit followed: the bright green of kiwis, the russet orange of papaya, with mangoes and pineapple adding different hues of yellow as I placed them all over her body and along her arms.

She'd long since stopped taking glances out over the crowd, her body gradually relaxing as I continued. A beautiful smile appeared as I held up a purple pansy, moving to tuck it behind her ear.

"Flowers aren't simply meant to be stuck in a vase," I said as I began to fill in any blank areas with a variety of blooms. "Some blossoms such as a rose have a subtle flavor that is fruity. Others, like the pansy are minty. Violets and sage are sweet. But one of my favorites is the hibiscus which has a cranberry-like flavor and when you drop a bud into a glass of champagne, they bloom before your very eyes." As I spoke, I tucked more flowers into her hair. By the time I was done, she was covered... except for her nipples.

She gave a soft moan as I grinned and picked up something no chef would ever admit to using, her eyes growing wide, her fingers twitching to close against the red rose petals I'd placed in her palms while I shook the can. I knew that it was considered a culinary aberration, but I wasn't going for purity... I was going for effect. And when I turned the can upside down and held the tip a fraction of an inch above her nipple and pressed the nozzle, I was rewarded by a deep moan as the thick whipped cream covered the hard little bud, forming a nice white mound. I lifted the can and plucked one fat, dark red cherry out of the bowl on the last tray. Placing it in its bed of cream, I repeated the steps a second time before finally stepping back.

Lifting the last berry, I held it up and said, "Happy Valentine's Day to the most beautiful centerpiece ever created." Bending down, I gently kissed her, enjoying the slight quiver of her lips against mine. Pulling back, I said, "Open." After her lips parted, I placed the heart-shaped strawberry between her lips. "Now, no biting. A good hostess knows that to eat before her guests have had their fill is the epitome of rudeness."

It took but a couple of seconds, but I knew the very moment she remembered that we weren't alone. A sound that had my cock jerking, once again protesting its confinement, came from her, as I bent down again. "You look incredible. Relax and allow yourself to revel in the experience." Kissing the tip of her nose, I stepped away, turned to face the crowd, and waved a hand over her body. "Bon appétit."

CHAPTER 11

 arnegie

PERHAPS I SHOULD HAVE FELT HUMILIATED AT BEING ON DISPLAY, NAKED beneath a plethora of food, as people accepted Ronan's invitation to dine... on me. When his intention had become clear as he laid the first shrimp my body, I was sure I'd die of embarrassment. Yet when he tilted the shell to my lips, the innuendo that we weren't discussing an oyster quite obvious, all I could think about as the liquor coated my tongue, was that pearly drop of pre-cum oozing from the slit of his cock that I was so desperate to taste. I'd actually forgotten about the crowd as he placed his items. And now, as he issued the invitation to come dine, and I looked up to see people smiling down, I realized it wasn't ridicule I saw in their eyes, their smiles weren't derisive... they were admiring.

As the first man bent forward and gently took a piece of sushi between his teeth, lifting it from my body, I knew I'd be a liar if I said I felt ashamed. As his warm breath wafted across the patch of skin now exposed with the removal of the bite… as his lips closed around the offering in pleasure, I felt… something I never expected.

Arousal.

Others followed, some people using their mouths, others their fingers to make their choice, and I felt every breath, every lick, every touch. Every little nibble had my arousal growing. I saw every smile, every look of enjoyment and I heard every soft moan of appreciation of the morsels they enjoyed. It was heady to know these strangers did not see me as some sort of deviant who ought to feel mortified.

But the most incredible acknowledgment I made was to meet Ronan's eyes and see the pleasure in them, knowing that it wasn't pride of his work in preparing the smorgasbord. It was gratification in seeing that I was enjoying the scene he'd created for me. I had no idea how much time passed as people moved away and others took their place, but looking down my body, I saw that the food was slowly but steadily disappearing.

"How fun." I turned to see a beautiful blonde standing at my side, but her eyes weren't on me, they were on Ronan. "Trust a chef to come up with something so incredibly creative."

"And delicious," the man beside her said, plucking a flower from my body and offering it to her. "It matches your eyes." And it did. When she turned to accept the bite, I saw that the violet he'd chosen matched a pair of the most beautiful eyes I'd ever seen.

"I hope you're enjoying it as much as our guests seem to be," a man who stood on her other side said and I realized the three weren't just members of the club… they owned it.

With the berry still in my mouth, I could only nod, the truth of exactly how much I did flooding through me. There was only one way I could enjoy this more and that would be if Ronan removed his clothes and joined me on the bar…

As if my thoughts had been spoken, the trio smiled and moved away, their departure acting as some sort of signal; the remaining diners offering their compliments to the chef and following. My eyes met Ronan's as he bent forward.

I whimpered as his lips closed around the cherry sitting on my left nipple, slowly drawing it into his mouth. After eating the pitted fruit, he used the tip of his tongue to take long strokes through the mound of cream. And when he moved to my other breast, eating that cherry as well, licking every bit of the whipped cream from my flesh, my arousal skyrocketed. I began to quiver when he lifted his eyes to mine as he ever so slowly closed his teeth around the chilled bud of my tight nipple. When he bit down, my entire body convulsed. His head lifted and he grinned, reaching up to trace the corner of my mouth. It wasn't until he put his finger to his lips and he licked it, that I realized I'd bitten into the berry he'd placed in my mouth, the sweet juice now flooding across my tongue.

"Delicious, isn't it?" he asked, taking the masticated berry from me, taking a bite before feeding me the other half. As I swallowed and nodded, he continued, "But not what I am truly craving." Straightening and taking hold of my hips, he swung my body around, my legs dropping off the edge of the bar on one side, my head off the other... until he pulled my ass forward as he had when I'd been on the exam table. With my head now supported, I was able to watch him run his fingers up my legs, bits of berries and flower petals clinging to his hands as he positioned the soles of my feet on the edge of the bar.

"What I want to taste is that little berry that is yours and yours alone. The one you carry with you at all times. The pearl hidden, protected, by those sweet petals of your cunt. The one that I know is as ripe and plump, as red and juicy as the cherries that decorated your tits."

Oh sweet Jesus. Who talked like that? Who said things that should have made me feel degraded and yet made me feel like the most desirable woman on earth?

"There is always that one serving a hostess sets aside, the one she knows is the best... the sweetest. Open your legs, Carnegie. Open them wide and invite me to feast on your pussy. Ask me to lick your cream from your slit, to suckle, to taste, to nibble your sweet berry until you explode."

Gone was the woman I had been earlier when Madison had called my name in the theater. Gone was the shy woman who'd almost

467

denied herself the experience of being with this man. Gone was the one who was too caught up in what others might think to allow herself to be free to experience life to its fullest. In her place was a woman who wanted nothing more than to surrender to this one man. Knowing he was watching, knowing he wanted me, I obeyed, opening not only my legs, but reaching between my thighs, I slid my fingers through the slickness to open the lips of my labia, offering him the very morsel he desired. The first spasm came as his nostrils flared and his eyes darkened. Looking down my body and between my legs, I had the perfect view of his crotch. I saw his thick cock pulse beneath his pants and knew that he had more control than anyone I'd ever met. He was denying himself yet again to pleasure me... and with that truth, I lifted my eyes to meet his gaze.

"I am yours, Ronan. Please take what you wish. Please, feast on my pussy."

His lip curled as he smiled and lifted my legs to place them over his shoulders. Sliding his hands under my ass, he raised me to his mouth. The moment his tongue made its first flick over my clit, I slid my fingers through the silver at his temples to clutch the thick black strands of his hair.

"Oh... oh God," I moaned as he drove his tongue deep inside my pussy, lapping up my cream, his fingers tightening against my buttocks, holding me in place as the sensations of his tongue, lips, mouth and teeth drove me higher and higher until I was sure I could go no further. When he drew his tongue from my slit only to drop it lower, to lick across my perineum and then to circle my anus, I knew the sounds coming from me were nonsensical. Pleas and moans mixed together into a mantra of passion that only two could understand.

It was wrong. Pressing your tongue into someone's ass was not something good boys did. Squirming—not to get away but to press toward that tongue—was something only the slutty girls did and yet I didn't care. One hand slid from beneath me and fingers began to play with my pussy as he ate out my ass. My hips rocked forward and back as if I were fucking myself on his tongue and his fingers that were now plunging in and out of my pussy. My hands moved to claw at his shoulders as my head tossed from side to side, my back arching.

"Please! Oh God, Ronan! I'm going to... Ronan!" I screamed as my world went supernova, and I learned that not only is it possible to see stars inside, but those stars exploded into bursts of the most indescribable colors as shockwaves ran through every inch of my body. My toes pointed as my heels drummed against his back, my hands reaching over my head to clutch the edge of the bar as if I needed an anchor to tether me to the earth as he forced another climax from me by taking the entirety of my clit into his mouth and biting down, grinding the nub between his teeth and tongue as I flew to the heavens once again, another scream filling the room.

I had no idea how much time had passed before I realized that I was no longer lying on the bar but was cradled on Ronan's lap.

"Welcome back," he said when I lifted my head off his chest to look up.

"God... what... I don't know what to say but, wow. And thank you. And I'm sorry."

He chuckled, bending down to kiss my forehead. "Wow is good, you're welcome and you have absolutely nothing to be sorry for."

"I passed out—"

"*La petite mort*," he corrected. "You experienced the little death which, Carnegie, is about the best compliment a sub can give her Dom."

"It was amazing, but... I wanted more." When his eyebrow arched, I giggled. "Not more for me... well, yes, for me, but for you too. I wanted to taste you... your cock. I wanted to feel your cock inside my mouth and my pussy."

Tightening his arms around me, he stood and began to walk. It wasn't until we reached the theater that I realized I was still as naked as the day I was born. I had no idea where my clothes were and for some reason, I couldn't bring myself to care.

Ronan didn't set me on my feet when we reached the roulette wheel.

"Are you sure she has the strength left to hold the ball?" Madison asked, attempting to sound concerned and yet her amusement was obvious as she pressed the ball into my hand.

"Funny girl," Ronan said, guiding my hand to hover over the wheel. "Go ahead, babe. Make a wish and drop the ball."

"For the love of all that is naughty, please, please land on something that guarantees I'll finally get into your pants!"

Madison gave a strangled laugh even as Ronan chuckled and I let my hand open. As it bounced about, Madison looked at us, her head shaking. "Girl, we've gotta meet for coffee. Like soon. I can't wait to hear how you can possibly look so fucking satisfied if you've not even been fucked."

I laughed and said, "You've got a date," turning my attention back to the wheel as it began to slow. When the ball finally dropped, I could feel my face flaming as I looked from the activity to Ronan. "Well, I suppose that is a way to assure your pants come off or at least open to give me a glimpse of your cock, but that is so not what I meant."

"It's fine," Ronan said without so much as a flinch.

"Oh, good, you picked it as a hard limit," I said, relief flooding through me.

Madison shook her head. "Sorry, but he didn't and since neither one of you entered *Water Sports* as a hard limit, I'm afraid—"

Looking at Madison, I said, "If I were a spiteful person, I'd cancel our date."

"Well, if it helps, you've got less than an hour before eleven when Roulette Night is officially over."

"Then we'd better get on with it," Ronan said. Turning, he carried me out of the theater for the last time. Before I could think of a way to get out of this activity, he grinned down at me. "Don't worry. I'm a chef, remember?"

"What does that have to do with... you know—"

"It means I am a pro at taking an old dish and resurrecting it into something so different you forget the original definition."

I had absolutely no idea how that helped, but if the truth be told, I really wasn't thinking about what he said. I was wondering how the hell I'd missed marking this as a hard limit.

CHAPTER 12

onan

I'D AGREED TO PARTICIPATE IN THIS AUCTION AS A COURTESY TO EMMA, and yet it seemed that she was the one who had done me a favor. I'd played with women before, but never had I ever enjoyed myself as much. There was just something about the woman in my arms. She was so innocent and yet so willing to explore. I'd seen the doubt in her eyes, heard the hesitation in her responses but as we'd scened, she'd opened like the flowers I'd scattered over her naked body. And when she'd stared into my eyes, holding her pussy open and invited me to feast, I'd almost come in my pants like some untried teenager.

But what I loved the most was her absolute trust that I was going to keep her safe, that I'd not allow anything to hurt her. Seeing her look up at me now, I was determined to fulfill the wish she'd made on the stage.

I didn't set her down until we reached the destination that had popped into my head the moment that ball had settled into the pocket of the wheel. Carnegie looked around and then back up to me, the little lines across the bridge of her nose as she scrunched it told of her confusion.

Keeping my arm around her, I said, "Are you okay to stand on your own?"

"Yes, I'm fine."

Releasing her, I dropped my hand to unbuckle my belt, and she reached out and put her hand against the wall. As I lowered my zipper, she moaned, but when I pulled out my cock, her eyes widened and I saw her legs begin to tremble. I was instantly at her side, my arm around her again.

"Whoa, babe. Breathe, I've got you."

"I'm okay," she said, her voice as shaky as her legs. "Just... just please get it over with." She straightened, stepped out of my hold and turned to face me, giving me a last look before her eyes closed.

Fuck... she was glorious and it had nothing to do with her nudity. It was her courage, her determination to submit with poise even when the act she expected was as far from dignified as one could imagine.

She stood as still as a statue, a stone sculpture, and though the marble was marred by bits of rice, dots of caviar, and spots of different colors where fruit had left its juices, she was the most beautiful goddess I'd ever seen. She didn't move a muscle as I stripped off the remainder of my clothes until I was as naked as she. Stepping forward, her quick inhalation told me she was aware of my presence, but she didn't flinch and her eyes didn't open... not until the splash hit her.

I was ready, slipping an arm around her again, but not to simply steady her this time, but to pull her to me as the stream flowed over both of us from the rain showerhead above our heads. When I was sure she wasn't going to fall, I loosened my hold to sluice my hand over her slick skin, removing the remaining evidence of the appetizers I'd decorated her body with. When her skin was once again clean, I reached past her and turned off the faucet before taking her hand and stepping away from the shower area to lead her down into the pool. I walked out until I was waist deep before stopping and dropping my hand to her waist.

"I thought you were going to… to pee on me."

"The activity dictates *water sports*," I said. "And since I've got the *water* part covered"—I reached down to stroke across the very top of her breasts that were bobbing on the surface—"all we need to do is satisfy the *sports* element and that, babe, is where you come in."

"So, you want what? To have a race?"

"No," I said, reaching out to take her hand and drawing it beneath the water. I watched her eyes as she smiled and wrapped her fingers around my cock.

"You want me to jerk you off?"

"No, I want you to suck me off," I said.

She nodded, but released my cock and attempted to turn. When I didn't move my feet, she looked up at me. "Um, aren't you going to get out or at least sit on the edge or something?"

I shook my head. "Sports are meant to be a challenge. They are meant to improve your physical condition, to increase your strength, to push your boundaries. You'll suck my cock right here."

Looking down, she said, "But your cock is under water."

"It is," I concurred, moving my hands to her shoulders. "You're not afraid of water?" She shook her head. "You can swim?" A nod gave me my next line. "Then, Carnegie, I suggest you take a deep breath."

She took several breaths, each a bit deeper, inhaling slowly and then exhaling. Finally, she took another, and with a final look at me, slipped beneath the water's surface. On her first attempt, she only managed to take the head of my cock in her mouth for the barest moment before she popped back to the surface.

"I'm afraid that's not a qualifying entry."

Pushing her mass of hair off her face, she said, "Consider it a false start. But… wow, you're really big."

I grinned. I mean, what man wouldn't when given such a compliment by a beautiful woman. Another breath and she went under again, managing to take me back into her mouth and this time, I felt her tongue sliding along my cock a couple of times before she broke away, and came up again.

"I keep drifting away," she said. "Can you help hold me down?"

I'd never had a problem holding a woman to my cock when dominating her, but never had I done so where water was involved. I took a few steps forward to lower the level. "I will, but I'll only hold your shoulders. You won't be able to speak a safe word so when you need to breathe, simply release your hold. I'll help you up."

Nodding, she took some more breaths and went down again, this time with my hands on her shoulders helping her to kneel on the pool's bottom. Her hair fanned out to float around her as she bent forward and took my cock into her mouth again. Her lips sealed around the head and her tongue began to take short licks as she suckled. It wasn't the best blowjob I'd ever gotten, but it was incredible simply because she was submitting to my request. And, to be honest, I was so primed at having held back that I knew it wouldn't take long to make me come. She'd come up for air, her hand continuing to move up and down my shaft as she filled her lungs before returning to her task. The third time she surfaced, I said, "I'm going to come. I know you can't swallow underwater, so pull off—"

"No, I want to taste you. I'll hold it in my mouth until I come up."

Holy shit! What could I say to that except, "All right."

It only took her lips tightening around me once again and a little unexpected scrape of her teeth before my cock jerked to shoot the first jet of my cum into her mouth. I was ready to pull her off and up at the first sign of distress, yet she held on to my thighs and took me even deeper, keeping her mouth on me until I was done. She lost a bit of my seed as she had to open her mouth to release me, the water diluting the evidence. Once she stood before me, she swiped her wet hair off her cheeks and lifted her chin to meet my eyes.

"Open," I said.

Her lips parted and she opened her mouth wide, a pool of white cream sitting in the cup of her tongue. My cock jerked, hardening again despite having just emptied into her mouth. "Swallow," I said. Her mouth closed and she swallowed before the tip of her tongue came out to trace along her lips as if to make sure she didn't miss a single drop.

"Fuck, you are incredible," I said, yanking her to me and lowering

474

my head to crush my mouth against hers. "Congratulations, you win the trophy for the sport of underwater cock sucking."

"I don't want a trophy or a medal around my neck," she said, wrapping her legs around my waist as I lifted her to carry her out of the pool.

"What do you want?"

"Your cock in my pussy… now!"

That definitely worked for me. Grabbing a condom from a bowl on a table, I dropped it into her hand, grabbing a small packet of lube as she ripped her package open with her teeth. She was already rolling the condom over my cock as I moved toward the first place that offered a bit of privacy, which happened to be the sauna. The moment the door closed and the heat hit us, I heard her moan.

Pressing her against the wall was iffy as I worried the surface was too hot. Instead, I sank down on the smooth teak bench and without needing encouraging, she reached for my cock, lifting a bit to guide me to her entrance and began to sink down.

"Oh my God," she moaned as my cock forced her pussy to open, to stretch to accommodate me. "So big… so good."

I helped her, my hands on her hips pulling her down, impaling her inch by inch until finally her ass sat on my lap. Planting her hands on my chest, she began to rock up and down, back and forth, finding a rhythm that had her eyes closing, her back arching. Her breasts filled my hands as I squeezed the plump mounds, playing with her nipples, rolling them between my fingers, each twist and tug drawing a moan from her. Our skin grew slick with the heat, the steam rolling over us as she continued to ride me. I slid a hand behind her, drawing a finger down the crevasse of her ass to find her anus, the tight pucker resisting my finger's entrance into her dark little hole. Her moan had my cock jerk inside her, yet I was not done… would not be satisfied until I'd claimed every hole.

"Let me in," I ordered. When instead she tensed, I pulled my hand free and slapped her ass… Once, twice, three times… hard. "I don't have my belt, but I owe you a half dozen strokes. If you don't wish to make it a dozen, then relax and ask me to put my finger in your ass."

By the time I was pressing against the little pink star again, all it took was a firm tap to feel her relax. She'd stopped rocking on my cock and that wouldn't do.

"Keep riding my cock and ask me to finger fuck your ass. Ask me to help it open, to stretch you before I replace it with my cock."

The steam was thick but not so impenetrable that I couldn't see her eyes widen. The instant contraction of her pussy walls around my cock told me she might be nervous, but the idea of having her ass fucked turned her on. "Ask me, Carnegie."

"Please… put your finger in me."

"Where?" I asked, pressing just enough to feel the give of her tissues without penetrating her.

"My ass."

"Why?"

"Oh God," she whispered. "To… to stretch me. Finger fuck my ass, please."

"Good girl," I said, pushing harder and breaching her ass. "Ride me, Carnegie. Ride my cock and my finger."

She began to rock again, back and forth as I worked on preparing her. Two fingers soon filled her, the heat, the sweat, her cream providing the lubrication needed to open her. I slid them free only to add a third, working them slowly inside her.

"I-I can't… it's…. oh God, it's too much."

"It's not," I assured her. Her mind might protest, telling her it was impossible to think of opening further or perhaps attempting to convince her that anything with *that* part of her body was taboo, but her body was telling the truth. Her nipples had drawn into tight little pebbles and her pussy continued to spasm, her cream leaking to add even more lubrication to that from the packet I'd torn open. Pulling my fingers free, I lifted her off my cock, loving the whine she gave. I stood, moving behind her and guiding her to plant her palms on the seat where I'd sat.

"Spread your legs and lift that gorgeous ass," I said, pressing my palm against her back, encouraging her to present her ass. With my free hand, I ran my finger around her opening before pushing inside

476

her ass again. "Every inch of you is mine. Every hole is mine to lick, to play with, to fuck with my tongue, my fingers and my cock. So, Carnegie, what am I going to put right here?" I asked, thrusting a bit harder.

"Your cock," she said without hesitating.

"And then what?" I asked, pulling my fingers free and spreading the last of the lube over the condom that was already slick from her pussy juice.

"You're going to fuck me."

"Fuck you where?"

"My ass. You're going to fuck my ass."

"That's right. I'm going to fuck your ass and you are going to come for me aren't you?"

"Yes… yes, sir."

It was the first time she'd called me sir. For the first time in my life, I recognized it not only as a title offered to a Dom, but an offering of respect, of trust, of submission on a level I'd never truly contemplated before this moment. Bending forward, I turned her head to the side, looking into her eyes. "Just like on the bar, allow yourself to feel, to embrace every sensation." At her nod, I gave her lips a soft kiss. Straightening and positioning my cockhead at her entrance, I began to press forward, forcing her anus to open, the preparations making it easier and yet still the stretch required had her legs trembling, her breath hitching between soft mewls, her body stiffening.

"Push back," I instructed, a hand on her hip guiding her back. "Put your face on your hands and lift your ass higher." I held still, the earlier blowjob allowing me to go slow, to allow her time to adjust as I continued.

"God, you're so tight," I said. I loved every soft yip, whine, moan and gasp as my cock slowly disappeared inch by inch into her hot little ass. When my balls finally slapped against her pussy, I bent forward again. "Good girl. You took every inch. How do you feel?"

"Full," she said softly. "Very full."

Pushing the mass of her hair aside, I kissed her neck, feeling the walls of her ass spasm around my cock. Taking a nip, I kissed and nibbled my way down her spine as I straightened. Sliding my hands under her, I played with her breasts, squeezing them gently before giving them little slaps that had them bouncing and her moaning and arching back. Wrapping one arm around her waist, I drew her up until her back was pressed against my chest, the new position driving my cock deeper.

"Oh... oh fuck," she moaned.

"That's the plan," I said, her groan most likely meant as derision for my tasteless joke, but it did nothing except have my cock swell inside her, filling her even fuller as I began to piston my hips.

"Hands around my neck," I instructed when hers lifted to interfere with my plucking, twisting and pulling on her nipples. Lifting her arms, she obeyed, the position exposing every inch of her glorious breasts and those sweet nipples to whatever I wished. And I wished to fuck her... hard. Every thrust upwards drove her onto her toes and every withdrawal had her flat on her feet again. It was a dance that was our own, the sounds of flesh slapping against flesh mingling with the soft cries and moans of a woman finding intense pleasure in the gift of her submission. My hips snapped forward as my fingers dropped from her nipples to her pussy.

"Oh, God, please." The sound of her moan was delicious and yet suddenly she gave a different cry when the door opened.

I ignored the intrusion, not allowing her to drop out of the pleasure. Sliding my fingers through her sex, I opened her plump, slick lips to circle her throbbing clit. It didn't take long for the first mini contractions to start, each one felt as the walls surrounding my driving cock grew tighter.

"That's it. Come for me, Carnegie. I want to feel your walls squeezing my cock. I want you to come while I'm fucking your ass. I want you to explode while my dick is buried deep in your tight little hole." Taking her clit between my index finger and thumb, I pinched them together, flattening the sensitive bundle of nerves as I drove my cock deep into her bowels.

I didn't need a trophy or a medal. My reward was her primal scream, her fingers practically ripping a clump of my hair out by the roots as every muscle in her body contracted. The walls of her ass were like a vise around my cock, making it almost impossible to move, milking me, forcing my release to come as well. I shouted her name, my cries of pure bliss joining hers as I filled the condom with my cum while hers covered my fingers as I continued to stroke her pussy.

With a final cry, she shuddered, releasing my hair as she bent forward, planting her hands on the bench again, breathing hard and giving soft little mewls as I pulled from her ass a bit quicker than I wanted but I was afraid she might pass out again. After disposing of the condom, I pulled her to me as I turned to sit, drawing her onto my lap.

"Perfect timing," came a disembodied voice from the direction of the door. "It's 11:05, but I didn't have the heart to stop you before you finished."

"If you want me to think you're kind-hearted, you'd turn around and forget we're in here," I said, recognizing the voice as belonging to Elijah Keaton, the Dungeon Master for Black Light.

He laughed. "Sorry. Not only can't I do that, but at the risk you might slip something into my next hamburger, I'm actually doing you a favor. It's unsafe to stay in this heat for too long. I've dropped your clothes outside the door. Oh, and should I assure the bosses that you enjoyed our little game?"

"You should leave before I decide to kick your ass," I said, listening as he chuckled, pulled the door open and stepped out.

"I don't want it to be over," Carnegie said, her head lifting from where it had been pressed against my chest.

"Who said it's over? I not only owe you a session with my belt, but I've yet to sink into you while you're wearing those incredible fuck-me heels," I said as I stood, letting her slide down my body until she settled on her feet.

"But he said we had to leave."

Guiding her to the door, I opened it and stood on the threshold as the steam billowed out before dissipating around us. Looking down, I brushed her hair over her shoulders. "Babe, Roulette is over, but that doesn't mean we are. We'll simply move to my place to continue our play. I've a lot more to teach you."

"You do?"

"Yes, so much that I'm afraid it will take far, far longer than a few hours. But don't fear, I'm in the perfect profession to make sure you're well fed between lessons. How does that sound?"

Her smile was huge as she looked up at me, her eyes sparkling as she gave me her answer. "How about we start with a demonstration on how it is possible to share a midnight snack without having to cook a single thing. Ever heard of sixty-nine?"

The End

ABOUT THE AUTHOR

Maggie Ryan is a *USA Today* and #1 international best selling author in the USA and UK. Often found in Top 100 authors on Amazon and is a Multi-award Winning Author in Victorian/ Historical, Western, and Contemporary Erotic Romance.

Take something sweet, drop in a bit of spice, mix with a dash of taboo and what do you get? A story that will take you on a journey. I love the thought that fiction offers a world of endless possibilities. I hope you will curl up in your favorite chair and take the journey with me. Happy Reading!

Connect with Maggie on:

- http://www.authormaggieryan.com
- Follow her on Twitter: @authormryan
- Email: maggie.ryan.writes@gmail.com
- Facebook: https://www.facebook.com/authormaggieryan/
- Amazon Author Page: https://amazon.com/author/ maggieryan

CHERISHED

A Black Light: Celebrity Roulette Novella

By

Sue Lyndon

CHAPTER 1

*S*erena gasped at the contents of her inbox. She clutched her phone harder and inhaled a deep breath. The chatter from the brunch crowd in the trendy outdoor café faded into the background.

Holy shit. Holy motherfucking shit.

She placed her phone down and reached for her mimosa. Her hands shook as she managed a few sips. The drink settled her nerves, but only a little. Excitement continued pumping through her, so fast she felt as if her heart might burst out of her chest. If she was alone in her house, she would squeal and jump up and down. But as a well-known heiress out in public during Sunday brunch in L.A., she didn't dare make a scene. The last thing she needed was her face splashed across the tabloids again with another ridiculous headline.

Tapping on her phone to illuminate the screen, she studied the email, just to be sure she wasn't dreaming the whole thing up.

She read it over and over, reveling in each victorious word.

Congratulations, Ms. Hawthorne! You are the winner of the charity auction for Trenton Banks. We look forward to seeing you at the Celebrity Roulette event at Black Light West on Valentine's Day. Please arrive before the 7:00PM start time.

If you are no longer able to participate, a runner up will be selected to take your place. Please reply to this email confirming your attendance.

Her heart skipped a beat.

Trenton Banks.

Trenton-*oh-my-god-I-want-to-have-his-babies*-Banks would be hers. For an entire evening. And not just any evening, but a very, very kinky one. Heat pulsed between her thighs and she squirmed in her seat, exhaling a shaky breath. She pushed up her oversized sunglasses, shoved her phone aside, and reached for her mimosa. Once she finished it and the waiter brought her another one, along with the tomato frittata she'd ordered for herself and the fruit plate she'd ordered for her friend Gwen who was already thirty minutes late, she compiled a mental list of everything she had to get done during the next three days to prepare for her big night.

A trip to Magnolia's Spa was first on her list, for a full day of massages, waxing, facials, exfoliation, and aromatherapy. She also needed the perfect outfit, the perfect hair, and a killer mani pedi. She wanted to look her best for Trenton. Her pulse raced faster when his handsome face flashed in her mind.

Her phone buzzed and she peered at the screen. She frowned at the text from her friend Gwen.

Sorry, love! I am 2 hungover 2 make it! Drink a mimosa for me tho!

Typical Gwen. Serena wasn't surprised, but with the upcoming night at Black Light occupying her mind, she wasn't too upset her friend couldn't join her this morning. Now she had more time to think and plan and…overthink.

She took a small bite of the frittata and tried to ignore the anxieties that were threatening to dampen her excitement. She couldn't help but wonder if Trenton Banks would remember her. They'd shared a *moment* a couple of years ago, one that had had a lasting impact on her. One that left her unable to stop thinking about him and crashing parties she thought he might attend, if only for the chance to talk to him one more time.

As the voices from the brunch crowd and passing cars faded

further into the background, she relived every second of the fateful night she'd met her celebrity crush.

Serena navigated through the party, heading for one of the balconies she'd spotted earlier. On her way through the crowd, she grabbed a glass of champagne off a passing waiter's tray. Before she stepped outside, she scanned the party for signs of her boyfriend, Amos. She hadn't seen him for at least a half hour.

Where the hell was he? He had a bad habit of temporarily ditching her during parties.

Since it was New Year's Eve, he'd promised to stay by her side all evening, joking that he didn't want to risk not being the one to kiss her at midnight. Now that he'd broken yet another promise, his joke no longer seemed funny and part of her didn't care if she wasn't standing next to him when the ball dropped.

Relief filled her to discover the balcony empty. She moved to the railing and peered across the illuminated pool area below. Christmas lights twinkled on palm trees surrounding the perimeter of the large backyard. During lulls in the noise of the party, she heard the occasional crash of ocean waves hitting the shore. Maybe if she couldn't find Amos before midnight, she'd walk down to the beach and ring in the New Year by herself. Why not? The beach was a better option. A thousand times better than finding herself surrounded by a houseful of semi-acquaintances who might as well be strangers.

She sighed and squinted against the lights of the surrounding houses and streetlights, trying to make out the moon and stars. As she turned her head and tried to focus, she caught movement in her peripheral vision.

Great. She wasn't alone, after all. A couple stood beside a tall potted plant in the near darkness, kissing one another and grinding their hips together. Jealousy surged through her. She wished Amos would grab her and kiss her like that. But he never did. Not even when she donned a short, tight red dress like she wore tonight.

When the couple shifted away from the plant and further into the light, she glimpsed the man's hair—a familiar shock of frosted blond locks, spiked tall in the middle.

No no no. It couldn't be.

"Amos?" His name escaped her lips in a disgusted hiss.

"Shit!" The man pushed his redheaded companion away slightly, holding her out by her arms, and stared straight at Serena with wide eyes. "What the fuck are you doing out here? I thought I told you to wait by the dancefloor, babe."

"Don't call me 'babe.'" Her stomach dropped to the floor.

The redhead looked from Amos to Serena, her expression growing agitated. "You said you didn't have a girlfriend, you asshole." With that, she spun on her heel and stalked back into the party, leaving Serena alone with Mr. Cheater Fuckington.

"I can't believe this." She gripped onto the railing for support. "I'm such an idiot. My friends warned me about you, but I didn't listen."

"Babe." Amos gave her a charming smile as he moved fully into the light. "Come here." He opened his arms and beckoned her to hug him. She didn't move a muscle. "I'm sorry. It's just that she has very large breasts, and well... you know how much I like a busty woman. It was a mistake. One little slip. I swear it's never happened before. You're my girl," he said. "Only you."

"We're over," she said, "Now, if you don't mind, I'd like to be alone." She needed a few minutes to get her emotions under control before she left the party for good and walked down to the beach. The crashing waves called to her over the noise of the party, promising solitude and safety.

"Fine," he said, running his fingers through his spiked hair. "I'm gone. I was planning on breaking up with you after the holidays anyway."

His words stung, but she bit the inside of her mouth to keep her lips from quivering. She blinked fast a few times, not wanting to give him the satisfaction of seeing tears in her eyes. But he'd already turned his back on her. He walked into the party and immediately put his arm around the first woman he came across. The blonde smiled up at him, no doubt excited that Amos Badd, heartthrob of the early 2000s boy band, Bad Badd Boyz, had decided to pay attention to her.

Serena turned to gaze over the pool area, only to give a gasp when a male figure approached her from the other side of the balcony. And not just any male figure. A very famous one. She felt her eyes widen as her stomach flipped.

Famous action movie star Trenton Banks was walking up to her. All six feet seven inches of him. To her surprise, a concerned look covered his face, worry lines forming on his forehead as compassion flared in the depths of his sexy dark eyes.

"Excuse me, miss, but are you okay?" He gave her a brief smile and gestured to a seating area in the shadows, on the opposite side of the balcony from where Amos's make out session had just transpired. "I was sitting over there and saw the whole thing. I didn't mean to eavesdrop, but...well, I was kind of hoping you'd toss your champagne in Amos Badd's face. I absolutely detest his music. It's a sin against mankind."

Laughter built in Serena's chest and she finally let it loose. Oh, it felt nice to laugh. She grinned up at Trenton, appreciating his joke, even if she personally liked most of Bad Badd Boyz's albums. "Don't worry about the eavesdropping." She glanced down at her drink. "Damn, you're right. I should have soaked the bastard."

He placed a hand on her arm, the concern in his eyes deepening. "But seriously, are you okay?"

"I'm fine. Really. It came as a shock, even though all the warning signs of being a major fucking player were there." She ran a hand through her hair and glanced at the twinkling palm trees as they swayed in a gentle wind. "I kept ignoring them because I thought...well, I guess I thought if he fell in love with me, he would finally change his ways. Sad, huh?"

"It's not sad, and if it makes you feel better, I know the feeling. My last girlfriend cheated on me. It's a shitty feeling and I'm sorry it happened to you —on New Year's Eve, no less."

"I'm sorry to hear that. Why do people have to suck?" She shot him what she hoped was a comforting smile, and to her delight the corners of his mouth creased just a little. He didn't grin often in his movies, she noted. He chased down bad guys and beat the shit out of them, but the serious nature of his typical movies didn't leave much room for smiling.

Did he recognize her? She wondered. She wasn't nearly as famous as him, but sometimes their names graced the same tabloids. She didn't want to be pretentious and ask if he knew her name.

What was he doing at a New Year's Eve party hosted by Blue Inspire Records, though?

Had he come with someone?

"Um, it's almost midnight," she said with a glance through the windows at the large lighted ball in the middle of the main party room, a miniature replica of the ball in Times Square. "You'd better go find the person you came with, if you want to be with them when the ball drops." She took a sip of champagne, needing to hide her expression. She didn't want him to see the disappointment on her face when he departed the balcony.

But he didn't turn and leave. He remained next to her, his hand still gently touching her arm. The breeze picked up, sending the scent of his expensive cologne to her nostrils. She inhaled deep, wishing she could lean against him and let him hold her while the ball dropped.

"I came alone," he said, "and I'd like to remain on the balcony with you. Unless you wish to be alone."

Hope rose in her chest. But she quickly told herself she was being silly to think Trenton Banks was attracted to her. He was simply being nice, trying to comfort a woman he'd just witnessed getting dumped on a holiday. His reputation as a good guy in real life really preceded him.

"Miss?" he asked when she took too long to reply.

"Please stay," she said, and she realized he most definitely didn't know who she was. He'd called her 'miss' twice now. She tried not to let that wound her.

"All right." His dark eyes twinkled and he moved closer, until she could feel the waves of heat from his huge, muscular body.

"Ten, nine, eight, seven..." The crowd within the house started counting down.

During the countdown, Trenton held her gaze, not once blinking or glancing away. For the briefest second, she thought he might kiss her. How ridiculous, she scolded herself.

He doesn't even know your name. Why would he kiss you?

But when the ball finally dropped, he did in fact kiss her, though it wasn't the kind of kiss she had expected. Instead of leaning down and pressing his lips to hers, he gathered her close and placed a soft, lingering kiss to her forehead.

The world stopped spinning and even though Serena saw fireworks exploding in the sky from the corner of her eye, she didn't hear the booms or even the cheering that must be going on inside the house. For several long moments, it was as if Trenton and Serena were the only two people left on Earth.

"Happy New Year," he said, stroking the side of her face, causing goosebumps to rise all over her body.

"Happy New Year," she replied.

"Come on." He placed a hand on her lower back and turned her to face the party, "I'll walk you out of here and put you in a cab."

Five minutes later, she watched him wave goodbye to her from the middle of the street while the cab pulled away. Once he was out of sight, she settled into her seat and touched the spot on her forehead where he'd kissed her. Tingles spiraled through her limbs. Her legs suddenly felt like jelly and she was glad to be sitting down.

Trenton Banks, of all people, had kissed her forehead at the stroke of midnight.

And when his lips had pressed to her flesh with such gentleness, she'd felt warm and fuzzy inside, as well as...cherished.

Oh, how she hoped she saw him again.

"Miss, is something wrong with your meal?" The waiter's concerned voice pulled her back to the present.

She glanced around, almost surprised to find herself seated in the outdoor section of her favorite brunch spot, the place packed and the noise of the brunch crowd louder than she remembered. When she shifted slightly in her seat, the same delicious pulses that had affected her earlier flared hotter. Thoughts of Trenton Banks never failed to make her feel all sorts of things. Excited, nervous, hopelessly aroused...

"Miss," the waiter said again, "could I bring you something different?"

"Oh," she said, looking at her nearly untouched plate. "This is quite good. No need to bring anything else. Just the check please so I can leave as soon as I'm finished." She flashed him a smile and his eyes filled with relief. He produced the check, wished her a pleasant day, and departed the table.

Serena enjoyed the rest of her brunch in a trancelike state, imagining the fun she would have with Trenton during Celebrity Roulette. She doubted he would remember her from that night. It had been dark and both of them had been drinking. Well, she assumed he'd been drinking. She hadn't actually seen him consume any alcohol.

It was probably best he didn't remember her, lest he think she was some weird lovestruck stalker who just happened to have deep enough pockets to win an evening with him at Black Light West.

Maybe they would spin for *bondage* or *spanking* or *oral sex*, she thought with a wry grin as the mounting heat in her sex made it impossible to sit still. She certainly wouldn't mind if Trenton—who, lucky for her, happened to be a dom—tied her up, took her over his knee for a spanking, or held her face in his hands while she sucked his cock.

Thankfully, his hard limits were the same as Serena's—blood play, needle play, and water sports. While she was a new member at Black Light and didn't have a lot of experience in all the kinks they could possibly spin on the roulette wheel, she was up for the challenge of trying something new with handsome, dreamy Trenton Banks who had once kissed her forehead and made her feel like the most special girl in the entire world, if only for one night.

She almost laughed aloud when she recalled her shock over finding his name on the Celebrity Roulette silent auction list. She'd been visiting Black Light for only a month and had never run into him there. She hadn't had the slightest clue he was a dom or even dreamed that he might be a member of the exclusive club.

Talk about luck. Or maybe, fate.

She replied to the email from Black Light, confirming her attendance. The second she hit *send*, a fresh batch of nerves fluttered to life in her stomach. What if this was all a big, horrible, impulsive mistake?

Trenton Banks, aka Mr. Big Macho Movie Star, whom she'd had a crush on since her early teenage years, was twice her age and probably far more experienced in the BDSM scene than her. She swallowed hard and reached for her mimosa.

What had she gotten herself into?

CHAPTER 2

*T*renton sat at the bar in Black Light West, thankful to be back in familiar surroundings after two months of filming in Australia. When his friend Jaxson had asked if he wanted to celebrate his grand return by participating in a charity auction *with a twist*, Trenton had readily agreed. It's not like he had anything better to do on Valentine's Day, and the prospect of being matched with an eager submissive who'd won him in an online auction had been too good to resist.

Now here he sat, nursing an Old Fashioned, thirty minutes before the start of Celebrity Roulette. His blood heated and his cock stirred in his jeans, his anticipation over the evening to come growing with each passing second. He wondered who had won him for the evening and cast a curious glance over his shoulder, but he didn't catch anyone watching him. He turned around and took another sip of his drink.

Based on his MF pairing, he supposed a spoiled socialite had likely placed the highest bid. Maybe even a wealthy divorcee or widow. This was Los Angeles, after all. But that was no fucking problem. He would enjoy playing with a spoiled little submissive, making her blush, making her obey, and punishing her when she failed to follow his instructions.

But Christ, he really fucking hoped they spun intercourse as one of their activities.

Vaginal or anal, it didn't matter.

After spending the last two months filming in a remote part of the Australian outback, he was ready to fuck a submissive woman completely senseless. Whoever the winner was, not only would she get her money's worth, but she would be sore between her thighs for days.

If he hadn't returned home to a mess involving his younger brother, he would've had time to visit Black Light already and satiate his needs. But the first week back he'd had to bail Chuck out of jail and drag him to a rehab center upstate. Once Trenton returned to L.A. from that unexpected trip, he spent several days looking in on Chuck's wife and kids, making sure they had everything they needed and assuring them that Chuck would get sober and come home soon. He only hoped he wasn't lying. He was paying for Chuck's rehab and wouldn't let his brother's wife and kids go without. Beyond that, there wasn't much Trenton could do, and he hated the fucking helplessness of the situation.

Downing the last sip of his Old Fashioned, he resolved to push all thoughts of family troubles from his mind this evening. He needed to stay focused on the submissive woman who'd placed the winning bid on him, where his control and domination would be welcomed. Leaving the bar area, he slowly made his way through the opulent rooms of Black Light. He greeted acquaintances he passed, some of them actors who'd starred in movies alongside him.

When he reached the large movie theater where festivities would begin, he spotted a pretty young woman with flowing blonde curls leaning against the wall, sipping a glass of champagne. She wore killer heels, a tight mini skirt, and a skimpy halter-top that shimmered in the light of the decorative sconces. Her stomach was flat and toned, her legs were long and lithe.

Who was she? A spectator come to watch Celebrity Roulette? Or a participant?

Despite her revealing outfit, there was an innocence about her that intrigued him. Perhaps it was the lost look in her eyes, a spark of loneliness so subtle that most people wouldn't notice it. She wasn't mingling with anyone, and he got the sense that even though she was obviously a member here, she still felt out of place. He had the ridiculous urge to stroll up to her, take her in his arms, and promise her she was about to have an enjoyable evening.

His pulse quickened when he realized she looked familiar. Had he met her before? Was she an actress whose name he couldn't remember? He racked his brain but came up empty.

Just as she lifted the champagne glass to her lips, her gaze locked with his. Suddenly, she gagged on her drink and started coughing. She turned her back on him and coughed harder.

After grabbing a glass of water off the tray of a passing waiter, Trenton approached the woman and offered her the drink. "Here you go. Drink this. It'll help."

Her deep blue eyes widened and her mouth parted slightly as she stared at him, giving him the same awestruck look women who ran into him in public usually gave him. Sometimes he hated this particular look, but on her he fucking loved it.

He took the champagne from her hand and replaced it with the water, again urging her to drink it. With her face reddening further, she tilted her head back and took a long, drawn out drink of the water. Once she finished, she only gave one last tiny cough.

"Thank you," she said. "The bubbles must have gotten to me. I don't drink champagne often."

"You're very welcome." He paused to fully appreciate her beauty. She really did have the most stunning blue eyes, and it took all his self-control to keep himself from moving closer and running his hands through her hair. "Have we met before?"

She shook her head vigorously. "Nope, I don't think so." A fresh flush spread up from her neck to cover her entire face. "Well, I mean I know who you are, Mr. Banks, but we've never actually met before. It's nice to, um, meet you."

He gave her a brief but warm smile. "May I ask your name?"

"Serena." An alarmed look took over her lovely features. "I mean, *Sunshine*. My play name is Sunshine."

"It's nice to meet you, Sunshine." Secretly, he was fucking thrilled to know her real name. Even if only her first name. Serena. Little Serena Sunshine.

Fuck. What was he doing? In minutes, he would learn who'd won him for the night. Openly ogling another woman right now was most definitely a dick move. The winning submissive might be watching him right now. But fuck if he couldn't help giving Sunshine another admiring look, his gaze sweeping from her head to her toes and taking in every glorious curve of her toned little form.

He took a deep breath and returned his eyes to hers, delighting in the blush that stained her cheeks. What he wouldn't give to play with her for a few hours. Perhaps he would run into her on another night and they could share in a scene. His blood heated at the thought. In his experience, the shy, innocent looking ones always came the hardest. He'd bet the earnings from his last movie that her panties—if she was wearing any—were soaked through by now. Judging by the hitching of her breath and the dilating of her pupils, his nearness had an effect on her.

Little Serena Sunshine would be his. Maybe not tonight. But soon.

"I have to head up to the stage now." He returned her champagne back to her, his fingers grazing hers for one delicious, tense second. "Perhaps we will run into each other later."

"Yes, Mr. Banks, perhaps we will."

He entered the movie theater and went to stand close to the stage near some of the other contestants. He recognized a few musicians, as well as a baseball player and a model. A nice variety of celebrities, he decided.

Trenton checked his watch. Five minutes until start time. His pulse raced and he inhaled a deep breath, feeling a surge of power at knowing that he would soon meet his submissive female for the night.

But the sudden sound of a woman crying out in pain pulled his attention to the opposite side of the movie theater. He turned to see a crowd of people forming around someone on the floor. Alarmed, he

497

peered at the scene, only to see the baseball player in front of him rushing into the crowd.

"She tripped her on purpose!" a tall woman standing a few rows back yelled, pointing at a smirking dark-haired woman who was sitting near the scene and holding an umbrella. "I saw it! She stuck her umbrella out and tripped her!" Several other spectators called out, confirming the accusations.

Apparently, the crowd was gathered around a woman on the floor who'd fallen, and the baseball player moved between them and knelt on the floor, though Trenton couldn't see the hurt woman. A shouting match soon erupted between several DMs and the accused woman, whose voice hurt Trenton's ears as she screeched out her denial. The crowd grew larger and Trenton had a difficult time seeing or hearing what was going on. Eventually, the baseball played carried the injured woman out of the theater and Miguel, who Trenton vaguely remembered was head of security, escorted the protesting dark-haired woman from the movie theater as well.

Jaxson, one of the owners of Black Light, quickly brought order to the room. "Sorry for the early drama, folks. I promise the rest of the night will have less of an 'assault and battery vibe' and more of a 'naughty sub gets punished' feel."

The crowd chuckled and everyone soon returned to their seats and spotlights illuminated a stage in front of the screen. A few seconds later, a pretty blonde who looked full of energy stepped up, holding some index cards and a short leather crop. Trenton thought she looked vaguely familiar but couldn't quite place her.

Fuck, what was it with him and pretty blondes and not remembering their names?

Jaxson, Chase, and Emma followed the blonde onto the stage, and Trenton finally recognized her as Madison Taylor, Club Manager for Runway, the popular club located above Black Light, although she was dressed much differently than she usually did. Rather than wearing typical L.A. designer clothes, tonight she wore a tight black leather outfit with high heeled boots that gave off a dominatrix vibe.

At the 7:00 start time, Jaxson gave a quick welcome speech. They soon introduced Madison Taylor as the Mistress of Ceremonies for the evening. Jaxson lowered the microphone and moved to the side next to Chase and Emma, and the peppy blonde soon moved in front of the mic and beamed at the crowd.

"Good evening, ladies and gentlemen, and thank you for coming. Like, I know it's hotter than hell with us jammed into the theater together, so let's get this show on the road so we can all spread out." She turned to the celebrities to finish her thought. "And I know you're all very anxious to find out who has won the honor of playing with you tonight." She proceeded to give a quick run-down of the rules, which Trenton had already memorized from the materials on the member's website.

The first three pairings were announced and the activity wheel spun for each one. With each one, he got more on edge wondering when it would be his turn. He was happy he didn't have to wait too long.

"Our next celebrity contestant is the one, the only, Trenton Banks! As we are all aware, Trenton has starred in dozens of action movies. If you haven't seen at least one of them, then shame on you!"

The spectators cheered as Trenton made his way onto the stage. Though he was used to people staring at him, particularly in public, despite all his fame and wealth he couldn't help but experience a twinge of self-consciousness. Aside from award ceremonies, he hadn't actually stepped on a stage, in front of so many eyes, since his early days as an actor. He reminded himself that despite the title of the event—Celebrity Roulette—tonight he was just a man and he could be his dominant self without the pressure of remembering his lines. His only concern tonight was his submissive, and whoever she turned out to be he planned to take damn good care of her.

Madison's boots clicked on the stage as she walked closer and glanced at a card in her hand. "The lucky submissive to place the winning bid of fifty-two thousand dollars on Trenton Banks is...Sunshine! Come on up, Sunshine, and you can spin the activity wheel."

Sunshine. His heart raced. Little Serena Sunshine who couldn't drink champagne without coughing had placed the winning bid. Yet outside the movie theater, she'd given him no indication that she was the winner.

As the naughty little girl approached the stage, taking slow, small steps as if to keep herself steady, his blood heated and his cock stiffened in his jeans. He moved to the steps to assist her onto the stage, reveling in the feel of her tiny hand in his large one.

"Nice to see you again, Sunshine."

"Errr...hi, Mr. Banks." She blushed profusely and avoided his gaze, as if embarrassed by the reminder of their first meeting only minutes ago.

But had it really been their first meeting? He could swear he'd stared into her breathtaking blue eyes at least once before. But when? And where? Fuck his sleep deprived brain.

A shudder ran through her as he pulled her close. He wrapped an arm around her and guided her to the roulette wheel where Madison was waiting.

"Ready to spin?" Madison asked with a dazzling white smile. "I'm, like, so happy you two matched up. You look so cute together! Don't they look cute together, folks?"

More applause and cheers rang out.

"We're ready to spin, Madison," Trenton said, anxious to discover which activity they would enjoy together first.

Madison passed Sunshine a marble and winked at them. Then she gave Sunshine the go ahead to spin.

Trenton released his hold on Sunshine, allowing her enough space to spin the wheel and toss in the marble. As they watched the wheel spinning, he placed his arm back around her and enjoyed the catch of her breath when he did so. Why had she bid on him? Was she a fangirl? He hoped she liked the real him and didn't expect him to put on a big-macho-guy-life-of-the-party show for her. He was a dom and he liked women very, very much, but he wasn't the characters he played in his movies. In real life, he was more laid back and quieter.

The wheel came to a stop on...*ABDL*.

Trenton's cock hardened further.

Fuck yes. He would enjoy this one.

He glanced down at Sunshine, only to see a look of mild confusion spreading over her lovely features. But she soon plastered on a polite smile, as if to prove she was happy with the activity.

"*ABDL!*" Madison announced into the mic. "And that isn't on either of their hard-limits list so have fun!"

Several loud whoops came from the crowd.

Trenton escorted Sunshine off to the side, where the other paired couples were standing, keeping his arm wrapped tight around her. A surge of protectiveness for the little blonde pummeled through him. As the remaining pairings got underway, she fidgeted beside him.

Finally, she peered up at him from underneath thick dark eyelashes. "So, um, *ADBL*. Is that one of your favorite activities?"

"It's *ABDL*, not *ADBL*," he gently corrected. When the confusion in her eyes from earlier returned, he wondered how experienced she was. "Sunshine, do you know what *ABDL* stands for?"

Her eyes widened, then she bit her bottom lip and glanced away. "I-I…" Her voice trailed off. "No, Mr. Banks, I do not. I'm sorry, I hope you aren't disappointed. I confess I sort of skimmed over the list of activities and simply focused on checking off my hard limits, which as it so happens are the same as yours. But I'm a fast learner and I've very much enjoyed the last month I've been a member of Black Light."

A newbie. All the blood in his body rushed to his cock. No wonder there was an innocence about her. She was in way, way over her head. With a bit of arrogance, he mused how lucky she was to have won the night with him, rather than some of the other less experienced celebrity doms standing on stage.

He leaned down, placing his lips to her ear. "*ABDL* stands for *adult baby diaper lover.*"

She gasped and turned to peer directly at him. "It stands for *what?*"

"*Adult baby diaper lover,*" he repeated. "My my, Sunshine, look at you blushing. I think you're looking forward to having Daddy tend to all your needs, including diapering your cute little bottom."

CHAPTER 3

*H*oly fuck. Serena could scarcely breath.

Adult baby diaper lover.

She'd heard of the kink before, but she'd never realized it went by an abbreviation. When she'd seen *ABDL* on the roulette wheel, she certainly hadn't put two and two together. There were a lot of kinks on the wheel with which she was only vaguely familiar.

When she visited Black Light West, she typically enjoyed roleplaying with the doms. Teacher/student was her favorite scenario. And last week, she'd enjoyed a lengthy boss/employee scene, during which she was scolded for not answering the phones properly, bent over a desk and spanked with a ruler, then fucked long and hard for being such an errant employee. *A sore bottom and a sore pussy will help remind you to take your duties more seriously,* her *boss* had told her, and heat pulsed in her sex at the remembrance.

Oh, how she liked to become lost in such a scene and pretend she was someone else. For a few precious hours, she wasn't Serena Hawthorne, heir to the Hawthorne Hotel empire with a reputation for being a party girl. She was someone else. Anyone else—preferably someone who didn't have to worry about having her picture snapped every time she left the house. She supposed a man as famous as

Trenton Banks, who appeared in the tabloids far more often than her, could understand her feelings in regards to publicity. From what she could tell, he tried to go incognito whenever he went out in public, but the paparazzi still managed to recognize him from time to time.

Her stomach flipped. Would he really diaper her bottom?

Shame coursed through her and she couldn't help but squirm in place. Arousal quickened in her core, the molten waves of desire making it hard to think. At least, judging by the heated gleam in his eyes as he promised to tend to all her needs and diaper her, he seemed excited by the prospect of an *ABDL* scene.

Despite her embarrassment over not only the activity, but her lack of knowledge as well, the pulses affecting her between her thighs grew stronger with each moment. Her nipples tightened against her pleather halter top, the stiffened peaks chafing against the material with each rapid inhale.

Trenton's breath wafted against her ear again. "For the remainder of the evening, you are to call me 'Daddy.'" He tightened his hold on her, causing little shudders to afflict her. His nearness, not to mention the intoxicating scent of his masculine cologne, the very same scent he'd worn on the balcony, scattered her senses. If not for his support, she feared she might lose her balance in her ridiculously high heels. "Baby girl, I want to hear you say it now. Call me 'Daddy.'"

"Da-Daddy," she uttered. Warmth rushed through her.

"I hope you plan on being a good baby girl this evening." He placed a finger beneath her chin and forced her gaze to his. "If you misbehave, Daddy will have to spank your little diapered butt."

A small noise of desire escaped her throat, a low moan that she couldn't help. She laced her fingers together in an attempt to still her trembling hands. Trenton Banks was her dom for the evening. And not just any kind of dom, but a Daddy Dom. She would be his baby girl, forced to wear diapers and allow him to tend to her most intimate needs. Heat rushed her face and she tried to pull away from his penetrating stare, but he grasped her chin between his fingers and wouldn't let her look away.

"Now, I have a question for you, baby girl." The serious tone of his voice made her quiver in place. "Have we ever met before? I mean before tonight?"

"No, Daddy. Never." The lie tasted bitter, but she couldn't admit she had a total crush on him after one little meeting a few years ago. Or that she'd had a little crush on him even before that fateful night. She also didn't want to admit to stalking headlines about him, seeing all his new movies on opening night, and lying awake in bed dreaming about *that kiss*. She was a bit embarrassed that he knew the exact, exorbitant amount she'd bid on him.

"Are you sure? You look very familiar and for the life of me, I just can't place you." He studied her with an intensity that made her head swim with endorphins.

"I'm sure, Daddy," she replied. Crap. Maybe she should've told the truth. But it was too late now. She didn't want to anger him, especially when he'd already promised to spank her if she misbehaved.

Once the final pairing took place, Serena had a difficult time focusing on what the MC was saying. From the corner of her eye, she saw the paired contestants moving towards the exit, but Trenton was still holding her chin in his grasp and staring into her eyes. *Please don't recognize me*, she thought. *I'm nobody. Tonight, I only want to be your baby girl.*

Daddy/baby girl. Their *ABDL* scene would basically be a form a roleplay, she told herself. She relaxed somewhat and breathed an inward sigh of relief when Trenton released her chin and guided her off the stage with one hand pressed to her lower back.

Half of the audience members had already departed the movie theater. Luckily, it wasn't too crowded as they navigated their way outside. Despite her party girl reputation, the truth was, Serena didn't like large gatherings of people in closed spaces. She wanted to have fun and be what she was supposed to be at her age—a carefree young heiress—if only to feel normal for a little while, and she therefore attended all the best parties in L.A., pretending to be what everyone thought she was supposed to be.

Unfortunately, the search for acceptance had driven her into many foolish situations over the years, and for as long as she could remember, she had never felt quite normal. The desires she had, the cravings that afflicted her, often left her worried that even if she carefully played the part of a rich heiress who had a side business designing handbags, that one day her entire world would unravel and she would be exposed for a fake.

A fake *what*? A fake person? She didn't really know. She only knew that at least once a day she experienced a deep sense of drowning, a sudden surge of worry that she was the biggest fucking imposter of her social set and one day everyone would find out. Her parents. Her friends. The goddamn tabloids.

Pretending to be someone else was her escape, the last safe place in her world.

"Where are we going?" she asked Trenton as he guided her through the sprawling mansion.

"To wardrobe first." He eyed her outfit. "You look good enough to eat in that, but you don't look like a baby girl." He clasped her hand, just as a daddy might hold his little girl's hand, and gave her an affectionate look that warmed her insides.

Cherished. The word flitted through her mind. That's how he'd made her feel on the balcony. Even now, when he gazed at her with such tender care, she felt cherished beyond all measure. No man had ever looked at her with such loving warmth. She swallowed past the burning in her throat as they walked through the main play area, where her gaze was briefly drawn to a redheaded submissive being placed in painful looking nipple clamps by the celebrity dom—whose name escaped Serena at the moment—that she'd won for the evening.

What kind of outfit would Trenton—*Daddy*—put her in? She flushed from head to toe. What if he made her wear nothing but a diaper? The very thought left her heating further with shame, even as her panties grew damper and damper.

Oh God, even though she definitely had a kinky side, she still felt out of her element as Trenton spoke with Amber, an employee in wardrobe, telling her he wanted to dress Sunshine in a cute little girl outfit and a diaper.

The dark-haired woman smiled. "We have a few adorable little girl dresses to select from, but the diapers are kept in the nursery, so you'll have to go there next, though I assume that's where you'll be playing anyway." She grinned wider. "Follow me."

They followed Amber to a rack containing over a dozen colorful dresses in a little girl style, most of them with big puffy sleeves and adorned with ruffles and lace.

"Of course, if you decide you want to put her in a onesie or a pair of drop seat pajamas, we have those in the back. But there should be some extras in the nursery too." She lifted her eyebrows at them in a cheerful manner. "It's necessary to have extras of those in the nursery. Sometimes baby girls and baby boys have accidents and need a quick change of clothes."

To Serena's relief, Trenton selected a short light pink dress that flared outward and contained several layers of petticoats built into the skirt.

"This dress right here will do just fine," Trenton said, holding the garment up. "Come on, Sunshine, let's go to a changing room and get you out of that outfit. It's much too grownup for a baby girl like you." He shot her a scolding look that set flutters off in her tummy.

～

TRENTON ESCORTED SUNSHINE TO A CHANGING ROOM AND HELPED HER sit on a stool, knowing she would appreciate some relief from walking in those painful looking heels. He hung the dress up on a hook and gave her a pointed stare.

"I want you to be the best baby girl you can be, Sunshine, and stay right there with your hands folded in your lap. Don't move and don't you dare try to undress yourself. Daddy will be back soon."

With Amber's help, he selected white panties with ruffles adorning the butt, short white socks with matching lace ruffles on the ankles, and a pair of black Mary Janes. He also grabbed a bottle of water, a hairbrush, two elastic hair ties, and two pink ribbons. Gathering his haul, he strode back to the dressing room.

What he discovered when he pulled the curtain back nearly caused him to drop the contents in his arms to the floor.

Sunshine, still seated on the stool, had her legs spread wide apart in front of the mirror. Though she hadn't removed any of her clothing, it appeared she was trying to inspect the crotch area of her panties in her reflection. She gasped upon his entrance and quickly righted herself on the stool, folding her hands in her lap as if she hadn't just been looking at her own crotch.

"Baby girl," he said in a stern tone, placing the items down on a small shelf. "What were you just doing? You weren't trying to pleasure yourself, were you?"

Her face reddened. "No-no! I wasn't touching myself, honest!"

"I told you not to move, young lady, only to find you with your legs spread wide in front of the mirror. You disobeyed your daddy and I expect you to tell me what you were doing." He crossed his arms over his chest. "Now, explain. Before I lose my patience and give you more smacks on your little bottom than I'm already planning."

"Please, no spankin', Daddy!" she said, her voice softer than earlier as she seemingly fell into the role of his sweet but sometimes naughty baby girl. His cock went rock hard. "I-I was only lookin' to see if my pa-panties were wet."

"Did you have an accident?"

She shook her head back and forth, looking horrified at the prospect. "No, Daddy! I'm a big girl and I don't have accidents. But my panties feel very wet and I-I'm not sure why." A look of pure innocence sparkled in the depths of her blue gaze.

He was so stunned by her adorable playacting that for a moment he couldn't think of a response. Not only that, but the expression 'hard enough to cut steel' currently applied to his cock. God, what he wouldn't give to plunge into her tight little wet pussy right now.

Not yet, he chided himself. *You're her Daddy and she needs proper care and tending.*

He knelt in front of her and took her hands in his. "Hm. So your panties feel wet and you don't know why? Tell me, are your privates aching right now?"

Her breath caught in her throat, a delicate and sexy noise that heated his blood further. "Yes, Daddy. My privates have never felt so achy before. Is-is there something wrong with me? Oh no, am I sick?"

Indulging her, he placed a hand on her forehead. "You feel quite cool to me, baby girl. But we'll still take your temperature when we get into the nursery, just to be sure. Now, spread your legs for Daddy and show me where you're aching."

She obeyed, pushing her mini-skirt up as she forced her legs wide apart to reveal the thin scrap of black material that barely covered her pussy. He reached for the wet spot on her panties, dragging his fingers up and down this part of her. She moaned and squirmed during his inspection.

"Your panties are soaking wet, baby girl." He met her eyes and gave her a look of reassurance. "But you needn't worry. Daddy will help get you all cleaned up. Of course, you will still be punished for moving. When I tell you to sit still, I mean sit still. You will learn to be an obedient baby girl this evening, even if I must wear my hand out administering your discipline."

"Oh, Daddy. But I don't want a spankin'." She reached back as if to shield her bottom, even though she remained seated. Fuck, she was adorable. And his for tonight. All his.

"Oh, you're getting a spanking, baby girl, and that's final. But first, let's get you dressed in more proper attire." He lifted her to her feet and reached for the hem of her halter top. "Lift up your arms, please." Once she obeyed, he pulled the garment over her head, folded it, and placed it in one of the garment bags provided in the room. To his delight, her firm rounded breasts greeted him. She wasn't wearing a bra, and he didn't plan to put one on her either. As his baby girl, she wouldn't be permitted to wear such a grownup item.

Next, he turned her around in order to unzip her mini-skirt. He pushed it down and caught his first glimpse of her bare bottom, as she was wearing a thong. No wonder the fabric barely covered her crotch.

"Turn around and place your hands on my shoulders, baby girl." Once she complied, he drew the thong and mini-skirt down her smooth, shapely legs. The first glimpse of her bare sex made him groan. *Fuck yes*. She had the cutest little pussy lips, and as he knelt to pull the thong and mini-shirt fully off her, urging her to lift her feet one at a time, he noticed the glimmer of arousal coating her inner thighs.

As carefully as he had undressed her, he proceeded to help her into the cute white panties, ruffle socks, girlish pink dress, and Mary Janes. Next, he sat her in front of the mirror and fashioned her long, wavy locks into pigtails, complete with a decorative pink ribbon tied around the base of each one. A deep blush suffused her cheeks as she watched him style her hair and every now and then he heard her breath catching in her throat. It was the sexiest fucking sound he'd ever heard, though he suspected hearing her moan his name would top it. Fortunately, they had three hours of playtime, and he planned to make careful use of each minute. Time with his baby girl was precious.

She was precious. With each touch, she flushed a darker shade of pink, her eyes shining bright with a mix of longing and curiosity as they caught his in the mirror. He wanted nothing more than to shower her with hugs, kisses, and his undivided attention.

"You look adorable, baby girl." He smoothed his hand through one of the pigtails and moved closer behind her, allowing the full hardness of his erection to rub against her back. Leaning against him, she squirmed in her seat. "Are your privates still aching?"

"Yes, Daddy." She twirled the end of one pigtail around her finger, still holding his gaze. "Even worse than before."

Christ, did she have any idea of the effect she had on him? His cock had never felt so hard, and his heart thumped faster as his blood heated anew. She might not have any experience with *ABDL* kink, but in his eyes, she was already perfect at it. Innocent yet eager, she would be his sweet little baby girl tonight and he would be her firm but loving daddy.

He opened the bottle of water and handed it to her. "Drink the whole thing, please."

She gave him a funny look. "But why? I'm not thirsty, Daddy."

Lifting an eyebrow in censure, he said, "Trust that Daddy knows best and drink all the water, Sunshine. I suggest you listen. You don't want to find out what happens when you blatantly disobey an order from your daddy."

CHAPTER 4

Serena finished the water and handed the empty bottle to Trenton. No, not Trenton, but—*Daddy*. Tonight, he was her daddy. She observed as he shoved the rest of her clothing and heels in a garment bag, wondering why he'd made her drink an entire bottle of water. She'd only had a little champagne earlier in the evening, but now with all the water she really hoped she didn't have to interrupt their *ABDL* scenes to visit the bathroom.

Unless...

Oh, God. Her tummy flipped.

Did Daddy plan to make her pee in a diaper? The very thought left her awash in shame, even as the arousal between her thighs deepened to a ceaseless pulsing. Her brand-new white panties were likely already soaked through.

He placed his hands on her shoulders and turned her to look into the mirror again. He stood over a head taller than her, his bulky six-foot seven frame enfolding her much smaller one.

"You are the cutest baby girl I've ever seen." The warmth in his voice made her melt.

"Th-thank you, Daddy." Calling him Daddy felt natural and right.

He turned her in his arms and pressed a gentle kiss to her

forehead, so reminiscent of the kiss on the balcony that for a few moments, she couldn't breathe. When he pulled away, he stared down at her with suspicion gleaming in his dark eyes.

"Are you absolutely certain we've never met before tonight?"

"Yes, I'm sure, Daddy." *Oh no.* The curious look in his eyes didn't dim, causing her stomach to clench. What would he say if he suddenly remembered their first meeting? Her bottom cheeks tingled at the prospect of receiving real discipline from him, for a reason more serious than moving slightly out of her ordered place in the dressing room.

"Time to head to the nursery," he announced.

On their way out of wardrobe, he passed her bag of clothing to Amber for safekeeping and they emerged into the main play area. The redheaded submissive from earlier no longer wore the nipple clamps. Instead, she was bound to a spanking bench, a glazed look in her eyes while her dom struck her bottom repeatedly with a soft leather flogger.

A small crowd gathered and started to follow Trenton and Serena to the schoolroom, where the nursery was located in a small room in the back. As he guided her into the schoolroom, she noticed Jazz and Michael, one of the pairings for tonight. They'd rolled a *schoolgirl roleplaying* scene. Michael sat behind the large teacher desk, wearing a strict expression as he stared down Jazz, who was dressed in a short plaid skirt and tiny white top, her black hair fashioned into braided pigtails. When they'd rolled for the *schoolgirl roleplaying* scene, Serena had felt a stab of envy as she stood next to Trenton on the stage.

"It's not polite to stare at people, baby girl," Daddy said in a scolding tone as he urged her closer to the nursery. When she spied several cribs and changing tables through the doorway, she halted in her tracks. At that moment, to her great mortification, she felt an urgency in her bladder. She really shouldn't have had the water on top of the champagne.

When Serena still didn't move, Daddy picked her up as if she weighed nothing, holding her on his hip. She laced her arms around his neck, peering at him as a heated flush stole through her. "Sorry, Daddy. I-I'm a little nervous."

"It's normal to feel nervous before you try something new. But I want you to know that Daddy is going to take very, very good care of his baby girl. I promise to keep you safe tonight." With that, he carried her into the nursery, closing the door behind him, though the observation window remained open, and a small group of spectators soon gathered there.

Serena had never had a huge audience before while at Black Light or any of the other BDSM clubs she'd attended, and a sense of vulnerability swept over her. But one glance into Daddy's warm gaze helped melt most of her anxieties away.

She wasn't alone. Not tonight.

She had her daddy.

He carried her to the changing table, and a whimper escaped her when Daddy placed her on the cool padded surface. Her heart raced. *Oh God*. When she'd imagined the various activities she might experience with Trenton Banks tonight, being diapered by him hadn't even crossed her mind.

Trembling, she gazed up at him, admiring how handsome he looked tonight in just a snug green t-shirt and jeans. Nobody could pull off such a casual ensemble and look as hot as him. The shirt hugged his bulging muscles and his chest, revealing his defined pectorals. She had the sudden urge to jump off the changing table, rip his shirt off, and run her hands up and down his bare flesh. But she didn't dare make so bold a move. Daddy was in charge, not her.

He lifted her legs and the skirt and petticoats of her girlish dress fell back. Pressing two fingers to the crotch area of her panties, he made a deep noise in his throat. "You're soaking wet, baby girl. Is all this moisture for your daddy?"

She had the urge to cover her face, but she forced her hands to remain at her side. "I, um, yes, Daddy." What else could she say? Since the second she'd taken her place by his side on stage, she hadn't been able to control the incessant throbbing between her thighs, a building heat that threatened to consume her. No man had ever had such a profound effect on her. In his presence, she became a molten mass of hormones, hopelessly aroused and aching for his touch.

She remained still while he drew her panties off, pulling them down her legs and setting them aside. His gaze focused on her bare, freshly waxed pussy lips. Grabbing a baby wipe from a warmer, he commenced rubbing the cloth through her wet pussy lips, removing the traces of her arousal. With a fresh wipe, he cleaned the moisture that had escaped to her thighs.

"We have to get you nice and clean." He gave her a kind, playful look that instantly put her at ease. He didn't think this kind of scene was gross or weird. The passion flaring in the depths of his dark eyes, behind the warmth he was showing her, revealed he was actually enjoying himself. She surrendered herself to his care and found that she enjoyed his intimate attentions as he finished cleaning her off.

But her heart commenced racing when he retrieved a thermometer and jar of salve from under the changing table. He flipped the jar open and pressed a button on the thermometer.

"Um, Daddy? What's that for?" she asked, nodding at the jar.

He hoisted her legs higher and spread her behind apart, giving her bottom hole a gentle tap with his finger. She flushed and squirmed, but he tightened his hold on her, not allowing her to move more than a smidge. "Be good," he chided. "That is salve for your little hiney hole. To help ease the thermometer into your tightness."

"But I'm not sick, Daddy!" She wiggled more, only for him to ignore her protests and place a cool dollop of salve directly onto her bottom hole. She gasped at the sensation of him spreading it around her pucker, and squealed when he briefly inserted the tip of his finger, coating her most private entrance thoroughly with the salve.

The thermometer came next, and she tensed her cheeks together as he pushed it inside.

"Tensing up will only make it hurt, baby girl, and Daddy doesn't want to hurt you. Relax those cheeks."

By some miracle, she managed to soften her behind, though she winced when he finished pushing the thermometer all the way inside.

She didn't engage in anal play often—hadn't in months, in fact—and the slim object felt large and intrusive, just as his fingertip had.

What if they rolled *anal intercourse* later in the night? She whimpered, trying her best to be a good girl for Daddy while he twisted the thermometer around a few times before slowly withdrawing it from her bottom. She'd considered listing *anal intercourse* as one of her hard limits, but in the end she hadn't. The idea of anal turned her on, but taking a big hard cock in her ass for real—she shivered at the imminent prospect and hoped luck remained on her side.

"Hm. No fever, just as I suspected, though I'm glad we made sure. My baby girl's health is very important to me." He set the thermometer aside and retrieved a diaper from a shelf next to the changing table, holding it up for her inspection. A pattern of various fairytale princesses covered the bulky white diaper.

"You're going to look adorable in this," he said. "Daddy's cute little baby girl."

TRENTON LIFTED SUNSHINE'S LEGS HIGHER AND PLACED THE DIAPER beneath her bottom. But he didn't close it yet, as he still had to properly chastise her for moving out of position in the dressing room. Giving her a stern look while still holding her legs up in one hand, he said, "This is for your disobedience in the dressing room. Do you remember? Daddy instructed you to sit still, but you didn't."

Her eyes widened and she tried to shield her bottom, but he shooed her hands out of the way. "Please, Daddy! No spankin'!"

Ignoring her pleas, he proceeded to apply ten quick but sharp smacks to her behind. During her punishment, she squirmed and whimpered with each slap. Once he delivered the final slap, he wasted no time in fastening her diaper closed.

Sunshine glared at him, crossed her arms over her chest, and stuck her lower lip out in the cutest pout.

"Baby girl, I suggest you wipe that look off your face now." He lifted an eyebrow at her. "That is, unless you want Daddy to take your diaper off and give you a longer, harder spanking? Little babies who pout end up with very ouchie bottoms."

"Sorry, Daddy." The pout melted away. She soon gave him a regretful look followed by a shy smile, and her arms fell to her sides.

"Much better." He patted her diaper clad bottom and lifted her off the table. "Upsie daisy." Once she was on her feet, he grasped her hand and led her to a bright multi-colored playmat.

From the corner of his eye, he noticed the crowd in the window had grown larger. Many of the voyeurs seemed to be moving back and forth between his scene with Sunshine and the scene in the schoolroom, where he heard Michael, a regular at Black Light, issuing an order to the spirited little singer he'd won in the silent auction. From the tone in his voice, it sounded as if Jazz wasn't being the most cooperative submissive.

Repressing a smirk, he gave Sunshine a gentle push to the floor. She sat on her bottom and peered up at him with a questioning look, as if waiting for his instructions. Her golden pigtails rested over her shoulders, the large pink bows at the base of each pigtail much too large for her petite features, but he thought she looked endearingly cute. She took a deep breath and started playing with the lace ruffles edging one of her socks.

"Sunshine, Daddy wants to see you crawl." His cock throbbed hard in his jeans as he imagined her obeying this particular command. Fuck, he couldn't wait. "Get on your hands and knees and crawl around the mat like a sweet little baby girl. Make sure you move around in circles so Daddy can have a nice view of your diapered bottom."

She released a deep breath and slowly, very slowly, moved onto her hands and knees. Her face flushed a deep pink, and when she started crawling the skirts of her short dress fell forward. Still crawling, as she turned to complete a circle, he had a perfect view of her cute diapered butt.

"Good girl." He grabbed a dolphin stuffed animal from the toy bin, walked in a circle around her, enjoying the sight of her on her hands and knees, then handed her the toy. "Baby girl, I need to request an item from one of the DMs. While I do that, I want you to stay here and play with your dolphin." He stroked a hand over one of her pigtails, then gave it a playful tug.

Sitting down with her legs spread wide on the play mat, she hugged the stuffed animal to her chest and nodded. "Okay, Daddy." The trust in her beautiful blue eyes astounded him, causing his breath to catch as he rose to his feet. One evening with Sunshine wouldn't be enough. He hadn't even kissed her properly yet and already he knew he'd want more. Why the fuck did she look so familiar? *Serena.* That was her first name. Her real name. But who was she?

Before he left her to find a DM, he knelt down one last time to place a kiss to her forehead. He felt her melting as his lips pressed to her flesh and he inhaled the intoxicating scent of her—a mix of her perfume, her natural aroma unique only to her, and the faint hint of her arousal that still hung in the air.

When he pulled back from the kiss, a stark sense of déjà vu spiraled through him.

"New Year's Eve," he said.

She gasped and horror filled her eyes.

More fragments of the memory fell into place. The party at Blue Inspire Records. On the rebound at the time, he'd gone to the party alone because his record producer friend, Andre, had pleaded with him to make an appearance. After some polite mingling with guests, he'd found himself out on a balcony, staring at the night sky and lost in his thoughts. On the other side of the balcony, he heard the sounds of laughter and realized he wasn't alone, but he took a seat in the shadows and nursed his drink. Moments later, Sunshine had appeared, staring across the pool area with a sad look that had moved him. He'd had the urge to approach her and take her in his arms even before her confrontation with her cheating boyfriend broke out.

Once the boyfriend and the other woman departed the balcony, he'd been drawn to her side like a moth to a flame—an apt expression, given her play name that undoubtedly reflected her brilliant blonde locks—unable to keep himself hidden in the shadows. He'd tried his best to comfort her and when the clock struck midnight, the urge to kiss her overwhelmed him. But how could he kiss a stranger he'd just witnessed breaking up with her boyfriend? And so he'd kissed her forehead, chaste and gentle, holding her briefly in his arms while fireworks exploded around them.

"New Year's Eve," he repeated, tipping her chin up and forcing her gaze to his. "We met before today, Sunshine, and you *know* we met."

She hugged the dolphin tighter and gave a faint shrug. "I dunno, Daddy, I-I..." Worry and regret filled her features and she gulped hard. "Maybe-maybe we met once before." Her confession escaped as a whisper and her eyes danced around as she attempted to avoid looking directly at him.

"Baby girl, I expect answers when I return. You have some explaining to do. I asked you twice if we'd already met, and both times you told a fib. Daddy doesn't like it when his baby girl tells fibs." He stood and stared down at her. "I'll be back."

Walking quickly through the nursery and schoolroom, he stuck his head outside and asked Miles for a vibrating wand. Within moments, Trenton returned to the nursery with the requested item in hand.

"This is for good baby girls." He held up the wand. "And if you want Daddy to make the aching in your privates feel better, you had better start behaving and explain why you told a fib. Why would you claim we've never met before, Sunshine?"

"I'm sorry, Daddy, it's just that I..." Her voice trailed off and she buried her face in the stuffed animal, curling her body in on itself as she tried to shut him out.

With a sigh, Trenton moved to a large rocking chair placed near the mat. He patted his thigh. "Come here, baby girl, and sit in your daddy's lap." When she started to rise, he shook his head and said, "No walking. Crawl to me like a good little baby girl."

An adorable, shy expression spread over her face, but she soon obeyed. With her long pigtails nearly touching the mat, she crawled toward him on her hands and knees. Once she reached him, he lifted her up and cradled her in his lap.

"It's time for Daddy to have a discussion with his baby girl."

CHAPTER 5

Oh God. Why had she concealed the truth?

Daddy knew about her fib and he looked none too pleased.

And yet, in his arms, her world felt right. Even when he wasn't happy with her. Beneath the disappointment in his eyes, she glimpsed his tender regard for her.

Who would've guessed a big, bad macho guy like Trenton Banks possessed such a tender, caring daddy-dom side?

Of course, he had a firm side too.

When she wiggled in his lap, her bottom still stung from the spanking on the changing table. Shame washed through her when she cast a quick glance at the window where over a dozen people were gathered to watch their scene. With her legs held in the air and her privates on display, she'd been spanked in front of an audience.

She sighed. The spectators were probably about to witness another spanking.

"Sunshine," he said in his firm daddy voice, "look at me." His no-nonsense tone sent a ripple of unease through her.

With great reluctance, she met his dark gaze, wishing she could shrink small enough to disappear in a crack in the floor. His disappointment gutted her. She should have told the truth, no matter how silly or embarrassing it seemed.

"Why did you claim, more than once, that we had never met before tonight?"

She exhaled a shuddering breath and braced herself for his rejection. Surely he'd think her ridiculous for crushing on him all because of the innocent kiss to her forehead on New Year's Eve. It was one little moment. That night, he hadn't even asked her name. He hadn't offered his name, but he didn't have to. A man like Trenton Fucking Banks didn't have to introduce himself anywhere.

"I'm waiting, baby girl, and I expect an answer."

"This is going to sound silly, Daddy." She cringed, imagining his response when she finished explaining herself. "I only joined Black Light a month ago. I didn't know you were a member here and had no idea you were a dom, but when I saw you were on the silent auction list, I just had to bid on you. Not only that, but I had to *win*."

"Go on." He gave her an encouraging nod and rubbed her back, comforting her in the midst of her shameful confession.

"You see, I had a little itty bitty crush on you when I was a teenager, but I kinda sorta developed a *huge* crush on you after that night. When you stayed with me during the countdown to midnight and kissed me on the forehead...well, it made me feel special. It was the nicest thing anyone had done for me in a long, long time."

His eyes twinkled with pleasure, as if her confession pleased him. She didn't understand how it could. Despite having already met once, they were still practically strangers.

"But even if you had a crush on me, why not admit we'd met before, baby girl?"

"Because the kiss happened over two years ago and I didn't want you to think I was some silly, lovestruck fangirl or borderline stalker!" When he failed to comprehend how bad she had it for him, she took a deep breath and forged on. "I became obsessed with you! I went home and binged all your movies, over and over. I even started attending lots more parties than I usually attend in L.A., all in the hopes of running into you. So, you see, I am kind of crazy. And lucky you, you get to spend the whole evening with me."

"Did you ever hide in my bushes with binoculars?"

"No, Daddy."

"What about sneak into my house and steal my underwear?" He waggled his eyebrows at her in a teasing manner, causing her to laugh.

"No, Daddy." She could see where his line of questioning was headed, and she already understood his point. Okay, maybe she wasn't *crazy* crazy. Just your average lovestruck socialite with too much money to spend on silent auctions featuring handsome celebrities.

"Baby girl, you're not crazy. You're adorable and I'm glad you won me for the evening. If the rest of our time tonight goes as well as I suspect it will, I have a feeling we'll be seeing more of each other."

Whaaaaa? If not for his snug hold on her, she would've tumbled to the floor. Her heart raced and her hands felt clammy. She breathed faster, feeling as if she couldn't take in enough oxygen. "You really mean that, Daddy? You don't think I'm crazy?"

"Of course I mean it, and no I most certainly don't think you're crazy." His expression turned serious, his eyes darkening as he raised his brows at her. "But I still intend to discipline you. Telling fibs to your daddy is a big no no."

She lowered her head. "Sorry, Daddy. I know I'm in trouble."

He rose with her in his arms and moved to the center of the playmat. A tremor ran through her. How would he punish her? Another spanking? Would she get to keep her diaper on?

"I want you on the floor, head down, with your bottom lifted high in the air, baby girl." He let her down and got on his knees beside her, guiding her into the ordered position. Humiliation coursed through her when she turned on her hands and knees, tucked her head down, and lifted her bottom high. He pressed on her lower back, forcing her diapered butt to jut out in an embarrassingly awkward fashion as her skirts fell forward.

"Please not a hard spankin', Daddy. I'm sorry, and ev-everyone's watching."

"I don't care who's watching. When you're naughty, Daddy will always bare your bottom and give you the punishment you deserve, no matter who happens to be nearby. Let them see what happens to disobedient baby girls."

She whimpered and buried her face between her arms, praying this chastisement would be a quick one. Still pressing on her lower back, he cupped her bottom with his free hand. Then he gave her diaper clad butt a firm smack. Even through her diaper, she felt the sting. Her tummy clenched with increasing nerves. How badly would it hurt when he finally bared her bottom?

He continued on, landing over a dozen smacks as she tried her best to remain in position. Remorse over her lie, which Daddy had mercifully called a fib, built in her chest. To her utter shock, tears soon burned in her eyes, though they weren't wrought from the pain of her spanking.

Perhaps she had jumped the gun when she joined Black Light, given her vast inexperience. She'd thought she knew a thing or two about BDSM, but she hadn't even recognized some of the activities on the roulette wheel, including *ABDL*.

She had only received a personal invitation to join after meeting Kitty Kat, a member of Black Light, in a BDSM club on the other side of L.A. After Serena had confided to the young woman that she was pretty sure the paparazzi had followed her to the club, Kitty Kat had slipped her a card with her phone number and cryptically told her she knew about a better, very secretive BDSM club that Serena might be interested in joining. The two women had met for lunch a few days later and Kitty Kat told Serena about Black Light West—without mentioning the actual name of the club until Serena expressed great interest in joining and promised she was good at keeping secrets.

The sting built on her bottom cheeks and she shifted forward, only for Daddy to force her back into position. What if she didn't really belong here? Daddy might not think she was crazy for having a secret crush on him, but what if he thought she didn't belong here? What if he preferred a more experienced submissive?

Her musings were interrupted when he opened the sides of her diaper and pulled it off her, exposing her bare bottom to his punishing blows. He wasted no time in delivering the first spank to her naked behind, giving her a series of rapid smacks as he alternated from left to right cheek.

Despite the pain and her continued embarrassment, searing hot desire pulsed between her thighs. If only Daddy would stop spanking her and touch her privates. She needed his touch soon or she would combust, or perhaps lose control and reach underneath herself to stroke her own pussy.

He paused and caressed her smarting bottom. "You need to be honest with Daddy at all times, baby girl, even when the truth embarrasses you. Telling fibs is wrong, and I want you to be my good girl. Do you understand?"

"Yes, Daddy, I understand, and I'm very, truly sorry. It won't happen again."

"Five more smacks, baby girl."

TRENTON ADMINISTERED THE LAST PART OF HER DISCIPLINE—FIVE QUICK but hard smacks to the lowest curve of her cheeks, where her thighs merged into her bottom. She cried out and whimpered, but to her credit, she didn't move out of position. Such a good baby girl.

He massaged the red marks on her behind for several moments before fixing her diaper back in place. Outside the perimeter of the nappy, a slight glow of redness showed on her otherwise pale flesh. He ran his fingers over this part of her skin.

"Even though you have a diaper on, anyone who looks at you from behind will know you just had your bottom spanked good and hard by your daddy."

She peered over her shoulder at him, and to his surprise he glimpsed tears in her eyes. None had fallen down her cheeks yet, but the telltale glimmer of tears was clearly evident. She gulped hard and blinked fast, as if trying to get her emotions under check.

The urge to comfort her became all-consuming, and he gathered her in his arms and carried her back to the rocking chair, where he cradled her against his chest and whispered words of comfort into her ear.

"All is forgiven, sweet girl. Daddy's not mad at you."

He rubbed her back and held her close, reveling in the feel of her soft warm body in his embrace. He never wanted to let her go. Though she wasn't familiar with *ABDL*, it seemed this scene was coming naturally to her. She'd thrown herself into it with her natural sweetness and her desire to please him as her dom for the night.

He'd been on the rebound the first time he'd met her. And, as life often had a funny way of coming full circle, he was once again on the rebound. His last girlfriend had broken up with him via a phone call while he'd been filming in the outback. She'd met someone else— another fucking actor—and said she couldn't wait for him anymore. All the rage he'd felt at her betrayal melted away as he held sweet Sunshine in his arms. All the hurt in his heart calmed, including his worries about his brother. For the first time in a long time, Trenton was at peace, and he had Sunshine to thank for it. He hugged her tighter and kissed her forehead, knowing how much she loved the gesture of affection.

If she belonged to him, he would kiss her forehead a hundred times a day.

Fuck. He couldn't help but think of the future. A future with Sunshine. Would she think he was moving too fast? Hopefulness had shone in her eyes when he'd said he suspected they would make plans to see one another again.

When the clock struck eleven and Celebrity Roulette came to an end, he could not fathom spending the night without her by his side. He'd rented one of the private bedrooms upstairs in the mansion, and while he hadn't originally planned to bring a guest to his room, he for fucking sure did now. Once he had her alone in the private bedroom, he would get more of the truth out of her. Like her full real name. She was someone with money and he felt like an ass for not knowing who she really was, but asking her the question during their scene wouldn't be appropriate.

But God, how he wished he knew, if only to understand her better.

He wanted to know everything about her. The story of her life up to this very minute. Was she another actor's daughter? A socialite? Or maybe a movie producer's daughter? Whoever she was, she obviously had money—enough of it to blow a huge chunk on a celebrity auction.

She remained still in his arms at first, though soon she started squirming. He smiled inwardly, lust spiraling through him as he anticipated the next part of their scene. Over thirty minutes had passed since they'd entered the nursery, but he wasn't ready to spin for a new activity yet. In fact, he wanted to keep her dressed as she was all night long.

She looked positively adorable and entirely fuckable in her cute baby girl clothes, her golden pigtails gleaming in the overhead lights.

Sunshine. She was indeed sunshine through and though. *His Sunshine.*

"I like holding you, baby girl." He inhaled the scent of her lavender shampoo, unable to get enough of her. He imagined he could fuck her a thousand times in a row and still not get his fill. He would always want her as much as the first time.

"I like it when you hold me too, Daddy." She withdrew partway from his embrace to peer up at him. "This scene isn't as strange as I thought. I-I was worried I wouldn't be able to handle it. But I'm enjoying myself."

"Remember those words when I'm changing your diaper soon, baby girl."

"Huh?"

"You're squirming around. I know you have to pee."

Her eyes grew wider than ever before. "No, Daddy!" She sounded truly shocked. "I-I couldn't possibly."

"You can and you will. But first, Daddy wants to watch you come." He produced the vibrating wand and placed it between her legs, overtop her diaper. He turned it on a medium setting and watched as she flushed.

"I don't think—oh!" She gyrated her center against the wand and a look of rapture filled her eyes.

"Come for Daddy, whenever you're ready, baby girl, and that diaper of yours will be very, very wet by the time I change it."

Shudders racked her body and her eyes fluttered shut. She came hard and fast, clutching onto him as she pushed her center against the wand, riding the waves of her first orgasm of the night. He turned the wand off, set it aside, and cradled her in his arms.

After a minute, she opened her eyes and pointed at the doorway near the corner. "Um, Daddy?" Breathlessness tinged her voice. "Isn't that a bathroom? Please, Daddy, can I pretty please use the potty?" She gave him a pleading look, her cheeks still pinkened from her recent exertions.

"I'll give you a choice, baby girl."

"What kind of a choice?"

"Pee in your diaper and let Daddy change you, or go pee in the potty with your legs spread wide while Daddy stands there and watches you. And yes, if you choose the second option, you can expect me to wipe your privates for you afterward. Either way, I'm going to be tending to your needs and cleaning you up after you pee. Then I'll put a fresh diaper on your cute little butt."

"But I wanna go pee all by myself, Daddy. I'm a big girl."

"You're a *little* baby girl," he said in a matter-of-fact tone while giving her nose a playful tap, "and you are not allowed to go potty all by yourself. Pick one, or Daddy will pick for you."

"I-I choose the second option," she said after a long pause.

His cock leapt and pressed hard against her bottom. He'd never watched a submissive pee before, but the prospect of sharing in such a private act with Sunshine, even though it embarrassed her, left him sweltering in the confines of his shirt and jeans. He couldn't fucking wait.

Rising with her in his arms, he carried her to the bathroom and stood her in front of the toilet. "Lift up your skirts so Daddy can take off your diaper, please."

After a mournful glance at the bathroom window behind her where the spectators were relocating, she slowly gathered the layers of her dress up, until the fabric and sheer white petticoats were bunched in her arms.

"Good girl." He removed her diaper with deft movements and shoved it in a nearby diaper receptacle. Just as she tried to sit on the potty by herself, he grabbed her around the waist and lifted her up, placing her on the toilet seat. "Be sure to spread your legs wide. Daddy wants to see *everything*."

CHAPTER 6

Oh God, oh God, oh God.

How could she pee in front of Daddy? Somehow, she'd thought this option would be the least embarrassing, but now she second guessed her choice. Maybe wetting herself in a diaper wouldn't have been so bad, after all. Too late now.

"Baby girl, you barely have your legs spread. I suggest you obey Daddy. And gather your skirts higher up, too. I want a perfect view of your smooth pink privates while you go pee."

Gulping, she forced her legs wider apart and hoisted her dress higher. Her face heated. She couldn't recall a time in her life when she'd felt more humiliated and exposed. But despite her utter shame, the hot pulses between her thighs deepened with each second. Somehow, someway, knowing Daddy was about to watch her pee prompted her arousal to soar to new heights.

The crowd outside the window grew larger and she closed her eyes, wanting to pretend this moment was only between them. She tried to focus on emptying her bladder, hoping she didn't get a case of stage fright. She didn't wish to unintentionally disobey him. Not so soon after a punishment. As she squirmed on the toilet seat, she winced at the soreness on her bottom cheeks. Daddy spanked hard!

"Relax, baby girl, and let it come. Be a good girl and pee for Daddy." He sounded closer than before, but she didn't dare open her eyes, lest she lose her concentration. "Go ahead. You can do it."

At last, she felt herself going and soon heard the trickle of her pee in the toilet. Once she finished, she peeked one eye open, only to see Daddy standing in front of her holding a rolled up ball of toilet paper. He graced her with a warm smile.

"Good girl, Sunshine. Daddy is proud of you for going potty."

If someone had told her Trenton Banks would utter those very words to her this evening, she would have thought they were lying. Yet his words caused her to flush with pleasure. She liked making Daddy proud and vowed to obey him to the best of her ability for the remainder of the evening.

With all the tenderness she had come to expect from him, he wiped her privates in a slow, gentle manner, then tossed the tissue between her legs and helped her stand up. He flushed the toilet and gave her a wink, while she stood still as her skirts fell back into place with a whoosh. He proceeded to help her wash her hands, even going so far as to dry them for her.

But as much as she loved this scene, she couldn't help but think about what kind of fun they might enjoy on the next spin of the activity wheel. Her pussy throbbed harder. She ached for him, wished he'd bend her over the sink and plunge his cock deep inside her. She'd detected the hardness of his erection beneath her bottom as she sat on his lap earlier, and a quick, casual glance at the front of his jeans confirmed his arousal remained. He wanted her too.

As if reading her mind, he said, "Let's go get a fresh diaper on you, little girl, and then we'll go spin for a new activity. How does that sound?" He cupped her face, his eyes beaming with warmth.

"Okay, but…why do I need a fresh diaper if we're spinning for a new activity?"

He leaned down, putting his gaze level with hers. The heat of his breath wafted across her face. "When I wiped you just now, baby girl, I discovered your privates were very, very moist with your arousal. You need to wear a diaper to keep from making any messes." He held her out by her shoulders, looking her up and down. "And you're keeping the dress on for now, as well. Socks and shoes, too. That is, of course, until we spin for an activity that requires you to get naked."

Ten minutes later, a freshly diapered Serena stood on stage, watching as the roulette wheel spun in circles. Her pulse skittered and Trenton squeezed her hand, as if sensing her nervousness and wishing to help her calm down.

But did it really matter which activity they rolled?

She trusted him. He'd helped her enjoy an *adult baby diaper lover* scene—something she would have never tried on her own accord—and she'd left the nursery feeling not only turned on, but deeply cherished.

"Oral sex!" Madison announced with a wink. "You two have fun. Oh, and you must have enjoyed that *ABDL* scene. You guys, like, stayed there forever! It's already 9:45! Love the dress, by the way, Sunshine. You look so adorable."

"What do you say, Sunshine? She just paid you a very nice compliment," Daddy said. Or should she think of him as Trenton now? She was so confused. Though their *ABDL* scene had ended, she still wanted to call him 'Daddy.'

"Th-thank you, Madison," she uttered, embarrassed that she'd needed the prompting.

"Come along, baby girl," he guided her off the stage, "and we'll find a room."

She repressed a yawn as they navigated through the spectators and guests in the main play area. Trenton put his lips to her ear. "I expect you to open just as wide when you take my cock in your mouth, baby girl."

"Yes, Trenton," she replied through her yawn, grinning as her excitement built.

He squeezed her hand and drew her into an empty room usually used for cool-downs, with a bed. It didn't contain a window, but the velvet curtain normally across the doorway was pulled open, and Trenton made no move to close it.

"If you still want to call me 'Daddy', you can. In fact, I would like it very much." He lifted her onto the bed and sat beside her, holding her close to his side. "I still want to call you 'baby girl.' That was the hottest scene, hands down, I've ever enjoyed in a club."

"I-I would very much like to keep calling you 'Daddy.' Thank you. But...*really*? The hottest scene? We didn't even have sex. You didn't even get your, um, cock played with. Not even a hand job, Daddy!"

He cupped her face. "Doesn't matter. It was hotter than hell." He leaned closer, until his lips rested but an inch away from hers.

Anticipation curled in her tummy. The murmur of the crowd faded and time seemed to stand still.

Clutching her face harder, he leaned in to kiss her.

She moaned against his lips and shuddered. *Yes, yes, yes.* After years of dreaming of this moment, it was finally happening. And it was even better than in her imaginings.

His stubble rubbed against her face and she whimpered as he deepened the kiss. When he finally pulled away, she was left breathless and unable to stop squirming in her diaper. Her pussy throbbed and the pain from sitting on her freshly spanked bottom only increased her arousal.

"I'm going to taste you now, baby girl, and you're going to spread your legs and let Daddy do it." He nodded at the pillows. "Lay back on the bed."

Complying with his demand, she rested on the pillows and kept still while he removed her diaper and tossed it aside. "Soaking wet, just as I suspected." He peered up at her over the length of her body, his eyes glimmering dark in the muted light of the decorative sconces lining the walls.

She quivered, aching beyond belief for his attentions.

When he touched his tongue to her clit, she clutched the covers and cried out.

HIS BABY GIRL NEEDED TO COME AND TRENTON WAS FEELING MERCIFUL.

He shoved two fingers into her tight pussy, pumped them in and out in a slow but deep rhythm, and circled her clit with his tongue. She came after a few moments, and that was fine by him. No sense drawing it out when she'd been such a good baby girl during their last scene and earned it.

But the next time he ate her pussy, he would fucking feast on it for an hour before he allowed her to come.

Someone outside the room clapped, but Trenton didn't even glance over his shoulder to see how many spectators had gathered. His only concern was Sunshine.

She remained on the bed, panting and wearing a blissful expression.

"That was...wow, Daddy." She tried to sit up, only to fall back on the pillows. "Gah! Blood rush." She clutched her head and giggled.

He gathered her close to his chest, holding her tight in the aftermath of her release. But her hand soon drifted to the bulge of his erection tenting his jeans. She shot him a saucy look, her lips quirking and her eyes twinkling with mischief.

"I believe, Daddy, that it's my turn now."

He moved to the side of the bed and unfastened his jeans. "Get on your knees, baby girl, and beg for it. Beg for the privilege of sucking your daddy's cock." His voice came out strained and raspy.

She knelt before him on the floor, watching with wide eyes as he released his cock. The sharp, shuddering inhale of her breath made his manhood throb harder, primal lust taking over.

"Pl-please, Daddy. May I please suck your cock?" She licked her lips in a seductive manner and tilted her head to the side, playing with one of her pigtails.

"You may." He tensed in anticipation when she leaned forward, her mouth open and her pink tongue darting out. He groaned when she licked the tip of his shaft—*holy fuck*—and his head spun as she tried to take the fullness of his erection into her mouth.

Winding her pigtails around his hands, he gripped her hair and guided her up and down over his shaft. She moaned around him, the vibrations driving him wild, and took him deeper at his urging. Occasionally, she gagged, but the bastard in him loved watching her struggle to accept his size. He could be a gentle daddy sometimes, but other times he could be rough and demanding.

As the tip of his cock hit the back of her throat, she suddenly sucked harder and swallowed. The suction and increased pressure became his undoing, and he soon came hard down her throat in great, pulsing torrents. Holding onto her pigtails, he groaned his release and watched to make sure she swallowed.

She did. She gulped down every last drop like a good girl. He stroked her head and praised her, and he felt her melting under his touch.

"Are you sure that was good, Daddy?"

"Very." He'd just told her so, but worry still clouded her gaze. "Why would you think it wasn't good? I came hard, baby girl, straight down your throat, and I enjoyed every second of it." He rubbed a finger over her swollen lips.

"It's just that...well, someone once told me I wasn't that great at it."

Anger flared in his veins. "Was it that cheating asshole from the balcony?" he asked, putting away his cock and zipping his jeans.

"Maybe."

"He's an idiot, baby girl." He lifted her and circled his arms around her. "But his loss is my gain. I only wish I'd given you my number that night, or at least asked you for your name."

"Why didn't you ask for my name? I've always wondered."

"Because I figured you didn't recognize me, and I didn't want to have to reciprocate on the name thing. I'd gone to the party as a favor to a friend, and I'd spent the better part of the night getting fawned over by strangers. I enjoyed speaking with you because you didn't get all weird and ask me to sign a napkin or take a selfie with me."

"I see. So you'll never agree to take a selfie with me?" She laughed.

"I'll make a fucking sex tape with you, if you want." He chuckled and hugged her tighter. "Now come on, baby girl, let's go spin one last time."

Apparently, several other paired couples had the idea to spin at the last minute too. When they arrived at the stage, they had to stand in line behind four couples. Trenton checked his watch. Ten thirty. Still time for another scene. Despite having just come down Sunshine's throat, his cock hardened in his pants at the idea of sharing one last scene with her. He didn't care what they rolled, as long as she remained with him, allowing him to guide her and bring her to pleasure.

As luck would have it, five minutes later, they found themselves back in the same room they'd just departed, having rolled *vaginal intercourse*. Trenton stripped Sunshine completely naked, admiring her curves and her pert breasts. His need for her flared so hot, he shed his clothes in record time, so quickly that his eagerness drew a few chuckles from the spectators gathered in the doorway.

He reached for Sunshine's hands and pulled her close. "Daddy is going to pound into you long and hard, baby girl."

Desire sparked in the depths of her gaze. He guided her into position on the bed, deciding to claim her missionary style. When he pushed his cock inside her, he wanted to look into her pretty blue eyes, wanted to watch her every little expression while he gave her a proper fucking.

And so he did.

He kissed his way down her body, worshipping every inch of her, every delicious curve, tasting the saltiness of her flesh. Finally, when she undulated her center against him and tried to impale herself upon his cock in an adorably desperate manner, he grabbed a condom from a bowl on the bedside table and suited up.

He gripped her hips and surged forward, plunging to the hilt in one quick drive. *Oh yes. Fuck yes.* He set a rapid pace of pounding into her. The headboard banged on the wall with each hard thrust.

She gave a strangled moan and spread her legs wider, inviting him to surge into her deeper and deeper. He fucked her faster, with a strength he didn't know he possessed, until the spasms of her own release prompted his to descend upon him in a rushing wave of ecstasy. Dark spots dotted his vision, his orgasm claiming him with a violence that left him disoriented.

Fuck, he had never come so hard in his life.

After he regained his senses enough to stand, he disposed of the condom and rushed back to bed, where he gathered Sunshine to his side.

~

SERENA BASKED IN THE AFTERMATH OF YET ANOTHER ORGASM. SHE'D never come before without a vibrator's assistance or without a man touching her clit directly, but somehow, simply being fucked by Daddy had done it. She snuggled deeper into his comforting embrace, enjoying the tickle of his chest hair on her face.

"I could hold you all night," he said, kissing the top of her head. "Tell me, I need to know. What's your name? Who *are* you?" he asked in a tone so low none the spectators could hear.

"Serena Hawthorne," she whispered back.

"Hawthorne," he repeated. "As in the hotel chain? You must be Ethan Hawthorne's only daughter. You-you design handbags, if I'm not mistaken. I got one for my mother last Christmas."

"Yep, that's me. Sorry I'm not as famous as you," she said with a giggle. "Though I must confess I'm a little offended you didn't recognize me the first time we met."

"Allow me to make it up to you," he said, kissing her neck.

Just outside of their room one of the dungeon monitors called out "Time." It was eleven—and the end of this year's Celebrity Roulette. Sunshine tensed in Daddy's arms.

"Hey," he said gently, giving her a gentle squeeze. "This doesn't have to end."

"I-I'm glad you want to see me again, Daddy." Relief filled her. She smiled and snuggled deeper into his chest.

"I meant tonight," he replied. "*This* doesn't have to end yet *tonight*. I rented a private bedroom upstairs and I would very much like you to join me, Sunshine."

"Join you?"

"Yes, I want to hold you all night."

"That sounds...perfect. Thank you, Daddy." The prospect of spending the night in his arms left her spirits dancing with joy.

Stroking her cheek, he stared at her with such intensity that she imagined he was trying to memorize the flecks in her eyes. No one had ever stared at her with such heartfelt longing, such profound reverence. It knocked the air from her chest.

"I'm glad you stalked me," he said, "because this was an evening to remember." A smirk touched the corners of his lips.

"What? We already established that I didn't stalk you. Remember? I never hid in your bushes and I never stole your underwear!" She giggled when he suddenly sat up and pulled her into his lap. "Daddy! We're supposed to be leaving!"

"We will, baby girl. After one more kiss."

The End

ABOUT THE AUTHOR

USA TODAY bestselling author Sue Lyndon writes steamy D/s romance in a variety of genres, from contemporary to historical to fantasy. She's a #1 Amazon bestseller in multiple categories, including BDSM Erotica and Sci-Fi Erotica. She also writes non-bdsm sci-fi romance under the name Sue Mercury. When she's not busy working on her next book, you'll find her hanging out with her family, watching sci-fi movies, reading, or sneaking chocolate.

- Website: www.suelyndon.com
- Facebook: https://www.facebook.com/AuthorSueLyndon/
- Twitter: https://twitter.com/SueLyndon

JAZZED

A Black Light: Celebrity Roulette Novella

By

Lesley Clark

CHAPTER 1

*T*he applause was still ringing in her ears as Jazz left the stage. Damn her manager for talking her into yet another pre-tour concert. She was supposed to have some time off before leaving for her six-month tour, yet she didn't seem to know how to say no when he asked her to always do more. She went to her dressing room and fell into the puffy chair they had provided for her.

Who would have thought at the age of twenty-six, she would be tired? Not the kind of tired that came from a crazy night out with friends, but the type of exhaustion that cuts all the way to the core. She understood exactly what the saying 'bone tired' meant and felt it nearly every day. She was living the dream she'd set out to live when she was a teenager in the middle of BFE Ohio. There she was only seen as that 'weird emo kid' who dyed her hair black and wore too much eyeliner. Hell, eight years later she still had pitch-black hair, but now people thought it was cool — even if she couldn't remember what color her hair was under all that dye.

They had spent the last few weeks getting ready for her upcoming world tour. Before that, she had been touring the US. *When was she not on tour?* That might be easier to name. Singing was still all she wanted to do, but everything else that came with it wore her down. She was famous and couldn't go anywhere without being recognized but was still lonely.

Lost in her thoughts, she was unsure how much time had passed when Jamie nudged her shoulder. "Hey, Jazz, where in the hell are you? I've been trying to get your attention for the last ten minutes."

Jamie was her best friend and the one person who had been with her from the beginning. The emo girl and the fairy boy who never quite fit in Johnson's Fork, Ohio. The funny thing was, she wasn't the emo girl they made her out to be, not that many ever took the time to look deeper.

"I'm a little tired, Jamie. We only have a few weeks until we leave again. Damn, this break was so short we might as well not have had a break at all." Not to mention she couldn't remember the last time she had allowed herself to submit to a man. The only time her mind was truly quiet was when she was on her knees, but her schedule and well-known face made it nearly impossible to simply show up at a club without the fear of being found out.

"Baby girl, I think it's time to slow this train down a little. You're wasting away to nothing. You aren't taking care of yourself. If I didn't tour with you, I think you wouldn't make it home. But hell, I'm no Dom, baby, and that's what you need-someone to spank that cute little ass." Jamie was such a cocky shit.

"Do you want to repeat that? I'm not sure the reporters outside heard you."

Jazz protected her privacy like a guard dog, but Jamie didn't really care if anybody knew what he was up to. Once they'd escaped Ohio at the age of eighteen, he'd sworn he would never go back into hiding himself again. She often wished she could be as brave.

"If you bend over, I'll take the stick out of your ass for you. I might not smack it like you want, but maybe I can free it up for the surprise I have for you." The gleam in his eyes scared her because she knew he was capable of some devious stuff.

"What are you up to? I know you too well, and you don't say things like that unless you have a reason, so spill." He knew her better than anyone, and it had been way too long, which meant he was probably plotting to get her laid. But Jamie didn't acknowledge any boundaries, so she could be in trouble if she didn't find out what he was up to and put a stop to it if she could.

"Come on, sweets. Let the guys finish packing up. I'll take you home, and we can order in while I show you the surprise I have in store for you." Jamie slung his arm around her shoulders and led her to his car

"I'm not even going to argue with you. I'm ready to get out of these clothes." She climbed in, and he started the car.

"I'd help you with that, but you know I don't swing that way. You simply don't have the right parts." He chuckled at his own joke.

"Hardy har har, you missed your calling. You should've been a stand-up comic." Though her life would suck without him.

He pulled into the underground parking under her building. While she'd dreaded adding yet another concert before her tour, at least her manager had scheduled it in Los Angeles where at least she could sleep in her own bed. Her condo was on the seventh floor, and Jamie's was right down the hall, which worked perfectly for them. They took the elevator straight to their floor, and Jazz felt as if she could breathe for the first time that day. She was in the one place where nobody asked anything of her. But, in truth, even that didn't help shut her mind off. The side of her that needed to submit was going without, so her brain always seemed to be going without a break.

"Baby girl, go grab your laptop and meet me in the living room." Jamie headed there without waiting for her to respond.

"Bossy much? At least let me get changed first. I'll be there in a few," she mumbled as she went to her bedroom to change into comfy cotton pajamas before doing what he wanted. Grabbing her laptop from its place on her desk, she carried it to the living room where she settled in her favorite spot on the couch. It actually fit her small frame perfectly. The end table held her favorite things, starting with her e-reader. If she couldn't submit to a man, then at least she could read and daydream about it. Exactly why she really wanted to get this over with, so she could go back to reading the dark romance she'd started last night when she should have been sleeping. Tonight, she had a date with a hot book and her BOB.

"What the hell do you need my computer for? You have one that can rival any in the State Department." *What was he up to?*

"I did a thing." He flashed a cocky grin. "Now, you know I love you, so you aren't allowed to be mad at me. And if you get mad, you aren't allowed to stay that way." He opened her laptop and logged in without bothering to ask for her password. He managed her life, so he knew her log-in information and everything else. But he had never steered her wrong, so she wasn't concerned about it.

"That does not sound good. What the hell have you done?" She didn't know whether to be pissed or worried, but at the moment worried was winning out.

"You haven't been with a man in so long, I swear that you must be all dried up. We can't have that, so I took matters into my own hands." *Did he seem nervous?* "Do you remember me mentioning Runway West?"

"It's that new dance club. I hear it's really popular. What about it?" She couldn't go somewhere like that without causing a riot, and he knew that.

"There's a private BDSM club in the basement. The security protocols are crazy. It was designed for people like you." His words hung in the air, and she had no idea how to process them.

"So, you're saying there's a place I can go play and be safe about it? I mean, we all can't be free to play like you are."

He frequented several clubs in the area, but Jazz was too worried about being found out to go with him.

"I am saying that, and there's more. They're having a special event on Valentine's night, and I signed you up." And there it was—what he worried she'd be angry about.

"What have you gotten me into?" She folded her arms across her chest in a huff.

Jamie continued typing into her laptop for a moment, and then turned it to show her the Black Light website. She focused on the words Celebrity Auction on the screen and grabbed her computer, pulling it onto her lap. It wouldn't do her any good to go off the rails without knowing the entire story. After reading the information, she was speechless, so she waited for him to explain.

When he remained silent, she choked out, "Explain."

"You and I both know you need a Dom. You might be scared of what that would really do to your crazy life. Hell, you might actually have to show yourself to someone for the first time in years. You would have to open yourself up to trust someone other than me. But I can't stand watching you wither away into nothing anymore. You don't take care of yourself. You work, you tour, and you read those naughty books you think I know nothing about. That's not a life. This is only one night, but it's time you start doing something for yourself, and if you won't, then I will." The tight set of his jaw told her he meant business.

"I'm not saying you're wrong, but what does that have anything to do with this?" She pointed to the screen, still unable to understand exactly what she had read.

"I signed you up for the auction. Doms will bid for the privilege of spending the evening with you. The roulette game is cool. Every thirty minutes, you get to spin the wheel for a different kink. You may get a chance to step out of that very little box you've put yourself in."

"What if it's a kink I don't want to do?" She couldn't even believe she was considering this.

"You get to choose five things that are off the table for you, and if they're spun, then you get to spin again. I already did your paperwork and did the deciding for you. Hell, I know you better than you do."

"I'm pretty sure you've lost your damn mind. Are you telling me that you not only signed me up for some crazy night of debauchery, but you decided on my hard limits for me as well?" He was right about how well he knew her, but this was a bit too far even for him.

"I left things pretty open, sweets. I just know how you are about water, so I kept that one-off limits, and of course no golden showers. Otherwise, you are just gonna have to trust me." He had that grin of his on his face.

Dammit he knew he had her in his trap.

"But I can't do this. People will find out."

"I call bullshit. You know I would never put you in danger like that. Didn't you see it's a celebrity auction? You're not the only famous person who will be participating. They will protect you, and I'll be there in case you need me — though I don't think you will. We fly out the next day, so this is the perfect time for you to take a night for yourself, no strings."

Shit, this was going to happen, and she had a feeling things were going to get very interesting. Worst case, she could use her safe word and get the hell out of Dodge. Best case, she could have a great night where she could shut her brain down for a few hours... and if she managed an orgasm or two, then she'd be the big winner. "Why the hell not? You already signed me up. Let's do this."

CHAPTER 2

$\mathcal{M}$ ichael was bored. Sure, his practice kept him busy. Being one of the few psychiatrists in the area who specialized in what the world considered 'alternative lifestyles' meant he'd always have an active work life. Hell, L.A. was home to every alternative lifestyle there was. This, however, did not help with his overall boredom with his life. The weekly poker game with the guys was great. He had enough money to do what he wanted when he wanted without having to worry about anything, and yet he couldn't escape the feeling something was missing.

He went to the club and played with the unattached subs there, and he enjoyed himself when he did, but lately even that left him feeling unfulfilled. He had never wanted to even think about committing to one woman. In fact, he considered that to be one step closer to the grave. But, lately, that seemed to be the trend among his friends. So many of them were getting married. Except, they didn't seem to think of it as settling down. They actually seemed happy, content, fulfilled — which was more than he could say for himself.

The boredom led Michael to Black Light's website to see what they had coming up. Maybe there was something going on that would get him out of this monotony he was feeling. After all, Valentine's Day was in a few weeks, and though he didn't want to be tied down, it would be nice to have a soft little subbie to spend it with.

As he was concentrating on his computer, his best friend, Troy, strolled into his office like he owned it. Well, technically that was half-true since they shared the practice. "Hey man, what ya up to?"

"Just checking out what's happening at Black Light."

He and Troy had both been active Doms for many years. The first trip to a club was all it took, and he was hooked.

"Did you see the Valentine's roulette thing they're doing? It seems interesting. If I weren't taking Becky to Atlanta to see her family, we would be there to enjoy the festivities. You know how she loves to watch." His gaze shifted and glassed over. *Yep, he was visualizing his sub in some naughty situation.*

"I was reading about it. They're doing a celebrity auction for charity with a game of kink roulette." He was reading the description without paying much attention to the fact Troy had come around and was peering over his shoulder at his computer screen.

"Do you really think you could leave it up to the spin of a wheel to tell you how you get to play with your sub? Seriously, I've never known you to give up control in any area of your life, especially play." His friend was all but daring him to put his money where his mouth was.

"Are you saying I'm not creative enough to roll with the wheel? Seriously?" It was insulting. Sure, he liked to control his life, but the idea of being able to pull out his naughty creativity made it a hard opportunity to pass up.

"It's not your creativity I'm doubting. You plan your scenes in advance. You leave nothing to chance. It's who you are. I'm just not sure how much you'll enjoy yourself if you don't have time to plan. Why not team up with some sweet little club subbie for the night? You might have more fun." *Leave it to Troy to always play the devil's advocate.*

"Don't you have somewhere to be? I'm sure Becky is waiting at home for you with something special. Why don't you get the hell out of here and let me finish what I'm doing," he grumbled. It wasn't really a request.

"Fine, I'll go. Don't say I didn't warn you." Grinning, he turned and left Michael's office.

Michael wished he could have argued with his friend, but he was right. He was known to plan everything to the last detail, but maybe that was his problem. He continued to do things the same way every time. Hell, that's probably why he was in such a rut. Could he step out of his comfort zone as a Dom and go for the spin of the wheel? It could be totally amazing or a total cluster fuck.

He continued skimming the website until he found the list of celebrities who were up for auction, and immediately recognized several of the people staring back at him from the screen. Francesca was the first face he recognized. She had a reputation for being quite the brat in her everyday life, if the magazines were to be believed. Though he loved turning a sub's ass bright red, he never really enjoyed the brats. Being bratty just never did it for him, so he continued down the list.

After several minutes of researching his options, a pair of stunning green eyes called out to him. There was a sadness to them he wanted to fix despite the fact that he knew nothing about the beautiful woman. Her name was listed as simply 'Jazz.' He didn't immediately recognize her, so he went on to read all of the information they had about her, which wasn't enough. He needed more. Despite not understanding why he was so interested, he decided to move on to the other submissives listed.

As he made his way to the end of the list, his mind wouldn't let go of the sad green eyes. Nobody else grabbed his attention in the same way. Since they didn't tell him enough about her, he opened another browser and searched 'singer Jazz', astounded at the number of results he received. The first site he opened told him about her career. It seemed she was a singer who edged toward the harder side of rock. This surprised him. Yes, her hair was obviously dyed the shade of black it was, but she had a young, innocent quality that didn't make him think hard rock.

She was in her early twenties, which was younger than he typically was attracted to. At thirty-nine, he never wanted to be mistaken for a woman's father. But, none of that mattered as he continued to get lost in this woman's gaze. If he reacted so strongly to just a photograph of her, there was no telling how attracted to her he would be when they met face to face.

He realized he was thinking in terms of when, not if. That fact alone was exciting to him. The last thing in the world he felt when gazing at her was boredom, so he knew he would do whatever it took to win a night with the green-eyed pixie.

He went back to the Black Light site and found the sign-up form for the celebrity auction. Though he was already a member, there was still extensive paperwork required. With the wheel choosing their scenes, he was given the opportunity to list five hard limits, but he didn't need all of them. No golden showers was an absolute for him, but otherwise he was open to the many choices listed.

After filling out his information, he found where he could place his bid. There was no way to tell how high they would go, so he needed to consider carefully what to bid to ensure he got what he wanted.

Money wasn't an issue for him. He could retire and still have enough to live several lifetimes without worrying about money. It was for charity, so he could write off any donation he made. He was trying to justify how much he was willing to spend to get what he wanted, because every fiber of his being wanted this woman.

He typed in his bid without any regrets. If he won the auction, it would be the best fifty thousand dollars he could imagine spending. He knew that this amount was probably a little excessive, but there was no way he was taking a chance with the pixie. In fact, he would keep an eye on the auction site. He was willing to pay what it would take. What was the point of working as hard as he did if not to spend the money on something he wanted?

After placing his bid, he left the Black Light site. He didn't know how, but he knew this was exactly what he needed to break him out of his rut. He could spend an amazing night torturing the raven-haired sub, and then say goodbye at the end of the night. No muss, no fuss.

Navigating to his favorite toy site, he decided to order some new tools for the occasion. As he checked out the different items he could add to his bag, he clicked on the medical portion of the site Seeing the exam tables with stirrups attached gave him some naughty thoughts about what he could do with the lovely sub.

He ordered several items before shutting down the computer for the evening. Glancing up at the clock, he was surprised by how much time had passed while he'd planned his Valentine's night at Black Light.

All he needed was for all the stars to align.

With a spring in his step, that had been missing for longer than he cared to think about, Michael grabbed his jacket and locked up his office before heading to his SUV. He needed to get home to release some of his nervous energy in his gym.

With the pixie in his future, he couldn't wait for Valentine's Day.

CHAPTER 3

*J*azz stayed quiet on the drive to the club. Jamie, on the other hand, talked non-stop. It seemed he was beyond excited to see the inside of Black Light. "Girlfriend, what's wrong with you? You're finally going to have a little fun after months of nothing but work and travel. I'm sure you must have elicited a bidding frenzy with that beautiful face. Did I misread the situation? You could always back out you know." The words came out in a rush as they always did when he was worried about his friend.

"No, you know me better than anyone else on the face of the planet. I do need this, but, honestly, I'm a little nervous. What if there's no chemistry? Whoever the Dom is, he spent a lot of money for the night with me. I don't want to let him down." She glanced down at her hands as she continued to pick at her thumbnail. If she wasn't careful, there would be nothing left of it before they even arrived.

"Look at my Jazzy, submissive to the very core. Listen, think of tonight as a game. Three spins of the roulette wheel. You have a chance to step out of your comfort zone in a safe place. Hell, the amount of scrutiny for everyone who steps through the door has to be up there with trying to gain access to the Pentagon. I'm surprised they didn't ask for a DNA sample to go along with our medical tests." He ran off on a tangent which made her giggle as she peered out the window, seeing Beverly Hills pass by.

"What does any of that have to do with what I was talking about," she chuckled

"Sorry, the train continued down the tracks without me. I was trying to say they will protect your privacy, so you can let go a little. If you're put in a situation you aren't comfortable with, then use your safe word. It isn't like you need the free month. And, I'll be there as a spectator, so if you need to get out of there, all you need to do is tell me, and we're gone." He was always taking care of her. She needed to see this through if for no other reason than so he could have a night off.

"You know, you're right. It'll be great to have a night I can shut it all off and let go. I want you to enjoy yourself, too. You won't be able to do that if you spend the whole damn night worried about me. So, I'm ordering you to let go and have a little fun. I know you love watching. You're such a voyeur."

"True, I do enjoy watching the scenes, but you'd best believe that I'll be avoiding yours. You may be my BFF, but that's a little close for comfort." He winked at her. She knew he would stick with her if that was really what she wanted, but she didn't want that at all.

As they hit Rodeo Drive, she knew they were getting closer, and a herd of elephants rumbled through her stomach. She had decided to give herself over to what the night might bring. She felt excited and only slightly nervous wondering what the roulette wheel would give her and who her mystery Dom would be. She hoped like hell she would be attracted to him.

After turning off Rodeo, it wasn't long before they turned into a long driveway with double gates and a security booth. The drive was surrounded by trees. When they pulled up to the gate, security asked for their ID cards. Jazz pulled hers out of her wallet, seeing her legal name and thinking that it had been a while since she had thought about it. People asked her all the time what her real name was, but to her, Jazz was as real as it got because it was who she was. When she handed it along with her confirmation email to Jamie, she noticed a slight tremor in her hand. Damn she needed to get hold of herself before she entered the club.

The drive ahead to the mansion that held the club was breathtaking. She realized immediately that privacy was the main point, but all the trees and quiet was also calming. After a short distance, they took a smaller driveway to the left and followed it around until they reached another security checkpoint and handed the large-framed security man their invitations.

"Welcome to Black Light. If you'll continue to follow the path, it will lead you to the parking area." He waved them to continue their journey and turned toward the next car that was making its way toward them.

"I sure hope you're ready because this night is going to be awesome." Jamie reached over and squeezed her hand. His lopsided grin told her that he was more than ready to get the night started. He took his hand back and drove them the rest of the way to the parking area. She was surprised by how many cars were already there, because she'd been worried they might be too early, but that concern flew out the window.

After parking, Jamie took her hand and escorted her across the brick walkway and through the door that led them to an area with lockers and yet another security person behind a podium. "Welcome to Black Light and Happy Valentine's Day. If you could please hand me your invitation, I would appreciate it." *Well, isn't everyone here so polite.* They handed their cards to him while peeking around the small area they were in.

"Very good. Now, a few housekeeping items. As you hopefully saw on your application for tonight, no electronics are allowed in the club, and there are no exceptions." He reached under the podium and she heard a clicking sound behind her. When she turned, she noticed one of the lockers had popped open. "Please place all electronics in the locker. You can pick them up when you leave. Feel free to place your jacket there as well." He nodded toward the locker, encouraging her to do as he asked.

Jazz placed her purse with her phone in the locker and started to untie the belt at her waist, pulling off the trench coat she'd put on prior to leaving for the club. Turning, she met Jamie's eyes as he placed his phone and wallet in her locker. It didn't matter how many times in the past he had seen her like this, it was still not comfortable. She could amble around naked for the entire club to see, and it wouldn't bother her, but the red leather corset with matching mini skirt and thong showed a lot of skin, and she felt bare next to him.

"The club uses the traffic light system for your safe word. Are you familiar with this system?" the security guy asked.

She nodded, appreciating that they were upfront in dealing with safety.

He went on. "Though many of our couples use different safe words, the word red is universal and will stop your play while one of the monitors comes to help. Remember, red stops everything, including Roulette for the night. So, your Dom has more than enough incentive to only give you what you can handle."

"I understand." Jazz took a deep breath. She was really doing this.

"If you're ready, welcome again, and enjoy yourself." He gestured toward a door behind them. Jazz took a deep breath and followed his direction, making her way into the club with Jamie.

She stepped into the main area and glanced around. It could have been any crowded bar in the city but for the fact that so many people were scantily dressed. Sure, in a mainstream club you might see short skirts and crop tops, and lots of corsets. People dressed in leather ambled around chatting as if they were fully dressed. What did surprise her was the number of suited up men. Sure, a bare chest was sexy, but a man in a suit did something to her. What she didn't see around the club was judgement. Though everyone was doing their own thing, no one seemed out of place. Her muscles relaxed, and her breathing calmed.

She was home.

Jazz looked across the room and saw a man gawking at her. No, staring was more like it. She was used to people staring when she was out, but this was different, and it gave her the creeps. She turned away immediately and found herself looking into the eyes of the most beautiful man she had ever seen. Seeing him, she understood the term 'take your breath away' for the first time, because that was exactly what he did.

"O.M.G. Talk about man candy," Jamie said. "Damn girl, he can't keep his eyes off you." His words drew her attention away from the dark-haired man and back to her best friend.

"Please, Jamie, you exaggerate," she said, though she secretly hoped Jamie was right. That gorgeous man screamed Dominant to his very core. Hell, her panties were a little wet from merely seeing him across the room. What would happen if he touched her?

"Exaggerate? Turn back around and look." He turned her so she was facing him across the room and he was still checking her out. But, unlike the other man, this man made her lady parts stand up and pay attention.

She pulled her gaze from him and searched for where the roulette spin would happen. Her email verification had said it would be in the theater. Was there anything this club didn't have? As she started toward the theater, someone bumped her from the side. She turned to see the creepy man from across the room. "You should have been mine," he mumbled under his breath as he continued without even excusing himself.

"What an asshole." Leave it to Jamie to say what she was thinking. "Listen, baby girl, I'm going to let you go in there and see what your night will hold. I'll be out here wandering around seeing what kind of trouble I can get into. There's a silent auction going on, and I want to check it out." He was giving her the space she needed, while letting her know he would be around if she needed him. Just another reason they were best friends for life.

"Enjoy yourself. I'm not the only one who hasn't been getting what they need with the schedule we've been keeping. I'll be fine. In fact, I have a feeling tonight will be amazing." She squeezed his hand and headed into the theater, finding a seat toward the back so she could see not only the stage but also the Doms and subs gathered there. Though she didn't consider herself a voyeur, she loved being a people watcher. She wanted to watch everyone come in before it was time to start. She knew she would have to move to the front eventually, but this gave her a chance to watch without being the center of attention.

$\sim$

SHE WAS HERE. WHEN MICHAEL SPOTTED HIS GREEN-EYED PIXIE ACROSS the room, it took everything in him not to cross over to her and carry her out caveman-style. He had to take a deep breath to center himself because seeing the pixie in person took his breath away. Her pictures simply didn't do her justice. Her hair was the darkest black he had ever seen, which made her eyes pop even more.

She seemed a little unsettled, gazing toward the other side of the room, and he didn't like that at all. But when her gaze shifted toward him, her eyes lit up. She obviously liked what she saw, and he loved that. *That's right, Pixie. Tonight is ours.*

He let his gaze wander around the room and his inner Dom start to settle, knowing he would be coming out to play soon. When he turned back toward Jazz, he noticed some jackass bump into her, and he seemed to linger for longer than necessary. Then she frowned and placed her hands around her waist. He wanted to go over there and physically remove the man from her presence. After he left, she turned and talked with her friend before giving him a kiss on the cheek and moving in the direction of the room where the roulette spins would take place.

"Michael, it's been a while since we've seen you. I'm glad you decided to join our little game of roulette."

He turned to see Jaxson behind him, following his gaze across the room before he added. "That was some bid you placed. I have to say I'm surprised you chose Jazz. She seems different from most of the subs you play with."

He really was a nosy bastard.

"I didn't realize you were such a voyeur. I always thought those two subs of yours kept you too busy to be watching the rest of us." He smiled at his friend, letting him know that he was yanking his chain.

"But, yes, she is different. I don't know what it is about her, but the thought of not having her tonight was something I couldn't accept." That was as much as he was willing to share.

"Oh, this night keeps getting better and better. You're going to be in so much trouble, and I for one can't wait." Jax chuckled and walked away shaking his head

Michael entered the theater, and immediately searched for his Pixie. He found her sitting in the back of the room watching her surroundings. What drew his attention was the way she picked at her nails. Was she nervous, or was it simply a habit? It occurred to him that she didn't know who would be topping her tonight, but he was grateful to know she would be his. There was no way he would be able to handle watching her submit to anyone else until he had his fill of her. They had yet to speak to one another, but he couldn't deny the spark when their eyes met. Tonight would certainly be interesting.

All of the celebrities were corralled near the front of the theater, but Michael couldn't have named a single one. Not that he didn't follow popular culture, but he couldn't pull his eyes from the beautiful green-eyed pixie. Her eyes continued to dart from person to person all over the room. It appeared neither of them were paying any attention to Jax on stage. He could've been announcing the end of the world, and Michael would have had no idea. Eventually, he finished the speech he was giving and a pretty woman in a leather cat suit stepped up to finish the explanations and start the night.

"Next up, we have Jazz! Lead singer of the rock band The Scarlet Letter!" When Madison finally announced it was Jazz's turn, she was ringing her hands. If he didn't know better, he might have thought she had no experience with this at all.

This is going to be so much fun.

"And our winning bid of fifty thousand dollars came from Dr. Michael Adams!" As Madison announced him as the winner, Jazz sucked in a deep breath, her eyes as wide as saucers.

He took his time moving up the steps to the stage, walking until he was close enough to tower over the petite beauty. "Hello, Pixie."

"Time to spin!" Madison called out over the speakers as she

pressed the ball into Jazz's hand, although his pixie hadn't taken her eyes off him yet.

The roulette wheel started to spin, but Jazz was holding the ball without moving and so he moved her hand over the wheel and let the ball drop. She finally seemed to snap out of her daze, staring at the whirling kinks until the ball finally came to rest at—

"Like, their first scene for the night is *teacher/student role play*! I'm sure that will be fun!" Madison laughed, but Jazz looked stunned as those perfect green eyes met his again.

Without waiting, he grabbed the back of her neck and leaned in to whisper in her ear. "You're mine, my little pixie. My name is Michael, but you can call me Sir."

She shivered and took a deep breath.

That's right. Now you know who will master you tonight.

CHAPTER 4

*R*ole play. They seriously wanted her to role play, and as a schoolgirl. What the fuck? She'd run as far as she could the day she graduated, and she did not want to think about those days again. Why in the hell hadn't Jamie put this shit on her limit list? She should have forced him to show her the application he'd filled out. Now she had to see it through, because she would be damned if she would wimp out before the night even started.

"You're going to be so adorable in pigtails and a schoolgirl uniform," Michael grinned at her.

"I'm sorry, did you say pigtails?" She hadn't even considered that. Now she was imagining herself as Britney Spears, dancing and singing with braids. *Like that would ever happen.*

"What's a great school girl fantasy without pigtails and a pleated skirt so short your ass peeks out?" He was enjoying this way too much. "I am so looking forward to getting to know you, Pixie." Placing his hand on the small of her back, Michael led her out of the theater. She loved how settled it made her feel.

"I'm curious, Sir. Why do you keep calling me Pixie? You do know I'm called Jazz, right?" She couldn't help the hint of sarcasm that leaked into her voice. She knew she was on the shorter side, but she didn't like to be reminded of it.

"We officially started the night the minute they spun that wheel, which means you are mine for the night. You need to watch the tone in your voice before I forget all about the game and turn you over my knee right here." They had stopped, and he was staring down at her with his arms across his chest. "To answer your question, the moment I laid eyes on you and your beautiful green eyes, I knew you were going to be my pixie." He stood straight, and his hazel eyes darkened to a smoky topaz. They were captivating when they were light hazel, but when they darkened, they were mesmerizing. He cocked his right eyebrow, telling her she had been lost in her thoughts for long enough.

"I'm sorry, Sir." This was not how she wanted to start the night, so she knew she needed to rein in her attitude, and quickly, or the spankings she had been wanting would not be the sexy kind at all.

"You're forgiven. Let's go find your costume. We have a classroom to get to." He actually winked at her. She thought both the playful and dominant sides of him were hot. *Damn this man is sexy.*

He led her through the pool area, and it appeared the night had already begun for several other members of the club. There were people both in and out of the water in varying stages of undress. In the corner there was a small stage that she was sure would be in use before the night was over. But what caught her attention was the fact that her best friend was kneeling next to a man she recognized, but couldn't quite place. She would have to file that away and ask him about it later.

When they rounded the corner leaving the pool area, the first door they came to was already open, and she saw that it was a closet of sorts full of all kinds of costumes. *This should be interesting.* A woman came into view with a big smile on her face.

"Good evening, Sir. How can I help you this evening?" She didn't hold his gaze, making Jazz wonder if she was a submissive working in the club. "I am here for anything you might need, and I mean anything." The woman glanced at him and winked. *Is she blatantly flirting with him right in front of me? It looks like I just might have to kick a little ass tonight.*

"Yes, we want a schoolgirl outfit for my submissive," he put his arm around her waist in a clear sign of ownership. "I want her to have a plaid pleated skirt with a white button up, hair in double braids. And, she won't need any panties for this scene."

Michael had a very specific idea about what he wanted, that much was clear.

He turned to Jazz with a smirk. "I want you to go to the changing room and get ready. You know what I want, so I don't expect there to be any issues when you come to the classroom down the hall to find me. When you get there, sit in the desk in the middle of the first row and wrap your feet around the legs of your chair. I want to see your pretty pussy from my desk at the front of the room. You have ten minutes before I will come for you and trust me you do not want to allow that to happen." *Holy shit, this was so much hotter than she imagined when teacher/student showed up on the roulette wheel.* "If you have any doubts, that means you are to wear what I assigned and only what I assigned." He turned and left her with her mouth hanging open.

"You are one lucky girl," the employee said. "I'll go get your outfit. Give me a sec. You're a small right?"

Jazz nodded, still unable to find her words as the other woman went in search of her costume. She didn't know how long it took her to come back, but she was grateful she had the correct clothes when she returned.

"Here you go. She passed her the clothes and held up a couple of ribbons. "I assumed you might need these as well. If you want, I can throw your hair up in the braids really quick. Should only take me a minute." Her genuine smile made Jazz feel bad about assuming she was making a play for her Dom.

"That would be amazing. I have no clue how to do it," Jazz replied and took a seat. "What's your name, anyway? You're being so sweet, and I don't even know your name."

"My name is Annie and I have to admit I am a big fan. Your rock

562

style is so much smoother than most of the harder stuff that's out there, and I love it."

Jazz loved meeting fans, but now she had to worry about being outed this was not the time or place. *Just great.*

"Wait, I saw you stiffen up. There's no reason to worry about me. I would never put your business out there, but if you're concerned, remember that everyone here has signed an NDA. I simply couldn't afford to out you even if I wanted to." She patted her shoulder. "All done, and if you don't want to start out with a punishment, you might want to hurry. You only have a couple of minutes left."

"Thanks so much!" Jazz jumped up and ran to change her clothes. The skirt was so short that her ass cheeks really were hanging out like Michael wanted. *No walking away now.*

When she stepped into the classroom, there he was sitting at the 'teacher's desk,' looking down at some papers spread across the wood in front of him. He didn't budge when she came in. She ran into the room unsure of how much time she had, but knew it had to be close as she was hooking her feet as instructed. Then he glanced up. His intense gaze made her so wet, it dripped down between her legs to the cold, hard, plastic chair. *Great, I left a wet spot for all to see.*

"I'm glad to see you made it, though I was looking forward to what would have happened if you hadn't."

SHE WAS THE PICTURE OF PERFECTION, THE NAUGHTIEST SCHOOLGIRL HE had ever laid eyes on. She'd tied off the shirt, leaving the buttons undone and the sides of her beautiful breasts on display in the sexiest way. She had obeyed his instructions, giving him a clear view of her pussy, which was glistening in the light. Jazz may not have been excited about role play, but her body couldn't lie to him.

He shuffled papers around, trying to remain in the scene while he got his thoughts together. His dick was hard as titanium, making his pants tight under the desk. He met her gaze, and her hooded eyes brought him back into the moment. "So, I am Mr. Adams, and I will be watching over detention today. I hear you have been a very naughty girl. It says here your name is Jazz. I know that cannot be the name your mother and father gave you. What is your real name, girl?" Michael really wanted to know her name, and this was the perfect way to find out.

"My name is Jazz." The stubborn set of her jaw told him her answer was not about the game they were playing. She really didn't want to tell him. *To hell with that.* Now, he needed to know.

"Excuse me, young lady. I asked you a question that I expect you to answer. What is your name?"

"I did answer. It's the only answer you're going to get," Jazz replied, completely calm. She added, "Sir," before he had the chance to respond.

"Adding sir doesn't change the fact that you did not answer as you were instructed, little girl." He searched around the desk, noting the ruler sitting right in front of him. Yes, it would do nicely. Leaning back in his chair, he stared into her mesmerizing gaze.

He waited to speak again until he saw her start to squirm in her seat, obviously uncomfortable with the silence.

"All right, young lady, if that's how you want to play this, get up and go to the chalkboard at the front of the room. Start at the top and write the sentence 'I will obey my teacher' over and over until I tell you to stop. If you stop before I instruct you, I will turn you over my knee and spank you. Unless I ask you a question or instruct you otherwise, you are not to speak. Do you understand my instructions?" He had thought his dick couldn't get any harder. He was wrong. Watching her slide out of her chair and shuffle toward the front of the room was a practice in torture. He needed to get control of himself quick. The chalkboard was behind him, so he continued to face the front, hearing her pick up a piece of chalk from the metal tray.

He stood from his chair and pushed it under the desk before turning to see her on her toes reaching to write her lines at the top of the board, which accentuated her tight little ass perfectly. The round globes peeked out of the bottom of her skirt, just begging to be spanked. "Did you forget something, little girl? I asked you a question.

Do I not deserve the respect of an answer?" He grinned at the shudder he saw run through her. One quick smack on the ass and she yelped "Yes sir"

Taking a step forward, he pressed himself against her back, allowing his rock-hard cock to settle between her ass cheeks. She hesitated where she stood for a moment, and he thought he was going to be able to get his hands reddening her ass faster than he'd believed. But she took a deep breath and started to write again. She was in this with him.

"That's right, little girl. You keep writing like the good girl I know you are, even if you chose to disobey and not answer my question." He reached around and unbuttoned her shirt slowly. The chalk screeched a little on the board, but she continued as he untied her shirt where it was knotted around her waist, leaving her breasts hanging out.

He trailed his fingers up each side with a feather light touch, feeling her take in a deep breath as he did, but she still didn't stop writing. "Your skin is so soft, my sweet," he whispered in her ear right before nipping at her earlobe. "I can't wait to turn this soft, white ass red when you disobey, and I have no doubt you will."

Because he would make sure she did.

He wasn't above cheating if that was what it would take to get what he wanted, and what he wanted more than anything in that moment was to redden her ass. As she continued to concentrate on her lines as if her life depended on it, he continued his attack, dragging his hands up to her breasts. Slowly, he stroked around her nipples before taking each one between thumb and forefinger and pinching with enough force to make her moan as he bit down on her neck.

She was the sexiest thing he had ever seen, and, at least for tonight, she was his. "You like that, huh? Well, naughty little schoolgirls don't get their pleasure that easily. I could put you out of your misery, if you would just answer my question. What's your name, young lady?" He squeezed again, this time a little harder than the last, knowing instinctively she could handle it.

"My name is Jazz, Sir" was her breathy response. Such a stubborn little subbie. He thought she would stop her lines at this point, but her chalk stayed in motion on the board. The letters were not as neat as they had been when she started, but he could still read them. She was not going to make this easy on him.

He let go of her nipples, and she whimpered. Making mental note to remember how much she seemed to like her breasts played with, he stepped back so they were no longer touching. Jazz seemed to lean back, searching out his touch. Yet, her chalk continued to write.

Michael reached down and caught the zipper of her skirt, slowly inching it down, prolonging the moment. When he had her skirt unzipped as far as it would go, he ran his hand inside and down the crack of her ass until he reached her rosebud. When he circled his finger around the sensitive area, she shuddered. He didn't attempt to breach her tight hole, but instead just lingered around the perimeter, enjoying the feel. She continued to write, but much slower than she had been, and her breathing slowed. She was obviously affected by what he was doing, which meant it was time to pull out the big guns.

Maybe not his big gun, but still effective.

Pulling his hand away, he jerked her skirt to the floor before getting down on his knees. It was time for some up close and personal time with her pussy. Tapping her right ankle, she lifted her foot so he could tug the skirt out of the way. Repeating it with her left, he removed her skirt. Her safety was important to him, so he needed to make sure she didn't fall, and it gave him such a lovely view.

After removing the skirt, he reached up and parted her pussy lips. *Beautiful.* Before thinking about it, he took a swipe with his tongue. Her taste exploded in his mouth, and she shifted from foot to foot, widening her stance. With his right hand, he took her clit between his fingers, and pinched with enough pressure to test another of her limits.

Her pussy wept for him exactly as he had hoped it would. He was rewarded by her response when she dropped her hands and stepped back slightly. She was obviously trying to control her reaction to his ministrations.

Letting go, he rose to his feet so that he was standing in front of her now that she was no longer facing the chalkboard. Reaching up, he grabbed her hair tightly and pulled back, forcing her to look up at him.

"Oh, you tried so hard to be good little girl, but you broke the rules. That means I get to put you over my lap and turn that pretty ass of yours bright red." He couldn't hide his smile.

This was exactly what he wanted them to get out this scene.

She blushed at his words. She definitely had experience but wasn't jaded like so many of the other club subs. Michael took her hand and pulled the chair from the desk. Sitting down, he led her until she was sitting in his lap.

"My little pixie, you are so beautiful. Since you almost made it before breaking the rules, I'll be kind to you." Reaching up, he stroked her cheek, still flushed and lovely, but her eyes narrowed. "Be careful that you remain respectful to your teacher, or I might not be so forgiving with regard to your punishment. I'll spank you first with the ruler. After all, this is a punishment. Fifteen swats with the ruler followed by fifteen with my hand. I will change the rules and let you be as loud as you want as long as you are respectful." When she continued to stare at him without responding, he grabbed her knee with some force. "Do I not deserve some gratitude for my kindness, little girl?"

"Oh, of course, Mr. Adams. You are a wonderful and kind teacher. Thank you for being lenient with me. This is the first time a teacher has spanked me, and I'm a little nervous." She made a show of biting her bottom lip, playing up their scene for all it was worth.

"As it's your first time, I hope for your sake that you don't repeat your offenses and require harsher punishment than I'm going to give you. I want you to stand and take the ruler from my desk and give it to me." He put out his hand and waited for her to place the ruler in it, watching as she rose gave him a peek of her ass again. Once she handed over the ruler, he continued. "Lay across my lap and ask me to begin your punishment."

She took no time to follow his directions. Yes, his little pixie wanted this as much as he did.

"You're not allowed to come without permission. In fact, that's a rule that will remain in effect for the rest of the night." He counted in his head, waiting for her reaction. One... two... but he never made it to three, because she raised her head.

"What? I must have misheard you." Her voice was tight, showing she was close to the edge.

"Hmm, already forgetting your manners." He waited to see the understanding light in her eyes.

"I'm sorry, Sir. I forgot myself for a moment." She grinned and batted her eyes at him. This subbie was going to be trouble for him in the best possible sense.

"Forgiven, but to clarify, no, you did not misunderstand. If you want to come tonight, you will only do so with my permission, which I may or may not give." Saying nothing else, he pointed toward the floor and she lay back over his legs, grabbing his ankle to hold herself steady. He placed his hand on her thigh, pulling it out so that her legs were spread the way he liked it.

With the ruler, he took his first stroke, a light tap as far as he was concerned. The scream that came from Jazz's mouth told a different story. But that didn't deter him as she hadn't used her safe word. He landed his second stroke slightly higher, but it reached across both cheeks, leaving a nice red stripe. Then he continued with the next thirteen in quick succession because he wanted to get his hands on her ass, with her moaning and squirming the entire time.

Setting the ruler on the desk, he reached out and stroked her ass. Her skin was warm to the touch, and sensitive if her wiggling around in his lap had anything to say about it. He stroked over her ass until he reached her cunt. He couldn't resist stroking her pussy just once, and he was rewarded when he brought his hand back, as it glistened with her juices. Damn this woman was everything he could want in a sub.

He bit back the thought, so he could keep his attention right where it belonged. "Well, well, well. My little student seems to love having her ass reddened if her wet pussy is any proof. Fifteen more swats then we will be finished." He smacked first her left cheek and then her right, careful not to smack in the same place twice. They had not been together long enough for him to know how much she could take. After the second slap, she moaned, writhing over his legs — but not because of the pain. The third and fourth slaps landed on each sit spot, which brought him so close to her pussy he could feel the heat coming from it. She was so close, and he wanted to see her explode in his arms.

"One more spank, and we're done. You may come when I spank you, but if you don't, then you'll have to wait for the next scene." Before she could respond, he pulled his hand back and spanked her pussy with enough force to set her off like a rocket. She screamed his name along with a lot of unintelligible garbles. He left his hand on her pussy and enjoyed the pulsation coming from it as he teased her with light caresses. Her juices ran down onto his black dress pants. He didn't care. In fact, he would wear it like a badge of honor.

When she started to come down from her orgasm, he lifted her until she was sitting on his lap. Holding her close, he enjoyed the feeling of her small frame in his arms.

This woman was dangerous to him.

When she started to shake in his arms, he grabbed the blanket he had stashed in the desk drawer along with a bottle of water and bar of chocolate. When he wrapped the blanket around her, she cuddled in closer, placing her face up to his neck. Opening the water bottle, he shook her slightly. "Pixie, I need you to wake up and drink some water." He brought the bottle to her lips as her eyes fluttered open, reminding him of a butterfly's wings. She sipped the water as he held it to her mouth. When she had her fill, he placed the bottle on the desk and a piece of chocolate to her lips. She followed his nonverbal instruction and opened her mouth, moaning when the chocolate hit her tongue. It only made him want her more, but this moment wasn't about that.

Michael held her for several minutes while she came down from her endorphin high. When she eventually sat up, she looked him in the eyes then leaned forward and kissed him. It took him completely by surprise because he'd never had a sub make a move like that before. He may have been surprised, but he wasn't bothered at all by the turn of events. Holding her tightly, he deepened the kiss, tasting her and the chocolate as their tongues danced. Eventually, they both needed to come up for air and he pulled back, taking a moment to gaze at her beautiful face.

"You're going to be trouble little pixie," he said and leaned in with a quick nip of her bottom lip. Standing up, he placed her gently on her feet. Once she was steady, he patted her on the ass and smiled when she yelped.

"Go ahead and get dressed in your personal clothes. Then we'll head back to the wheel of wonders to see what we will get to do next." And he was anxious to see what would happen.

"Yes, Sir," she responded. Her voice was soft, almost shy.

"And, Pixie, you might as well leave the panties. You won't need them for the rest of the night."

CHAPTER 5

$\mathscr{A}$s Jazz left, she couldn't get over her pull toward Michael. She had been on the road the majority of her adult life, and though she was no virgin, she was also not as experienced as most her age. If she was being honest with herself, sex was something she had always been able to take or leave. But, during the last hour, she'd been given something she wasn't sure she could give up. She may not even understand it, but she didn't have time to worry about that at the moment. She needed to get dressed so they could spin again, then she'd find a way to enjoy the night and walk away without looking back.

After dressing in her own clothes, sans panties, Jazz came around the corner to see Michael in conversation with another Dom. Though she didn't know him, it was obvious by the way he carried himself that he was definitely a Dominant and, of course, they all stuck together.

She took advantage while Michael was distracted to watch him. He was a handsome man, and his eyes were nothing short of magnetic His brooding expression was something she was rapidly getting used to, but as he laughed at something his friend said that went away, and he seemed almost carefree. As much as the submissive in her loved a dark, brooding Dom, the woman in her fell a little for the smiling man.

She shook off her thoughts when she noticed he was looking at her with that grin she was rapidly growing to like.

Oh, she needed to be very careful with her heart — or he'd steal it.

"Little Pixie, were you going to stand there all night, or did you plan to come over here and let me put my hands on you?" His look became mischievous, and she obeyed without a word, stopping next to him while he said goodbye to the man he had been speaking with.

He didn't introduce them and, in this instance, it didn't bother her at all.

"Are you ready to see what treats the wheel has for us next?"

"Yes, Sir." She nodded, still trying to find a way to keep her heart in check. They went to the theater for their next spin, and she noticed there were more than a few people there watching the movie they were playing on the big screen. But she could hear the sounds of slapping, screaming, and sex. She was ready to see what would be coming next, though she was a little nervous.

When the wheel landed on medical play, her throat dried, and if she hadn't been leaning against Michael in that moment her knees would have given out — she would have been a puddle on the floor. It wasn't a kink she had participated in before, and it was honestly a little scary. She peered up at Michael and noticed right away that he wasn't nervous. In fact, he reminded her of a kid who had gone into the toy store after being told he could have whatever he wanted.

"I was hoping the wheel would land on medical play. I get to put my schooling to good use." If possible, his eyes lit up even more. He turned to one of the employees and asked, "Can you please get my bag from the locker room and have it brought to the exam room?" The young man nodded and left before Michael turned back toward her.

"You know, I haven't had the chance to ask what it is you do for a living?" She had been curious but too distracted by the sexy play to even go there.

"I'm a psychiatrist. Dr. Adams is going to give you a thorough examination." He wagged his eyebrows as he placed his hand on her lower back and led her back to the same hall as the classroom. She didn't even notice any of the people around her. In fact, the club could have fallen down around her feet, and she still would only have noticed him.

When they approached what she assumed was the exam room, she glanced up and saw a couple leaving, and she couldn't help but stare at the man leading his sub. She knew him from somewhere but was having trouble remembering where from. He reached out and shook hands with Michael.

"It's all yours. We were a bit messy, but I've made sure it's all clean for you." Once he spoke, she realized who he was, and she had to admit to herself that she was a little starstruck. He was that famous chef, Ronan Bellington. She had eaten in his restaurant once, and to this day, it was the best meal she had ever eaten.

"Thanks. I'm sure we'll be messy, too," Michael answered and turned to wink at her.

The woman standing next to Ronan blushed. "Have fun," she said to Jazz.

Michael led her to where a folded, white hospital gown lay on top of the paper covering the padded leather top of the exam table. "I want you to change into the gown. Fold your clothes neatly and set them on the chair against the wall. When you're finished, sit on the end of the table and wait for me. You are to remain silent unless I ask you a question. Do you have any questions for me before we begin?" Gone was the easygoing Michael, replaced by the intimidating Dom who had won her for the night.

"No, Sir. I understand what you want." She looked down where he had taken her hands in his, realizing that she had been picking at her nails again.

"Nervous is okay, but I don't want you to be scared. I'll take care of you. Now, please do what I asked before we have to start the fun with a punishment instead." He swatted her ass as she turned away to comply with his orders.

Undressing, Jazz slipped her arms into the gown, reaching behind her to tie the strings at the neck before sitting on the table.

Her trepidation reminded her of her first visit to the OB-GYN. Her mother had made her go at the age of fifteen to get on birth control assuming that. because she was different, she was sexually active. Sure, she dyed her hair black, and she loved rock music, but she never understood how this equated to sexually active to her mother. 'Little slut' were the words her mother had used when she'd talked to the doctor. It had been mortifying. but in no way different than things had always been with her mother. It was why she so often avoided going to the doctor unless she had no choice. But she hoped tonight would replace those memories with much better ones.

She fidgeted while she examined the room, listening to the crinkle of the paper, trying not to let her nerves get the better of her, as Michael approached.

"Good evening. I am Dr. Adams. I will be doing your exam today. What is your name?" Michael wore a lab coat and had a stethoscope hung around his neck as he studied a clipboard.

"Hi, my name is Jazz." She couldn't decide why he kept asking, but he was going to get the same answer every time.

"So, that's how we're going to play it? Okay, *Jazz*, we will be doing a full physical exam today. I need to make sure you are healthy enough for the strenuous work you do." His eyes narrowed.

She didn't understand his need to know her name, but if she shared that part of herself, wouldn't she be sharing everything? Sitting on the exam table, she waited for his next instructions. He had told her not to speak, and if she couldn't give him everything he wanted, then she could give her obedience in this.

"Very nicely done, little Pixie." He stroked the back of his hand down her cheek, making her feel small in his masculine hands. Reaching behind her neck, he untied the hospital gown and let it fall, leaving her breasts on display. "Lie back on the table so we can start your checkup."

As he helped her get settled, he reached under her ass and

extended the table slightly, so she had a place to rest her legs. It felt nice, but she knew that wouldn't last long.

"The first thing we are going to do is a breast exam. Breast health is so important." Pulling her gown farther down, he took it off her arms, but her pussy remained covered. He began by placing his hands on her left breast and massaging it.

It was actually relaxing, which surprised her. She wasn't sure what she expected, but this wasn't how she'd thought he would start.

"Your breast tissue feels good, no lumps noticeable," he said, maintaining a clinical tone. She was relaxed enough that she wasn't prepared when he pinched her nipple between his thumb and forefinger with enough force that her head came off the table, and she cried out. "I thought you understood the rules, little one. You are to remain silent unless you are asked a question. Did I ask you anything?" There was that eyebrow hiked again. *Cocky bastard.*

"No, Sir, you did not. You just took me by surprise." Though she wanted to continue, she stopped with that, knowing anything more would be asking for trouble.

"I will let it pass, but only this one time. Let's continue, shall we?" he asked as if he really wanted an answer, which she knew damn well he did not. "Now, where was I?"

He bent over and placed her nipple in his mouth, licking and sucking. She started to wonder if she could get off simply by him playing with her nipples, because if anyone could make her, it would be him. Then he bit down hard enough to cause a sharp pain, but before her brain could make sense of the feeling, he was licking and sucking again. *Damn this man is good.*

Moving to her other breast, he continued with his slow and methodical approach. Licking, sucking, biting. Before long, she was writhing enough the paper sheet crinkled loudly under her. She had no clue how long they continued like this before he removed his mouth from her breast with a *pop.* "Beautiful pink areolas, nice firm breasts, looks good."

He kissed his way down her stomach, pushing her gown away as he went, stopping short of her pussy. *Damn him.* She must have made a noise, because he lifted his mouth from her and raised his eyes, looking straight at her.

"Growling will not get you what you want, Pixie." Straightening, he came around the end of the table, and she couldn't help wondering what he had in store next. He reached around her left leg and pulled something out from the underside of the table. It took her a minute to understand what she was seeing. A stirrup. She sucked in a breath, watching him pull out the second stirrup.

Panic rose with the onslaught of bad memories. No matter how many years passed, the cruel things people said always found a way to come back to her. She was on the verge of yelling out 'red' when Michael grabbed her hand.

"Pixie, breathe with me." His voice was calm. When she didn't immediately comply, he squeezed her hand and spoke louder. "Jazz, look at me." That brought her back to the present.

She released the breath she hadn't even realized she had been holding.

"Before we continue, I want you to explain to me what just happened." His voice allowed for no argument.

"Being in this room brought back some unhappy memories. I guess I got lost in them a little. No big deal." She tried to brush it off, so they could continue with their night. She was not ready to let it end like this.

"Do you honestly think I'm going to accept that explanation, Pixie? If so, you couldn't be more wrong. I will ask you one more time before we call it a night. What happened?"

He wasn't playing. He would end their time together, and she was not willing to let that happen. "When I was young, my parents were not what you would call... kind. My mother assumed I was a slut and forced me to go to the gynecologist. Based on what my mother had told him, he assumed I was already sexually active. Let's just say that as a virgin, I was a little emotionally scarred by that visit." She picked at her thumb nail and closed the distance between her knees. She was having a difficult time staying in the moment.

"Did he touch you inappropriately?" His hands fisted, his voice low and dangerous.

"Honestly, at the time, I wouldn't have known. I was innocent. I was only fifteen years old. Hell, I had never even kissed a boy. Looking back, he didn't touch me in a bad way, but he was the first to see and touch me, and he wasn't kind about it. Please don't end the night. The memory took me by surprise for a minute, but I swear I'm okay."

She would be so disappointed to stop now.

MICHAEL COULDN'T STAND THE SADNESS IN HER EYES. HE REFUSED TO allow ghosts of her past to interfere with what they were building. He needed to get her out of her own head; it was that simple.

"Have you not been to the doctor as an adult? Your medical forms said you are currently on birth control. Did you not undergo a vaginal exam when they prescribed it?" he asked. He needed to know what he was dealing with before moving forward.

"I did. I wasn't exactly comfortable during the exam, but I just tried not to pay attention and made it through. I think that is why it took me by such surprise when the feelings and memories hit me. I've been on the road for so long and I can't exactly pick up a Dom in the different cities I visit. I had someone who topped me a couple of years ago, but it was just for play. There were no feelings involved. I think I underestimated the emotional aspect of tonight."

"Okay, Pixie. That asshole is not invited here tonight. It's just you and me here, or we need to end this now. Do you understand?" He waited for her answer. If she wanted it over, he would take her to one of the chairs by the pool and cuddle for the rest of the night. What he wouldn't do unless she demanded it was let her go before the night was over.

"I understand, Sir. He is gone, they both are. The memory took me by surprise, that's all." It seemed she was as invested in this evening as he was. He was determined to replace those memories with something so wonderful that she would never think of the asshole again.

"Okay then, lie back." When she did, he decided to change his plans. He picked up her discarded hospital gown and folded it in on itself. When he was finished, he had created a makeshift blindfold. He went to the head of the table and laid it over her eyes. "Do not lift your head from the table. If you raise your head, and the blindfold I made for you falls off, then I will assume you want to end the scene." He knew she would find this a difficult order to follow, but it was the best way he could think of in the moment to get her out of her own head.

"Yes, Sir," she whispered, her voice strained. Her head moved slightly, and he wondered if she was rolling her eyes under the gown, but he wouldn't call her on it. Now was not the time. It was time to pull out his toys and have a little fun.

He unzipped his bag, and when he looked back at his Pixie, he could have sworn he saw her shiver at the sound. Jazz really was a perfect fit for him. He was beginning to think one night would never satisfy the need he was developing for her. Digging through his bag, he was looking for one of his favorite toys and it only took him a second to find it. He loved the weight of the five-wheeled Wartenberg wheel in his hand. He started by rolling it across the arch of her left foot with the slightest touch and she jerked back. *Oh, my Pixie is ticklish. I'll keep that in mind.* He was glad her eyes were covered, so she couldn't see his amusement. He moved to her other foot, this time adding pressure, and she moaned.

His eyes sought her pussy to find it weeping, the spicy scent of her arousal rising to his nose. She may have been nervous about this kind of play, but her body obviously liked it. If his dick could have gotten any harder, it would have. By the time he pulled it out, he was sure his zipper would leave an indent.

He ran the wheel up the inside of her right leg with the slowest pace he could manage. She squirmed under his touch but managed to stay quiet the entire time. After making it past her knee, he ran the wheel back down, this time on the outside of her leg. Moving to her left leg, he added slightly more pressure.

"Oh please," she whispered, so softly he wasn't exactly sure what she said.

"Hmm, little Pixie. I know I told you that you aren't allowed to speak. What should I do?" This time, she didn't respond with the exception of biting her lower lip. He continued rolling toward her mound, and when he reached the apex of her legs, he leaned forward and took a deep breath, savoring her scent. Her clit was peeking out from between her labia, screaming at him to dive in.

Who was he to deny what his pretty little pussy wanted?

He ran his tongue from right above her anus until he reached her clit where he flicked up and down. He lifted his head and she attempted to follow as her hips lifted from the table. "Naughty girl. You'll take what I give you. No chasing orgasms."

She groaned her response, her skin flushed with a slight sheen of sweat. She was right where he wanted her.

"However, I am feeling magnanimous today. If I push you over, you may come at will. I'll even let you make noise. Just remember, no talking." He didn't have the patience to wait to see her in the throes of passion. Walking over to the sink, he placed his wheel next to it to be cleaned. Then he pulled out his TENS unit from his play bag. *Yes, this will do nicely.*

He returned to where she was lying, ready to see her come apart in his arms. Leaning in, he took her mouth like a man starved. This was no gentle get-to-know-you kiss. This was the kiss of a man who knew what he wanted and was going to take it no matter the cost. When he became dizzy from the lack of oxygen, he raised his head. Her mouth was heaven and he couldn't wait to feel it wrapped around his dick... but this was about her.

LYING THERE ON THE EXAM TABLE, HER PAST WAS THE LAST THING ON HER mind. Actually, the only thing on her mind at the moment was the orgasm she had yet to have. This man had absolute control of her body and mind, and she couldn't have enjoyed it more. After that mind-blowing kiss, her thoughts were a jumbled mess. First, he took away her ability to see, then instructed her not to talk — now he made it impossible to think straight.

He didn't speak as he kissed his way down her body, and it required every ounce of willpower she had not to writhe under his touch. When he reached her breast, he spent time licking and caressing it before continuing down her body. Every nerve cell was alive and firing. Pretty soon she would explode, and it would be everything.

Once he reached her pussy, she prayed to every deity she could think of that he would give her what she needed to push her over the edge. One touch in the right place would be all it would take, just one. But he was in no rush to give her what she craved so desperately. In fact, he bypassed her pussy completely and continued to kiss down her leg until he reached her foot, not stopping until he kissed the tip of her big toe.

Cold air hit her body when he stepped away, and she nearly cried. How could he even consider leaving her this way? Though she tried to conceal her disappointment, the whimper that escaped her lips gave her away. She could have sworn she heard him laugh. *Asshole.* His lab coat brushed her bare hip as he passed, making her want nothing more than to rip the gown from her eyes. She needed to see what he was doing. Maybe not needed, but she sure as hell wanted to.

"I can see the tension radiating off of you. Does my little Pixie need something from me? Sure seems like it," he mumbled to himself as he worked on something she couldn't see.

"Let's see how you like what I have planned next." He started placing what she thought might be stickers in a place where no sticker should go, first on one side of her labia, then on the other. She was closer to using her safe word than she'd ever been, so she took a deep breath to center herself. She had to consider whether she trusted him. Though she had only just met him, for some reason she did, so she waited to see what he had planned, suspecting it would be epic.

"I know you must be dying to know what I'm doing. You will

figure it out in a minute, I'm sure."

She heard him doing something beside her and waited, though waiting was the last thing she wanted to be doing.

"You have been so good my little Pixie, that I plan to reward you richly. Thank you for your trust." Before she could contemplate his words, she heard something she couldn't place before feeling a slight prickling feeling which turned into a deeper buzzing in her core. *What in the hell?*

"What is that?" she asked before she could stop herself. *Damn I'm in trouble.*

"Hmm, I thought I was clear on the expectations, yet you broke the rules. I guess that means you don't get the privilege of coming when you want to. Now, you have to wait for my instruction before you do. If you come without permission, I promise you will not like what happens." His finger ran up the inside of her thigh.

Damn and double damn. This is hell.

"No worries little Pixie. I won't make you suffer too long."

She could hear the laughter in his voice, and the next thing she knew, the buzzing turned into a constant throb. She needed to come more than she needed her next breath.

"Pixie, your little clit is so engorged. It's begging to come. Should I let you? Have you earned it?" The buzzing intensified, vibrating throughout her entire body.

This was both heaven and hell at the same time.

"Come now," he ordered while smacking her pussy, and the impact sent her over the edge. She screamed until her voice cracked, forcing her to breathe. Michael removed the cover from her eyes, and tears streamed down her face, while her eyes remained closed. "I'm going to remove the pads. I know you feel sensitive, but it's safer to remove them now than to wait."

She felt tugging as he removed the stickers from her labia, and if she'd not just come harder than she had in her life, she might have been upset that he had placed them in the first place. *Damn that hurts.*

After he was finished, he wiped her clean with a wet cloth, but she couldn't bring herself to open her eyes, because if she did, would the spell be broken?

He lifted her and carried her to the other side of the room where he sat in a large chair before wrapping her in a large blanket. "Here sweetheart, drink this."

She opened her eyes to find him holding a bottle to her mouth, and the water was so refreshing she had to force herself not to gulp the cold liquid. He took the bottle away.

"Open up." He tapped her bottom lip, and, when she opened her mouth, he placed a piece of chocolate on her tongue. She held it there, allowing it to melt, and the bittersweet taste brought her joy. She snuggled in, feeling floaty and safe in his arms. He continued alternating water and chocolate while she cuddled closer, wishing she never had to move from this spot. She'd thought she needed a Dom, but maybe she just needed *this* Dom.

She didn't know how much time had passed before she became more alert to the room around her. Opening her eyes, she was grateful she hadn't let her past get in the way because she would have missed out on a wonderful experience.

"Pixie, we need to get moving. How are you?" His voice was gentle, kind, as he stroked her face with his finger as if she were a precious gift.

"I'm good, though I feel badly for you, Sir," she replied. His shaft under her ass was hard as steel.

"No need for that. I'm exactly where I want to be."

She wanted to see what he was packing because she was sure it had to be something to behold. But she realized in that moment her bladder was full and wiggled in his lap.

"I am going to clean up our mess. Go get dressed, then meet me back here, and we will head out for our final spin." He kissed her on the cheek before standing and placing her on her feet.

Her emotions were all over the place, and she was grateful he was giving her a moment to herself. Jazz went to the restroom, dressing inside before returning to see Michael throwing away some cleaning wipes and zipping up his toy bag. She stood in the doorway, watching him move around the room. He was so handsome she wanted to jump his bones, which was a new feeling for her, and she wished it was possible to have more nights like this.

"So, were you going to just stand there and stare?"

"Maybe a little." She was glad the feeling was light. The beginning of the scene had been so heavy with her emotional baggage, but she was happy they had both been able to let it go.

"We have time for one more spin. What do you say we go out there and make that roulette wheel our bitch?"

CHAPTER 6

*A*s he led her toward the theater, Jazz saw a scene playing out on the stage in the main room. The Dom was looping his sub with long ropes and tying intricate knots in a beautiful pattern. She stopped, entranced. "What is that?"

"Ahh, that is called shibari." He pulled her into his side and kissed the top of her head. The Dom wrapped the rope under the sub's breasts causing them to lift higher as if they were seeking his touch. Then the sub was turned as her Dom continued to work, and Jazz noticed something silver coming up from her ass and ending at the small of her back. She leaned in to try and investigate.

"What on earth?" She knew better than to judge another's kink, and she never did, she just wanted to understand what she was seeing.

"Ahh, you saw the anal hook. It's a specialty of his."

"I'm sorry, did you say anal hook? I've never even heard of that before." She couldn't decide if she was interested in learning more — or running as far and fast as she could. She was leaning toward the running, but then she turned to see that Michael was very curious about what was happening on the stage.

"Yes, it's an anal hook, and I have always been interested in using one in play."

"I didn't realize you liked anal play. Though I'm not a Dom, I would be happy to shove one up your ass if that is what you want." She knew she was deliberately being disrespectful, but the thought of him wanting to do that to her was not something she could handle at the moment.

"You already know that's not what I meant. I have been learning shibari, and you would look beautiful in ropes with a hook in your ass." He crossed his arms and waited, daring her to continue to sass him, but she was smarter than that. "You're lucky we have a limited amount of time tonight. I don't like harsh punishments, but I will always punish for disrespect. This is your one and only warning."

"You aren't serious that you want to do that to me tonight? What if we roll anal play?" Would he push her to the point where she used her safe word? She wasn't opposed to anal sex, but that looked like anal on steroids.

"I guess we shall see what the roulette wheel has for us." He winked at her. *Cocky bastard.* He placed his hand on the small of her back to lead her to the theater for the final spin of the night. It was beginning to feel like his hand belonged there, and she loved it.

"I'll just pray we don't spin anal or bondage, I guess then." She hadn't meant to say that out loud, and she wasn't sure she actually had until she heard him chuckle beside her.

"I can't say I agree with you, but I'm ready to see what comes next." They returned to the wheel where this time they rolled *vaginal intercourse.*

This actually scared her more than anything else they could have spun. She had been feeling more and more connected to Michael as the scenes went on, but when the night was over, she would have to leave. If she became any more attached, she would have a hard time walking away. She needed to remain detached.

Easier said than done.

"Looks like your prayer was answered, little Pixie. But then again, so was mine." He leaned in and took her mouth in a quick, passionate kiss. When she managed to get her brain back online, she considered his comment. Hell, she'd been given the two best orgasms she had ever experienced, and he had yet to receive any relief. No wonder this was what he wanted.

"I cannot wait to feel your silky heat wrapped around my cock." He grabbed her hand and pulled her through the main bar area, through the velvet curtain, and past the pool at a quick rate. She barely registered the fact that the sub she had been watching earlier was still bound in ropes and sucking her Dom's dick. That was the last thing she saw as they left the area and headed down the back hall.

She wondered where they were headed when they reached the end of the hall right outside of the dungeon. Jazz had to admit to herself that she was slightly nervous. Why would they need to go to the dungeon?

"Stay with me, Pixie." He pulled on her chin until she was met his gaze. "This is you and me. Remember, nobody else is allowed here with us." His tone left no room for arguing as he nodded toward the couch that sat across the hall from the dungeon. She was surprised to see the couch empty and looked around to see where everyone was. This part of the club seemed to be where all the voyeurs collected to watch the happenings going on in this area of the club.

"Yes, Sir," she whispered. Something about him made her want to submit to him in every way.

"I love the sound of that, little Pixie." He leaned over and brushed his lips across hers before leaning back to look at her beautiful face.

"Sir, can I please do something for you?" She continued looking up into his handsome face, because she wanted to taste him. She had never really liked giving blow jobs. In fact, she considered herself pretty bad at it. But, with this man, she wanted to try. She wanted to make it amazing for him. After catching a quick glimpse of the restrained sub on the stage, she wanted to give him that.

"What would you like to do for me, little one?" When others had referred to her as little, it always seemed like an insult, but with him, it made her feel soft and sweet.

"I want to taste you, Sir. Please let me make you feel as good as you have made me feel…" *She shouldn't be this emotional.*

"I would love that, my Pixie. However, when I come, I want to be

586

in your sweet pussy. You will stop when I tell you, is that clear?"
Damn his voice was pure sex. She had climaxed twice already this
evening, and his dominant words had her dripping wet again.

"I understand, Sir." She would take what she could get.

"Take me then." He stood like a statue, daring her, and she would
live up to it.

She nodded and gracefully lowered herself to her knees in front of
him. When she reached up, taking his leather belt in her hands and
easing it open, calm washed over her. She unbuttoned his dress pants
and gently pulled them down, careful not to catch his erection. He
was huge and hard behind his boxer briefs, just begging to be
released. Though she had never been the girl who loved to give head,
she wanted nothing more in that moment than to bring him pleasure.
She looked up at him, wanting to make sure he was still pleased
with her.

He stroked the top of her head, conveying without words his
desire for her to continue.

She grasped the band of his boxers and pulled them down over his
erection. The sight of his cock took her breath away. It was a thing of
beauty, long and thick with veins running down the sides, and she
couldn't wait to have him inside her. But first, she leaned forward and
licked a drop of precum from the tip, then licked down the shaft until
she reached his balls. The taste was salty, but she liked it, wanting
more. She took one of his balls in her mouth and sucked with a little
force making him moan in response. The sound pleased her, making
her want to do more. She enjoyed knowing he liked what she was
doing—kneeling before this man bringing him pleasure. Licking her
way back up his cock, she reached the tip that continued to leak and
flicked her tongue over it, feeling powerful. Why had she never
enjoyed this before?

Maybe it needed to be him.

"Enough. Take me in your mouth," he growled, his control slipping
slightly.

She placed her mouth around the head, no small feat considering
how thick he was, then inched forward until he reached the back of

her throat and she started to gag. Pulling back all the way to the head, she caught her breath before descending again.

She held no misconceptions about what was really going on. He was in charge, though he gave her the illusion that she was controlling what was happening. What made her feel powerful was watching him give himself over to what she was doing and seeing how much it affected him.

~

Her mouth was pleasure beyond anything he had ever experienced. He could stay there all night, and never want to leave. She was hesitant, at first, but when she got her rhythm he felt as if he might lose himself in her. He placed his hands on either side of her head, holding her still, and started to rock. Within a minute, he was fucking her face and made no apologies for it.

When she swallowed around his head, it required every bit of self-control he had not to explode down her throat. He stepped back pulling out of her sweet mouth with a *pop*. She followed, and it seemed she didn't want to stop either. "I told you I want to be in your pussy when I come, and that's what I meant."

Reaching down, he removed his pants and underwear before going over to the small table beside the couch where he grabbed a condom from the drawer. He knew the rules. Though everyone was required to provide proof that they were clean, all men in the club had to wear a condom. For the first time since losing his virginity at the age of sixteen, he thought of what it might be like to take a woman without one. He had a feeling if he ever did, he would never want to be with her wearing one again.

He sat down and beckoned her forward. Jazz shuffled closer, looking at her hands, picking at her thumbnail, until she stood between his knees. *Was she nervous after all they had shared?* He couldn't let that happen, so he knew he needed to get her out of her own head again. Michael brought his hands up her legs, starting at the back of her knees and trailing up to the globes of her perfect ass. Reaching

588

under her hot leather mini skirt, he grabbed her cheeks and squeezed, happy she had obeyed him and didn't have anything in the way of what he wanted. He trailed his way down the crease until he reached her tight hole. Ever since he saw her reaction to the scene on the stage, all he could think about was taking her ass. That wasn't going to happen tonight, but there would come a time he would get her ready and make her want it.

As the thought settled in his mind, he froze, shocked. Nothing after tonight was promised. Hadn't she been clear about her busy life? For all he knew she lived across the country. He had to get control of his thoughts and stay in the moment like he forced her to do, and not waste the time he had with her.

He pushed his finger slightly into her, and she moaned her pleasure. He didn't go past the first knuckle because if he did, this would go a completely different direction than what they were given by the spin of the wheel.

He brought his hands around and unbuttoned her skirt. As he lowered her zipper, he let the skirt drop to the floor so her arousal could not be hidden. Her juices glistened on her upper thighs and when the smell of her arousal reached him, he could almost taste it on his tongue. She was as hot about what was happening as he was. "Pixie, you smell so good." He ran his left hand through her slit and brought it to his nose before taking a deep inhale. When he placed his finger to her lips, she opened her mouth and sucked in his finger with the same enthusiasm as she had his cock. He felt his balls tighten up with the visual it presented.

Pulling his finger from her mouth, he tore open the condom. Rolling it on his cock was almost painful. If he didn't release in her hot little body soon, he would surely die.

"Come here, Pixie," he beckoned. She had remained so quiet, he needed to make sure she was okay with what was happening. He was the Dom, so that meant her wellbeing was more important than anything, including his dick. "You're quiet. Tell me where you are."

"I'm green, Sir," was her only response.

"Not good enough, Pixie. Before we go any further, you need to tell me what is going on in that beautiful head of yours." He would walk away before he would take her without knowing where her mind was.

"Can't we just have sex without you psychoanalyzing me, Doc?" she snarked. He couldn't believe how quickly her attitude had changed.

He put his hands on either side of her waist and placed her on his lap with a knee on either side of his hips. They sat there, face to face, with his cock nestled between her labia as he grabbed the hair at the base of her neck forcing her to meet his gaze.

She wouldn't be able to hide this way.

"I am going to ignore the attitude for a moment. You will tell me what's going on, and you'll tell me now. If you choose not to, then understand there will be consequences, after which you will end up telling me anyway. So, save yourself and start talking." This wasn't supposed to be that kind of scene, but this felt like more than a scene. His Dom senses screamed at him to get this right.

When she tried to keep her gaze from his eyes, he tightened his grip on her hair. "Please, little one. Tell me what's going on, so I can fix it."

When she finally met his gaze, she sighed. "I don't know if I can do this," she said without continuing.

"What can't you do, sweetheart?" He stroked her face. Her beautiful eyes were sad. He was missing an important piece of the puzzle.

"I came into tonight looking for a bit of fun before I leave on tour. Somehow, at least for me, it seems to be turning into something more..."

"Oh, little Pixie. I knew the moment I laid eyes on you that this would be something more, though I couldn't have imagined just how much." He leaned in and placed a soft kiss on her mouth, which she deepened the moment his lips touched hers. Without thought, he regained control of the kiss, holding her in place. She returned his passion easily, giving herself to him as he closed his fist in her hair, and her body finally relaxed. Though she seemed confused about her

590

emotions, her body wanted this. When he pulled her head back, her breaths were shallow and rapid.

"I want to submit to you in a way I can barely understand. It scares me, but that… that is the truth, Sir." That was all he needed to hear. He was going to give them both what they needed in the moment, and they would figure out the rest later. He lifted her and brought her down on his dick. She was so tight he needed to lower her at an achingly slow pace, so he didn't hurt her. When he was finally fully sheathed, he stopped. He needed a moment to gather himself, because once he started, he wouldn't stop again until neither of them knew their own names.

"Oh, please, Sir. I need you to move or I might die." She panted as she attempted to move to give herself what she wanted, but he was having none of that.

He tightened his hands on her hips and held her in place. "Naughty girl. You are not in charge of what's happening here, and if you try that again, I'll take you to the edge over and over again and never let you fall over. Is that clear?" He gritted his teeth, using all his willpower to remain still.

"You must have fucking nerves of steel, Sir."

He needed to move more than he needed his next breath. "Not at all, little Pixie. I just need to make sure you are stretched enough that I don't hurt you. I want you to put your hands behind my neck and lock your fingers together. Do not let go, and do not come until I tell you to. Am I clear?"

She locked her fingers behind his neck and answered, "Yes, Sir."

That was all it took for him to let go. He pounded into her pussy with enough force to lift her from his lap before slamming her back down again. He did it over and over, and the more he gave her, the more vocal she became. "Please, Sir! Please let me come!"

"Almost, my sweet. Hold on for me. You can do it." He pounded her, because he thought his dick might explode at any moment, and he would welcome it. When he could take no more, he yelled out, "Come, my Pixie, now!" He let go, coming with a force that took his breath away.

Within a moment, she screamed, and her pussy started to squeeze his dick which made his orgasm amplify in intensity. In all of his years, he had never orgasmed like this and wished he could find a way to prolong it. Her pussy contracted in waves as her orgasm went on.

When they finally came down, she fell into his chest with her head on his shoulder. He opened his eyes to see that several people had stopped to watch them, not that he cared.

He didn't know how long they sat like that with his softening cock still inside her before she lifted her head from his shoulder. When he saw her smile, he leaned in and licked the seam of her mouth, and she opened to him without resisting.

CHAPTER 7

*A*fter several minutes, he pulled back. "Pixie, we need to clean up."

Moving was the last thing on earth she wanted to do. Michael leaned away from her to pick up something from the table by the end of the couch. He opened the water bottle and took a large drink before handing it to her.

"You need to drink. I don't want you to get dehydrated."

She grabbed the bottle in both hands and drank it until it was gone, while Michael stood and discarded the condom. After cleaning himself up and dressing, he knelt in front of her and cleaned her up. She didn't know where he got the cloth, and she couldn't bring herself to care. She remained quiet while he finished and helped her put her skirt back on after pulling her to a standing position.

She'd known the end of the night would come, but damn it had happened too fast. Everything she thought she knew about herself was in question tonight. She turned toward Michael and had a hard time thinking about walking away, but that was exactly what she had to do. She was leaving in a couple of days and would be gone for six months. This was simply not the right time to consider starting something, and she wasn't sure he would want that anyway. Hell, this had to be the emotional shit that came from submitting after so long, at least that was what she tried to convince herself of while he cared for her. She would find a way not to cry.

Shit, she needed to get ahold of herself and fast. When he finished cleaning up, Michael grabbed her hand and led her back toward the main area of the club. This was the first time he took her hand, and she wasn't sure how she felt about that.

He didn't speak until they got to the bar area where he led her to a table and helped her with her chair before asking, "What would you like to drink, little one?"

"Water," Jazz answered, wanting to keep her head clear until she could find Jamie and get out of there. Then she would go home and get shitfaced. That sounded like a plan.

When Michael returned to the table, he opened the bottle of water and set it down in front of her, while he had what she thought might be a double scotch. He placed his hand on hers and stroked her knuckle with his thumb. It was an oddly comforting gesture, considering the fact that there was not an inch of her that he hadn't touched.

"Pixie," he started, before taking a deep breath. "I don't even know your real name, but tonight was amazing, and I'm not prepared to let you leave without knowing what you want to happen. I want more. I don't know what that looks like, but I do not want tonight to end. But I'll warn you, I am not easy. There will be no secrets between us. I will want you to belong to me. I will want to take care of you, even though I'm aware you can do it for yourself." He held her gaze. His hazel eyes had grown darker as the night had gone on.

As much as she wanted to jump in his lap and accept what he was offering, that wouldn't be fair to either of them. She was leaving and would spend the next six months traveling the globe. These tours always exhausted her to the point where she had nothing left to give. She had been considering taking some time off afterward.

Maybe they could meet up after she got back?

"Michael." It felt right to call him by his name for this conversation. "I'm not gonna lie. This night has been eye opening for me, but it wouldn't be right for me to promise you something I can't deliver. I'm leaving in a few days to go on tour, and I'll be gone for close to six months. We can't start a relationship that way. There is no way it could work."

How could she feel so sad over someone she just met? This whole thing was crazy.

"Let me clarify what you're saying so there is no misunderstanding. Are you saying you would consider what I am offering, but you won't because of the fact that you're going to be gone for several months?" He kept his tone even so she couldn't really tell what he was thinking.

Jazz decided to go ahead and be honest. "I guess what I'm saying is that if I wasn't leaving, I would absolutely want to see where this would go. I feel connected to you in a way I haven't experienced before. But, none of that changes the fact that I am leaving."

"I don't see it as the stumbling block you do, Little Pixie. I understand long distance relationships can be difficult."

"Wait." Before he continued, she needed to get her point across. "I cannot do a long-distance relationship with the life I live. It's not difficult, it is impossible."

"I understand. How about I give you my contact information? We can be friends, keep things light. You will come home, and when you do, if you aren't in another relationship, then you have to give me a chance. How does that sound? I refuse to let you go tonight without you at least knowing how to get in touch with me." His voice trembled.

MICHAEL WAITED TO SEE HOW SHE WOULD RESPOND. THIS WAS ONLY supposed to be for one night, but he was finding it difficult to even think about letting her go.

"We can email. It would be a good way to get to know each other with less pressure." She seemed hopeful as she said the words. He released the breath he didn't know he had been holding.

"And there is always the phone. I'm up early, so, depending on where you are in the world, we can talk before you go to bed. I would rather tie you to my bed, but this will do until you get back, Jazz." Damn it felt weird calling her Jazz. No matter what happened, she would always be his green-eyed pixie.

She stood and went to the bar, leaving him wondering what she was doing. If she was his, she would need to learn to communicate a little better, but he would never want her to lose her spark. She returned with a white paper bar napkin and handed it to him. When he glanced down at it, he noticed she had written a phone number and email address on it. "That is my cell and my email."

"Hey, sweets, you ready to get out of here?" The man he had seen her arrive with was standing behind her — *damn him.*

"Michael, this is Jamie. He is my bestie and keeps my life on track. He also has terrible timing." She didn't seem any happier to see her friend than he was.

"You are one hot piece of man meat," he said and stuck his hand out to shake. He carried a bag in the other one. Michael stood and took his hand, maybe squeezing slightly harder than necessary.

"Thank you." At least he was gay, so Michael wouldn't have to kick his ass for having the nerve to be close to his Pixie. "It's nice to meet you."

"Doms are always so straight-laced, aren't they?" He laughed in Jazz's direction. "Oh, girl, you should see all of the goodies I won at the auction. Looks like you weren't the only winner tonight." He shook the bag he held.

" Jamie, can you give me a minute? I'll meet you by the lockers." She leaned up and kissed his cheek, making Michael crazy. It didn't matter if he was gay or not.

Jamie winked at him before walking away. *Asshole.*

Jazz came around the table and hugged him. She wasn't the kind of sub that waited to see what he was going to do. She embraced him tightly and laid her head against his shoulder.

As he held her close, knowing their time was up, he leaned in and kissed her cheek. As he started to let her go, she hugged him even tighter.

"Jessica," she whispered. He pulled his head back so he could look her in the eyes. "You wanted to know my given name. It's Jessica, though nobody has called me that in years. I couldn't leave without you knowing the real me." The single tear that fell down her cheek nearly did him in.

"You'll come back. We will have our chance to see what we can be." Maybe if he used his Dom voice, it would be true.

"You make me want to believe."

He leaned in and kissed her mouth, knowing he would not be able to again for far too long. When he pulled back, he took a step away because if he didn't, he wouldn't be able to let her go.

She turned away before he could say anything else, and he sat back in his chair before he chased her out of the club. *Damn.* He was the Dom, and he wasn't the type to get all emotional and shit, but here he was. Troy would have a field day if he knew what Michael was thinking.

Once she was gone, he looked around. Alone again.

He needed to get the hell out of here. Would it be totally inappropriate to text her? *Who the hell cares?*

Michael hurried to the locker room to get his things and headed out to the parking lot. Once he reached his car, he slid into the driver's seat and brought up his cell phone. He entered the number she had given him and texted what was on his mind. *J, you are mine. It is only a matter of time, which will make your submission all the sweeter. See you in six months.* He started his car and before he put it in drive, his phone alerted him that he received a text.

It simply said *Yes, Sir.*

The End

ABOUT THE AUTHOR

Lesley Clark is first and foremost a wife and mother. She has been married for 26 years to a wonderful guy. She has 2 beautiful daughters who have both kept her on her toes since entering this world. Lesley has been a RN for the last 14 years and truly enjoys taking care of her patients.

Lesley writes stories with hot alpha men and sexy sassy ladies that will keep you on the edge of your seat from start to finish.

Connect with Lesley:

Website: www.thelesleyclark.com

Facebook: https://www.facebook.com/thelesleyclark

Author FB Page https://www.facebook.com/lesleyclarkauthor

Twitter: https://twitter.com/thelesleyclark

Instagram: https://www.instagram.com/thelesleyclark/

Bookbub: https://www.bookbub.com/profile/lesley-clark

Goodreads: https://www.goodreads.com/author/show/17954607.Lesley_Clark

CONTROL

A Black Light: Celebrity Roulette Novella

By

Dani René

CHAPTER 1

aelin

ONE WEEK BEFORE CELEBRITY ROULETTE

MY PHONE VIBRATES ON THE TABLE BESIDE ME, BUT I IGNORE IT. MY friends would be sending me messages about the latest parties in the city since Valentine's Day is coming up. Perhaps I should go, find some hot guy to fuck, but that's not what I need.

Flipping through the pages of the glossy magazine, I get to the article I wanted to read. Even though I know what it's going to say, I still allow myself to wallow in the jealousy that burns me each time I see him in the tabloids. There's nothing of interest in the songs he played in the latest show, or which city, country, or town he's visiting next. I know all this already.

The man in the interview has haunted my most illicit thoughts for long enough. I've known him for years and to this moment from the first time I saw him, he's hated me for reasons unknown to me. As much as I taunt him, he's never once confessed why.

When I glance at the half page spread, it sends me spiraling into the cloud of jealousy that always follows when I see him with other women. But, there's nothing I can do because I have no claim on him. The images I can't tear my gaze from are large, filling up most of the page. It's not that I don't like seeing *him* on the pages of my latest tabloid, it's the fact that in every one of these color or black and white shots, he's not alone.

I look at each image in detail, taking in his clothes, how he's smiling, and in some I notice he's not. His eyes shimmer even on the pages and I can't stop myself from grinning like a damn fool. I'm no fangirl, but there's always been something about Jed and his command of a crowd that's caught my attention.

I've been to a few of his concerts and watching him up on stage is an experience like no other. His hazel eyes are accentuated by the dark shirt in one of the photos, piercing me through the camera lens. The color only magnifies those thick lashes that seem far too long for a man.

His golden hair shines in the low lights of the nightclub he's vacating with a woman on each arm. They're both staring at him like he's a god, and I can't deny it—he's chiseled and sculpted from porcelain, making him look like the Greek god, Zeus, well-known for his thunder strike and his erotic escapades.

Flipping the page, I notice one of the women caught on camera exiting his hotel only hours after the previous shots were taken. My heart thuds painfully as I wonder just what he did with her. Shaking my head, I sigh, shutting the magazine and throwing it on the lounger beside me. He's always fucked with my head, but with each passing month, and every time I see him, it only gets worse. The more time I spend around him, I only want him more. And when he's not here, I miss him. It may sound stupid to miss someone like him, but I do. And I think he wants me. When he met with Dad a month ago, before his tour, I was almost certain he wanted me.

I caught him staring at me as I walked by the office window, but as soon as he had finished and stopped outside to take a call, he offered me one of his scowls, and I realized it was purely my mind playing tricks on me.

Picking up my phone, I scroll through the messages, ignoring all the party invites to find a message from Laurence, one of the men I'd been seeing for the past few years. Even though I want Jed, he's never made a move, or given me a clear indication that he didn't actually hate me. His gazes burn through me, and the permanent scowl on his face is the only evidence that he even acknowledges that I exist.

After each time he's been here, with his anger always directed at me, I decided it was time I grew up and attempted to move on from my silly *crush*. In my struggle to find someone who likes me for me, I've found myself with Laurence who's offered me clarity on what it is I truly need to find satisfaction.

Sadly, I'm still utterly enamored with the asshole who thinks I'm a stupid little girl. I open the message to read it, sitting up as I re-read the words on screen.

Black Light is having a Roulette event. Would love to play if you're up for it?

Tapping out a *maybe* and hitting send, I lie back and close my eyes. The sunglasses shading my eyes do nothing to stop the harsh glare of orange hitting my lids, and I know its time for me to head inside and get ready to meet Darcy and Melissa at the café for a late lunch.

My eyes flutter when the golden glow disappears from my skin, and I open them to find my father looming over me like he always does when he's angry at me for some reason or another. Generally, it's because I've fucked up, other times, it's because he's stressed at work about not landing a new client, which comes with the territory of being one of L.A.'s best celebrity agents.

"Kaelin," my father's grumble steals me from the thought. "James is out picking up a new client that I have a late meeting with today. He won't be back for another couple of hours and I need you to do something for me." I watch as my father drops the keys to his Bentley on the table beside me. "Would you collect Jed from the airport? I've sent him a message to inform him you'll be picking him up."

"Why can't one of the other—"

"For God's sake, Kaelin," Daddy grunts. "Can you for once do as you're told?" His green gaze burns through me, causing my defenses to rear back, ready to retort, but I know I need to pick my battles with my father. It's been years of our back and forth and his frustration isn't new to me. But it's the job he's sending me on.

His reddening face is evidence that I'm annoying him. As usual. Since my mother walked out with Daddy's last client not long after I turned twenty, I've been on the receiving end of my father's mood swings and it's not eased up. It's been three years since that day, yet he doesn't want to move on. Sometimes I wonder if he's holding out hope that she's coming back. I know she won't.

Even after being married to him for so long, and Daddy Dearest giving her all he could, the moment a young rock star flirted with her, she ran off with him. Perhaps she was going through the female version of a mid-life crisis. Daddy bought a Maserati, and mom decided younger men were better than a family.

"What time is he arriving, Dad?" I question coolly.

He sighs. "Look, I'm stressed, I didn't mean to get angry." His wrinkles deepen when he scrunches his face. "Jed's flight lands at five," he tells me. That's two hours from now, which means I have time to shower and get ready.

I wanted to move out the moment I could, but deep down, I knew I'd miss being in the home I grew up in. Also, with me helping my dad every now and then, it's easier to be here. Once my mother left, the house was big enough that I didn't see him as often as I thought I would and at times it feels as if I'm living here alone.

"Fine, I'll be there to pick up your precious rock star." I sigh. Picking up Jed is not something I'd like to do, not because I don't want to see the man I'm practically in love with, but because each time Jed and I are in the same room it feels as if I can't breathe.

"You're not wearing that to go to the airport," Daddy waves his finger at my bikini and I can't help but roll my eyes at his retort.

"I'll get changed and leave in time to get him." Rising from my seat,

I sidle by him, offering him a small smile that is filled with the confidence he drummed into me from a young age.

I wonder how this new client can be more important than his own daughter. Sadness grips my chest and I swallow back the tears. He hates to see me cry, not like other dads are with their kids, where tears make them want to protect their children. No, Roger Le Blanc, the infamous agent is nothing like that. He just doesn't want to give in to the guilt that weighs so heavily on him. His heartbreak is my problem even though I could never control my mother.

"Thank you, Kaelin," he responds to my back, but I don't look at him. I don't turn to meet his guilt-ridden expression. It's the same every time he loses his shit with me and I'm a grown woman who doesn't need to take shit from him anymore. If he wants me to move out, I'll do it.

Perhaps I'll move to another city, where people aren't as fake as they are in Hollywood. Living in Beverly Hills, I've grown up with nothing but lies of the rich and famous. The women have fake tits and plastic smiles, and my dad decided it would be a good idea to get me used to a lifestyle of decadence. He thinks love is bought with extravagant gifts, expensive meals, and holidays to Europe — but that's not me.

He doesn't know those are the last things I want or need.

No.

What my father doesn't know is I have a secret of my own. One that's going to get me sated when I walk into the one place I can be who I truly am. Once I pick Jed up from the airport, perhaps I'll drop him off at his house and head down to the exquisite club where I've found solace—Black Light— for a scene with a handsome Dominant.

My bedroom is furnished in white and beige—all soft colors along with a pale blue and pink. My king-sized bed is large enough and I'm sure I could fit a football team on it. With a blue and white comforter and scattered cushions in various shades of pink, I love throwing myself on the mattress and closing my eyes.

I would do that, but I have a more pressing matter.

The Black Light Valentine Roulette event.

Settling at my desk, I lift the lid of my laptop and click on the website for the club. If what Laurence said is right, there'll be information about the upcoming event on there. Last year they had an amazing evening in D.C. I told my father I was going on a road trip with the girls, but Laurence took me to the club and even though I only observed, I knew it wasn't enough.

I wanted to participate.

He was the one who taught me. Our agreement was clear, we were not in a relationship, and we could find another person to play with at any time. For me, it was perfect because I was allowed to explore without being tied down, so to speak, to one man.

This time I want to be one of the lucky girls that gets to spend the night with a Dominant and lose myself in submission. I found my solace in kneeling — three years ago when I met Laurence, when I realized what freedom it offered — and never looked back. Laurence isn't my Dom, but he's there at times when I need a scene. Our friendship turned into a mentorship, and he's been training me with all sorts of scenes and toys, and he knows my heart is with one man. Only, I've never mentioned that man's name to anyone.

I'd never found someone I wanted to fully submit to. Even after all these years of learning about the lifestyle, I know there's so many more avenues I haven't even tapped into. Granted, I have my hard limits. I know what they are because some of the things I've tried just don't turn me on in any way. But I have always kept an open mind for softer limits, things I'd be willing to try if the right Dominant wanted to explore them with me.

The event is celebrity-based this year which only makes me giggle. Scrolling through the names and images, I recognize most of the men and women who are up for auction. When they see me, they'll know exactly who I am, as some of them are Daddy's clients. The advantage is they can't tell him I've been there. It's the main reason Black Light is so popular with this crowd, the NDA and anonymity that comes with being a member.

As the page reaches the end, my heart catapults, slamming against my chest. The name glares at me from the screen, stealing my breath and my fingers quiver above the keys of my laptop.

Jed Major.

He's a client of Black Light?

Furrowing my brow, I click on his profile. Staring back at me is the man who's been a star of my fantasies ever since I can remember. He was the only person I ever thought of when I first found pleasure with my fingers between my thighs. His photo with a short biography is set out on the page, along with a word that sends a cool tingle down my spine — Dominant — and a list of five limits that he's not willing to try.

"Fuck," I whisper to myself. Jed is being auctioned to anyone willing to pay a small fortune. I notice all proceeds will be going to a charity, which is perfect. My heart skitters up and into my throat as nerves set in. *Would he even know I'm a submissive?* I allow my gaze to linger on his limits again, some match mine, and I know it's now or never. He's here, within reaching distance for the first time in my life and he won't know until I'm announced as a winner on the night.

Jed will have to play a scene with one lucky bidder and I'm confident it will be me. There's no way I can lose to some other woman, or man. My fingers tremble as they fly over the keys of my laptop to put my bid through.

I need him.

I want him.

Since the moment I laid eyes on him I knew I would never crave another man like I do Jed. But I was always the little girl that wasn't old enough. At sixteen, I crushed hard on the older man, but now, I'm twenty-three and he can't deny me anymore. I've seen the way he looks at me—those deep hazel eyes that shimmer with flecks of gold and a hint of heated desire underneath the anger that, for some reason, he's always tampered down.

He makes me feel as if I'm an annoyance to him, and I've wondered if perhaps he was angry because of something my dad said, or something I said. I thought the moment I turned eighteen, he might see me differently. Perhaps not as a teenager, but as a woman. Once again, I was wrong.

Hitting send on my bid, I smile because I'm looking forward to winning this. I read up on the deadline, and ensure I have a reminder on my phone to check the bids every couple of hours. Even though I know there won't be any other person that can outbid me I'm not taking any chances.

I shut my laptop and head into the attached bathroom to turn on the shower. Once I've stripped, I step under the spray and close my eyes. Since Jed is a client of Black Light, perhaps he's always been scared of taking a chance on me because he's worried I'd be freaked out by it.

Not everyone understands. That's for sure.

But now he'll know he has no reason to push me away. That means he can give me what I need.

The thought of his hands spanking me harshly, causing me to whimper and beg for more is all that fills my mind. I wonder what it would feel like being bound by him, being pleasured and taunted by those fingers that can strum a guitar to perfection.

Would he play me like an instrument?

Would he draw it out like an erotic symphony using my body for his pleasure?

I picture myself kneeling for him as my hand snakes along my curves to my pussy, and I can't help teasing myself at the fantasies of what that man will do to me. I dip two fingers inside my body, taunting my need for release, and as I find pleasure, I cry out Jed's name like I have done so many times before.

Soon, Jed Major, very soon.

CHAPTER 2

 ed

THE WHEELS OF THE PRIVATE JET HIT THE TARMAC AND I SIGH KNOWING I'll soon be home. The tour has taken its toll and I'm prepared to let Le Blanc know I'm done with this shit. Yes, I enjoy the music, performing, but I want a time out. I can finally reap the rewards after five years of working my ass off. It's only February and I'm ready to take the year off. Endless hotels and faces I'll never remember are a blur and I'm ready to put the experience to rest for a while. Women who throw themselves at me are becoming rather monotonous.

If my career ended tomorrow I wouldn't even care, because there's no longer a love for the music from my fans. Most of them are more concerned about the fact that I'm still single. Which is why my band normally finishes off the set with numerous items of underwear in their pockets.

I love women. That's no secret. But there is no longer a challenge.

They throw themselves at me which doesn't hold my interest. Every country I perform in, each city I step foot inside, they're there, clearly offering themselves to me like a buffet dinner. I don't want them. And even though there are times I've let myself indulge, they mean nothing to me.

With every woman I've been inside, there's only one who lingers in my mind every day. The one beauty I've pushed away since the moment I met her. And that's what puts me at ease being back in L.A. Knowing I'll be able to ease the tension with a scene at Black Light calms me.

The other reason I'm eager to step off the plane is the problem—seeing my agent's daughter. The sweet girl who's turned into a sultry, seductive woman overnight is the one person I can't have—Kaelin Le Blanc.

It's time for me to sit down and focus on writing the new album and spending some time at my favorite club—Black Light.

I haven't been there in a long while, and now that I'm back from Europe, I can safely say I need a scene. That's one of the reasons I can never act on my feelings for Kaelin. She's twenty-three now, there's no longer a danger of her being too young for me, but if she knew what I needed sexually, she wouldn't be so quick to offer herself up.

When I got the email from Jaxson and Chase inviting me to be one of the celebrities on the auction block this year, I agreed. Not because I want the recognition, but because it will be great to get back into the scene after spending far too long on the road. And since all the money will be donated to a charity chosen by the owners of Black Light, it's a great cause. Lord knows I don't need it.

Once the door slides open, I'm off the plane in seconds. Security guards, along with my entourage, follow me through the airport and into a secure lounge where I'm able to wait for my ride.

But as soon as I enter the space, I see her.

Long blonde hair hangs in waves down her back. Her short and sensually curvy frame is hugged by a dress so tight it looks painted on. Her ass has the perfect curve of a peach and I can't help groaning at the thought of seeing her porcelain skin stained blood red. I'd love to mark her, to make her scream, whimper, and beg, but she's off limits in more ways than one.

And that's the other reason I've pushed her advances away.

She may not throw herself at me like my fans do, but she does flirt. There have been so many times over the past few years that I wanted to give in but didn't. I've given her the cold shoulder, making her believe I hate her. I have my reasons. She'd run a mile if she knew I was a sadist. A Dominant that would make her cry and scream while I filled her with my cock.

My sexual needs run darker than most, and I'm turned on by things that would have the little princess hiding from me every time I entered her home. I can't help smiling at the thought of chasing her through the house, catching her and pinning her down on that pretty blue and white bed while she squirms beneath me.

It's always taken all my restraint to stay away from Kaelin, and right now, her twenty-three year-old body is more temptation than ever before. She's legal. She's fucking beautiful. And I'm dying to see how she'd look kneeling before me while her wide eyes tear up while I'm forcing my dick down her delicate throat.

"Jed." She smiles when she notices me sauntering up to her.

I don't offer her a friendly greeting because I love seeing her knocked down a peg. Humiliation is one of my kinks, seeing how those shimmering eyes gloss over with tears makes my dick throb. The princess before me is far too spoiled, and sometimes, girls like her enjoy the rough more than the kindness I could offer her.

"Where's my driver?" The deep grunt of my voice is enough to give her gorgeous smile a tilt and her face turns almost sad. I say almost because there's still a fire dancing in her eyes which makes me want to see how much she'll take from me.

My question causes her lips to turn into a sour pout. She waves her hand in the air behind her when she responds. "He's helping my dad with something." Dropping her arm to her side, I watch as her cheeks turn a bright shade of pink.

"Fine, let's go. I'm tired." Sauntering by her, I ignore the soft clicking of her heels behind me. Those shoes would look amazing on my bed while her legs are spread wide as I spank her cunt with my leather belt. *Could she handle the pain?* I'd love to find out. I glance over my shoulder at her before noticing how she's drinking me in with those big green eyes.

Shaking my head from the errant thoughts, I sigh in relief when I notice she's driving her father's Bentley. Her tiny Porsche is bright pink, and I didn't feel like squeezing into those seats today. I pull open the back door when I notice her bodyguard exiting the passenger side. He's one of the men I've seen around the Le Blanc mansion when her father's had parties. He's like a fucking watchdog. Perhaps it's jealousy that courses through me knowing he spends more time around her than I ever can. I've never given into that emotion with Kaelin because she's been off limits all the time I've known her.

I settle in the backseat and watch her from behind. She doesn't meet my gaze, but I know she can feel my glare burning into her. The engine purrs to life and I shut my eyes, wanting to get some rest, but I know I can't do that until I'm in my own home, my own bed.

"So, are you happy to be back?" Her question filters through the space toward me and her sweet voice makes my body shiver with need. I don't respond. With my eyes on hers, I reach for the button of the divider and press it. I recall the *on the go* meeting I had with her father in the back of this car, he told me he needed privacy when clients were with him, so he had it installed. Chuckling softly, I notice her frown on her face as her eyes disappear from view.

I enjoy seeing her overly confident demeanor shift into unsure nervousness when I anger or frustrate her. It's something that I've perfected over the years of knowing sweet little Kaelin. I only do it because I know I'll never see her the way I truly want—lost in passion, in the euphoria of submission. The place I can take her with a mere lashing of my belt, or my flogger, or even my cane. She'd be the most exquisite piece of art, spread for me, begging for more, or less. Anything to have me give her the gift of release after edging her for hours.

But that can't happen.

Never mix business and pleasure.

Her father is one of the top agents in L.A. and losing him would be detrimental to my career. All I need is a scene with a beautiful woman this weekend to unwind and stop my mind running riot for the pretty girl in the driver's seat.

A while later, we're pulling into the driveway of my home. The house that sits on the property overlooks Los Angeles, has five bedrooms, three bathrooms, a cinema, and two studios where I spend most of my time. The Olympic-sized pool is out back with a smaller cottage at the back of the main house where my guests can change.

I push open the door once she's killed the engine. By the time I'm out of the car, the bodyguard that seems to follow her around like a shadow has taken my luggage from the trunk. Her heels click behind me and I realize she's following me up to the entrance. I can't have her in my house because the moment she steps foot inside, I'll want to pin her against the wall.

"Thank you," I tell him, leading him up to the door which I unlock. Once he's placed the suitcases in the foyer, he makes his way back to the car. It's not until he's in the passenger seat do I meet those big green eyes. "Have a good day."

"Why do you have to be such a dick?" Kaelin bites out, shocking me with her little outburst. Normally she's shy and insecure, but seeing her fire only makes me want to bend her over and spank her even more than I did before.

"Your sassy mouth should respect it's elders, *Princess.*" I return her fire with some of my own. Leaning in, I inhale her fragrance. The gentle scent is nothing like I expected, not floral and girly at all, more like a spicy cinnamon which reminds me of those warm pastries I ate in London during the cold winter days.

I've spent time around Kaelin before, but I never allowed myself to really take her in. Mainly because the moment I met her, I was new to the industry, and her father had promised me fame. Call me a cold-hearted bastard, but that meant more to me than getting my dick wet. The other reason was far more responsible of me—I didn't want to go to jail for fucking her at sixteen.

"I'm no princess, *Rockstar.*" She bites out the last word, spat with a vengeance that makes my dick throb in my jeans. "I'm trying to be friendly."

615

"Don't try. I'm not a man you want to be nice to."

She folds her arms across her chest which pushes up those perky tits and I can't help my mind wandering down a dark road. Imagining them all bound in rope while I whip them until she's screaming bloody murder, which makes me almost come in my pants. "Oh? And what are you then? An asshole?" Her words drag me from the dark.

"I should scare you." My warning is clear when my voice lowers. "I'm a man who does extremely bad things to pretty girls. I'll make you cry and when I see your eyes glisten and hear those pouty lips beg me to stop, I'll smile and continue because it will make my cock hard. Innocent girls shouldn't poke dangerous animals."

"Men shouldn't play up their abilities," she bites back with fiery venom.

I close the distance between us, but she quickly moves backward until her body has nowhere else to go. The banter has my body thrumming with need, my palms itch and tingle with the urge to feel her flesh burn with the sting of slaps. Reaching for her, I grip her neck, pressing her against the wall behind the door where her bodyguard can't see me.

Her breathing hitches and her pupils dilate, shocking me still for a moment. She's caught between me and the solid surface and I'm certain she can feel my erection attempting to fight its way out of my jeans.

Is she turned on by this?

"My abilities will leave you a broken fucking mess for weeks. You'll feel me inside you for months and every man that attempts to fuck me from your body will fail miserably." My promise is illicit, but I can't stop myself. My lips feather along her chin, my tongue snaking out to taste her smooth skin. "And every time you touch your pretty little cunt it will be me you want inside you."

This earns me a soft gasp that has me leaning in further toward her. "Jed—"

"Now go home like a good girl," I tell her, leaning into her small frame. My mouth finding the shell of her ear as I whisper my threat,

"Or I'll have to bend you over right here and see how pretty your ass looks when it's welted from my thick leather belt."

Her tiny hands push against my chest, and I step back, allowing her space. "You're insufferable." Her words cause me to chuckle, but what she doesn't know is that I wasn't lying because God help me, I do want to mark her.

I watch her race to the door and out to the waiting car. Once she's in the driver's seat, she glances my way once more before the vehicle is winding down the drive and out the open gates. I stand there for a moment, watching the large metal barriers that keep me inside and leave her out there in the world where I ache to go to her and make her mine.

This is ridiculous.

Running my fingers through my hair, I shut the door and head into my kitchen. I need a beer, and I need to forget all about Kaelin Le Blanc.

CHAPTER 3

 aelin

HE'S AN ASSHOLE.

I knew this. It's certainly no secret that Jed is nothing but a man whore, however, what he doesn't know is I'll be the one he's spanking in a few days. Which reminds me, I need to check on my bid. If someone has outbid me, I need to up my game. I'm not losing my chance at having my one night with him.

Even though he's denied me all these years, I'll make sure I win, and when I step out of the crowd on Valentine's Day, I want to see the shock on his face when he realizes the one woman he's always said no to is the one woman he'll have to have.

His warning is still ringing in my ears, reminding me of why I should walk away, but also confirming how much I want him. Yes, Jed may have spooked me somewhat, but there's something about the way his veiled threat did things to me. My thighs squeezed together, my panties drenched at his promise, because that's what it will be, a promise that he'll have a chance to make good on.

What Jed doesn't realize is I like being spanked, being flogged, and feeling the bite of leather against my skin. He thinks he's scared me off, but he's only made me more curious about all the things he can do to my body.

Once I reach home, I pull into the parking space where Dad loves to keep his Bentley and exit the vehicle. I don't acknowledge the man who follows me around like a fucking shadow as I head into the house. The silence that greets me is deafening as I make my way directly to the kitchen.

Opening the fridge, I grab a bottle of water and make my way upstairs to my bedroom. As soon as my ass hits the chair, and my laptop is open, I click on the website and pull up the bids. A few smaller ones for Jed have appeared, but mine is still the winning bid.

Smiling, I sit back and stare at his photo. His hair is stylishly messed up, his eyes twinkle with mischief and the corner of his mouth is lifted in an all-knowing smirk. The confidence that oozes from that image alone is all you need to know about the rock star himself.

Opening the bottle, I take a long gulp, wishing the liquid would cool me down, but nothing will. My nervousness is at an all-time high. Would he deny the scene? When he sees me step up as the winner, would he refuse to play with me?

THREE DAYS BEFORE CELEBRITY ROULETTE

GRABBING MY MUG OF COFFEE FROM THE COUNTER, I HEAD OUTSIDE with a magazine. The latest entertainment news has Jed on the cover once more. His smiling face looks back at me, and I flip it open to find the article.

As much as I try to focus, I can't. It's been four days since I put my bid in. It's also been four days since Jed landed and I haven't seen him since our little altercation in his house. I wanted to challenge him, to take him up on his offer. But with my bodyguard sitting in the car, I couldn't.

My fingers itch to look at the bids. To check if I won, but I don't. I know they closed the bids today, so we'll know who the winners are soon enough. My stomach is tight with anxiety, curling like a sleep serpent.

My eyes scan the words on the page, reading about the man I want to be with. I try to convince myself I just want one night, but that's a lie. No, I want so much more from Jed.

An alert on my phone has my gaze snapping to it. A new email arrived in my inbox and I quickly open the program on my phone. The subject line has my heart skittering wildly in my chest as I read it. I won. I'll be the woman who Jed has on the night of the Roulette event. In three days' time, I'll walk up to the stage and I'll take one of the most intense gambles of my life.

Shit.

Hurrying inside, I'm shaking as I sit down at my laptop and open it. But it does nothing to calm my erratic heartbeat. Clicking on the email to open it, I scan the letter informing me of how the evening will work. It's only a few hours that the event will run and within that time, I'll be in a scene with the man who offered me an illicit promise only four days ago.

The thought lingers for a long while as I stare at the congratulations from the owners of Black Light. I go through the rules once more, hoping to commit them to memory, but I know nothing will stay in my mind — only the thought of submitting to Jed.

Closing the lid of my computer, I pick up my phone and flop on my bed. Tapping out a message to Laurence, I tell him I'll be at the event, but I've bid on someone for a scene.

He doesn't respond and I wonder if he's jealous. The three years we've been playing together, he's taught me so much, but he never once told me I couldn't be with someone else. I know he fucks other women, he's been in scenes with other submissives as well and I'd never felt an inkling of jealousy, not like I feel when I see Jed pictured in a magazine with some fan that's hanging from his arm.

I'll need to get an outfit. Something sexy, but sophisticated. I want Jed to see me as a woman, not the little girl who's had a crush on him since she can remember. I want him to remember me once the scene is over—that thought makes my heart hurt. I never thought I would love him, or even *could* love him, but I wonder deep down if one night will ever be enough with Jed Major.

Pushing off the bed, I open my walk-in closet and step inside. Clothes from every designer adorn the rails, hanging off plush material hangers to keep the garments safe. Taking note, I flip through them without interest. Nothing catches my eye and nothing fits the idea of what I have running through my mind.

Leaning against the cabinet door, I slide to my ass as I wonder where I'm going to find something that's seductive and sophisticated. I pull a drawer open, grabbing the black lace panties along with an underwire bra that matches. Both are soft and sexy, with just a peek at what's beneath.

The perfect tease.

I plan on breaking all of Jed's control and he's going to have to give in to what I know is between us. I can't wait to see just how the hidden animal he keeps composed around me bares its teeth.

VALENTINE'S NIGHT

TONIGHT IS *THE* NIGHT. THE MOMENT I WALK INTO BLACK LIGHT AND show Jed just who I really am. Only one thing matters, that he sees me as a woman, a submissive, not as the daughter of his agent. I'm no longer off limits, and tonight, control will be in his hands.

As the material slips over my curvy frame, I keep my eyes closed, not wanting to see myself just yet. Jed's face is at the back of my eyelids like always, and I pray to all the gods out there, that he'll look at me tonight and smile.

It's strange, but when you spend most of your time fantasizing about someone, they become this figment of your imagination. They're no longer real, but more like a god themselves. Even though most of the articles I've read about him have confirmed he's one of this generation's 'Rock Gods', I've realized there is so much more to him.

His anger—which is generally directed at me—is nothing more than him holding onto restraint. It's him denying what we both feel. Inhaling a deep breath, I finally open my eyes. Even though my nerves are scattered and electric at the thought of what's about to happen tonight, I can't help smiling. It's a small one, but I notice it on my lips.

I stare at my reflection, at the submissive before me.

I'm a woman who craves the dominance of a man, and I'm no longer scared to ask for it.

Pivoting, I take in my appearance. The full-length mirror offers me a view of what he'll see as soon as his gaze lands on me tonight. The dress I chose is black silk and the cut is figure-hugging. A low neckline offers a tiny glimpse of my cleavage, which with the help of my bra is better than it normally is. My average B-cup breasts aren't big by any means, but the way the dress fits and the lace of the underwire offers support, I look like a grown woman, rather than a nervous young girl.

The back of the dress is the reason I chose this one from the silver rails of options. A string of pearls zig-zags left to right, holding the material together making this mid-thigh silk dress sophisticated, yet sexy. To complete my outfit, I've chosen a pair of four-inch pumps which will put me at chin height to Jed.

My hair is pinned in a messy bun at the back of my head, while the earrings I'm wearing hang in thin diamond strings to my shoulders. Elegant, classy, and sexy.

Even though I've kept my make-up light, my eyes are darkened by the liner, as well as the mascara that offer length to my lashes. My lips are glossed with a shimmering pink and I've lined them with a slightly darker dusky rose to offer a fuller effect.

Smiling to myself, I grab my purse and head out the door to my fate.

CHAPTER 4

 ed

I NOTICE HOW BUSY THE CLUB IS AS SOON AS I STEP INSIDE.

It seems the Roulette event will be a bigger hit this year. I missed the event in D.C. last year and I'm looking forward to seeing who I'm playing with tonight. It feels like coming home the moment I allow my gaze to roam the crowds of people who are all here for the same thing.

To feel normal without judgement.

Settling on a stool at the bar, I order a drink from the barman. My signature whiskey with one block of ice is the only drink I ever have when I'm playing a scene. Even though the limit is two drinks, I would rather keep a clear head if I'm going to be playing with a stranger.

My gaze lands on a pretty woman on the opposite end of the bar and I wonder if she is one of the bidders. Perhaps even one of the winners. Her long blonde hair reminds me of Kaelin, but her face is nothing like the fiery girl who's had my attention since the moment I laid eyes on her. This woman is much older, and her tits are much bigger, probably fake, and that immediately has me turning my attention away from her.

I swallow my drink and head into the theater where we're all being corralled for the main event. As soon as I step into the space, I take in the immaculate room. There are men and women standing around, chatting, holding their drinks as they work the crowd.

I recognize a few of the famous faces as I head toward the area in front of the stage where everyone else has been gathered. Madison, along with the trio who own the club, step on stage to begin the announcements.

Jaxson smiles as he gives the opening welcome speech, and even though I'm used to being up on stage in front of crowds, there's tension in my shoulders at the idea of walking up there. But I know it has more to do with who I'll be spending the evening with.

A moment later Madison, the MC who looks cute in her leather ensemble, starts to explain the event and its rules. I already know them all, I must have read over the email they sent twenty times on the flight home.

I shouldn't be nervous, I'm a Dominant, I can step into a scene with any woman and be at ease, but it's the unknown that turns my stomach. Normally, I choose the submissive, and this time I have no choice. And I know I can't refuse to play, no matter what. As some of the other celebrities get paired off, I scan the room but there are too many women looking my way to guess who may have bid. At least I'll get to burn off some of this energy, even if it's not with someone I'd choose.

"I can't tell you how excited I am to call the amazingly talented rocker Jed Major up to the stage as our next celebrity Dom! You know him as the front man for Original Sinners." Applause rings out with her announcement, and I take a deep breath.

Smiling as I step on stage, I meet Madison's gaze as she smiles up at me. Even though she's in heels, I still tower over her.

"So good to see you here this evening, Jed," she says with a grin, her cheeks pinken with shyness and I'm tempted to see how well she takes to a crop on her pert ass.

"Thank you." I offer a small nod before casting my gaze forward. The crowd has gathered, and I can hear the whispers from women who are in the front row. Any one of them could be my sub for the night. I allow myself to imagine each of them kneeling for me, but none of them really do it.

Focusing on the lights, I imagine I'm up on stage and my fans are calling to me, requesting another song, begging for an encore. But tonight, my fingers will not be making music with my favorite guitar. No, this evening I'll be strumming a beautiful woman to orgasm, over and over again, until she's spent, and her legs have turned to jelly.

"All right," Madison says into the microphone. "And the winner with a bid of $85,000 for a night with the amazing Jed Major is..." Madison looks down at her cue card, but I can't steal a glance at the note since she steps away from me to make way for the winner. "Kaelin Le Blanc!" When she calls out the name, my world spins wildly on its axis before tilting and I suddenly feel drunk, or high, or *something* because I'm sure I'm hearing things.

"What?" My voice is one of shock, but her smile never falters. When I glance at the crowd once more, there, inching closer to the stage is the woman of my wet dreams, my fantasies, and the one woman I never thought I'd see inside a BDSM club.

"Congratulations," Madison grins at Kaelin who shyly smiles and nods. "You're welcome to step up to the wheel and take a spin on your activity for the night." Everything is far too loud. My ears ring as Kaelin's big green eyes meet my gaze.

Her expression matches mine—shock. I'm not sure she was expecting to win, perhaps she was, but didn't think about her actions until the moment she was called up on stage. I observe her body language as she reaches for the little white marble Madison offers. Her attempt at not trembling fails miserably as she takes the small object. Her nervousness enamors me even more.

My eyes are glued to the ball as it drops, bouncing from one kink to another. They spin—round and round and round—until finally the wheel slows and my body is rigid as I hold my breath.

Clink. Clink. Clank.

The wheel stops.

Her body turns rigid.

And I smile.

Wild Card.

It's my choice. I can decide anything, and she has to go along with it. Although, I'm not an asshole, I'll never do anything to actually hurt her in any way, but something has just popped into my mind and that's the scene I plan on giving sweet little Kaelin.

The activity we've landed on offers me all the control on what we do. Her limits will be given to me, those are her no-go areas, and I'll never break those, but other than that everything is fair game.

"And it's a *Roleplay Wild Card*—Dom's choice!" Madison tells the crowd gleefully as she announces the activity the ball has landed on since none of the crowd can see it for themselves. "Wishing you both a fun-filled evening," the woman tells us as we're ushered off the stage, but kept in the theater as we wait for the go ahead. Since we have to wait until everyone has been paired up, we're able to watch the rest of the winners meet their celebrities. My head is spinning with ideas for scenes, remembering long-suppressed fantasies, and still trying to process that Kaelin Le Blanc not only plays at Black Light, but bid on *me*. It feels like it takes forever, standing in silence next to Kaelin who keeps almost speaking before stopping herself — but finally we're released.

"A drink first," I tell her abruptly, wondering if my aloofness will cause her to rethink this. Granted, I've spent the better part of five years thinking about having her in a play room with me. Seeing her bend to my will, but now that she's here... I know I can never be gentle.

She's so small. Delicate, and I'm afraid I'll break her.

A slight nod is her only answer and that heats my blood. She's going to have to learn to speak. I want words. Which brings me to the conversation that will need to happen before we enter the room the scene will take place in.

When we reach the bar, I glance at Kaelin. "What would you like to drink?"

"I'll just have a soda please," she says in a sweet tone that's got my cock responding.

Turning to the bartender, I order two sodas and settle on the stool offering her the one opposite me. I want a drink, a strong one, but I can't lose my head with this girl. I shouldn't even be with her — with this beauty.

"Why are you here?" My question has her gaze snapping to mine.

"Why can't I be here?" Her feistiness is beautiful, intoxicating, and I want more of it.

"You being in this club means you're a member. Which also means you're not new to this."

Kaelin lowers her gaze to the glass, spinning it around on the coaster that has the Black Light logo printed on it. She nods even though I didn't ask her a question.

"And you bid on me because?"

This time, she does meet my inquisitive stare. "Are you blind, Jed?"

I can't help chuckling as I lift the glass to my lips. She watches as I take a long gulp of the cold, fizzy drink, then set it on the bar. "If you keep that sassy mouth working tonight, you'll be crawling out here on your hands and knees in a fucking collar."

She sighs, knowing I'm going to win no matter what she tells me tonight. I'm the one in control and the sooner she gives in and submits, the easier it will be. "I've liked you for years, since I was sixteen. Having the chance to be with you was something I couldn't pass up. When I saw your name, I put in a bid that couldn't be outmatched."

Nodding, I ponder her response. I know she's liked me all this time and hearing her finally admit to it boosts my ego. Not because I need it, but because it's Kaelin. She doesn't realize how special she really is.

"You look beautiful," I tell her finally. Lifting my hand, I gesture for her to stand. When she does, I allow my gaze to linger on her curvy figure. My cock jolts when she turns, and I notice the pearls that zig zag across her back. Tanned, smooth skin peeks at me from between the lines that crisscross and I'm tempted to tug the pearls until they're tiny jewels at my feet.

"The dress is new, but what's underneath isn't."

"Darling, the dress is not what you'll be wearing tonight," I tell her as I lean in. "Finish that soda, it's time for you to experience just who the real Jed Major is."

She shivers at my words and I know it's time. I lead her with a slight touch to the base of her spine with my fingertips. The sparks that shoot through my arm at the contact are evidence enough that I want this girl. I've craved her for a very long time.

We make our way through the curtain and over to the costume area. It doesn't take long for me to spot the outfit which will be perfect for our evening. The way her slight curves will fill out the small skirt and white shirt, I know seeing her dressed up will have my cock painfully hard all night.

She watches me pick up the hanger with the outfit on it. I choose the socks, the shoes, and offer her a wicked smirk. The rosy blush that darkens her cheeks makes heat burn through my veins. This is something I've wanted for so long, and I can't wait to take the sassy little pet into the play room.

"Come."

She leans close to me as we make our way back toward the play areas. Her hiss is low, filled with frustration. "I'm not wearing—"

"This isn't a discussion. It's a scene, if you don't like it, then you're welcome to leave, and I'll just take another submissive into the play room." Her mouth gapes at my rudeness, but she couldn't have expected me to be nice to her. Not after all these years of me pushing her away.

Finally, Kaelin shuts her mouth, following me without so much as a peep. If only we could banter all night. As soon as the thought comes to me, I shove it away.

Moving into the main floor of the club, I'm happy to find one of the semi-private cool-down rooms still vacant. I know the rules of the game insist that we not close the curtain, but tonight it will be the perfect place for our first scene.

As we step into our semi-private room, I'm enamored by her excitement and allow her to look around. She may not show it outwardly, but I can read her like I would any other submissive that walked into a play room with me.

"This is..." she murmurs, then her words taper off when she turns to me. "This is a *wild card*." Her expression changes to a mix of emotions—shock, anxiety, and excitement.

"It is indeed," I tell her, settling myself in a chair that overlooks the small space. I steeple my fingers under my chin, noticing the shiver that trails through her body when my heated gaze lands on her. "Tonight, you'll be my toy, my submissive to use for pleasure—mine. And when I deem you ready, you'll find your release. I control you, your pleasure, and your body."

Her stare is enough to have me bending her over right now, but I need to keep calm. This is new for me and her. Being with Kaelin is nothing like any submissive I've ever been with. No. Kaelin Le Blanc is fresh faced and so fucking innocent, but I want to defile her in every sadistic way possible.

"And when you give me that submission completely, I'll dominate your mind, right down to your very soul. Apparently, this is what you've wanted for years, and now that you're finally here, I can't wait to see what you make of my... needs." I shift in the armchair, watching her tremble and shiver. It's breathtaking seeing her in my world, in the one place I can be myself.

"You know I'm not scared of you," she tells me. When she lifts her chin, I know I'm in for it. Her body is clearly vibrating with need, with frustration, and all I want to do is release her from the bindings that hold her hostage. This life may not be for everyone, but for those who are in it, it's so clear when they need a scene. The tension that holds them captive is not for pleasure, it's their prison. And all I want to do is unlock Kaelin's cage.

CHAPTER 5

 aelin

He nods. "I know you're not scared of me."

A smirk adorns his handsome face. His ankle leaning on the opposite knee as he sits back and observes me. I can tell by the confidence in his posture he knows exactly what I'm feeling. Even though we're in a semi-private room, in the middle of a crowded club, I only notice him. Jed is alluring in every sense of the word.

He's dressed in black slacks. It's the first time I've seen him in anything other than his signature torn jeans. His shirt, also black, is stylish with the top three buttons undone, offering me a peek at his smooth tanned skin beneath. The tattoos that adorn his chest are mostly hidden, but when he moves I get a glimpse of the ink that snakes its way to the left side of his neck.

He crooks his finger, calling me over to him, and my feet obey. He pats his knee, before ordering, "Kneel at my feet."

I allow myself to drop to the plush carpet. The position causing me to look up into his desire filled orbs.

"Are you ready?" His voice is low, dark and dangerous, and I'm not sure if I should run away from him or into his arms. I never pegged my nerves to take hold of me so much. All my most sensual fantasies have come to life and now I'm a little uncertain as to what I've gotten myself into. I lean closer to him, needing to feel the heat of his body near mine. When I lay my cheek on his thigh, my erratic heartbeat calms somewhat, but I'm nowhere near relaxed yet.

I nod. "I'm ready." My voice cracks slightly, and he notices. Of course he does, he's a Dominant and he's known me for what seems like forever. He should notice every nuance, every nervous tick because he's seen it all before.

"There are three safe words," he tells me, taking my hand in his. "Red, yellow, and green," he says as his thumb circles my palm. The whispered words cause goosebumps to rise on every inch of my skin.

"Yes, I know the safe words." I lift my head to face him once more, needing to look into his handsome face and see the desire that's always been there. It's for me, only for me.

He lifts his hands, cupping my face, holding me steady and I'm thankful because I feel dizzy. "If you need to stop, you tell me, I want to hear the safe word. Do you understand?"

"Yes, I understand." My voice sounds more confident than before, and this seems to please him because he offers me a grin.

Once he releases me, I feel the heat on my cheeks. Blushing as I always do for him, I lower my gaze to his chest in an attempt to focus on anything other than the thrumming between my legs. Knowing we will have an audience soon makes me shiver with anticipation as to what he has planned for me. That's the least of what's making me so nervous. Knowing that, in a few minutes, I'll be naked and at his mercy — that's what's got my body trembling.

I don't turn to face the mirror, only wanting to see every inch of Jed, the Dominant. To offer him the one thing I've wanted to give him from the moment I first met him—me. He gestures for me to stand as he sits back, relaxing into the armchair.

"Strip."

It's one word, but it holds the weight of the world in it.

"If you don't, I'll have to do it for you."

"Is this why you're so bossy?" I question, stalling for a moment before I place my hands on my hips. I'm not sure where my courage comes from, or why I'm defying a Dominant in a scene, but I am.

He rises without responding, stalking toward me, he grips my neck in one hand, squeezing until my fingers fly up to claw at him. That's when he tilts his head to the side, a smirk curling full lips as he regards my flailing form. "This is what you like. Isn't it?"

I don't respond, I don't need to because he knows he's right. When we were at his home, he saw it, the desire and need for what he's doing. He looked right through me in that moment and I knew he knew.

"You love me holding you down, pinning you against a wall." As he speaks, he walks me backward, and soon I'm held between two hard surfaces—his toned body and the wall.

"Jed—"

"It's Sir," he grits out through clenched teeth. He's barely holding on. His restraint is a taut thread about to snap and I wonder just what lies beneath. "In this room, when we're in a scene, you will address me appropriately."

"Sir, please?" I'm not sure what I'm asking for, but his free hand finds the hem of my dress, pulling it up to my waist. He doesn't relent on my neck, holding me steady while his fingers gently stroke the material of my panties.

"Mm, someone's all wet and needy already," he observes with a wicked grin. His fingers taunt me, circling my clit through the material and heat pools between my legs. I'm drenching my panties. "Is this what you wanted, pet?" he questions as he continues his assault on me. My knees wobble, and I'm certain if he wasn't holding me up, I'd be on the floor.

"You will be dressed in a uniform," he tells me easily and the smirk on his face is nothing short of victorious. He motions to the padded table, the blue and white skirt, with a white button up shirt, and knee high blue white socks await me. There's a deep blue tie which matches the color in the skirt, and I know exactly what he's role playing today—me in my school uniform.

"You can't be serious," I bite out, pivoting to meet his gaze.

"Oh, Kaelin..." He smiles. "You'll find that this is something I don't joke about. When I'm here in this club, or any other club like it, I never joke. My dominance is something I take very seriously." His expression is devoid of any smile now. "And if this is something you'd like to run from," he taunts. "I'll understand."

"I'm not walking away. If that's what you want me to wear..." I smile up at him, offering him a sweet, sultry, yet innocent grin. "I'll do it."

Walking toward the table, I slowly pick up the items and examine them. It's as if he knew my size. They're a perfect fit. Or they will be once I change into them. Jed settles in the chair, waiting for me to do it right here, in the room. If he thinks this will deter me from wanting him, he's so wrong.

Pushing the straps of my dress down, I step out of the material and I hear the soft intake of air from him when he notices my underwear. I move to put on the uniform, feeling more and more illegal as I turn to face him once I'm dressed.

This is exactly how I would have been all those years ago when I'd fantasized about him and he knows it. The asshole is messing with me because he knows how much I've always desired him. He sits for a long while merely taking in every inch of me dressed up like a school girl. The corner of his mouth lifting slightly, his eyes burning a blaze through me. His tongue darts out as he slowly, meticulously, licks his lips.

"Is this what you looked like when you fingered your pretty cunt thinking about me?" he questions, causing me to blush furiously. My cheeks are hot, burning up because of Jed. He doesn't make a move to come to me. He admires me from afar like I'm nothing more than a painting he has hanging on his wall. I'm something he wants to own, and somehow, that both hurts and heals me at the same time.

"Maybe," I respond coyly.

Once more, he calls me to him with a crook of his finger. When I reach him, he points to the floor. "On your knees for me, little one."

I'm positioned between his spread thighs, noticing how muscular they are in the slacks he's wearing. His hand grips my throat while the other mauls my tits. Even though he's choking me, holding me hostage, I can't stop myself from taunting him by licking my lips, wetting them until they're glistening with saliva. Years have passed and all I can think of is him spanking me, fucking me, owning me. *Would he want to own me?*

"Tell me, pet," he growls an order as if its law. "Tell me how much you wanted my cock in your pretty teen cunt?" I open my mouth, but before I can respond, his thumb presses against my tongue, holding it down, my mouth forming an O shape. The fire that flares behind his beautiful eyes seem to blaze as if an inferno is lashing against a forest. "Suck."

Wrapping my lips around his digit, I suck it into my mouth, deep as he forces it into my throat. I choke, the sound a soft gag and it makes him grin like a schoolboy who just found his first Playboy magazine. He continues assaulting my mouth and, right then and there, I wish it was his cock violating me.

Spit drips from my chin when he finally pulls away from me. He grips the tie, lifting me as he rises from his chair. He leads me to the table as if I'm a dog on a leash. I stumble behind him, slamming into his body when he suddenly stops.

"Tell me, pet..." He smirks. "I want to hear how wet you used to get thinking about me." Humiliation burns my cheeks, because he's right.

"I used to... I mean..." I don't know why it's so difficult to admit my feelings, my emotions.

"This is me," he confesses. "The asshole you wanted to give your virginity to. That's what you wanted. Isn't it, little one?"

"Yes..." I murmur honestly because I can no longer lie to him, to myself.

"Did you think of me when your boyfriend bled your little cunt of its virtue?"

I can't find the words to admit just what I want him to do to me, but I don't need to because Jed spins me around and pushes me onto the table. The padded top at my chest, my hips bent, and my ass offered up to him as a sacrifice.

"Tell me," he growls.

"Yes, yes, I did." Tears fall from my eyes, trickling down my cheeks. It's not sadness that's making me cry, it's the need for more. I want him to make me cry, I want him to claim me.

I claw at the leather in an attempt to play the role he wants from me. And just like he promised, he doesn't let me get away. A screech falls from my lips when he grips my ankles, pulling me back to position. We're fighting, and I realize, we did land on the roleplay wild card. On a roleplay. Smiling, I feel my nipples tighten with want. I need pain. I want this violence that thrums through my blood heating it with desire.

My skirt is ripped down my legs and a stinging spank lands on my ass, left, then right, again and again. Jed's lost in the darkness of our scene. He's holding me down, his hand pressing me into the padding while the other delivers the punishment I've been aching for all this time.

With every squeal, every plea, I shudder. My body is burning hot with passion so fierce, it ignites me from the inside out. My stomach tightens when I realize I'm so close to orgasm. I'm lost in pleasure when the pain stops, the spanks cease and my gaze snaps wide. Turning to peek at him over my shoulder, I find him staring down at me, his smile is beautiful.

"You will only come when I command it," he tells me in a tone that confirms there will be no debate on when I orgasm. He's in control, and I wouldn't have it any other way. "Take your shirt off before I fucking rip it off."

I move quickly, because I can tell from the look on his face, he's not lying. I allow the white material to pool at my feet, not moving to pick it up. Jed stares at me for a long while, his gaze trailing up and down my almost naked frame.

"Bra, then panties," he commands me.

My trembling fingers unhook my bra, and it joins my dress on the floor beside me. Next, I push my panties down my legs, stepping out of them, I rise. I'm about to add them to the pile of clothes beside me, but Jed holds out his hand.

I place the damp material on his waiting palm and gasp when he lifts them to his nose. Inhaling deeply, I watch his eyes flutter as he takes in my scent. His heated gaze snaps to mine, the corner of his mouth tilts. "You watching me, baby?"

"Yes, Sir." The words are raspy, and I attempt to clear my throat, but it's no use. I'm far too turned on watching him sniff my panties than I ever thought I could or would be.

"Who knew the little Kaelin was so filthy?" He smiles. "Lie back on the table, spread your legs for me."

I obey. I can't *not* obey him. Once I'm in position, he stares at the juncture between my legs, the wetness is all for him and I'm certain he's enjoying knowing what he does to me. His hands move for his belt and I shiver. A small smile plays on my lips when he looks up.

His dark brow arches in question before he asks, "You like when I make it hurt, don't you"?

"Yes, Sir."

"I'd love to spend a whole day with you doing this, but you realize we only have a limited time, don't you?"

I nod, and gulp nervously when he pulls the leather from the loops. "Y…yes, Sir."

"And you want this?" He waves the leather in the air, his hand gripping the object so tight, veins pop on his hand which only serve to turn me on even more.

I nod quickly in an attempt to beg wordlessly for him to spank me with the belt. I've been whipped before, and I came hard from the pain. I crave it.

"Good. We're going to use every minute tonight. I've got a lot in store for you. When I told you earlier you'd never forget me when I fuck you, I meant it."

"Th…thank you, Sir." My response has him grinning as if he's just signed another multi-million-dollar record deal. And I commit it to memory because I'm sure this will be the first and last time I ever spread my legs for the famous rock star.

"Tell me where to start, pet," he muses, trailing the leather over my naked body. The coolness of the material causes me to shiver in anticipation. "You choose, and remember, it's the only thing you'll choose tonight—thighs, breasts, ass, or that beautiful cunt? Choose."

He allows the leather to lick at my pussy, and my hips lift involuntarily. Even though I haven't yet voiced the words, my body is begging. It's pleading. "Please, Sir, start with my pussy."

"Excellent choice, pet." Another heart stopping grin curls his lips. "Open your legs as wide as they go, I'd like to devour you with my eyes while I turn that pretty little cunt a dark shade of pink before I fuck it."

"Yes, Sir."

CHAPTER 6

ed

HER BODY TREMBLES ON THE PADDED TABLE AND I WISH I HAD A blindfold, but then when her wide eyes land on me, I decide against it. Raising the belt, I bring it down on her inner thigh earning me a yelp which makes my dick jolt. It's ready to drive into her body, but I have so much more for her.

I offer her another swat on the opposite thigh, causing her to whimper. Her hips rise up in an attempt to wiggle away from me, or toward me, I'm not sure because desire has overridden my mind and all I can think about is claiming her.

Soft red welts rise on her porcelain thighs and I finally allow the leather to lick against her pussy in a harsh swat that earns me a blood-heating scream as her fingers dig into the leather beneath her. I wait for her to scream *red*, but she doesn't. A gentle smile glimmers on her face and I know she's ready for another which, I deftly deliver. Her trembles are intoxicating as her body undulates on the table.

"Please, Sir," she begs, her voice raspy with emotion, with need so fierce it grips me by the throat. "I need more."

Dropping the belt, I reach for her, tugging her from the table by her wrist. Once she's standing, I spin her around and bend her over. The pert little ass I've been ogling for years is right here, mine for the taking.

"Tell me, pet," I command her as I lean into her body, cocooning her with mine. "Tell me how you used to touch your pretty little cunt thinking of me." I know I'm taunting her, humiliating her, but I can't stop myself. I've forgotten all about the crowd that's most likely gathered to watch. All that exists is me and her.

"I... I..."

"Did you run home from school and finger yourself? Did you imagine my thick fingers stealing your precious virginity?" My words force a shudder through her as my fingers work their way between her legs. Kicking her ankle with my foot, I spread her open.

"Sir, Jed, please?" Her pleas fall on deaf ears. She wanted this. I know she'd been fantasizing about it for years, and to be honest, so have I.

"You wanted to play with fire. Are you scared of being burned now?" I smirk down at her and plunge two of my fingers into her tight heat, pumping in and out, slow and steady, just enough to have her moaning loudly. The sound of her need is music to my ears. I strum her like I do my guitar. When I feel her walls pulse around my digits, I halt all movement earning me another mewl of frustration.

My cock strains against my zipper, urging me to finally claim her, but I wait. Although my restraint is wavering with every whimper, I focus on giving her everything she's wanted for so long. Pulling my wet fingers from her cunt, I circle the tight ring of muscle of her ass.

"No, please, not there," she pleads. Turning her head, she peeks at me from over her shoulder, her gaze dark with lust, with a fire so hot it burns me when I slide one finger into her ass.

"No? Are you sure? Because your pretty little cunt is begging for me." My smile turns her cheeks a deep red and I see the guilt in her expression. She can't deny it. I work her hole open, adding a second finger. "Look at how much you need me to fuck you," I tell her as I scissor her open. "These holes are hungry for my dick. Aren't they, pet?"

"Fuck," she hisses through clenched teeth when I grip her neck, cutting off her air just enough for her ass to tighten around my digits. Her hand flies between her legs as her hips lift to offer her access and soon, she's playing with her clit.

Her body is spasming wildly at the intensity. I wish I could spank her right now but working her into a frenzy is beautiful. It's the most exquisite thing I've ever seen. Her walls clench, my dick is close to spurting in my boxers as she cries out in pleasure, her body squirting all over my slacks as she drenches me in her release.

I pull my fingers from her quickly. Grabbing the foil packet from my pocket before shoving down my pants, along with my underwear, I sheath myself in the condom. Fisting my dick, I stroke it as I rub it along her glistening cunt. The softness and heat of her is too much and I have to close my eyes to keep the image of painting her with my seed from my mind or I'll come far too soon.

"Is this what you wanted?" I taunt, the heat of her turning me into an animal needing to drive inside her, owning and claiming her. "Tell me, pet."

"Yes, it's what I've always wanted," she finally admits, and I can't hold back anymore. Slamming into her, I feel the heat of her tightening around my dick. Her cries echo around me as I rain down swats on her thighs, on her sweet little ass that's turning a deep shade of red with my handprint.

"You're mine now, pet," I tell her as I slide out, then slowly move in again. "Such a tight little pussy." I growl, gripping her hips, I hold her down on the table. Our bodies locked together like chords of a song that becomes a melody. And we move together like a symphony of passion and yearning.

I pull out and then with the slightest movement, tease inch by inch back into her. A whimper falls from her lips—sweet and innocent— but when her body pulses around mine, there's nothing more I want than to violate her in the most sinful ways.

"Please, Sir," she pleads with me.

"Tell me what you need."

"You, I want you. All of you." I can't hold back any longer. I slam into her, causing her body to shudder and tremble as I fuck her mercilessly. I feel it the moment she tightens, the instant her body milks me. And I give it to her. Allowing my seed to spill and I know I'll never want another woman on my dick, or in my arms.

CHAPTER 7

aelin

He doesn't relent. His hands grip me, they hold me so tight it's as if he's trying to keep me close, but I know it's not that. It can't be. My father will never allow me to be with him.

I'm still shaking when he leans in and holds me. His body cocooning me with its heat, calming my erratic heartbeat that reminds me I've just been fucked by Jed Major—heartthrob and man-whore extraordinaire—but also, a Dominant who I want to submit to.

We lay in silence for a moment, and my mind is running riot on what's going to happen next.

"Are you okay?" Jed questions, his lips stealing a kiss on the nape of my neck causing a shiver to travel through me. He doesn't stop, making his way down my body, slow and steady. The feeling is sensual, making me weak in the knees. He rises, leaving me on the table when he slips from my core. The feeling of emptiness hits me suddenly and I move to stand up, turning to face him.

"Yes." Meeting his gaze, I smile up at him. Taking in the man who's just showed me more pleasure than I'd ever experienced in my life. "I didn't think you'd..." I wave my hand in the air between us, unsure of what to say. I may not be a teenager with a crush, but he makes me feel like one.

"You didn't think I would want you?" He arches a brow at me, his questioning gaze burning a hole right through me, hitting deep in my soul where I've hidden my feelings for him. "You really didn't think that all this time I wanted nothing more than to saunter into your room, push you up against the wall and kiss you until your knees give out?"

I shake my head. "No, all these years you've acted like you hated me."

"Darling," he smirks. "I've wanted you since the moment I saw you. I've fought my feelings—what I've wanted—because of who you are, who I am. Us being together would put you in the spotlight." He holds onto my arms, gripping me tightly as if he wants to shake the truth into me.

"I don't care about that. I've been in the spotlight since I've been born. My father wanted that life for me, even though I didn't, but with you..." I sigh, shaking my head. "I want this, Jed. I want us." This time, when I meet his searing gaze, he sees it, something between us clicks and I know without a doubt I'm about to embark on something I never expected—a relationship with Jed Major.

He leans in close, his lips whispering over mine as he murmurs, "I want you in another scene, I want more of that pretty little cunt coming all over me. Do you want another roll on the wheel?" His words cause my stomach to flip wildly.

I nod slowly, acknowledging that no time we have together could ever be enough. I know the rules are we're meant to be in scene for longer, and another scene will give us more time to explore each other and stick as close to the rules as we can.

"Kiss me, pet," he orders, his voice deep and gruff.

Our lips touch, the heat of his kiss causing my thighs to squeeze together. Jed's tongue licks along my lips, and I allow him entry. We duel, the taste of him intoxicating more so than anything else ever has. When he pulls away, his eyes shine with need.

"Want to watch a scene before we see what else we can spin on the wheel?" he questions easily.

"Yes, let's be voyeurs." I grin.

"Mm, my little pet loves to watch?"

My cheeks burn with guilt at the truth. "Yes, sometimes I do." I right the dress I was wearing when we arrived while Jed zips up his slacks and buttons up his shirt. Once we're ready, he offers me a smirk.

"Ready?" he questions, gesturing with his head toward the door.

Nodding, I smile at Jed who looks at ease inside Black Light. I wonder if this is where he's more himself than on stage. I want to ask, but I don't get a chance when he slides an arm around my waist and tugs me deeper into the club, toward one of the viewing areas in the back hallway. When we come to a stop, there's a beautiful woman bound and gagged, being flogged between her legs, on her breasts, and my body trembles in response.

"Is that what you want?" he questions from behind me as his hands trail along my body. I can't answer because I know if I do, he'll fuck me again. Right here for everyone to see.

When I turn to look at him, I see it in his eyes. Everything inside me says that he's telling the truth, but deep down, I know he's spent his life as a man-whore, fucking his fans at every tour stop. If he walks out of here tonight and forgets about everything that's happened between us, I'm not sure I could survive that. I cast my gaze toward the scene playing out. The erotic sensuality of how blissful the woman looks makes me crave more. Another scene where I'm bound and flogged, where my ass is caned until I'm drenched with need to be fucked.

"Look at me," Jed orders from behind me, and I obey. I have to, because he commands obedience with only a few words. "I want to delve into that pretty little head and find out just what you're thinking."

"You've had a single life for—"

He breaks my words with a kiss, his lips molding to mine as he licks along the seam of my mouth. When I open on a soft moan, he takes advantage and slips his tongue along mine. We dance to the music of our hearts, knowing that this isn't wrong. It's what I've wanted, what he's wanted, and there's no longer any doubt when he pulls me flush with him.

"I have been," he admits easily. "But I never had anyone I wanted. Every woman was a distraction from the life of a rock star. Stop second guessing shit."

"I'm not second—"

"Then enjoy the evening with me, and we'll take it from there." He insists, his gaze turning dark and I wonder just what's going through *his* mind right now.

The two people on the other side of the window pane play out their scene, and I can feel him taunt me, touch me in ways I'd only dreamed of, but I know exactly what it is and there's only one way to fix it.

Pushing away from Jed, I lace my fingers through his and pull him back through the club towards the theater. Once there, we step up onto the stage to find the wheel spinning. There's a couple up watching the object turn with a click of the ball, looking nervous, and I'm certain it's their first time together. I recognize him, an actor from the newest blockbuster. I'm about to step forward when hands grip me tightly and I know I've been caught.

"You sure want another spin on the roulette wheel?" Jed's question is playful and I wonder if he's trying to distract from the serious conversation only moments earlier. And my eyes are already scanning the kinky options available. I want more. I'm hungry and greedy for him. I've waited for years to get the opportunity to be with him, and now that I have him, I'm not walking away. I need my fill of Jed, and he's going to give it to me. We've only been through one scene — one intense, erotic scene — and if I can show him I can handle his darkness, his hunger, I'm sure he'll change his viewpoint of me.

Perhaps for once, he'll see me as more of a woman than the

teenage girl who's had a crush on him for far too long. I can satisfy him, and I intend to make him see it tonight.

"Listen to me," the deep, low grumble comes from behind me. Even in this position, as woman and man, he's a Dominant. He's a man, not one that could easily be swayed by my half-truths, not like the boys I go to college with. No. Jed Major is a man who will never take my fiery, stubborn demeanor and accept it. He will pull the truth from me one way or another, and to be honest, I would prefer the latter.

"I'm listening," I tell him, but I don't turn to him. I can't face him because, if I do, I'll fall into his spell and then I know there's no way of returning to the normal world because I'm owned. I'm his and there's nothing that can tear me away from the man I know I love.

"I don't play by half measures, pet. I'm not going to give you candlelit dinners or walks in the park. I don't do shit like that. What I do, and what I enjoy, are far beyond what you can grasp." He doesn't sound like he's joking. The MC's voice, the crowd that seem to murmur and mill around the roulette wheel, everything—everything fades into nothing and all that exists is me and Jed.

"Then show me."

CHAPTER 8

 ed

Her voice cracks slightly, but she rights herself and I can read the tension running through her. She's nervous, but that's all right because I'm going to show her just how much she can take. I want to test her limits, make her feel things she's never experienced in all her young life.

We take a step closer to where the wheel has come to a stop on the kink for the couple who look almost tortured at what they're playing out.

"Another spin?" Madison questions with a smile and I nod.

"Yes, my sweet pet would like to test another kink," I inform her, allowing Kaelin to move forward and stand beside the wheel. I want it to land on something naughty, something that will have her trembling beneath me. Madison reaches for the wheel and tugs, just before Kaelin drops the small marble in the wheel. The colors blur as it spins, and I watch the ball bounce in anticipation. My body already humming at the thought of what's to come.

Her eyes are glued to the object as it slows... click... click... click. When the marble finally comes to a stop, I notice her inhale a deep breath before looking at me. A smile plays on my lips, satisfaction clear in my expression when she blushes at our newest kink—*Edge Play*. One of my favorites. Watching her squirm and tremble at the cool steel against her skin will be my drug of choice. Getting high off seeing her eyes widening as she watches me taunt her.

I hold out a hand to Kaelin who slowly slips hers in mine. With a wave at Madison, I take my pet through the club, taking in the people who are all watching scenes, having drinks, but the only thing on my mind is getting Kae bound to a St. Andrews Cross while I tease a blade over her naked flesh.

We make our way into the dungeon, one of the fantasy rooms along the back hallway and find Miles, the DM who will apparently be watching over the scene. He offers a nod in greeting which I return. I met him a while ago when I first started frequenting Black Light, and he loves blades just as much as I do.

"I want you naked," I tell Kaelin, whispering in her ear.

Her gaze meets mine and she nods slowly. I stand back, watching her as she slips the dress off. I should've kept her in a school uniform for the night, but enjoy watching how the material of the dress she wore for me falls to the floor is just as sexy as the uniform.

Her underwear is next, and soon, she's standing before me, her head bowed, her eyes on the floor, and her hands behind her back like a good girl.

"Look at me," I order in a deep, low tone. She obeys easily, beautifully. "Give me your hand." Once again, her dainty little hand slips into mine. I lead her over to the cross against the wall and position her facing me, just how I need. Binding her ankles, then her hands.

Seeing her open for me, at my mercy has my cock hardening in my slacks again. There are implements to use set out and I have a number of choices for the *edge play*. Picking up one of the knives which have a black handle, with a thin sliver blade, I lift it in front of my face.

Twisting it left and right, the metal glints in the low lights of the room.

"Are you ready, pet?" A slight nod, but she knows I want to hear her. "Words. Or I'll whip you before we do this."

"Please," she begs, and I know she wants the whip licking against her skin. A little masochist. And I want to give her everything she needs. "I want it all. I'm ready, Sir."

Miles groans, watching us, and I wonder if he's as turned on by her as I am. I love an audience, and it seems Kaelin does too. The spectators are slowing down, stopping just outside our room, and I can't help but wonder if they'll stick around for the whole show.

With a smile, I trail the blade over her lips, painting each one with invisible ink. Her mouth opens slightly, her breathing comes in short bursts and her pupils dilate at the movement.

I notice her tremble when I reach her chest, turning rings around her hardened nipples. The little buds peak, needing my mouth to suck on them, but I ignore the craving and continue my way down her stomach, pressing slightly into her belly button.

I step forward, our bodies inches apart. "Are you still wet, pet?" I question with an arch of one brow. Her tongue darts out, wetting her plump lips.

"I am, Sir." Her confession is enough to have me rock fucking hard. I'm ready to take her, I want to claim her right here in front of the audience. But I don't. Stepping back, I allow the knife to tease its way down her thighs, missing her pretty cunt. The scent of her intoxicates me, and I want so much to lean in and lap at her core.

I trail my way up her other leg, then place the blade flat against her mound. She pulls in a deep breath, her body rigid when I press the sharper edge to her flesh. It's not hard enough to cut, but I can see the smooth porcelain skin indenting from the pressure.

"Look at how pretty you look all flushed and needy," I taunt her, allowing my fingers to stroke her lower lips. A whimper falls from her mouth, but she doesn't move. I would never hurt her, but there's always that fear in a submissive in a scene with blades.

I lower the knife against her flesh, the arousal glistening on the metal and my cock throbs wildly at the sight. Fuck, this is more than I can take. I want her again. Once the steel is drenched in her juices, I rise and place it on her lips, painting them with her need for me.

"Taste yourself," I command, and she does. Her tongue laps at the metal causing my dick to fight against my zipper. She smiles, licking up the juices I've offered her, and I can't stop myself from leaning in to kiss her.

With the knife behind me, I press my body against hers, spearing my tongue into her heat, licking and dueling with her own tongue, tasting her arousal. The sweet musk making me never want to stop. I want her. I will have her. The world and press be damned because this girl is mine.

"I want to fuck you again. Right now," I murmur against her lips. When I take one step back, ensuring there's distance between us, I twirl the blade in front of her again and allow it to lick her skin, just the way I want my tongue to dance across her flesh. I want to draw every melody from her, making her cry out, beg for more.

Pressing the tip against her nipple, I'm tempted to push further, but I don't. And when I pull away, she mewls like a kitten who's hungry. My sweet pet is starving for a whipping, for a fuck, she wants me to fill her up with all I have to give, and I will, very fucking soon.

CHAPTER 9

aelin

I'M DRENCHED.

I'm shaking.

My gaze flits to the doorway and I see Laurence watching. His eyes are locked on my bound body, a slight smirk plays on his lips when he sees Jed taunting me with the blade. He never wanted to do this with me, but I know he would've enjoyed it.

The sleek silver metal traces circles around my nipples again and again. My knees are buckling and I'm thankful I'm tied against the cross or I would've fallen to my knees. Jed presses the sharper edge along my thighs, scraping it against my skin causing goose bumps to rise up against every inch of me.

He doesn't speak, merely makes pretty patterns with the object against me and I know I'll have thin red welts from the knife. He continues painting me a picture with his need. I want nothing more than for him to fill me once more, to slide inside me and make me his, but his concentration is on the edge play.

When he finally rises, he slips two fingers into my pussy, causing me to cry out in pleasure. I'm so wet the sounds of my arousal echo in the room as Jed fingerfucks me ruthlessly. I want him to hurt me, I want him to make it ache. And the smirk he's giving me as he touches me tells me soon enough, I'll be screaming his name again.

Jed leans in, whispering in my ear as he fingers me, "I wish it landed on fisting, I want to shove my hand inside you, I want you to feel me for fucking weeks while I make you cry and scream. Then I'd cane your pretty little ass, until the only thing you'll want and crave is me."

"Please, Sir," I moan as he circles my clit with his thumb, two of his fingers still deep inside me, pumping in and out, causing my body to shudder with the need to come. I want to feel my orgasm take over, but the moment I pulse around his fingers, Jed stops.

He pulls his hand from me, lifting his shimmering fingers and shoving them into my mouth, deeper until he hits the back of my throat. The blade he's holding presses against my chest, trailing up to my neck. I feel the sharpness, but I know it's not breaking skin. He could, I know he could, but I trust him. He wouldn't hurt me, and that's what I know in my heart.

He starts his assault on me again. My body thrumming with need for the release he's holding back from me. The steel against my skin heating from the want emanating from me. Jed's eyes darken as he watches me move closer and closer to release.

The moment I near it... he stops.

"Please, Sir, I need to come."

Shaking his head, he grins, looking every bit the Adonis he is. "Not yet," he tells me. "As much as I'd like to make you come all over my cock again, I think I'll be nice to you since you begged me so beautifully." His words grip my heart so tight, and I hope they'll never let go. He enjoys this, controlling me, controlling every aspect. As he pulls away from me, I watch him stalk to the cabinet, setting the blade down. Once he's done, he nears me, helping me from the cuffs.

I can't help but smile.

"Thank you, Sir," I flutter my lashes, flirting with him as he lifts me against his body, setting me down at the padded table and pushing me chest down on the smooth surface. The chill of the leather on my skin causes me to shudder.

He leans over me, his body cocooning me with heat which coils low in my belly. "You're going to take my cock again with all these people watching. They'll know you belong to me."

From behind me, I hear the sound of ripping foil. I'm about to glance over my shoulder when suddenly, he slams into me. My pussy tightening around his thick length as he pulls out and drives back in.

He can't be far off his own release, because the more he thrusts into me, the higher I fly. My body shakes and trembles. His hand fisting in my hair, tugging me backward until I'm arched toward him. The crowd watching can see my tits bounce with every plunge, and I can hear the sound of our slapping skin surrounding me.

Sex hangs heavily in the room and I can't help edging to the cliff, wanting to fly off and soar while I have Jed inside me. His lips find purchase on my shoulder, his teeth grazing the skin and I cry out as pleasure rips through every nerve inside me when he bites down, marking me.

His other hand is on my hip, holding me down, making my pussy pulse around his cock. The grunts of his pleasure vibrated through me as he fucks me into oblivion.

"Come for me. Show them all who you belong to," he growls in my ear. An order, one I don't take lightly because my eyes roll back in my head when Jed circles the tight ring of muscle of my ass, dipping his thumb into me. The movement has stars bursting behind my eye lids and I'm lost in a cry of pleasure that's drawn directly from my soul.

I feel his cock thicken and I know he's close. A moment later, his pleasured roar echoes in my ears. He slows his movements, his cock slipping from my drenched center and I'm limp on the table before him.

Moments pass. Then he's helping me up. My legs are shaky. My mind is a whirl of pleasure and I glance up into those beautiful orbs that hold me hostage before he quirks a grin at me.

"I'm taking you home, pet." There's a promise hanging in those words, one that makes me grin. He places a kiss on my lips and moves about the room picking up my dress, and grabbing my shoes.

Ever so gently, Jed helps me get dressed. Even after that scene, he's sweet and caring as he takes my hand and leads me from the play area. Eyes are on us as we head toward the main area of the club, and I can't help but blush from the thought of everyone seeing me get thoroughly fucked.

I'm not sure how long we've been inside the dungeon room, but when we finally make our way to the bar, all I want to do is sit down. My legs are wobbly, and my whole body is alive with want. Every nerve ending is sparked with desire and there's only one man who can ease the ache—Jed.

"We'll have one drink, then we're leaving," he tells me. "If they say we didn't play enough, fuck it. I'm going to take you home and devour you on my bed before I fuck you on every available surface in my house."

"I have a feeling Jed Major doesn't want to share me with anyone else for much longer," I tease with a smile, already imagining just what else he might have in store for me.

"You're absolutely fucking right I don't want to share you right now," Jed says, flashing that smile I've seen in so many magazines. We're seated beside each other. His eyes on me, and that's when I see the promise in them. It's us. We're going to do this.

"No backing out now, rock star," I tease.

"I'm not the one who should be worried." He offers me a cocky wink as we get our drinks and I know I'm in for it. I've never been one to back away from a challenge. And Jed is stuck with me because I've waited far too long to ever walk away from him.

"I can never worry when I'm with you."

"Good girl," he winks, clinking his glass with mine.

Smiling, I bask in this new journey I'm about to embark on and excitement spills from me in that moment when I realize, I finally got the guy.

The End

ABOUT THE AUTHOR

DANI RENE is an international bestselling author and proud member of the Romance Writer's Organization of South Africa (ROSA) and the Romance Writers of America (RWA). She is a fan of dark romance that grabs you by the throat and doesn't let go. It's from this passion that her writing has evolved from sweet and romantic, to dark and delicious.

CELEBRITY ROULETTE CONCLUSION

Livia Grant & Jennifer Bene

Unfortunately... the night has to end, but keep reading to find out what happens when Celebrity Roulette is over!

*J*axson stepped out of the men's locker room just in time to see Mark, one of their temp dungeon monitors, plowing what looked like one of the part-time waitstaff they'd brought in for the event. At least, he thought it was one of the servers based solely on the scraps of uniform Jaxson could see from his particular angle. Mark had the fit server bent in half — head down, ass high — over the back of one of the cushioned chairs. Even in the dim lighting Jax could see the white knuckles of Mark's grip on her naked hips as he ruthlessly slammed his cock into her so hard and fast that the chair supporting them was starting to scoot across the dungeon floor.

Christ, his own cock felt strangled in his too-tight slacks. As if watching the debauched scenes of the roulette couples all night hadn't been torturous enough already, catching this impromptu live porn show had him sorely tempted to unzip his pants and stroke one off on the spot.

"There you are, Jaxson. We just finished a sweep of the club and found a few couples hadn't quite... well... finished celebrating Valentine's Day yet. Remind me to have Nalani and the crew wipe down the sauna extra good. Bellington and his sub are still in there wrapping up." Elijah grinned as he started into his report before he realized Jaxson's attention was on something else behind him.

Elijah turned in time for the two men to witness the grand finale happening just a dozen feet away. The high pitch scream of the coming woman was drowned out by the shout Mark released as he finished pistoning, finally slumping over the bare back of the well-fucked woman now recovering under him.

Elijah chuckled. "Poor Mark. I think we're all anxious to finish up so we can go take our sexual frustrations out on a willing sub, but he had it especially bad tonight."

"How's that?" Jaxson asked, reaching down to reposition his hard-on in his slacks in an attempt to relieve the building pressure.

"I had him stationed in the Red Light District. It was busy back there tonight, what with Adam Butler and his partner on their marathon sex and punishment scene and the glory holes in near constant use. Mark was literally inches away from the action for three hours straight. He already told me an hour ago when I stopped in to check on him that he planned on fucking the first person who said yes after the game ended and he was off duty."

Jaxson chuckled. "Looks like it didn't take him long."

"I didn't think it would, but that reminds me. I really need Nalani and her crew to use extra care when cleaning that small room back in that hallway. There's a ton of body fluid spray on the floor and walls and we're gonna need a better way to ventilate back there. Mark's gonna have to fumigate the clothes he's wearing to get the sex smell out. Good thing he's single. No woman would believe he hadn't cheated on her coming home smelling like he does."

Now that the show was over, Jaxson turned his attention back to his Dungeon Master. Having helped to bandage Nolan Boeing's bleeding knuckles earlier, Elijah nodded in the direction of the nearby men's room. "How's Nolan holding up?"

Jaxson answered truthfully. "Better than I'd be under the circumstances. The bleeding stopped, but I'm pretty sure his bruised ego's gonna take longer to heal."

Elijah shook his head. "Yeah, well I can't say I'm surprised how things turned out. Piper Kole is one icy bitch."

Jaxson turned his gaze on Elijah. "Careful. Any male Dom who acted as dominant would be considered a strong Dom. I don't want us treating her any differently just because she's a woman."

"I resent that. I never treat the Dommes any differently. I'd call Egan, Ronan, or Trenton a bastard too if they'd left their submissives tied down and just walked out on them at the end of the night. It wasn't cool."

Jaxson sighed. "Yeah, well, on that we can agree."

A flurry of end-of-the-night activities were going on all around them as the house lights started to brighten and the pounding music suddenly came to a stop. Someone had obviously made it back to the club's control room.

Jaxson was anxious to get the hell out of there — not only because they had the house all to themselves that night, but more importantly, watching dozens of couples in kinky scenes all night had his cock at permanent full-staff. He needed to stick it into one of his lover's holes — the sooner the better.

"Listen, we have a few things to debrief on. I left Chase and Emma in the theater with Madison. Let's head back there. Miguel will be joining us after doing rounds."

As the men headed through the velvet curtain, he picked up on the thumping beat of the music still banging away at Runway directly above them. They'd purposefully kept the dance club open an hour later to help stagger the departures of their many guests on the property.

They met Madison, Emma, and Chase coming out of the theater. The mischievous grin on his husband's face turned Jaxson's already hard cock to rock. Christ, they needed to get the hell out of there.

"We were just heading to the bar for a nightcap since we know you can't leave yet," Chase explained.

If it were up to him, they'd already be naked in their bedroom. Glancing at the whir of activity still going on around them, he knew Chase was right. They couldn't leave... yet.

"Fine, but let's make it quick. I have plans for you two," Jaxson warned.

Emma slid next to him, wrapping her arm around his waist as they headed to a table. "I hope those plans include me pumping. My dress is getting wet from my leaks."

Chase reached around their wife from the back, squeezing her full breasts suggestively. "Oh, there will be a lot of pumping going on," he teased suggestively.

Damn straight.

Jaxson knew Emma wouldn't be able to really relax though unless she knew her babies were doing well without them for the night. "Did you call to check in on the twins?" he asked as they picked their seat.

"Yep. Alicia was fussy earlier, but they were both asleep a few minutes ago when I talked to the nanny."

Jaxson was relieved. "Good. Then you have no excuses for being distracted tonight when we get you naked and on your knees," he teased.

Ignoring the sexual undertow of the room, Madison plunked down into one of the chairs with a huff. "Like, my feet are killing me. I should have broken in these boots before I had to stand in them for hours. I wish I'd brought a change of clothes down with me," she complained.

They all fell into chairs, Emma snuggling into Chase's lap looking like she was fading fast. It spurred Jax to speed things along.

"So, talk to me. How much did we clear tonight?"

Elijah sat next to him as he answered. "Too early for final numbers, but the food and beverage total alone was fantastic. Without the drink limit for most of the people in attendance, booze sales skyrocketed."

Madison jumped in. "I'll do another count tomorrow when I've got my laptop, but we need to boost the amount from the couples auction by about twenty-five grand since technically we sold Chef Ronan twice."

"Yeah, but we can't charge Stephanie for Carlos Ferrara since they spent the night in the emergency room. Has anyone heard how she's doing?" Elijah asked.

"The guy I sent with them to the hospital called twenty minutes ago. They released her. It was just a sprain with some heavy bruising. No broken bones," Miguel, their head of security, answered from behind Jaxson. He'd snuck in at some point.

Jaxson took a swig of the beer the bartender had put in front of him before adding, "We dodged a bullet there. I hope they throw the book at the lady crazy enough to try that stunt."

"Well, unless we want to make a big stink about it, I'm pretty sure the Beverly Hills Police will cut her loose if they haven't already. I mean, sure, we have witnesses, but who's gonna want to testify against her?"

"Any of our employees who witnessed it, that's who. And I'm pretty sure Carlos Ferrara is pissed enough to testify. Don't let them drop this. I want to make an example out of her," Jaxson instructed.

"Got it, boss. I'll call the chief of police and bug *him* for a change."

That wasn't the only security concern Jaxson wanted answers on. "How the hell did a recording device make it to the main floor of the club. After last year's debacle in D.C., we spent a goddamn fortune on detection gear. Do you have any idea how lucky we are that Lincoln Porter is a trained bodyguard and knew that water bottle was a camera? Scarlett A would have sued us in a hot second if those images of her naked at a BDSM club hit the Internet, and rightly so."

Miguel moved across from Jaxson, making the look of regret on the head of security's face easy to spot. "I'm so damn sorry, Jax. I pulled the security cameras from when the asshole arrived. The sensors caught the device, and my guys searched him, but when they just found the water bottle and sex toys in his duffle bag, they passed him through."

"Well screw that. Effective immediately, we're gonna be like the fucking TSA. No outside food or drinks allowed past security. I pay you a shit-ton of money and I need you to keep up on the newest gadgets on the market if we're going to stay one step ahead of these assholes. It's inevitable. Black Light's success is putting us at risk. Enough people know about the club that eventually reporters are gonna come at us with everything they've got to be the first one to get images of our members in compromising positions."

"Got, it boss. We'll double down to make sure it never happens again," Miguel offered sincerely.

Jaxson hated to tell him, but keeping Black Light both successful and secret were competing goals. The more popular the club became, the harder Miguel's job would get.

"Give Connor Lambert a call. The fucker who snuck the camera in signed an NDA. I want to make his life a living hell for not taking that seriously."

"Yeah, well, he was talking about pressing charges against Lincoln for punching him," Miguel added with a sour look on his face.

"Let Connor deal with that too. That's why he's on retainer."

Jaxson's iPhone appeared in front of his face just as Miguel's gaze moved to somewhere above his head.

"Thanks for the use of your phone. I texted myself that contact info." Nolan Boeing's voice was shaky as he dropped the phone on the table in front of Jaxson.

"Sit down. I'll buy you a drink. I think you deserve one," he offered.

"Naw. I want to get home and put some ice on... never mind. Oh, and Jonah Carter called like three times while I was getting dressed. You might want to call him back."

Nolan hadn't even finished his sentence when the phone started ringing again. Cash Carter's face filled the screen. The injured Dom didn't stick around, heading towards the door as Jaxson answered with a gruff, "Yeah. Now what?"

"Fuck you, man. I'm doing you a favor tonight, remember?" Cash groused.

"Yeah, yeah. You're an entertainer who loves being in the spotlight. And you're a sadist who got to watch people get punished and fucked all night. I'm having trouble feeling too sorry for you."

His friend's good-natured chuckle at the other end of the phone told him Cash wasn't really angry.

Jaxson pressed him further. "It's after two there. I thought you'd be upstairs pounding out your sexual frustrations on that wife of yours by now."

"That's why I'm calling."

"You have a daughter. I'm pretty sure you know how it works by now. Peg A in slot B."

"Fuck you. I thought you'd want to know someone pulled a damn fire alarm in Runway after the club closed. We all had to evacuate the premises. It was *not* convenient. Sami and I were just getting comfortable for the night, if you get my drift."

"Who the hell did that? Was there really a fire?" Jaxson raised his voice, alarmed.

"Nope. Security cameras caught some drunk punk pulling the one right outside the men's room. Blake turned the footage over to the police, but the asshole was long gone by the time we had his picture."

Chase was waving at Jax, trying to get him to share the details. He held his finger up, letting his husband know he'd fill him in later.

"So are you back in the building now?"

"Yep. I was stupid enough to leave without my phone when we had to evacuate. I just got back upstairs to my phone. I know I could have used Maxine's or Spencer's, since they were both outside with us, but they were busy making sure everyone was accounted for and had enough coats and blankets since it was cold as fuck out. I told them I'd let you know and they said they'd call you later with a full report."

"All right, thanks for calling, man. Tell Sami I'm sorry your fun got interrupted. Hopefully you can pick up where you left off."

"No such luck. Since we left Natasha with the nanny for the night, she promptly fell into bed and asleep the second we got back up to your loft. I'm gonna have to either stroke one off in the shower or go to bed with blue balls."

"And how is that different from any other night?" Jaxson added. The men had discussed the hardships of fatherhood many times.

"Tonight was supposed to be our night without the kid!" Cash complained.

"Same here. In fact, this call is cutting into my time with my subs," Jaxson teased, glancing to his right. "Emma is falling asleep right now. I need to go. Later."

He hung up on his friend, pressing the group around him to wrap things up. "What else? I want to get out of here."

Madison piped in, "The silent auction."

"What about it?"

"It was, like, a huge success. We made almost seventy-five grand more just selling BDSM gear and furniture. It's given me lots of ideas for how we can do something like it up at Runway."

"Fine. We can talk about it later," Jaxson urged. He didn't want to deal with anything but the most important things tonight.

Elijah spoke up next. "What the hell happened in the theater about an hour before the event ended? I heard a lot of chatter on the radio, but I was stuck in the back hall and couldn't make it up front."

All eyes turned to Madison who was turning a nice shade of pink.

"What?" she asked defensively.

Chase teased her. "You know what. Lincoln wasn't the only one throwing punches tonight. How does it feel knowing you had two guys fighting over you?"

"They weren't fighting over me." She paused before adding, "Okay, maybe they *were* fighting over me, but since I'm sitting here all alone, clearly neither of them won me."

Jaxson saw the crease of disappointment on her forehead. He'd missed the excitement, but Chase was more than happy to regale them all with the story.

"At first I thought you were friends with the guy who came up on the stage with you, but when he started pawing you and pulling you into a kiss and I saw you were trying to push him away... man, I was pissed. I stood up to head to the stage, but BAM! McLean jumped up there and had him pinned against the wall in two seconds flat."

Jaxson chuckled. "Trevor is a big guy. I'd have loved to see him scaring the shit out of the guy. Anyone know who he was?"

"He was a friend of Carlos Ferrara. He got stuck here when Carlos left for the hospital. Seems he spent too much time at the bar."

"Well, I'm glad McLean had our backs protecting Madison, but she shouldn't have been in danger in the first place."

"I wasn't in danger. I can handle myself." A sadness came over the MC's face as she added, "I have to since I'm on my own."

"Like hell you are," a deep voice boomed from the entrance.

Jaxson didn't need to turn to see who had arrived. If he hadn't already recognized Trevor McLean's voice, the surprised joy lighting up Madison's face would have told him who had joined them.

"I thought you left," Madison accused.

The burly bodyguard to Khloe Monroe was already next to

Madison's chair when he answered her. "I did. I took Ryder and Khloe home and came back."

"Why'd you do that? You forget something?" Madison asked, a smile creeping over her lips.

He would have towered over her even if she wasn't seated at the table, and they stayed trapped in a staring contest for a few long seconds before Trevor finally answered. "Yes. I forgot that I have the next thirty-six hours off and I'm not in the mood to spend them alone. So, if it's okay with you, I'd like us to get the hell out of here."

Madison's face broke into a broad grin, yet she still teased him. "I'm not sure. I'm still working."

Jaxson was about to tell her she could leave when McLean took matters into his own hands. He leaned down to pull Madison to her feet before leaning down and lifting her onto his shoulder, ass in the air as she squealed with surprise.

McLean turned to Jaxson. "Ms. Taylor may have been in charge of tonight's event, but if it's okay with you, I'd like to take her upstairs and show her who's really in charge."

Jaxson had to fight the urge to smile as he answered, "That would be entirely up to Madison. Consider her officially off-duty for the night."

The spunky blonde was thrashing over McLean's shoulder, but Trevor's quick swat to her leather-covered ass settled her down. "What do you say, Madison? You want to leave with me?"

Her muffled, "Hell yes! It's about time you asked me!" brought a round of laughter from everyone present.

Before he left, Trevor announced, "Madison put in a really long day today. She is officially calling in sick for tomorrow. She'll be back on Saturday."

Damned if McLean didn't even wait for a reply. He just turned towards the back staircase behind the bar, heading up to the suite Madison had claimed for the night.

Emma was obviously still awake enough to take notice. "That was so romantic! He carried her off like a caveman."

Chase pushed to his feet, taking only a second to lean down and throw Emma over his own shoulder, mimicking how McLean had carted off his woman.

"If I'd known it turned you on, I would have started carrying you over my shoulder before now!" Chase teased her as she flailed.

"Put me down! I'm way too heavy! You're going to hurt your back!"

Jaxson and Chase's eyes met in a flash, both knowing immediately they couldn't let their wife's outburst go without a punishment. She'd just broken their longest standing rule. She wasn't to ever put herself down because of her curvy figure.

Jaxson quickly stood, hugging his lovers in a way that subdued Emma's struggles. "That's more than enough, young lady. You seem to forget that Chase and I don't take kindly to you talking poorly about your weight." Jaxson paused as Emma groaned loudly. "Chase, take our girl home and get her stripped. Let her pump if she needs to, but I expect you both naked and her strapped down to the spanking bench in the bedroom by the time I get there. We're unfortunately going to have to fit a punishment in before we can have any fun tonight."

Emma's chuckle from her upside-down position made both her husbands smile. "Oh, don't you dare pretend there's anything unfortunate about this at all. Your cocks are hard as rocks right now just thinking about it!" she said.

Jaxson stepped back far enough to land an open-palmed smack on his wife's perfectly round ass. It was hard enough his hand ached. "That may be true, but don't pretend your pussy isn't dripping wet right now just thinking about all of the fun we're gonna have. Now go, Chase. I'll be ten minutes behind you."

"Yes, sir. Please hurry or I might be tempted to start without you." Chase's grin was like sunshine as he turned and headed towards the exit.

He made his decision in a flash. "Fuck it. Elijah and Miguel, you guys can handle anything else that comes up tonight."

He turned long enough to pick up his phone from the table. Nodding to the smiling employees around the table, Jaxson bid them goodnight. "Thanks for all your work tonight, everyone. It was a big success. I'm outta here."

Jaxson took off at a brisk walk. As successful as the night had been, he couldn't wait to get their private Valentine's Day celebration started.

The (Sort of) End
There is always more Black Light to enjoy!

GET A FREE BLACK LIGHT BOOK

Enjoy your trip to Black Light? There's a lot more sexy fun to be had. All of the books in the series can be read as standalone stories and can also be enjoyed in any reading order.

Get started with a FREE copy of **Black Light: Rocked** today. Your fun doesn't need to end yet!

BLACK COLLAR PRESS

Black Collar Press is a small publishing house started by authors Livia Grant and Jennifer Bene in late 2016. The purpose was simple - to create a place where the erotic, kinky, and exciting worlds they love to explore could thrive and be joined by other like-minded authors.

If this is something that interests you, please go to the Black Collar Press website and read through the FAQs. If your questions are not answered there, please contact us directly at: blackcollarpress@gmail.com

WHERE TO FIND BLACK COLLAR PRESS:

- Website: http://www.blackcollarpress.com/
- Facebook: https://www.facebook.com/blackcollarpress/
- Twitter: https://twitter.com/BlackCollarPres
- Black Light East and West may be fictitious, but you can now join our very real Facebook Group for Black Light Fans - Black Light Central

BLACK LIGHT SERIES

Did you enjoy your visit to Black Light? Have you read the other books in the series? They can all be enjoyed as standalone books read in any order.

Season One

Infamous Love, A Black Light Prequel by Livia Grant
Black Light: Rocked by Livia Grant
Black Light: Exposed by Jennifer Bene
Black Light: Valentine Roulette by Various Authors
Black Light: Suspended by Maggie Ryan
Black Light: Cuffed by Measha Stone
Black Light: Rescued by Livia Grant

Season Two
Black Light: Roulette Redux by Various Authors
Complicated Love, A Black Light Novel by Livia Grant
Black Light: Suspicion by Measha Stone
Black Light: Obsessed by Dani René
Black Light: Fearless by Maren Smith

Black Light: Possession by LK Shaw

Season Three
Black Light: Celebrity Roulette by Various Authors
Black Light: Purged by Livia Grant
Black Light: Defended by Golden Angel
Black Light: Scandalized by Livia Grant
Black Light: Charmed by Jennifer Bene

Season Four
Black Light: Roulette War by Various Authors
Black Light: Brave by Maren Smith
Black Light: Unbound by Jennifer Bene and Lesley Clark
Black Light: Branded by Kay Elle Parker

Season Five
Black Light: Roulette Rematch by Various Authors
Black Light: Bred by Shane Starrett
Black Light: Wanted by Maren Smith
Black Light: Worthy by Stella Moore
Black Light: Saved by Raisa Greywood

Season Six
Black Light: The Menagerie by Maren Smith
Infamous Trio Boxed Set by Livia Grant
Black Light: Cured by Vivian Murdoch
Black Light: Gamble by Livia Grant (Fall 2022)
Black Light: Disciplined by Livia Grant (Fall 2022)
Black Light: Protocol by Shane Starrett (Fall 2022)
And many more planned!

Season Seven
Black Light: Roulette Finale by Various Authors (Coming Feb. 2023)

www.ingramcontent.com/pod-product-compliance
Lightning Source LLC
Chambersburg PA
CBHW052338020726
47503CB00001B/20